PRAISE FOR GARRETT LEIGH

“Emotional and brilliant...”

ALL ABOUT ROMANCE

“Tastefully erotic ... more smart than smutty...”

PUBLISHERS WEEKLY

“Powerful and compelling...”

FOREWORD REVIEWS

SKINS

THE BOX SET - VOL 1-4

GARRETT LEIGH

For my foxes, as ever, with love...

DREAM

CHAPTER ONE

"YOU DIDN'T HAVE to run out on us."

Guilt surged through Dylan Hart as he pressed his face against the cool glass of the train window, his phone plastered to his other cheek. "I'm sorry, babe. I just need some space, okay?"

Eddie sighed. "I'm sorry too. I wish things were different."

"No, you don't." Dylan forced a chuckle. "You and Sam are perfectly happy wrapped up in each other. We can party as much as we like, but at the end of the day, I'm an add-on you don't need."

"Don't say that."

"Why not? It's true."

Crickets. Dylan suppressed a sigh of his own and squeezed his eyes shut. "Look. Me and Sam have been close for a long time, but we never messed around much until you came along. Sam's into me because you are, and I'm okay with that, but—"

"You need more, don't you?"

"Yes." Dylan hadn't realized how true it was until he said it, but once he had, the reality that he had to quit his sexual addiction to his two best friends gut-punched him. He leaned forward in his seat, like he could curl his body against the pain. He'd been in love with Sam for years, and now Eddie too, but where did it end? "Eddie," he whispered, "you've got it made with Sam . . . he loves you so much. Let me go find a piece of that for myself, eh? Before we all get hurt."

He hung up before Eddie could reason with him. She was upset, he could tell, but it was for the best. Sam would take care of her, like he always did, and Dylan would take care of himself.

Dylan changed trains at Highbury and then again at Stratford. By then it was getting dark, and he almost convinced himself this was his usual commute home and he hadn't left a piece of his heart in Vauxhall.

But the feeling didn't last as he got off the train in Romford, and he drifted out of the station with a black cloud for company. Outside, a queue of traffic was being held up by a funeral procession, complete with a horse and carriage. Dylan stared at the coal-dark horses, mesmerised by their grace. Old school cockney funerals were common around Romford, but the spectacle never lost its dignity. He observed the procession as it passed—the undertakers and the family walking slowly behind—and wondered where they were headed. The Sacred Heart, perhaps? Dylan's grandfather was buried there.

The procession passed. Dylan snapped out of his daze and made his way to his apartment in the old Railstore complex. He hadn't been home for a few days, but the converted flat was exactly as he'd left it—cluttered and yet distinctly empty. He glanced at the L-shaped couch and recalled a night he'd spent on it a few weeks ago, wrapped up with Sam and Eddie, their legs tangled together as they slept off an evening of fucking and friendship. He'd miss those nights.

He turned his back on the living room and trudged to the bathroom, his nerves beginning to tingle with the urge to wipe the slate clean. *No. It's too soon.* But was it? How did you measure something like that?

Dylan had no idea and continued to wrestle with it as he stripped his clothes and abandoned them in a pile by the bath.

A hot shower did little to soothe his disquiet, and by the time he should've been winding down for the night, he had itchy feet that he couldn't ignore.

Forgoing dinner, he slipped into his favourite tight jeans and a fitted dark shirt and headed out with only one thing in mind: *I want to be someone else for a while.* Or at least a different version of himself.

He took a cab to the outskirts of town. The nondescript building by the motorway junction appeared lifeless as he got out of the car.

"Are you sure you want to be here, mate?" the driver asked, though he didn't seem to particularly care.

Dylan paid the man and allowed himself a small grin. "Oh, I'm sure. Have a good night."

He shut the door and walked towards the old coach house. With its painted over windows, it looked abandoned, but as he got closer, the faint thump of EDM reached him, and his pulse picked up to match the beat.

The signage was as discreet as the rest of the building, but the wording never failed to get Dylan hot: *Lovato's—a place for every fantasy.* So far, it had yet to let him down. He paid the entry fee and signed in, and then made his way to the downstairs cloakroom. Usually, he'd hit the bar first, but he wasn't in the mood to wait today. His non-fuck with Sam and Eddie had set him on fire, and he couldn't rest until he'd done something— or someone—to dampen it down.

By the stairs, the door to one of his favoured haunts was open. Despite his focus on reaching the basement rooms, Dylan glanced inside. The row of cubicles was affectionately known as "the truck stop" and the scene that greeted Dylan was a perfect endorsement—men and women alike stood with their underwear around their ankles while burly men screwed them from behind. One guy was sprawled on the pseudo bathroom counter, his legs in the air while his missus did him with a strap-on. Dylan caught his eye and winked. Perhaps he'd join them later, if he could shift his dark mood.

He left the truck stop behind and descended the stairs. The corridor leading to the basement rooms split in two, and he took the left fork to changing rooms that were quiet compared to the pleasurefest upstairs. Pounding music slowed to a dirty dubstep beat, and Dylan let the headier vibe seep into him as he stripped his clothes and stashed them in a locker.

With a towel around his waist, he bypassed the glory hole pit and approached Seamus, who was guarding the bunker rooms. "What ya got for me?"

Seamus appraised Dylan with his usual inscrutable stare and handed him a strip of inky-black fabric. "Go to the end. I've got a cracker for you."

Yeah, yeah. But Dylan had been frequenting Seamus's lair long enough for the surly Scot to know what he liked, and the rush of what was to come stirred Dylan's dick to life. He entered the last bunker in the corridor and dropped his towel by the raised mattress that took the place of a cosy bed. The room was barren to a layman's eye, but Dylan approached the utilitarian chest of drawers like he was in his own home and selected his box of tricks with little conscious thought. Just rubbers and lube today—the plugs and glass dildos could wait.

Dylan draped his towel over the liquid-proof mattress and then sat on the edge and fixed the strip of fabric Seamus had given him over his eyes. Blindfolded, his pulse kicked up again. He licked his lips and counted the beats as he positioned himself on the mattress—chest down on his hands and knees. He palmed his aching dick just once and then raised his hand to signal that he was ready for whatever walked through the door.

"ANGEL! LONG TIME, NO SEE."

Angelo Giordano slid onto a bar stool and nodded at Carl, an old friend of sorts, though they'd never seen each other outside of the club. "It hasn't been that long."

"No? Seems like forever since I last saw your pretty face."

"Piss off and get me some water."

"You don't want a Peroni?"

"Nah. Fuck that." Angelo had drunk his fill of crappy Italian beer at his father's wake, and his empty stomach was still protesting. "Water's fine, mate. Honest."

"Suit yourself."

Carl slunk away to the fridges on the other side of the bar. Angelo watched him go, admiring his perfect porn-star backside. Carl was good fun and they'd played together many times in the past, but as Angelo ran his gaze over his broad shoulders and thickset thighs, he felt nothing. He wasn't here for familiar; he'd come for the unknown.

A bottle of water appeared in front of him. Carl squeezed Angelo's wrist and moved on, because that was the other good thing about him: he knew when to leave people alone.

And Christ, Angelo wanted to be alone, but he had one last thing to do before he locked himself away for the rest of the week; a last itch to scratch before he gave himself over to the black cloud that had followed him all the way home from New York. Was still following him, two months later.

He spun around on his stool and surveyed his surroundings. The bar was situated in the middle of the club, equidistant from most of the play areas. At this time of night, things were starting to heat up and spill over from the more popular rooms. Angelo's first cursory glance picked up an acquainted couple screwing over a table, a snake pit of women on the floor, and a dude clearly getting the blowjob of his life from the bear of a man on his knees at his feet.

Heat pooled in Angelo's groin. He thought about joining the couple on the table, of claiming his space behind the man and fucking him while he banged his wife, or shoving his dick in the bear's mouth and hitching a ride on what looked like some damn fine head. But he didn't move because both options were dances he'd danced before, and he wasn't in the mood for another waltz.

Angelo drained his water bottle and slid from his stool. Instinct drew him to the stairs that led to the basement rooms—his favoured place to play when his mood was this dark—and he joined the short queue of others who fancied a mystery tour. At the front, he found Seamus, a beast of a man who watched over the basement rooms like every participant was his own child.

He tipped Angelo a wink. "Looking fly, brother. Do I need to go through the checklist with you?"

"Probably not, but I know you want to."

Seamus chuckled and went through his safety list before stamping Angelo's hand, branding him as the only player who'd walk into whatever followed with his eyes wide open. "Bunker five," he said. "I gotta feeling you're going to like what you find."

Angelo rolled his eyes. Seamus was a terminal optimist, and his script never changed, regardless of what Angelo found on the other side of the thick steampunk door. "Whatever. Cheers, mate."

He left his shoes with Seamus and padded barefoot down the industrial-styled corridor, the metal floor cold against the soles of his feet. The play bunkers were soundproofed, what went on behind the heavy doors audible only to Seamus and the pay-by-the-hour observation galleries, but Angelo sensed the heat emanating from each room he passed and let it seep into him and merge with the building anticipation roiling in his gut.

Bunker five was at the end of the corridor. Angelo paused with his hand on the door and psyched himself up for what he might find. In the past, he'd screwed all kinds of people, but dear God, he wanted to fuck a man tonight—needed it. *Craved* it.

Pansexual be damned, some days, only a man's touch could take the pain away.

Angelo opened the door. Blinked a few times. And then a rush of relief hit him so hard he had to steady himself on the doorframe.

Whoa. Jackpot.

He sucked in a breath, and the smouldering desire in his gut did a happy dance. It had been a while, but the thrill of opening the door never got old, and this time he'd struck gold—literally. The slender young man waiting for him on the bed had a halo of fair hair and pale skin that would look awesome with Angelo's handprints welded into it. And beyond that, he was *ready*. Blindfolded and splayed out on his hands and knees, the man had left condoms and lube beside him—his message clear. He wanted to be fucked, and Angelo was over the damn moon to oblige.

Dropping his clothes as he went, he stalked around the raised mattress, his dick already hard. His plan was basic, already spelled out by his mysterious companion, but he paused by the man's head, intrigued by his lips. Pillowy and full, the temptation to slide his cock between them was strong, but the metal floor biting into his bare feet stopped him. People didn't come to the basement rooms for that—they came for the anonymous oblivion that Angelo *craved*.

Angelo returned to where the man clearly wanted him most. He reached for the condoms, and the man shivered as Angelo tore the foil wrapper open and then tossed it aside. Angelo rolled the condom on, jacking himself a couple of times before he turned his attention to his partner in crime and his willing hole. The lube was the stretchy kind that was fashioned on real come. It dripped out of the bottle in long wet strings and onto the man's cleft, sliding down his thighs. The man shuddered again, but Angelo made no move to comfort him. *Nah.* The basement rooms weren't about getting up close and personal; they were about getting down and dirty, and Angelo was more than ready.

He pushed lube into the man's hole with his thumb, absorbing the delicious answering moan. Words were rarely exchanged in encounters like this, but there were a few that Angelo was obliged to utter. He eased his thumb further inside the man and leaned over him, his nipples brushing the man's smooth back. "Safe word is *fox*. Don't be shy about using it."

The man gasped out a laugh. "I won't."

His voice was deeper than Angelo expected, and the gravelly words went straight to his dick. He withdrew his thumb, lined up with the man's hole, and pressed inside with as much care as he could muster with his blood roaring a symphony in his ears. The man was tight and hot and slick with lube. And more than that, he wanted Angelo's cock and widened his stance to take all of him in one slow slide.

"Fuck yeah." Angelo stopped for a moment, reeling from being balls-deep inside a man. He took a breath, and then a strange sensation washed over him, and he lurched forward before he caught himself, hands flailing as he fought the urge to run his hands all over the man's smooth back. *What the hell?*

That was a new one. When he'd played in the basement rooms before, he'd never thought about really touching whoever he'd been railing. Had never taken much notice because that was the point—a hook-up that took anonymity to the extreme, where sex narrowed to the lightning bolts of pleasure shooting through his dick. But he wanted to touch this man, wanted to squeeze those slim hips and let his palms roam that flawless back.

Wanted it. Craved it.

Fuck it.

Under the pretence of steadying himself, he laid a hand at the base of the man's spine. A jolt of electricity surged up his arm, and a strangled groan escaped him. "*Shit!*"

"Yeah?" The man arched, his chest dropping to the mattress, his hole clenching, and then he drew himself off Angelo's cock, before spearing back down on it, again and again, setting the rhythm that Angelo had played out in his head before he'd lost his bloody mind. Over the moody electronica, the slap of skin on skin grew louder as the man ground back on Angelo's dick, meeting Angelo thrust for thrust as Angelo regained the ability to screw him coherently.

The club faded away—the music, the hum of the crowd, and even the eyes that were bound to be watching them from the secluded observation points. The roll of the man's hips grew more erratic, and Angelo was right there to take up the slack. For long minutes it seemed that their heady encounter would be a quick one, but then the reason Angelo had come to the club returned to him, and the desire to take control won out.

He gripped the man's hips, slowing his movements, and then stilled him entirely as he took the man's arms and pinned them behind his back. Angelo paused a moment to give the man a chance to squirm or protest or give any sign that he didn't want Angelo to bang his brains out. There was none, and Angelo briefly pictured them with their positions reversed. With the man on top doing everything to Angelo that Angelo was planning on doing to him. *Wow.* That was new too. Angelo rarely bottomed. It had been years.

Angelo spat where they were joined, adding to the lube already there, and tightened his hold on the man's slender hips. He started slow . . . but deliberate, dicking out the man with targeted stabs of his cock. The dizzying heat burned his veins, and he knew the moment he'd found the man's sweet spot. The velvet warmth clamped tight around his dick, and the man cried out, balling his hands into fists and pushing back on Angelo in a blatant demand for more.

Like that, is it? And fuck if Angelo could deny him. As if he wanted to. He picked up the pace, shoving his dick home with as much rhythm as he could manage with their slick bodies sliding together. Over and over, he drove his cock deep, panting, growling, and flicking his head from time to time to keep the sweat from his eyes.

Edging had always been Angelo's jam, and it seemed he'd found the perfect partner for his favourite game. He fucked the young blond to the other side of the mattress, and it was only when the man was perilously close to sliding off that he grasped his hips and yanked him back.

On their third go around, the man let out a ragged moan, and Angelo's cock pulsed in warning. Heat rocketed through every vein, and his skin burned. Another odd urge to touch his companion swept over him, and then the desire to flip him over and pound him face-to-face. Except they wouldn't be face-to-face, because the unwritten rules of the basement rooms prophesied that they should stay like this—back to chest and invisible.

Angelo had never been one for rules.

He flipped the man over, revealing a lean, toned chest that was the stuff of Angelo's fantasies. He'd played with plenty of big guys, but when he was alone in bed, it was bodies like this that kept him awake—soft and lean . . . delicate, and yet crying out for a brutal railing.

Angelo yanked the man closer and pushed his legs apart. "Name."

"What?"

Angelo leaned over the man, his lips a hairsbreadth from that slender neck. "Give me a name."

"Dylan."

Clubs like this were full of people playing under an alias, but a distant instinct told Angelo that this was real. *Dylan.* Yeah, he liked that. He dug his fingers into Dylan's thighs and drove back inside him. Dylan let out a piercing moan, and Angelo took it as a cue to give it to him hard, all the while transfixed by his cock stretching Dylan out. It was a beautiful sight by itself, but combined with Dylan's pliant body and guttural moans, Angelo was gone.

Dylan's cock was poker straight and rigid on his sweat-sheened belly—somehow he'd known that he didn't have Angelo's permission to touch it.

Angelo wanted to touch it.

Squeeze it.

Suck it.

On a good day, he could've fucked and sucked Dylan at the same time, but today wasn't a good day, and he settled for leaning back on his heels, raising Dylan's hips off the mattress, and screwing him so hard that his moans turned to shouts and then desperate yells as he started to come.

Angelo rode the wave as Dylan convulsed and plastered himself with jets of come, but then things got hazy. His vision darkened to the point where he might as well have been wearing the blindfold. He busted so hard he saw stars, and for a long moment, the reality of his so-called life faded away.

He was dimly aware of a smattering of applause as he chased the last shocks of release. Beneath him, Dylan was splayed out, panting and clearly exhausted. Completing a hat-trick of weird thoughts, Angelo pictured himself collapsing beside him and then spooning up against his back, melding their laboured breaths until they fell asleep.

Idiot. Angelo hadn't shared a bed with anyone that way in years, and he wasn't about to start now. Ignoring the urge to stroke Dylan's golden hair back from his sweaty face, he pulled out and lightly punched his shaky thigh.

"Cheers, mate. Thanks for the ride."

CHAPTER TWO

DYLAN BALANCED his precious coffee mug on his stack of paperwork and resisted the urge to kick the photocopier. It took a herculean effort and he growled expletives under his breath. *Why does nothing in this place ever work?*

Helen, the office manager, glanced up from her own teetering pile of files. "Bad day already? It's barely ten."

"Is two hours not enough for everything to go horribly wrong?" Dylan gave up on the copier and chanced the temperamental scanner instead. "I've got three new DRO cases to set up and no way of duplicating the paperwork."

"I've called someone out for the copier. Have you tried next door? They offered to help yesterday."

Dylan scowled. Setting foot in the nearby Council offices was like asking the child catcher for a ride, but with his next appointment due in ten minutes, he didn't have much choice.

He staggered back fifteen minutes later, avoiding eye contact with the mutinous huddle of pissed-off clients in the waiting room. "Sorry," he said to Helen. "I had to play nice with that creepy receptionist."

"Uh-huh." Helen passed him the appointment schedule. "Your ten fifteen is in room five. Remember to keep it to twenty minutes for your initial assessment. We're overrun right now."

Dylan didn't need reminding. He was the only full-time debt advisor at Stratford Citizens Advice Bureau, and his workload was so biblical that he hadn't had time to even glance at the notes from his next client's telephone consultation. *Brilliant.* If there was one thing worse than having too many clients, it was walking in blind to an appointment.

He grabbed a new notebook from his desk and made his way to his waiting client, trying not to smirk as he recalled the last time he'd entered a room with a big fat number five on the door. It had been a week since his trip to Lovato's had reset his sexual energy, and despite missing Sam and Eddie, the burn of whoever had turned him inside out remained hot and strong.

So strong, in fact, that he'd gone to bed every night since and jacked off imagining the man with the strong hands and smooth voice. Picturing how he'd lifted Dylan from the bed and flipped him over. Remembering how he'd growled as Dylan had come so hard his eyes had watered for hours after. Lovato's had always been a healthy escape, but whoever had railed Dylan that night had come through in more ways than one. It was the first time Dylan had ever regretted playing with a blindfold on too. *I wonder if—*

Get a grip, dickhead.

Dylan clutched his paperwork close to his chest, and with another considerable effort, pushed all thoughts of his basement encounter aside. He opened the door and swept into the consultation room, moving straight to the battered desk to power up the ancient PC. As the advice database loaded, he finally faced his client. "Hi, I'm Dylan—"

Jesus fucking Christ.

Dylan's words died on his lips as he met the liquid gaze of the most beautiful man he'd ever seen. Slim and dark, the man had neat hair and sculpted cheekbones, warm olive skin, and both ears pierced. Black jeans clung to his perfect legs, and a white T-shirt revealed slender forearms that made Dylan drool until he was drawn back to the man's eyes.

"Uh, yeah . . . anyway." Dylan fumbled for the notebook he'd dropped on the table. "I'm one of the debt advisors here. I haven't got all your details to hand right now, but if you give me a minute—"

"What did you say your name was?"

"Pardon?"

The man leaned forward. "Your name. What is it?"

"Dylan."

Silence. The man stared hard enough for Dylan to squirm in his seat. He dropped his gaze to the files in front of him, flipping through the pages until he found the client's information. *Angelo Giordano.* The name was familiar, though Dylan couldn't say why. He scanned the notes the telephone advisor had made, listing personal and business debts and a recent family bereavement. The advisor had suggested a DRO or an IVA or possibly bankruptcy, and it was Dylan's job to figure out which option was best for the client. For *him*, the gorgeous man who was still scowling at Dylan. "I'm sorry about your father."

"What?"

"Your father," Dylan repeated. "It says here that he died recently?"

The man blinked, and the intensity in his glare faded a touch. "We buried him a week ago. That's why I'm here."

"To run his business? The deli at Gallows Corner?"

"You know it?"

"I do. Romford's my hometown."

"I bet."

"Excuse me?"

The man blinked again and seemed to shake himself slightly. "I mean, it's mine too. That's why I came to this office, so I wouldn't see anyone I know."

"Makes sense. It's why I work in Stratford." Dylan speed-read the man's information again. "But I'm not sure how much I'm going to be able to help you today. We don't offer commercial business advice here, so anything related to the deli will need to be set aside."

"It's all related to the deli."

Scepticism warred with Dylan's massively unprofessional preoccupation with Mr. Giordano's legs. Some of the personal debts listed were years old, and from what he could tell, Mr. Giordano's salary as a dancer—*oh God, kill me now*—had largely disappeared into paying enormous interest charges on unsecured loans and late payment fees when he'd fallen behind. Mr. Giordano had been in financial trouble long before his father died, and taking over the family deli had pretty much reduced his income to zero.

Ten minutes later, Dylan read through the notes he'd made. "As the business is in your mother's name, it counts as neither an asset nor a responsibility. Which is good and bad. You're not liable for its debts, but you can't borrow against it to consolidate your personal loans either."

"I know."

Dylan glanced up. It was the first words Mr. Giordano—*Angelo*—had uttered for a while; he'd apparently drifted off as Dylan had filled in financial statements from the paperwork spread out between them and had stopped responding to Dylan's observations. "Your wages from the deli are a hundred pounds a week?"

"Yup."

"And you don't have any other income?"

"Nope."

"Okay." Dylan completed the last of the forms. "Well, as you're probably already aware, your personal debts, and the repayments on them, vastly outstrip your current means, even with your living expenses as low as they are while you're living in your mum's garage."

"Right."

Dylan waited until Angelo met his gaze before he went on. "The deli belongs to your mother, and so I'm going to refer you—and her—to an organisation that can help with your business debts."

"What about the rest of it?"

"Honestly?"

"I didn't come here to be lied to."

The growl in Angelo's voice did odd things to Dylan. For a moment he was briefly transported back to the basement rooms where a voice like that had come with a firm grip and an expertly aimed dick. "You have no assets or leftover income each month, and your debts come in at just below twenty grand. The best advice I can give you right now is to apply for a DRO—a debt relief order—that would be in force for twelve months, after which, your debts would be wiped. It costs ninety pounds and will affect your credit score for six years, but unless you foresee your circumstances changing anytime soon, it's your best option."

Dylan sat back in his seat as Angelo digested the information. It had been a strange consultation—one-sided, mainly, as the beautiful man had fluctuated between gazing into space and staring so intently that Dylan's teeth itched. Angelo's financial situation was dire but fixable. What Dylan couldn't work out was how it had got so bad in the first place. The deli had been a victim of gentrification, but Angelo Giordano had earned good money in his previous job and he didn't strike Dylan as a man who'd be careless with cash. A brave assumption, perhaps, but Dylan had a decade in debt relief, and he'd bet his right arm that a big piece of the puzzle was missing. "What did you do for work before the deli?"

"Hmm?" Angelo glanced up from the financial assessment Dylan had slid across the table.

"Your previous job," Dylan said. "What was it?"

"I was a dancer."

"I know that. I meant what kind of dancing."

"Ballet."

"Seriously?" Dylan blurted before he caught himself. With his pierced ears and dark beard, Angelo didn't fit Dylan's naïve idea of what a ballet dancer would look like. "That's amazing."

"It was," Angelo said flatly. "But I'm past it now."

"Past it? Too old, you mean?"

"Something like that." Angelo's dark gaze flashed with an emotion that cut Dylan to the bone, but it faded fast, like it had never been there at all, and he broke the spell by tapping his elegant fingers on the desk. "So what happens next? Do I need to sign something?"

"Uh . . ." Dylan opened a drawer in the desk and retrieved a DRO pack. "Applications for debt relief orders can only be made by an approved intermediary, and I can't do it for you here because you live in Romford."

"So?"

"You're out of area," Dylan explained, though he couldn't explain why it was killing him. "I have to signpost you to the Romford office."

"Then why did you give me an appointment here?"

"Because we'll see anyone who walks through the door, but our options are limited when it comes to making DRO applications. It's policy to refer you to the office closest to you."

"That place is shite."

Dylan couldn't deny it. Aside from not wanting to know the financial woes of his friends and neighbours, it was the notorious disarray of the Romford office that had led him to take the position in Stratford. But his hands were tied. "I'm sorry."

"Why? Not your fault, is it?"

"No, but it seems unfair that you came here for help and all I can do is pass you from pillar to post."

Angelo stood. His gaze was directed at his feet as he seemed to manoeuvre himself with more care than necessary, but when he looked up, the dull haze had faded, and in its place was a malevolence that was almost frightening. "Don't worry about it, mate. Twenty minutes on the train is nothing. Besides, it ain't like you walked in here and fucked me, is it?"

Dylan blinked. "What?"

"You heard me." Angelo pushed his chair back and walked to the door. "Thanks for your help today, *Dylan*, but I gotta say, you did more for me a week ago when I railed you at Lovato's. You have a nice day, now."

WANKER. Angelo pressed his fists into his eyes, like he could unsee the horror he'd left on Dylan's face when he'd walked out on him with legs that had only just made it outside before they'd given way. He'd barely made it to the train station.

Serves you fucking right.

Of course it did. The first rule of Lovato's was that there was no Lovato's, and yet Angelo had taken it to Dylan's work and thrown it in his face. The gravity of his own woes had outweighed his shock at recognising Dylan, and then his treacherous temper had intervened, and he'd hurt the man who'd haunted his fantasies all week long.

Angelo stretched his aching legs out in front of him and made a half-hearted attempt to massage the pain out of his thighs. For a while it seemed that he'd be spending the night on the bench he'd collapsed on when he'd stumbled off the train, but eventually he found the energy to get up and trudge the two miles back to Gallows Corner, trying not to dwell on the fact that Dylan knew he couldn't afford the bus.

At the deli, his mother was waiting for him, already drowning in the lunchtime rush. "Angelo! Where have you been?"

Angelo pushed passed her and grabbed his apron from under the till. "I told you, Ma. I had to go to Stratford for some business."

"What business?"

"What do you think?" Angelo snapped before the guilt at having left his mother alone in the deli all morning kicked in. "I went to Citizens Advice, remember?"

Theresa Giordano frowned. "What do you need to go telling our business to strangers for? Your father would turn in his grave."

"Then he should've paid the damn bills when he was alive."

Angelo regretted the words as soon as they were out of his mouth, but it was too late. His mother's eyes filled with tears and she turned her back on him, leaving him to face the rest of the day on his own.

It was late by the time Angelo made his escape. The Giordano house was a mile away, but the walk seemed to stretch on much farther. Angelo was so tired he felt sick, and the long stagger to the tatty garage he called home seemed like it would kill him.

He was halfway there when a figure hopping off a bus caught his eye. His heart stopped and then restarted with a painful thud. *Jesus. Twice in one day?* Surely not. But as Angelo fell into step behind the slim blond, the back of his head grew more familiar. After all, he'd spent the best part of their first encounter staring at it.

Angelo wondered where Dylan was going. He'd said that he lived opposite Romford's Citizens Advice Bureau, but that was in the wrong direction for Angelo's home, and there was no need to follow him . . . right?

He was half a mile out of his way before he saw reason, and

by then the converted Railstore development where Dylan likely lived was at the end of the road. Angelo thrust his hands into his pockets and thought about turning around. But he didn't. He trailed Dylan all the way to the entrance doors, intending to walk straight past, but a startled exclamation from Dylan halted him in his tracks.

A pile of folders and paperwork hit the pavement. Angelo turned right at the moment that Dylan looked up. Their eyes met, and in the murky light of the early autumn evening, Angelo's world stopped. His heart raced, and his breath caught in his chest, and no coherent thought graced his brain as Dylan stared at him, his blanched skin and red-rimmed eyes caught in a devastating mix of shock and horror. "What the hell are *you* doing here?"

Any hope that Angelo might've had that Dylan hadn't connected his vicious parting words with the dick that had slammed him in the club evaporated. He swallowed and took a hesitant step forward. "Um . . . I live here."

"Your mother's house is a mile in the opposite direction."

"So? Doesn't mean I have to spend all my time there, does it?"

"No, but I'm pretty sure there's laws against stalking people, so I suggest you find somewhere else to be."

Dylan gathered his things from the ground and turned to his front door, jabbing a key at the lock with shaking hands. Angelo retreated and watched from a respectable distance, but when Dylan dropped his keys, the daft twat that had followed Dylan from the bus stop in the first place sprang to life again, and even his fatigue-addled legs betrayed his sanity.

He scooped up Dylan's keys and jammed the biggest one in the lock. "There you go."

"How is that fucking off?"

Despite the aggression lacing Dylan's tone, the way his voice wrapped around the words erased the torturous morning they spent together in the stuffy Citizens Advice office and took Angelo back to the start—back to the basement room where the first he'd seen of Dylan was his leonine body, arched and ready.

Ready for me.

"I'm sorry."

"For what?" Dylan snapped. "Turning up at my work? Blasting me with shit that should've stayed at the club? Or following me home?"

"All of it . . . except, I didn't turn up at your work on purpose."

"No? So why did you sit through a twenty-minute interview without saying something then? That's messed up to the nth degree. Now, get the fuck away from my house."

Dylan crunched his key in the lock and opened the door. He marched inside and the door swung shut in Angelo's face.

Defeated, Angelo backed away, the ache in his body returning with every step. Somehow, being close to Dylan had distracted him from the reason he'd wound up back in Romford without a penny to his name in the first place. He sank down on yet another nearby bench and put his head in his hands. Jesus. What the fuck had he just done? If Dylan had any sense, he'd call the rozzers. And being carted off by the police would just about top off Angelo's day—week, month. Fuck it. The whole damn year had been shit.

The temptation to slump down on the bench and fall asleep was strong—it wouldn't be the first time he'd slept outside—but it began to rain, and Angelo was perversely glad of the chill that came with it. The wind rattled through his tired bones and matched his mood. He took a deep breath and stood, but a hand closed around his arm before he could take a step.

"Why are you here?"

Angelo turned. Dylan was behind him, dressed in ripped jeans and an Iron Maiden T-shirt. It was such a contrast from the smart casual he'd worn to work that Angelo simply stared, as transfixed as he'd been when he'd found Dylan naked and waiting for him.

"Well?" Dylan shoved his floppy blond hair out of his face. His wrist was covered in distressed metal bracelets and grungy festival bands. His hand was elegant and smooth. Angelo wanted to kiss it.

He stepped back, raising his own hands in surrender. "I said I was sorry. I had no idea you'd be at my appointment this morning, and I only followed you when you got off the bus in front of me to apologise for losing my shit at you. I'm not a fucking stalker, and I'm *sorry*, okay? You'll never see me again, I swear."

"Angelo—"

"Mate, I'm embarrassed enough. Don't make me say it again." Angelo turned on his heel and walked away as the heavens opened in earnest. The clusterfuck his day had become felt surreal, and despite being sick of his own four walls, he couldn't wait to get home and pretend it had never happened. Hell, he'd even give up on the memory of fucking Dylan if it meant he could escape the cold impatience in Dylan's eyes now.

"Angelo, wait."

Angelo kept walking. Fat raindrops soaked into his clothes and ran down his face. His one remaining pair of Nikes squelched in the puddles. But still he recoiled when Dylan grabbed his arm. "Get off me."

"Why? You followed me all the way home and now *I'm* supposed to leave *you* alone?"

"You told me to fuck off, so I'm fucking off."

"So why did you get in my face in the first place?"

"I already told you."

"I know, but *why*? Why do you care how I felt about what you did in the office? It's not like we ever had to see each other again."

"Isn't it?" Angelo cast a pointed glance around them. "We

live in the same town. We'd have run into each other eventually."

"Would we, though? My dad has lived on Faringdon Avenue for twenty years and I've never seen you before. I even used to buy lunch from the deli when I worked at Jack's Barber Shop. I can picture your father, your mum . . . even someone I think is your sister, but never you."

"That's because I wasn't there."

"What? Never?"

"Not since I was fifteen."

"Why not?"

"What do you care?" It was oddly satisfying to throw Dylan's question back in his face, and it seemed that Dylan had no better answer for it than Angelo.

"I don't *understand* . . . I don't get it."

Angelo wiped rain out of his face. "Get what?"

"How this fucking happened!" Dylan's shout rang out, but no one looked their way, and after a moment, he tugged on his hair again. "Look, I've been going to the club for a couple of years now, and there's no way that the other night was the first time you've fucked someone in the basement rooms—I can always tell—so it seems a little messed up that you screw me once and then turn up everywhere I go a week later."

Angelo's brain didn't work as fast as it used to, especially on days like this that wouldn't just end already. "Are you asking me if I engineered fucking you and then stalked you ever since?"

"I don't know what I'm asking. I'm just confused. And freaked out. I've never seen anyone I've played with outside of the club."

"Neither had I until this morning."

Dylan stared at Angelo, his bloodshot eyes suddenly more intense than ever. "Don't lie to me."

"Why would I lie? If I really am a stalker, I'm a pretty shit one, given that you know everything about me and my family. No mystery there, mate, is there?"

"I guess not."

"Right." Angelo started to move away.

Dylan caught his arm again. "Don't go."

"Why not?"

"I don't know." Dylan's grip on Angelo's arm tightened. "Because it's raining?"

Angelo laughed for what felt like the first time in a year. "If you're worried about getting wet, it's a little late for that." He gestured at their drenched clothes and shivered. "I gotta get home before I bloody drown."

A bus rumbling past drowned out Dylan's reply, and his feet moved in the wrong direction. Belatedly, Angelo realised that Dylan was tugging him in the direction of his flat. "What are you doing?"

Dylan speared him with a determined frown. "I'm taking you home."

"I live over there, remember?"

"I meant my home."

"Why?"

Dylan yanked on Angelo's arm a little harder. "Because we don't know the answer to that question. Now come the fuck on."

DYLAN CLOSED the door behind them and leaned back on it, watching as Angelo turned a slow circle in the hallway, his gaze flicking around the mesh of urban and vintage décor.

"This place is nice."

"This is the weirdest day ever," Dylan countered, and it truly was. For years, he'd kept most facets of his life separate, but today they'd collided and his brain had caught fire.

"*. . . you did more for me a week ago when I railed you at Lovato's.*"

Was that true? Thinking back over their meeting that morning, it probably was. *Brilliant. So you're a better shag than you are a debt counsellor. Guess Angelo can use a fuck-hot blowjob to pay his overdraft then.*

Dylan shook his head to clear it, struggling to match the Angelo, who'd apparently chucked him all over the basement room mattress, with the exhausted man he'd found in the interview room that morning. Both versions of Angelo Giordano were *gorgeous*, but what had happened in the eight hours since Angelo had dropped his bomb was all kinds of screwed up.

And now Angelo was in Dylan's house. *What the hell do I do now?*

A hundred questions burned on Dylan's tongue, but none seemed right. Water dripped from both of them onto the hardwood floor. Dylan watched the puddles grow until a violent shiver wracked Angelo's slim frame and spurred him into action. "I'll get some towels."

He dashed to the airing cupboard and retrieved two towels, tossing one at Angelo when he returned to the hallway and pointing at the kitchen. "Come through."

Angelo's presence behind him was like a live hand grenade, and the silence that drowned them was too loud. Dylan flicked the switch on his wireless speaker as he passed. The Cooper Temple Clause drifted out, smooth and low, heady and deep, and did nothing to ease the scratchy friction in Dylan's veins.

"The 'Murder Song'? Are you sure it's not you that's the mad axe murderer?"

A dry chuckle caught in Dylan's throat. He opened the fridge and found his last two bottles of Polish lager. "Here. It tastes like piss, but I make lousy coffee."

"I'm sick of coffee. Been brewing it all day."

Dylan had forgotten that. The deli that belonged to Angelo's family made the best paninis in east London, but Dylan couldn't picture him slaving over the press or wrestling with the ancient coffee machines it was famous for.

For better or worse, he could only feel Angelo's hands all over him, gripping him, lifting him while his thick cock drove every last drop of—

"How long have you lived here?"

Dylan blinked and handed Angelo a bottle. "Six months. I lived in Vauxhall for a few years before that."

A small smile fleetingly warmed Angelo's face. "So you weren't around this way for a while then?"

"Um, not as often. Why?"

"Because that explains why we didn't run into each other at

the club. I worked there for a year a while back, before I moved to New York."

"I thought you said you hadn't been here since you were fifteen?"

"No, I said I hadn't worked in the deli since I was fifteen. I danced with the English National Ballet for four years—worked at the club for some of that. It kept me out of trouble, believe it or not."

"Get in trouble a lot, do you?"

The ghost of a grin returned, laced with the kind of self-loathing Dylan had often seen in Sam when he talked about his childhood. "I'm not in trouble *now*," Angelo said. "Or am I? You still look pretty pissed off."

Dylan schooled his features. "I'm not pissed off. I'm fucking bemused. Aren't you? What were you thinking when you recognised me this morning? Come to think of it, *how* did you recognise me this morning?"

Angelo licked his lips, his tongue moving slowly . . . sensually as it moistened the skin. Dylan was mesmerised and caught off guard when Angelo answered him.

"It was your voice."

"But we didn't speak at the club."

"Yes, we did. I told you the safe word and you said you wouldn't need it, and then, uh, later . . . you told me your name."

Heat flooded Dylan's veins. His memories of Angelo fucking him were vivid and raw, but he'd forgotten the brief words they'd shared, distracted by Angelo's hands and the current they'd seemed to carry that night. "You don't look anything like I thought you would."

Angelo tilted his beer and took a long pull, his elegant neck working as he swallowed, his mouth glistening as he lowered the bottle. "I can't decide if you think that's a bad thing or not. You're hard to read."

That was rich coming from him, but Dylan let it slide,

preoccupied by the idea that Angelo believed that revealing himself—however bizarrely it had occurred—was somehow a disappointment. Was he fucking serious? It was the fact that he was so goddamn hot that had freaked Dylan out in the first place. The bear of a man he'd imagined hadn't materialised, but the moody, lithe dancer leaning against his kitchen counter was the stuff of wet dreams. "It's not a bad thing. I'm just having trouble believing you're real."

Angelo chuckled. "Back at ya. I couldn't believe my luck when I found you waiting for me in the bunker. It's been a long time coming."

"Yeah? Do you go downstairs a lot?" Dylan picked at the label on his beer bottle, hoping his question appeared innocuous.

Angelo eyed him, perhaps sensing that his bland tone hid the startling reality that whatever answer he gave would turn Dylan inside out all over again. "I hadn't been to the club for more than a year before the other night. I can't deny that the basement rooms are familiar—I helped set them up—but it's been a while since I used them."

"You set them up?"

Angelo shrugged. "Kind of. Tammy, the owner, did a secret ballot of the staff a few years back, asked us to describe our ultimate fantasy. Mine got picked out of the hat."

It's not just yours. Dylan rubbed his temples. There was so much he wanted to ask Angelo, but the abrupt collision of too many worlds was giving him a migraine. "Let me get this straight: You worked at the club when you were dancing in London, then you moved to New York and only came home when your father died?"

"That's about the size of it."

"What happened to your money? You have massive loans, but they're not student debts, so I don't understand."

"Why are you asking about that? You're not my advisor

anymore, remember? You sent me back to the shithole across the road."

The air shifted, but Angelo's obvious irritation did nothing to ease the building desire in Dylan's gut. "I did that before I knew who you were, but that doesn't mean I don't care."

"I don't want you to care."

"No? So what do you want? Why are you in my house?"

Angelo put his beer bottle down and folded the towel Dylan had given him into a neat square, setting it carefully next to the empty bottle. "I'm in your house because you asked me to be. *You* never told me why."

He had a point.

Judas Priest shattered the heavy air between them before Dylan could answer. He reached for his phone, and Sam's scowling face flashed up on the screen. Dylan swallowed thickly. Until Angelo, only Sam had ever made him feel this way—like his skin belonged to them and not him. Like he couldn't breathe until he touched them again. *Fuck this.* He silenced the call and set his phone face down beside Angelo's towel. "I don't know what I want."

"Well it ain't to talk to whoever just called. Isn't a debt collector is it? 'Cause they were calling me 24/7 before I binned my phone contract."

"It's a friend, actually, but I can't talk to him for a while."

"Because you love him?"

Dylan snapped his eyes up to find Angelo gazing at him, his molten eyes shrewd, like Dylan's every thought made perfect sense to him. "He's my best friend."

"Is he straight?"

"Mostly."

Angelo smirked. "That's the worst. Queer enough to hook up, but too straight to give a shit afterwards?"

"It's not like that."

"No? So how is it?"

Dylan wouldn't know where to start, which was just as well, as it seemed that Angelo's question was rhetorical. He stepped into Dylan's personal space. For a moment Dylan wondered if he would kiss him, but he didn't. His fist touched Dylan's shoulder, and then he was gone. The front door banged a few seconds later, leaving Dylan to contemplate how he'd feel if he never saw him again.

———

HELEN BROUGHT a plastic cup of sludgy instant coffee to Dylan's desk. "I can see you're upset that your mug got broken."

"Hmm?" Dylan glanced up from his pile of financial statements. "Oh, thanks, but I'm okay, really. It was just a mug."

Helen raised an eyebrow. "So why the long face? You've been quiet all week."

I'm pissed off because the best fuck I've ever had came into my life in the most fucked up way possible, and I can't see a way of fixing that. And by the way, he's a client. "I'm a bit tired. I went to The Pit at the weekend. Haven't quite recovered yet."

That got rid of Helen. She was the nicest woman in the world, but Dylan's passion for grungy metal music baffled her.

He went back to his paperwork and was instantly lost in the reason he'd been scowling all morning: He'd fucked up. Angelo's paperwork had come back from the Romford office with a glaring snag that threatened to derail the plan Dylan had worked out with his Romford counterpart. A year ago, Angelo had made a payment to the deli, prioritising the family business over creditors he'd owed thousands to for longer. It would seem a small point to a layman, but Dylan had seen DROs refused for less.

"*Do you want to call him?*" the Romford advisor had asked, eager to get out of giving a client bad news. But Dylan had shut her down. His connection to Angelo was screwed up enough, and the sooner they took Angelo's financial dire straits out of it, the better. *Right. Because you'll be BFFs after.* And removing himself from Angelo's case didn't stop him worrying. Angelo had said little in his interview with Dylan, but the notes from his telephone consultation painted a picture of a desperate man with nowhere left to turn. Without the DRO, his creditors would hound him into the ground, and then what would he do? It had been six years since Dylan had endured his first client suicide, but it haunted him, even now.

The rest of the day passed in a haze of client meetings and phone calls to ruthless creditors. Dylan had learned to handle himself over the years, but he was still pretty strung out by the time he left the office. The train home from Stratford was packed with fellow commuters glad to escape the rat race for the weekend. Dylan tried to hitch a ride on their muted enthusiasm, but it was a lost cause. Over the summer, he'd spent most weekends with Sam and Eddie, and with that option out, he didn't feel like facing his dad.

That left locking himself away in the flat for two days straight, which sounded ideal after a long-arse week, but he knew he'd be climbing the walls by Saturday night. *You could always go to the club—*

But he nuked the idea before it took hold. Playing at the club had been his happy place in recent years, but the shitstorm with Angelo had changed that. Part of Dylan wished they'd never fucked that first time—that someone else had railed him and then disappeared out the door, never to be seen again. But it was a very small percentage of his brain. The rest of him, and definitely his dick, would give just about anything to confine what had happened between them to the four walls of the heady bunker room. That way, Dylan could've gone back and taken a chance on Angelo coming back for more.

Yeah, because when it came down to it, that was all this was. A fuckhot play session that had spilled out into real life, right?

On the cramped train, Dylan almost believed it, but then he found himself walking the long way home from the bus stop and slinking past Giordano's Deli. On his first go around, Angelo was nowhere to be seen, but as Dylan crossed the street under the pretence of ducking into Waitrose, his creepy behaviour paid off. Angelo was at the serving counter, handing someone a wrapped package and a paper cup of the kind of coffee that Dylan dreamed of when he was stuck in the office.

He trailed to a stop, blocking the supermarket's entrance. Angelo was dressed in skin-tight black jeans that clung to his slim hips and dancer's calves. A plain white tee with rolled up sleeves sat perfectly on his leanly muscled torso, covered by a forest green apron that probably made his dark eyes gleam. *Damn it.* The week since their last chance encounter had done nothing to ease the burn in Dylan's veins, the ache in his chest, and the heat in his blood. Angelo Giordano was so fucking beautiful it *hurt*, and only the muttered exclamation of someone behind him broke the spell.

Reluctantly, Dylan tore himself away and braved the Friday night crowds in Waitrose—harried yuppie parents who'd forgotten to buy dinner on their lunch break and loved up couples planning a cosy night in. When he emerged a little while later, clutching a ready meal for one and a bottle of gin, the deli was closed and Angelo was gone.

DYLAN MADE it to Saturday afternoon before he turned stalker again. A weekend with no plans meant running the bazillion errands he'd spent weeks avoiding, which gave him an excuse to wind up loitering outside Giordano's. At least, that's what he told himself when the irony didn't choke him. And as luck would have it, or not, Angelo was there this time and looked up at just the right moment to catch Dylan staring at him from across the street. *Brilliant.* To walk away would have appeared more stalkerish than ever, so he swallowed his pride and crossed the road.

Angelo came outside to meet him. "What are you doing here?"

"I live here."

Angelo's rare smile made a brief appearance. "No, mate. That's me."

"You don't live at the deli."

"No? Sure feels like it this week."

"Business booming?"

"Something like that. My sister has gone back to uni, and having my mum here is more hassle than it's worth."

"You should sell it."

Dylan instantly regretted his bluntness, but Angelo merely nodded. "Tell that to my entire family, I dare you. 'Cause I've been trying for years and all it's got me is a seat at the kiddie table at Christmas."

"Do they know how much debt it's in?"

Angelo shrugged. "Probably not, because then my mum would have to admit that my father gambled our piss-poor profits down the swanny when he couldn't keep up with the Starbucks down the road."

Ah. So that was it. Dylan had been ruminating over what had happened to what little profit Giordano's had turned in the last few years, because it hadn't gone on staff salaries. Angelo took home next to nothing, and his father before him had paid himself even less. It was on the tip of Dylan's tongue to ask if Angelo's own missing money had gone to his father, but then he remembered that discussing Angelo's debts outside of the office was a massive breach of confidence. Fuck's sake. What was it about this bloke that obliterated Dylan's common sense?

"Anyway . . ." Dylan started to turn away. "I'll let you get on."

"Okay."

Angelo didn't move, and the sensation of his eyes boring into the back of Dylan's head made Dylan's every step feel ridiculous, like he was walking away from a friend he hadn't seen in years.

And he couldn't do it. He was three feet away when he stopped and turned. "Um, are you going to the club tonight?" An infinitesimal twitch in Angelo's eyebrow was his only reaction. Dylan shifted his weight from one foot to the other and fidgeted with his shopping bag. "I mean, because I might, and I'm not your advisor anymore, so—"

"So what? You want me to fuck you again?"

"Would that be bad?"

Angelo glanced over his shoulder. In the few minutes Dylan had been wasting his time, a queue had formed at the panini counter. He started to back up, and for a mortifying moment, Dylan feared he wouldn't answer, but then he fixed Dylan with the arresting stare he'd imagined all along, way back before he'd known that the strong hands holding him down belonged to Angelo.

"I might be there," Angelo said. "If I am, you'll be waiting."

He was gone before Dylan could deny it.

<hr>

THE CLUB HAD NEVER FELT SMALLER. Dylan saw Angelo in every corner and crevice, even though he'd been inside for more than an hour, surreptitiously watching the door, and Angelo had yet to arrive.

If he was even coming.

Dylan took a deep swallow of his ill-advised Jägerbomb. The booze was having little effect on his nerves, and the Red Bull had made him jumpy enough that he didn't notice the beast of a man dropping onto the bar stool beside him.

"Hey, man. You wanna play?"

Dylan cast a glance at the man. Big and brawny and covered in a fuzz of body hair, he couldn't have been further from Dylan's fantasies if he'd tried, but his smile was lovely, and Dylan knew just the man to send him to. "Not tonight. Have you met Ron over there, though? He was a little lonely a while ago."

A small white lie. Ron was never lonely, but there was always room for one more in his all-man scrum. Dylan watched the man take his place in the fold and then turned away. Ron's orgies were legendary, but Dylan was holding out for something far more intimate, and as the clock struck ten, he forced himself to take a chance.

Downstairs, Seamus greeted him with a knowing smile—or at least as close to a smile as he ever got. "Back so soon?"

"It's been two weeks."

"Aye, funny that. Well, let's see what the night brings you." Seamus relinquished the blindfold and directed Dylan to the very first room in the corridor.

Dylan's heart clenched. What if Angelo didn't find him there? What if he requested bunker five on the assumption that Dylan would be there? *What if he doesn't come at all?* If Angelo didn't show, Dylan would take the cock of whoever walked through the door in his place—a thought that made his entire body tingle—but the muted thrill had nothing on the fire Angelo had left burning a fortnight ago.

He'll come. He has to.

Dylan undressed and then let himself into the dark basement room. He tied the blindfold and positioned himself on the bare mattress, absorbing the brutal jolts of hope running through him. *Come on, Angelo. I'm waiting for you.*

And wait he did, for what seemed like hours. He counted his thumping pulse as his dick hardened and waned with each turn of his brain. Nerves rarely troubled him when it came to sex—in the club or out in the real world—but on his hands and knees, waiting for the fuck of a lifetime, he could barely breathe.

The door opened and the faintest hint of a cool breeze tickled Dylan. Goosebumps broke out on his heated skin, and anticipation zapped up his neck, buzzing through his scalp as his companion dropped their clothes on the floor.

What little breath Dylan had caught in his throat, and he shuddered, sure he felt a ghost-like hand brush his shoulders. Warmth bloomed in his chest and spread through every nerve. His gut told him that the light-footed man prowling around him was Angelo, but until they touched and the stars exploded, he couldn't be sure.

Strong fingers threaded through Dylan's hair, yanking his head back. "Safe word?"

He came.

Dylan gasped. "Fox."

"Say it. I'll hear you."

Angelo's voice was like a drug, and Dylan's nerves faded away. He leaned into Angelo's touch, and the charge where their skin touched sent pulses of desire hurtling through him. *Fuck, yeah.* He remembered this—the crazy current that made him dizzy. Heady and addictive, he couldn't get enough, and his cock throbbed in anticipation of what was to come. Would Angelo take him hard and fast like he had before, or were they in for an entirely different ride?

A million scenarios spun through Dylan's mind, but his world narrowed when Angelo's hands gripped his arse, his dick gliding along the seam like it was made for him, like it was dying to get inside. Angelo, apparently, wasn't playing around.

Teeth scraped along Dylan's spine as Angelo leaned over him, and the rustle of a condom wrapper pierced the air. Dylan braced himself for the blunt intrusion of Dylan's cock, but it didn't come. Instead, the strong hands he remembered lifted him clean off the mattress and tossed him onto his back.

Dylan groaned and spread his legs. Rough play had always got him hot, but knowing that it was Angelo chucking him around like a rag doll? *Damn.* His balls were already drawn up so tight he worried they'd never come down. His dick ached too, and his hands twitched, craving friction. But he didn't move. Angelo hadn't commanded him to stay still, but he didn't have to. Dylan submitted because he *wanted* to. He splayed his arms wide and offered himself to Angelo. "Fuck me."

"Quiet."

Angelo's palm connected with Dylan's thigh. The slap was playful, but Dylan gasped all the same and arched his body, desperate for more. Angelo struck him again, harder this time, and Dylan moaned out, long, loud, and pleasured.

Yes. But he didn't dare say it.

Hit me. Use me. I want it.

The spanking went on for a while, each strike soothed by Angelo's warm palms. Dylan cried out each time. By BDSM standards, their play was light, but by the time his dick was welcomed into Angelo's sinfully hot mouth, his senses were in overdrive. *Shit. I'm gonna come!* But before he could bust, Angelo eased off, edging out Dylan's climax like a pro.

"Not yet," he whispered in Dylan's ear, his breath hot against Dylan's cheek. "This is gonna last, baby."

Baby. Dylan hated sappy terms of endearment, but hearing it drip from Angelo's devilish tongue sent shivers down his spine. He tensed his stomach muscles and raised his hips off the bed, still stubbornly leaving his arms spread wide.

I want to kiss him.

The revelation caught him off guard, though it shouldn't have. He'd wanted Angelo in every context where they'd encountered each other—even the office, where Dylan had imagined Angelo fucking him over the battered MDF desk.

Angelo gripped Dylan's thighs, and a groan tore out of Dylan. His body was crying out for Angelo to be inside him, but a renegade army was enjoying Angelo's touch too much to give it up without a fight, and he trembled as the battle raged inside him.

Touch me. Fuck me.

And the longer Angelo kept him waiting, the less he cared about what came next.

Just give me something . . . please.

The aching void Angelo had left behind last time deepened. Dylan ripped his arms from the mattress and made a clumsy grab for Angelo's hips, yanking him closer until Angelo's cock nudged him, and cool lube trickled onto his tingling flesh.

Angelo's low chuckle rumbled through Dylan. "So impatient," he muttered. "I'm gonna have to be firm with you."

"Do it," Dylan gasped out, and the answering burn of Angelo's cock pressing inside him blew his mind.

Angelo fucked him senseless. Nonsense fell from Dylan's lips as he fell slack beneath the brutal assault of Angelo dicking him out. Over and over, Angelo drilled Dylan's prostate, and Dylan could barely stand it. He went to pieces, thrashing his head from side to side, his cries loud and strained. Edging was apparently Angelo's party trick, and Dylan was so crazed by the need to bust that he almost didn't notice Angelo lifting him once again.

The cold metal wall against his spine came as more of a shock, and the rush of blood to the head had him lolling like a rag doll in Angelo's unswerving grip. He wrapped his legs around Angelo's waist and held on for dear life as Angelo speared him again, and the change in angle was enough to shatter what was left of his tenuous control. Four deep thrusts and he came undone, spilling between them in jets of wet heat. His climax was blinding, his moans delirious, and only Angelo's ragged shout kept him in the present.

The warmth of Angelo filling the condom was nearly enough to send Dylan over the edge again. He convulsed in

Angelo's arms and squeezed his bound eyes shut as Angelo carried him back to the mattress. Angelo laid him down and briefly pressed their foreheads together, and the club faded away. For a long moment, they simply breathed together, and Dylan imagined that Angelo would stay with him, that he wouldn't step away, retrieve his clothes from the floor, and leave Dylan alone with his laboured breaths and racing heart.

But Angelo left.

THE KNOCKING on the garage door came and went as the morning drifted into the afternoon. Angelo dozed through most of it, curled up on the couch that doubled as his bed, but eventually, Theresa's patience wore thin, and she let herself into his garage lair.

"Why are you still in bed?" she demanded. "Your uncles are visiting today. They want to talk about the business."

Angelo cracked his eyes open, shielding them against the light Theresa had let in with the open door. "Unless they want to buy it, I'm not fucking interested."

Theresa met his cursing with a string of her own Italian expletives. "You're no help to me when you're like this. You're just like your father."

Angelo could believe it. Silvio Giordano had been a constant source of disappointment to all who knew him, and it was clear by the way his mother was looking at him now that she felt much the same way about her son. "I'm tired, Mum. Can we do this later?"

"You're always tired. Perhaps if you came home at night instead of staying out drinking, you'd feel better. It's no wonder you're not fit enough to dance anymore."

Fuck you. Angelo sat up, ignoring the wave of nauseating fatigue that threatened to send him straight back down again. "I'm retired. What did you expect me to be? A fifty-year-old ballerino?"

"You're twenty-eight."

"Right. Did you want something? Because I've got shit to do."

The conversation had no destination. Theresa treated him to a final glare before she turned on her heel and left. The bang of the garage door rattled Angelo's aching bones, and he lay back down, retrieving the TV remote and his phone from the concrete floor. His phone was of little interest to him—he'd run out of data on his PAYG SIM days ago—so he switched the TV on and stared at the news channel until sleep claimed him again.

Dawn the next morning found him alone in the deli, taking deliveries and setting up for the breakfast rush. Despite sleeping most of Sunday away, his legs were still dead weights, and he was practically on his knees when he sensed a familiar presence behind him.

Dylan.

Angelo turned slowly, half convinced his exhaustion-addled brain was playing a cruel trick, but for once the universe was on his side, and Dylan's tentative smile felt like a light summer rain. "Hey."

Dylan's grin amped up a notch. "Hey. I wasn't sure if you'd be pleased to see me."

"Why would you think that?"

Dylan shrugged. "Stalker, remember?"

"I followed you to the club on Saturday."

"What? Literally?"

"Well . . . no, but you said you'd be there, and I wouldn't have gone otherwise."

"No?" Dylan leaned forward with his elbows on the table.

"That's odd, 'cause I've been asking around about you, and apparently 'Angel'—that is you, right?—is a man of extremes. You either disappear for months on end or show your face every week."

"How do you know I'm not in a disappearing phase?"

"Because you hadn't been seen all year before the first night we met."

"First night we met, eh?" That was one way of describing it. Angelo's arms throbbed with a darkly familiar pain, but convincing himself that it was a hangover from holding Dylan against the wall had got him out of bed that morning. "Well, I'd go back to the stalker bullshit if I could be bothered, but if I'd had the time, I'd have asked around about *you*, so I guess I can't complain."

"I'm too intrigued to care if you complain or not."

"Intrigued?" The door opened behind Dylan. Angelo glared at the potential customer, willing them to fuck off already so he could lose himself in a conversation that was making him hot all over. "There ain't much about me to be intrigued about. Fucking in the club is my jam, and I'm a miserable bastard in real life."

"Are you? Or has life kicked you in the nuts?"

Dylan stepped aside without waiting for an answer, and with a cruel twist of fate, the customer behind him had a long list of orders for the estate agent's office down the road. Filling them took the best part of fifteen minutes, and by the time Angelo was finished, Dylan was gone.

He trudged home that evening in a warped funk—torn between the buzz of Dylan's unexpected visit and the reality that whatever was simmering between them would likely fizzle out once Dylan realised that Angelo was a disaster in just about every way possible. Besides, it wasn't like he had plans to stick around. Convincing his mother to sell the deli would take time, but as soon as it was done, Angelo was gone. Where to, he had no idea, but Romford was as dead to him as Silvio Giordano.

In the garage, he found a stack of debt collection letters and a bowl of rigatoni ready for him to chuck in the microwave. It was about as close to an apology as his mother ever got, but he couldn't stomach it. He tossed it in the bin with the letters, bowl and all, and went to bed.

The next morning, Dylan was waiting for him on the street with the morning papers.

"Wow. Okay. Maybe you are a stalker after all." Angelo unlocked the deli and waved Dylan inside. "Did you want something? Or are you just checking I haven't topped myself?"

"Why would I think you'd do that?"

Angelo shrugged and started pulling stools from the tables. "You've got that look that social workers give you when your school tells them you're depressed, and I haven't exactly shown you my happy side."

"Do you have one?"

"I did once."

Dylan lifted a stool from the table. "Where did it go?"

"Dunno. But I do want to know why you're here." He gestured at Dylan's metal tee and jeans combo. "You're clearly not working, so why are you even awake?"

"I like early mornings."

"Freak."

"Yup. But you already knew that."

It was true, but what little Angelo knew about Dylan had nothing to do with daylight. "Seriously. Why are you here?"

Dylan took the last stool from the last table. "I don't know, to be honest. You looked like shit yesterday—"

"Thanks."

"—so I was worried that Saturday wasn't as good for you as it was for me. And then I realised how fucking self-absorbed that was and figured there might be something actually wrong . . . you know, something real."

This rambling version of Dylan was nothing like the poised professional Angelo had met in the debt interview, and he was glad of it. The brief, random moments he'd spent with him outside of the club were like another world, and the bullshit that had brought them together seemed a lifetime away. Angelo smiled and drifted to the kitchen, trusting that Dylan would follow.

He couldn't describe how he felt when Dylan trailed him and hopped up on the counter, lounging there like he'd done it a thousand times over. *Christ, I could fuck him right now.* And the sensation briefly won the battle raging in his treacherous body.

But Dylan's fast sobering expression ruined it all. "So . . . ," he pressed. "Are you okay? We're not supposed to discuss your financial stuff anymore, but I can listen if you want to talk?"

Angelo scowled. Despite Dylan's assurances that he could get his personal debt wiped, a phone call from the shitty Romford office had fucked it all up, and the looming prospect of bankruptcy was the last thing he wanted to talk about. "I don't want to talk about that."

"Okay."

The defeat in Dylan's voice did odd things to Angelo's gut. He paused in the process of retrieving ciabatta loaves from the freezer and went to him, positioning himself between Dylan's thighs with little conscious thought. "I don't want to talk about it because I'm not in the headspace right now. Maybe we can another time?"

"If you want to. We can pretend it's not happening if it makes you feel better. I'm not your advisor anymore."

"And you only were for about five minutes, right?"

"Right." Dylan licked his lips as Angelo leaned closer. "Now I'm just a playmate."

Playmate. In recent years, they'd been the closest relationships Angelo had forged, but something—*everything*—was different about Dylan. The man who'd waited for him in the club wasn't the same man who gazed at him now, and Angelo had no idea what to do next. His heart screamed at him to kiss Dylan, to wrap his arms around him and chase down the warmth Dylan's presence had teased him with so far, but then what? Dylan was the sun, but Angelo was dead inside.

A delivery driver pounding on the back door broke the spell. Angelo drew back as Dylan stared holes in him, unable to look away until he wrenched the door open.

A stack of fresh fruit and vegetables awaited him. He signed the invoice, mentally calculating how much he'd need to take today to honour it, and shut the door.

Dylan appeared at his side. "What do you do with all this?"

"Wash it. Cut it. Put it on the plates and in the bags."

"With the paninis?"

Angelo cut a glance at Dylan. "Yes. Why?"

"Because you open in half an hour, and I'm guessing that you don't have time to prepare all this and do everything else by yourself unless you have someone coming in to help you?"

Angelo rolled his eyes. "Like who? I've pretty much banished my mum, and you know we can't afford to pay any extra staff."

"That's what I thought." Dylan took his wallet, keys, and phone from his pocket and set them on a nearby shelf. "Pass me an apron. I'll give you a hand."

Angelo would've been less surprised if Dylan had suggested they fuck in the freezer, but shock could be a wonderful thing, and he passed Dylan an apron before he'd truly comprehended what was happening.

For the next half hour, they worked in companionable silence. Well, Dylan worked. Angelo meandered around the deli, completing jobs he rarely had time for, all the while watching Dylan move around the kitchen like he was some kind of angelic apparition.

"You've worked in a kitchen before."

It wasn't a question, but Dylan nodded anyway. "I've helped my mate at his café in Vauxhall before. Spent all summer there when I was a student."

"Is this the mate whose calls you won't answer?"

A guilty flush crept up Dylan's neck. "For your information, I called him back, but it seems he doesn't want to talk to *me* now."

Angelo couldn't imagine why anyone wouldn't want to talk to Dylan, but he kept quiet as he claimed the cured meats Dylan had prepared and took them out to the service counter. After all, he barely knew the man. Perhaps he was as much of an arsehole as Angelo.

Right. Like that's even possible.

Angelo started the coffee machine, checked the milk supplies, and unlocked the front door. He went back to the kitchen, expecting to find Dylan getting ready to leave, but found him scrutinising the ancient recipe cards tacked to the walls. "Are these still current?"

"Um, I suppose? Can't say I've looked at them since I was about six."

"But your menu is the same, right? That's your hook . . . that it's been the same for fifty years?"

"Something like that, though we upgraded the panini press about a decade ago."

If Dylan heard the bitterness lacing Angelo's words, it didn't show. He took a last look at the recipes and then retied his apron. "Good, then I should be able to help you serve. You'll have to teach me the coffee machine later, but I can handle a panini press."

"Are you serious?"

Dylan shrugged. "As serious as I am about anything when

I'm not at work or getting my dick sucked at Lovato's. You need help, and I'm free. If we're going to be friends, it stands to reason that I should do you a solid."

"Who said we were going to be friends?"

Dylan picked up the last tray of tomatoes and swept past Angelo into the deli. "I did, sunshine. Now come and show me how to turn this thing on."

IT WAS PROBABLY the most bizarre Monday Angelo had ever lived through. Dylan moved like a whirlwind, working the panini press, clearing tables, and washing up things that hadn't been washed in months, while Angelo looked on. Working with Theresa drove him up the wall, but with Dylan's help, the day was like a holiday.

It was gone three by the time Angelo forced himself to make Dylan go home. "You've rocked my world, but I can't let you work for free. That shit ain't right."

Dylan smiled. "I enjoyed it. Being stuck in an office all day is making me old."

"Spend a week here, then talk to me about feeling old."

"Would that help?"

"Fuck no." Angelo shook his head before Dylan could start getting any ideas. "It might get me home before seven, but my conscience would kill me. Thanks, mate, but you've done enough."

Dylan let it go and took his apron off. He folded it into a complicated triangle that looked like it belonged in a hotel and set it on the counter. Angelo passed him his wallet, phone, and keys, and Dylan pocketed them absently, his gaze distant as he chewed on his lip.

Angelo pinched Dylan's cheek, his thumb lingering for

longer than was entirely necessary. "What are you scowling about?"

"I'm not scowling."

"No?" Angelo gave in and let his fingers ease the frown lines from Dylan's usually sunny face. "Why do you look like a Chihuahua chewing a wasp then?"

"It's bulldog chewing a wasp, dickhead."

Angelo grinned. "Yeah, but you're too small to be a bulldog."

Dylan's arms gently circled Angelo's waist. "Says you."

It was Angelo's turn to glower. He was taller than Dylan by a mere inch, and they were evenly matched in weight, though Angelo's muscles were more defined . . . for now. Until that moment, he hadn't given much thought to the aesthetic consequences his inactivity would have on his body, but with Dylan so close, and so fucking beautiful, vanity kicked him square in the gut.

He let his hands drop and stepped out of Dylan's personal space. "Thanks for today. Not having to play nice with customers has done me a world of good."

"Yeah, I can see that peopling gets on your nerves."

Angelo snorted. "You're being kind. It's a wonder I've never decked anyone during the lunchtime rush. Hungry yuppies get on my tits."

"Hmm, well, your people skills work just fine with me."

The vague innuendo nearly sent Angelo straight back to the hypnotic haven of Dylan's loose embrace, but the sound of the front door opening brought him to his senses. He left Dylan alone and mechanically brewed cappuccinos while Dylan waited in the kitchen, but on the fourth jug of frothy milk, he sensed Dylan leaving. The backdoor closing was another kick to his gut, and it wasn't until he found Dylan's note on the fridge that an alien thrill of another impromptu encounter returned.

Here's my number. Call me.

DYLAN SWITCHED his phone to silent and set it face down on the beer-slick table. Logic told him to jam it in his pocket and forget about it, but he wasn't quite there yet. His phone had been ringing all day . . . and he'd been ignoring it all day. The party line was that he was at work and unable to take personal calls, but the truth was that he had no desire to speak to his dad, his landlord, Sam, or, indeed, anyone that wasn't Angelo. *Fuck that noise.*

And of course Angelo hadn't called since they'd spent the day together at the deli on Monday, and given that it was Friday now, it didn't seem likely that he would. Which had left Dylan in the worst mood ever—an unfortunate thing for his long list of clients. And for his bank balance when he'd ditched a solitary train ride home in favour of hitting the pub. A few Friday night pints had seemed like a good idea then, but by the time eight o'clock had rolled past, taking the last bastion of his sobriety with it, he'd changed his fucking mind.

Shame he couldn't undrink four pints and an ill-advised round of Sambuca shots, though he was kind of glad for the booze buffer when a familiar hand closed around his shoulder some time between should've gone home o'clock and fuck it, let's get wasted hour. "Go away, Sam," Dylan slurred.

"Right. 'Cause that's how it fucking works."

Sam's trademark growl had nothing on Angelo's perfect contradiction of smoothness and grit, but it compelled odd feelings in Dylan all the same. He allowed Sam to tow him outside and dump him on a nearby bench and then looked up with a sneer that Sam would be proud of. "What brings you here, sweet friend?"

"What do you think?" Sam's expression was hard. "You've been playing cat and mouse with me for weeks, and I needed to make sure you were okay."

"You couldn't just stalk my Facebook like a normal person?"

"I'm not a teenage girl. You could've just answered the phone."

"I called you back."

"Once. At nine o'clock in the morning when you knew I'd be at work."

Dylan rolled his eyes, aware that he was being a prick but somehow unable to stop. "What's your point?"

Sam's glare burned nuclear. "Are you taking the piss?"

"No, mate. I'm deadly serious about this fucking ridiculous conversation. It's not like I haven't told you that I want some space."

"You didn't tell me shit. You told Eddie."

"Same thing."

"Is it? Last time I checked, we were still individuals, and it ain't Eddie you've been best mates with for all these years."

Reality began to creep into Dylan's drunken haze. In the rare moments when he hadn't been obsessing over Angelo, he'd felt guilty for explaining himself to Sam through his girlfriend, but not enough to do anything about it—like pick up the phone.

He stared at Sam, suddenly hit by all that they'd shared, good and bad. They'd worked together at Sam's grandfather's greasy spoon and cried together when Sam's beloved grandmother had finally died. They'd partied all over London—Sam keeping Dylan company on the many, *many* nights he just *couldn't* sleep—and survived the times Dylan had scraped Sam off the kitchen floor and nursed him out of a diabetic coma. Didn't Sam deserve better than a second-hand phone call? "I'm sorry."

Some of the fight left Sam and he sank onto the bench beside Dylan. "I don't want you to be sorry, I want you to be okay. You know I'd never hurt you, don't you?"

"Of course." It was true. Sam had never lied to Dylan or led him on. Dylan had walked into everything that had happened between them with his eyes open. "I'm just not as okay with it as I used to be."

"Why not?"

Now there was a question. Dylan wrestled with his beer-addled brain and tried to verbalise a coherent answer. "I guess seeing you and Eddie so happy reminds me of what I don't have."

"You want a girlfriend?"

Dylan shrugged. "I'm more into lads at the moment, but I do know that I'm pretty tired of sleeping alone."

"Then stop banging people in sex clubs and get out into the real world—"

"Hey—"

"Don't." Sam held up his hand. "You always end up going mad in that place when you've got a cob on about shit, so don't even try to deny it."

"You sound mad northern right now."

"I'm from Leeds. Deal with it." Sam ditched the fierceness he'd arrived with. "Look, I get what you're saying, okay? And you know there's been times when I've wished things were different, but I can't change who I am."

"I know that. I've never asked you to."

"Then what do you want from me?"

"Nothing."

"Nothing?"

Dylan shrugged again. "Well, I suppose I could go for some pierogi next time Pops is making some."

Sam's glower returned like it had never been gone. "That's not what I meant."

"I know, but it's all I have right now, and I'm hungry, so . . ."

Sam sighed, defeat seeping out of him like smoke from a dying fire. "If I buy you a kebab, will you promise to stop dodging my calls? I respect that you need to take a step back, but I can't handle worrying about you. You're my best mate, and I miss you."

"I miss you too." Another inconvenient truth. It would've been easier if Sam had rejected him, turned him down that first time they'd shared a drunken kiss, and they'd never spoken of it again. But it hadn't played out that way. Sam was the best friend Dylan had ever had, and life without him was *hard*. "Can we get battered sausages instead?"

Sam finally smiled. "Sure."

* * *

IT WAS the wanker side of midnight by the time Dylan made it home from Stratford. After a sneaky fried dinner with Sam, they'd taken the scenic route to the station via a few more pubs. At moments, it had felt like old times—like nothing had changed—but when they'd parted ways, they'd both seemed to know that it would be longer than two weeks before they saw each other again.

At home, Dylan threw himself onto his bed. His night had taken an unexpected turn, and despite sinking even more beer after Sam had tracked him down in his favourite Stratford haunt, he felt surprisingly sober. *Fuck my life.*

Restless, he rolled over and pulled his phone from his pocket to stop it digging into his hip. That he'd remembered to grab it from the wet table before Sam had yanked him out of the pub was a miracle, and he hadn't looked at it since. If he had, he'd have seen the three missed calls from Sam and one from an unknown number.

Dylan sat up, his heart turning a sudden, drunken cartwheel in his chest. He'd used his phone for business when he'd worked at the bank and still got calls from random overseas numbers, but this was a UK mobile number. *Angelo?* Dylan didn't fancy the disappointment if it turned out to be Nanna pocket dialling him from an ancient handset she'd bought on eBay, but hope still started a rave in his veins.

He swiped at his phone and brought up the call log. The number taunted him and his thumb pressed CALL of its own accord. Stomach in his mouth, Dylan activated the speaker and stretched out on his front, his chin on his folded arms. It occurred to him far too late that it was after midnight, and the line crackled to life before he could correct his mistake.

"Yeah?"

Dylan's breath escaped him in a whoosh. "Angelo? Is that you?"

"Um . . . yeah, I think so. I just woke up, so it's hard to tell."

"Shit. Sorry." Dylan cringed and grabbed his phone. "I can ring back tomorrow—"

"Nah, it's all right." Angelo cut him off and then yawned before he went on. "I was kinda hoping you'd call."

"Yeah?"

"Yeah. It's been a long week, and, uh, is it weird that I've missed you?"

Warmth spread through Dylan from his scalp to his toes. "Maybe, but that makes me a weirdo too, because I've missed you."

"It doesn't feel like we've only met six times."

"Wow. Is that all it is?" Dylan rolled over and dropped his phone on his chest. "Are we counting the club?"

"It'd be four without it."

The mere thought of their club encounters sent Dylan into overdrive. His skin tingled and heat flooded his groin. "I guess numbers don't mean much."

"Not in this context."

Absorbed as he was by his Angelo-themed buzz, Dylan picked up the bleakness lacing Angelo's tone. "I shouldn't ask if you've heard from the DRO advisor."

"So don't."

"Um, okay?"

Angelo sighed. "Sorry. I'm just sick of thinking about it. I took my mum to that business advice centre today, and they told her she should sell the house and downsize if she wants to keep the deli, and she basically had a fucking breakdown. She doesn't seem to understand that this is the last chance she'll have to make the decisions herself."

"Is there enough equity in the house to bail out the deli?"

"And then some. She could get a bungalow down the road and forget all about it."

"What about you? Where would you live? I'm assuming you'd still run the deli for her if she paid the debts off?"

"It was never my plan to stick around, but it's not like I've got anything else to do."

"And you could hire some staff?"

"I'd have to. Working it on my own is fucking killing me."

Dylan didn't doubt it. His impromptu shift at Giordano's had been *busy*, and he couldn't imagine how Angelo coped by himself at the weekends. "Do you think she'll sell the house?"

"After this morning? Not a chance in hell."

"Damn. So what are you going to do?"

Angelo didn't respond straight away. Dylan listened to him breathe and closed his eyes. If the context of their conversation had been different, Angelo's gentle exhales could've sent him to sleep. Maybe. If sleeping was something that ever came that easy. As it was, Dylan settled for a gentle meditation and wondered if his heart was beating in time with Angelo's.

"So . . . ," Angelo said.

Dylan opened his eyes. "Hmm? Sorry, I mean . . . yeah?"

"Are you drunk?"

Was he? He'd felt pretty sober when he'd come home, but Angelo's voice did strange things to him. Had done since the very first time. *Huh.* Perhaps he was drunk on Angelo.

The thought made him chuckle. "I've had a few," he said when he'd composed himself. "I'm not twatted, but if you need financial advice, we should probably talk again in the morning."

"I didn't call you to talk about that."

Relief warred with concern. "No? Well, you can, if you ever need to. I can't give you professional guidance, but I can be your friend."

"Is that what we are? Friends?"

And then some. But Dylan couldn't define the pull he felt for Angelo, the ache in his bones when they were apart, and the crazy-hot current when they were together. "We can try. Though I should warn you . . . apparently I'm not too good at separating friendship from fucking, so . . ."

"Are you talking about the BFF again?"

"How did you guess?"

"Because you get all melancholy and shit whenever he comes up."

"Jealous?"

"Curious, actually."

"Why?"

"'Cause you fuck like a fella who's trying to get something out of his system."

"Says you."

Angelo chuckled darkly. "Okay. Let's not go there, eh? Seems like we've both got some ghosts to escape."

"And friends can help each other out with that, right?"

"Yes. They can have dinner together too . . . I mean, if you fancy it?"

Dylan fancied more than just dinner, but it seemed a healthy place to start. He arranged to meet Angelo at Giordano's after closing time the next day, and they exchanged slightly awkward goodbyes. When Angelo had hung up, Dylan stared at his darkened phone screen, like he could see through it to Angelo's brooding eyes and lose himself in them. They'd set their date for early evening, but Saturday was club night, in Dylan's nocturnal life, at least. Would Angelo want to go to Lovato's after?

The possibility excited and horrified Dylan in equal measure. A dirty night out with Angelo set him on fire, but could he watch Angelo fuck someone else? Turn them inside out with his dick while Dylan stepped aside? He had no right to think not, but as he closed his eyes in the hope of at least a few hours sleep, he was sure of nothing but the fact that the prospect of seeing Angelo again, in any capacity, had given him a near permanent boner.

CHAPTER SIX

ANGELO CAST a critical eye over the makeshift picnic he'd cobbled together and regretted being so honest with the first woman he'd spoken to at Stratford Citizens Advice Bureau. If he hadn't made that damn phone call, then Dylan wouldn't know that he didn't have a pot to piss in, and perhaps Angelo could've found a way to take him on a real date.

Date. Right. You think he's gonna stick around when the best you can offer him is a fucking cheese sandwich?

A knock at the door interrupted whatever despairing cynicism was coming next. Angelo took a deep breath and untied his apron before approaching the locked deli doors like they were the only thing between him and an unexploded bomb. The prospect of seeing Dylan had kept him upright through a brutal Saturday lunchtime, but now he was here, Angelo's efforts to make the walk across town worthwhile seemed pretty pathetic.

The temptation to hide in the freezer was strong, but his phone rang in his hand before he could duck away from the front door. *Dylan.* Angelo answered the call with a swipe of his thumb. "Hold up. I'm coming."

"Come quicker."

"Brat."

"Only for you."

Angelo ended the call and unlocked the door.

On the other side, Dylan was leaning against the wall, looking a lot more sober than he'd sounded the previous day, though his shadowed eyes told the tale of a late night. "All right, mate?"

"Am now." Angelo found a smile from somewhere and plastered it on, and the longer he stared at Dylan, absorbing his silky soft hair and spirited gaze, the easier it was to hold on to. "Come in."

Dylan slipped past him into the deli. "Oh wow. You made food?"

"It's just some leftovers really. We can—"

"Fuck no. We're staying in." Dylan zeroed in on the antipasti Angelo had laid out and popped a green olive into his mouth. "I was going to suggest pizza, but this is so much better. I was drooling over these artichokes the other day."

Dylan's enthusiasm was so heartfelt that Angelo couldn't contain his widening grin. Truth be told, he was sick to death of Italian food and everything it represented to him, but he'd eat a bazillion marinated tomatoes if it made Dylan smile like that. "There's not much focaccia left, but we can make paninis if you like?"

"Prosciutto and mozzarella? With basil and anchovies?"

Angelo laughed. "Sure. Whatever you want."

And like magic, any awkwardness that might've hung over them faded away. Dylan ate everything Angelo put in front of him and encouraged Angelo to eat far more than he would've if he'd been alone.

"You're going to make me fat," he muttered, patting his stomach.

Dylan's gaze lingered on Angelo's abdomen. "Doubt it, mate. Your body is awesome."

The ever-present fatigue in Angelo's muscles begged to

differ, but he pushed the shadows away. "It's all leftover from my dancing days. I don't know how much longer it will stick around."

"You don't dance at all anymore?"

Angelo shook his head. "I don't have time."

It was mostly true. There were studios around Romford that he could've trained at, but arsing around in front of a mirror would never be the same as performing on stage, and he didn't even want it to be. The days when he could barely move were easier to take when he wasn't missing as much.

Dylan seemed to accept his half answer as he stole the last slice of salami and wrapped it around a caramelised pear. He studded it with Gorgonzola and popped it in his mouth and then speared Angelo with a curious gaze.

Angelo shifted in his seat. Dylan was the master of small talk, but he was sometimes at his loudest when he said nothing at all. "Fuck's sake," Angelo growled. "What?"

"Just wondering."

"Wondering *what?*"

"What you look like when you're dancing. I mean, you move like a lion, so I know you're graceful as fuck, but I'm trying to picture you with your legs all pointing up in the air or something, and I can't."

Neither could Angelo anymore, but he understood Dylan's curiosity. Previous lovers had always been intrigued by his profession and fascinated by the things his healthy body could do. "I'm pretty flexible, or at least I can be when I'm fit, and I'm strong too. Male dancers do a lot of lifting."

Dylan nodded slowly, still chewing. "That makes sense. The way you threw me around in the club had me looking out for some giant, hairy bear."

"Giant?" Angelo laughed and it chased away some of the tension in his shoulders. "You think only big men can be strong?"

"Not anymore."

The sudden heat in Dylan's eyes went straight to Angelo's pulse, quickening it and warming his blood so fast that it roared in his ears. The urge to jump Dylan was overwhelming, but he swallowed it. Choked on it. And slid from his stool. Tight jeans were no good for stretching, but the pair he wore were so old that they had little resistance left. He braced himself and then cautiously lifted his foot from the floor. Extending his leg was easier than he expected, and lengthening it out felt *good*—natural—and the ease with which he stretched it up and behind his head surprised even him.

Dylan's expression was a fucking cartoon. "Wow. That's incredible."

"Not really." Angelo held the pose until his abandoned muscles protested and then slowly returned his leg to earth. "I've been doing that since I was nine."

"Still wow. I can barely do the Macarena."

"I did a show in Barcelona a few years ago that included those moves."

Dylan laughed, then his expression turned curious again. "Did you travel a lot when you were dancing?"

"Yeah. Europe, mainly, until I got the gig in New York." Angelo reclaimed his seat. "I didn't appreciate it, though. You don't when you think something is going to last forever."

Dylan rested his elbows on the counter and cupped his chin in his hands. He'd grown a slight beard since Angelo had last seen him, and it suited him, setting off his grungy T-shirt and the skull pendant hanging around his neck. Dylan seemed to be more metal every time Angelo saw him, and today he looked like a rock star.

"What's your deal with the club?" Dylan asked. "I know I've only, uh, seen you there twice, but you're a different person there."

The last part wasn't a question, but Dylan was so on the

money that Angelo nodded. "It's a release for me . . . a healthy one. I'm a miserable git, in case you hadn't noticed, but playing at the club gives me some control back."

"Has it always been that way?"

"Nah. When I first went there, it was because I'm a bit of a perv."

"Makes two of us." Dylan licked his lips, and the air between them thickened again, heavy with the weight of what had brought them together three weeks ago in bunker five.

Angelo's world narrowed to Dylan and the way he'd felt clamped around Angelo's dick. He sucked in a breath as Dylan leaned forward but pulled away milliseconds before their lips touched. "I need a drink."

He stood and went to the till and rummaged in the cabinet below. The grappa was exactly where his father had left it, the bulbous shot glasses stacked beside it. He retrieved the bottle and two glasses and slid them across the counter.

Dylan picked up the bottle and studied the label. "Grappa, eh? I haven't drunk this stuff since a staff jolly to Athens a few years ago."

"Citizens Advice has office parties in Greece?"

Dylan chuckled. "No, we barely have teabags. I worked in banking before I joined CA. Still in the debt sector, but it was less compassionate and pretty fucking oppressive. I ditched it a few years ago."

"I'm glad."

"Yeah?"

"Uh-huh. I want you to be happy."

Dylan stared, and for a fleeting moment, Angelo wished the ground would swallow him whole, but then Dylan reached out and covered Angelo's hand with his own. "I want you to be happy too."

Why? But Angelo didn't say it. Reeling from the sensation of Dylan's palm on his knuckles, he used his free hand to thumb the cork out of the grappa bottle and pour two meaty measures.

He passed one to Dylan. "Bottoms up."

Dylan smirked and brought the glass to his lips, and any hope that Angelo may have had of lowering the temperature in the room was dashed as Dylan's throat worked to swallow the fiery liquor.

I want to fuck his mouth.

As if Angelo had spoken aloud, Dylan dropped his glass on the counter and tightened his fingers around Angelo's. "So . . . are we gonna take this date to the club, or what?"

"You want to?"

Dylan shrugged. "I wasn't sure when I thought about it earlier, but I think it would be good for us. There's a lot going on. Let's clear the air."

That Dylan already understood how Angelo's convoluted brain worked made Angelo's soul sing. Could they play in the club and build on whatever was brewing between them in real life? With anyone else, Angelo would've called it a day weeks ago, but Dylan wasn't like anyone else he'd ever hooked up with. The way their worlds had combined was bizarre but somehow felt right. "I really did just intend on feeding you dinner."

"And you have," Dylan said with an impish grin. "Now come up the road and feed me your cock."

***

DYLAN'S SKIN tingled as he dried himself off from the shower in Lovato's opulent bathroom. He'd left Angelo at the bar already turning heads. And Dylan couldn't blame the potential playmates who'd zeroed in on Angelo the moment they'd entered the club. Angelo was beautiful any day of the week, but something had shifted in him as they'd stepped over the threshold—his shoulders had squared and his chin had risen, and there was a confidence in him that was lacking in the outside world. In the club, Angelo became *Angel*, and Dylan couldn't wait to play with him.

If someone else hasn't got there first . . .

But his fears proved groundless when he returned to the bar. Angelo was alone and nursing an amber shot of Jack Daniels.

Dylan swiped it and knocked it back, letting the burn seep into his bones, stoking a fire that was already well lit. He cast a glance around the club. It had filled up while he'd been in the shower, and it was pumping now. The music had been ramped up, and the moans of nearby playmates barely carried over the sultry dubstep beats. Dylan bought more drinks and slid one Angelo's way.

Angelo stared at it. Dylan nudged him. "What's wrong?"

"I can't buy you one back. I only had a tenner in my pocket."

"But you paid for me to get in," Dylan protested. "That's worth a couple of bevvies."

A ghost of a smirk threatened Angelo's earnest expression. "I didn't pay. Perks of being an ex-employee."

Dylan cast his gaze around the club again, picturing Angelo weaving among the tangles of writhing bodies, delivering drinks, and clearing glasses. Clocking off early and joining the fray. He hadn't been sure how he'd feel about watching Angelo play with someone else, but now that they were in the club, it was all he could think about. Getting fucked in the basement rooms had sated Dylan's darkest fantasies, but there was more—always, always more. He'd felt Angel rise in Angelo, but he hadn't *seen* it. *I need to see it.*

At this time of night, the club's dance floor was basically a blowjob pit. Cast in shadows from the colourful spotlights, Dylan couldn't see much, but a hot bloke going to town on a fat dick caught his eye. The dude had skills, and Dylan wondered how he'd look with his lips wrapped around Angelo's cock. How *Angelo* would look as he got deep throated.

The man finished up with his playmate a little while later. Dylan sidled closer to Angelo, who was playing his role of the quiet brooding top to perfection. "You wanna play?"

"With you?"

Dylan jerked his head at the man who was meandering vaguely in their direction. "And him. I wanna see him suck you."

Angelo raised an eyebrow and necked his drink. "What are you going to do?"

"Watch. Touch. That okay with you?"

"Are you going to let me fuck you after?"

"I'd imagine so?"

"Then you'd better wave him over."

The man seemed to be heading towards them now anyway. Dylan chanced brushing a kiss to Angelo's neatly stubbled jaw and then turned his attention to the approaching man. He took a step away from Angelo and slipped seamlessly into the other dude's personal space. "Hey. What's your name?"

"Rhys," the man replied without hesitation. "You?"

"Dylan. And this is my friend—" Dylan tugged Angelo forward—"Angelo. Would you like to join us?"

The pleasantries didn't last long. Rhys was clearly an experienced player, and he was on his knees within a few minutes.

Dylan plastered himself to Angelo's side as Rhys swallowed Angelo's cock. He pulled Angelo's shirt over his head and then fused his lips to Angelo's left nipple. The quickening thud of Angelo's heart echoed in his ear, and as he bit down, Angelo's answering groan sent him into overdrive. He stripped his own clothes and moved around Angelo. *God, I want to fuck him.* But he dampened the craving—for now—and dropped down beside Rhys. "Care to share?"

Rhys treated him to a wet grin. "Have at it."

Dylan didn't need telling twice. He claimed his place at Angelo's feet, and Angelo tasted *amazing*. Dylan slid his mouth up and down, flicking his tongue like a precome-crazed lizard, and it was only the need for oxygen that forced him to pull back.

He drew his mouth from Angelo with a *pop* and gazed up at him. Angelo returned his stare, his eyes hooded as Rhys feverishly sucked his cock, his cheeks stained with a heady flush. He leaned back on the bar and raised an eyebrow, the challenge clear. *What ya got next for me?*

Dylan smirked. *Wait and see.*

He stood and relished the distant buzz that came with the sensation of dozens of eyes on him. The thrill of being watched wasn't as sharp as it had been when he'd first come to the club a few years ago, but he made a show of retrieving a condom from his jeans anyway—for Angelo, as much as their audience.

Angelo's eyes widened, and Dylan winked, even as his pulse jumped in anticipation of what he'd had in mind since he'd spotted Rhys sucking cock on the other side of the room.

Dylan tugged Rhys to his feet and brought his lips to his ear. "Can I fuck you?"

Biting down on his slick bottom lip, Rhys nodded. "Condom?"

Dylan dangled the rubber between them. Rhys plucked it from his fingers and took Dylan's hand, leading him to a nearby couch. The leather was cool against Dylan's heated palms as he bent Rhys over the arm of the sofa. He closed his eyes and imagined that he was sliding his dick into Angelo. His balls jumped, and his soul cried out for the man he was fast becoming utterly infatuated with.

Like Dylan had called his name, Angelo was suddenly behind him, his chest to his back, urging Dylan on as he started to fuck Rhys with long, hard strokes, giving Rhys everything he craved from Angelo.

"Yeah," Angelo murmured. "I've been dreaming of

watching you fuck someone, and you're even hotter than I thought you'd be."

Consumed by Rhys clenching tight around his dick, Dylan didn't have it in him to be so coherent. He pulled out of Rhys and tugged him over onto his back. He drove inside him again, and Rhys threw his head back. "Fuck!"

Angelo chuckled and smacked Dylan's arse. "Damn, my dick's so hard I'm gonna bust all up your back while you fuck him."

Dylan imagined Angelo's hot come splattering on his skin and a bolt of raw pleasure shot through him. He threw a hand out and clawed at Angelo's muscular thigh. "Do your worst."

Angelo made an appreciative noise in Dylan's ear and then disappeared, taking his leg—and all that was tying Dylan down to the world—with him. Dylan clenched his teeth and fucked Rhys faster, bending over him so that their sweat-slicked chests slid together.

"Where did your friend go?"

"Dunno," Dylan gritted out. "He—"

But Angelo returned before he could finish, pressed up against the backs of Dylan's legs, his slicked, condom-covered cock probing Dylan's hole. The intrusion was sudden, and it *burned*, and the pain was everything. A sharp cry escaped Dylan and he fell forward as Angelo chased him down and seized his hips, fucking into him and pushing him deeper into Rhys.

The sensation of Angelo taking control and fucking them both was mind-blowing. His rhythm started slow but built to a rough ride. Dylan matched his pace, and Rhys came quickly, shooting on his belly before rolling away.

Dylan was absently aware of his goodbye kiss, but with Angelo still nailing him, it didn't resonate. He bent his legs to take Angelo deeper. Angelo hit his prostate and all bets were off. Dylan moaned and clutched uselessly at the leather sofa. "Harder."

"What was that?"

"*Harder.*" Dylan grabbed Angelo's leg again, pulling him impossibly closer. "Make me come."

A gravelly groan escaped Angelo. "So fucking hot. I could bang you all night."

I wouldn't stop you. But speech was beyond Dylan. He let go of Angelo's leg and threw his arms out in front of him, flattening his torso and raising his hips. Angelo's response was instant, and the brutal dig of his cock was blinding. The club melted away. White noise filled Dylan's ears and snow obscured his vision. His hole clenched, and the first strains of release rocketed up his spine.

"Jesus Christ!" Angelo steadied him, his voice cracking. "You gonna come?"

Dylan could only gasp and finally—*finally*—grip his own weeping dick and jerk it desperately in sync with Angelo's spearing thrusts.

Heat sluiced through Dylan like a rampant wildfire. He shouted, arching his back, his nerves as tight as an archer's bow, and come shot out of him, spurting all over the already slick couch. "*Oh!*"

The masochist in him cried out for more, and Angelo responded with a flurry of final strokes before he pulled out and ripped off the condom.

Red-hot splatters of come hit Dylan's back. Angelo's guttered exclamations were half drowned out by the carnival going on in Dylan's senses, but Dylan absorbed every grunt and moan like they were his own and was pretty much catatonic by the time Angelo yanked him upright, wrapping his arms around Dylan's trembling body so tightly that Dylan forgot how to breathe.

"Open your eyes," Angelo whispered. Dylan obeyed, and

Angelo's strong hand gripped his chin, his fingers digging into Dylan's jaw, nails scratching through the fine layer of fair stubble. "Look . . . everyone's watching."

Dylan stared at the dozens of eyes trained on him. Where their rapt attention had seemed distant before, now it seeped into him, throwing a last handful of kindling on the fading flames. He searched for Rhys but couldn't find him in the dancing shadows of the club. Would he recognise him after tonight? Did it matter? As Angelo bit down on his earlobe, he lost the ability to decide.

The heat faded eventually. Angelo half carried Dylan to the showers and washed him like they'd been lovers for years while Dylan stared, mesmerised, and tracked a bead of water as it trickled down Angelo's strong chest. There was so much he wanted to say, but he didn't speak a word until they were dressed and outside. "Are you hungry? I could murder some dodgy chicken."

Angelo shook his head. "I'm pretty much done for the night."

"You sure?" Dylan tried to temper the flare of disappointment. "King Chook is on our way home?"

"On *your* way home, maybe."

Angelo's expression was hard to gauge, and he didn't give Dylan much chance to try before he dropped his gaze to the floor. They started walking to the junction where they would go their separate ways if Dylan couldn't persuade Angelo to come home with him. Dylan thought about taking Angelo's hand, but it didn't seem to fit. Their only physical contact had been in the club, and away from its safe embrace, Angelo seemed a different man. *Angel* melted away with every step, and Dylan didn't know how to bridge the gap. "Are you sure you're not hungry?"

Silence. Dylan slowed and realised Angelo was already trailing behind. "Angelo?"

"Hmm?" Angelo glanced up from his apparent preoccupation with his shoes. "Sorry, what?"

Dylan stopped walking entirely. "What's the matter?"

"What?"

Dylan reclaimed his place in Angelo's personal space. "What's the *matter*?"

"I'm fine."

"Really? 'Cause you look like you're about to keel over."

Angelo's lovely face twisted into a scowl. "Piss off."

It was nothing Dylan hadn't endured from Sam, but Angelo's sudden change in mood still stung. "Is something wrong?"

"*No.*" Angelo pushed past Dylan and stalked to the taxi rank that was just beyond the junction.

With better ideas in short supply, Dylan followed and joined him at the kerb. "Do you want to share a cab?"

"Nah. I'm going to walk."

"Walk?"

"Yeah. I'm not going the same way as you, remember?"

"Um. Okay. I'll call you soon?"

"Sure."

It would've been easier if Angelo had slapped him. The night they'd shared had been fucking magical, and the cold sullenness marring Angelo's features now made no sense. The date had been his idea, and he hadn't protested when Dylan had suggested moving things to the club. They'd left in high spirits, and nothing had happened to explain Angelo's sharp mood change.

A million questions danced on Dylan's tongue, but the moment to ask them passed as Angelo flagged down a black cab and opened the door, jerking his head for Dylan to get in. *Fuck no.*

Dylan ripped the door from Angelo and slammed it shut. "Are you taking the piss? That's all I get? A club blowout and taxi for one?"

Angelo shrugged, his once-expressive eyes dull and devoid of any emotion. "What do you want? We're not married."

Wanker. Embarrassment washed over Dylan. Had he completely misread this? Had Angelo's only motive for asking him out been a third go-round at the club? Ten minutes ago, Dylan would've been sure that the answer was no, but as Angelo thrust his hands in his pockets, he wasn't sure of anything except the need to get as far away from this bullshit as possible. "You know what, mate? Fuck you."

CHAPTER SEVEN

ANGELO STAGGERED to a nearby bench as Dylan stormed away, his biker boots thudding against the damp pavement, and every step like a kick to Angelo's gut. He watched Dylan disappear into the drizzly night and then dropped his head into his hands.

It was a while before he found the energy to take stock of the fatigue that had hit him like a train the moment he'd stepped outside. The wrong kind of heat had spread up from his toes and into every joint, and suddenly it was all he could do to put one foot in front of the other.

Pathetic. He took a deep, shuddering breath and considered standing up, but the thought of what would come next kept him down. With no money for a cab, his only option was to stumble back to the club and beg Carl for a lift home, but it would be hours before Carl was done working.

So he dropped his head again and fell into the kind of doze unique to the illness that was burying him alive.

"ANGELO? MATE? YOU AWAKE DOWN THERE?"

The unfamiliar voice roused Angelo, and he looked up to find himself staring into the earnest face of the rugby player Dylan had nailed in the club. His name escaped Angelo, but whoever the man was clearly had a better memory.

"Angelo?" he said again. "You okay?"

Angelo licked his dry lips. "I'm fine."

"Sure about that? 'Cause I'm a paramedic with the LAS, and you look like shit."

"LAS?"

"London Ambulance Service."

It didn't mean much to Angelo, and the desire to be left alone gifted him a faint surge of resilience. He found a grin from the pit of his miserable existence and plastered it on his face. "I'm all right, mate. Honest. Just had a skin full."

Dylan's fuck buddy didn't seem convinced, but Angelo had run out of energy to care. He uncurled his aching arms and retrieved his phone and made a show of absorbing himself in absolutely nothing until his would-be rescuer moved on.

Silence enveloped Angelo again. His phone slipped from his fingers and clattered to the ground. He stared at it, searching for the drive to pick it up and see if the screen was cracked, but nothing happened. The throb in his joints amped up, and nausea crept into his dulled consciousness. He straightened his legs and tried to picture them extended and strong, stretched out behind him as he flew through the air. The scenes that came to him seemed a lifetime ago—a lifetime that held someone else's dreams.

"Angelo?"

Angelo blinked. His fatigue-fogged brain had been known to play tricks on him, but never with anything pleasant. He shook his head, and a sound that was somewhere between a groan and a sigh escaped him. As if Dylan would come back for him. As if he'd ever speak to Angelo again, let alone kneel in front of him and take his hands.

"*Angelo*." Dylan squeezed Angelo's hands hard enough to bend the bones. "Seriously, if you don't talk to me, I'm going to get someone from the club, okay? You can't stay here like this."

The white spots obscuring Angelo's vision cleared, and he met Dylan's wide eyes almost by accident. "What?"

"Come on," Dylan said. "Talk to me. You can't just sit here."

Angelo laughed, but the lack of humour in it apparently alarmed Dylan enough for him to scramble to his feet and put his arms around him. The sensation was beautiful, and Angelo leaned into him, chasing down the warmth that skimmed the edge off the cramps seizing his tired muscles.

Dylan held him close for a long moment, his fingertips grazing the back of Angelo's neck with feather-light strokes that almost sent Angelo to sleep, but then he pulled away and took Angelo prisoner with his earnest gaze. "What's *wrong*? Are you ill?"

"I—" Angelo shook his head. "I can't move."

Dylan cupped Angelo's face, his thumbs now working their magic on Angelo's temples. "Why can't you move? Do you need an ambulance?"

"No! No—I just—I need to get home."

"Okay." Dylan released Angelo and stood. He said something that Angelo didn't quite catch and then disappeared.

Angelo slumped down, prepared to accept that he'd never been there at all, but then Dylan was back and draping Angelo's arm around his shoulders and helping him stand.

"There's an Uber over there. If I help you, can you walk?"

Angelo honestly didn't know, but short of spending the night on the bench, he had little choice but to try.

DYLAN UNLOCKED his front door and manoeuvred Angelo inside. The bedroom was the closest place to deposit him, and

Angelo didn't react at all until Dylan had eased him onto the bed.

He gazed around Dylan's bedroom with a bewilderment that made Dylan's heart weep. "I don't live here."

"I know," Dylan said. "But you didn't answer me when I asked you where you do live, so I brought you to my place."

"You know where I live. It's on all those forms I filled in."

"I don't have those forms. I'm not your guy for that anymore, remember? And even when I was, I didn't memorise your exact address."

Angelo braced himself on the bed and leaned forward. Dylan wondered if he was going to be sick, but only a shuddering sigh escaped him. Dylan unzipped his boots and kicked them aside and then went to Angelo and took his hands again. "I can call another cab if you want? Get you home? Or you can stay here for the night and I'll look after you."

"Look after me?"

"Yes—if you'll let me. Whatever's going on, Angelo, you shouldn't be by yourself." Angelo said nothing, and Dylan took his silence as acquiescence. "Lie down, mate. I'll get you a cuppa."

Dylan retreated to the kitchen and pottered around with the kettle, leaving Angelo to acclimatise. He hadn't seemed particularly averse to sleeping in Dylan's bed, but the possibility that he was too fucked up to protest didn't leave Dylan's mind. Absently, he brewed strong sweet tea and took it back to the bedroom with a packet of Jammie Dodgers.

Angelo hadn't moved and was staring at his feet. Dylan set the tea and biscuits on the bedside table and knelt at his feet again. "Need some help?"

"I don't know."

"How about I help you anyway?"

Angelo sighed. "How about the ground just swallows me whole?"

"You've fucked me seven ways from Saturday three times now. The world isn't going to end if I take your shoes off for you. I've got plenty of trackies you can sleep in; we're about the same size."

"Will you stay with me?"

It was Dylan's turn to blink. "Hmm?"

Angelo mauled his bottom lip with his teeth. "I don't want to be in your bed without you."

Dylan hadn't given his own sleeping arrangements much thought, but leaving Angelo alone hadn't crossed his mind either. He squeezed Angelo's leg. "Of course I'll stay."

He helped Angelo out of his shoes and jeans and then dressed them both in soft sweatpants. Crawling into bed together felt a little surreal, but once they were settled—facing each other, hands clasped—reality kicked in, and the reason they were huddled up in Dylan's bed returned in the form of Angelo's soft, pained groan.

"Shh." Dylan rubbed his shoulder. "It's okay."

Angelo shook his head slightly. "It's not."

"It is. Just tell me how to help you."

"You can't help me."

"I can try."

"It won't work."

"You won't convince me of that until you tell me what's wrong."

Angelo closed his eyes. For a while, Dylan took it as his cue to mind his own business, but then Angelo apparently returned to the present with another soft sigh. "I have ME."

"ME?" Dylan's brain worked to recall where he'd heard the term before. "Is that like chronic fatigue syndrome?"

"It's the same, as far as I know. Just a different name."

Dylan scanned his brief encounters with clients who suffered from CFS. He hadn't had one for a while, but the last woman he'd had to visit at home because she'd been unable to get out of bed. "How long have you had it?"

"A year or so. I've got some rare, fucked-up version of it that comes and goes . . . relapsing and something or other. I can't remember." Angelo's words slurred together, and he closed his eyes, his face a study in pained concentration. "Relapsing and remitting. I suppose I'm lucky. Most people with ME are like this all the time."

"Do you feel lucky?"

"Only with you."

Dylan smiled and rolled onto his back, gently coaxing Angelo close enough to lay his head on Dylan's chest. With the lights low and the duvet tucked around them, Angelo finally relaxed. Dylan carded his fingers through his hair and hummed an old Iron Maiden song, and Angelo fell asleep.

IT WAS NEARLY dawn when Dylan eased Angelo off him and slipped out of bed. All night, he'd laid with Angelo and listened to him breathe, all the while itching to grab his phone and google the ever-loving shit out of whatever was making Angelo flinch in his sleep. At six a.m. he could wait no more.

In the kitchen, he boiled the kettle for more tea that no one would drink and logged into his MacBook. The NHS page on CFS/ME came up at the top of the search and he clicked on the link. A list of symptoms for myalgic encephalomyelitis came up: Extreme exhaustion, muscle and joint pain, brain fog—confusion, memory issues, slow thinking—and blurred vision. Migraines, depression, and crippling viral symptoms. Any combination was possible, including all at once, and the list of treatments was woefully short, both in content and success.

Dylan swallowed thickly. Angelo's life was hard enough, but with *this*? Jesus. It was a wonder the man was still standing—*but he isn't standing, is he?* Dylan took a deep breath and clicked on another link, and another, and another, but none made him feel any better. Angelo's condition was brutal and cruel, and even if he recovered from this relapse, another would never be far away. *This can't be it.* But the more Dylan searched, the more disheartened he became, and he gave up in the end and returned to bed.

Angelo hadn't moved, and he didn't stir as Dylan slipped back under the covers. Dylan pulled the duvet up around him and held his hand. *I'm sorry this has happened to you.* But what now? For all the research Dylan had done on Angelo's symptoms, he'd forgotten to look up what he could do to help.

Common sense told him to let Angelo rest for as long as possible, feed him, and keep him hydrated. Comfort him and do whatever he could to make his life easier. But would Angelo let him? Dylan would have to wait for him to wake up before he knew that.

Which didn't happen until midmorning. Dylan was considering breakfast when he felt Angelo's gaze on him. He turned his head and met Angelo's weary stare. "All right?"

Angelo blinked slowly. "I think so."

That he hadn't moved a muscle was telling. Dylan cupped his chin, stroking his cheek with the pad of his thumb. "Do you need some painkillers? I've got some paracetamol floating around somewhere?"

"Allergic. Makes me sick as a dog."

"Ibuprofen?"

"Nah. I can't do NSAIDs anymore. Gave myself a fucking ulcer with them last year."

"That sounds horrible."

Angelo winced. "It wasn't pretty, but it was my own fault. I knew I was taking too much, and to be honest, it was the wake-up call I needed, even if it did bankrupt me—" Angelo broke off with a yawn. "Shit, sorry. I should probably go."

"Do you have to be somewhere?"

"No."

"Then stay," Dylan said.

"That an order?"

Dylan hadn't meant it to be, but if his unintentional firmness made Angelo smile even a tiny bit, he'd roll with it. "Yes. I'm going to make some breakfast, and bring it in, and the only place you're going is the bathroom . . . if you need to, uh, I can help you if—"

Angelo's scowl cut him dead. "Dude, I can hold my own dick."

Fair enough. Dylan slid out of bed. "Whatever. There's plenty of towels and a spare toothbrush in the cabinet. Help yourself to anything you need, okay? I'll be back with bacon butties."

He left Angelo alone for a while and busied himself in the kitchen. Grilling bacon and buttering bread didn't take all that long, but he took his time, giving Angelo some privacy, though he kept a sharp ear out when the shower turned on. Angelo had barely been able to walk the night before, and Dylan had practically carried him home. The thought of him falling was terrifying, and Dylan's hands shook as he poured yet more tea. *How did this happen so fast?* Angelo had seemed fine all night—his devilish grip on Dylan's sweaty body as strong as ever. Unless Angelo was the world's best actor, it didn't make any sense. Armed with bacon, he put the question to Angelo when he returned to the bedroom.

Angelo shrugged. "Sometimes it creeps up on me and I can manage it, but it hit me like a train yesterday. I was fine in the club, but it's been a long week, you know? Maybe I should've just watched."

He broke a tiny piece off the doorstep sandwich Dylan passed him and chewed slowly, water from the shower still glistening on his flawless back. *How does he look so fucking edible right now?* Dylan had no idea, and unbidden, his brain took him back to the club, to watching Angelo get blown by Rhys—his fat cock sliding past Rhys's full lips, his clenched fists and snatched breaths.

Stop it.

With a herculean effort, Dylan pushed the club aside and sat next to Angelo on the edge of the bed. "Is the ME why you had to retire from dancing?"

"Yeah. You can't dance if you can't stand up."

"Sorry, I shouldn't have asked, I'm just . . . I don't know, curious, I guess? I knew I was missing something when you came to the office in Stratford."

Angelo coughed and set his half-eaten sandwich on the bedside table. "That was a good day, believe it or not."

Dylan swallowed the last bite of his own breakfast and with it, another barrage of questions. The desperate need to know as much about Angelo as possible was burning him up in all the wrong ways, but he'd pushed enough. Angelo was wrecked, and he owed Dylan nothing. "It's pissing down outside. I was planning on staying in bed with *Peaky Blinders*. You game?"

"You want me to be? I'm not good company when I'm like this."

"Then sleep." Dylan slipped his empty plate beneath Angelo's and claimed a mug of tea that he was *definitely* going to drink this time. "It's a big bed, mate. Plenty of room for two."

Perhaps Angelo would've taken more persuading if he hadn't been so clearly dead on his feet, but it didn't seem to matter as they huddled up together again. Dylan flicked Netflix on the TV, but neither of them looked at it and instead faced each other.

"I got diagnosed in New York," Angelo whispered. "I had a tiny surgery on my knee in the summer break, but the anaesthetic never went away. It was like it had latched onto my bones and wouldn't let go. We were gearing up for a huge run of *Swan*

Lake and I kept falling over. My balance was so fucked that they thought I had a brain tumour. Sometimes, I wish I had."

It was the most he'd ever said at once. Dylan absorbed every word but could only think of one of his own. "Why?"

"Because my health insurance would've covered that, and I might have been able to salvage something of my life."

"Shit." Dylan whistled. "You didn't have cover?"

"For cancer, MS, narcolepsy, epilepsy, and everything else they tested me for, but not ME. It cost me thousands of dollars to get a diagnosis, and when I couldn't afford to see any more doctors, I started on the painkillers and energy drinks to keep me upright. It was supposed to be a short-term plan while I saved up to get treatment, but it didn't work out like that."

"The ulcer?"

"And the rest. Even without it, I was a mess. It got so bad that I couldn't roll over in bed. I slept for, like, a month before I got evicted from my apartment, and by then my contract at the ballet company had been terminated."

"They sacked you?"

"Of course they did. They were never going to pay me for hibernating."

"Don't make light of it. They should've looked after you."

Angelo sighed. "I had a benefits package with my contract, but ME was excluded. Like I said, if I'd had MS or something else, it might've been different."

"That's awful." Dylan felt sick. "And then you had to come home to your family's mess?"

"Uh huh. I was here for a few months before my dad died. And you know the rest."

"They don't, though, do they?"

"What?"

"Your family. They can't know or they wouldn't let you work yourself into the ground." Dylan didn't need Angelo's silence to confirm it. He reached for the tea he'd brought for Angelo. "Sit up a bit. You need to drink something."

Angelo didn't protest as he propped himself up on his elbow, and Dylan held the mug to his lips until most of the tea was gone. "I never told anyone except my bosses at the company. I never got round to making many friends over there, and there was other shit to worry about when I came home."

"I get that," Dylan said. "But you can't live like this. That deli is going to kill you if you keep working the way you are. What does your doctor over here think?"

"Dunno. I haven't been."

"You haven't seen a doctor in the UK?"

"What's the point? Doctors can't help me."

"You don't know that."

"Don't I? My bank balance says different."

Dylan let it go—for now. The bitterness had gone from Angelo's voice, and he'd revealed more in the last ten minutes than he had in the whole time they'd known each other. Besides, he was fading fast, his face so weary that Dylan's soul wept for him. An invisible magnet drew him close to Angelo—so close that their noses touched, and then before he could comprehend the bloom of warmth in his belly, his lips found Angelo's in a sweet kiss.

It wasn't the kind of kiss he'd imagined when he'd thought of seeing Angelo again after their club encounters. The heat was there, but it was tempered by worry and exhaustion and a flurry of other emotions that Dylan couldn't quite decipher. Angelo kissed him back, moving his lips like a softly whispered dream, and it seemed like a lifetime had passed before the need to breathe forced Dylan to pull away.

His hands found Angelo's face like they had so many times since he'd brought him home, and Angelo stared at him with watery eyes. "Sleep," Dylan said quietly. "I'll be here when you wake up, I promise."

CHAPTER EIGHT

ANGELO ACCEPTED Dylan's outstretched hand and stepped carefully out of the shower. "Thank you."

Dylan scowled, only the thin layer of scruff on his jaw stopping him looking like a stroppy teenager. "I still think you should call in sick."

"Call who?"

"I don't know . . . your mum?"

"My mum is sixty-eight and can barely see the labels on the milk bottles. Closing the place is better than leaving her to open up by herself."

"So close the place."

Angelo didn't answer. If Dylan didn't know by now why he couldn't close the deli, then the last month meant nothing. Losing a day's takings would mean he couldn't pay his suppliers, and then he'd have to live with pushing them into a financial hole too. *Fuck that.* His own mess was enough.

Dylan wrapped a towel around Angelo. "I know you can't stay home. I'm just worried about you."

"I'm—"

Dylan tapped his fingers against Angelo's mouth. "Don't tell me you're fine. Silence is better than bullshit."

Angelo pursed his lips, swallowing the denial that would've likely earned him far worse than a boyish scowl. The twenty-four hours he'd spent with Dylan was mostly a blur, but the memory of Dylan pretty much carrying him home from the club was already haunting him. He dried his face and braved a glance at his reflection in the mirror and then looked back at Dylan. Big mistake. Angelo had slept the whole of Sunday away, waking late in the evening to Dylan feeding him soup and imploring him to stay another night. It had seemed like a good idea at the time—more than that—but now Dylan looked as tired as him, and the guilt was almost enough to put Angelo back on his arse.

Almost, because he had a deli to open, and apparently Dylan was coming with him.

"Don't you have your own job to go to?" Angelo asked at the front door. "'Cause you aren't exactly dressed for a day of foaming milk."

"Are you taking the piss out of my office get up?"

As if. Dylan was wearing tight grey trousers and a fitted black shirt that seemed as though it had been made to have his compact body poured into it. Even through the fog of a lingering relapse, Angelo wanted to jump him. "You look awesome."

"Right."

"It's true." Angelo was dressed in the same clothes he'd been wearing Saturday. Dylan had washed them, but he still felt like a tramp. "Anyway, I've got to go, so if you really are coming with me, you can tell me your dastardly plan on the way."

Turned out there wasn't much to Dylan's plan. He had to be in Stratford by nine and so could only stay an hour to help Angelo in the deli. And that was more than enough. Dylan's unobtrusive way of taking care of Angelo had kept him sane when he'd been flat on his back, but Angelo couldn't live with disrupting Dylan's life more than he already had.

"Are you going to be all right?" Dylan asked.

Angelo looked up from the bread he was arranging on the shelves. "Yeah."

"Sure?" Dylan took his apron off and came to Angelo's side. "You don't look well."

"Thanks."

"Don't be a dick."

"I can't change who I am, mate."

Dylan grinned. "Uh-huh. Good job I like your dick, but seriously. Call me if you need me, okay? I'm not that far away."

Being even a foot from Dylan felt like a fate worse than a slow death, but they both knew that Angelo wouldn't make that call. "I'll be fine. I *have* to be. But I'll miss you, if that makes you feel any better."

"It does." Dylan stepped impossibly closer. "But it doesn't make it any easier to leave you."

Angelo dropped the focaccia he was holding as Dylan stole another one of those kisses that stopped the world turning. Their lips brushed and then fused together, soothing the residual aches in Angelo's battered body. The roof could've fallen in while Dylan caressed Angelo's tongue with velvet strokes.

But it was over too soon. "I'll find you later?" Dylan asked.

Angelo nodded. "I'd like that, though I'll probably fall asleep on you again."

"I'm not complaining," Dylan said. "It's not like you snore and drool."

"No?"

Dylan shook his head. "Nope. You didn't move a muscle. If it wasn't for your chest moving, I'd have thought you were dead."

They were morbid words to part on, but Angelo's first customers arrived for their coffee fix, and Dylan had a train to catch. He pecked Angelo's cheek, and then he was gone, leaving

Angelo to face the day alone—a scenario that wasn't unusual but suddenly seemed harder than ever.

He struggled through the morning rush and then locked the doors for ten minutes just before the lunchtime. His head was pounding, and his legs were like lead, but the cloud of despair that usually came with the worst ME symptoms was noticeably absent.

Angelo forced a banana down while he fiddled with his phone, poaching the Wi-Fi from the bank across the road. A WhatsApp message popped up with a photo attached. The sight of Dylan lounging at his desk, pulling a stupid face, warmed him from the inside out. Over the weekend, they'd shown each other so many sides of themselves, but this was the Dylan that Angelo craved most—not the power bottom who drove Angelo fucking insane in the club, but the sunny, down-to-earth dude with the perpetual smile. The man who stole Angelo's breath with his gentle kisses and eased him to sleep with soothing hands. *I miss him already.* Was that even possible? The ache in Angelo's heart said yes.

The rest of the day passed in a dizzying blur of coffee and scorched cheese. Angelo was scraping the panini presses down when his body gave up the ghost. In the past, he'd have forced himself to keep going, but it wasn't in him today. He braced himself on the counter and bowed his head. Prickly heat crept through his joints and tingled his skin, but conversely, he was cold. A shiver passed through him. *Damn, I need to sit down.* But before he could move, sinuous arms wound around his waist from behind, and warm lips grazed the back of his neck. *Dylan.*

Angelo's legs trembled, but for once it wasn't fatigue claiming his balance. Dylan's touch brought him back to life, and he leaned back into Dylan's embrace, melting against him. "You're here."

"I am," Dylan murmured. "I locked the doors too. Did you forget?"

"Maybe I left them open for you."

Dylan chuckled. "Maybe, but I've locked them now, so how about we clean this place up, then go get some dinner?"

"You're obsessed with food."

"I'm obsessed with *you*."

Dylan's voice had tied Angelo in knots from the start, but combined with Dylan's hands snaking under his flour-dusted T-shirt, never more than it was right now. He gripped Dylan's hands and squeezed them. "I'm up for dinner. But you're not cleaning this place. You've done enough for me today."

He braced himself for a row, but Dylan merely kissed Angelo's cheek and then perched on a counter stool, apparently engrossed in his phone while Angelo finished closing the deli down.

"I just need to mop," Angelo said. "Then I'm done."

"Okay."

Dylan didn't look up, and so Angelo mopped around him and chucked every other stool up on the tables. When he was done, he swiped Dylan's phone from the counter and then braved making a grab for Dylan too. Dylan felt heavier than he had in the club, and Angelo's muscles screamed in protest, but he barely felt the pain as Dylan's whoop of laughter rang out.

"Put me down!"

"Nope." Angelo carried Dylan carefully across the wet floor and into the kitchen where he deposited him on the counter. "I didn't want you to slip," he said in the face of Dylan's mock outrage.

"Right." Dylan smoothed his hair. "So you went caveman on me? I'll remember that."

"Yeah?"

Dylan dropped his hands and hooked Angelo closer with his legs. "Yeah. There's going to come a time when you don't have the upper hand, you know."

"I thought we just spent all weekend like that?"

"As if. Angelo, I'm never going to think any less of you when you're unwell. It's part of who you are, but it doesn't define you."

Angelo hid his face in Dylan's sweet-scented neck. "You sound more adjusted to it than I've ever been."

"It's not me that has to live with it," Dylan said. "But I'm used to grouchy hot dudes with life-changing illnesses. My mate is diabetic."

"The one you hook up with?"

"*Used* to hook up with. I quit a while back. Got a little crowded, you know?"

"But you still love him?"

Dylan sighed. "That's the second time you've asked me that, but . . . yeah. Of course I love him—he's my friend—but messing around together was never about love until his missus came along."

"And then he ditched you?"

"Far from it. If anything, we were tighter . . . for a while, at least. I miss him."

Angelo wrapped his arms around Dylan and held him close. He'd been trying to get a handle on Dylan's feelings for the friend he'd brought up multiple times. Jealousy tickled his veins, but he pushed it aside. "I'm sorry."

"What for?"

Angelo shrugged. "For being a liability when you need a mate?"

"You're not a liability. And we *are* friends, even if you don't appreciate what you've done for me since we met."

"I literally have no idea what you're talking about."

Dylan pulled back, his sunny face twisted in a glare that went straight to Angelo's cock. "Pay attention then. I was miserable when I came to the club that first time. I'd walked out on the best friends I've ever had because I couldn't stand seeing them so happy together, and I was scared, depressed, and fucking lonely. Then I met you, and I stopped wishing things could be different."

Angelo wanted to seal Dylan's words with the kiss that he'd been craving all day, but then he pictured himself stumbling into Dylan's bed and sleeping like a dead man. "I wish you'd met me two years ago."

"Why?"

"Because I was a different person then."

"I like you as you are."

Angelo shook his head, like he could block out the reality that had hounded him out of America with pure denial. "You shouldn't."

"Well, I do." Dylan wriggled out of Angelo's embrace and slid off the counter. "So you can either come home with me and spend the night or you can piss off and wallow in self-loathing. Either way, we're going for dinner first."

THEY SQUABBLED over who paid for dinner, and for once Angelo came out on top. He took Dylan to Romford's best-kept secret and bought two polystyrene trays of Greek gyros for less than a fiver.

Dylan ate the chargrilled, garlicky chicken like sin, licking his lips and sucking on his elegant fingers. Angelo barely tasted his own dinner and instead passed the time imagining wrapping his own tongue around various parts of Dylan's anatomy.

"I've been reading about chronic fatigue syndrome today," Dylan said when he was done driving Angelo *insane*.

"You didn't have any real work to do?"

"I had plenty, but ME is something our office has come across often, but not ever truly understood, so I figured it would help lots of people if I read up on it."

Angelo knew Dylan well enough by now to believe that he

was entirely serious. "What good is you being an expert on my bullshit to anyone else?"

"Plenty. We have plenty of clients who can't work because of conditions like ME and fibromyalgia. If we can persuade creditors—and the government, actually—to take them more seriously, then sufferers will be a lot better off. Imagine if I could persuade your credit card lenders to wipe your debts?"

"That won't happen. You think they give a shit that I can't dance in tights anymore?"

"I'm using you as an example, a bad one, I know, as your shit hit the fan across the pond, but still. Don't heckle me. I'm tired."

Angelo nudged Dylan's foot under the tiny plastic table. "I'm not heckling. I guess I'm just embarrassed that you know all my darkest secrets. The only time I feel halfway human compared to you is when we're in the club."

Dylan's eyes flashed. "Are you serious? You run a town-centre deli single-handed all the while battling a debilitating condition with no support whatsoever, medical or otherwise. I couldn't do what you do, Angelo. I have to go kip at my dad's for a week when I catch a cold."

"I don't believe that."

"Well, you should. I know it pisses you off when I bring up Sam, but you're just like him in this sense. Stubborn as a fucking mule."

"It doesn't piss me off when you bring up Sam."

"No?"

The challenge in Dylan's electric gaze was clear. "That's a shame. It would piss me off if you had a friend you'd been lusting after for years."

"Why?"

"Because I want you all to myself."

"You have me all to yourself—" Angelo's hand twitched. The muscle spasm ran up his arm and into his shoulder, leaving a trail of pins and needles behind. He glowered at his arm and braced himself for the tingling to spread.

Dylan touched Angelo's arm. "What's wrong?"

"Nothing."

"You know my bullshit filter is the latest model, right? So it'll be quicker for both of us if you just tell me you're not interested."

"What?"

Dylan withdrew his hand. "I'm kinda throwing myself at you here—in real life, not in the club. If I'm making a twat of myself, just say."

Angelo's arm shot out and grabbed Dylan before his brain formulated a coherent response. "It's—fuck—it's not that. Jesus, no. If anyone's a twat here, it's me."

"It's okay if it is. I can take it."

"I know you can."

Dylan responded to the innuendo with a devilish smirk, but his humour was fleeting, and he frowned as he threaded his fingers through Angelo's. "What's wrong, then? Are you in pain?"

Angelo shook his head. "Not exactly—it's hard to explain."

"Try." Dylan popped a can of Lilt open with his spare hand and poured it between two paper cups. "I want to understand."

Why? But Angelo didn't say it. Dylan's earnest empathy was beginning to seep into him and penetrate the armour he needed to get through each day. "My legs are buzzing. I don't think that's the technical term, but I don't know how else to describe it."

"Buzzing?"

"Like the nerves are short-circuiting. It doesn't hurt, but I wish it did. I can deal with pain, but this shit freaks me out."

"Can you move them?"

Angelo shrugged. "It makes it worse, though. It's fatigue that makes the muscles jump, but it doesn't feel like that when they're like this. It's like this cruel illusion of energy . . . it's the worst symptom that I get." Acknowledging the false life in his legs seemed to make it more real. Angelo let go of Dylan and clamped his hands down on his tingling thighs. "It sounds so stupid when I say it out loud.

"It doesn't sound stupid to me. Sam—" Dylan stopped and covered his mouth.

Angelo rolled his eyes. "I thought we'd established that it was cool for you to talk about him?"

"Maybe I wish it wasn't."

"Why?"

"So then I'd know that you were as crazy about me as I am about you."

Angelo didn't know what to say. Dylan was the only light in the mammoth tunnel his life had become, and he spent every waking moment thinking about him. But what did it mean? Where could it go? Angelo was a mess, and Dylan deserved the whole fucking world. "I am crazy about you, but—"

"Don't." Dylan moved his palm from his own mouth to cover Angelo's. "Don't say whatever negativity you're about to come out with. Just let things be, okay? Give yourself a chance."

Angelo had no answer to that. He nodded slowly as Dylan dropped his hand. "I think I need to go home."

"My place or yours?"

The temptation to crawl back to Dylan's pristine bed was so strong Angelo could taste it. "Mine. I need to get myself together for the rest of the week."

Dylan smiled. "Okay, mate. I'll walk you."

CHAPTER NINE

DYLAN TOSSED his phone on the bed that still smelled of Angelo, glad that it landed screen side down. It was Thursday—three days since Angelo had kissed him outside the derelict garage he apparently slept in, and apart from a couple of vague WhatsApp messages, Dylan hadn't heard from him. Though, what he'd been expecting, he wasn't entirely sure. After all, Angelo hadn't exactly professed his undying love.

Undying love? What are you? Fucking twelve?

Dylan kicked off his shoes and lay down on his bed. Despite knowing better, he reclaimed his phone and opened WhatsApp. Angelo hadn't been online since the arse crack of dawn, and though Dylan knew he was likely still working, it was hard not to worry . . . at least when he wasn't convincing himself that it wasn't even his place to henpeck a dude he'd pretty much only just met.

But still. Dylan worried. How many times had he assumed that Sam had gone to bed early, only to find him half dead in the morning? *Too many.* Dylan shuddered, and his thumb hovered over the Call button, but his phone buzzed before he could press it, and he jumped a mile.

The phone flew out of his fingers and sailed over the side of the bed, landing on the hardwood floor with a sickening clatter. Dylan scrambled to reach it and toppled onto the floor, thwacking his knee on the radiator just in time for the call to ring out. He grabbed the phone and turned it over. *Angelo.* Dylan's heart skipped a beat. He called straight back, but it went to voicemail without even ringing. He tried again and again, but the calls didn't connect.

Restless, he hauled himself off the floor and went to the kitchen. His dad had brought over a pie from the butchers the day before, but he ignored it in favour of a big bottle of fruity cider—the shit kind that tasted like Vimto. He has halfway deep in it and peeling tiny bits of the label from the bottle when his phone rang again.

He jumped on it like a starving man. "Angelo?"

"It's me."

Relief rushed out of Dylan in a whoosh of breath. "Sorry I missed your first call. I threw my phone by accident, then fell off the bed trying to catch it."

"Erm . . . okay? Are you drunk?"

"Nope. Just a twat."

"Fair enough." Angelo didn't sound convinced. "I'm sorry I haven't called you sooner. I didn't have any minutes left on my phone, and I keep crashing out as soon as I get home."

"How are you doing with that? Do you feel better?"

"Actually, yes. I've been locking the door for an hour every morning to take a nap in the stock room, and I think it's helping."

Dylan pictured Angelo trying to get his head down amongst the vats of olive oil and giant jars of sundried tomatoes. *This isn't right.* "What about your legs?"

"Well, I haven't cut them off and hurled them under a bus yet, so I suppose they're all right."

"Gallows humour, eh?"

"Well, I am on Gallows Corner, babe."

Babe. Jesus. This dude kills me. It had been a long time since a male lover—if Angelo could even be defined as that—had called Dylan *babe.* On the rare occasions his dirty nights in with Sam and Eddie had spilled out into a stolen kiss or touch from Sam, it had always been *mate* or *brother,* and the emptiness Dylan had felt then now made sense. "What are you doing tonight?"

"Accounts. I'm trying to get my mum to sit down with me, but she ain't having none of it. Makes me want to start smoking again."

"When did you quit?"

"Eight years ago," Angelo said around an ironically timed cough.

"Wow."

"I know. Not sure what that says about me or her."

Dylan went to the fridge and opened it, staring blindly inside at the contents before he grabbed another cider. "Do you want to maybe meet up later? We could get a drink, or . . ."

"Or what?"

"I don't know. Go to the Thursday night gangbang party at the club and have crazy-mad sex? What are we doing here?"

Angelo laughed, which made Dylan feel a little better about the determined bunny boiler who fell out of his mouth every time he spoke. "I have no idea what we're doing. You told me to let things be, so that's what I'm doing. I'm stuck with my mum tonight, but if you want to do something tomorrow—drink council pop at the bus stop or sit on a park bench, 'cause that's all I can afford right now—I'm game for whatever."

"So you're not going to the club?"

"Are you? Because I'm pretty sure I'm game for that too."

The romantic in Dylan wanted to ditch the club and take

Angelo out for dinner. Get a bottle of wine and leer at each other over spicy food until they stumbled home to bed. But the realist in him knew that Angelo would never agree to a night out on Dylan's wallet, and as much fun as the bus stop sounded, the club would do far more for Angelo's fragile self-esteem.

Besides, going to the club wasn't exactly a hardship. Fuck no. It was the best offer Dylan had heard since the last time, and they made loose plans to meet near Lovato's the following night. And after they'd hung up, Dylan took a shower with a grin and boner he wouldn't touch until he had his mouth around Angelo's cock.

THE CHANGE in Angelo was startling. Dylan watched him spring over a bench as he approached the club, and for the first time truly saw him as the incredible athlete he'd once been. He stepped out of the shadows and into Angelo's path. Nerves shivered through him and he opened his arms, willing Angelo to step right into them.

Angelo did exactly that, and his embrace warmed Dylan's bones. "Hey."

"Hey yourself." Dylan inhaled Angelo's scent and brushed his lips along his darkly stubbled jaw. "You look good."

"Says you."

"What does that mean?"

Angelo stepped back and speared Dylan with a heated stare, running his gaze over Dylan's skinny jeans and grungy vest combo. "I'm never sure which skin you're gonna show up in."

"Yeah, 'cause that clears it right up." Dylan rolled his eyes. "And you're one to talk about skins. Am I partying with Angel tonight or has Angelo come out to play?"

"You tell me. Angel ain't something I've ever called *myself*, is it?"

He had a point, but as they made their way to the club, Dylan couldn't help noting every inch of the mask as it descended over Angelo's features. He knew that Angel would burn him alive when they played, but what did that mean if Angelo wasn't there too? Did it even mean *anything*? At this point, Dylan had no fucking idea.

Inside the club, a man who knew *Angel* by name waved them past without taking the entrance fee, and though the club was as familiar to Dylan as his mother's house, walking in with Angelo felt like the first time all over again—the lights were lower, the bass line deeper, and the eyes that followed them to the bar pierced holes in his back.

Angelo bought drinks with a screwed up tenner, and Dylan swallowed the urge to push Angelo's money aside and swipe his card over the contactless payment machine.

"Next round's on me," he said.

Angelo scowled. "Yeah, yeah."

Perhaps they wouldn't get that far. Dylan claimed his beer bottle and glanced around the club. It was early yet and some corners were quiet, but it didn't take long to spot Rhys on his back with his legs in the air, getting pegged by a girl who reminded Dylan of Eddie. For a moment, he imagined that it was her and that she was thrusting her big black strap-on into Sam and that Sam was loving it, warming himself up to take Dylan's cock. How different would their lives have been if Sam's sexuality had been more flexible?

But even before the question had solidified in his mind, he knew the answer. Their lives would've rocked out exactly the same because Sam's sexuality was irrelevant. Eddie was his soulmate and Dylan his friend, and no amount of dick could change that.

Angelo tapped Dylan's temple with his own icy-cold beer bottle. "Who are you thinking about?"

"What makes you think I've got anyone else on my mind?"

"Because you've got that orgy-BFF scowl on your face."

Dylan wondered when he'd become so transparent, or perhaps his mind was just open to Angelo. "Do you really want to talk about Sam again? It feels like all we ever do."

"When we're not discussing my shit show, you mean."

"Don't be like that."

Angelo shrugged. "It's true. You've seen all my dirty laundry and listened to my tales of woe, but I don't know much about you apart from that you dress like a banker by day and a metal-head by night."

"And that I used to have threesomes with my best mate and his missus."

Angelo glowered and swigged his beer, his expression a world away from the last time Sam had invaded their conversation. "I can't see you in a mosh pit. You're too . . . I dunno. Nice?"

"I'm nasty enough to bend over in a fuck club," Dylan retorted. "And I can't see you pirouetting to *Swan Lake* either, but that's my problem."

He hadn't meant to speak so harshly, but Angelo's only reaction was a slight twitch in one eyebrow, and Dylan sighed. "The bad luck in your life doesn't define you, Angelo."

"No?"

"No. Nor does the fact that you can pretty much make me come just by looking at me, but I reckon there's a lot more to both of us, eh?"

Angelo said nothing, and frustration rippled through Dylan. Complex individuals crossed his path all the time, but he'd never met anyone as hard to read as Angelo. They'd come to the club to play, but the air between them was heavy, weighed down by something that Dylan couldn't quite decipher.

He necked his beer and reached for Angelo's hand just as Rhys came up to them, his grin a mile wide. "Evening, gents."

Angelo pulled his hand away milliseconds before Dylan managed to grasp it and stepped back to make room for Rhys. "All right, mate?"

His tone was flat, his face devoid of the smirk he'd greeted Rhys with the last time they'd met, but Rhys didn't seem to notice. He barely glanced at Angelo, and his friendly gaze zeroed in on Dylan.

"I was hoping I'd run into you again."

"Oh yeah?" Dylan regretted downing his beer and settled for picking at the label. "Why's that?"

Rhys shrugged. "Why do you think? I haven't been fucked that good in years."

Angelo snorted and turned away, signalling to the barman for another drink. Dylan glared at his back. How could someone so beautiful be so damn maddening?

Rhys cleared his throat. "So, are you two up for some company tonight?"

Dylan shot Rhys a surprised glance. Despite the three-way fuck that had gone down the last time they'd met, when he looked at Rhys, all he could see was the concern in his face when he'd caught up with Dylan at the taxi rank. "*It's none of my business, mate, but your boyfriend doesn't look well. You might want to head back and give him a hand.*"

Dylan had dashed back to the club too fast to correct Rhys's assumption.

"I'm going to take that as a no then," Rhys said when Dylan failed to respond, and Angelo seemed intent on ignoring the both of them. "Have a good night, guys."

He was gone before Dylan found his tongue, disappearing into the shadows of the club to find someone else to play with and leaving Dylan to contemplate Angelo's back. He moved closer to the bar and nudged him in the ribs. "That was rude."

Angelo flicked him a dry stare. "What was?"

"You didn't have to blank him."

"Who?"

"Rhys. The bloke who sucked your cock last week." Dylan reached around Angelo and helped himself to one of the beers Angelo had bought. "He's also the reason that I came back to the club to find you."

"I don't want to talk about that."

Dylan rolled his eyes. "Jesus. When did you flip your twat mode on?"

Angelo's gaze darkened, but the twitch of his lips gave him away, and he let loose a rueful grin. "Sorry. I guess I'm used to playing the solitary Dom when I come here. I don't do small talk."

"Just fuck and run, eh?"

"Don't knock it."

"I'm not. But you didn't have to ghost Rhys. He seems like a nice bloke."

"You want to fuck him again?"

"I—"

Angelo cut Dylan off with a kiss that was nothing like the sweet-lipped make-out sessions they'd shared in the real world. Crazy-hot, biting, and demanding, it wiped Dylan's mind clean of any coherent thought, turning his legs to jelly before Angelo broke away with a sinful smirk. "Because you can if you want . . . but I'd kind of counted on not sharing you tonight."

"Oh yeah?"

"Yeah." Angelo pulled Dylan close and wrapped his arms around his waist. His graceful body moved in time with the moody dubstep beats that had ramped up while they'd been at the bar. "I felt like shit that this was the only way I could take you out, but now that we're here, I can't help picturing all the ways I can make you come."

Dylan shivered and leaned against Angelo, their lean

ripples and curves moulding together like they were always meant to. Angelo was sex on legs at the best of times, but as he led Dylan in a slow dance that entwined their bodies until there wasn't a scrap of air between them, Dylan was dizzy with want. His legs buckled, but Angelo kept him from dropping to his knees.

"Not here. Let's go to the chambers."

Another shudder passed through Dylan. The chambers were where the BDSM happened. Much of it was too heavy for Dylan's taste, but he trusted Angelo and followed him across the club like a moth chasing a flame.

They ditched their clothes in a locker and then made their way to the chambers. The darkened dungeon-style rooms were busy, the air thick with ecstatic cries and the slap of leather on flesh. Dylan's pulse quickened, and he dug his nails into Angelo's palms.

Perhaps sensing his nerves, Angelo pulled Dylan in front of him and pointed to a vacant play bench. "Just you, me, and a rope. Whaddya say?"

Dylan stumbled slightly and licked his lips. His gaze fell on a length of silk that was draped over the black bench. "Can we use that?"

A heated sound rumbled through Angelo's chest. "Fuck yeah."

Dylan snagged the silk and then straddled the bench. The heady rush of anticipation left him giddy, and he raised his arms, submitting himself to Angelo and letting his mind fall into that magical place where his thoughts were blocked by pure sensation.

Angelo tied the silk around Dylan's wrists like a fucking fisherman. In his delirium, Dylan imagined him on a boat, his beautiful face lashed by wind and rain, dressed in whatever fishermen wore. He laughed—a choked-out sound that betrayed his hyped-up state of arousal, and Angelo's answering frown was laced with humour too.

"Something funny, Dylan?"

Dylan shook his head as the silk bit into his flesh. "No . . . *Angel*."

Angelo's expression darkened. "Don't call me that. I've told you it's not me."

It must have been at some point in Angelo's life, but naked and bound and at his mercy, Dylan let it go. After all, they'd already both conceded that they came to the table with more than one skin.

He let Angelo flip him over and hitch his tied wrists to the convenient hook at the end of the bench, and braced himself for the breach of Angelo's fat cock—"Fuck!"

The gentle lapping at his hole caught him off guard. His entire body jerked, and the force of it nearly sent him toppling over the side of the bench. Angelo's iron grip steadied him, but the tongue probing Dylan's hole didn't falter. Angelo teased him with tickling licks and driving thrusts until Dylan was sure that he'd come from that alone.

He gave himself up to a violent shudder and groaned, his voice cracking into a plaintive cry. Somewhere nearby, he heard a chuckle—Rhys, perhaps—but he didn't care how desperate he appeared to anyone watching because he *was* desperate. Their relationship outside of the club was complex and undefined, but this? *Yeah.* This was goddamn primal, and Dylan had never doubted the fiery burn that kept him awake most nights.

Angelo pulled back and bit the fleshiest part of Dylan's inner thigh. The sharp pain stopped Dylan's fast-approaching orgasm in its tracks but did nothing to calm the storm in his veins. Angelo yanked Dylan's hips higher and dragged his fingernails down Dylan's spine. "What do you want, Dylan? Want me to eat you out or fuck you into oblivion?"

Anything. Everything. "Fuck me," Dylan gritted out. "Please."

Angelo groaned. "God, I love it when you beg. Makes me lose my head."

"*Please.*"

Angelo's hands left Dylan, and Dylan mourned the loss of his electric touch, but the void didn't last long. Cool lube trickled over Dylan's hole, and a condom wrapper fluttered to the floor. The blunt intrusion of Angelo's cock finally came, and despite every nerve demanding it, the stinging stretch knocked Dylan off balance again.

"Easy." Angelo's voice was soft and devoid of the authority that chased away Dylan's senses. "I've got you."

Dylan gasped, his lungs burning, and more shudders racked him. Angelo started to pull out, and Dylan fumbled desperately for any part of him to cling on to. "Don't stop, don't stop."

But Angelo withdrew, and the knot securing Dylan's wrists fell away. Dylan resigned himself to face-planting the bench, but as his body collapsed, Angelo caught him and somehow cradled him in his lap.

"Easy," Angelo said again.

And again, and again, until Dylan's breath was no longer snared in his throat. He sagged against Angelo and stared up at him through blurry eyes. "I'm sorry."

"What for?"

Dylan didn't have an answer. He shook his head, and Angelo caught his chin, forcing him to meet his gaze.

"I'm never going to force you, Dylan. You're safe with me. You know that."

Of course Dylan did, and he had no explanation for the bizarre panic that was still having a party in his gut. He took a shaky breath and closed his fingers around Angelo's wrist. "I know I'm safe."

"Then what is it?" Angelo hunched his shoulders, shielding

Dylan from anyone who may have been watching the cluster-fuck their playtime had turned into. "Was it the ties? I figured you were okay with shit like that."

"I *am*," Dylan said. "It wasn't the fucking . . . I don't know what it was. It's never happened before."

Angelo stared hard at Dylan, like his gaze could pierce Dylan's soul and decipher the truth. "You don't seem the panicking type."

"I'm not."

"Do you wanna get out of here?"

Dylan absorbed the sensation of Angelo's arms caged around him, of his fingers stroking his face, and shook his head. "I want *you*. Please?"

For a long moment, he feared Angelo would refuse him, but then the worry clouding Angelo's eyes faded, and he smiled. He released Dylan and moved like a stretching cat, lying back on the bench, his sheathed cock still rock hard as he folded his hands behind his head. "If you want me, Dylan. Take me."

Well, okay then. Weird panic bullshit be fucking damned, Dylan was getting on that dick. And as he pushed Angelo's chest and straddled his waist, the accompanying rush of power cleared his foggy brain. He still had no idea where he and Angelo were headed with this madness, but for now, he had the reins.

He eased himself down on Angelo's cock, bracing himself on the bench frame, intending to take it slow, to string the ride out until neither of them could take it anymore, but his body had other ideas. Adrenaline took over as he ground down on Angelo, lapping up Angelo's grunts and groans. He clenched around Angelo's dick and rode him hard, his sweat dripping onto Angelo's chest, the ache in his thighs building with every rush of pleasure.

Angelo arched his back and brought his hands to Dylan's

hips, deepening the angle. His moans grew louder and higher in pitch, and for the first time ever, Dylan had the upper hand.

He gripped Angelo's throat, squeezing, gentle at first, but then rougher as Angelo's dick pulsed inside him. "You like that? You gonna come with my hand on your throat and your dick buried in my arse?"

Angelo's eyes rolled back, and Dylan's brief control slipped. He slammed down on Angelo one more time, then came with a ragged cry, splattering Angelo's ripped abdomen. "Fuck!"

"Oh God." Angelo threw his head back, pressing his perfect neck into Dylan's hand, and his release seemed to come in waves as Dylan squeezed his throat.

It felt like they were both coming forever, but eventually, Dylan collapsed on Angelo's chest, smearing himself with come and sweat before he remembered that it was Angelo who'd had his air supply cut off.

"Fuck." He sat up sharply. "Are you okay? Did I hurt you?"

Still panting, Angelo shook his head and touched the reddening marks around his neck. "Nah, I like that shit when I'm with someone I trust."

"You trust me?"

Angelo met Dylan's gaze with a ferocious stare that seemed out of context with the mellow post-coital vibe descending on them. "Of course I do. You know who I am. Can't think of anyone else who ever has."

Dylan opened his mouth, but any answer he may have given was cut off by Angelo's hand covering his lips.

Angelo shook his head. "Don't. Just give me tonight. Please?"

As if Dylan could refuse Angelo anything when he looked at him the way he was now. In the blue lights of the club, Angelo's eyes seemed almost black, and Dylan fell head first into their vortex. The night was closing in on them. All they had—all they needed—was each other, right?

IT TOOK Dylan approximately six seconds to persuade Angelo to get a cab home with him, but it felt like the longest six seconds of his life. And then the taxi ride passed in a blur of heated stares and aborted sentences. Dylan's blood sizzled from their club encounter, but even that wasn't enough to give him the balls to ask for another round.

Lucky for him, Angelo was way ahead of the game. He held Dylan back with one arm and paid the driver with the other and then yanked him out of the car. Cool air hit Dylan's heated skin, and a residual shiver rattled through him. A heartbeat behind, Angelo wound his arms around Dylan's waist and buried his face in Dylan's neck.

Dylan leaned into him and waited for the shift in their dynamic—for the inferno to fade and them to slip seamlessly back to the slow burn of friendship. Remembering what had happened the last time they'd left the club together, Dylan nuzzled Angelo's cheek. "All right?"

In answer, Angelo swept him off his feet and spun him around, and Dylan would never stop being in awe of his strength. "Shouldn't I be asking you that?"

Dylan rolled his eyes. "I told you—I'm fine. I didn't have dinner before I came out. Maybe that fucked me up."

Angelo didn't look convinced, but Dylan wasn't in the mood to persuade him. That would mean talking about whatever had upset his equilibrium in the club, and Dylan had a buzz that he intended to carry them all the way to bed. "Are you going to kip at mine?"

"You want me to?"

"Yes."

Angelo shot Dylan a sideways glance. "Okay, but we need food and showers before we get all dirty again."

Dylan's heart skipped a beat. "You want to get dirty again?"

"Uh-huh." Angelo's expression was comically serious. "If I'm going to spend the night, I want to do more than sleep this time."

Dylan wound his arms around Angelo's neck as Angelo set him back on the ground, their lips still a hairbreadth away from the kiss he craved so badly. "You won't get any arguments from me."

"Good."

The way Angelo's voice wrapped around the single syllable had echoes of Angel, but Dylan pushed it away. It was *Angelo* who had lain back on that bench and given himself up to Dylan, and the slight snarl on his face now turned Dylan's every thought to a liquefied mush. *God, I want him.* And the idea of Angelo fucking outside of the club—in Dylan's bed, on the couch . . . on the kitchen worktops—was so beguiling that Dylan swayed on his feet.

For the umpteenth time that night, Angelo steadied him. "Come on," he said. "Let's get inside."

Dylan didn't need telling twice. He grabbed Angelo's hand and towed him to the front door. He fumbled with his key like he'd drunk ten pints, but eventually, he got it unlocked and led them to his flat.

Inside, the pressing need for a shower outweighed his desire to tumble Angelo straight into bed. He pressed two bottles of beer into Angelo's hands and pushed him towards the bedroom. "Five minutes."

"We need food," Angelo said. "Or no fucking."

It was clear that he meant it, so Dylan jerked his head to the kitchen. "Raid the fridge then. Just make sure you're naked when I get back."

He took the quickest shower known to man, but rinsing sweat and dried jizz took a few minutes. When he got out, the flat was quiet and still. He wrapped a towel around his waist and padded into the bedroom, nearly tripping over Angelo's boots. On the bedside table was a plate of sandwiches that looked far more appetising than the contents of Dylan's fridge deserved and a bottle of beer. Angelo had ditched his T-shirt and unbuttoned his jeans, the trail of dark fuzz on his belly disappearing invitingly beneath his underwear, and Dylan gazed at him, his cock springing to life again.

God, he's gorgeous. It was a crying shame that Angelo was already fast asleep.

ANGELO WOKE up in his underwear and covered by Dylan's clean-scented duvet. The bed was so much more comfortable than the couch he slept on at home, that he allowed himself a moment to pretend he didn't have to get up and go to work. Then he realised he was alone.

He sat up and instantly regretted it as his head spun, letting him know that he was in for a day of dodgy balance. "Dylan?"

Damn it, his voice was pretty fucked too. Luckily, it didn't have to travel far. Dylan popped up at the edge of the bed, a pair of black-framed glasses perched adorably on his perfect nose. "Hey."

Angelo blinked. "Hey. What are you doing down there?"

"Catching up on some emails."

"Seriously? What time is it?" Angelo swung his legs out of bed, praying that they'd hold him up on the first try. "I have to get to the deli."

"Easy," Dylan said. "It's only five thirty."

"Oh." Angelo relaxed and set his feet gently on the hardwood floor. "What are you doing up then? You don't have to work today—" Angelo broke off with a coughing fit.

Dylan left his laptop on the rug and crawled onto the bed

behind Angelo, pressing his warm chest to Angelo's back until Angelo was done hacking. "I couldn't sleep and I didn't want to disturb you."

"Fat chance of that." Angelo leaned back into Dylan's embrace. "I don't even remember taking my clothes off."

Dylan chuckled. "You started. I helped you out after you passed out on me."

Through the ever-present fog, Angelo tried to recall the latter part of the previous night, but all he remembered was wanting to punch Rhys in the face for no reason other than the fact that he had a body that worked. And Dylan having a mid-fuck panic attack in the BDSM chambers.

Angelo turned in Dylan's arms and regarded him. Despite the insanely hot play session that had followed, he couldn't shake the sensation of Dylan shaking beneath him for all the wrong reasons, and the dark circles now beneath Dylan's eyes didn't help. "Are you okay?"

"Of course."

"Sure about that? 'Cause you kind of look like I feel."

"And how do you feel, Angelo?"

"Tired and like I've been hit by a bus."

Dylan's brow furrowed. "That's not good."

"Actually, it's not that bad. Some mornings I'm still under the bus."

"I wish I could help you feel better."

"You do." Angelo pushed Dylan's messy hair away from his face. "If I was at home right now, I'd be so fucking miserable that even opening my eyes would hurt."

"Your state of mind has that much impact on your physical wellbeing?"

Angelo shrugged. "Some days."

Dylan looked like he wanted to ask more but merely put his hands on Angelo's bare shoulders and massaged them so soothingly that Angelo was halfway back to sleep before he remembered that he had to get to work.

He stilled Dylan's magic hands with a groan. "I've got to get moving."

"You don't have time for a blowjob?"

"Huh?" Angelo's eyes flew open.

Dylan smirked. "That woke you up."

"Unfairly, so if you're taking the piss . . ."

"Would I do such a thing?"

"The fact that you're not on your knees yet incriminates you." Angelo grinned and dodged Dylan's playful swat.

"Please." Dylan pushed Angelo's chest until he was lying flat and crawled over him, his face inches from Angelo's. "We're not in the club right now, so I'm not getting on my knees for anyone, but I'll still make you come in three minutes flat."

"Three minutes, eh?" Angelo's morning wood solidified, tenting his underwear, and he folded his hands behind his head in the same pose as he'd adopted last night when Dylan had ridden him into oblivion. "Reckon I can make time for that."

"Game on, then." Dylan ripped Angelo's underwear down his thighs and took his dick in his mouth in one smooth motion. Angelo's tip hit the back of Dylan's throat and the banter died a fiery death.

"Jesus fucking Christ." Angelo arched his back, and his muscles screamed with tension, his balls already drawn up tight. "I'm putting money on two minutes."

Dylan dragged his lips wetly up Angelo's dick and chuckled but cut himself off by plunging his mouth down again. He sucked Angelo fast and deep, his lips fused tight around Angelo's shaft, his teeth scraping gently with the perfect amount of pain.

And it was the right kind of pain too. The aches in Angelo's body faded, replaced by spine-tingling sensation. He'd always been a sucker—*ha*—for good head, but Dylan's mouth clamped around his dick was something else, particularly while he was still half asleep, his mind at that meandering point where it was easily distracted. Removed from the real world enough that he didn't think, only felt.

Angelo's stomach muscles clenched, drawing his head up from the bed. His neck flexed, and a jolt of discomfort rippled through the tendons, but the throb in his cock outweighed the pain, and a guttural groan tore out of him.

The two-minute deadline passed, and then another minute, and another. Edging was Angelo's party trick, but it seemed that Dylan had picked up a few tricks of his own. Over and over, he brought Angelo to the brink, only to ease back just enough to drive Angelo *insane*.

Angelo's body curled off the bed and he clenched his fists. Dylan slid his hands beneath Angelo's thighs and lifted him slightly. His fingers splayed out over Angelo's buttocks, teasing the sensitive flesh behind Angelo's balls, pressing . . . probing.

"Fuck, fuck, fuck—" Angelo's hands flew to Dylan's head, and he locked his fingers in Dylan's silky hair as he drove his hips up, fucking Dylan's mouth with rapid, short-fire thrusts. Dylan moaned around Angelo's cock, and the hummed vibration pushed Angelo over the edge. He released his death grip on Dylan's head to give Dylan a chance to pull back. "Shit. I'm gonna come."

But Dylan didn't pull back. He opened his mouth wider and took Angelo impossibly deeper, swallowing every jet of come as Angelo shot down his throat.

Angelo collapsed, slack and panting, his heated skin sheened with sweat. He clumsily grasped Dylan's hips as Dylan moved quickly up the bed. Dylan straddled Angelo, jacking himself furiously, his expression caught in the throes of a fast approaching orgasm. His breath came in tortured moans, and then he started to come, his head thrown back, his dick pulsing, and wet warmth painted Angelo's chest.

"Damn." Dylan fell forward, his damp hair flopping into his face.

Angelo pushed it back and pulled Dylan down, capturing his lips in a slow, sensual kiss that went on and on until Dylan broke away to breathe.

"Whoa. That went on a bit longer than two minutes."

Angelo laughed breathlessly, but the phantom clock in his brain sobered him way too fast. "I want to stay here and fuck you, but I've really got to go."

Dylan sighed and slid off him. "I know. I put a clean towel out for you in the bathroom if you want to take a shower."

Angelo shot a pointed glance at his come-smeared abdomen, then forced himself upright. His limbs felt light and loose as they bathed in the rush of endorphins, and a hot shower would hopefully prolong the sensation, but he didn't want to leave Dylan.

He stood and held out his hand. "Shower with me?"

TWO HOURS after the best start to a day that he could remember in recent years, Angelo's morning was fast descending into the day from hell. He'd arrived at the deli to find his mother already there with his least favourite uncle in tow, faffing around with signage displays that didn't mean anything when they couldn't pay for the coffee beans. He'd only just managed to get rid of them when the bailiffs turned up.

"I can't pay you anything," Angelo explained for the fifth time. "I don't own the place."

"I understand that, mate," the bailiff said. "But we're going to need some kind of payment today or we'll have to remove goods."

Angelo sighed. Deep down, he'd known this was coming. The financial plan the business advice centre had put together had been sound, but it had depended on selling off equipment, using cheaper suppliers, and raising prices—all things his mother, backed by good old Uncle Gino, had refused to do. "If you remove goods, we won't be able to trade."

The bailiff was sympathetic but ultimately unmoved. He listed the contents of the deli and then took a seat at the counter while Angelo placed a dozen unanswered calls to the Giordano family home.

It was midday when the bailiff ran out of patience. Angelo watched with mixed emotions as the deli was packed up and loaded into the back of a transit van. Half a century of his family's history was winging its way to an auction house, and he'd always figured that when it happened, it would take a part of him with it.

As it was, he felt nothing except a vague sense of panic that his sole remaining source of employment had gone too.

Dazed, he locked the deli and walked home. Under the unseasonal sunshine, he found Theresa in the garden having coffee and biscotti with his uncle, aunt, and three teenage cousins.

"What are you doing here at this hour?" Gino snapped. "Theresa told me that you've been closing the deli during the day and it's got to stop. How do you expect to get out of this mess if you aren't putting the hours in?"

The unfairness of it was almost funny. Angelo leaned in the back doorway and shook his head. "Enough bullshit. I couldn't trade if I wanted to. The bailiffs have been and cleaned us out."

Theresa lamented to God in Italian and clutched her hand to her chest. Aunt Carmella rushed to her side while Gino stood and stepped forward, his large frame towering over Angelo.

"What do you mean they've cleaned us out?" Gino said. "You let thieves come in and take your father's business from under your nose?"

"Not thieves. Bailiffs. Sent by the high court by suppliers we haven't paid. Some might argue that makes *us* the fucking thieves—and by 'us' I mean me and Mum. It's got fuck all to do with you."

Angelo spoke quietly, as exhausted mentally as he was in every other capacity, but Gino's face reddened like Angelo had called his wife a whore. "Nothing to do with me? My father built that business from a pot of piss and then my brother killed himself keeping the doors open. You run it into the ground and tell *me* it's not my concern?"

Angelo glanced at Theresa. They'd never been close, but familial loyalty had kept Angelo in Romford, flogging the dead horse his father had left behind. Or had it? Was he giving himself too much credit? After all, it wasn't like he'd had any better offers.

Gino shoved at Angelo's shoulder. "Don't glare at your mother. I'm talking to you."

Angelo's gaze shifted to where Gino had touched him. Was still touching him. "Get your hands off me. Dad ballsed the business up all by himself. And she"—Angelo pointed at Theresa—"has done nothing but bury her head in the sand. I'm the one who's been stuck behind that counter for the last four months. If I hadn't been, it would've been over a lot sooner."

"Four months?" Theresa finally looked up. "Four months, Angelo? I needed you home four *years* ago. Where were you?"

"You know where I was and what I was doing. And Dad took the money I sent home to him. So don't give me any indifferent, uncaring-brat bullshit." Angelo fished the keys to the empty deli from his pocket and tossed them past Gino's head and onto the glass garden table. "All you can do now is sell the place as a going concern and then hide any leftover cash from this money grabbing bastard." He jerked his head at Gino.

Gino spat on the ground. "I should put you over my knee and teach you some manners."

"Try it." Angelo wrenched Gino's hand from his shoulder

and sneered. "And don't think for a minute that I don't know why you're hanging around Mum like a fucking disease. If you weren't as stupid as you look, you'd have encouraged her to sell the moment she got power of attorney when Dad was ill. That way you could've got your hands on the cash long before I came home."

"You little fucking faggot."

Angelo laughed. "Right. And you're not? Me and Paolo found your porn stash when we were kids and it was pretty obvious that you like cock as much as I do."

Gino's huge fist connecting with Angelo's ribs and then his stomach should've surprised him—shocked him. But it didn't, even though it had been more than a decade since Gino had last struck him, and what came next seemed to happen in slow motion. The weight behind Gino's blow sent Angelo crashing into the doorframe. The back of his head hit the wood with a dizzying thud, but Angelo barely felt it as the punch to his stomach stole his breath.

He doubled over, and an odd calm settled in his veins. For a moment, he thought he would pass out, but then adrenaline kicked in, and his own Giordano temper roared to life.

Angelo lunged at Gino and rained hits on his head and chest, his fists blurring in the sunshine, his speed making up for the weight disadvantage.

Gino grunted, caught off guard, and fell backwards, stumbling into the glass table and knocking it to the floor.

Someone screamed. Gino kicked out and his boot slammed into Angelo's ribs again. The sickening crack poured petrol on Angelo's fury, and the long-neglected masochist in him—the one who'd danced on the international ballet circuit through a dozen ME relapses—sprang forward again. Bones crunched against his knuckles and blood flowed. More screams. And then desperate hands yanking him back.

"Angelo! Stop it. You'll kill him."

Angelo struggled against the hands that held him, but the fight drained from him as perspective returned. The patio was a wreck, and so was he.

Gino was on his arse by the broken table, blood dripping from his mashed-up nose, his left eye already swollen. Angelo stared at him and felt nothing. And the numbness frightened him. His family had always been dysfunctional, but even on the other side of the world, he never felt so detached.

His cousins released him. Angelo's arms dropped to his sides, and pain throbbed in his ribs, spreading fast to the renegade nerves in his back. Nausea roared in his gut. He swallowed it down and looked at Theresa—at his *mother*.

She turned her back on him and crouched at Gino's side, leaving Angelo to stagger to his garage bedroom alone.

He locked the door behind him and sank to his knees by the tiny basin. His stomach heaved, and he threw up. When he was done and had cleaned himself up, he fell back in a heap, clutching his injured ribs. Past experience told him they weren't broken, but his weakened muscles didn't support his body as well as it used to, and he knew he was in for some fuck-awful bruising.

Brilliant. Angelo sucked in painful breaths and crawled to his makeshift bed on the couch. Lying down was worse than sitting up, but Angelo was *tired*, and the buzz he'd left Dylan's place with that morning was long gone.

He didn't remember falling asleep, and the darkness he woke to some time later unnerved the distant part of his brain that was aware that it had been early afternoon when he'd last been awake. The prickling sensation that something had woken him bothered him too. He sat up, wincing as the bruises forming on his ribs made themselves known. The garage was quiet and still, and *dark*, the only light coming from the strip of light below the shutter door that was rarely opened.

Sometimes it rattled in the wind, treating Angelo to a

chilling breeze that he'd never noticed when he'd slept in the garage as a child. He shivered now and the nausea he'd passed out with lingered, and his chest burned too. Perhaps that had woken him. But then the garage door shook again, far harder than any wind had ever shuddered through it.

What the fuck?

Angelo stood and shuffled to the door. There was a tiny rust hole in the top corner. Stretching to peer through it hurt like the devil, and he didn't relish the prospect of brawling with Gino again. Angelo's anger had long faded and he simply didn't care enough to fight anymore.

But it wasn't Gino shaking the door and calling his name.

Angelo lunged for the handle that raised the door. It seemed to take a lifetime for enough space to appear for him to duck beneath the door, and by the time he stumbled out, Dylan was already walking away.

"Hey!" Angelo limped after him. "Dylan! Wait!"

Dylan stopped walking but didn't turn round. Angelo caught up with him and grabbed his arm, but Dylan wrenched it away. "So you're not fucking dead then?"

Angelo flinched, like the fury in Dylan's voice had hit him. "What?"

"I was worried," Dylan said. "You didn't respond to any of my messages, and when I stopped by the deli, it was closed and the shutters were down. I tried calling, but you didn't answer me that way either."

Shit. In the shambles Angelo's day had become, he hadn't given his phone a second thought. Through the ever-present fog in his brain, he pictured it clearly on the prep counter where he'd left it when the bailiffs had told him to wait outside. When they'd handed him the keys to the empty deli twenty minutes later, he'd forgotten all about it, too intent on getting home and throwing the keys in Theresa's face.

It hadn't occurred to him that Dylan would be worried.

Guilt burned hard in Angelo's gut, matching the inexplicable fire in his lungs. He fumbled for Dylan's hand, the words to explain himself jumbling in his mind as he tried to form them into a coherent sentence, but Dylan evaded Angelo's touch.

"Look," he said. "I don't know what's going on between us—even though we've had a gazillion conversations about it—but I thought we were at least friends."

"We are—"

"Bullshit!" Dylan snapped. "If we were friends, then you'd have picked up your phone or at least sent me a message to tell me to mind my own business. You wouldn't have me running across town in my pyjamas to check you weren't dead."

Angelo looked at Dylan's Spiderman clad legs. With his hi-top Pumas, he was so adorable that a smile escaped Angelo before he could stop it, and for the second time that day, he was sent stumbling by someone else's hand.

Dylan shoved him hard. "Don't fucking laugh at me."

"I'm not—"

"You are. And you know what? That makes you a bit of a dick."

Angelo regained his footing, acid dancing in his chest as pain lanced his ribs. "I've never claimed not to be a bit of a dick, but I'm sorry I dragged you out here, okay? I had a shit day, and I left my phone in the deli."

It was the vaguest explanation in the world and Dylan clearly knew it. He shook his head and stepped back, and when he spoke again, the rage was gone, replaced by flat despondency. "I can't do this with you. Maybe it's my fault because I keep falling for blokes who have a million other things to worry about before they get to me, but I just can't do it anymore."

Angelo's heart scraped a dull summersault in the pit of his stomach. "What do you mean?"

"I mean this." Dylan gestured between them. "I'm tired, Angelo—tired of losing my shit every time someone I care about doesn't answer the phone or goes dark on me—" Dylan held up his hand to keep Angelo quiet. "The reasons don't matter anymore, mate. It's my fault; you never promised me anything. I just—I can't do this with you again. I feel like I'm stuck on a loop."

"Dylan—"

"Nah." Dylan shook his head. "I *can't*, okay? I need some space. Maybe I'll see you at the club some time."

The thought of only seeing Dylan in the club—of those snatched and wonderfully sordid encounters being their only interaction—nearly sent Angelo to his knees. He reached out for Dylan, but Dylan was already walking away. In his mind, Angelo called out to him—called him back and promised to be a better man, but when he took a breath, there was nothing there.

Because Dylan was right—especially in the things he'd left unsaid. Angelo was a mess, and Dylan deserved so much more.

CHAPTER ELEVEN

DYLAN STARED MOROSELY at the bottom of his fourth
pint. It was Wednesday night—a school night—and he was well
on his way to being proper fucking bladdered.

He was lonely too, but that was nothing new. Even partying
at The Pitt all weekend had done nothing to lift his mood, as
he'd spent most of his time explaining Sam's absence.
Goddammit. It wasn't like they'd ever been joined at the hip.

At least he'd managed to keep his dick in his pants, though.
As he tracked a familiar bloke at the bar, he was struggling to
decide if a period of self-imposed celibacy was worth the hassle.

Go home, dickhead. But as hard as he tried to make himself
move, nothing happened, save Rhys looking round at just the
wrong moment and spotting him at his solitary sulking post.

"All right, mate?"

Dylan stared at the table. "Yup. You?"

"Not bad, not bad." Rhys dropped into the seat beside
Dylan, nudging aside Dylan's abandoned work bag. "Where's
your fella?"

"My what?"

Rhys winced. "Oooh, like that, is it? Damn. I'll get the
beers in."

He got up again and went to the bar. Dylan absently watched him move—the roll of his broad shoulders, the swing of his trim waits. The devil in him craved the oblivion of fucking Angelo out of his system, and he knew Rhys would likely make a willing accomplice for a jaunt across town to Lovato's's biweekly orgy club, but pride and Sam's voice echoing in his fuzzy head kept him quiet. " . . . *stop banging people in sex clubs and get out into the real world . . . you always end up going mad in that place when you've got a cob on about shit . . .*"

Fuck off, Sam.

Rhys came back to the table with a couple of pints and four shots of what smelled suspiciously like Sambuca. Dylan groaned and dropped his head to the table. "Jesus. Haven't you got work tomorrow?"

"Nope." Rhys slid half his bounty Dylan's way. "I'm not back on shift until Saturday, which means I've got all night to cheer your miserable arse up."

He spoke without innuendo, and Dylan was grateful. It was rare that he came across playmates from the club in the outside world, and—Angelo aside—it had always been awkward. Sexual attraction and a genuine rapport weren't the same thing, and Dylan was often left wondering why he'd fucked them in the first place.

But Rhys wasn't like that. He was treating Dylan like they were old friends, and right now he was exactly what Dylan needed.

"So," Rhys said when Dylan didn't respond. "What's going on with you and the fella? Angel, ain't it?"

"His name is Angelo, actually. And he's not my fella."

"No?" Rhys cocked an eyebrow and necked a Sambuca shot. "Coulda fooled me. I had you two down as an old married couple."

"I wish." Dylan choked out a bitter laugh. "Shit. Did I say that out loud?"

"Sounds like you've got it bad, brother."

Dylan couldn't deny it.

Rhys clapped a rough hand on his back that was nothing like Angelo's smooth touch. "Come on, mate. Chin up, eh? Maybe he's just a bit screwed up and not feeling a relationship right now."

Dylan looked up sharply. "What makes you think he's the one that's screwed up?"

"I didn't say he was," Rhys countered, his tone mild. "I'm speculating based on the piss poor information you've given me so far."

Dylan maintained his glare as long as he could, but a rueful chuckle escaped him anyway.

Rhys laughed too, but then his expression sobered to the one Dylan dimly remembered from the night Angelo had collapsed outside the club. "Look, it's none of my business, but the bloke clearly has something going on right now, and when shit like that gets real, everything else suffers. If something has gone wrong between you two, it might not have anything to do with the way you feel about each other."

"You didn't seem so wise when I had you bent over that couch." Dylan sank half of his beer and considered Rhys over the rim of his glass. A vague memory of him revealing that he was a paramedic hazed through his beer-addled mind—and it *was* vague. That night, Dylan's concern for Angelo had over- whelmed just about everything. "Can I ask you something?"

Rhys shrugged. "Sure. Like you say, you've bent me over a couch and fucked me sideways, so what else is there?"

"Lots of things, I'd imagine, but I'm not talking about the club."

"Right," Rhys said. "You're talking about Angelo. What's that got to do with me?"

"Nothing, I just—" Dylan stopped. Was he really about to

betray Angelo's confidence to someone they'd fucked about with in the club?

Rhys nudged Dylan with his elbow. "I get it, mate. Serious head on now. Ask me anything, okay? I'm good with discretion . . . comes with the job."

"I don't where to start."

"Try the beginning."

"Fucking comedian."

Rhys grinned. "I try."

"Try harder," Dylan grumbled, but he took Rhys's advice and traced his time with Angelo back to the point where he'd first realised there was a problem. And it wasn't at the beginning—it was the night he recalled every time he looked at Rhys. Always. Everything came back to that. "Angelo's not well," he said eventually.

"I kind of figured," Rhys said. "What is it? MS or something?"

"ME, actually."

Rhys whistled through his teeth. "Man, that's nasty. I'm not surprised he was on his arse after the railing he gave you that night."

It was the last thing Dylan wanted to hear, but after spending the last month with Angelo, he wasn't surprised either. "I don't know much about it, but that isn't even the problem—at least, it's not the problem between us. I think it's a communication thing . . . as in, he doesn't communicate, and I can't cope without some kind of constant verbal vomit . . ."

Dylan trailed off as he realised his booze-loose tongue was kind of telling the story for him.

Rhys said nothing. Just waited patiently for Dylan to go on.

"I just don't know where I am with him, and that's like a flashpoint for me," Dylan said. "Bad memories, you know?"

"You got dicked on before?"

"Not really. It was my fault."

"And you think you've let that fuck things up with Angelo?"

"Maybe." Dylan dragged his finger through a puddle of beer on the table. "But he doesn't talk to me. I mean, I get that he feels like crap all the time, I really do, but he doesn't *talk*—he just fucking stares at me until I lose my shit."

Rhys eyed Dylan and rolled himself a cigarette. "You know chronic fatigue syndrome is way more than the name suggests, don't you?"

"What's that supposed to mean?"

"That it's more than feeling a bit knackered."

"I know that," Dylan retorted. "I looked it up when he first told me."

"Then you should know that he's probably finding it hard to keep up with you. Mentally, I mean. No offence, but you talk a thousand miles an hour. Even without brain fog, it's taking me a minute to compute what you're saying."

It wasn't the first time Dylan had been accused of having a motor mouth. He pursed his lips as Rhys stepped outside for a smoke and pondered Rhys's theory. Rhys only knew *Angel*, the confident top who turned Dylan inside out in the club, but somehow he knew that Angelo just wasn't fucking *well* enough to deal with Dylan's needy bullshit.

Dylan pictured Angelo's face when he'd rattled his garage door and pulled the plug on their brief and yet-so-*consuming* relationship. At the time, he'd found Angelo's expression frustratingly bland—like he just didn't give a shit—but had he completely misread Angelo? Was it less that he didn't care and more that Dylan was simply asking too much?

"I'm guessing I haven't done much to cheer you up then." Rhys dropped back into his seat. "You look like you're about to off yourself."

Dylan threw his last shot of Sambuca down his throat. "I'm not suicidal, just a wanker. I read about brain fog on the NHS website, but I didn't consider how real it was."

"Why would you?" Rhys said. "It's not your reality. I only know so much about ME because my brother is a physiotherapist and talks about it all the time. It's a hideous illness . . . kinda mysterious too. It's different in every sufferer. My bro had one patient who hadn't walked in two years. Another that couldn't focus enough to use a computer anymore. It's brutal, man."

Dylan's head hit the table with a dull thud. "I'm such a cunt."

Rhys rubbed his shoulders. "I doubt it. Angelo being ill doesn't give him a license to treat you like shit, and it might be that *he's* the cunt."

"He's not a cunt," Dylan slurred, but he lost the rest of his sentence to his elbow sliding off the table, and by the time he'd righted himself, the Sambuca had kicked in and coherent speech had left the party.

Rhys swayed in his seat too, apparently as rat-arsed as Dylan. "Well . . . whatever else we say about the man, he fucks like a beast."

Dylan nodded slowly. "Yeah. Yeah, he does."

WORKING through a hangover had been the norm for Dylan a few years ago, but he liked to think he'd grown up a bit since the days of partying all weekend and heading into the office on Monday morning on barely an hour of sleep. But Thursday morning found him praying to the porcelain God and wishing he'd never been born. *Dramatic?* Maybe, but it didn't feel that way on a train ride that seemed to go on for days.

In the office, he slumped at his desk and skimmed through his email. His neglected inbox was overflowing, and he had no one to blame but himself. It took till lunchtime to work through the backlog, and of course there *had* to be another snag in Angelo's DRO application. *Is there anything I haven't fucked up with him?*

An hour on the phone revealed that it was a clerical error in the Romford office.

"Who's the case manager?" the woman on the phone asked. "Is it you or the advisor in Romford?"

Dylan gritted his teeth and scanned the mess of paperwork again. He couldn't take Angelo's case back—not now after all that had happened between them—but his conscience wouldn't let him leave Angelo at the mercy of the Romford office. Wincing, he gave them Helen's name and hung up just as she appeared at his desk. "I gave your name on an out-of-area DRO case," he blurted before he could give in to the urge to hide under his desk.

"Oh?" Helen raised an eyebrow. "Any particular reason."

Lots of reasons, but Dylan went for a painfully casual shrug. "Romford were fucking—er—messing it up, and this client needs a break. I'll do the paperwork, I swear. You'll just have to sign it."

Helen was a stickler for rules, and Dylan knew that she'd insist on overseeing the case, but with the chaos he was currently residing in, that likely wasn't a bad thing. He waited for her lecture and for her to then move on, but she perched on the edge of his desk and put a hand on his shoulder.

"What's the matter, Dylan?"

"Hmm?"

Helen fixed him with the kind of look his dad had given him every time he'd cried over his mother's moonlight flit. "You seem a little distracted, and it's not like you to pass casework off. I usually have to pry it out of your hands."

"I'm tired," Dylan said. "I've not had much sleep this week."

"Insomnia bothering you again?"

Dylan shrugged. "Maybe."

Helen stared at him for a long moment, perhaps waiting for

him to squirm and break like he had done in the past, when his problems had been limited to needing a little more kip.

But Dylan didn't break. Not this time. He'd spilled his guts to Rhys and woken up on the couch feeling worse than ever. He didn't have it in him to revisit the reasons why. "I'm fine, honest. I'm gonna sleep all weekend, I promise. And I *will* do that case-work for you."

"I'm not worried about the casework, Dylan. I'm worried about you. I know you'd never let your personal issues affect the clients, but we've got a hectic phase starting from tomorrow with the TC renewals. If you're not up to it, I need to know."

Shit. Dylan had forgotten that Tax Credit renewal season was coming up—a wonderful eight-week period that left vulnerable clients at the mercy of a woefully inadequate system. He suppressed a groan. "I'm up to it. Are we ready for the first wave of claim stoppages?"

"Are we ever? Award notices went out on Monday and I've drafted extra volunteer advisors for each day, but there are going to be some cases that only you and I can deal with, and that's on top of your regular workload."

"I know." Of course he did. Thirty-five per cent of his cases from last year were still open, thanks to a series of criminal government fuck ups. "I can stay late tonight and prepare some gateway packs?"

"Only if you feel up to it." Helen stood. "A few extra hours tonight won't do us any good if we lose you on sick leave. I mean it, Dylan—it's time for some self-care."

She left him to it, taking Angelo's paperwork with her. Dylan was relieved to see the back of it—Helen had forgotten more about debt regulations than he'd ever know—but guilt still scratched his insides. Dylan had failed Angelo in many ways, but he couldn't live with himself if he didn't square away the DRO. After everything, it was the least he could do.

Dylan stayed late at the office and boarded the train home as it was getting dark. His blistering hangover had faded as the day had gone on, but his head still ached, and he was bone tired. For once, his empty bed was calling him, and he was half asleep when he stepped up to his front door a little while later and walked smack into Sam's chest.

"Jesus!" Dylan reared back, rubbing his forehead. "What the fuck are you doing here?"

Sam shrugged, and Eddie appeared behind him, her wild strawberry-blonde hair blowing in the wind. "I made him come," she said. "We've got something to tell you."

"You couldn't have called?"

Sam snorted. "Right. Like you ever pick up the phone these days."

More guilt lanced Dylan's veins. Was his behaviour towards Sam and Eddie really so different to what he'd accused Angelo of? "Sorry. Shitty week. You coming in?"

Apparently they were. Dylan led them to the kitchen, avoiding the living room where they'd spent their last encounter in Dylan's flat—naked and entwined on the couch, Dylan fucking Eddie from behind while she went to town on Sam's cock. The recollection had excited him way back when, but he wasn't in the mood for a trip down memory lane.

He went to the fridge and retrieved the milk, giving it a safety sniff before he risked boiling the kettle. "I'd offer you a beer, but the smell of it would probably have me puking on your shoes."

"Hanging?"

Eddie's gaze was concerned, but it was Sam's stare that made Dylan squirm. He turned his back on them and filled the kettle at the sink. "I'm dying. Getting blotto on a school night is always a bad idea."

"Must've been a heavy night," Sam said. "You look trau-matised."

The word was so fitting that Dylan laughed, the sound

unnaturally loud in the quiet kitchen. "Something like that. But I don't want to talk about it." He faced them again. "You said you had something to tell me. If you're pregnant, I'm not playing godfather. I hate kids."

Eddie cringed. "Pregnant? Are you serious?"

"I'll take that as a no then."

"And then some." Sam slid onto a stool at the breakfast bar, looking like he'd always been there, which he pretty much had until Dylan had wimped out on that friendship too. "We'd have to see each other to get pregnant, and Eddie's been on tour for a month."

Fuck. Dylan dumped the kettle on its stand and flicked the switch. "I'm sorry, I forgot. I'm such a shit friend. Dude, you should've called me."

Sam rolled his eyes. Another man would've repeated the fact that he *had* called Dylan, over and over, but Sam had little patience for conversations that went in circles. He pulled Eddie close and buried his face in her hair, leaving Dylan for her to deal with.

"We're moving," Eddie said.

"Okay." Dylan had expected this. Sam and Eddie had lived in Sam's crappy studio flat while she'd finished uni, but it was far too small to accommodate them long term. "Are you going to rent in Vauxhall or try further out?"

Eddie disentangled herself from Sam, and they exchanged a glance. "Actually, we're going to move to Warsaw with Artur. I scored a place in the Polish National Orchestra. A first chair. It's at the back, but still."

Dylan didn't know jack about orchestra hierarchy, but he knew how hard Eddie had worked to reach the top of her game in London, closing out her time at Goldsmiths University as leader of their prestigious orchestra. "Wow. That's awesome."

"Really?" Eddie bit her lip. "You don't have your awesome face on."

Dylan abandoned the kettle and claimed his own stool at the counter, his legs wobbling as he sank down. "Sorry. I'm just a bit shocked. I'd figured that you'd be on the move when you graduated, but Poland? Damn."

"It's been a long time coming," Sam said. "Pops wants to take that bloody urn home, and he wants to show me where he came from before he's too frail."

Dylan's heart constricted. Sam's grandparents were *his* family—he still mourned Sam's wonderful grandmother—and the thought of losing his grandfather too . . . shit. He couldn't bear it. "Artur's okay, though, right? There's nothing you're not telling me?"

"He's fine," Sam said. "Just aware of his own mortality. But it's more than that for me. I want to do something with my life while Eddie's tearing the world up with her violin, and I can't do that flipping eggs in Vauxhall."

"But you do it so well," Dylan retorted with a ghost of a grin he didn't really mean. "Vauxhall won't be the same without you."

"It'll be all right. That bakery opened by the river last summer and turned the whole borough on its head. Can't move for hipsters sitting on the pavement with their fucking sourdough scones now."

Dylan laughed. "I know the owners of that place. At least, I used to."

"Meet 'em down the sex club did you?"

"Not quite."

Sam shook his head. "I don't want to know."

"I do," Eddie said. "Dylan always has the best sex stories."

"Yeah, but we didn't come here to talk about sex, babe. That ship has sailed, remember?"

Eddie's expression was so comically downcast that a real belly chuckle escaped Dylan. He got up and rounded the counter and took her in his arms, squeezing her tight in a hug that felt far too much like a goodbye to keep him laughing for long. "We can't fuck anymore, Eddie, but you've still got first scoop on all my escapades, okay?"

"I'd better have." Eddie sniffed and squeezed him back. "We're going to miss you."

"I'll miss you too. I already miss you, actually." Dylan sensed Sam behind him and let Eddie go, turning to embrace his best friend. "When are you going?"

"Erm . . . tomorrow," Sam mumbled into Dylan's shoulder.

"What?" Dylan squirmed and tried to back off, but Sam held firm.

"Don't," he said. "This is hard enough. I can't handle a long farewell, mate."

Neither could Dylan. He held Sam until it didn't make sense to hold him anymore.

And then he said goodbye.

CHAPTER TWELVE

THE A & E doctor pressed his gloved fingers under Angelo's arms and frowned. "Take a breath for me?"

Angelo inhaled a shaky breath, willing his body to stay upright as the devastatingly hot doctor examined him. Seriously. When did British hospitals start getting doctors who looked like him? He thought about snapping a sneaky picture with his phone but then remembered that it was still locked in the gutted deli, and not vomiting became his priority.

"Lean forward, buddy."

Angelo leaned forward. The doctor's hands glanced over his bruised ribs, and Angelo winced.

"Almost done," the doctor said. "You look like you're about to pass out on me. Is the pain that bad?"

"Not in my ribs." Angelo fought his heavy eyes. "My head. And my chest."

The doctor said something, but Angelo missed it and fell forwards. His head hit the doctor's shoulder and he stayed there for a little while. The bloke smelled nice, though not as nice as Dylan. No one smelled like Dylan.

"All right," the doctor said. "I'm going to lay you down and take some blood. Breathe the oxygen, okay? It'll help."

Help with what? But Angelo was too far gone to form the words. Someone else in the room—Theresa, maybe—spoke and then came closer, gripping Angelo's hand. But he pulled away, even though he was dimly aware that something had changed between them. A needle pierced his skin and the nice smelling doctor touched cold metal to Angelo's bare chest again.

"Angelo, buddy . . . look at me."

No.

"Angelo." Theresa shook him. "Listen to the doctor."

Listening and looking weren't the same thing, but Angelo forced his eyes open, squinting against the harsh overhead light.

"Good," the doctor said. "How is your breathing?"

Angelo shook his head. "I—I don't know."

The doctor seemed to accept the non-answer, like perhaps he was expecting it. He removed his stethoscope from Angelo's sternum. "I'm sending you for a chest X-ray, but I think you may have pneumonia. It's quite common in patients with chronic fatigue syndrome, and you might've been carrying it for a while."

Angelo's head swam as he glanced at Theresa. Her face held no surprise—clearly the ME wasn't new information to her—but Angelo had no idea when that had happened. He coughed and fire spread through his chest. His eyes watered and his skull throbbed, and it was all he could do not to vomit on the hot doctor's vintage Nikes.

Almost.

After, he settled for passing out. And he came round some-time later to Theresa holding a plastic cup of stale water to his lips.

Angelo pushed it away. "I'm fine, Mum."

"You are not fine, Angelo."

Like you care. But he bit back the retort and thought hard, sifting through his pain-clouded mind. *Why is she here?* And the only explanation came from his scattered memories of how he'd wound up in A & E in the first place. The mother of all headaches had ended with an afternoon on the kitchen floor before Theresa had discovered him. He remembered staring up at her, his head spinning and his vision fogged, half expecting her to step over him, but then the air had shifted, and in a blur of gentle hands and flashing lights, she'd suddenly become his mother again.

The doctor came back to Angelo's bed. "Your X-rays show pneumatic infection in both lungs."

"Does that mean I have pneumonia?"

"Yes. Like I said, it can be quite common in ME patients."

"Why? Is my immune system fucked?"

"It's not that simple," the doctor said. "There's a lot of research that says the immune system is actually hyperactive when challenged in ME patients and becomes unable to shut down once the danger is passed."

Angelo heard the words but failed to compute the meaning. "I don't understand. I can't—I can't think straight."

"I know." The doctor laid a kind hand on Angelo's arm. "ME does horrible things to cognitive function when you're not well, eh?"

"I thought it was my ribs making me breathe funny."

"I don't think so." The doctor sat Angelo up and listened to his chest again. "The bruises are a few days old, and your X-ray shows no injuries to the bones. That also wouldn't explain why you're so ill. I'm still waiting for your bloods to come back, but I can tell by looking at you that you're anaemic, and your white blood cells are probably all over the place."

"Can I go home?"

"No. Your oxygen levels are too low. I'm admitting you to a ward upstairs and you'll likely be in for a few days."

Angelo lay back down, what little fight he had left all but gone. The doctor disappeared and Theresa took his place. She claimed Angelo's hand and stroked his face. Her touch felt cold and alien and ten years too late, but Angelo let it happen anyway. With Dylan, the deli, and now his damn fucking lungs giving up on him, their fractured relationship was all he had left.

"SO THIS IS where they stashed you, eh?"

Angelo glanced up blearily. After three long days on the crowded hospital ward, the doctors and nurses were all starting to look the same, but this bloke was vaguely familiar.

And gorgeous.

Ah. It was the hot doctor from the emergency department, and by the look on his face, he'd been waiting too long for Angelo to answer him. "Um, I s'pose so. What are you doing up here?"

"Checking on a few patients. I'm heading back up north in the morning."

"You're not from around here?"

The doctor shook his head. "Nah. I got drafted in for a specific incident and ended up getting stuck for a few days. London ain't my bag, man."

Angelo nodded slowly. The haze in his brain had lifted as his oxygen saturation had improved, but the ME fog remained, and laced with morphine, it was thick enough for him to take a moment to figure out how to verbalise what he wanted to say. "Thank you."

"What for?"

"For helping me. A specialist physiotherapist came to see me this morning. Harry something or other. He's coming again tomorrow."

The doctor glanced at the notes hanging from the end of Angelo's bed. "Harry Foster. He's a mate of mine, actually, so I called in a favour. He's the best physio in the business for conditions like yours, but you'll need to register with a GP if you want to continue seeing him."

"I know. My mum's on it."

"Good. Listen, ME is brutal, but there's plenty you can do to manage it—to give yourself a better quality of life. Find things that make you happy and hold onto them."

Angelo coughed, which didn't hurt as much as it had a few days ago. "Is that a treatment plan?"

"It's the only one you're going to get from me." The doctor returned Angelo's notes to their place and held out his fist. "Take care, mate."

And then he was gone. Angelo stared after him and shifted on the bed. Inactivity had done wonders for the infection rampaging through his immune system, but his muscles were fucked—seized up, jittery, and crampy. Brief periods of standing helped. Angelo hauled himself upright and eased his legs over the edge of the bed. It took a moment for his ankles to take his weight and the IV in his arm got tangled, but eventually, he was stable enough to shuffle to the window.

He gazed out over the city, the one positive of his corner bed. Without the view, he'd have lost his mind entirely, and the twinkling lights of a city that never slept grounded him now, soothing the scrape of anxiety that plagued him every time he pondered what the hell he was going to do. He had no job, no money, and soon he'd have no home either, at least not one that didn't involve sharing a retirement flat with his mother.

Fuck that. Angelo had felt pretty close to death over the last few days, but continuing to live with Theresa in any capacity would be a damn sight worse.

An obnoxious buzz pierced the quiet of the near silent ward. Angelo jumped and turned around faster than his healing equilibrium was totally comfortable with. He put a hand to his chest, absorbing the rattle that came with each breath and the thud of his startled heart. It was the middle of the night, and he was surrounded by snoring old men, so why could he hear a buzzing iPhone?

As the thought meandered through Angelo's mind, his gaze fell on a grubby white cable. He blinked and tracked it to the broken chest of drawers by his bed. Beside the ever-present jug of lukewarm water lay his own battered phone, plugged in and charging. *What the . . . ?* Angelo stared at it, scrabbling to recall Theresa's afternoon visit, which was the only logical explanation for the phone's reappearance in his life. She hadn't stayed long, but Angelo didn't blame her for that. He'd spent most of his time in hospital, sleeping, coughing, and throwing up, and in his brief moments of lucidity, he'd had no idea what to say to her. So he'd said nothing. And she'd left but not, apparently, before plugging in his long-abandoned phone.

He shuffled back to his bed and sat down before tentatively reaching for his phone. The cracked screen was alive with the messages Dylan had sent him the day the bailiffs had cleaned out the deli, but there was nothing since. Angelo deleted the messages without reading them and wiped his voicemail. The hurt in Dylan's eyes that night was all the reminder Angelo needed for just how badly he'd screwed up.

He set the phone down and, worn out by his jaunt to the window, curled up on his bed, wishing he had another pillow to wedge between his knees and some food that didn't smell like reheated linoleum. That he was hungry was progress, but he still felt like carving his lungs out and flinging them at the wall.

Angelo closed his eyes, but despite the quiet of the ward and the ever-present weight of exhaustion, couldn't sleep. He stared into the darkness for a while, and then shifted his attention to his dormant phone. *Don't.* But he reached for it anyway and searched for a Wi-Fi connection. A café downstairs had an open account. Angelo logged on and opened WhatsApp. A single message buzzed through the shaky Internet connection. It had been sent an hour ago and simply read *I'm sorry.*

It was from Dylan.

Angelo's heart skipped a thudding beat. He sat up, rubbing his face, willing his mind not to be playing a cruel trick on him. And when he looked again, the message was still there . . . and Dylan was online.

With shaking hands, Angelo attempted to tap out a reply. Nonsense filled the screen, and panic that Dylan would go offline before he typed anything coherent sent him into a coughing fit. Dying inside, he did the only thing he could think of and snapped a picture of the IV in his arm.

The photo hurtled into the abyss before he could check himself, and a reply from Dylan buzzed back almost instantly.

D: *WTF? Are you ok?*

Damn it. Angelo wrestled with his treacherous focus and painstakingly composed a reply.

A: *Pneumonia. Probs ME related.*

D: *Shit. Has that happened before?*

A: *No. Might have had it a while without realising tho*

Dylan didn't reply straight away. Angelo lay back and squinted at the screen. Perhaps talking would be easier than typing, but then again, even breathing was a ball ache right now. Besides, it was the middle of the night, and despite the cacophony of snoring going on around him, he didn't want to disturb anyone.

His phone buzzed again.

D: *Are you in Queens?*

A: *Yup. Shit hole.*

D: *All hospitals are.*

A: *Yeah.*

D: *Are you on the respiratory ward?*

A: *No. It was full, so they put me on some spillover ward*

D: *Bluebell?*

A: *Yeah.*

Angelo closed his eyes, willing away the dizziness and

accompanying stabbing pain behind his eyes, then forced them open and texted again.

A: *Bluebell A, I think. There's two.*

D: *Bluebell B is for children. Um . . . are you game for visitors?*

Angelo sat up again. The flutter that had danced through his burning chest when he'd first seen Dylan's message suddenly had bigger feet.

A: *Would you come?*

D: *Of course. I miss you.*

A: *I miss you too.*

And God, it was true. Life had imploded in so many ways over the past few weeks, but the wreckage of his relationship with Dylan had taunted Angelo more than anything. Everything hurt, but the cracks in his heart hurt the most.

Dylan didn't reply to Angelo's last text, and Angelo took that to mean that their conversation would perhaps continue in the morning. He plugged his phone in again and lay back down, pondering the possibility of Dylan coming to see him. Visiting hours started at ten, but Dylan would probably be at work then. The evening session was at six. Would Angelo be able to stay upright in the shower before then?

He'd bloody well try.

DYLAN PULLED a chair up to Angelo's bed. In the dim light of the quiet ward, he looked asleep, but the ward sister seemed to think he'd been awake a few minutes ago. Dylan found his hand, bruised and swollen from the IV jammed in the back. Jesus. *How the hell did this happen?*

Angelo's elegant fingers seemed to wrap instinctively around Dylan's before his eyes fluttered open. The surprise in his tired gaze was obvious. Dylan caught his shoulders as he struggled to sit up, easing him back down and stroking his face.

"Shh. It's just me."

Angelo took a breath that turned into an obviously painful cough. Dylan rubbed his chest and reclaimed his hand, squeezing gently until he was able to speak.

"You came," Angelo whispered.

Dylan smiled. "I did."

"What time is it?"

"A little after three."

"In the morning?"

"Yup."

"But—how? I mean, how did you get in here?"

Dylan slid his chair impossibly closer and shrugged. "I went to school with the ward sister, and she's let me in a few times to see Sam when he's been admitted here."

"Orgy BFF?"

"That's the one, though there won't be any orgies for a while. He moved to Poland yesterday."

Angelo cocked an eyebrow. "He did? Wow. You're going to miss him."

It wasn't a question, and Dylan didn't deny it. How could he when it was so true? "Anyway. I kind of figured that as you were awake an hour ago, you were probably having trouble sleeping in this place, so I might as well visit you straight away. I can come back in daylight if you like—"

"Don't go." Angelo tightened his grip on Dylan's hand. "I'm having a hard enough time believing that you're really here as it is."

"I'm here, mate."

Angelo closed his eyes, and for a while it seemed that he'd fallen asleep. Dylan took the opportunity to look him over, taking in the dark smudges under his eyes, the marks and bruises on his arms from needle sticks, and the oxygen mask hanging within easy reach. Coupled with the IV and the unmissable rasp in Angelo's chest, it was clear to see that he'd been—and likely still was—horribly ill.

"Are you okay?"

Dylan blinked to find Angelo very much awake and staring at him. "What?"

"Are you okay?" Angelo repeated. "You look traumatised."

Dylan forced a low laugh. "Maybe I am. And maybe I deserve to be. I should've been here when you were admitted, not rocking up however many days later in the middle of the night."

"Three days," Angelo said with a weary sigh. "And as much as I appreciate the sentiment, I'm glad you weren't here when they brought me in. I was a mess, and I'm pretty sure I puked on some hot doctor in A & E."

Dylan winced. "Really? Yeesh. Why is it always the hot ones?"

"I dunno. He was nice, though. He came to see me up here and referred me to an ME physio."

"That's good. It's about time you had some help with it—" Dylan stopped. "Sorry, I'm not here to lecture you."

Angelo smiled tiredly. "You're not lecturing me if you're telling the truth. I might have got pneumonia anyway, but it probably wouldn't have been this bad if I'd been in a better state beforehand. The doctors here reckon I'm anaemic as fuck and totally run down."

Dylan could believe it. The hand Angelo had been dealt was brutal, even without chronic illness thrown in on top. "What happened to get you here? I feel like I've missed a lot."

"You have, but it's not your fault, so wipe that guilt shit off your face."

"Guilt shit?"

"Yeah. That frown you get when you're blaming yourself for everyone else's problems. I saw you do it at work that first time I saw you in Stratford. You ran through the waiting room like a walking migraine."

Dylan laughed and then clapped his hand over his mouth, remembering the ward sister's warning about keeping quiet. "That's pretty much my life when I'm not in The Pitt or Lovato's, and I haven't been to either for a while."

"The Pitt is that mysterious metal club you've never taken me to, right?"

"Yeah. Why? You wanna go?"

"Sure. I can dig a mosh pit. When I was with the EBC, we performed with Mötley Crüe at Glastonbury. It was proper mental. I loved it—" Angelo broke off with a harsh cough that went on and on.

Dylan passed him some water and helped him drink, then eased him back down, frowning when Angelo winced. "What's the matter? Apart from the obvious."

Angelo shifted onto his side. "My hips are killing me. I need to wedge something between my legs— Don't fucking smirk. I'm serious."

Dylan swallowed a grin and stood, searching for something to help. He opened and shut a few battered cabinets but came up blank. "What about a pillow?"

Angelo rolled his eyes. "You think I haven't thought of that? I asked for one yesterday, but I was asleep when the pillow fairy came around."

"Pillow fairy?"

"She didn't tell me her name."

"She could've left it anyway, even if you were asleep."

"I think you have to sign something. Stop you nicking them."

"That's fucking ridic—" Dylan caught himself mid-rant again. "Never mind. I'll just go ask Jade for one."

"Jade?"

"The ward sister."

"Blonde with tattoos?"

"That's her."

Dylan briefly deserted Angelo and cadged a pillow from the nurse's station. When he got back, he helped Angelo get comfortable and then covered him with the thin hospital-issue blanket. "Still cold?"

Angelo shrugged. "I'm all right."

"Yeah, yeah." Dylan unzipped his beloved Judas Priest hoodie and held it out. "Borrow this. It's clean, I promise."

After a fleeting standoff, Angelo took the hoodie, and the faded gunmetal grey was awesome against his light olive skin, and warm too, if his contented sigh was anything to go by. "Thanks. I've only got the clothes I came in with and some random shit my mum found in the loft."

"Your mum?"

"Yeah. She's retraining as a parent but forgot that I'm not sixteen anymore."

Angelo said it with humour, but Dylan sensed the tale simmering beneath his wry grin. "What's been going on with your family? The deli's been closed for a week now."

"Damn. Is it that long?" Angelo pulled his hood up and propped his head on his folded arms. "The bailiffs turning up feels like yesterday."

Bailiffs. That made sense. Dylan had been waiting on a hammer blow to hit the Giordano family business from the start. He poured Angelo more water and gestured for him to continue.

"There's not much to it, really," Angelo said. "One of our suppliers took us to the small claims whatsit and sent high court bailiffs to collect what they were owed. Add in costs and the fact that all our stuff was so ancient that it wasn't worth squat, and they pretty much cleaned us out."

"What happened next?"

Angelo's expression darkened. "I was on my own when they

came—obviously—so I locked up and went home. My mum and my uncle's family were there talking bullshit about how I hadn't tried hard enough to make the business work."

"That's—"

"I know, I know." Angelo found Dylan's hand. "And for once I didn't let it go. I threw the keys at my mum and got lairy with my uncle. It kicked off and we had a bit of a punch-up."

Dylan whistled. "Awkward. How bad did it get?"

"I broke his nose, and he fucked my ribs up." Angelo pulled Dylan's hoodie and his T-shirt up to reveal ugly bruising on his torso. "But it was a good thing, I suppose. My mum finally figured out that Gino was manipulating her and sacked him off."

"That's good." Dylan couldn't tear his eyes from the bruises. He reached out and tugged Angelo's clothes back down. "So you're getting on better with your mum?"

"It's hard to tell. I haven't spoken to her much, but she did peel me off the kitchen floor and bring me here, so I can't complain too much."

"The kitchen floor?"

"Yeah. I don't really remember, but apparently the oxygen in my blood was really low and I passed out."

Dylan shook his head slightly to disperse the images of Angelo unconscious and helpless on the floor. "Sounds like you're lucky she was there."

"I am, and she's visited every day since. Oh, and she's put the house on the market too. She's downsizing to a retirement flat in Peterborough."

"Peterborough? Why on earth would she want to go there?"

"Because it's dirt cheap compared to round here and full of Britalian's like her. Either way, it's what she needed to do all along; she's just a week too late."

"Wow." Dylan let out a whoosh of air. "Sounds like your whole world is upside down. What are you going to do?"

"I don't know. Nothing's going to happen fast, so I guess I'll stay put until she moves then see where I'm at. She said she'll give me some money to help me find a place around here if I want, but I'm not relying on that."

"You can't take money from her," Dylan said. "Not if you want your DRO to stand. You'd have to pay your creditors in full before you have anything for yourself."

"I know. I'm still fucked, aren't I? I haven't even got a job."

Dylan's mind went into overdrive, scouring his brain for the cases he'd worked on where debt relief orders had been revoked. "That might work in your favour. If we can get your GP and your physio to write letters confirming your condition, the receiver might let the order stand."

"We?"

Dylan flushed. "I—er—took your case back from Romford. It's my boss's name on it, but we're working on it together. Your order came through a couple of days ago."

Something akin to relief coloured Angelo's tired face. "Thank fuck for that. Romford are clowns."

"I can't argue with that. Just keep the office informed, okay? We can't help you if we don't know what's going on."

"Story of my life," Angelo muttered.

Dylan grinned. "And mine. Oh, and if you ever meet my boss, Helen, don't tell her that we've been fucking. It's kind of inappropriate."

"Fucking. Hmm." Angelo squeezed Dylan's hand again. "Is that what we're doing?"

Of course it wasn't. Dylan had been in love with Angelo pretty much from the start, but so much had happened—and not happened—since then that it was hard to see the light. "I don't know what we're doing, but I do know that I was wrong to hassle you for commitment when you had so much shit going on."

"That's not fair," Angelo protested. "You didn't ask me for

commitment—just some friendly communication, and *I* messed that up, not you."

"Not deliberately, though. I thought I'd got my head around what ME means for you, but I was wrong, wasn't I? I had no idea how badly it was affecting you—um—mentally, if that's not a totally offensive way to put it."

"It's not. I wish I could've explained it better so you knew it wasn't that I didn't care, but please don't feel bad. None of this is your fault, Dylan."

Dylan traced a careful finger over Angelo's knuckles. "I never gave you a chance to explain, and for someone who gets paid to listen, that's pretty unforgivable. And it's something I've been guilty of before—letting my imagination have a fucking rave. Maybe I've got mummy issues."

He tried for a laugh, but it came out too bitter to see Angelo smile in return. Angelo stilled Dylan's fingers. "You've never told me about your mum. Was she a bitch?"

"No idea. She ditched me and my dad when I was two."

"You don't remember her?"

"Nope."

"I don't believe you," Angelo said softly. "But that's okay. We don't have to know everything—understand everything—to move forward. Sometimes, we have to let things be."

"We've said that before and look where we are."

"We're here," Angelo said. "Both of us."

Green shoots of hope flared in Dylan's belly. Every part of him screamed to lean forward and kiss Angelo's chapped lips, but Angelo's increasingly heavy eyes stayed him. Despite a desperate need to be as close to Angelo as possible, it was probably time he left.

Perhaps sensing the war going on in Dylan's convoluted brain, Angelo brought Dylan's hand to his lips and kissed his fingers. "Don't go."

"I'll have to eventually."

"I know, but not yet . . . please? Stay a bit longer?"

Dylan couldn't refuse. Didn't want to. He disentangled his hand from Angelo's and cupped Angelo's face, stroking his darkly stubbled cheek with the pad of his thumb. "You do something to me."

"Do I make your heart feel like it's stuck on a spinning top?"

"Yeah, actually. You do."

"Good." Angelo's eyes closed. "Because that's how you make me feel too."

Dylan felt suddenly lighter, like he always did in Angelo's rare moments of sentiment. "You know I'm not talking about the club, don't you? I mean, the things we've shared there have been amazing, but that's not why I'm sitting here."

Angelo opened his eyes with a barely audible sigh. "I know you didn't come here to fuck me, Dylan. And I know that's not what you got so upset about. I do kinda get the feeling that playing in the club is . . . Shit, I've lost my words. Uh, cathartic, maybe? You always seem calmer after."

"I'm not calm before?"

"I don't know. But I need to learn if we're going to get better at this."

He's so fucking right. Dylan sucked in a deep breath, Angelo's warm skin against his palm tying him down to the world. "I'm a pretty anxious person—in case you haven't noticed by now." He choked out another harsh chuckle. "I don't mean to be, but my brain works a million miles an hour, and sometimes I can't catch it before it's fallen off a cliff, you know?"

"I remember that feeling," Angelo said softly. "It's been a while, but I remember it. And I was a selfish prick when I was well—probably still am. I can't imagine how it must be to be like that when you care more about other people than yourself."

"What makes you think I'm so selfless, eh?"

Angelo shot Dylan a hard look. "Every moment we've ever spent together."

"Bollocks. Maybe it's just you I'm sweet on."

"So it's a coincidence that you waited for your BFF to find his soulmate before you stepped away?"

"An unintentional one." But was it? Dylan had lost many nights to worrying about Sam. Had that changed when he'd met Eddie? Or had he got caught up in fucking them both as a way of holding on? "I don't know. Sam was too easy to fret about, and angsting over shit is like an addiction sometimes. I know I'm not doing anyone any good, but I can't stop."

"How do you feel about Sam moving to Poland?"

"Sad. Relieved. Lonely." There were other emotions that Dylan couldn't quite decipher. "But I don't worry about him so much anymore. Eddie takes good care of him."

"Who takes care of you?"

"What?" Dylan looked down to find that Angelo had somehow hauled himself upright again. "What do you mean?"

"I mean that you spend all day at work fixing people's problems, then you go home and keep doing it. What about *you*? When does it stop, Dylan?"

A thousand words passed through Dylan's mind, but none of them fit. He leaned forward and pressed his forehead against Angelo's. "When you're inside me."

For a long moment, Angelo simply stared, then a slow smile spread across his face. "That's sweet, and the world comes to a standstill then for me too, but you've got to have other ways of taking a break."

Dylan sighed and reluctantly pulled away. "I'm working on it."

"Are you?"

"No, but I've got plans to."

Angelo rolled his eyes. "I s'pose that'll do for now. I'm not exactly in a position to be doling out life advice."

"You should probably lie down," Dylan observed. Was it his

admittedly overactive imagination, or had the rasp in Angelo's chest got louder? "Jade told me not to tire you out."

"Was she taking the piss?"

"I don't think so, and we should probably humour her. She threatened to put Sam in restraints once."

"I like that shit." But Angelo lay back down all the same, though his smirk remained, glinting through his obvious fatigue like a devilish beacon. "Can I ask you something?"

Dylan covered Angelo with the blanket. "Sure."

"When did you first realise that you like fucking in front of other people? I spent a decade on tour with a hoard of horny queer teenagers, so it came with the territory, but it must've been different for you."

"Your way sounds fun."

"It was, and I'll tell you about it sometime, but I'm too tired now. I wanna hear you talk."

Dylan smiled, as much for the memories as for Angelo. "It was a long time ago—back when I was a student. I was working—"

"As a waitress in a cocktail bar?"

"Shut up. As a kitchen porter in a student canteen, actually, but that's hardly the point. Anyway, I got friendly with one of the owners, and after I'd left the company, we met up again and ended up shagging . . . and, uh, his fella saw us doing it."

Angelo whistled. "He caught you?"

"No, it wasn't like that. They had a cool-as-fuck open relationship, and he never bottomed, so he got a kick out of watching Cass top other blokes."

"And you got a kick out of him watching you?"

"Yes."

"Wow." Angelo let out a long breath. "I was worried that my dick was broken, but that little anecdote has woken it right up."

"Oh yeah?"

Angelo yawned around a painful cough. "Yeah. Don't worry, though. I'm going to save it for you."

There was so much Dylan wanted to say, about possible uses for Angelo's rejuvenated libido and *so much* more, but Angelo was done. He faded out so fast it was hard to imagine he'd been awake and talking, and all Dylan could do was hold his hand just a little while longer and then leave him to his dreams.

ANGELO LAY BACK on his childhood bed—the one he'd finally consented to sleep in now Gino was out of the picture—his cracked phone pressed to his ear as Dylan's husky voice soothed his soul—a nightly occurrence since Dylan had appeared at his hospital bedside ten days ago.

"So basically," Dylan concluded a story that Angelo had only managed to half follow, "I'm a little bit drunk . . . and horny, so I'm going home."

"Fucking hooligan."

Dylan laughed. "I try, but it's Saturday night and my partner in crime is still benched."

It took Angelo a moment to realise that Dylan was talking about him, and a rush of warmth made him glad that Dylan couldn't see the flush staining his cheeks. "I don't know when I'll be up to the real world again."

"You're not feeling any better?"

"Actually, I am. Apparently passing out in the kitchen is my thing now, but this time I came round feeling like a new man."

"I can never tell if you're being sarcastic or not."

Angelo snorted. "It's usually a safe bet that I am, but for

once I'm serious. I woke up hungry and breathing like a normal person instead of Darth Vader. It was weird."

"Good weird, though, right? Oooh, hang on. I'm getting off the train."

Angelo waited while Dylan got off the train and swiped his way out of the station. His absence seemed to go on forever—the longest ten seconds of his life—and he let out a long breath when Dylan came back on the line.

"Are you tired?" Dylan asked. "I can leave you to it if you like?"

"No!" Angelo said quickly—*too* quickly. "I told you, I'm feeling good. I just miss you . . . I wish we were stumbling off the train together."

"Oh yeah?"

"Yeah. I want to see you."

Dylan sighed. "I want to see you too. I just figured you needed some space to get better and sort things out with your mum."

Angelo couldn't deny that if Dylan had been around over the last ten days, Theresa wouldn't have got a look in, though he was glad Dylan hadn't seen his more undignified moments. "Mum's asked me to go to the solicitor with her tomorrow. And she's been feeding me to death. I'll be a walking lasagne by the time you see me."

"I doubt that. Your bod is still killer."

"That's the worst joke I've ever heard."

"Sorry." Dylan sounded anything but. "Gallows humour, remember?"

"Piss off."

Dylan laughed and a pleasurable shudder rattled through Angelo. He remembered the first time he'd heard Dylan laugh in the club—in the basement room where it had all begun.

"So . . . ," Dylan said. "What do you want to do? I guess you're not up for going out yet?"

"Actually, I could do with a change of scenery, but I'm still skint, so—"

"Come to mine."

"Um . . ." Angelo wanted to. *Fuck*, he wanted to. But Dylan spoke again before Angelo could.

"Pretend I didn't say that."

"You don't want me in your place?"

"Angelo, I want you everywhere, and that's the problem. We've been fucking all this time and not paying attention to stuff that actually matters. We've got to change it up if we want to live better."

Live better. It was the exact phrase Harry the friendly physio had tossed out when he'd visited Angelo at home that morning. And Dylan thought he didn't know jack about what Angelo needed?

"Listen," Dylan said when Angelo failed to respond *again*. "Leave it with me, okay? I've got a mental week coming up, but I'll think of something. I want—I *need* to see you. I'll figure it out, I promise."

It was on the tip of Angelo's tongue to remind Dylan that figuring everything out wasn't his responsibility, but he let it go. He'd do whatever Dylan asked, be anywhere if it brought them together anytime soon.

They said goodnight and hung up. Angelo plugged his phone in and swallowed the palm full of vitamins and supplements Harry had recommended. It would be months before he saw any meaningful results, but as they slid down his throat, he felt better already. Tacit complicity in his own recovery was apparently the greatest tool of all.

ANGELO TURNED the small white box over in his hands. "You bought an iPhone?"

Theresa shuffled some paperwork. "If that's what it's called. It looked the same as that broken thing you spend your days staring at, so I got you a new one."

There were three things about those two sentences. First, that his mother had noticed his newfound preoccupation with his phone; second, that she cared; and third, that she'd done something about it. He couldn't remember the last time she'd given him anything that wasn't a bowl of pasta.

Not that he was complaining about that.

The phone, though . . . "Thanks, but I can't afford to put credit on a phone right now. I only use the one I've got because it's logged into next door's Wi-Fi."

"The one I bought has a contract."

"What?"

"That's what they called it in the shop. Data things and minutes."

"Mum, I can't have a contract either. My finances are all tied up in the DRO I told you about this morning."

That had been a fun conversation. To an outsider, Theresa's reaction would've seemed cold, but Angelo was beginning to know her better than that again. Naively, he'd thought that she'd listened.

Theresa tucked the folder of papers relating to the house sale into an envelope. She labelled it in neat block capitals and set it aside.

Then she folded her hands in front of her and fixed Angelo with a look he didn't quite understand. "While you were in hospital, I went to see the business advisor."

"In Dagenham?"

"Yes."

"The one you called a *puttana*?"

"Don't pick at me, Angelo. I'm trying to talk to you."

Resisting the urge to roll his eyes, Angelo sat back in his seat at the kitchen table and pushed his half-eaten lunch away. "Sorry. Go on."

"So, I went to see the advisor and discussed with her the sale of all our assets."

"*Your* assets."

"*Angelo!* Let me speak, child." Fire flashed in Theresa's dark eyes. "That was precisely why I went to this woman when you weren't here. I've had enough of you men thinking you can talk for me."

Angelo said nothing; merely gestured for Theresa to continue while he fought to keep his own temper in check. How could she accuse him of talking for her when she'd been intent on saying nothing at all for so long?

"The house will be sold," Theresa said. "And the business too. Our debts are vast, but there'll be money leftover for me, for you, for your sister—"

"Mum—"

Theresa held up her hand. "I know that you can't accept it right now, Angelo. Despite what you think, I *do* listen to you, but I want you to know that I will put your share aside until you are able to use it. Also, there is an investment fund that your father paid into for a while when you were younger. I think he had forgotten about it—though I'm sure Gino knew it was there—and I'd like you to have it."

"Have it?"

"Yes, to live on while you recover and to pay you back for your work *and* the money you've been sending to your father all these years. I had no idea about that until the advisor went through the accounts with me."

Of course she hadn't. Silvio Giordano had been much better at keeping secrets than he was at anything else. "Mum, that's amazing of you to offer me money, but it's the same as the left-over money from the house and business sales. I can't accept it unless I use it to pay my creditors."

"I know, Angelo. And I've thought of that. I've set up a monthly payment into a cash account in my name. It has a debit card"—Theresa slid a VISA debit card across the table—"and a chequebook, and the monthly payments should be enough to feed and house you for a year if you want to stay in Romford when I move."

Angelo opened his mouth. Shut it again. Of everything Theresa had done for him in the last fortnight, this was the most unexpected. Damn, a month ago, she didn't know how to put petrol in her own car. There were snags in her plan—he'd have to pay his rent in cash and live somewhere where utilities and furnishings were included—but it was still a lifeline, and the permanent knot of tension in his chest eased a touch.

"The phone is in my name," Theresa said when Angelo failed to respond. "I got your sister one too so she calls home more than once a year."

"I don't know what to say."

"Then perhaps we've done enough talking for one day." Theresa stood and gathered her paperwork. "You are a stubborn boy, and for that I blame myself and your father both, but I also know that we failed you. I told that poor business advisor far more than she wanted to know, and she asked me only one thing. Do you know what that was?"

"Um, no?"

"She asked me why you were as ill and alone here as you had been on the other side of the world, and I was so ashamed of the answer that I left." Theresa laid her hand briefly on Angelo's shoulder. "Take the phone, Angelo, and the money. And perhaps we'll all sleep a little better tonight."

Theresa swept out of the kitchen, leaving Angelo alone with a debit card and a brand new iPhone. He stared at both for a long moment, and then reached for the phone. Chewing on his lip, he inserted the new SIM card and powered up the phone. While it was booting, he retrieved Dylan's number from his old phone, along with Harry's contact details, and entered it all into the new phone. Then he dropped the battered handset in the bin, torn between the long-forgotten excitement of playing with a new gadget and the guilt of enjoying it while his creditors went without their payment.

Get a grip. It's not like you owe a little old lady for her bread. Those insurance companies ripped you off in the first place. Thousands of dollars for a simple blood test? Angelo's hands shook. Back then, he'd been so desperate to get better that he'd have paid a million dollars for whatever those quacks had suggested. Now? Fuck. Now he was happy to wake up with the ability to walk to the bathroom.

Stop fucking wallowing.

He picked up the new iPhone and scrolled through the app store, installing Instagram and Facebook and logging into his long-dormant profiles. Facebook was as vacuous as ever, but he'd always enjoyed Instagram—seeing people's lives, however staged, through the tiny lens of a phone camera. Most of the profiles he followed were dancers and performers. He ignored them and clicked on the search icon, typing in Dylan's name in various forms until he scored a hit.

Damn. Angelo scrolled through Dylan's feed, taking in the black-and-white catalogue of what was clearly a colourful life. Parties, concerts, friends . . . and maybe lovers. Was that the Dylan that Angelo knew? As he took it all in, he wasn't quite sure.

Dylan's infamous BFF—*Sam*—was impossible to miss, though. Tall, dark, and handsome, he had the air of a brooding rock star, and even if he turned out to have the personality of a dead fish—unlikely, but it made Angelo feel better—it was easy to see why Dylan had fallen for him.

Christ, I'd let him fuck me.

The thought warmed Angelo's blood. He tapped out of staring at Sam and followed Dylan's profile, hoping that Dylan would return the favour and take a much-needed glimpse at the life Angelo had left behind. Somehow, it seemed easier than explaining it a thousand times over.

He didn't have to wait long. His phone chimed with a flurry of notifications a few minutes later. Dylan had followed his profile and sent him a private message.

D: *Tell me it's really you*

A: *Who would pretend to be me???*

D: *Good point. But still. Caught me off guard*

A: *Sorry*

D: *Nah. It's awesome. I'm drooling over how bendy you are*

A: *Was*

D: *Are*

A: *Whatevs. I'm still wearing your hoodie btw . . . and I'm drooling over your BFF*

D: *IKR?*

A: *Yup*

D: *You make me hotter, tho*

A: *For real?*

D: *You know it*

A: *I want to see you*

D: *When?*

Angelo paused. Up till now, Dylan had been coy about meeting up and Angelo hadn't had the energy to push, but this felt different. The buzz in Angelo's veins was tangible, pleasurable, and he knew they'd been right to wait.

And that he couldn't wait any longer.

A: *Whenever ur free*

D: *I'm free tonight*

ANGELO STOOD on the front steps of the smart semi-detached house, his hand hovering over the heavy doorknocker.

What the fuck am I doing? But for once, no answer was forthcoming from his usually vocal subconscious.

He took a deep breath and knocked on the door, half-expecting it to be instantly wrenched open by a stern giant version of Dylan. But, of course, it wasn't. Dylan had invited Angelo to his father's house, but he hadn't given any indication that his father would actually be there.

Footsteps sounded in the hallway. A fair-haired shadow appeared in the glass of the door, and then it opened, and Dylan was right there.

Angelo drank in every inch of him, from his messy hair to the fair stubble that made him such a perfect combination of delicate masculinity. His long legs in the skinny jeans that matched Angelo's. His Metallica T-shirt. And his eyes. His perfect fucking eyes.

It took Angelo a moment to realise that Dylan had opened his arms.

"Come here." Dylan grabbed Angelo's hand and yanked him forward, enveloping him in the kind of embrace he'd dreamed of since they'd last been together. "God, I've missed you."

"I've missed you too," Angelo mumbled against Dylan's chest. "You smell so good."

Dylan laughed. "I shouldn't. I've been to the gym and I haven't had time to shower."

"You go to the gym?" That was news to Angelo and a reminder that they still had much to learn about each other.

Dylan released him and stepped back, coaxing Angelo over the threshold. "I don't go often because it's full of wankers, but a bit of half-hearted exercise sometimes helps me sleep."

"What's been keeping you awake?"

"The usual." Dylan shrugged. "Missing you and fretting about the mountain of work waiting for me each morning. It's still tax credit season, so the office is nuts."

"Tax credits?"

"Long story. Come through and I'll tell you all about it."

Darting his gaze around, Angelo followed Dylan through the house to a large kitchen that was strategically lit by spotlights built into the low wooden beams. "Wow. This is cool."

"My dad's a sparky."

"An electrician?"

"Yeah, so he did most of the house himself."

"Nice."

"Tell him that. He rips it all out every couple of years and starts again. Drove me up the wall when I lived here."

Angelo glanced around again. "Is your dad here?"

"Not yet. He'll be in the pub till dinnertime."

The mention of dinner made Angelo's stomach growl—a new phenomenon since Theresa had become obsessed with feeding him. The more he ate, the more he wanted to eat, and it felt good.

"You look well, by the way," Dylan said. "Better than when I last saw you."

Angelo winced. "That can't have been pretty. I was off my tits on morphine."

"I couldn't tell."

"Liar."

"It's true. Hey, do you eat curry?"

"Huh?"

Dylan chuckled. "My dad would live on fish and chips if I didn't cook for him every once in a while. I'm making a ruby. You game?"

It was the best offer Angelo had heard since the last time Dylan had asked him if he was game for something. "Can I help you cook?"

"If you want," Dylan said with a shrug. "There's not much to it."

Still, the motions of moving through a kitchen felt

natural—*right*—even if the kitchen was unfamiliar. They worked side-by-side, grinding spices and browning chicken pieces in a huge pot. The air around them was warm, soothing, and Angelo slipped into a contented daze.

A little while later, Dylan slid his arms around him from behind. Angelo leaned back and arched his neck to look at him. Their lips were millimetres apart and Angelo longed for one of those kisses that set his world on fire, but Dylan simply smiled and knocked their heads gently together. "It's got to simmer for a while now. Let me stick the rice cooker on and we can go chill."

Chilling turned out to be a cold beer and lounging on the most comfortable sofa in the world.

"It's the same as the one in my flat," Dylan said.

"Is it?" Angelo tilted his head back and closed his eyes. "I've never been in your living room."

"No, I suppose you haven't." Dylan sniggered.

Angelo cracked an eye open to meet his smirk. "I don't know what you're giving me that look for. We haven't fucked at your place."

"I'm sure we will."

"Are you?"

Dylan shrugged. "Yeah. I know we're keeping things cool at the moment, but we'll get back to the mad sex at some point."

"So why aren't we having mad sex right now?" Though Angelo couldn't deny that it would take a crane to move him off the marshmallow-like couch.

"*Because.*" Dylan sat up and swung a leg over Angelo's waist, straddling him with his sinfully long legs. "There's a lot going on, and I want whatever happens between us to be more than a co-dependent horn-fest. That's why we're here and not at my place."

Angelo gripped Dylan's hips, trying not to picture what had happened the last time they'd struck this particular pose. "Codependent hornfest? Does that mean you've been using me for sex?"

"No!" Dylan swatted Angelo gently upside his head. "It means that we got the screwing bit down early and messed everything else up."

"Hmm. I think you spend too much time trying to figure things out."

Dylan shrugged. "You're probably right, but I really want to get to know you better, and I can't concentrate on that when you've got your dick in me."

It made sense, even if Angelo didn't like it. Not that he had the energy to keep up with Dylan right now. "I get it. We need to find our feet in the real world before we go out to play."

"I'm not talking about the club."

"I know." Angelo ghosted his hands up Dylan's sides, noting that he didn't seem to be the least bit ticklish. "I meant in every sense. You know me for who I am now, but I'm still getting used to it. The club gave me a way to go back in time—to block out my reality—and I need to let that go, at least for a while."

Dylan nodded slowly. "I *love* playing with you in the club, and I'd never want to give it up, but I want to fuck the real you."

"The real me, eh?" Angelo's hips flexed of their own accord, and heat pooled in his groin. "What about the real *you*? Are you gonna surprise me?"

Dylan smirked and leaned in close, but the front door banged an agonising millisecond before his kiss reached Angelo. "Shit. That's my dad."

He sprang lithely from Angelo's lap and landed like a cat. Angelo was too jealous of his easy agility to consider the heavy footsteps in the hallway, and so the startlingly good-looking man who appeared in the doorway a few seconds later caught him off guard.

Angelo scrambled to his feet as the bearded silver fox clapped Dylan on the back and sniffed the air.

"Jalfrezi?" the man Angelo assumed to be Dylan's father asked.

Dylan nodded.

"Good." Dylan's father grunted, nodded at Angelo, and then he was gone, his boots on the wooden stairs the only reassurance Angelo had that he hadn't imagined the whole thing.

"Wow." Angelo sat back down. "He didn't say much."

"He never does. Trust me, he'll scarf his dinner in two seconds flat, check that I'm still using condoms, and then lock himself in the cellar with his model airplanes until it's time for bed."

"Model airplanes?"

"Yeah. Dad's not good at doing nothing."

"Sounds familiar." Angelo cast Dylan a pointed look.

Dylan stuck his tongue out. "I'd rather be like him than a flake like my mum."

"You think your mum's a flake?"

"I don't care if she's a flake anymore." Dylan tilted his head towards the kitchen, gesturing for Angelo to follow him. "My dad's not exactly tactile, but he was a good parent—and he *wanted* to be a good parent, which is half the battle won, right?"

"I suppose. My dad was a selfish prick."

They moved into the kitchen. Dylan took the lid off the pot of curry and gave it a poke. "Let's forget about the both of them then. Hey, do you think this is done? I can never tell with chicken."

Angelo peered into the pot. "It's done."

"How do you know?"

"Because the thigh bones are loose. My parents didn't teach me much, but I can cook pretty well."

"We should probably get married then," Dylan deadpanned. "Because that's literally all I want out of life—great sex with a shit-hot cook."

Angelo laughed. "What would your dad say about that?"

"Not much. He's down with the queer stuff, but he's a total prude. Actually, I think he's more uncomfortable when I bring girls home."

"Oh yeah?" Warmth spread through Angelo again. "Do that a lot, do you?"

"No. I haven't brought anyone other than Sam here in years, and Dad was always a bit iffy about him because he thought us being so close stopped me meeting anyone else."

"Thought he didn't say much?"

Dylan opened a cupboard and retrieved a stack of artfully chipped bowls. "He has his moments—oh hey, speak of the devil."

Angelo turned as Dylan's father entered the kitchen. Dylan grabbed the older man's arm and tugged him forward.

"Dad, this is my friend, Angelo. Angelo, this is my dad, Mick."

Mick Hart was broader than Dylan—taller too—but their features were the same even down to the natural shape of their facial hair. Mick's smile was easy, despite the gruffness he clearly wore like a second skin, and his handshake warm and firm. "Nice to meet you, son. Come take a seat. My stomach thinks its throat's been cut."

He preceded Angelo to the kitchen table. Lacking any better ideas, Angelo followed him and slid into a funky chair that wouldn't have looked out of place in a Camden bar. Mick poured himself a glass of wine from the bottle on the table, then offered it to Angelo.

Angelo shook his head. "I can't drink at the moment. Antibiotics."

"That's a bugger," Mick said. "Haven't got the clap, have you?"

"Dad!" Dylan banged the bowls down on the table. "How do you find a way of asking that every time you meet one of my friends?"

Mick chuckled and swigged his wine like it was cheap lager. "You know I'm only joking, son."

"Of course I do. It's the only joke you have."

Dylan huffed and stomped back to the stove. He was back a moment later with the curry, and as he'd predicted, Mick inhaled his food and disappeared again, thumping Angelo on the back and taking the wine with him.

Angelo sat back in his seat, pleasantly full from his first non-Italian meal in weeks. "That was short and sweet."

"Always is." Dylan picked at his food. "He likes you, though."

"How can you tell?"

"Because he offered you his wine."

Angelo snorted. "Bollocks. That was the most pointless interaction ever."

"No interaction is pointless, Angelo."

"Ain't it?"

"Of course not." Dylan pushed his bowl away. "People don't have to talk to express themselves. I knew that before I met you, but somehow I forgot."

"Is this your way of telling me that I'm a shit communicator?"

"More like it's my way of telling you that it doesn't matter and that there's plenty of things that I'm shit at too. Perhaps I don't listen enough."

"Listening is your job."

"Right. And I hear the same problems recycled over and over again. What are the chances that I've stopped paying attention?"

Angelo frowned. "Are we still talking about the same thing?"

"Oh, I don't know." Dylan stood with a sigh and gathered the dirty bowls. "I guess I'm a bit frazzled at the moment."

Angelo trailed Dylan to the sink with the curry pot. His legs had gone to sleep, but for once the persistent tingling didn't bother him. "You were going to tell me about tax credit week at your work. Is that what's stressing you out?"

"Mostly. It's worse than January when the credit card debts kick in."

Angelo gestured for Dylan to explain and hustled him sideways so he could get to the sink and turn the taps on.

Dylan looked as though he might protest, but after a fleeting standoff, moved aside. "Tax credits are a wage top-up the government pays to low-income households. Recipients have to renew every summer, which inevitably leads to total chaos. The system is shambolic and makes no sense even to me, and I've been on every craptastic training course under the sun."

"So it takes a while for renewals to go through?"

"*If* they go through." Dylan opened the dishwasher and began to stack it with the rinsed crockery Angelo passed him. "Delayed renewals don't matter so much because claimants continue to get paid. It's when a renewal gets lost, fucked up, or cancelled that things get shitty. People get pretty pissed off when they can't feed their kids."

"I'll bet. I heard someone yelling at one of your colleagues when I came in that first time."

"Yeah, that happens a lot at this time of year. Clients expect us to fix everything for them, but when we're dealing with a broken system, we just can't do it."

Angelo washed the curry pot and set it on the draining board. "At least you're there for them at all. Where would they go otherwise?"

Dylan shrugged. "I'm there because I get paid to be. Most of the other advisors are volunteers."

"They pay you for a reason. And I know for a fact that you work way beyond your nine-to-five, so take that look off your face."

"What look?"

Angelo dried his hands and stepped into Dylan's personal space, swiping at his frown lines with his thumb. "You're always so worried that you're not doing enough."

"How do you know that?"

"Dunno. But I ain't wrong."

Dylan didn't deny it. Angelo let his hands travel to Dylan's soft hair and toyed with the silky strands. They seemed to be back in that vortex where the air between them was ever shifting, tying them closer, bonding them. How was it possible that he'd lived a whole lifetime without Dylan?

No answer was forthcoming from his subconscious, or Dylan, and the moment passed. Angelo's hands dropped to his sides, and Dylan turned away.

By the time the kitchen was cleaned down, Angelo was flagging. Eagle-eyed as ever, Dylan slipped an arm around his waist and guided him to the living room, laughing when Angelo fell face first onto the squishy couch.

But his expression sobered quickly. Angelo sat up and patted the space beside him. "What's up?"

"Hmm? Oh, nothing."

"Liar."

Dylan poked his tongue out. "Am not."

"Yeah, you are."

Dylan sighed. "It's hard to explain."

"Try? Please?"

"It's just that even though you're tired and still recovering from the pneumonia, and I know the ME never goes away entirely, I can see how much better you are."

"And that upsets you?"

"Yes. Because it reminds me how wrong I got it before."

Angelo was lost. He leaned against Dylan when he finally sat down and lolled his head on his shoulder. "I don't understand."

"When we met at the club a few weeks after you first told

me about the ME, I thought you were better, but I know now that you weren't, that you were still struggling."

"Oh." Angelo could barely remember the last few weeks he'd worked at the deli and couldn't imagine how he'd fooled Dylan into thinking he was anything close to okay. "Well, that's my fault, isn't it? Not yours. How would you have known any different when I was so used to keeping it all to myself?"

"I don't know," Dylan muttered bleakly.

Angelo sighed. That Dylan cared for him so much had proved a lifeline, but Dylan didn't deserve to be angsting over it like this. "I'm always going to struggle. There are things I can do to feel better, but I'm never going to be like I was before."

"Like you were on your Instagram profile?"

"Yeah, 'cause the Internet constitutes reality." Angelo sat up and glared half-heartedly. "No, in general, not just the narcissism I chose to share back then. And what I actually mean is that I don't want you to worry about things we can't change."

Dylan chewed his lip. "Are we going round in circles with this?"

"A bit—" Angelo broke off with a yawn that made his head spin. "But that's *my* fault. I'm getting better at talking, I swear."

Dylan smiled and coaxed Angelo to lie down again, stretched out on the magical sofa, his head in Dylan's lap. "You're better at it already."

Angelo chuckled hazily as Dylan moved his fingers over his scalp. "I've been practising with my mum. She keeps trying to give me money. Did I tell you she gave me a phone and a debit card in her name to use for a while?"

"No, but you probably shouldn't. The less I know about stuff like that, the better."

"Should I make her take it back?"

"That's not for me to say, but as we're in my dad's house and not my office, I'm going with no. You need to live, Angelo, not just survive."

Survival had been all Angelo was capable of for so long that Dylan's words took a while to sink in, and by then he was half asleep. With his head in Dylan's lap, he listened to Dylan humming along to Kerrang! and dozed until instinct told him it was time to go home.

Dylan walked with him, his arm comforting and solid around Angelo's waist, keeping him upright in more ways than one. They stopped at the end of the driveway and Dylan pushed him gently against the wall. "When can I see you again?"

Angelo shrugged, breathless from the walk or maybe the fact that Dylan's lips were mere inches away. "Whenever you're free. It's not like I've got much on."

"I'd argue that you have *way* too much on." Dylan's grin was a beacon in the gloom of their dark corner. "But it is pretty cold so I guess I can't strip you."

"If you wanted to strip me, you should've said before we left your dad's place."

"I was trying to be good."

"Stop."

Dylan laughed. "Maybe next time. I'm working late tomorrow, but I'll call you. Maybe we can grab a drink or something?"

Angelo nodded, but fatigue had caught up with him and his head bobbed alarmingly. "Sounds good. If you're gonna kiss me tonight, though, you'd better do it now before I'm too tired to remember it."

"You want me to kiss you?"

"Is that a real question—"

Dylan's lips cut him off, crashing against his with the sweet force that Angelo had been dreaming of. He pushed Angelo ever tighter to the cold brick wall and shoved his hands under Angelo's jacket and T-shirt, his smooth, warm palms gliding over Angelo's tingling skin, and Angelo caught fire. He fell slack in Dylan's arms, all the while kissing Dylan back with a wild, wretched groan. Why had they wasted the night talking when they could've been doing *this*? Why were they outside in the cold, wrestling with layers of clothes, when they could've been rolling around on a bed—any bed—Dylan's, his own, even a plastic-covered mattress at the club?

Angelo groaned again and fumbled desperately for any part of Dylan that he could reach, pulling him impossibly closer. Reason abandoned him, and he'd have been on his knees in a heartbeat, swallowing Dylan whole if Dylan hadn't broken their crazed kiss.

"I should go," Dylan said, panting.

"I don't want you to."

"I know." Dylan flexed his hips pointedly, grinding their crotches together, his cock as hard as Angelo's. "But I still should. You're exhausted, and we've got all the time in the world to get back to fucking."

Dylan was wavering, Angelo could tell, teetering on the edge of doing the right thing or giving into the fire that was making him tremble as hard as Angelo. Another grind, another kiss and he'd crumble. Theresa slept like the dead, she'd never hear Angelo leading Dylan upstairs and fucking his brains out on his childhood bed, especially if he pressed his hand over Dylan's mouth, a club-born fantasy that could easily find a home in the real world. *But . . .*

Angelo closed his eyes and banged his head softly on the wall behind him. Dylan was right. If they fell into bed now, they'd crawl out right back where they'd started. They both needed more.

Besides, as active as his imagination was, the reality was that right now he'd be lucky to climb the stairs on his own, let alone with Dylan wrapped around him, and sleep was the only thing calling his name that would truly get an answer.

He kissed Dylan one last time, sweeping his tongue over

Dylan's lips, biting down hard enough to make them both groan. And then he pulled away. "You'll call me tomorrow?"

"Yes. As soon as I'm done."

Angelo nodded slowly. "Okay. Guess this is goodnight then."

"Uh-huh."

Dylan stepped aside, and Angelo forced himself away from the wall. Turning his back on Dylan was torture, and each step toward the house lanced his heart with pain, but he didn't look back. Couldn't. Because one more look at Dylan would've crumbled his resolve to dust.

Fuck. I love him.

CHAPTER FOURTEEN

DYLAN SCANNED the notes he'd typed up for his last client of the day. To his frazzled brain, they didn't make much sense, but he was hoping that would change when he looked them over tomorrow.

With a weary sigh, he began the slow task of shutting down the ageing PC. It hummed and rattled like a dying helicopter, signalling that it would take a while to close all the open applications, so he turned his attention to his phone. Two messages from Angelo lit up the screen and his heart skipped a beat.

A: *Are you nearly finished?*

A: *Fuck it. I'm gonna come meet you*

Joy roared in Dylan's ears. He spoke to Angelo every day, but it had been nearly a week since they'd last seen each other. Dylan's extended working hours meant he'd get home too late to catch Angelo awake, and *God*, he missed him. His fingers flew across his screen as he tapped out a reply.

D: *You sure? I'll be done in half an hour*

A: *Perfect. I'll be there*

Dylan set his phone down, excitement battling an irritating rush of anxiety as he fought the urge to tell Angelo to stay put and wait for him. *Trust him, remember? He wouldn't come out if he didn't feel up to it.* Angelo seemed to have good and bad spells, but he'd been working hard with his physiotherapist and testing himself a little more each day. And even when his body wouldn't play ball, the change in his personality was startling. His smile, his laugh—even when he was tired—were both so genuine that Dylan dreamed of them every night he wasn't lucky enough to see Angelo in person.

"You're grinning like a maniac again."

Dylan jumped as Helen came up behind him and dumped a stack of files on his desk. "Huh?"

Helen laughed. "The grinning, Dylan. You've been at it all week."

"Have I?" Dylan cringed. "Sorry. Just in a good mood, I guess."

"That's not something you need to apologise for. I take it you're sleeping better?"

"A bit. I'm freaking out less about work too. We've cleared most of the backlog, right?"

"Most of it," Helen agreed. "You know what it's like, though. We're bound to get—"

The office door opened, cutting Helen off. Tony, the volunteer who often manned the waiting room, poked his head in. "We've got an overflow."

"How many?" Helen asked.

"Three. Shall I tell them to come back tomorrow?"

Helen glanced pointedly between the three of them—one for each still waiting client—and Dylan's heart sank. Another client meant an hour of extra work, at least . . . an hour that Angelo might not have left in him after a long day of physical therapy.

He felt like crying as he composed the message to Angelo.

D: *Last minute client. Gonna be another hour at least. Go home. I'll find you x*

He didn't have time to wait for a reply.

With a heavy sigh, he grabbed what he needed and trudged to the waiting room to retrieve a client. Tony had already taken one, so he nodded at the stocky man holding card number two. "If you'd like to come with me?"

He led the man to the room at the end of the corridor and waved him inside. "Take a seat. I'm Dylan, one of the advisors here. Can you tell me why you're here today?"

The man sat down and unbuttoned his coat. He reached inside and withdrew a machete. "I'm here for my fucking money, mate. How about you?"

FEAR DID strange things to time. And time was a strange thing when fear didn't manifest itself the way you might have expected it to. Dylan sat on the floor of the consultation room, his back to the corner, his hands on his knees, following the instructions of his apparent hostage taker to the letter.

"Does this phone come off the table?" the man asked gruffly.

"Depends what you want to use it for." Dylan pictured his own phone lying useless in the next room. "Do you think you could put your knife away?"

"Nope. I'm not doing anything you say until you ring those bastards up and tell them to pay my missus her money."

"What money?"

"Her family allowance, innit? Six months she's been without it and you cunts have done nothing about it."

Dylan eyed the grubby machete that was still on the desk within the man's easy reach. "Family allowance doesn't exist anymore. Do you mean child benefit? Or tax credits, maybe?"

"I don't bloody know what it's called, do I? All I know is we got a bunch of letters telling us we'd had too much money, then they stopped putting our money in the bank. Six times my missus has been down here and you cunts done nothing. Now the council want to take our house. Where the fuck are my kids gonna live?"

The man spoke lowly, but the flat tone in his voice frightened Dylan more than if he'd been shouting and throwing things around. This man wasn't hysterical—he had a plan . . . a plan that involved Dylan and a machete. "What do you want me to do?"

"Phone them up."

"Who? I can't resolve your situation if I don't know who you're dealing with."

Anger flashed in the man's eyes. He banged his fist on the table, making the machete jump and slide closer to him. "Just call them!"

He threw the phone to Dylan and then stood—grabbing the machete—and moving across the room to stand over Dylan. "I've got the number right here, so don't try any funny business."

A scrap of paper drifted down towards Dylan as the door to the room opened. Tony stared in like a rabbit caught in headlights.

"Fuck off!" the man roared.

"Um . . ." Tony stuttered. "Dylan has a phone call in the next room. Could he step out for a minute?"

"No. He's staying here until he's sorted this mess. Don't open that door again or I'm gonna hurt someone, I swear."

Clearly lacking any better ideas, Tony disappeared, the door closing with a quiet click. Dylan eyed it and wondered if he was fast enough to scramble through the man's legs and make a run for it, but a steel-capped boot connected with his shin before he could weigh it up.

"Dial," the man growled.

Footsteps in the corridor spurred Dylan into action. He grabbed the piece of paper the man had tossed down to him and studied the number, recognising it immediately as the tax credits call centre. "If I call this number, we'll be on hold for ages. There's another one I can use that's just for Citizens Advice centres and goes straight through."

"You think I'm stupid?"

"No." Dylan swallowed the fear bubbling up from his gut. "I think you're in a hurry, and the quickest way I can help you is by calling a direct number. It's on a clipboard in that drawer over there if you want to check it yourself."

More footsteps and voices sounded from the corridor. Fabric brushed against the door and Dylan pictured Helen frantically trying to see through the tiny glass panel. *Don't open the door, woman. Dear God, don't open the door.*

The door remained closed. Dylan held eye contact with the man and nodded again at the desk drawer. "The number is in there."

Keeping the machete trained on Dylan, the man backed up to the desk and opened the drawer. The clipboard with the telephone directory on it was right there, and he threw it at Dylan's feet. "Don't fuck about, mate. I'm not in the mood."

Dylan inhaled a shaky breath and took the phone off the hook. "I'm going to need your name and national insurance number—your wife's too, if the claim is in her name."

"What?"

"I need your information. I can't negotiate a claim if I don't know who it's for."

"Are you taking the piss?"

"No." Dylan put the phone back in its cradle. "You've given me the number for a tax credits call centre. Who's on the claim? You and your wife? Just her?"

"I don't know."

"Can you call her and find out?"

Dylan offered the man the phone and, for a split second, thought he'd take it, but then something changed in the man—

something snapped—and the phone was kicked out of Dylan's hands.

It sailed sideways and hit the wall, fracturing into three pieces. The man bellowed like an angry bull, then set about destroying the room while Dylan cowered in the corner. A chair flew past his head, scraping his knuckles, and the desk splintered as the man kicked and stamped at anything that crossed his path. The machete zipped through the air, slashing at the noticeboards, and Dylan covered his head with arms, waiting for the blade to bite into his flesh.

"I'm done with this," the man shouted. "Someone's gotta pay."

CHAPTER FIFTEEN

POLICE CARS ZOOMED past Angelo one after another—three, four, five, six. And then vans too, three of them. He sat up on the bench he'd crashed on when he'd got Dylan's message, unease prickling his sensitive skin. Police activity wasn't unusual in the city, but as a string of ambulances followed the police vehicles, something—everything—felt off.

He stood, adrenaline fizzing in his veins, and tracked the vehicles as they disappeared into the distance. Stratford wasn't as familiar to him as Romford, but the blue lights were heading in the same direction as Angelo had been when Dylan's text had stopped him in his tracks, and as far as Angelo knew, there was nothing at the end of that road but a kebab shop and a disused pub.

His phone buzzed. *Dylan.* He ripped the phone out of his pocket, but the message was from Harry, confirming an appointment for the following week. Angelo swiped it away and opened WhatsApp, clicking on the ever-growing chat thread between him and Dylan. The reply he'd sent to Dylan's last message remained unread, and Dylan hadn't been online since he'd told Angelo he'd been delayed. The rational part of Angelo's brain told him that Dylan was simply with a client, but a monster of panic dug in the other part, seizing control of Angelo's imagination. He'd only ever seen that many police cars before when the Tube had been bombed a decade ago, but the world had changed since then. Bad shit happened all the time, especially in London. *What if—*

No. Angelo shook his head to clear it, almost laughing at himself, though the knot in his chest made that impossible. Since when had he been a fucking drama queen? Why would he bother when life kicked him in the tits regardless? *Dylan's fine.* But even as he thought it, the nerve-jumping anxiety having a party in his gut rebelled. *He needs me.*

The realisation hit Angelo like a truck and made no more sense than the cold sweat beading on his tingling skin, but his soul knew it was true.

Running hurt Angelo's knees, his hips, and his back, but he barely felt the pain as he tore down the street, chasing the sirens still wailing in the distance. He dodged commuters heading for home and early evening drinkers already stumbling outside the bars. Ahead, flickering bursts of blue light lit up the evening sky, and Angelo's heart dropped as the police cordon came into view. A wall of emergency vehicles was blocking the road that Dylan's office was on—nothing and no one was getting through. And no one wanted to, if the crowds of people running away from the area were anything to go by.

Angelo crashed into a woman as a million catastrophic scenarios flashed through his panicked brain. He grabbed her arms, and somehow they both stayed upright. "What's going on? Why have they closed the road?"

"Terrorists," the woman hissed. "Probably those dirty Muslims again."

Angelo didn't have time to challenge the blatant racism. He let the woman go and tore past her, elbowing his way upstream until a policeman caught his arms and lifted him clean off the ground, propelling him five paces back before he set him down.

"Can't go down there, mate," the policeman said. "Road's closed."

"Why?" Angelo forced himself not to fight the policeman's hold. "What's happened?"

"An incident. We need to clear the area, so go back to the train station and go around."

"I can't go around. My friend's in there."

"In where?"

"The Citizens Advice office."

Something flickered in the policeman's eyes and chilled Angelo to the bone. "What's your friend's name?"

"Dylan."

"Dylan what?"

Angelo's mind went blank. He'd seen Dylan's surname on the neat stack of post he kept in his kitchen by the kettle, heard it when he'd met his father, but as hard as he tried, couldn't recall it. He shook his head. "I can't remember."

"Can't be that good a friend then," the policeman snapped. "Head back to the station and go around."

"No—you don't understand. I can't remember because there's something wrong with me, not because I don't know it."

The policeman hauled Angelo to one side, impatient scepticism deepening his frown. "Look, mate, there's some serious shit going on here. I ain't got time for any nonsense."

"It's not nonsense. I—" Angelo's words stuck in his throat. Brain fog short-circuited his ability to string a sentence together and he fumbled desperately for his wallet. The shiny plastic card the ME nurse at the clinic had given him that morning was at the front. He pried it out and passed it to the policeman. "I can't get my shit together to explain myself, but I'm not wasting your time. My friend Dylan works in the Citizens Advice Bureau—he's a debt advisor there—and I need to know if he's okay."

The policeman took the card and studied it, his expression

as impassive as his impatience would allow. "How well do you know your friend?"

"What?"

"Your friend," the policeman repeated. "How close are you? Do you know his family?"

Panic like Angelo had never known roared in his ears. Faint and dizzy, he grabbed the policeman's arm. "He's my boyfriend."

<hr>

THE OPTIMISTIC DECLARATION didn't get Angelo very far. The policeman led him through the cordon but then dumped him in the back of an open police van and ordered him to stay put, and with armed officers as far as the eye could see, he had little choice but to do as he was told.

Eventually, a plain-clothed officer came to find him. "Angelo Giordano?"

Angelo slithered out of the van. "Yes. Where's Dylan? Is he okay?"

The officer held up her hand. "ID?"

Angelo passed over his ancient provisional driving licence. "Where's Dylan?"

"He's safe," the officer said. "A few cuts and bruises, and he's a bit shaken up, but he'll be okay."

Relief rushed through Angelo and cleared his mind, blowing away the haze of panic that had left him so dizzy. "What happened?"

"A client brought a machete into the office and triggered a terrorist alert. We have him in custody now. Dylan and his colleagues are at the council offices next door. I'll take you there now."

Dazed, Angelo followed the officer through the eerie closed-off streets. The need to get to Dylan outweighed every emotion somersaulting through him, but as they got closer to the second cordon, perspective came back to him. Was Dylan expecting him? Or would he flip his shit when the police announced Angelo as his boyfriend in a room full of his work colleagues? *Shit.* What if Dylan wasn't even out at work? What if—

"He's in the last room on the right." The officer touched Angelo's shoulder and turned him gently in the right direction. "The team in there are expecting you."

She probably meant her smile to be reassuring, but Angelo felt sick. He'd barged his way into this part of Dylan's life under false pretences and seemingly couldn't stop. His legs moved of their own accord and carried him into the nondescript building and down a dreary corridor. A policeman at the end took his name and pointed to a closed door. Angelo touched the handle and resolve crashed into him. If Dylan was angry that he'd lied to get to him, Angelo didn't care—couldn't care—because nothing mattered except putting his hands on Dylan and knowing for sure that he was okay.

He opened the door. At first, the small room appeared empty, but then he saw Dylan sitting on the floor in the corner, bruised and bleeding arms a cage around his head. "Dylan?"

Dylan looked up slowly, his gaze hooded and heavy. "Angelo?"

Angelo crossed the room and dropped to Dylan's side. He pulled Dylan close and wrapped his arms around him, holding him so tight that he didn't know where Dylan ended and he began. "I'm here, baby. I've got you."

DYLAN WAS WRECKED. "Please, Angelo. I just want to go home."

"I know, I know." Angelo held him tight. "I'll get you out of here, I promise."

But escaping turned out to be easier said than done. It took a while for the paramedics to check Dylan over and then for him to convince the police to let him leave, and by then, the reopened streets were overrun with press.

They snuck out a side door and jumped into a waiting cab. Dylan said nothing on the journey back to Romford, and by the time they pulled up outside Dylan's place, his trembling outshone Angelo's, even on his worst days.

Alarmed, Angelo swiped the cab driver's machine with Theresa's debit card and hauled them both out of the car. He patted Dylan's pockets for his keys and let them into the flat. Safely inside, he leaned back on the front door and released a long breath. The hint of colour returning to Dylan's cheeks eased the worry banding his nerves, but it wasn't nearly enough.

Dylan toed off the grey plimsolls he wore to work, his gaze fixed on the floor. Angelo went to him and took his hands. "Do you want some tea?"

"How did you know?"

"What?"

"How did you know where to find me?"

"The police told me. I—um—said I was your boyfriend."

Dylan stared blankly. "They never mentioned that. Just said that someone was waiting for me. When they said your name, I thought I'd imagined it and my dad would come waltzing in."

Angelo chewed his lip. "I'm sorry."

"What for?"

"I don't really know."

A ghost of a smile flickered across Dylan's drawn face. "If it's for telling the police you're my boyfriend, you can stop that shit right now—unless you didn't mean it, of course. Then you can go fuck yourself."

There was no malice in his tone. Angelo squeezed his hand and stepped into his personal space, pressing their bodies together, his chest so tight against Dylan's that he felt his hammering heart. "I don't know how to be a boyfriend. I've never had time, until now. But there's nothing I won't do for you. You know that, don't you?"

Dylan shook his head slightly. "I don't know much right now. My brain's fried."

And as Angelo lost himself in Dylan, the truth of that statement made itself known. He'd seen Dylan panic before—in the club when his hands had been tied—but this was different. This was *worse* because Angelo didn't even halfway understand it. "Will you tell me what happened today?"

"The police didn't?"

Angelo kissed Dylan's forehead and then stepped back, tugging Dylan towards the kitchen. "Just that a client had come into your office with a machete. It was all over by the time they told me that, though, and you seemed so freaked out when I got there that I just wanted to get you home."

"I'm glad you did." Dylan let go of Angelo and drifted past him to the kettle. "I was losing my fucking mind."

I could tell. But Angelo said nothing. Just watched as Dylan made tea with shaking hands and waited for him to talk.

"I don't know who he was," Dylan said eventually, still mechanically stirring over-brewed tea. "I went through the records after they took him away. He'd never been in before, nor had his wife, though he seemed to think she had."

"His wife?"

"Yeah. That's why he was so angry. Her tax credits had been stopped and they were losing their house . . . at least, that's what he said."

Angelo searched his brain for what Dylan had told him about tax credits over the last few weeks. "This was the government thing you were worried about?"

Dylan nodded. "It's always chaos, but it's never kicked off like that before. He hardly touched me, but I honestly thought he might kill me before the police tasered him. And then I thought that *they'd* killed *him*, and somehow that was worse."

"Why?"

"Because he was desperate, not evil, and that isn't his fault." Dylan dropped the teaspoon on the counter and turned his back on the tea. "He wasn't my client, but he could've been. Do you know how many cases I couldn't fix this week? How many people face months with sanctioned incomes because there was nothing I could do for them?"

"Um . . . no?"

"Neither do I, because I lost count. Shit, I need to call my dad. And why the hell am I still shaking?" Dylan stared at his trembling hands.

Angelo was beside him in an instant. "You're shaking because what happened today scared you. But none of it was your fault. You didn't create the system, and you can't solve everyone's problems when the world is so messed up."

"But I'm supposed to be able to help the people who walk through that door. That bloke got *tasered* because he hit rock bottom and lost his head. How is that fair?"

Angelo had no answer to that because the last twelve months had kicked the shit out of him. His only blessing was that his bad luck had brought Dylan into his life, but the man who'd been tasered? That he'd hurt Dylan made Angelo want to kill him, but an eye for an eye made everyone blind, and none of it was fucking fair.

Dylan shuddered. Angelo put his hands on his face and let his agitation crackle through his own nerves, like he could take it all away. Dark smudges under Dylan's eyes told Angelo that he was exhausted, that he needed to sleep and forget this day ever happened for a while, but as he held Dylan and absorbed his excess energy, he realised there was no way Dylan was sleeping anytime soon. "Call your dad."

"Okay." Dylan stared at his phone.

Angelo took it off him and found Mick's number. The call went to voicemail, and when Dylan shook his head, Angelo typed out a text message instead.

D: *If you see the news, don't worry. Home and safe with Angelo*

Dylan smiled. "Home and safe. I like the sound of that."

"Me too. I think you should show me round your place, though."

"What? Why? You've been here before."

Angelo shook his head. "We talked about this at your dad's place. I've slept in your bed, used your shower, and I know where the kettle is. Show me the rest."

Perhaps it was the break in the cycle that Dylan needed. He shook himself slightly and then led Angelo out of the kitchen. "I forget that our relationship is totally abnormal because being with you is like breathing . . . I can't imagine not doing it."

He spoke absently, but the sentiment hit Angelo like a truck all the same. "I can't really remember not having you in my life, either. I know I fuck up pretty much every day, but I'm as crazy about you now as I was from the start."

"We started in the club with my arse in the air." Dylan opened the door to his living room. "And you've been on my mind ever since. Ain't we romantic?"

"Fuck that shit. Who wants to be romantic?" Angelo stuck his head in the living room. As promised, the couch was the same as the one at Dylan's father's house, and the urge to flop down on it was strong, but Dylan wasn't ready to crash yet, and Angelo would be awake when he was if it killed him. "You don't spend much time in here."

"How can you tell?"

"Because it's tidy."

"Fair point. And you're right. Any evening I'm at home, I tend to flit from one room to another. I'm easily distracted, in case you hadn't noticed."

"I hadn't noticed because I don't think it's true. You have much better focus than me—you must have, to deal with all that bullshit DRO paperwork. I reckon you're just crap at relaxing."

"Says you." Dylan tugged Angelo away from the living room. "You were working 24/7 at the deli."

"Not quite. And look where it got me—on a geriatric ward with a mask strapped to my face."

Dylan's fingers tightened around Angelo's. "I hate thinking about that."

"So don't." Angelo tapped Dylan's temple. "Stop thinking at all. What's in there?"

Dylan followed Angelo's gaze to the last door before the bedroom and bathroom. "Nothing."

"Nothing?"

"Yup. It's empty. Look." Dylan opened the door to what was indeed an empty room—a *beautiful* empty room with the same wood floors as the rest of the flat and an original window from the old Railstore. In daylight, it would've bathed the room in natural light. Right now, Angelo could see the stars, and it took him back to the happy-clappy pain clinic he'd spent all afternoon at.

"Have you got a lamp?"

"What?"

"A lamp," Angelo repeated.

"There's one behind you. Why?"

Dylan broke off with a shiver. Angelo rubbed his arms and kissed his forehead again and then looked around for the lamp. "I want to show you what I did today. Go and put your pyjamas on."

"My pyjamas?"

"Or sweats. Whatever."

"You're weird."

But Dylan sloped off to the bedroom anyway while Angelo unplugged the lamp and carried it into the empty room. With it plugged in and emitting exactly the glow he'd been after, he searched out the wireless speaker from the kitchen and set that up in the spare room too.

Dylan came back as he was linking his phone to the speaker. "Temple of the Dog?"

"Chris Cornell was my jam when I first realised I liked blokes as much as girls. I had a thing for his hair."

"Bit young for nineties grunge, aren't you?"

"Never too young for something you like, mate."

Dylan sat on the floor beside Angelo and tilted his head to one side. His eyes were still bright with stress, his limbs tight, his hands clenched, but his characteristic shrewdness was back. "You're different."

"Different to what?"

"To how you've mostly been since I met you."

"You're going to have to explain, because that doesn't make much sense." Angelo set his phone aside and widened his legs to a straddle, leaning forward and testing his tired muscles. "But first, I want you to help me with something."

"You're asking for help?"

"Yup. I've spent all day relearning how to relax my muscles, and I'm worried I'll forget it by morning. If I show you, it might stick in my mind."

If Dylan saw through Angelo's breeze-block-lined attempt at subtly, it didn't show. He nodded absently and mirrored Angelo's pose, legs spread wide, his elegant feet naturally pointed. Caught young enough, perhaps he'd have made a hell of a dancer. He certainly had rhythm.

Angelo leaned forward, flattening his chest to the floor, and reached for Dylan's hands. "Breathe in deep and let it go as you stretch out."

"Does this count?" Dylan leaned down a fraction. "Because that's about all I've got. I don't bend like you do."

"How d'you know if you haven't tried?"

Dylan winced as Angelo gently pulled him lower. "Sadist."

"You usually like that side of me."

"Yeah, well. Maybe I'm in the mood for something more gentle."

But he didn't complain as Angelo coached him through the simple series of stretches. The routine was low impact—an easy ask for a healthy body, but though Angelo's flexibility had survived the ravages of ME, he couldn't hold his arms and legs up for long.

Dylan had less reach but far more stamina. Angelo stood beside him, guiding him, and coaxed him to hold the stretches as long as possible. "Breathe," he whispered. "Longer on the exhale and your body will relax by itself."

It took a while for the calm forced on Dylan's body to filter through to the rest of him, but Angelo sensed the moment it had. Dylan's shoulders dropped, his eyes fluttered closed, and his death grip on Angelo's hands loosened.

He sucked in the first deep breath that didn't catch in his chest and let it go with a low moan. "Oh God."

Angelo rubbed his back, sliding his hands under Dylan's softly worn T-shirt, losing himself in the smooth skin he found beneath. He wanted to pull Dylan into his arms and bury his face in his neck, sink his teeth into the tender flesh there. Maybe even ease Dylan's sweatpants over his slim hips and then his own, and when they were both naked, chase away the shadows likely still lingering in Dylan's eyes.

But he didn't move, save his hand still rubbing soothing circles into Dylan's back. Even if he'd had the energy to jump Dylan, it was the wrong thing to do. Dylan needed a friend, and Angelo was too in love with him to be anything else right now. "Do you want to go to bed?"

Dylan opened his eyes, and as Angelo had feared, the crazed horror had faded, but the disquiet remained. "Bed?"

"Yeah. It's late and you're exhausted."

"So are you."

"Actually, I feel pretty good."

Another faint and yet wonderful smile brightened Dylan's tired face. "Really? That's awesome. I thought physiotherapy would make you worse to start with."

Angelo shrugged. "Yes and no. I *am* tired, but I don't feel like I'm going to die when I close my eyes. My legs hurt, but I trust them to hold me up. Little steps, I guess."

Dylan nodded slowly. "You've mellowed. That's what's different about you."

"If you say so." Angelo reached out to brush Dylan's hair off his forehead, but his hand lingered of its own accord, drawn to its natural place cupping Dylan's cheek.

Dylan turned to face him and leaned into the touch. Then he twisted his hands in Angelo's T-shirt and yanked him close, kissing him with a ferocity that belied the Zen-like glow of the room but fit with the grungy beat and mournful vocals filtering out of the music system.

Despite his best intentions, Angelo was gone. He held Dylan tight against him and kissed him back, fighting Dylan for dominance until he'd backed him into the doorframe.

Dylan gasped and kissed Angelo harder, but the impact lanced Angelo's treacherous body with just enough pain to bring him to his senses.

He broke the kiss and pressed his forehead to Dylan's, panting. "We need to go to bed."

Dylan's grip on Angelo held firm. "Not necessarily."

Angelo laughed but shook his head. "No. Really. We do. I want you so much, but not like this—not when your brain is in bits and I'm too tired to think clearly for both of us."

"I'm okay, Ang—"

Angelo covered Dylan's mouth with his hands. "You're too good at making yourself okay for other people, and I don't want you to do that for me. You need to let me take care of you for a while. Will you let me do that . . . please?"

For a long moment, Angelo feared that Dylan would refuse. And that he'd let him, and they'd fall into each other for all the wrong reasons.

Then Dylan took Angelo's hand from his mouth and kissed his knuckles. "Only you."

CHAPTER SIXTEEN

DYLAN WOKE to rare November sunshine streaming through his bedroom windows. The daylight startled him—it had been a while since he'd last slept past dawn, and at this time of year, most mornings were dreary and wet. Rubbing his face, he rolled over, chasing the warmth of the body beside him and fully expecting to find Angelo asleep.

Wide brown eyes startled him for a second time. "You're awake."

Angelo blinked. "So are you."

Any response Dylan may have made caught in his throat. Angelo was always gorgeous, but right now he was beautiful—he was everything—and Dylan couldn't look away. Couldn't resist the invisible magnet that drew them together. He reached out and touched Angelo's face, scratching the dark stubble on his jaw, rubbing his thumb over the shadows beneath his eyes. *He hasn't slept.*

Guilt burned in Dylan's gut. Last night was a conflicting blur of numbness and razor-sharp anxiety, but he remembered the gentle way Angelo had coaxed him through those stretches, even though it was clear that his own body had given up the ghost for the day. And then how he'd led Dylan to bed, laid him down, and held his hand, talking about anything and nothing until Dylan had somehow fallen asleep. "Angelo—"

But there was nothing he could say. Could only feel. Could only touch. Could only lose himself in Angelo with the kind of kiss they should've been sharing from the start. Dylan's heart thundered as Angelo kissed him back with his whole body, shoving the sheet aside until skin found skin and pressing them so tight together they both gasped. The first night they'd been together at the club flashed through Dylan's brain. Angelo had been dominant then, but so much had happened since; their dynamic had shifted a hundred times and never settled in the same place twice.

Right now was no different. Dylan shoved Angelo in the chest and toppled him backwards, and Angelo fell without struggle, splaying out on the bed, his arms wide, like he knew what Dylan wanted before it had solidified in Dylan's own mind.

Dylan crawled over him, covering Angelo with his body. Just their underwear separated them, and as he kissed down Angelo's torso, pausing at every rip of his abs, he made short work of stripping them both. Angelo's cock seemed to find its own way into his mouth, but Dylan didn't linger there for long. Couldn't, because the primal craving heating his blood was fast taking over.

He pulled Angelo down the bed so their faces were level. Angelo's eyes were hooded and bloodshot, but the fire in them matched Dylan's. "I know what you want," he whispered.

"You always do." Dylan hooked a cautious arm under one of Angelo's knees, raising it and bringing it slowly to Angelo's chest. "I don't know if it's something you want too, though."

"Try it and see."

"Are you sure?"

In answer, Angelo shifted onto his side and pulled Dylan behind him. "I pictured this the first time we fucked. Like I knew this moment would come. Don't be too gentle. I need to feel you."

It was all Dylan needed to hear. The unseasonal sunshine had faded, but it didn't matter. They had enough warmth and light of their own. He lubed up and rolled a condom on and then pressed inside Angelo so slowly that he almost busted right then, ending this dream before it had truly begun.

But Angelo's ragged groan grounded him, perhaps the way Angelo always had, whether either of them knew it or not. Angelo felt incredible wrapped around his dick, hotter and tighter than anyone before him . . . men, women, and everything in between; all faces Dylan couldn't remember now. Didn't want to. Didn't care to. Because there was no one in the world for him but Angelo. Body, heart, whatever. They'd shared a playground, and now they shared a soul.

Dylan fucked Angelo long and deep, heeding every subtle signal and cue Angelo gave, every gasp and whispered moan, until it seemed like they'd been this way forever—limbs entwined, torsos sliding together with shared sweat, their lips fused like they'd never been apart.

But then something changed. The air shifted, and every-thing was suddenly hotter. Angelo rose up on his knees, his chest to the mattress, and pushed back on Dylan. "*Harder.*"

As if Dylan could refuse. As if he wanted to. He gripped Angelo's hips and banged him harder, *faster*, the only sound in the room the slap of their flesh and their guttural cries. He was so close that his shaking thighs barely held him up, and he yelled as Angelo tightened around him. Angelo's hands curled into fists and he cried out, arching his back and coming with a shudder that pushed Dylan over the edge.

He shot inside Angelo, his dick pulsing so hard an irrational fear that it would explode sent him tumbling to the side, an intelligible noise that was halfway between a laugh and shout bursting out of him. His chest heaved, lungs burning, and his vision blurred, but his mind was clearer than it had been in a long time.

Clear enough to eventually pull himself together and wrap his arms around Angelo's shaking form. "You okay?"

Angelo was breathing too hard to answer. Dylan withdrew fast and rolled him over. Anxiety clawed its way up from the depths they'd chased it to, but when he found Angelo's eyes, they were bright and laughing, despite his obvious discomfort. "Give me . . . a minute. I'm fine, honest."

He wasn't fine, but they'd both learned the tough way that he rarely would be. Dylan cleaned up as best he could and then retrieved the duvet from where it had been kicked to the floor. He got back into bed and laid his hand on Angelo's chest, absorbing the tremors as they racked Angelo's body. "Shit. Did I hurt you?"

"As if you could."

Dylan bit his tongue and settled for ghosting his hands over Angelo's twitching muscles, swallowing a sigh of relief when Angelo's breathing evened out sometime later. Fucking him like that had been incredible, but seeing Angelo in pain would never stop tearing him apart.

"Stop fretting," Angelo mumbled. "I'm fine."

"I know you are, babe. Rest, it's okay."

Whether Angelo heard him or not, Dylan couldn't tell, as he was pretty much asleep a moment later. Dylan watched over him for a while, tracing patterns on his glorious skin, and counting his heartbeats, but then his phone buzzed too incessantly for him to ignore, and he reluctantly snuck out of bed to deal with it.

In the kitchen, Helen's name flashed up on the screen, and Dylan's heart juddered as he realised that he hadn't given last night's events a second thought since his lips had touched Angelo's. He answered the call. "Helen?"

"It's me," she said. "I've been calling you all morning. You had me worried when you didn't answer."

"Sorry." Dylan moved automatically to the kettle and flicked it on. "I was asleep."

"Really?"

"That so hard to believe?"

"Recently? Yes, actually, it is. You didn't go out last night, did you? The paramedics told you to rest."

"And I did. I slept till—" Dylan checked the time and calculated roughly how long he and Angelo had been fucking. "Shit. I slept till nine. I haven't done that in years." He spoke to himself as much as Helen as his mind drifted back to the crazy twenty-four hours that had brought him to this point. She was halfway through a sentence when he realised that she was speaking again. "Sorry. What?"

"The client from yesterday," Helen said. "You were right: he wasn't one of ours. Romford had his family's case on file, but they'd archived it by mistake. The tax credit sanctions were from last year, and no one had done an assessment to see if they could afford the repayment plan."

"Romford." Dylan abandoned the kettle and sat heavily on a stool. "Why is that office a permanent pain in my arse?"

"I'm actually more worried about your leg. The paramedics said you were in for a nasty bruise."

Dylan's gaze flickered to the shin that had taken the impact of the raging man's steel-capped boot. He'd been so wrapped up in Angelo since he'd woken up that he hadn't thought about it. Looking down, the blackish bruise seemed rather small as he recalled the pain he'd endured at the time, but he welcomed the faint throb now. Without it, it would be too easy to pretend that yesterday hadn't happened. "My leg is fine. I don't think he wanted to hurt me."

"I think you're right," Helen agreed. "But the fact remains that he did. He brought a machete into the office and threatened you with it—even if he didn't say the words. The police will want a statement from you at the very least, so you might want to draft something while it's fresh in your mind."

The only thing fresh in Dylan's mind right then was the tight heat of Angelo clamped around his dick, but he knew his hyperactive mind well enough to know that even Angelo couldn't distract him from yesterday's events forever. "Is the man okay? He went down like a sack of shit when they tasered him."

"The hospital released him into police custody this morning, but that's all I know. I just wish there was something we could do to help his family. If he goes to prison, they'll be without his income too."

Dylan concurred and then, after agreeing to take a week off work, hung up on Helen with a heavy heart. Yesterday had been so pointless in so many ways it was tough to swallow, and despite Helen's best intentions, they both knew there was absolutely nothing they could do to make that right.

He returned to bed, craving the comfort of Angelo's skin on his. To his surprise, Angelo was awake, lying flat on his back and staring at the ceiling. Dylan recounted Helen's call to him, and Angelo absorbed it with little comment.

Then he sighed and coaxed Dylan into his arms. "You didn't even know this guy. None of this is your fault."

"I know that. It just all got so messy when it didn't need to."

"Doesn't everything?"

Dylan kissed Angelo's chest. Then he sat up slightly and wove his fingers into Angelo's hair. "How are you doing? You didn't get much sleep."

"I'm okay," Angelo said. "Tired, but wired. It's weird, actually. My brain feels clearer than it has in a long time."

"That's good. You told me in the hospital how much the brain fog frightens you."

"Did I? I don't remember."

Dylan remembered everything about that night—how terrifying it had been to see Angelo so ill, but conversely, how he'd come away from it feeling like they finally had a chance. "You want to stay in bed today?" He lightly scraped his fingers over Angelo's scalp. "To rest, I mean. We could Netflix and chill?"

Angelo shook his head. "As much fun as that sounds, I've got to get up. That's what I've learned this week—that if I can move, I *have* to, however much it hurts. Muscle memory, you know?"

Dylan didn't, but he took Angelo's word for it and helped him up with a smile that Angelo didn't miss.

"What are you grinning about?"

Dylan shrugged. "You. It's so amazing that you feel as terrible as you did before, but you're somehow coping with it so much better. What's your secret?"

"Education." Angelo stood and stretched so elegantly that Dylan nearly tackled him to the bed again. "I was so scared when I first got ill that I stuck my head in the sand. If I hadn't, I'd have known then what I've learned this week about ME, and I'd probably feel a whole lot better."

"What's next for you, with your recovery, I mean?"

"Graded exercise. Slow and steady, a little bit each day. I don't think I'll dance again, but I can utilise the way my body is already conditioned to move."

More stretching that turned Dylan's brain upside down. Again, he recalled their impromptu yoga session in the spare room last night. "Perhaps you could teach."

"What?" Angelo looked at Dylan from between his legs. "Teach who?"

"Other people with ME. You were so good with me last night—so patient. And you did it instinctively."

"That's because I like you." Angelo came upright. "I've done mentoring before at ballet companies, and I hated it because ninety-nine per cent of people on this planet annoy me."

Dylan let it go. Angelo would need an income eventually, but did that matter right now? As he watched Angelo's naked form disappear into the bathroom and debated following him, he couldn't quite decide.

LATER THAT DAY, it turned out not to matter at all. Angelo's mother called while they were walking slow loops of the park and gave Angelo some news that turned his fortunes the right way up.

"She's sold the business?" Dylan guessed from the one side of the conversation he'd heard.

Angelo nodded, his eyes bright. "Yeah, and then some. Apparently a couple of blokes turned up this morning and bought the building, the equipment we had left, and even our fucking name. She said they might go to the auctions too and scoop up all the vintage stuff the debt collectors took."

"Oh my God. That's incredible. I thought the house would go first."

"Me too." Angelo stopped walking and abruptly dropped onto a nearby bench. "And I thought we'd end up giving it away for peanuts too—just to get rid of it. But these guys have offered the asking price and a shedload more to keep the name above the door. I can't fucking believe it."

The financial nerd in Dylan cried out for specifics, to know what this truly meant for Angelo, but concern for Angelo in the here and now won out as Angelo shook his head, dazed, and clearly overwhelmed.

Dylan knelt in front of him. "This is good news, right?"

Angelo stared at his blank phone screen. "It's more than that. My mum's splitting the profit from the business three ways between her, me, and my sister. It's a lot of money, Dylan . . . like, life-changing. I don't know what to do with it. I feel fucking sick. Is that weird?"

"You're probably in shock." Dylan rubbed Angelo's knees. "It's a big change from when we first met."

"Can I cancel the DRO?"

"You'll have to," Dylan said. "You won't be eligible when the money comes through. Will you have enough to clear your debts?"

Angelo laughed. "Um. Yeah. Twice over. And I'll be able to pay rent for a year while I get my shit together."

"Rent where?"

"I don't know. Wherever's closest to you."

"To me?"

Angelo's humour faded. "You're doing that freaky question thing."

"That freaky question—" Dylan stopped and tried again. "I don't know what you mean."

"It means I'm trying to tell you that I can afford to live near you for the next twelve months because I'm ridiculously fucking in love with you, and the blank look on your face is terrifying."

Dylan's heart thudded to a stunned and wonderful halt. "You love me?"

Angelo groaned. "Oh God. Stop. Please. Of course I love you. I've *always* loved you—been in love with you—whatever. I've just been too fucked up to do anything about it. How can you not know that?"

Dylan had no answer because he did know it. How, he had no idea, but out of everything they'd been through in the last few months, the sudden certainty that Angelo loved him nearly sent him to his knees. "I love you too. More than that. I'm fucking crazy about you."

"Just plain crazy, more like," Angelo grumbled.

But the joy in his tired eyes was unmistakable and did something to Dylan that he couldn't describe. "Do you want to hear something else crazy?"

Angelo sobered. "Depends. That you love me back has pretty much done me in for the day."

"Move in with me."

"What?"

"You heard." Dylan rose out of his crouch and climbed carefully into Angelo's lap, straddling his waist and pressing their foreheads together. "Move in with me. Pay half my mortgage and use the spare room for your physio, and maybe, when you're back on your feet, we can look to buy a new place together."

"I don't know if I'll ever be well enough to do that. What if I relapse to the point that I can't get out of bed for a year? What then?"

"Then I'll go back to paying the mortgage by myself until you're better."

"What if we get a bigger mortgage that you can't afford on your own?"

"I'm a debt advisor. Do you really think I'd let that happen? That I'd ever let us get into a position where I couldn't look after you?"

"You shouldn't have to look after me." Angelo's fingers tightened around Dylan's wrists. "It's not fair."

"Nothing's fair. But we've got each other—we *love* each other. Surely we should embrace that and face whatever life throws at us together? Angelo, I want to live with you. I want to go to bed with you every night and wake up with you every morning. We can handle the rest—you know we can."

Whether Angelo truly knew it or not was hard to tell, but he wore his crumbling resolve on his sleeve. "If we're gonna do this, you've got to slow down. I can't spend the rest of my life watching you worry yourself into the ground. That hurts me as much as me being ill upsets you."

"But you can help me with that," Dylan said. "Teach me to

relax and break the cycle? I know you can't see it, but you've done just as much for me as I have for you. If yesterday had happened to me six months ago, I'd be drunk now . . . and I'd stay drunk all weekend until I had to go back to work on Monday and pick up all the pieces."

"You wouldn't have taken the time off?"

"Nope. Not a chance. But being with you has made me realise that the quiet isn't something to be afraid of. That I can take control of it and make it work for me."

Angelo chuckled softly. "How you've taken all that from me constantly flaking out on you, I don't know. I think you're insane for wanting to live with me. Even without the ME, I'm a moody bastard."

"You think I can't handle a moody bastard?"

"I know you can handle me, Dylan." Angelo's voice dropped an octave. "Perhaps that's what I'm afraid of."

Hope bloomed in Dylan's heart as Angelo's humour returned. "Is that a yes?"

Angelo smiled like the rare winter sun hazing the park. "Of course it's a yes. I know I'm shit at showing it, but you and me together, despite all the bullshit that got to the table before us, is everything I've ever wanted. Shit, didn't even *know* I wanted."

Dylan couldn't argue with that. They still had much to learn about each other, but their love was real, and so were their dreams.

DYLAN STARED across the crowded rock club, his gaze drawn, as ever, to the graceful form that stood out among the sea of sweaty bodies. Angelo was dancing with Eddie, lifting her high above his head, his strong arms holding her firm as her laughter rang out over the thrashing music.

Sam watched them too, his expression hard to gauge. "Should I be jealous?"

"Of what? His moves? Probably. But if you're worried he's gonna crack on to your missus, don't bother. We're in the wrong club for that."

Sam laughed. "Don't mention that bloody sex club to Eddie. You know she'll want to go."

"That a bad thing?"

"Fucked if I know, but I ain't man enough to deal with all of you."

Dylan laughed too, leaning on Sam and absorbing his familiar solidness. He'd fretted when Eddie had called him a few days ago to say she and Sam were paying London a flying visit, but his anxiety had proved baseless. Sam was happy and healthy, and the space he'd once owned in Dylan's heart now belonged so entirely to Angelo that it was hard to recall when life had been any different.

It helped that Angelo and Eddie got on like a house on fire. Both so beautiful and vibrant, Dylan could watch them move together all night. Had done exactly that, in fact, while he and Sam had got quietly drunk in the corner.

"When do you start your new job?"

"Hmm?" Dylan snapped his attention back to Sam. "Oh. Um, next week. I've got a few cases to close up in Stratford first."

Sam tipped the last of his beer down his throat. "Never thought I'd see you working in the Romford office. You always said you'd rather shoot yourself."

"I'm not going to be just working there, though. I'm running it—the financial department, at least. And they've given me a lot of scope to change things. It's worth it now that I can make a difference."

"You don't have to change things to make a difference. Sometimes you've just got to carry on."

Dylan thought of the years that Sam had put into keeping his grandfather's café open, the eighteen-hour days he'd worked without a second thought to the effect it was having on the rest of his life. In that, he and Angelo were exactly the same. "I hear you, but there's a real opportunity here to make things right. And it's closer to home so I can be there for Angelo if he needs me."

Sam said nothing to that, all too aware of what it was like to depend on those he loved most to take care of him. He'd been well the whole time he and Eddie had been in Poland, but who knew what was round the corner? Not Dylan, and living with Angelo's condition had taught him to take each day as it came. Worrying about tomorrow didn't make anything easier.

Besides, today was a *great* day, and as awesome as it had

been to spend it with Sam and Eddie, Dylan was itching for the next phase to begin.

Hot, sweat-sheened arms slid around him from behind. Angelo pressed a wet kiss to Dylan's cheek. "What are you smirking about?"

"I'm not smirking," Dylan protested as he turned around, though Sam certainly was until Eddie distracted him with a heated kiss of her own. "I'm just happy."

"Happy, eh? I'll take that. Have I done enough moshing for you yet?"

"You love it."

"I love *you*." Angelo swiped Dylan's beer and necked it. "And you've been pining for this place, admit it."

"Maybe," Dylan hedged. "I didn't think you'd be quite so into it, though."

Angelo set the empty bottle down. "Why not? I let you fuck me with Motörhead growling in the background, don't I?"

Behind Dylan, Sam burst out laughing. Dylan flipped him the bird over his shoulder and made an executive decision. He moved impossibly closer to Angelo, wedging his knee between his legs. "Careful. It's your turn to call the shots when we ditch this place, but I might change my mind and bend you over the bar."

Angelo smirked, seeing Dylan's bluff for exactly what it was, because they both knew that even if Angelo was more than a once-in-a-blue-moon bottom, Dylan was waaay too thirsty to switch up their sex club adventures. "Does this mean you're ready to go?"

Of course it did. They said goodbye to Sam and Eddie and left The Pitt, taking advantage of the heady summer air to save money and walk across town. They held hands, like always. Nine months to the day since they'd first met, and it had yet to get old. Would it ever fade?

Dylan doubted it.

ANGELO FELL onto Dylan's chest, his muscles screaming, but for once the lactic acid in his legs was there for all the right reasons. He kissed Dylan's sweat-damp skin, trailing his lips up until he found Dylan's neck, and then he sank his teeth in, thrusting into him one last time. "Jesus!"

At home, his shout would've rung out and disturbed the neighbours. In Lovato's, though, only the crowd who'd chosen to watch the show reacted, and Angelo barely noticed them—too transfixed by Dylan falling apart beneath him. His arched back and flailing hands. His wild, guttural cries. One day, Angelo would get used to how beautiful he was.

But not today.

They peeled themselves off the mattress and slipped away from the masses into the private showers. Angelo finished first and sat on the bench while Dylan finished up, watching, awed and wondering, as had become his habit in the last few months. *How did I get so lucky?*

As if he'd ever know.

Dylan crouched in front of him, naked, his hands on Angelo's denim-clad knees. "Are you falling asleep on me?"

"Not yet. Just enjoying the view."

"In Romford? You need to get out more."

"Don't be a dick." Angelo poked his tongue out. "I want to ask you something, actually."

Clearly intrigued, Dylan grabbed a towel and wrapped it around his waist. "Not gonna propose, are you? Because I've already told you I'm not a marriage kind of bloke."

Angelo snorted. "You and me both."

It was true. On one of the many nights they'd sat up battling the evil tag team of Dylan's insomnia and the spasms in Angelo's muscles, they'd talked about anything and everything, learning what made the other tick, and solidifying their bond until it was absolute. They were different men, but their dreams were the same.

"Actually," Angelo went on. "I was going to ask you if you'd be my student for the day on Wednesday. I know it's your last day off before your new job, but it's my first assessment and I'm freaking out a bit."

Understatement. Freaking out wasn't Angelo's usual style, but Dylan wasn't the only one with new employment prospects. Angelo's ME-specific physio had panned out so well that Harry had suggested he retrain as a graded exercise therapist. In a moment of madness, he'd agreed and was now three months deep into his first year.

Dylan nudged Angelo with his shoulder. "Of course I'll be your student for the day. I don't know what you're fretting for, though. I know you don't like peopleing, but you're an amazing teacher. If it wasn't for you, I wouldn't be able to bend my legs behind my head like I did just now."

Angelo chuckled. "You're a quick learner."

Dylan laughed too, but the ever-present shrewdness in his gaze told Angelo that he'd seen right through him. "They'll give you another date if you're not up to working that day."

"Yeah, but what's the point in that? If I can't get myself healthy enough to go to work, how can I help anyone else?"

"By showing them that it's okay to have bad days. You know that exercise therapy isn't a blanket treatment. It's helped you massively, but it doesn't work for everyone—and it doesn't work all the time. That's what Harry tells you, and that's what you'd tell your patients, right?"

"I s'pose so."

"You *know* so." Dylan knocked Angelo's shoulder again. "Don't be so hard on yourself. Besides, you have just as much chance of having an amazing day. Like today. Did I tell you that I love you yet?"

And just like that, the malaise clouding Angelo's mind

cleared. Despite their surroundings and lingering heat of their playtime encounter, Dylan's gaze seemed innocent and pure, and Angelo lost himself in the smile that had turned his life upside down for the better. "I wanna get into bed with you."

Dylan held out his hand. "Then we'd better go home."

"Okay, but Dylan?"

"Yeah?"

"I love you too."

THE END

WHISPER

FOREWORD

Many thanks to my sensitivity reader, Packy, who gave me invaluable insight into his life as a settled Cornish gypsy. Also to Rosa, who triple checked the Roma details. Thank you for letting me into your world. And finally to my wonderful husband for sharing his gypsy family tree with me.

CHAPTER ONE

Joe

I watched the flaps of burst tyre flutter down the hill. The horsebox was a heap of shit—ancient and tired, like everything else in my life—but I'd been counting on the brake pads to give up on me first. A cheap fix, rather than a triple-figure repair bill I'd have to sell a kidney to pay.

Fuck's sake. I rounded the back of the horsebox and kicked what was left of the tyre. The impact rattled up my shin, but the pain wasn't enough to ward off the fast-approaching black cloud. Guilt, frustration, and plain old rage fought for dominance in my gut and guilt won out—for now. The tyre bursting was my fault, because the anger simmering in my veins had been there before I'd come to a skidding stop in a bramble bush.

I turned my back on the horsebox and crossed the sand-dusted road. The only pro I could find at breaking down so close to the beach was that there were plenty of pubs to keep me occupied while I waited for my friendly neighbour to tow me home. At least, I hoped Dex would be friendly after I'd called him out to rescue me for the third time this month. And he wasn't exactly my neighbour—his place was fifty miles away.

Still, he readily agreed to come and get me after I'd called him and begged for assistance. Dex was a man of few words, but he had a heart of gold and a rare smile I often thought about when I pretended his gentle giant of a fella didn't exist. Shame Seb was even nicer than Dex. It would've been easy to hate him. Distracting, too; something I was in dire need of as I set myself up at the nearest tourist-rammed pub with a pint of crappy shandy.

But as hot as Dex was, he couldn't keep me from my financial woes for long. Buying my piss-weak pint had emptied my pockets of change, and the maxed-out cards I'd left at home made my wallet so useless that I hadn't bothered bringing it out. If the abandoned mare I'd come out to collect had been alive, I'd have lacked the resources to rescue her.

"We'll find a way, son. We always do."

But that shit wasn't real. The man who'd uttered those words was as good as dead, and the mare? Fuck. At least I hadn't seen her emaciated body. My soul was running out of room for horses I couldn't save.

A heavy hand clapped me on the shoulder. "Well, look who it is. Jonah Carter's boy propping up the bar. Who'd have thought it?"

Great. New tension rippled through me, merging with the disquiet already there. I was a little ways out of town and holed up in a pub that most locals wouldn't bother to frequent at this time of year, but lately it didn't seem to matter where I went, there was always a wanker around the corner.

I set my glass down and shrugged the man's hand off me. A cursory glance revealed him as Dicky McGee, a one-time friend of my father's before his life had gone to shit. "What do you want?"

Dicky took the stool next to me, his brawny fists curled menacingly on the bar. "I want my money."

"So? What's that got to do with me?"

"I ain't seen your old man for weeks, so you'll have to do."

I laughed. Couldn't help it. Coming after me for money was almost as pointless as chasing Jonah. "You're barking up the wrong tree, mate. Even if I gave a shit—which I don't—I haven't got a pot to piss in."

"Likely story. Saw your ma driving around in that Transporter last week. Bet you've got a few of those tucked away on that big farm."

"Couldn't give them away if we had. That old thing is a heap of junk."

Dicky knew it was true, I could tell, and the taunting humour faded from his eyes, only to be replaced with resentment that mirrored mine whenever I thought of Jonah. Staring into a pint glass with a financial cloud of doom was his job, not mine, but his inability to think beyond his next bottle of whisky had ruined more lives than he'd ever know.

"Now listen here," Dicky rumbled, gripping my arm. "You tell your old man that I'm done waiting for my cash. If he don't show up at the Legion on Friday with full payment, I'm gonna—"

"You're gonna what?" I shoved his hand off me and slid from my stool, squaring up like I had been my whole life, one way or another. "What do you think you can do that I care about? 'Cause if you're going to knock him off, you'd be doing me a favour."

"Wouldn't get me my money, though, would it?"

Dicky had a point, but so did I. I didn't care what he did to my father for whatever failed scheme they'd cooked up between them; I just wanted him out of my face. "Whatever. Just piss off, yeah? I'm trying to have a quiet pint."

Someone behind me sniggered. I reckoned probably at my expense, until the scowl on Dicky's face said otherwise. His already ruddy skin reddened and he grabbed me again, shoving me against the bar. "Now listen here, you little poof. Your old man might be AWOL, but your ma is still right where he left her. If he don't—"

My patience snapped. I'd never been good with folk up in my personal space, and my mum was my flashpoint. I'd decked people for even looking at her wrong. Threatening her? Damn. My fists blurred. My knuckles crashed against the bristly skin of Dicky's face, and blood seeped through my fingers as his eyebrow split like an overripe peach.

He roared in response, lunging at me the way I wanted him to so I could punch him again—his gut this time, adrenaline surging through me as he went down.

My grandfather had taught me the world as he knew it, raising me from the hole Jonah had left me in. *Never kick a man on the ground.* I never had, and I didn't now, something I regretted in the seconds it took Dicky to get up—just margin enough for someone to come to his rescue.

I fought the arms that restrained me from behind, landing blows with my elbows before the burly man holding me back was joined by another, and then another. "Get the fuck off me."

No one paid me any attention, save Dicky, who got to his feet with a smirk. "You're as nutty as your old man," he scoffed.

But he was wrong about that too. Jonah was a worthless drunk who'd frittered our lives away, but it hadn't always been like that. And as far as I knew, he'd never laid a hand on anyone. Me? I had a record as long as my arm, and as the pub landlord appeared, phone in hand, it looked like it was about to gain an extra page.

HARRY

I helped my last client of the day to his feet—a client who had, over the eighteen months we'd been working together, become my student and eventually my friend. "You did great today. Those legs loosened up in the end, eh?"

Angelo shrugged. "Didn't feel like it. Thought my calves were going to snap."

"That's because you're still looking at yourself and expecting to see your body from three years ago."

He didn't deny it. Just sloped off to get his clothes. I watched him move, analysing the slight limp he'd developed in recent months. Angelo had been a world-class ballet dancer before chronic fatigue syndrome had ravaged his muscles and joints, and the longer we worked together, the more it hurt to see him on his bad days. "Come back."

"What?" Angelo glanced over his shoulder.

"Come back," I repeated. "I want to try something."

Angelo groaned. "Don't make me do more lunges. I'll puke on you this time, I swear."

It wouldn't be the first time a client had puked on me, but I was pretty sure Angelo could handle what I had in mind. Despite all his condition threw at him, his pain threshold was far higher than mine. And when he left the clinic a little while later, his hip moving better than it had in months, his smile wide and warm, I knew I'd miss him if I took my newly signed agent up on her offer of a summer writing retreat.

And it was a big *if*. For me, at least. Rhys—my brother—who met me at the juice bar across the road after work, couldn't see the problem.

"It's a few weeks, li'l bro. And it's not like it's a holiday. Your publisher gave you a deadline."

The mention of deadlines made my stomach clench before I forced myself to think positive. Eighty-thousand words exploring the value of mind over matter. Of what benefits positive thinking and mindfulness brought to recovery. By September. I could do that, right? Twenty-thousand words a month. Five-thousand words a week. How hard could it be?

Well, pretty damn hard, actually, I'd discovered when I hadn't factored in time for self-editing and rewrites. At my current pace, I'd be done by Christmas. Maybe. Which meant I needed a plan B.

"You should take a sabbatical," Rhys said. "You've barely had a week off from that clinic in five years."

"It's not the clinic I'm worried about. It's my patients. I can't just abandon them."

"You wouldn't be gone forever. Besides, you're not what makes their recovery viable—it's what's going on inside them, and that's what your book's all about, right? That we have more power over our minds and bodies than we realise?"

Damn my big brother and the stubborn paramedic logic he applied to the whole world except himself. He was the only person I could never reason with. "I don't even know where they want to send me. If it's the backside of nowhere, I'm definitely not going. I've got my private clients to consider too, and there's no one to pick up slack there."

"Of course there is. Farm them out to another clinic."

"I can't do that—"

"Yes, you can. It's not slacking off to take some time out to do other things. If you weren't planning on giving yourself a chance to actually write this book, then you shouldn't have signed the deal."

I shot him a half-hearted glare and toyed with the straw in my glass. The book deal had come out of the blue, and I'd let my immediate excitement get the better of me, assuming the fact that an agent had scouted me online meant that I could cobble the book together from stuff I'd already written and posted. But no such luck. The eighty-thousand words due by winter had to be original, and since I'd learned that tough reality, my muse had jumped ship, taking any and all of my inspiration with it.

"Show me the email they sent you," Rhys demanded. "They must've said something about where they're sending you."

I couldn't actually remember. I got thousands of emails a week and reserved my concentration for my patients. Wednesday was my busiest day, and I'd had a full list. Still, resistance was futile. I dug my iPad out of my bag and handed it over.

Rhys swiped at it until he found the right email. "They haven't got a particular place in mind. They're saying you can find your own and send them the bill."

"Really? Where on earth would I find a writing retreat?"

"That's not a positive mental attitude," Rhys chided. "And it's pretty short-sighted. Where do we find everything these days?"

I looked at him blankly.

He sighed and rolled his eyes. "You're impossible. I don't know how you run three successful enterprises when you're so bloody dense."

"I don't run three enterprises," I retorted mildly. "I work for the NHS. My blog and a handful of private clients are side projects."

"Side projects that got you a book deal you won't fulfil if you don't give yourself the time to write it. Shut your face a moment while I find you some place to hole up for the summer."

It was on the tip of my tongue to point out *he* was the one who hadn't shut up since we'd sat down together for the first time in months, but I couldn't be bothered. What was the point? Rhys was a force of nature when it came to other people's problems, and for this brief moment, I loved him for it.

"Why do you have the Airbnb app on your iPad when you only ever go to the clinic and the gym?"

"Hmm?" I blinked at Rhys as his words sank in. "That's not fair. I *do* have a life. If I didn't, I'd have time to write the book."

"I suppose that's true," Rhys said. "But I don't remember you leaving London recently."

"How would you know when you spend all of *your* time working or hanging around that sex club?"

Rhys flipped me off, but he was more right than I cared to admit. I settled for gathering our empty glasses with a scowl and retreating to the counter for more of the kale-pineapple-protein smoothies that would probably be my dinner.

When I returned to the table, Rhys slid the iPad to me. "Found you somewhere. It's on the coast and quiet."

"Which coast?"

"South-west. Down near Newquay."

"Newquay isn't quiet." I took the iPad and studied the room for rent he'd found on a Cornish horse farm. "It's full of surfers and teenagers."

"Not all of it," Rhys protested. "And I said it was *near* Newquay. Not in the town itself. The farm is further inland."

I studied the gallery of photos on the farm's profile. The scenery was stunning, and the room itself was gorgeous— wooden floors and beams, a large bed, and even a desk by the window where I could set up my computer to write.

"See," Rhys pressed when I didn't speak. "It's perfect."

It *was* perfect, but all the four-poster beds in the world didn't solve the issue of my packed patient list. But still . . . something drew me to the images scrolling across my iPad screen. I'd never been on a farm in my life, but there was no denying London was too brutally suffocating for me to get done what I needed to do. I had a choice to make: bite the bullet and take some time out of the real world, or stay home and let go of an opportunity I'd been damn lucky to get in the first place.

Common sense told me there were easier ways of making this happen. That I could simply cut down my hours at the clinic. Scale back my private clients. But a whisper of something I didn't quite understand argued that I had no business writing a book on the power of the mind if I couldn't reason with my own.

Rhys put his hand on my arm in a rare show of fraternal affection. "So? What's it to be?"

I shrugged and reached for my smoothie. "I'll think about it."

CHAPTER TWO

Joe

I walked out of the police station the following morning to find my sister, Emma, having a panic attack at the wheel of my battered VW Transporter. *Brilliant.* Like I needed a boatload more guilt on top of everything else.

Sighing, I wrenched open the driver's door and pried her sweaty hands off the steering wheel. "What are you doing here?"

"Someone had to pick you up," she muttered through chattering teeth. "George left for his friend's funeral last night, remember?"

Shit. "I forgot about that. Who brought Shadow down from the top field?"

"I did."

"How? He's got the wind up him at the moment. Pulled me over last week."

"I managed," Emma said. "Just. We've got no sugar left, though."

Her smile was tight. I pulled her out of the van and gave her a hug, enveloping her elfin frame in my much larger arms, taking care not to smother her. Emma was as strong as any man—

stronger—but she was fragile too, and I felt like a proper wanker for dragging her out when agoraphobia kept her on the farm for weeks at a time. "Seriously, girl. You didn't have to come out."

"Actually, I did." Emma pulled back and fixed me with a look that made me wish I'd drunk a hell of a lot more than half a pint of shandy before I'd got nicked. "You can't keep doing this, Joe. Mum's upset, and we're both terrified you'll get in real trouble one day. What's going to happen to the farm if you end up in prison?"

"Don't be daft." I released her and stepped away, hoping that she'd get in the passenger side and be done with it, but she didn't move. "Jesus. I didn't get charged with anything."

"But you still got arrested for fighting. Again. And what the hell for? What has Dicky McGee ever done to you?"

That she didn't know was oddly relieving. I'd worked hard to keep our father's mess from our doorstep, though my mum likely knew more than she let on. "It doesn't matter what he did —or what I did. It's done and no one's pressing charges. Can we just go home and get the stables done? I've got to fetch the horsebox home and cadge a spare tyre from somewhere."

Emma shot me another withering look that belied the anxiety still making her tremble. "The stables are done," she snapped. "And Dex brought the horsebox home last night. That's how we knew where you were—he rescued it from the tow company and they said you'd been arrested."

She turned on her heel and rounded the front of the van. The slam of the passenger door rang out in the empty car park and kickstarted a headache I could've done without. Guilt morphed into self-loathing, and the image of my mum fetching my father from the police station ran through my mind on a loop. I wasn't a raging pisshead, but that aside, was I a better man?

Not today.

I got in the van and turned the key in the ignition. A thousand apologies danced on my tongue, but I kept them in. Emma had heard them all before, and we both knew that words meant nothing in our family. Never had.

A mile away from the police station, she turned in her seat and put her hand over mine. "That mare died, didn't she?"

I nodded. "Didn't get to her in time."

"It's not your fault."

"Isn't it? We should've kicked those barn doors in and brought her home as soon as we knew she was there."

Emma shook her head. "You'd have got arrested for that, too, and charged with theft."

"She'd be alive, though."

"Not for long, and nor would our other old nags with you in prison. That's what I'm trying to tell you. Me and Mum—we can't handle the farm on our own. We *need* you. And so do the horses we already have."

My heart knew she was right, but it still hurt. "I wish the RSPCA wouldn't call us before they had a seizure order. It fucks with my head."

"Mine too." Emma's hand slipped from mine. "But we can't let it eat us whole. There's too much at stake."

Wasn't there always? I sighed and turned down the narrow lane that led to the farm. "We'll be okay. If I can't borrow a tyre for the horsebox, I'll sell the van."

"Dex lent us a tyre, but that's not what I mean. Not really, anyway. There's always a burst tyre, Joe. Or a broken fence, or a vet bill. When does it end? Mum's worried we'll lose some of the older horses if we can't pay for their care."

The thought of my wonderful mum—and Emma—worrying about losing our horses made me sick to my stomach. "We'll find a way. We always do."

"No, we don't. We just beat back the flames until the next inferno, and we're running out of water."

I snorted. "That's the worst metaphor I've ever heard."

"It's not a metaphor, dickhead. And even if it was, I'm still right. We're doomed unless we come up with something to bring more cash in."

I couldn't figure out why she was telling me this now, when it had been the case ever since our grandpa had died three years ago. The farm had been his, and the running of it a mystery to all but him. It was only after his funeral that we'd realised it had been in the red for decades. He'd left it to me, and it weighed heavily on my shoulders that things had got even worse ever since. "I don't have any bright ideas."

"I know. Which is why I've accepted an Airbnb booking for Grandpa's old room."

"What?" I swung the van into the yard with a screech. "How? And what the hell is an Airbnb?"

"It's an app where you can rent rooms out. We talked about this."

"Yeah, we talked about it, but I never agreed to anything. All Grandpa's stuff is still in there."

"Well, it shouldn't be," Emma said. "And he wouldn't want his room sitting there untouched while the farm goes down the toilet."

"Oh, and you think having a bunch of scuzzy tourists tramping through our house is going to save us, do you?"

Emma gave me the finger and got out of the van. I followed suit and trailed after as she stalked into the house. Our mum—Sal—was in the kitchen making sandwiches for the motley crew of locals who worked on the farm—Toby, Jemima, and Lacey, they filed in, eyeing me and Emma like we were unexploded bombs.

I couldn't blame them. Emma and I were chalk and cheese but cut from the same stubborn Carter cloth. Our rows were legendary. She threw things, I punched walls, and Sal cried until one of us saw sense. Usually Emma. Sense wasn't my strong point when my temper burned.

But I was right this time. The farm was inland from the coastal madness that descended on Newquay pretty much all year round, but summer was peak twat season, and I didn't want random out-of-towners fucking up my house. "It's not happening, Emma. I don't care what you've done. Undo it, and leave it alone."

Emma opened a cupboard on the rickety dresser and grabbed a handful of plates. She banged them down on the kitchen table without looking at me. "I'm not undoing anything. And it's not a bunch of randos—it's one guy, and he wants the room for the whole summer."

That stopped me in my tracks. "The whole summer?"

"Yes. Ten weeks. Payment up front. All we have to do is give him a kitchen cupboard and space in the fridge. We don't even have to feed him."

"How much are we charging him?"

"Fifty quid a night."

"*What?*"

"You heard." Emma took the heaping plate of sandwiches from Mum and dumped them on the table. "Fifty quid a night for ten weeks, Joe. That's three-and-a-half-grand. Enough to fix the tractor, the horsebox, and pay some of these goons."

She gestured around the table. No one looked up from their lunch, apparently disinterested now the storm had passed, and perhaps satisfied in the knowledge that no matter how dire the farm's finances ever were, they *always* got paid.

Eventually got paid.

Whatever.

"Who is he?" I demanded. "And why does he want to hole up here for ten weeks? Just because he's on his own, doesn't mean he's not a weirdo."

Emma sighed and noisily dragged a chair from under the table. "He's not a weirdo. Do you think I'm some kind of idiot? The app checked his credentials when he signed up, and he sent me a link to his blog when I accepted his booking so I could see who he was."

"Show me."

"No. I'm having my lunch. You can have a look later when you're done being an idiot for the day."

And that was apparently that. Defeated, I left the rest of them to their lunch and drifted out to the stables. Most of the horses were out in the fields, but a few of the most ancient knackers were in the stalls: Tauna and Carric, Noel, and my oldest four-legged friend, Mani. I whistled through my teeth and he came to his door, his whiskery nose searching automatically for the miniature hay cube treats I always carried in my pockets. I fed him a couple and knocked my head against his solid neck, my favourite place for brooding when the responsibility of the farm overwhelmed me.

But I couldn't hide in the stables forever. The morning's work had been done in my absence, but I still had a mountain to climb before I could catch up on the sleep my police station adventure had cost me.

I kissed Mani goodbye and left him to his life's work of chewing up his manger. First on my list was the broken fence post in the top field. On better days, I'd have driven the tractor up there, but that was broken too.

It was getting dark by the time I made it back to the house. Everyone had left for the day, even Sal and Emma had gone home to the bungalow they shared on the other side of the farm. I fed the cats, picked up the post, and found a covered plate in the oven. Then I took my dinner into the shambolic place we called a living room and ate in the solitary silence I often craved during the day.

Sal's chicken stew was amazing. The stack of red-topped bills, not so much. I flicked through them with growing unease, glad I'd left them until after dinner. Most could wait a few more weeks before things started getting cut off, but our feed supplier was running out of patience. I checked the farm's online bank accounts to see how many public donations had rolled in over the last few days. Not enough. It was never enough. There were many things we could live without—nice cars, new clothes, even electricity if we relied on the ancient stove for heat and cooking. But if we couldn't feed the horses, we were wasting our fucking time.

Depression settled over me in the dull haze I'd come to expect when I didn't have a pub brawl to distract me. When did it end? When we were homeless and all the horses destroyed?

I took the bills outside and chucked them on the manure heap. When I returned to the darkened living room, I remembered the blog of our impending houseguest. Emma had left it open on the farm's cracked tablet, but even the damaged screen couldn't hide the glossy city lifestyle of whoever the hell *Holistic Harry* was. His blog was crammed full of snazzy fitness shots and close-ups of grass-coloured smoothies, and it was clear that wherever he was coming from was a world away from life on the farm.

A few shots showed him lifting impressive weights in the gym. Despite myself, I zeroed in on his torso, taking in the bunched chest muscles and rippling abs. I'd always had a thing for hench dudes, but despite living in surfer country, it had been a while since a bod as hot as *Holistic Harry* had passed through my limited orbit. I wondered idly if he had a face to match, but sadly the few images of himself cut off at the neck.

It also disproved Emma's argument that checking out his blog proved who he was. There was a link to an Instagram account, but that shit was beyond me, so I checked out his biography page. His occupation was listed as a holistic physiotherapist and life coach. It meant nothing to me, but why would it when I knew nothing but the farm? Anything that wasn't horses —or surfing, back in the day—was a mystery to me, and I liked it that way. The bloke didn't sound like an axe murderer, but I was still bound to hate him.

HARRY

Google Maps cut out on me just past Newquay town centre. I switched to the sparse directions my host had sent me but began to despair as I passed rows and rows of surfer vans and beach shacks, hoards of glitter-faced teenage girls, and the boys in too-tight shorts who trailed after them.

None of it looked anything like the idyllic farmland I was searching for, and I began to wonder if I'd come to the right place. But then the road headed inland and the vibrant seaside community faded out. I turned down a succession of narrow lanes until I *finally* spotted the hand-painted wooden sign for Whisper Farm.

The lane to the farm was the tightest of all. My car was small, but I was sure it wouldn't fit and prayed I wouldn't meet a vehicle coming the other way.

My hands were sweating by the time I pulled up outside the tidy bungalow where I'd arranged to meet Emma Carter, my host for the summer. I parked up and got out, gazing around at the outbuildings and fenced-off paddocks. There was no sign of any stables, though. Perhaps I really had fucked up my navigation.

The front door of the bungalow opened and a dark-haired woman rushed out. I met her at the end of the path. "Are you Emma?"

The woman shook her head. "No, I'm Sal. I've been told to send you straight up to the main house to meet Joe."

"Joe? But I was meant to meet Emma?"

A shadow crossed the woman's weather-beaten face.

"Emma is more of an online person. It's Joe you need to deal with now you're here."

Okaaay. Nothing about this trip had worked out the way I'd expected, and I'd only left London this morning. Of course the woman I'd arranged to meet was MIA. It went hand in hand with the book of notes I'd forgotten to bring and the ominous rattle coming from my car. If I hadn't spent my whole adult life training myself to think otherwise, I'd have thought the world was against me. "Should I leave my car here? Or is there somewhere to park by the house?"

"Take the car," the woman—Sal—said. "It rains a lot here, and you won't want to be traipsing through the mud to fetch it if you want to go out."

Going out wasn't in my fun-packed schedule of tying myself to my laptop, but I thanked Sal anyway and got back in my car, making a mental note of her directions to the main house. I followed the dirt track through the fields, passing more paddocks and barns until I came to a small, stone house. A tall figure was waiting for me on the doorstep, smoking a cigarette and watching my approach with a gaze I could only describe as vaguely hostile.

Unnerved, I parked my car for a second time and got out, turning to face the utterly *gorgeous* man who had deigned to get to his feet. *Jesus. They don't make them like him anymore.* I proffered a shaky hand. "Joe?"

A cool, calloused hand gripped mine and shook it briefly. "Right. You the bloke renting the room?"

"Yes. I'm Harry."

"Holistic Harry?"

I blinked. "If you want to call me by my Instagram handle."

Joe shot me a dead-eyed glance, which was disturbing as I considered the riot of moody blues colouring his eyes. Vibrant and yet conversely lifeless. Was that even a thing?

"Um," I went on when Joe said nothing. "I'm here to rent

the room? I'd arranged to meet Emma at the bungalow across the fields, but Sal sent me here."

"Sal's my mum."

"She's nice."

"I know."

That he loved his mum enough to agree made me want to run my fingers over the strong, tanned forearms he'd folded across his chest. I adored my own mother and missed her desperately now she'd retired to Spain. It was only that she deserved to live out her days in peace and sunshine that eased the ache in my heart.

"Are you coming in or what?"

I blinked again to find that Joe had stepped back to the front door of the house and opened it. He was staring at me expectantly, and I was just, well, staring.

Idiot. I pulled myself together and followed Joe into the house, trying to break the instant fixation I'd developed with the back of his deeply tanned neck. His hair was inky-dark and stuck up in all directions, like he'd spent all day upside down, but it curled beautifully just below his ears, and the urge to stick my finger in a perfect spiral was so strong I shoved my hands in my pockets.

It had been a while since a bloke had caught my attention like that. The last time had been Angelo, but I'd got over it pretty quick when—aside from the obvious client-therapist issues—he'd talked about nothing but how in love he was with his gorgeous boyfriend. Even now, the light in his eyes whenever he mentioned Dylan stung. I was jealous—not of Dylan, but of them both. I wanted someone to burn for me the way they did for each other, and to feel the same way in return.

At least, some days I did. Others I just wanted to escape the rat race my life had become. Which brought me back to the large stone-floored kitchen Joe had led me to.

"This is the kitchen," he said unnecessarily. "Ma cleared a

shelf for you in the fridge, and you can have one of the cupboards. She cooks enough dinner for an army every night, though, so you're welcome to eat with the rabble."

"The rabble?"

"Staff."

"That's nice," I said absently, glancing around the homely space that was nothing like the sleek kitchen in my London flat.

"What is?"

"That you feed your staff. I'm lucky to get a mouldy water cooler where I work."

"Yeah, well." Joe scratched the back of his head. For a moment he looked directly at me. "It makes up for the peanuts I pay them."

I'd read up on Whisper Farm before I'd set off. Their simple website had them listed as a horse rescue charity, and for some reason I'd expected something . . . grander, maybe, than the ramshackle farm I'd seen so far. Animal rescue centres in London were slick operations—gift shops, fundraising booths, and marketing spiel on every corner. This place wasn't like that. There was nothing to indicate that it was a rescue centre. In fact, I hadn't seen a horse yet.

"Still awake?"

"Hmm?"

Joe was right in front of me. Again, his piercing gaze seemed to penetrate my soul. "I was saying that there's a bathroom upstairs that you can consider yours. It's attached to Grandpa's —to your room, and no one else uses it."

I didn't miss his slip. Nor the fleeting grief that crossed his face. And when he showed me upstairs, I saw why. The room I'd be renting for the next ten weeks was spotlessly clean and exactly as it had appeared in the photographs, but there were touches that the lens had missed—the rocking chair by the window, and the old school tobacco pipe on the ledge.

This room had been his grandfather's.

A stillness came over me as I deposited my bag on the bed. I didn't know why it mattered that Joe had frozen in the doorway, but it did. Something had happened here—in this room—and it had hurt him. And now I was going to spend the whole summer rubbing it in his face. "I don't have to take this room, you know," I said. "I came for the peace and quiet, so if there's a—"

"Something wrong with the room?"

"No. It's lovely, I just . . ." Just what? Made an assumption about his emotional attachment to it and figured I could make it all better? "It's fine. I just don't want to get in anyone's way."

"You won't," Joe said shortly. "Emma and my mum live in the bungalow, and no one else lives on-site."

"What about you?"

"I live downstairs."

Unless I'd missed a whole separate wing of the house, there was nothing downstairs but the kitchen, a living room, and a tiny walk-in shower, but I let it go. For all I knew, Joe spent every night with a girlfriend up the road, and it was none of my business.

And I wasn't even curious if that girlfriend existed.

LATER THAT DAY, after I'd unpacked my bag and set up my laptop at the large desk in my room, I wandered downstairs to ask directions to the nearest supermarket. Stupidly, I'd forgotten to bring a box of groceries with me.

Sal was in the kitchen, fussing with something on the stove. "There's a Morrisons up the road, but it's closed now."

"Closed? Ah, shit . . . it's Sunday. Damn. I took Friday off work so I'm all out of sync. Are there any smaller shops nearby that I could grab some supplies from?"

"Depends what you need." Sal heaved a huge pot of pota-toes to the sink and drained them. "The Londis in Holywell does a few bits, but old Dora's a pisshead. She doesn't stay open much past five whatever day of the week it is."

My stomach growled as it considered going to bed empty. Sal laughed and reached around me for a potato masher. "Daft boy. Eat with us. There's plenty to go around."

And there was. Sal put a giant pie on the table, with a mountain of mash and more peas than I'd ever seen. Gravy followed, and just when I thought she was done, a loaf of fresh bread appeared from the oven.

I expected a hoard of staff to roll in when she bellowed out of the back door that dinner was ready, but only four new faces pulled up chairs at the kitchen table: two teenage girls, Jemima and Lacey; an even younger boy called Toby; and an old geezer in his sixties who everyone, apparently, called Uncle George.

The two girls looked at me and giggled. Sal swatted them with a tea towel. "Ignore 'em. Boy crazy, those two."

I'd been accused of the same when I was their age, so I spared them a grin as I took a seat between Lacey and Uncle George. "Hey. I'm Harry."

"We know," Lacey said. "We saw your blog."

I cringed. "Oh god. Really?"

For all I had a six-figure following, it still surprised and unnerved me when my real life collided with the online mask. I rarely showed my face on my blog for the sake of my physiotherapy patients, but the rest of it was all me—my life, as I lived it. Sometimes I regretted splashing it all over the Internet, but then I'd remember that regrets cancelled out the lessons I'd learned from my mistakes.

Or something like that. Over the years, I'd learned that I was a better teacher than the mess in my head deserved.

I left Lacey and Jemima to their giggling and turned to Uncle George. "I'm Harry. Nice to meet you."

"George." The old man turned to face me and held out his

hand. "None of this 'uncle' nonsense. Can't think why this young lot harp on about it."

There was humour in his faded eyes that I'd hopefully understand over time. I peered at the newspaper he was reading. The headline alarmed me until I realised that the paper was a month old.

"Terrible business," George said when he saw me looking. "What humans can do to each other."

"Who cares what humans do to each other?" A new voice—female—came from behind me. "There's too many on the planet anyway. It's what humans do to horses that we care about." A petite, dark-haired girl who looked and spoke exactly like Joe slid into the seat opposite. She picked up a fork and pointed it at George. "And don't go lecturing me on empathy again. I've heard it all before."

"Then you should know it already," George returned mildly before returning to his paper.

The exchange was fascinating . . . and kind of lovely. In the city, anyone younger than thirty tended to stick together, like herds of sheep following the latest craze and trend. I couldn't remember the last time I'd eaten dinner with such a diverse age range. In fact, I couldn't remember the last time I'd eaten dinner with anyone that wasn't Rhys or Angelo and Dylan. Shit. When had I become such a loner? And how was that even possible when I never seemed to have a minute to myself?

Sal dished up. Perhaps my size had given her the wrong impression about my appetite, but I was a little horrified when she heaped my plate with more carbs than I'd usually eat in a week. I wondered if there was a dog around that I could pass some off to on the sly, but Joe's arrival distracted me from the ghost of my calorie-counting, protein-obsessed uni days.

He didn't look at me. Just accepted a plate as full as mine and dropped into the seat beside the new woman in the room.

She elbowed him. "All right?"

Joe grunted in response, apparently preoccupied with a stack of envelopes, so she turned her attention to me. "Hi, Harry. I'm Emma. I took your booking."

I smiled, hoping she wouldn't notice me hiding potato under my pie. "Nice to meet you. You were right about the room. It's perfect for writing. Lovely views."

In my peripheral vision, Joe's head jerked, but I forced myself to keep my eyes on Emma, noting that her eyes tightened a notch too. "It was my grandpa's room," she said. "He loved the big windows. Said he could keep watch over every creature on the farm."

"I love it, too," I said. "It's such a calming space."

Joe got up from the table, his chair scraping the flagstone floor. This time, I gave in and looked at him. His back was turned to me, but tight shoulders were my bread and butter, and the urge to put my hands on him was again so strong that I choked on the tiny mouthful of food I'd put in my mouth.

Emma's gaze flickered to Joe too, but her expression was unreadable. Perhaps it was a family thing.

I wiped my mouth and drank some water. No one seemed to have noticed my foot-in-mouth moment or that I was struggling to look away from Joe as he pulled a six-pack from the fridge and popped the top on a can of Stella.

He turned as abruptly as he'd left the table and offered me a can with a jerk of his chin. I shook my head. "I'm good, thanks, mate."

He grunted and gave the can to George. Then he picked up his plate and left the room.

His departure did odd things to me. Things I couldn't quite decipher, let alone explain. I'd met people like Joe before— aloof and moody—but I'd always seen a glimmer of something else in them. A light, perhaps. A way in. It had taken me weeks to get Angelo to talk when we'd started working together, but I'd absolutely believed that he would . . . eventually. Joe was different. Not a client or even a friend—but his silence still bothered me.

A little while later, Emma swapped places with George. "I'm sorry I wasn't there to meet you. I had grand plans to greet you with some homemade cake or something and show you around, but I bottled it at the last minute."

"Bottled it? Not that scary, am I?"

"No. It's not you . . . it's—never mind. I'm sorry you got stuck with Joe. He's not always so rude."

So I hadn't imagined it. Or the strange compulsion to defend him. "He was perfectly pleasant to me. Showed me the house. There was no cake, though." *Like you would've eaten it.*

Emma took a deep breath. Her hands were shaking enough to mirror the horribly familiar disquiet in my own gut. I stared at them, wondering if I was imagining the buzz of anxiety coursing through her, and pushed my half-empty plate away. Great. I'd been here five minutes and I was already having some kind of meltdown.

"Do you want to see the horses?"

I jerked back to the present. "What?"

"The horses," Emma repeated softly. "I can give you that tour now, if you like?"

I didn't know much about horses, but curiosity got the better of me, and lacking any better ideas, I nodded and got to my feet. "Lead the way."

Outside, I felt much better. The jitters I'd worked so hard to escape floated away on the summer breeze, and I gazed around the working yard with new eyes. Buildings I'd mistaken for barns were clearly stables, their half-doors open, revealing a horse or two in each one.

"We don't double many up," Emma said. "Most of them are too cranky to share, but Tauna and Carric bunk up together. They've never been apart."

"Are they rescue horses?"

"Kind of. They don't belong to us, though. They're Dex's. He's got a place in Plymouth, but it's too noisy for these old girls, so he keeps them here. Pays us enough for the space to keep the water on."

"Sounds like a good bloke."

Emma smiled. "He is. His fella has a Michelin-starred restaurant attached to their stables, so his place is rolling in it. Dex has bailed us out so many times I've lost count. The least we can do is take care of his girls." She clicked her teeth and one of the elderly horses ambled to the half-door. It fumbled its whiskered lips on the wood until Emma gave it a treat from her pocket. "Do you want to give her one?"

"Me?" I eyed the horse—Tauna, apparently—with a healthy dose of apprehension. She seemed gentle enough, but I'd never been this close to a horse in my life, and her teeth were *huge*. "Um, okay."

Emma passed me a cube of something grassy. "Hold your hand out flat and keep your thumb tucked in. If you don't want to do that, you can balance the treat on your fist."

Her gaze was playful, so I figured that only idiots took the second option. I held my hand out to Tauna, expecting her to come at me with her teeth, but of course, she didn't. She took the treat like it was made of glass and bumped my hand with her nose. A thank you? Who the hell knew?

Not me.

Emma took me around all of the stables and paddocks, including a couple of Shetlands who'd recently retired from the beach and a pair of donkeys who'd arrived from India a few months ago.

"Ronnie and Reggie," she said. "Joe and George think they're hilarious when they've been on the whisky, but the names stuck."

I couldn't help smiling as I studied the donkeys. "They're more delicate than I thought they'd be, and much prettier."

"Were you expecting Eeyore?"

"Probably." One of the donkeys came over. I was an expert at treat giving by now, so I held my hand out and fed it a grassy cube. "What's in the field with the hill?"

"Shadow. He's our only stallion, but I don't take visitors up there. He's too volatile."

"Hormones, eh?"

"Something like that. He was Grandpa's last horse from the old stud we used to have years ago. Never handled by anyone else. Even Joe struggles with him—" The landline phone attached to Emma's back pocket rang loud enough to send the donkeys skittering away. She reached for it, but it cut off. "Someone's picked up in the house. God knows who. Joe's horrible on the phone."

Emma stared out over the fields and paddocks. Her shaking had eased as we'd walked around, and she seemed calm enough now for me to take a chance. "Can I ask you something?"

"Sure."

"Sal said something about you being better online than in person, and you seemed pretty freaked out about meeting me today. Do you have an anxiety disorder?"

"Wow." Emma shook her head slightly. "You're the first person around here to ever work that out for themselves. It took me years to explain it to this lot." She jerked her head towards the house. "Not that they aren't sympathetic, of course."

"I think it's difficult to imagine if you haven't experienced it or studied it yourself."

"You've studied it? I thought you were a personal trainer?"

"I'm a physiotherapist, actually. PT is part of that, but the work I do is more holistic."

"Holistic Harry." Emma nodded.

I snorted. "That's my blog. And I started that as therapy for myself."

Emma's eyes widened slightly, but any response she may

have made was cut off by Joe coming up behind us, his face far more animated than I'd seen so far.

"Police on the phone," he said. "There's a pony loose at Crantock Beach."

"What?" Emma glanced around quickly. "It's not one of ours."

"That's not why they called. It's running riot and they need someone with a horsebox to come out and catch it. George is coming with me, but we'll need to put Ava in with Mani and get a stall ready."

"On it." Emma nodded like this kind of thing happened all the time. Perhaps it did.

Joe spared me a glance as he turned away, and I sucked in a breath. His dark blue eyes had been on my mind since I'd first seen them this afternoon, but they'd been flat then—dull, even. Now they glittered, alive with whatever it was that got him out of bed in the morning, and I couldn't look away.

I tracked him even after he'd turned his back on me and returned to the house. And I saw his face later that night when I closed my own eyes and tried fruitlessly to sleep.

CHAPTER THREE

Joe

The farm was never entirely quiet. At night, the horses called to each other, and the foxes screamed in the fields. Sometimes, I blocked it out and slept like a baby. Others, I lay awake all night, staring at the living room ceiling, but tonight turned out to be one of the nights when I didn't even make it to my makeshift bed on the couch.

Instead I walked our newest arrival around the yard, watching like a hawk for any signs of colic.

"Why?" Harry asked me from his perch on the doorstep—apparently he didn't sleep much either. "Stress?"

"Nah. Some tourists on the beach gave him their posh picnic—as in, all of it. Greedy fella's necked half of Waitrose."

"How did he end up on the beach in the first place?"

Now that was something I didn't know. The young male was in good nick—healthy and clean. Well fed. How he'd wound up galloping around Crantock Beach was a mystery, so I didn't answer Harry's question. His gaze on me as I looped the yard was unnerving, and I wished he'd fuck off already. I was *tired* and had less patience than usual for nosy questions.

The front door opened and closed, signalling that perhaps

Harry had taken the hint. I sighed and knocked my head lightly on the gelding's rump. He snorted cheerfully, like he had done since we'd caught him, and I scowled at him. "What are you laughing at, eh? We're gonna be up all night hiking round this shithole. Couldn't leave the sausage rolls alone, could ya?"

My grumbling earned me another good-natured grunt, and we set off round the yard again. Half my mind was on the dinner I'd abandoned in favour of ranting at the cats about broken tack, but the other treacherous half drifted to the stranger sleeping in my grandfather's bed. Despite poking around his blog, the dude who'd rocked up was nothing like I'd thought he'd be. For starters, I'd expected him to drive a wankmobile—a white Range Rover or a scraping-the-ground-lowered Subaru. Not a navy-blue Ford Focus. And his face didn't fit my assumptions either. His cut body had prompted me to picture some slick twat with a *Peaky Blinders* hairdo, not the rugged—he even had a *beard*—dark-eyed bear who apparently didn't like my mum's cooking.

And I wasn't sure how I felt about *that*.

The gelding and I had done another three laps of the yard when the front door opened again. I'd successfully ignored Harry when he'd first appeared around midnight, but as luck would have it—or not—this time, I was passing the steps as he was descending.

He was clutching a plate with a sandwich on and a chipped mug—*my* chipped mug—of coffee. "To keep you going," he said. "You seem like you're in for the long haul, and you didn't finish your dinner."

"Neither did you."

Shadows flickered in Harry's warm brown eyes, but he blinked them away so fast I wondered if I'd imagined them. Then I wondered why it mattered. Or *if* it mattered.

For some reason it did. "Sorry," I said. "I mean . . . thank you. I'll eat in a bit. Just got to get this idiot settled."

Harry nodded, his small smile as open as the rest of his features. "Are you going to be okay?"

Are you? "Of course. This ain't the first horse to do the overnight yard marathon, and sure as fuck won't be the last. Go to bed, mate. I'll see you in the morning."

Harry disappeared inside without another word, and I continued on my way with the gelding. My imagination tracked Harry's footsteps up the rickety stairs even as I turned my back on the front door and slipped back into the soothing pulse of hooves on the cobbled ground. I'd been alone in the house for so long it was hard not to see him as an intruder, but the arrival of his rent in the farm's bank account had swallowed most of my resentment.

His shy smile had swallowed the rest.

HARRY WASN'T in the kitchen when I wandered in from the fields the next morning, looking for breakfast and a couple of hours kip before morning muck outs began. His car was gone too.

Emma glared at me from the stove. "Scared him off already?"

"Would it matter? Got his money, haven't we?" I opened the fridge and retrieved the milk. "Where's Mum?"

"At the market, probably. It's Monday."

I frowned. "She didn't take the van."

"Maybe she walked."

It was possible, but Sal's favourite market was four miles away, and the skies had darkened overnight, eclipsing the sunshine we'd had the day before.

I poured myself a bowl of cereal and thumbed my phone to life. I'd tapped out half a text when a car pulled up in the yard.

Harry's car.

Harry and Sal got out, laughing like they'd known each other twenty-four years, not hours. Emma appeared at my shoulder and peered out of the window with me.

"That's cute," she said. "I think she has a crush on him."

I elbowed her in the ribs. "Not funny."

"I wasn't being funny. Mum deserves a bit of jam in her life. Why can't she have a toy boy?"

I suppressed a growl as Sal and Harry came inside carrying boxes of weird green shit that looked suspiciously like cabbage.

"Kale," Sal said when she caught my bemusement. "Harry said it's good for us."

I switched my glare to him, but he wasn't looking at me, his attention snatched away by one of the farm's semi-feral cats. "Don't be nice to them," I snapped. "We'll have them all in the house then."

Harry stopped petting the cat like he'd been burned.

Emma thumped my arm. "Right. Like you don't sleep every night on the couch with a dozen of them. Besides, they keep the rats away."

Harry finally met my gaze. "You sleep on the couch? Why?"

They were all staring at me, even Sal who'd given up on this conversation with me years ago. And Harry aside, they *knew* the answer, which should've made what I had to say easy.

But it didn't. I could ignore Mum and Emma for the rest of my life, but Harry's earnest gaze cut right through me. He didn't know why I'd slept on the couch every night since I'd moved back into the house five years ago, but he knew—somehow—how it made me *feel*.

Really? Telepathic now, are you?

But I was right. Every instinct that hadn't burned away in a life of disappointed cynicism sensed it down to the bone. And it infuriated me. *Who the fuck does he think he is?*

Irrational rage was a Carter trait and it flowed through my veins, bubbling out of me in moments when it was least helpful.

Like now. I dropped my bowl on the table, splashing the damn-fucking-cat, and picked up the van keys. "It's not fucking rocket science that I don't want to sleep in a dead bloke's bed. I'm going into town to get that head collar fixed. Don't call me unless someone else dies."

I stomped out of the kitchen and out to my van. It was low on diesel, but for once, there was money in the accounts—*Harry's* money—to fund a trip to the petrol station. The irony wasn't lost on me as I crunched the gearbox and rumbled out of the yard, and the faint shame crawling in my belly only irritated me more. The nervous horses in their stalls kept me from tearing off with screeching tyres, but I did it in my head.

It took a mile and a half for me to pull my head out of my arse, which wasn't bad as Carter tantrums went. My grandma would throw things at Grandpa for days when he got on the wrong side of her. I wasn't that bad—these days, at least—and *damn* if I didn't feel bad for growling at Harry.

I turned into town, avoiding eye contact with the bazillion out-of-town V-Dub drivers clogging up the roads. I told myself it was because tourists got on my tits, but truthfully, I was jealous. It had been a long time since I'd last chucked a sleeping bag in my van and headed to the beach without a care in the world, save where to buy bangers for the barbecue. My teenage dreams were long dead, and seeing yuppies from the city playing at a life that should've been mine pissed me off.

Filling the tank felt like sin, but I did it anyway. Who knew when the money would next be there? My phone rang when I got back in the van—it was the farm. I toyed with not answering, given the conditions I'd set out about calling me before I'd flounced off, but responsibility haunted me. "What?"

"Elaine just called," Sal said. "Dad's asleep in the street again."

"So?"

"So she wants someone to go and get him before opening hours."

"I don't give a fuck."

"*Joe.*"

Only my mum could lecture me with a single word. I put the phone on speaker and started the van. "What? You think I should peel him off the pavement and bring him home for lunch?"

"No. But I do think it's better if one of us does it rather than the police. We've had enough dealings with them this week, don't you think?"

I'd seen both sides of the rozzers this week, but I took her point. They'd only bring him back to the farm anyway if I didn't get there first.

"I'd go myself," Sal said when I didn't answer. "But you have the van."

"You're not going anywhere." I was done with my mum dealing with *his* shit. "Besides, I need to talk to him about Dicky McGee."

Mum exhaled, years of heartache and trouble lacing her sigh. "Please don't antagonise him. Or anyone else, for that matter. We've worked too hard to escape your father's messes to get dragged into his squabbles with Dicky McGee."

"Why am I traipsing down the Legion to pick him up then?"

"You know why, Joe."

Because whatever he's done, he's family.

Right. And I had a smile as sweet as Harry's.

Sal hung up, and I set off in the opposite direction to the tack shop. The Legion was on the other side of town, away from the tourist traps, and was rundown enough to constitute a proper shithole. Across the road was the cafe Sal's mate Elaine owned. She met me at the van.

"Sorry, luv. I just can't have my customers watching over a

vagrant while they eat their butties. Business is bad enough as it is."

I understood. If the horses that came through the farm brought rent payments with them, we'd be laughing, but life didn't work like that. We were full to bursting, with less resources to go round than ever.

With a heavy sigh, I refused Elaine's offer of breakfast and crossed the road to the heap of stained wool and corduroy that constituted my father. He was snoring, a pile of empty Tennant's cans next to him and an unlit roll-up dangling from his cracked lips.

I plucked it from his mouth and lit it, savouring the sticky loose tobacco that Grandpa had smoked too. Smoking was a filthy habit, but god, I loved it, even if stealing Jonah's leftovers made me feel dirty inside.

Loser.

I stuck the fag in my mouth and kicked out, my boot connecting with Jonah's shin. "Wakey, wakey."

He grunted and scratched his nose.

I kicked him again. "Oi. Wake *up.*"

Slowly, Jonah opened his eyes, revealing clouding irises that had once been a startling shade of blue. "Joe? Son?"

I hated it when he called me son. I hated *him.* "Just get up, will you? Elaine's doing her nut."

My father rose from the ground like an animated bag of shit. He glanced around and then up at the sky, gauging the time by the sun. "It's early."

"Yep. Did you go home last night?"

"Home?"

"Yeah. To the flat. Whatever. Please tell me you didn't sleep out here all night?"

Jonah shrugged. An admission, perhaps? Or maybe he simply didn't know. Either way, my patience with him was running thin. "Get in the van. I'll run you up the road."

I stomped back across the road without checking to see if he was following me. Chances were, he'd stay behind. Prop himself up on a bench until the Legion opened at lunchtime.

But the passenger door opened a minute after I'd got in the driver's side, and Jonah heaved himself into the van. "How's your mother?"

"Like you care."

"Come on now, son. There's no need to be like that."

I gritted my teeth and gunned the engine, tearing away like I'd wanted to when I'd left the farm with nothing but a flea in my ear. But I meant it this time. I'd had a dream once where I'd driven myself and my father off a cliff, to save everyone else from the both of us. Some days, that dream came back to me, especially first thing in the morning when I'd drive past the derelict shell of the old stud stables.

The drive to the bedsit where my father now lived was utterly silent . . . on my part, at least. He jabbered on like we were off down the beach to catch the waves, and I hated him a little bit more.

"How are you getting on with Shadow?"

I pulled up outside the bedsit. "Why are you asking me that?"

Jonah shrugged. "That horse needs a lot of work."

"Tell me something I don't know."

"Got a saddle on him yet?"

"As if." I stared at the betting shop across the road—my father's regular haunt when he wasn't pissing it up in the Legion. "He hasn't had a saddle on him in years, and I doubt he will again."

"Because you don't have time to work with him?"

"No—I get on him bareback when I can—but he doesn't want to be ridden by anyone who ain't Grandpa or you, and that isn't going to happen, is it?"

Jonah said nothing. Shadow had been Grandpa's horse, but

his brother, Dorn, had belonged to my father. The stallions had been like night and day—one black, one dappled grey. Their personalities too. Dorn would let anyone ride him, would eat apples from children's hands, and kiss their cheeks with his rubbery pink lips. We'd loved him like we'd loved Grandpa, but they were both gone, and we were stuck with Shadow who hated the whole world . . . except my useless drunk of a dad.

"You could always come by and pitch in," I said when the silence made my teeth itch. "With Shadow, I mean. It's all I can do to lead him down from the field these days."

"Thought I was banished?"

"You are when you're bladdered. Have a day off, mate."

"A day means nothing when the years are so long. You know that better than I do. Take care of the horses, son. They're blessed to have you."

My father's hand was warm on my arm, and then he got out of the van. I didn't watch him shuffle up to his scuffed front door, never did, but another sliver of my heart went with him with every doddery step. And *that* was why I hated him so much. Because as hard as I tried not to love him, in moments like these, I still fucking did.

I pictured Dicky McGee and wished I'd killed him.

And then I put the van in gear with a heavy sigh. I'd forgotten to grill my father about his latest fuck up, but there was a dozen Dicky McGees in this town. I couldn't kill them all.

SHADOW DANCED around the apple trees in the corner of the top field. I watched his elegant footwork as I hammered the final nails into the patched fence. In another lifetime, he could've been a show horse. Shame he was too good at shagging for us to geld him and sell him on to someone with the time and inclination to train him.

"As if you could ever sell him." Emma's scoffing from the last time I'd mooted the idea echoed in my head as I chucked my tools in the box. She was right, but that wasn't the point. Shadow was fit as a fiddle and relatively young. With Grandpa gone, he had no real place on Whisper Farm. Apart from the shagging, of course. His stud income had paid the hay bill last winter. *What more do you want from him? His leg to fall off?*

I leant on the fence and rubbed my face, pressing the heels of my grimy hands against my temples, like I could silence the conflict in my brain by pressure alone. *As if I could ever sell him.* But that didn't make me feel any less guilty about keeping a healthy horse in a stable that had been built for animals in need.

"All right, mate?"

I jumped and spun around, my hands falling from my face. Harry was behind me dressed in running gear, his broad shoulders wrapped in a pristine white T-shirt, his muscular calves a devilish vision in skin-tight black Lycra. "What are you doing up here?"

"Running. Emma said there was a good route through the fields now most of the horses are in."

"Don't go in this field." I jerked my head at Shadow. "He'll charge you."

Harry grinned. "She told me that too."

I nodded and waited for him to jog on, but he came to the fence and rested his cut forearms on the newly mended post. "He was your grandfather's horse?"

"Yes."

"I can't imagine an old man riding him. He looks wild."

"He can be, but Grandpa and my dad had a way with stallions. They bred them for a while."

Harry's gaze flickered to the wreckage of the old stud farm in the distance. Did he know that Jonah had razed it in a botched insurance scam? Had Emma told him that too? Jesus. The bloke had only been here twenty-four hours.

Lacking the words to match Harry's friendly curiosity, I whistled through my teeth. Across the field, Shadow stopped his prancing and looked at me. He wouldn't come—he rarely did—but the acknowledgement was progress, and Lord knew we needed some of that around here.

"He's beautiful," Harry said. "I've never seen a horse like him."

"Get many horses in London?"

Harry chuckled. "No. The closest I've ever been is Ascot, but I wouldn't go to something like that now. I can't deal with using animals for sport."

"Vegan, are ya?"

"No."

"Then you're a hypocrite," I said. "Just like the rest of us. There ain't no point bitching about the races when we're all eating bacon butties and swanning around in leather."

"I take it you're not a vegan either, then?"

"No. And I don't like racing—horses, dogs, whatever—so I'm lumping myself in that boat too."

"You can paddle. I'm not much of a swimmer."

"That's 'cause you weren't born by the sea. Newquay babies are born on surfboards."

Harry's tentative grin brightened a notch. "You surf?"

I shrugged. "It's not a world away from riding a horse."

"I can't do that either."

"Well, that we can help you with. Sold my boards on eBay, but we've got plenty of horses."

"You don't surf anymore?"

"No."

I braced myself for Harry to ask me why, but he didn't. He merely straightened up and fixed me with one of those piercing gazes that made me feel stark naked. "I'd like to ride. Emma said she'd teach me, but I won't hold her to it."

"You should. She's a good teacher. We had a slapdash riding school once, before, well . . . before things changed."

Harry nodded. "Then maybe you will again. Nothing stays the same forever, does it?"

I had no reply to that, but it turned out that I didn't need one. Harry touched his fist gently to my shoulder and moved on, jogging into the sunset and leaving a strange fire in his wake. It started where he had touched me and crept slowly through my veins, lighting up my nerves. The sensation reminded me of Deep Heat ointment, but better—*fuck*, this was better. And terrifying, because it had been a long time since a bloke had last made me feel like the world was on fire, and I didn't have time to nurture an unrequited crush on my houseguest.

I tore my gaze from Harry's retreating figure and rubbed my shoulder, staring hard at Shadow, like the big black horse could gift me my focus back. But even when he did, I didn't feel any better. Shadow had been Grandpa's horse, but he remained on the farm because of Jonah.

Because as long as Shadow was here, there was still a chance that my father would come back and be the horseman I saw in my dreams and the father he'd been before he'd burned our lives to the ground.

CHAPTER FOUR

HARRY

"Are you sure you don't want breakfast, sweetheart?" Sal waved her frying pan at me. "It's no trouble, honestly."

I backed away, clutching the green smoothie I'd managed to whizz up before she'd caught me and threatened me with a bacon sandwich. "Thank you, but I'm good. Got lots to do today."

"You say that every day," Sal retorted.

And she wasn't wrong. Despite being an early riser in the city, in the week and a half I'd been at the Farm, I'd been the last one up every single day—meaning it was a rare morning that I cobbled my breakfast together without having to dodge Sal's cholesterol train.

"It's true." I spread the hand that wasn't clutching the smoothie and took another step back. "I didn't come here for a holiday."

"Holiday? What's that? It's only the young ones around here have time for that nonsense." Sal finally disarmed, dropping her pan on the stove. "All right, luv. I've got the donkeys to do, but I'll bring you some tea in a little while."

It was a fair compromise now I'd convinced her that I didn't need three sugars dumped in the builder's brew she doled out every couple of hours, and I retreated upstairs, leaving my bedroom door ajar to save her the trouble of knocking. I went to the desk and opened my laptop. The planning software I'd been fudging the night before was there to greet me, and I nearly slammed the laptop shut again. The software was supposed to remind me of all the wonderful notes I'd left at home, but it had, so far, failed. *Chapter Two—Your Mind is a Machine.* What did that even mean?

I sat down and spent an hour or so trying to find out, but it was hard to concentrate at this time of day. Early morning meant mucking out, and the yard below was a hive of activity. Joe, George, Toby, and the girls—they were all there, except Emma. She didn't come to the yard every day.

Around ten, I needed a break. I shut the laptop, swapped my T-shirt for a compression vest, and laced up my running shoes. A protein bar topped up my liquid breakfast, and then I headed downstairs. Outside, I took a route that kept me away from the fields and took me into town. Road running was hard on my knees, but the scenery around the farm was gorgeous, and I'd made it all the way to Holywell by the time I stopped for a rest.

I stretched my legs out on a bench outside the little shop where the farm seemed to get most of its basic groceries—bread, milk, eggs. As luck would have it, Joe emerged a few minutes into my stop, a jumbo packet of sausages tucked under his arm.

"What the fuck are you doing here?"

I'd grown used to his bluntness by now. The way he barked out questions like you'd been put on this earth to irritate him. I didn't take it personally—anymore. I couldn't deny that I'd spent my first few days on the farm believing that he hated me. It had taken me a few days to see that he was rude to just about everyone. "Running. It's a beautiful day."

Joe squinted through the bright sunshine, narrowing his

ever-suspicious eyes. "I swear I saw you at the gate half an hour ago."

I checked my watch. "You probably did."

"You ran all the way here in half an hour?"

"Looks that way."

Joe stared me down—or, at least, tried to. I'd grown used to that too, and he reminded me of the semi-feral cats who lived around the house at the farm. The females were generally friendly if I tossed them a bit of chicken, but the tomcats remained aloof, glaring at me from a distance until I glared back hard enough for them to lose interest and wander off.

True to form, Joe grunted and walked away. He was at his van I hadn't noticed parked a few feet from the bench when he turned back. "It's my turn to make lunch. Are you about?"

Damn it. What was it about this family and feeding me? "Don't worry about me. I'll sort myself out later."

"With what? The three-hundred chicken breasts you've stashed in the fridge."

"Probably."

Joe opened his van and tossed the sausages inside. Again, I expected him to follow the bangers and drive off, but something drew me closer to him. I was a foot or so away when he turned, leaning back on the van, the sun that had been in his eyes before now casting a sinful shadow across his face. "How do you stay so big when you don't eat fuck all?"

I suppressed an age-old urge to fold my arms across my chest and hunch my shoulders. "I eat."

"I've never seen you."

"Liar. I had dinner with you last night."

"That boiled chicken breast shite you were eating? Fuck that."

I forced a grin. "It's good for fitness—high protein, low fat. I don't know how you eat all those carbs and stay so lean."

"Calling me skinny?"

There was humour in Joe's stormy eyes, but I denied it anyway. "No, I'm saying that if I ate like you, I'd be the size of a house."

"You are the size of a house."

"A softer house, then."

Joe laughed—really laughed, from deep in his belly instead of his usual gruff and reluctant chuckle. "You're a strange man."

He was one to talk, but I let it go with a shrug. "If you say so. I'm probably just jealous. I haven't had a sausage in years."

Joe stopped laughing. His eyebrows disappeared into his inky hairline, and his gaze flashed with something I couldn't quite decipher but yet seemed oddly familiar at the same time. A silence stretched between us—neither loaded or light. And then, *finally*, the innuendo of what I'd said hit home.

Shit. Was I about to get bitch-slapped with some homophobic bullshit? No one at Whisper Farm seemed interested enough to give a fuck about my queerness, and I'd assumed—given that most of them had referenced my blog—that it wasn't a secret. That it didn't *need* to be.

My heart skipped a beat. That wasn't unheard of in Joe's company, but it felt different now, and I took an unconscious step back before I caught myself. Fuck that. I was out and proud and pushing thirty. Was I really going to back down from this when I'd faced down—

Joe's long fingers closed around my wrist. "What's up with you?"

"What?"

Joe studied me, his eyebrows back in their rightful place. "You look hungry."

Even though we'd spent the majority of the last five minutes bickering about food, it was the last thing I expected him to say. "What?"

"Stop saying what. You're making me feel like I'm jabbering nonsense like my grandparents did." Joe released my wrist. "Just come home and have your lunch, will you? Ma's starting to think she can't cook, and that shit ain't right."

He got in the van and drove away. It seemed like he'd left in slow motion, but when I looked up from checking my arm for finger-shaped sear marks, it felt like I'd blinked and come awake to find myself in the strangest of places.

I started running again, instinct drawing me in the general direction of the farm. I'd intended to find a robust tree to use as a chin-up bar on my way back, but I got sucked into the hypnotic rhythm of my feet slapping the ground and was at the farm gate before I knew it.

It was too early for whatever Joe had planned for lunch, so I dodged the kitchen and found some trees by the donkey paddock. One of the donkeys—Reggie, I think—wandered over to stare at me while I completed six-dozen reps of chin-ups. My biceps were burning by the time I'd finished, and hunger rumbled in my gut. I'd learned not to ignore it in recent years, but I didn't fancy facing Joe again just yet. His moods—and mine—were giving me whiplash.

Lacking any brighter ideas, I shinned up the tree and picked an apple. I dropped out of the branches to find Toby waiting for me, apparently unconcerned with the houseguest climbing the trees. "Joe wants you."

"Why?"

"Dunno. Just said to fetch you in."

Brilliant. I trailed Toby to the house, cringing when he veered off in the yard and ducked into the feed store, leaving me to face Joe alone.

With a sigh, I went inside. Joe was in the kitchen, hacking up sausages at the table, an unlit cigarette dangling between his pillowy lips. "You rang?" I said.

"Your mum did, actually. She stayed on the line for a bit, but you took the scenic route to get here from monkeying around in the trees."

The fact that he'd been watching made me warm all over, almost eclipsing the guilt at pushing my mum's weekly email to the bottom of my to-do list. "Was she okay?"

"Aye. Seemed to be. I did check that it wasn't urgent, and I told her that your phone was probably dipping in and out of service. She said to check your email, eat your greens, and call her back when you can."

Joe kept his eyes on his sausages. Anyone else, I'd have pondered if they were taking the piss, but if there was one thing I knew about Joe, it was that he was an even bigger mummy's boy than I had once been.

"Thanks," I said. "My phone is playing up, and I keep forgetting to email her. I gave her the farm number for emergencies. Hope that's okay."

"'Course it is. Living here, aren't you?"

"I s'pose."

Joe leaned back in his chair and retrieved a net of onions from the vegetable rack behind him. "You're lucky my ma didn't take that call. If she found out you'd been blanking your old dear, she'd have your guts for garters."

"I haven't heard that saying in years."

"What saying?"

"Guts for garters. My nan used to say it."

"Yeah, well. We all talk like old women down here. Ain't got no slick city speak going on." Joe started chopping his mountain of onions and chucking them in a huge pan. "But feel free to use the farm phone to call your mum anytime. I can't promise it won't get cut off, but feel free all the same."

I couldn't tell if he was joking or not. I went with not, as every dinnertime seemed to be taken up by him and Emma squabbling about money. "Thanks. What are you making? Do you need a hand?"

"You want to help cook something you have no intention of eating?"

"I never said I wouldn't eat it."

Joe threw more onions in the pan. "Fair enough. Stick them bangers on the stove then."

I swallowed a poor attempt at humour and took the plate of hacked up sausages to the stove. A frying pan was waiting on the burner. "Is this for the sausages?"

"Yup. Fry them off, then I'll stick them in here."

I couldn't remember the last time I'd fried anything, and Sal's bemusement on the morning she'd caught me poaching my eggs flashed into my mind. *"What are you drowning them poor eggs for?"*

Joe appeared at my shoulder. "What are you grinning about?"

I didn't fancy admitting that I'd been daydreaming about his mum, so I shrugged and turned the gas on under the pan. "Just happy to be alive, man."

Joe's eyes narrowed suspiciously. "I reckon that kale sludge sends you bananas."

"What's wrong with being happy?"

"Nothing, it just probably means you haven't lived."

I wasn't in the mood to challenge that bullshit, and I knew Joe enough by now to know there was little point. He wore his cynicism like a second skin—spiky and tough—and didn't respond well to attempts to break through his walls. "If you say so."

The sausages hit the pan, sizzling and popping, fat leaching out of them. My stomach turned, but I tried to ignore it and then forced myself to when reasoning with my skewed logic didn't work. *I will not be hard on myself today.* The affirmation was an old friend, and one I used with my patients too, but today, Joe's close proximity turned out to be the push I needed to step away from the past.

He chucked his own huge pan on the stove and lit another burner. His shoulder bumped me, and I shivered. His dark eyes found mine. I lost myself briefly in the liquid depths, but I couldn't tell if he'd noticed my reaction to him. Joe was a perfect contradiction—thoroughly predictable and yet impossible to read.

Fat spat out of the sausage pan and splattered my arm. The sting broke the spell. I tore my gaze from Joe's and peered at the sausages, bracing myself for another ripple of disgust, but my stomach rebelled and growled, and for the first time in years, I stared at a puddle of saturated fat and wanted to eat it.

The sensation surprised me, but Joe didn't give me the chance to process it. He reached across me for the salt and his hair brushed my cheek, the nape of his neck inches from my face.

Not for the first time, I wanted to put my lips on him. Most days he was a complete twat, but in moments like these, when he wasn't glaring or snapping, he was so wonderfully human that I forgot myself.

"Sling them bangers in here."

"What?"

Joe nudged me, sending another jolt of electricity surging through my veins. "Give me the sausages."

I tipped the contents of my pan into Joe's, noting the healthy selection of vegetables he'd added to his onions while I'd been under his thrall—carrots, peppers, tomatoes—and trying not to recoil in horror as he lobbed in two cans of Heinz baked beans.

And failed, apparently. "What's the face for now?"

I schooled my features. "What face?"

"The one Ma gets when I flick broccoli at the cats."

"You don't like broccoli?"

Joe shuddered, and I swear I felt the vibration in my toes. "Fuck no. It looks like liquidised boy scouts when she cooks it."

I had noticed Sal's habit of boiling her veg like they'd been to Chernobyl and back. "It's nice when you treat it right."

"So are horses, but you still seem shit-scared of them."

He had me there. I'd only managed to befriend the donkeys so far, and that was mainly because they were so noisy and cartoon-cute that I couldn't bring myself to be afraid of them. "Which horse do you think is the friendliest? I've got a different answer from everyone so far."

At that, Joe smiled, revealing a set of teeth that were unfairly white, given the amount he seemed to smoke. "Let me guess . . . Emma said Tauna, George plumped for Noel, and the young 'uns said Flea?"

I laughed. "How did you know?"

"Because everyone has their favourites and their reasons for loving them. Tauna brings Emma out of her shell. Shame she's too knackered to ride, really, 'cause I reckon Emma would go anywhere with her. And George and Noel have been pals for life. George delivered that foal before I was born . . . oldest idiots here, them two."

"What about Flea?"

"He's a Shetland," Joe said. "And he eats Hula Hoops off your fingers. Of course the kids are going to go for him."

"So . . ." I watched Joe stir up what appeared to be an enormous pot of stew. "What's the real answer?"

"Mani," Joe replied like it was obvious. "He's a true elder. You ever feel like giving up on this shit, go see him and tell him I sent you."

It was a sweet offer, but as Joe threw a lid on his pan of mystery and left the kitchen, I knew it was one I'd never take up. Mani was *huge*, and more than that, I'd seen Joe in his stable late at night, his head resting on the horse's neck, his face buried in his mane. I knew jack about horses, but I knew a sacred bond when I saw one.

Mani was Joe's soul horse. Perhaps one day I'd find my own.

CHAPTER FIVE

Joe

"Come closer," I called to the young girls who'd come to the farm on a school trip. "Ava don't bite."

The gaggle of kids inched closer. Ava paid them no attention whatsoever and continued stripping a nearby tree of its bark, while I went on with my pre-packaged sermon on stable work. It was hard to tell who cared less: the kids, who just wanted to stroke the horses that were small enough to be cute, eat their lunch, and go home. Or me . . . who just wanted a nap.

Because, fuck, I was knackered. The escaped gelding from Crantock Beach—Buddy, apparently—had returned to his owners, but in his place had come two colts from an abandoned fairground in Swindon. Nursing the horsebox there and back and settling the weak youngsters into their stall had taken all night and most of the morning. I'd been on my way to bed when the minibus of bored tweens had shown up. Damn Emma and her bloody anxiety.

I didn't mean that.

Ava got bored with the tree and wandered off. I clicked my tongue and Mani came to me. The children took a collective step back, and the temptation to hide behind Mani until they went away entirely was strong, but the gazes of their watchful parents were burning a hole in the side of my head, and I reluctantly coaxed Mani forward.

"This is Mani," I said. "He's the tallest horse here."

"Do you ride him?" a young girl asked.

"Occasionally," I said. "He's quite old now, but he likes a turn around the field from time to time."

It was a far cry from the wild rides Mani and I had grown up on—galloping along the beaches at dawn, hurling ourselves over rocks and waves, and tearing through the woods and fields, trees and fences no barriers for two young boys with energy to spare. But life was different now. Mani was old, and I was *tired*.

But still, the call to ride, combined with the disbelieving stares of the visiting children, prompted me to retrieve some reins from the box I'd brought out from the tack room and fasten them on Mani. I'd rarely ridden him with a saddle, or even a helmet, but I got the feeling the watching parents would do their nuts if I didn't behave.

So I saddled Mani up and used the fence to mount him. I'd run out of words, so I turned Mani and took him on a slow loop of the paddock, easing him from a walk to a lazy trot. Beneath me, Mani's muscles bunched, ready for his smooth canter, but I didn't have time for that right now. "Sorry, old boy. I'll take you out later."

If I had time. Fuck it. I'd make time. Mani was born to gallop, even now, with his arthritic joints and knobbly knees.

Harry came out of the house as I trotted back to my starting place. He seemed taken aback to find the yard full of children, but to his credit, didn't run screaming back inside—he was a better man than me.

He was also on my mind far more than he should've been since I'd convinced him to eat the Carter sausage casserole a few days ago, so I decided to have a little fun. "Hey, Harry! Come here."

Harry moved his graceful bulk across the yard and came to the fence. "You rang?"

"I did. These lovely ladies here seem to think Mani is scary. What do you think? Pussycat, ain't he?"

Harry glanced briefly at the gaggle of girls and then at me, his gaze as friendly as ever, but with a tinge of wickedness that I didn't expect. "*You're* a pussycat, Mr. Carter. Not sure about Mani yet."

Wanker. I pursed my lips to contain my grin and slid off Mani. "There's an easy way to find out. I've been riding Mani since I was nine years old, but Mr.—" Shit, I couldn't remember his surname. Did he even have one? "Uh, Mr. Holistic, here, ain't never been on a horse's back. Think he should try now?"

The girls giggled as Harry took a step back from the fence, his eyes wide with mock horror that was likely more real than he cared to admit.

"Come on," I goaded. "You're as big as Mani, really. He's probably more scared of you than you are of him."

Mani wasn't scared of anything and Harry knew it. He glared at me, his back to the children, and I thought for a fleeting moment that he would walk away, leaving the joke on me.

But he didn't. He came back to the fence, laid his hands on the rail, and jumped over with a nimble grace that belied his broad frame. "If he runs off with me, I'm taking him back to London."

"Yeah, yeah." I beckoned him closer and brought Mani alongside him. "Stick this helmet on and put your foot on the fence."

Harry obeyed. I fed Mani a hay cube and murmured in his ear. He ignored me entirely, which was his usual code for compliance. Mani was a wicked ride, but the rest of the time he was simply too lazy to misbehave. I patted his neck. "Atta boy."

Then I turned to Harry. "Just grab his mane and vault up. Piece of piss—uh, I mean cake."

"Right." Harry took a fistful of Mani's mane. "You sure I won't hurt him?"

"You think I'd let you hurt my horse?"

Harry had no comeback to that. He tightened his grip on Mani's mane and heaved himself up onto Mani's broad back. The movement was light and easy, like I'd known it would be, and when Mani stayed stock still, staring disinterestedly into the distance, the apprehension in Harry's face faded.

He grinned and the sunshine beating down on us was suddenly brighter. "Hey, it's not bad up here. I can see Emma hanging the washing out at the bungalow and even the circus up the road. Who else wants to see?"

Spending an hour lifting kids on and off Mani hadn't been in my game plan, but it seemed that Harry had got my number. He'd played me at my own game and won. And my morning was all the better for it.

The minibus departed a few hours later. Harry helped me pack up the equipment we'd used and carried the box back to the tack room while I brought Mani into his stable for some water and a light feed in the shade.

I was fussing with his mane when Harry returned. "What was all that about?"

"All what?"

Harry rubbed Mani's neck like he'd been doing it his whole life. "Getting me up on this monster. I mean, it was fun—empowering, actually—but I didn't think it was your MO to fuck with people's fears."

"Why would you think that?"

"Because Emma hasn't left the bungalow all week, and you haven't tried to make her, even though everyone else has."

"Toby hasn't."

"Toby is equal parts terrified and totally in love with her."

"True that." There wasn't really room for Harry and me in the stable doorway, but somehow we made it work. His shoulder touched mine and I forgot about the long afternoon of hoof trimming that awaited me. "But to answer your question, I can't fuck with Emma's shit because I don't know how. The others know trying to help her won't work, but they do it anyway so she knows they care. I . . . I dunno. I don't see the point in rowing with her about something she can't change. It just makes her feel guilty."

Harry nodded, his gaze thoughtful. "What makes you think she can't change it?"

I looked at him properly. "What makes you think she can?"

Harry shrugged. "Experience. I work with a lot of MS patients, ME too. Many of them battle with anxiety and depression, I think much of it is because they can't visualise their situation ever changing—that they'll live debilitated and in constant pain forever."

"A physical illness isn't the same as an anxiety disorder."

"Not exactly, but they can share a psychology. I don't know enough about Emma's condition to make a judgement, but don't assume that nothing can change. Life can always be better, Joe."

Harry punched my arm and walked away. The impact of his fist was gentle, like his words, but I felt it for the rest of the day.

<hr>

IT WAS a rare morning that I slept past dawn, but on the third Sunday that Harry was with us—because that was how I apparently measured time now—it was gone nine by the time I rolled off the couch.

I stumbled into the downstairs bathroom and then into the kitchen. The smell of bacon lingered, but there was no one around, not even Sal, which accounted for the stack of dirty plates in the sink.

Chin-deep in a mug of tea, I wandered outside. And then blinked. *What the fuck?* Sunday often drew visitors to the farm, and so we tried to get the stables done first thing, but all the mucking out done this early was unheard of.

Most of the horses had been turned out to the fields. I checked on the ones that remained and found their stalls spotless too. "What's going on, eh?" I muttered to Mani, but he had no answer for me or any bright ideas about where everyone had got to.

I let him be and drifted across the yard to the tack room, noting that Harry's car was MIA too. It wasn't unusual for him to take my mum to the market in the week, but Sundays usually found him using the hay barn as some kind of assault course, and the realisation that he wasn't on the farm doing just that hit me kind of strange.

Puzzled, I set to work on the mountain of overdue tack cleaning, trying not to listen out for every engine that neared the farm. And failed, obviously, because I was waiting in the yard when Harry's car pulled up an hour later.

I opened his door before he'd turned the ignition off. "Your break discs are warped. I can hear 'em. And what the fuck is she doing in your car?"

Emma narrowed her eyes at me from the passenger seat, though it was tough for her to appear angry when her grin was a mile wide. "I heard the clunking too, so I showed him where Freddie's place was so he can get it fixed tomorrow."

"Freddie's place is three miles away."

"I know."

I opened my mouth. Shut it again. Emma had barely left the bungalow in weeks, but if she had the stones for helping Harry out, I had a whole fucking list of—

Harry put his hand on my arm as he got out of the car. The contact was brief, but enough to stop my inner tirade in its tracks. He found my eyes and tilted his head subtly to one side. I had no idea what he was trying to say, but figured it was something along the lines of "don't be a dick about this."

Easy for him to say. He hadn't been the only one driving every man and beast around for the last fuck-knew-how-many years. Roll on Toby's driving test—if only the little shit could pass it first time.

Harry took a box of green nonsense from the boot of the car and disappeared inside. I watched him go and then turned my attention to Emma as she got out of the car too. Not being a dick about whatever I was missing was tough, so I kept my mouth shut as she came up to me and slipped her arms around my waist.

"Don't be cross," she whispered. "I didn't know I could do it until I did it, and I don't know if I can do it again."

Of course she could do it again. She could do anything if she'd just fucking let herself. But I didn't say it, because what did I really know? Anger, resentment, grief—they were all my friends, but I'd been spared the debilitating anxiety that had plagued Emma for as long as I could remember. Sometimes I thought I understood, but I didn't. How could I?

I wrapped my arms around her, seeking comfort in her slender embrace, as much as I offered it to her. "How did you end up in Captain Harry's car?"

Emma giggled. "Don't call him that. I know you fancy him."

"What?"

"Come on." Emma turned a knowing, watery gaze on me. "You're so vile to him, it's obvious."

"I'm vile to everyone."

"Not like you are to him."

"Piss off." I glared down at her, picturing Harry's cut arms and kind eyes. "I don't fancy him. I don't fancy anyone. Dead inside, remember?"

Emma's humour faded. "No, you're not. None of us are. We've just had a bad time of it. Things can change, Joe. We don't have to be this way."

I heard Harry in every word and wondered just what he'd

done to convince her to get in his car. Then wondered why it mattered and where the fluttering in my gut had come from. Anything that rescued Emma from her bubble of introspection was fucking awesome. So why did I feel like crying?

Emma nudged me. "What's the matter?"

"Nothing." I shook my head. "Just woke up weird. And alone. It was strange finding everyone gone. What's up with that?"

Emma took my hand and led me towards the house. "I came over early because I couldn't sleep. Harry was up and offered to help around the yard. Then Lacey brought one of her mates down, and there didn't seem any point waking you. You're allowed a morning off, you know."

"That's not what you said a few weeks ago when you dragged me home from the police station."

"That's because you were acting like a twat, and you know what? Until today, I hadn't left the farm since then, so how about we forget that day ever happened?"

Fine by me. I trailed Emma into the kitchen and sat at the table. Despite my luxury lie in, I was still profoundly tired. I slumped with my head on my arms, watching Emma do her best impression of our mother, until Harry reappeared a little while later.

He didn't look at me, but his arm brushed mine as he passed me . . . I think, if the resulting goosebumps were anything to go by.

I sat up slightly, eyeing the bag of spinach he passed Emma. "What are you doing with that?"

Harry shot a grin over his shoulder. "Stick around and you'll find out. It must be my turn to cook for you by now."

He was getting better at eating the dinners Sal put in front of him. He pushed them around less, and he'd stopped hiding potatoes in his leftover pie, but that didn't make whatever he had planned for me any more appetising. "It's not that green slop you drink all day, is it?"

"Nope. But it will have green in it. Won't do you any harm to get some more iron in your blood if you are as knackered as you look."

He had me there. I put my head back down and observed him and Emma through hooded eyes as they moved around the kitchen like an old married couple. Somewhere in the back of my mind, I was jealous, but lacking the energy to figure out why, I pushed it aside and focussed on the parade of weird shit being tossed in the wok my mum had never used.

A plate of rainbow food was presented to me a little while later. "No bacon?"

Harry chuckled. "Nah, but I did fry your eggs to ease you into the spinach."

"So I see." Fried eggs, teeny tomatoes, and giant mushrooms all sat on a mountain of spinach. I wanted to bitch about it, but I was too hungry to wait and too dazed to figure out a way of denying how good it looked.

I inhaled it, obviously, much to Harry's clear amusement. He didn't gloat, but he didn't have to. And I wouldn't have cared anyway, because watching him eat a full plate of food without fretting over it was a fucking gift.

Emma ate too, and she didn't flee the kitchen the moment she was done. Damn. Was there something in the water?

I poured more tea from the chipped pot to make sure, forcing some on Harry just for the fun of it. Flicking sugar at him across the table had become one of my favourite games when mealtimes weren't taken up by invoices and bank statements. "Where's Mum?"

"On a date," Emma said.

"What?"

She sniggered. "Joke, I swear. She got the bus to Truro to

visit Aunt Deb like she does every other week, you numpty. What's with you today? You're starting to make me look sharp."

Emma *was* sharp. For the thousandth time that morning alone, her stolen future flashed through my mind. Anxiety, the farm, her loyalty to me—any one of them would've been enough to keep her here by itself.

Harry got up and did something with the ancient blender Mum had dug out of the attic for him. The screeching motor cleared my scratchy brain. His hand on my shoulder a few moments later rinsed it clean. "Take this," he said. "Top you up till dinner."

And then he was gone, leaving me staring into a travel cup of something purple.

Emma kicked me under the table. "Blueberries, I think. He did say, but I was too busy trying not to puke behind the mushroom stall."

"You went to the market too?"

She nodded. "Yep. Harry taught me some visualisation techniques and gave me a crystal to hold."

"A crystal?" This day just got weirder and weirder. "Did it work?"

"Maybe. I didn't die, so I guess that's something."

"Ain't it always?"

Emma smiled and pressed a spiky purple stone into my hand. "Try it and see."

"Close to death, am I?"

"You're the one who claims to be dead inside, Joe."

She had me there. I gave her the finger, and her fancy crystal back, and left her to the washing up. Out in the yard, there was still no one around, and I didn't fancy the gloom of the tack room. The sunshine we'd been blessed with all week had faded slightly, but the skies were still bright and the breeze cool enough for a ride. Mani's broad back called to me, but he deserved a rest day. Shadow was my other option, and for the first time in months, I felt patient enough to give him a chance.

I sloped up to the top field. Like he'd heard my thoughts, Shadow was by the gate, flicking his mane and blowing through his nostrils, his black eyes tracking me as I approached him with a saddle. Most horses responded to gentle mutterings and crooning as I saddled them up for work, but Shadow was different. True to his name, he preferred absolute quiet, and despite the cheery sunshine beating down on my back, the silence suited my mood.

Working with Shadow was exhausting. He fought every command, refused every turn, and kicked out at every little noise. Except when he didn't, and then he was wonderful . . . those rare moments of perfection that made every painful wrangle with him worthwhile. Grandpa had often said he should've been my father's horse for just that reason—that they both endured a fraction of the heartache they gave out—but I wasn't convinced that either of them could've survived the other.

Hell, the rest of us barely did, and after three hours with Shadow, I was about done with the world.

I unsaddled him and released him. He galloped away like he'd been in a cage all afternoon, only pausing to glare back at me reproachfully, even though he went half-mad when I didn't work him enough. That was the problem with clever horses—they needed constant stimulation or they became a beast who would kick you in the head just for something to do.

Perhaps he should've been *my* horse.

I lit a cigarette and ambled back to the house, daydreaming about Sal's Sunday roast and a hot shower. Maybe I was daydreaming about Harry too, but I blamed the spinach for that. Huh . . . spinach. A million Popeye jokes came to mind, but I pushed them aside as I pictured Emma in his car—relaxed and laughing. It seemed surreal, but the odd feeling in my chest wouldn't quit. I was proud of Emma, but there was also . . . guilt. What had Harry done for her that we hadn't? How could he have loved and cared for her more than we had?

The answers weren't there. Perhaps Harry would tell me. If he knew. Despite my propensity for being a dick, I'd learned enough about Emma's anxiety to know that it rarely made sense.

Leave it alone, boy.

Jonah's gentle voice kept me company up the path until the tell-tale goosebumps of Harry's close proximity prickled my arms. I glanced up, expecting to see him playing volleyball in the yard with Toby or sitting on the steps, scribbling in a note-book and generally getting in my way.

But he wasn't doing any of those things. Harry was with my mum by the feed store—standing in front of her, his body shielding her—as he went nose-to-nose with Dicky McGee and two of his friends.

CHAPTER SIX

HARRY

I was going to kill them—*all* of them. I didn't care that there was three of them and one of me, they were going down.

And they knew it too, if their hasty steps back were anything to go by.

Sal grabbed my arm. "Don't, Harry. It's okay. I'm sure Dicky didn't mean it."

I pried her hand loose and pulled her further behind me. It didn't matter if they'd meant it. I'd come outside to find three men surrounding her, backing her against the wall, demanding who the fuck knew what.

Fuck that.

I stepped forward. The guy at the front held up his hands. "Now look here. I don't want any trouble. Sal knows I just want my money, fair and square."

"Fuck off. You're on private property."

"So? Ain't my fault her old man has waltzed off with cash that don't belong to him, is it? I want paying."

His voice was rising, like he thought the louder he spoke, the more likely I was to give a shit about what he had to say.

Fucking joker. I *didn't* give a shit. We were inches apart now. He leaned forward a fraction, and I was done.

I threw him across the yard. He landed heavily on his side, rolled over, and fixed me with a look that could go either way. I glanced at his friends. They didn't move. Didn't look at me.

This bloke was on his own.

He got shakily to his feet. I braced myself to bounce him across the yard again, but suddenly Joe was between us, his hand on my chest, his face obscured by his lean, coiled shoulders.

"What the fuck is this, Dicky?" he spat. "I told you not to rock up here, you daft cunt."

Dicky—apparently—turned to Joe, though he kept his gaze on me. "I warned you, lad. Your old man owes me, so someone's gotta pay."

"And I told you that it didn't have jack shit to do with the rest of us. Get the fuck off my land."

"Your old man's for it if I see him."

"I don't care!" Joe shouted, but the smallest of tremors caught the words.

It was tiny, barely there at all, but I heard it, and so did Dicky. He smirked and, for a man who was more bulge than brawn, moved quickly into Joe's personal space, prodding him with a fat finger. "I'll burn this place down if I have to—what's left of it. I want my money."

I'd heard enough. I opened the door to the feed store and pushed Sal inside. Then I pulled Joe behind me too and lunged at Dicky again. "Get off the fucking land, arsehole."

He stumbled back into his friends. They gripped his arms and started to drag him away, but he fought them, and they let him go.

I was ready for him. A Land Rover I presumed was theirs was a few feet away. I propelled him towards it and he crashed into the side. "Get in."

"Piss off. Look at you, all muscles and faggy clothes. You his fucking boyfriend or something? Pair of fairies."

I laughed. It had been a hell of a long time since my sexuality had been used against me like that, and hearing it now in such clichéd terms was so fucking ridiculous that humour was all I had. "Just get in the car, mate. Before you get hurt."

Dicky's pals hit the Land Rover, one of them falling to his knees. I didn't have to look to know that Joe had put him there. Or that Joe was right behind me. Even through the haze that had descended the moment Dicky had come up on Sal, I felt Joe everywhere.

The man on his knees scrambled to his feet and got in the Land Rover. His mate followed, but Dicky remained.

Joe stepped around me and closed a hand around his brawny throat, pressing his elbow into his chest. "I don't care about your money. If you come on my land again, or even breathe near my family, I'll burn you alive. You got it?"

I believed him. And so did Dicky. He spat on the ground and reached for the door handle behind him. "Fucking pikeys, the lot of you. Always have been. Your pa hasn't heard the last of this."

Joe released him. Dicky got in the Land Rover and his mate gunned the engine. They roared out of the yard with a hail of gravel, leaving a cloud of diesel fumes in their wake. I tracked them down the lane and passed the bungalow and only let my breath go when I was sure they'd made it to the main road.

The haze evaporated, but in its place came the mess I'd been in the first time I'd ever raised my hands to someone. Nausea flared in my gut and spread out, its acid tendrils creeping through my veins like lava.

I spun around as Sal emerged from the feed store. She was fine. Joe's anger vibrated through me, but he was fine too. They were all fine. It was done. It was over, and I needed to get the fuck away from it all before I lost my shit all over again.

Joe touched my shoulder. I brushed him off and walked away from him, ignoring him when he called my name. If my car keys had been in my pocket, I'd have made my escape that way, but they were upstairs in my room, and before I knew it, so was I.

I shut my bedroom door and leaned against it, my heart thumping in my chest. Fighting wasn't my bag, but I was good at it—I'd had to be—and a sick part of me got off on it when I didn't keep myself in check. When I let myself be like *him*.

'Cause let's face it . . . it was in me, whether I liked it or not.

I closed my eyes, parroting the bullshit I'd fed Emma to get her out of the house. *"The only constant in life is change. And I'm ready for it."*

But was I? Until now, the farm had seemed a sanctuary from the real world—the last place I'd pictured myself squaring up to someone—but it was clear now that I'd been naive. Joe's family had drama just like everyone else. *More* than everyone else, if the scene in the yard was anything to go by.

A shudder passed through me. Those men had stood no chance of getting anywhere near Sal, even before Joe had appeared, but they'd meant business when they'd first arrived. If I hadn't been there, how far would they have gone? Would they still go? They'd threatened to burn the farm down if Joe didn't get to them first. Did they mean it?

Pondering that question reignited the anxiety dancing in my chest. I exhaled long and slow, trying not to fight the inevitable. A full-on meltdown was probably avoidable if I could get out for a run, but that would mean facing Joe and Sal, and I wasn't ready for that.

Not yet.

I went to my desk and forced myself to work. The words didn't flow, but I hammered them out anyway, until my cracked muse gave up on me. I was staring moodily at the nonsense I'd typed when a knock at the door made me jump. "Come in," I called, expecting Sal.

Joe slipped through the door and shut it behind him. He leaned on it in much the same way I had, but didn't close his eyes. Instead, he stared at me, curious—expectant, even—like *he* was the one waiting for an explanation.

"Are you going to tell me what that was all about?" he asked quietly.

I turned back to my laptop. "Shouldn't I be asking you that?"

"Not if you were paying attention. Pretty sure Dicky McGee told you all you need to know about my family drama."

"So, what else is there to say?"

Joe pushed off the door and came close enough that I could smell clean sweat and hay. "Whatever you want to tell me? I mean, I'm grateful that you twatted them, but I'm curious about the death moves. You wanted to kill him. Why?"

Somewhere in the back of my mind, I was disturbed that Joe had read me so easily, but I stood by my actions, however he'd interpreted them. I forced myself to look at him. "You wouldn't kill someone who put their hands on your mum?"

Joe's eyes darkened. "She didn't tell me that."

"Yeah, well. You know how it went down. He wanted money, she wouldn't give him any, so he got tricky with her. I moved him on . . . that's all. Guess he's lucky it was me, not you, eh?"

"Not necessarily. I had a row with him a few weeks ago. Got nicked for it. But he still came here and got in my ma's face, so I can't be that intimidating."

I begged to differ. The fact that a man as big as Dicky McGee had felt the need to come back with two equally large men said a lot, even if they had taken the pathetic route of harassing Sal. "Do you think they'll come back?"

Joe came closer still. He crouched beside me, his elbows on my desk, his forearms tanned and strong. "I don't know."

"Are you worried?"

"I'm always worried, but having an idiot drunk for a father will do that."

"Is he violent?"

"Christ, no. I wish he was. Perhaps I'd understand him better."

I laughed. Couldn't help it. "You'd understand your father better if he hit you?"

"You said violent. You didn't specify that it had to be towards me. Am I missing something here?"

He was missing the world—*my* world—but why would he want to share it with me? Why would anyone? I tapped a key on my laptop to bring it back to life. "Trust me, you're not missing anything. Is Sal okay?"

For a protracted moment, Joe stared at me, his eyes deep pools of something I couldn't escape. Didn't want to escape. But he sighed before I caught up with him, and the moment passed. "Ma's fine. She's used to dealing with my dad's mess. If you're okay too, I'm going to head out and try to get to the bottom of this bullshit."

"You're going after those blokes?" Tension rippled through me. The urge to kill had simmered down while I'd sat and brooded on where it had come from, but the thought of Joe fighting alone reignited the worst kind of fire.

He touched my arm, lightly at first, but then his fingers closed around my wrist, his thumb pressing against my pulse point. Sometimes I wondered if people could hear my thundering heart, but I didn't care if Joe heard it, if it outpaced his by a mile. How could I care about *anything* when the heat of his touch reached every part of me?

"I'm not going after Dicky," he said. "I want to, but I've

fucked up too many times to believe it will change anything. Besides, I can't get nicked again for at least a year."

"Got a record?"

"Little bit."

"But Dicky McGee's the one harassing you."

"Don't mean nothing in this town. We've got too much gypsy blood in us for the police to ever take our side."

Gypsy blood explained Joe's wild eyes and dark complexion, and as I glanced around my borrowed room, little clues that I'd missed made sudden sense. There was even a Romani trailer abandoned in one of the fields outside. How had I not made the connection before? "Your grandpa was a gypsy."

It wasn't a question, but Joe nodded anyway. "Roma. Came over from Bulgaria in the thirties. He was travelling with a circus, but when it all kicked off in Europe again, they couldn't go back. He trained horses in Norfolk for a while, then came here to work as a farrier."

"How did he end up with this place?"

"He won it in a card game. We've bought more land legitimately over the years, but this house is someone else's history."

"Sounds like you have plenty of history here."

Joe's eyes darkened again. "Too much. Listen, Sal's going to be downstairs for the rest of the day. Would you mind keeping an ear out while I go deal with my old man? I know it ain't your problem, but—"

"It's fine." Everything was fine while Joe's hand was still millimetres away from holding mine. "Your mum is safe with me."

"I know." And then he was gone, away and to the door before he looked back. "Hey, Harry?"

"Yeah?"

"Come have a beer with me later, if you're not too busy. Maybe we could both use the company."

I TOOK my role watching over Sal and the farm seriously. It was the perfect excuse to abandon my work and sit by the window. I watched George arrive on his rickety old bike, bring the oldest mares in for an ear inspection, and then push chaff through a machine that was older than he was. Some days I helped him bundle the chaff into bags, but I wasn't in the mood for even his quiet company today.

A little while later, Emma appeared in the lane from the bungalow. I tracked her as she came to the yard, comparing her slender frame and pale complexion to Joe's. They moved with the same grace; I couldn't imagine Joe creeping across the yard with the trepidation I saw in Emma now.

The decent fella in me thought about going downstairs to greet her. To smile at her and push a cup of tea into her hands like everything was okay. To help her forget the inexplicable terror that so often paralysed her. But I stayed upstairs and left her to Sal. Helping Emma with her anxiety was important enough to keep me up at night, but my brain was fixated on myself right now, and she deserved better.

In an effort to distract myself, I let my mind drift back to Joe, then immediately wished I hadn't because that was a vortex I could drown in all day long. I pictured him as I'd found him that morning, asleep on the couch, his face boyish and smooth—innocent, almost—then compared it to the Joe who'd hurled Dicky's accomplices to the ground, and then the Joe who sat up all night nursing a poorly donkey. It was hard to believe they were the same man.

At least it would've been if I'd been a different man myself.

Early evening, Sal knocked on my door and told me it was dinner time, but I didn't go down. I returned to my laptop and opened a blank document. I thought of Emma, and Joe, and everything they'd been through to make them such different people. After all, Joe's father was Emma's too, but the anger, the resentment, the raw pain was absent from her eyes when she spoke of him.

Why?

Four-thousand words later, I still had no idea, but an essay on the effect of personal relationships on the spirit was halfway done. I shut my laptop. I'd veered way off course, but the words I'd vomited out had legs. They had to, or I was wasting my time.

Something drew me back to the window. The gang had left after dinner, and the house and yard were quiet, but there was an energy in the air I couldn't decipher until I spotted movement in the top field. The sun was setting, casting a rosy glow across the horizon as Shadow cantered the perimeter of the field, his powerful legs and shoulders moving like liquid poetry. Joe was on his back, no saddle or helmet, his torso bare to the evening air. Even from this distance, I saw his strong shoulders and leanly muscled chest. He was glorious.

I watched him for a long time, enchanted. At one point, he seemed to return my stare, his flinty gaze and steely set jaw turning my insides to mush, but then Shadow whirled around again, and the moment passed, though the tremor in my heart remained.

Work drew me back to my desk eventually. Joe had been riding for hours and didn't look like he was going to stop anytime soon. I edited a few chapters from the book until I was sick of my own words, and then ventured downstairs. The kitchen was deserted, like it often was when the offer of free food was done for the day. The yard was quiet too, the horses in for the night, fed and watered. Only a goat that had randomly appeared a few days ago seemed to be awake, and it paid me no heed at all when I poked my head out of the front door.

Hunger brought me to the fridge. I opened it and surveyed the shelf that was apparently mine. Sal had left a covered plate that I considered removing and scraping into the bin, but I couldn't quite bring myself to do it. Perhaps I'd eat it later.

Right.

Another plate caught my eye. It had a Post-it stuck to the foil. *Joe.* I'd forgotten that he'd missed dinner too and, somehow, the reason why.

I grabbed both plates and stuck them in the warming oven—the farm didn't own a microwave—and then drifted back to the front door, scanning the fields for any sign of Joe.

There was none, and darkness had begun to fall while I'd dithered at the fridge. *Has he come in already?* I hadn't heard him, but I didn't always. Joe had a way of slipping undetected into his living room lair, and I'd noticed that people rarely disturbed him in there, and even then, it was only Sal and Emma.

Fuck it. I followed one of the cats into the hallway and took the open living room door as permission to peer inside.

Joe was sitting on the couch, an open bottle of whisky on the table, his T-shirt still missing-in-action. Sweat glistened on his beautiful chest, and his eyes gleamed like a wolf in the murky light of dusk.

He held up an empty glass and nodded to the space beside him. I hesitated for the briefest moment before I took the glass and sat down.

CHAPTER SEVEN

Joe

Harry drank whisky like he did everything else—artfully . . . thoughtfully, swirling it around in his glass before he tipped it down his elegant throat. Not that I was watching or anything.

"So," he said when we were three shots deep. "Did you find your dad?"

"Aye."

"And?"

"He's a bigger idiot than he was the last time I saw him."

"That's all you're going to give me?" Harry reached for the bottle. "I've been trying to figure out what he's done to owe that bloke money, but I can't think of anything sensible."

"There isn't anything sensible about Jonah, trust me." I scooped up my refilled glass, ignoring the devil on my shoulder who told me I'd probably had enough. "And the truth isn't particularly exciting. He bought a caravan on tick and then crashed it—and one of Dicky's dodgy cars—into the central reservation on the A30."

"Wow. What happened? Was he drunk?"

"'Course he was. My pa ain't often sober. He left everything there and walked home, so Dicky's boy got nicked for it too 'cause the car was in his name."

"He couldn't just say it was your dad driving?"

I shook my head. "That's not how it works around here. It's one thing to let me get done when the coppers turn up anyway, but we don't grass in our world."

"The gypsy world?"

"We aren't real gypsies anymore—and my ma is Welsh—but it's more than that. It's a local thing. We don't rat. We sort things out ourselves."

"Right." Harry necked his whisky. "By threatening your mothers and burning things down?"

"Something like that."

Harry scowled, but I kind of liked the sneer on him. After weeks of shy smiles and friendly grins, it was refreshing to know he wasn't perfect, even if his derision was probably justified.

I drank my whisky and eyed the bottle, contemplating a refill. My father's demons were never far from my mind when I got drunk, but some days I was able to push it aside, kick back, and forget that the end of the world was in my blood.

Today turned out to be one of those days.

I topped up my glass, Harry's too, reaching across him, my shoulder bumping his chest. His soft intake of breath made me shiver. I wanted to kiss him.

Whoa.

Where had that come from?

Fucking whisky. Even when it didn't push me into a fog of despair, it still sent me round the bend.

I sat back in my seat, my head spinning, and not from the booze. I stretched my legs out in front of me, massaging my thighs. My shoulders ached too, stiff from a three-hour ordeal with Shadow, and I knew my body was going to give me hell tomorrow. Still, that was what you got for leaving a horse like

Shadow unworked for so long. It was going to take months to get him back on track.

Harry nudged me, his elbow driving gently into my side with just enough force to rouse me out of my haze.

"Huh?" I blinked at him. "What?"

"I said, you look uncomfortable. Have you hurt yourself?"

"No."

"Sure about that? Because I can see the tension in your neck from here."

I scowled. Couldn't help it. "Got X-ray eyes, have you?"

"I'm a physiotherapist, mate, not a freak of nature."

He gestured for me to move closer and spin around. Against my better judgement, I obeyed. I braced myself for his touch but was sorely unprepared for the sensation of his hand sliding down my neck. He was tactile with Emma, with my mum . . . even George, but I didn't touch people carelessly, and so the dizzying relief that came with our contact now—the energy— left me breathless.

A strangled noise escaped me. Harry chuckled. "Better?"

Better than what? Whatever he was doing was magic— spreading down my spine and across my back, easing the burning tension in my shoulders—but what replaced it was *insane.* My chest tightened and my skin tingled. My vision blurred.

I closed my eyes and dropped my head. Harry upped the ante and pressed his thumbs hard into the pressure points in my neck. It *hurt,* but somehow my body knew the pain was productive, and I didn't flinch.

Another groan escaped me.

"Sorry." Though Harry didn't sound contrite enough to mean it. "Sleeping on this couch is probably messing with your entire body. Do you get a lot of neck pain?"

"Some. It's not usually like this, though. Riding Shadow

always fucks me up, especially when I haven't done it in a while."

"Would it be better with a saddle?"

He was watching me. I felt suddenly naked. I darted a gaze to my abandoned T-shirt, draped over an ironing board that no one ever used. To reach it, I'd have to stand up—to break the spell Harry had cast over my sore muscles.

I couldn't do it. "Even if Shadow would let me, I don't ride so well with all the gear. It doesn't feel right—too detached, you know?"

"I don't know anything about riding."

"What *do* you know about?"

Harry snorted. "Not much."

I didn't believe that, but I considered the things I'd seen Harry do and tried to compare them to riding a horse. "Would you rather run through the fields or on a treadmill in the gym?"

"The fields." Harry didn't hesitate. "I'd never run outside much until I came here. It's changed my life, I swear."

"Why—*fuck*, that feels good—I mean, how has it changed your life?"

Harry said nothing for a long moment, his thumbs still creating alchemy in my neck, then he exhaled a soft puff of air against my skin. "I guess it feels more natural to run outside, to feel the wind in my face, the sun, the rain. It's freeing."

"Uh-huh." I waited for the penny to drop, but Harry was silent again. He swapped his thumbs for the heel of his hand, and then I lost the ability to speak coherently anyway. I couldn't say how much time had passed when I finally got it back, but I did know that it was a split second after Harry removed his hands from my bare skin.

He leaned back on the couch. I did the same, angling myself to look at him, although I kind of wanted to scramble for my T-shirt. "So . . ."

"So?" Harry arched an eyebrow in a way I couldn't imagine

him doing if we were sober. "What are you staring at me like that for? Have you got some big burning question you want to ask me?"

"Not especially. I was going to ask you about where you come from . . . your family, your life in London."

"Oh."

"Sore subject?"

"No. I have a family—my mum and my brother. I grew up in Hackney, but we moved to Romford when I was fourteen. Rhys still lives there. My mum's out in Spain."

"Your dad?"

"Dead."

"Sorry."

"Don't be." Harry's eyes darkened. The shadow was fleeting but unmistakable. "I hated him."

Why? But I didn't ask. Didn't need to. Because the fire in his haunted gaze when he'd protected my mum suddenly made sense. "When did he die?"

"Four years ago."

"Was that freeing too?"

"A little." It was Harry's turn to reach for the whisky bottle. His hand shook as he poured double measures. "But I hadn't seen him in years, so it was surreal, actually. I didn't feel as much as I thought I would."

"What about your mum?"

"What about her?"

"Are you close?"

"Not so much anymore. I love her to bits, but life pulled a weird one on us. I was her shadow for years, then I just . . . wasn't."

"What about your brother?"

Harry smiled, the warmth of it melting away some of the tension. "He's my best friend . . . when I don't want to chin him."

I laughed. "With you there, mate, though I've made it this far without decking my sister."

Harry knocked his glass to mine and his grin widened. "So we're both pillars of restraint?"

I shrugged and tipped some whisky down, tracking it as it merged with the buzz already lacing my veins. "I try, though I reckon I dance too close to the edge some days."

Harry shifted on the couch, his smile gone like it had never been there at all. It was clear he'd had enough of the subject, and though I was screaming inside to learn more about him, I understood.

I rubbed my face. The whisky was starting to make me feel ridiculous. Like I should give him a hug or something. I settled for nudging him. "Thanks for breakfast. And the lie in. I know it was you who left me to sleep. Emma loves waking me up."

Harry shrugged. "I owed you a few meals, and I didn't see the point in disturbing you when I was awake anyway. Besides, I like helping with the horses. They're not as scary as they were —oh shit!" He scrambled off the couch. "I left the dinner in the oven."

He darted from the room, leaving me bemused until he reappeared with two scalding hot plates, filled with the kind of food he usually seemed terrified of. Sober me couldn't seem to hide my curiosity, but drunk me held my tongue. I claimed a plate and some cutlery and dug in while Harry did the same with a little more dignity.

"I haven't had a roast in years," he said after a while, his plate still half-full.

"Why not?"

He speared a roast potato and frowned at it in a way that I couldn't decipher. "My mum wasn't much of a cook when I was a kid, and then I kind of got out of the habit."

"Habit of what? Eating?" I threw the words out carelessly because they didn't mean anything to me, but as Harry's gaze met mine, it was horribly clear that they meant everything to him.

My dinner turned to dust in my belly. I forced myself to keep eating. And to say something—anything—to give him a way out of a conversation he clearly didn't want to have. "Mani likes you."

Harry blinked. "What?"

"Mani. He likes you."

"How can you tell?"

"Because he looks at you. He doesn't bother with everyone."

"Would it bother you if he didn't like me?"

"Yes."

"Why?"

The same reason it bothers me that you have as many demons as the rest of us. "Because he's always right."

Harry nodded slowly. "That's not what you wanted to say."

"Isn't it?"

"I don't think so. You want to know why I'm such a freak about food."

"You think I'd call you a freak?"

Harry looked at me. The whisky we'd necked had reddened his eyes, but the warmth was still there, despite the strain. "Sorry. My words, not yours."

"It's a fucked up word. Do you think Emma's a freak?"

"Do you?"

"Nah."

"You're good with her."

"No, I'm not. I want to shake the shit out of her." I put my plate on the cluttered coffee table. "I did once, when we were younger."

"What happened?"

"She hit me with a ladle and stayed in the house anyway."

A chuckle burst out of Harry. He slapped his hand over his mouth and shook his head. "Sorry. I'm just picturing it."

"Stop apologising. It's not you who fractured my cheekbone."

Harry winced. "Ouch. That hurts, doesn't it?"

"Yup. Nice shiner, though. I think she was secretly proud of it."

"I doubt that." Harry's smile faded. "She seems to feel very guilty about her condition."

My humour ran for the hills too. "I wish she wouldn't. She does more for this place than anyone. Without her, we'd have no website or online donations. And the freelance marketing she does from home keeps us fed some months."

"You all work hard, Joe."

I sighed. "I know, it's just never enough."

"What is? How do you define when you've done enough? Because it seems to me that it wouldn't matter how many horses you had here, there would still be more to keep you up at night."

He was more right than he probably knew. The RSPCA were monitoring a field of ponies ten miles away. It was only a matter of time before they called on us to take them in, and the prospect of turning them away cut me to the bone. "So, what are you saying? That there's no point in trying because we're doomed to fail?"

"I'm saying that you're too hard on yourself because you expect the impossible. Perhaps we all do."

"Did you fight him?"

"Who?"

"Your dad."

"Does it matter?"

Did it? I took Harry's plate from him and put it with mine. The booze in my blood roared to life and my body moved of its own accord. I straddled Harry, pushing him back on the couch, and pressed my forehead against his. "I don't know."

Harry took a breath, one of those, soft-sharp gasps that I'd started hearing in my sleep. I braced myself for his answer, but then he kissed me, and my mind was devoid of all else but the sensation of his lips on mine.

My hands flew to his face and I kissed him back, rising up on my knees, pouring everything that I didn't understand into everywhere we touched. Perhaps he hadn't meant to kiss me. And maybe I hadn't meant to return the favour, but right now, it was all we had.

Harry growled into my mouth and pulled me tight against him, his blunt fingernails scraping my bare back. I gasped and kissed him harder, my world narrowing to his chest and his heartbeat thundering a hairsbreadth away from the growing bulge in my jeans. *Too much. Too fast.* But I couldn't pull back. My lips were fused to his, my skin addicted to his bruising touch, and it was only the need to breathe that eventually forced us apart.

By then, Harry's T-shirt was somewhere behind me, his belt undone. I was shaking, and so was he. I tried to speak, but the words wouldn't come. So I kissed him again, losing myself in the rounded muscle of his beautiful torso—his smooth skin and ripped abs—and blocked out the fluttery sensation in my stomach. *What the hell are we doing?* But the bemusement in my conscience found no purchase either as I coaxed a low sound out of Harry with my tongue. Everything about him set me on fire, and what little control I possessed in spite of my father's dud genes was long gone.

Harry's belt buckle clanked against mine. I moved to rectify the fact that he was the only one with undone jeans, but he got there first. He ripped my belt away and unbuttoned my jeans. I braced myself for his electric touch on my dick, but it didn't happen. Instead, he slid his hands over my heated skin, his fingers digging in, and rocked up against me, the layers of denim between us the sole thing keeping me from embarrassing myself.

My heartbeat spiked and madness crept up on me. I snaked a hand between us and found Harry's cock. It was hard, and hot, and heavy, and the scrape of my palm along his length clawed a hoarse gasp from his throat.

"*Joe.*"

The way he said my name was everything, but as I gazed down at him, something changed. Perspective seemed to hit him first, and then come crashing into me, and the fierce compulsion to never let this end gave way to reality.

A shudder passed through me. I let my hand drop, and Harry brushed my hair out of my face like he could ease the sting of what I knew he was about to do. He stood with me still in his arms as though I weighed nothing, and deposited me gently on the sofa. He turned away. For a moment I feared that he'd leave without a word, but he stopped at the door, one foot in the hallway.

"I did fight my dad, but not until he'd hurt me enough that I'm still fighting him now. Don't try and make sense of these things, Joe. Just be the best man you can."

And then he was gone, and I was half naked on the couch with wet eyes and a raging boner.

CHAPTER EIGHT

HARRY

"What on earth are you doing up there?"

Emma wobbled precariously on the rickety ladder. "I'm looking for the bran mash. Tauna lost another tooth overnight, so she's going to need soft food from now on."

"Are you sure it's up there?" I steadied the ladder and gazed up at the cluttered shelves in the feed store. "It's not with the other sacks of, uh, stuff by the door?"

"I'm not sure of anything," Emma said. "Joe usually measures up the feeds, but he's not here."

I knew all too well that Joe wasn't around—I'd heard him tear off in the van at the crack of dawn—but I had no idea where he'd gone, and his kiss still bruising my lips kept me from asking. That and stopping Emma from breaking her neck. "Fuck this. Get down. I'll look."

Emma shot me a death glare but slid down the ladder anyway. "You're in a mood."

"Am I?" I climbed the ladder and heaved myself onto the dusty platform that served as the lowest shelf. "Can't say I'd noticed."

"Are you hungover? Because Joe was. He looked like shit when he stopped at the bungalow to give Mum some money."

That Emma trusted me enough to jabber on like I was part of the family warmed my bones, but the thought of Joe looking like shit turned my whisky-scarred stomach. I'd left him dishevelled and bemused on the couch, and gone to bed with the world and my dick on my mind, but I'd woken to a brain obsessed with only him, and the longer he was absent, the more distracting that became. "Was he okay?"

I didn't look at Emma, but I sensed her frown. "Why are you asking me that?" she said. "Has something happened between you two?"

"Like what?" I read the label on a half-empty sack and then discarded it. "There's nothing but oats and molasses up here."

"Grab some molasses and don't change the subject."

I passed Emma two tubs of molasses and climbed down from the platform, brushing dust from my clothes as I hit the ground. "I'm not. I just don't know what you mean."

"I mean the fact that you and Joe live in the same house but hardly ever speak. I can deck him for you if he's making your life miserable by being a grumpy little shit."

"He's not grumpy. He's—" He's what? I couldn't find a word that quite fit Joe. Mysterious. Raw. Kind. Funny. Rude. They all fit, but none told the whole story. "We do speak."

"Uh-huh." Emma eyed me. "I can still deck him. I'm sure he deserves it for one reason or other."

"Not going to break his cheekbone again, are you?"

Emma's face fell. "He told you about that?"

I nodded. "Last night. We had a few whiskys."

"Oh god. He's a nightmare when he gets on that stuff. He either thinks he's the funniest man alive or cries because he's worried that he's just like Dad."

"Is he? Like your dad, I mean?"

Emma's frown deepened. "That's a tough question. My brother's a complex beast."

I'd figured that much out for myself, and I had a complicated brother of my own, but I followed Emma to the tack room in the hope that she'd continue.

"Ah, here it is." She tugged a huge sack out from behind a teetering tower of saddles. "What on earth has he put this in here for?"

"He's complex, remember? You may never work it out." I took the sack from her and lifted it to my shoulder. "Where do you need this?"

"Back in the feed store. Poor old Tauna needs her breakfast."

We returned to the feed store. Emma mixed a bucket of bran mash and molasses with warm water while she pondered my question about Joe. "He is like Dad sometimes—impulsive and daft. They've got the same soft heart too, like Grandpa, but he's a better man than Dad . . . stronger, I guess. He works so hard, day in, day out, doing the same stuff over and over again, just to keep this place standing. Jonah doesn't have that in him. Never has."

She seemed to speak to herself as much as me. We took the bucket of overdue breakfast out to Tauna and her stablemate, Carric.

"Joe was wild when we were young," she went on as we rubbed the old mares patchy coats down with bundles of clean hay. "Mum couldn't keep him indoors. He was always off riding Mani or climbing up buildings and stuff. He loved to surf too, but then Dad started messing things up at the stud farm, and Grandpa got old. Joe picked up the slack, and he's been doing it ever since. As long as the farm is still going, I don't think he'll ever get his life back. And some days, I don't think he even wants it. I'm the anxious one, but Joe gets so down when he's tired. I think he's lonely, so I'm glad he has you, even if it is just for the summer."

Emma's speech was long and rambling, but I absorbed every word and filed them away in the "Joe" part of my brain. The part that had also taken up residence in depths of my heart I'd thought were barren. That Joe was ever lonely tore me up, but what could I do? I *was* only here for the summer, and I didn't have enough rope for the both of us.

THE PATTERN of Joe disappearing at dawn continued all week. By Thursday, I was beginning to feel a little paranoid. I sat at my desk, staring out of the window, texting Rhys periodically, though my mind was wholeheartedly on Joe. For the last three days, he'd come back around eleven, but it was midday now, and there was still no sign of him.

I licked my lips, as I had about a million times since our drunken sofa encounter, like I could still taste Joe on them. Part of me was embarrassed for practically throwing myself at him, but the majority of my Joe-themed daydreams were taken up with recalling the scorching heat of his touch that night and fretting over the fact that we'd barely locked eyes since.

Which was my fault as much as his. I'd taken to skipping Sal's dinners and eating alone when everyone had gone, and by then, Joe was often asleep—or, at least, I assumed he was. I didn't have the balls to stick my head in the living room. *Bloody idiot.* And I didn't understand why. My demons had plenty of lairs, but my sex life wasn't usually one of them. Not that I'd had sex with Joe. Or was planning to.

Shit. My brain felt like it was about to explode. I thought about going for a run or a drive, but for the first time in forever, I wasn't in the mood to pound the streets, and my car was still in the garage. Which left work. Lots of work. And I was already behind.

It was lunchtime when I heard Joe's van coming up the lane. I was still in my room but found myself at the top of the stairs as he pulled into the yard. When I got outside, Lacey and Jemima were piling out of the van, giggling and clutching brown envelopes.

Lacey leapt on me. "I got three As!"

"Um . . . Okay?" I gave her a hug and then set her back on the ground. "That's great. What for?"

"A-levels," Jemima said, coming up on me too. "It's results day. I got two As and a B, so I got into Exeter uni!"

"Wow. That's awesome. Where are you going, Lacey?"

"Liverpool," Lacey said. "Joe wrote me a character reference to help me get into veterinary school, and now I've got my results, I'm definitely in!"

The girls were on cloud nine. I hugged them both again and then retreated to the kitchen with Sal, who was making them a cake. "They've done really well."

"They have." Sal smiled fondly. "Don't know how, though. They spend all their time here when they're not at school. Their parents must've forgotten what they look like."

I laughed. The younger staff seemed to work when I was busy in my room, but I often smiled when their laughter floated up to me. They ran rings around Joe, and the brotherly affection he gave them in return was wonderful. "It was nice of Joe to take them to get their results."

"Tradition," Sal said. "He's taking Toby for his GCSEs next week. And I think the young 'uns like riding around in the van. Gives them street cred or whatever it's called these days."

I was willing to bet that it was the hottie behind the wheel that gave Toby and the girls the kudos in town, but I let it go. What did it matter? It had been a great day for the girls, and I was happy for them.

So happy, that the scent of whatever Sal was baking caught my attention. "What is that? It smells amazing."

"Banana cake—it's their favourite. Healthy, too, before you start lecturing me on saturated fat. It's got olive oil and everything."

"Not that bad, am I?"

Sal pinched my cheek. "'Course not. I'm only messing, luv."

But her words stayed with me all the same. Preaching good nutrition was part of my job—a vital part—but balancing that with old demons was hard, and if Joe's quizzical frowns around mealtimes were anything to go by, I was losing the battle.

Joe came in the kitchen. He didn't look at me. Just kissed his mother and slumped at the table. I wanted to rub his shoulders, his neck, his chest. More. But I settled for ignoring the urge to retreat to my room and sat down next to him. I half expected him to ignore me. His leg curling around mine under the table made me jump.

But *god* it felt good. I ran my finger down his forearm until he looked at me. I smiled.

And he smiled too.

***

"YOU CAN'T STAY UP HERE all day."

I glanced at Joe who was hovering in my bedroom doorway, like coming over the threshold would burn him alive. "I have to work, mate."

"It's nine o'clock on a Friday night. Give it a rest for the day."

"What do you care?" I was joking, but Joe's lazy grin dimmed. "I mean, who are you to comment on my unsociable working hours? You haven't stopped all day."

"That's because I dicked around yesterday playing chauffeur to a bunch of schoolgirls and failed to fix the boiler in the bungalow. Besides, I'm done now. And so should you be. Mum reckons you'll get square eyes."

Joe tapped his beer bottle on the door and jerked his head to the stairs. When I didn't respond, he rolled his eyes and walked away.

It was an hour before I was done enough with my work to shut it down for the day, and when I poked my head in the living room, Joe was asleep. For the dozenth time that day, I ached to touch him, to trace his chest with my fingertips, to bury my face in his neck, but when he seemed so peaceful, nothing on earth would have made me disturb him.

The landline phone by Joe's head rang, taking the matter out of my hands. He snapped awake, bolting upright so fast he nearly tumbled from the couch. "Jesus."

For a split second, our eyes met. The sleep-addled confusion in his expression melted my heart, but then the phone screeched again, and he turned away to answer it, swearing softly as he listened to whoever was on the other end. "We can't take that many. To be honest, we'd struggle to take two right now, let alone six."

My heart sank. It was a horse SOS, and by the slump of Joe's shoulders, a bad one. I considered leaving him to it—getting out his way and letting him do his job, but I didn't move, and I was beside him in a flash when he hung up the phone. "What is it?"

Joe looked at me, and the awkwardness of the last few days melted away. "Ponies. Six of them. There were ten, but apparently four of them starving to death is only just enough for a seizure order these days."

"Are they coming here?"

"They can't. I have nowhere to put them. We're full, Harry. I don't know what to do."

"You can't double up some of the others?"

"Not any more than they are already."

"What about the donkey paddock?"

"Where would the donkeys go?"

That stumped me. The donkeys were smaller than the horses, bar the Shetlands, and seemed to be the easiest creatures on the farm to look after, but they still needed food, water, and shelter. "What about the tack room? It's got a half-door, right? Empty it out and put the donkeys in there."

"Empty it out *where?*" Joe gestured around the cluttered living room. "There's no space anywhere."

"Put it in my room," I said. "There's loads of space in there."

"I can't do that."

"Why not?"

"Because that's *your* room. You've paid for a bed and some peace and quiet, not to drown in our mess. It ain't right."

I shook my head. "What's not right is leaving those ponies wherever they are when you have a solution to do otherwise. I know you won't do that, so let me help you, okay? It's not like I haven't had my money's worth of free food while I've been here."

Joe's eyes flashed like they always did when we talked about food, but he had bigger things to worry about right now. His frown deepened as he considered my offer, and I could almost see him moving things around the farm to accommodate six more horses. "All right," he said. "Let's do this, but it's temporary, okay? Until I think of something else."

"Fine by me." I stood, eyeing the clutch of empty beer bottles on the table. "What happens now? Is someone bringing the horses here?"

Joe snorted. "As if. That only happens when they get dumped at the end of the road. I'm going to have to ring George."

"What about Emma, or Sal?"

"They can't drive the horsebox."

"I'll drive it."

"What?"

I held out my hand and pulled Joe from the couch. "I'll drive."

"You can't. You need a category C licence for that beast, and there's a bunch of coppers waiting for us."

I retrieved my wallet from my back pocket and thumbed out my driving licence. "Read it and weep. Now let's go."

Joe scanned my licence with obvious scepticism but was in motion the moment he found what he was looking for. He made for the door, still clutching my hand from where I'd helped him up. "The box is round the back. Can you bring it down to the bungalow? I'll meet you there."

"Keys?"

Joe grabbed a set from the kitchen table and tossed them over his shoulder. Then he whirled around and kissed me fiercely, snatching my breath away. "Thank you. We'll have to make two trips to bring them all back, and it means the world to me that you want to help."

I smiled and touched his face, hoping he wouldn't notice my trembling hands. "Of course I want to help. Let's go, yeah? Sooner we go, sooner we're home."

Joe nodded. "Okay. But on the way, I need you to explain why you've got an HGV license gathering dust in your wallet."

It wasn't a particularly exciting story, but once we hit the road, Joe seemed fascinated by me driving lorries for ASDA in my uni days. "That's mad," he said. "Didn't you have enough to do with all your doctor shit?"

"I'm not a doctor. I'm a physiotherapist."

"And a writer."

"Pretend writer," I corrected. "I haven't finished the book yet."

"But you will. And Emma told me that the whole world reads your blog, so you must be good at it."

I scoffed. "Most of the world reads *The Sun*, and you can't tell me that's good writing."

"Don't put yourself down. I can barely write my name."

"That's not true."

"Isn't it?" Joe turned his dark gaze on me. "I pretty much sign cheques with a big fat X. I didn't go to school much—Emma has to type out everything for me."

"Yeah, well . . . there's plenty of things you can do that I can't. And every skill is worth more than people think."

Joe said nothing, and I wondered, as ever, what on earth he was thinking. But I didn't have time to ponder for long. The derelict farm he was directing me to appeared on the horizon, lit up by the flashing blue lights of police vehicles, and the time for small talk was over.

I parked next to an RSPCA van and we got out of the horsebox. I hung back while Joe talked to the inspectors and glanced around. The police were leaning on a gate, apparently disinterested, and another van from a veterinarian's practice was nearby. In the darkness, I squinted at the large black objects they were lining up. It took a minute to sink in that they were body bags.

Horror washed over me, and snatched conversations I'd overheard on the farm over the last few days clicked into place. Joe and Emma fretting over ten abandoned ponies. Lacey and Jemima cooking up farfetched plans to rescue them in the night. George grumbling about red tape and bureaucracy. But all of their fears about being too late had been realised. Four horses hadn't survived.

Joe came up on me, his face grave. "We need to get a move on. These nags are starving. Can you call home and check they're going to be ready?"

"Of course. Can I have—"

But Joe was gone again before I could ask him for the number. I dug my phone out of my pocket—apart from checking in with Rhys, I'd hardly used it since I'd been on the farm—and searched out the email that had Emma's mobile number in it. I called, praying that she'd answer. I'd only seen Sal when I'd picked Joe up from the bungalow.

Emma answered on the third ring, breathless and clearly stressed. "Harry? What is it? What's wrong?"

"Nothing, as far as I know," I said quickly. "Joe just asked me to call and see how Sal was getting on in the tack room. He wants to move fast with these ponies."

"Oh. Okay. You scared me. We've never spoken on the phone before, and I'm not very good at it."

I chuckled softly. "Neither am I, but don't worry. Joe's fine. He just wants to get home."

"I know Joe's fine if he's with you. I'm being silly. And you can tell him that we'll be ready for you. We've got most of the stuff out. It's all on your bed at the moment. Sorry about that."

"It's fine." I glanced across the muddy farmyard and spied Joe heading back my way with the first of the ponies. "We'll be there in half an hour."

"Drive safe, Harry."

"I will."

I put the phone in my pocket and met Joe at the back of the horsebox. "Are we taking three at a time?"

"Nah. The four strongest first, then the other two. I'm gonna have to go in the back with them to stop them keeling over."

I didn't like the sound of that but knew better than to argue with Joe about horses. He stood aside while I opened up the box, then led the ponies up the ramp. Another two followed, and then we were on the road, heading back to the farm.

Emma was waiting for us. George had appeared from some-where too. He took the ponies to get settled in the paddock.

Joe watched him go, then turned to Emma. "I need to call Dex."

"Dex? Why?"

"Because the next two aren't fit enough to go out in the paddock. The foaling stable is the only safe place for them, so I need him to take a couple of old-timers off my hands."

"*We* need him to. This isn't just your problem."

"So you'll call him?"

Emma flushed, her face pale, like someone had pulled the plug out of her complexion. I nudged her and held up three fingers, hoping she remembered the coping mechanisms we'd gone through the other day.

She stuck out her chin. "Of course."

It was a small victory, but when I saw the state of the remaining horses, I clung to it. the ponies were skin and bone, empty eyes, and bleeding gums. I asked Joe if they'd survive, and his hollow stare said it all.

I drove the box back to the farm while Joe stayed in the back with them. I took it slow, avoiding bumps and sharp turns, but he still looked traumatised when we pulled up. "Are you okay?"

He shrugged. "Not really. Holding two nags up for ten miles is a bitch on your shoulders."

I could believe it and made a note to check him over before we called it a night. But it soon became clear Joe had no intention of going to bed any time before sunrise. "I can't leave them in the yard by themselves all night. Someone's got to watch them."

The emaciated ponies had laid themselves down by now, collapsing in the first clean bedding they'd likely ever seen. Joe was hand-feeding one of them bran mash. Lacking any better ideas, I grabbed a fistful and held it out to the other one.

"You don't have to do that." Joe wasn't looking at me. "You've done enough already."

I manoeuvred myself to sit next to the pony, mirroring Joe's position with my back to the side of the box. "Just tell me what to do, and we'll get it done."

He didn't argue, and a companionable silence settled over

us. George checked in from time to time, taking a break from his own watch over the other four ponies, but no one said much until Emma brought tea and toast to us at dawn.

I was half-asleep by then. Joe shook me gently. "Go to bed."

"Hmm?" I blinked rapidly.

"Bed," Joe repeated. "Dex is on his way to pick Gerrard and Lily up. As soon as they're gone, I'll get these two set up."

Gerrard and Lily were the farm's hardiest horses—it made sense they'd be the ones to go—but my heart hurt all the same. It wasn't right that any of these horses were suffering, and it wasn't right that I snoozed in bed when Joe was still working.

I shook my head. "I'll stay till they're settled. Kind of attached to them now."

Joe frowned, and I braced myself for an argument, but he simply handed me a cup of sugary tea and went back to tending his sick pony.

I drank my tea, barely thinking about the tooth-rotting sugar content, and considered the mare I'd nursed through the night. I'd assumed she was old when I'd first seen her, but George—the farm's expert on such matters—thought she was juvenile . . . barely two.

"Hard life ages God's creatures."

Was he right?

I chanced a glance at Joe's face as he muttered nonsense to his sick pony and had to disagree. His eyes, haunted and wise, were older than his years, but his face was young. And that broke my heart all over again.

JOE'S FRIEND Dex arrived around eight.

"You'd better go inside," Joe said when we heard another horsebox rumbling up the lane.

"Why?"

"Dex don't like strangers, especially big, brawny ones. Go on. I'll explain after."

At this point, I was too tired to do anything but exactly what he said. I went inside and drifted upstairs, my bed calling to me despite my best intentions to stay awake until Joe called it a day.

Balls. The entire tack room was stacked up on my bed. Somehow, in all the excitement, I'd forgotten about that. Admitting defeat, I got in the shower. The tiny bathroom window looked out over the yard, and I watched as a newer, shinier horsebox than Joe's pulled up.

I expected someone equally shiny to get out, but a slight, dark-haired man jumped down from the driver's seat and gave Joe a friendly hug, before climbing straight into the box with the sick ponies.

Joe followed him, and they were in there long enough for me to wash my entire body. The hot water was starting to fade when they finally emerged, and I caught sight of Dex's face. *Christ.* He was stunning, all wide eyes and high cheekbones. Joe and Emma had spoken of him as though he was far older than them—a kind uncle who helped them out—but Dex didn't look much older than Joe.

I got out of the shower and peeped through the window some more as Dex went around the yard to greet the horses that hadn't been turned out into the fields. He stood with Tauna and Carric for a long time, his arms around Tauna, his face turned into Carric's neck. For some reason, I felt like crying and forced myself to finally turn away.

He left a little while later, taking Gerrard and Lily with him and the random goat who'd taken up residence in the yard. "He's not going to cook the goat in the restaurant, is he?"

Joe whirled around from where he'd been leaning on the gate. "How'd you know he has a restaurant?"

"Emma told me on my first night when she introduced me to the horses."

"Damn, that girl and her mouth."

"Is it a secret?"

"The restaurant? No, but Dex doesn't like people talking about him."

"Why? Is he a gangster or something?"

I was joking, but Joe didn't smile. Just shook his head and tapped his finger to his lips. I shrugged. "Is it a gypsy thing? A code of silence?"

"Dex is a Traveller."

"What's the difference?"

"Between the Roma and the Irish?" Joe shook his head again like I was the world's biggest idiot, and for once I agreed with him.

"Sorry," I said. "I'm so fucking tired. I do know the difference between the two . . . I think. Ask me again when I've had some sleep."

Joe grinned, though his exhaustion was obvious too. "I did tell you to go to bed."

"Yeah, well. I forgot about my bright idea to stack the tack room in there, so I might have to kip in with the donkeys."

"Fuck that. We'll figure something out . . . after breakfast. I'm so hungry my brain hurts."

Joe took my arm and tugged me inside. Sal was waiting with bacon sandwiches and more builder's tea, but she hustled us out of the kitchen and into the living room. "Get comfortable," she said. "No more work for either of you today."

"Nice try, Ma," Joe protested. "But the vet's coming at ten."

"No, he ain't. He called and said he can't be here until midday. George is setting up in the foaling stable, so I don't want you tramping about that yard until this lunchtime, got it?"

"Thought you were going to Cardiff today?"

"I am, but that doesn't mean I won't find out if you don't do as you're bloody told, boy."

Sal's words were firm, but her gaze soft. And she was apparently the only person that Joe didn't argue with. Or maybe he was simply too tired. He flopped down on the couch and waved her away. She kissed me on her way out. "Thank you for being here, luv. We couldn't have done this without you."

"Sal—"

But she was already gone.

"She's right, you know," Joe said from behind his hands. "George could've helped me get through the night, but then there would've been no one to watch the foaling stable today."

"You'd have done it."

"Aye, but it would've killed me. As it is, I don't know what I'm going to do when the girls go off to uni."

"Don't worry about that right now." At his subtle nod, I claimed the space on the sofa beside him. "One problem at a time. Get through the next few days first."

"Is that your professional advice?"

"No. My professional advice would be to quit smoking, eat your greens, and let me work on your back and neck before you spend the next twenty-four hours asleep, but we both know none of those things are going to happen."

Joe laughed softly and leaned into me, bumping our shoulders. "You can stick the first two up your arse, but the only reason I'm not letting you put your hands on me is because you're as tired as I am."

I couldn't deny it, though I'd have stayed up for days if it meant getting to touch Joe again. His flawless skin was hypnotising—addicting, and however many times I got to lay my hands on him, it would never be enough.

We ate our breakfast in silence. For once, Joe didn't shoot surreptitious stares at me while I ate, and I was glad of it. The bacon sandwich was amazing and I was doing pretty well at ignoring my carb phobia. Or perhaps *I* was the one too tired to argue, even if it was with myself.

Either way, I didn't much care.

And I cared even less when Joe took my empty plate and tossed it on the table. "Ma can probably make you a bed up at the bungalow . . . or, you could kip on here with me. Top and tail? I don't snore."

The proposal was tempting, and practical, considering the large L-shaped couch, but despite craving Joe's touch—craving *this*—what little sense my fatigue-addled brain had left told me that begging a bed off Sal and Emma was probably a better idea.

I opened my mouth to say as much, but Joe was closer than he'd been a split second ago, and for the second time that week, I was kissing him before I truly knew what I was doing.

The first time, Joe had taken control from his position straddling my lap, but now he submitted, falling backwards onto the couch. I followed him as easily as breathing, chasing him down and covering his body with my own. His arms snaked around my waist, holding me in place, and all bets were off.

I slid my hands under his T-shirt and deepened the kiss. He hooked his legs on mine, gasping, and I dove in harder. I'd never kissed a man like I found myself kissing Joe. Never felt a kiss so entirely. But I felt him everywhere—my skin, my veins, in every nerve. Tiredness faded away, and blood roared in my ears. I could've kissed him forever, if he hadn't broken away with a jaw-cracking yawn.

He groaned. "Sorry. I've been thinking about you like this for days . . . can't believe I'm close to sleeping through it."

His eyes fluttered closed, and warmth in my chest eclipsed the heat pooling in my jeans—stronger, even, than the desperate craving to have Joe's hands on my dick again. I wriggled around until I was beneath him, and coaxed him into using me as a pillow. "Rest, mate. It's okay. We can revisit this later."

"Promise?"

I wove my fingers into Joe's silky hair. "Promise."

CHAPTER NINE

Joe

I woke up alone, which was odd because I was pretty sure I'd passed out with my face in Harry's chest. Perhaps I'd dreamt it. But, no. When I stumbled out into the yard, there were still donkeys in the tack room and half a dozen emaciated ponies taking up space I didn't have.

Fuelled by coffee, I took a shower and then set to work reassessing the new arrivals. The vet would be here soon, but I needed a daylight idea of what we were dealing with. If the ponies were in as bad a shape as I'd feared last night, they'd be with us for the long haul, and that was a serious problem.

Besides, angsting over the ponies distracted me from looking for Harry around every corner. Seriously. What was it about that bloke and leaving me hanging on the couch? *He'd* kissed *me*, every time, goddammit.

The four ponies in the donkey paddock were doing well. George had fed them little and often, and they were enjoying the hay in the donkey shed. I checked their hooves and teeth and then left them to it. The two mares in the foaling stable were a different story. In the few hours I'd slept in Harry's arms, one of them had gone downhill.

I fed her more warm bran laced with the molasses someone had helpfully rooted out from wherever I'd stashed it. She didn't eat much—too weak—and I was trying to tempt her with some fresh green grass from Sal's garden when the vet arrived.

His assessment was bleak. He offered to put the mares down, but I wasn't there yet. Grandpa—and even my loser dad—had taught me that a horse would let me know when they'd had enough, and I'd never forgotten that lesson. Both mares were still looking me in the eye with the kind of determination you only saw in horses. That was enough for me, at least for now. It had to be, or my whole fucking life was a waste of time.

Dealing with the vet put me in a bad mood. More than that. A fog I couldn't shift settled over me, and I retreated to Mani's stable to get a grip on myself. It worked until Toby came to find me.

"Shadow's got a splinter in his leg."

I pulled my face out of Mani's mane. "What?"

"Shadow," Toby repeated. "You asked me to check the fields when I got here, so I did, and I saw Shadow was lame. I hid in the bush when he was eating and had a look. There's a splinter in his left shin."

Great. The vet had already left, and even if he hadn't, I didn't have the money to pay him for stuff like that. If Shadow had a splinter, I'd have to try and get it out myself, which meant bringing him into the yard when he was used to having the field to himself all day.

I took a deep breath of Mani's soothing scent and gave Toby my full attention, though I couldn't actually remember him arriving for work this afternoon. Couldn't remember anything except the dire state of the mares in the foaling stable and the intoxicating weight of Harry's body pinning me to the couch. "Sorry, kiddo. Tell me again from the beginning? And what the fuck are you doing climbing trees?"

Toby shrugged. "Harry showed me. It's fun."

"Fair enough." I trailed Toby to the top field. Shadow was about as far from the gate as he could get, but even from a distance, I saw him limping.

I whistled to him and shook a bucket of oats, but it was ages before he looked my way, and by then, Toby had got bored and wandered off. Standard practice, where Shadow's games were concerned. I was the only idiot stubborn enough to wait him out, but I wasn't feeling particularly stubborn today. Just weary and desperate to do something to heal at least one of the horses that relied on me.

Sighing, I vaulted the gate and ventured into the field, approaching Shadow with the bucket held out and my head down. He ignored me at first but then started to circle me, trying to catch me staring at him so he could charge me.

But I knew better than to look at him. I kept my back to him, turning as he cantered around me. I was dizzy by the time his appetite for oats got the better of him.

He stuck his nose in the bucket and ate as I examined the wound on his shin. The splinter was big but not that deep. If I could get some reins on him and lead him down to the yard, I could have it out in a couple of minutes. Stupidly, though, I hadn't brought any reins with me.

I fished my phone from my pocket to text Toby to bring some down and hang them on the gate, but it rang in my hand before I could switch it to silent.

Startled, Shadow reared up and knocked the bucket to the ground. Cursing, I cancelled the call without looking to see who it was, but it was too late. Shadow whinnied and grunted, his hooves stamping as he tossed his head, searching for the noise that had frightened him.

His body was a blur as he moved. I bent to retrieve the bucket and my phone rang again. Shadow shrieked, and I looked up just in time for him to spin around and kick me in the guts.

CHAPTER TEN

HARRY

Car mechanics always had the knack of putting me in a shitty mood, and Newquay's finest was turning out to be epic at it.

"Bad news," he said. "The parts came in, but they're the wrong size. We ordered some more, but they won't be here till Monday."

"You couldn't have told me that on the voicemail you left this morning?"

"I did ask you to call me back," the mechanic retorted mildly.

And the fact that he had a point pissed me off even more. Monday. Brilliant. I didn't particularly need my car, but hiking to and from the garage was something I could've done without today, and the fact that I'd abandoned Joe on the couch *again* for absolutely nothing frustrated the hell out of me.

I trudged back to the farm, pointlessly hoping that Joe had got up in my absence, done everything he needed to do, and returned to the couch. Today was typically British and grey, like summer was something that happened somewhere else, and curling up on Joe's beat-up sofa, snatching a few hours' sleep in between keeping the promise I'd made him would be a dream come true.

Fantasising about just how I would keep that promise kept me company on the three-mile walk, even when it began to rain and the dirt tracks leading to the farm became instant rivers of mud. The call to be wherever Joe was seemed so strong, I half expected him to be waiting for me on the doorstep, but of course he wasn't. The house was empty, and a cursory glance around the yard found it deserted too.

Deflated and wishing like a bitch that I'd called the garage back before assuming their half-cocked mumbled message meant my car was ready, I drifted to the kitchen. Sal's absence at lunchtime was obvious by the pile of dirty dishes in the sink. Sighing, I turned the taps on and looked around for a sponge. In the yard, a horse called out. A shudder passed through me, like someone had walked over my grave. I glanced out of the kitchen window, but there was still no one about.

Idiot.

I needed a nap, but my bed was still stacked with tack, and kipping on Joe's sacred couch while he wasn't around seemed all kinds of weird. Yawning, I settled for finishing the washing up and boiling the kettle. Coffee was on the list of things I rarely allowed myself, but if I had any hope of getting through the rest of the day, I needed it.

It took me a while to remember how I drank coffee, and the farm had every type under the sun squirrelled away in the cupboards. In the end, I picked the cheap brand that reminded me of my father, because by then, the two hours' sleep I'd caught on the couch had become inadequate enough to turn me into a masochist.

I was on my way to look in on the sick ponies when Toby burst into the yard, covered in mud, his face twisted in panic.

"Harry!"

I grabbed his arm to stop him barrelling into the tack room door. "Whoa. Where's the fire?"

"It's Joe," Toby gasped out. "Shadow kicked him. He can't get up. I—"

"Where?"

"Top field."

I took off running with Toby a heartbeat behind me. Dread laced every step. I knew jack about horses, but danger had always lurked around Shadow, even when Joe rode him so beautifully. *This is bad.* My heart knew it even before the top field came into view.

We reached the gate. Shadow was standing on the crest of the hill, storm clouds gathering in the sky behind him. He stamped his hooves and tossed his head, blowing like an angry dragon. He bent his neck and nosed at the crumpled body on the ground beneath him.

But Joe didn't move.

I grabbed Toby and pushed him towards the other gate. "Quick. Do something to distract that horse. I need to get Joe out of there."

"You can't." Panic reared in Toby again. "Shadow's guarding him. He'll barge you."

"Just do it. Where did Joe get kicked? His neck? His chest? His spine?"

Toby shook his head. "I didn't see."

Fear clenched my heart. If the impact of Shadow's hooves had injured Joe's spine or neck, I wouldn't be able to move him. And what if he was bleeding? Or worse? *Fuck.* I needed to get to him, and fast.

I pushed Toby again. "*Go.*"

He ran off, sprinting to the other gate until he reached the trees and swung himself up like I'd taught him a week ago. He called Shadow's name and shook the branches. Fruit began to tumble to the ground. Shadow turned his head, casting his baleful glare in Toby's direction. For a long moment, he didn't move a sleek muscle, and horror spiked in my chest. If I couldn't get him away from Joe, a vet would have to come, and—

A lighter voice sounded in the field. Emma's call was like tinkling bells, and Shadow ambled away like a soft summer breeze.

I took my chance and hurdled the gate, skidding across the wet grass until I got to Joe. He was moving—*thank God*—and trying to get up, but his arms wouldn't hold him. "Easy." I caught him. "Where are you hurt?"

"Stomach," Joe gritted out, rigid with pain. "Motherfucker stamped on my guts."

"Can you walk? I need to get you out of this field."

"I—" Joe's eyes rolled back in his head.

"Joe . . . *Joe*. Come on, mate. Stay with me."

He didn't respond, and as I wiped the dirt from his face, the blue tinge to his lips scared the shit out of me. I wasn't a doctor, but I knew the human body like the back of my hand, and whatever was going on inside his body was sending him into shock.

I scooped him up and carried him to the gate. Toby was waiting, a phone clutched in his hand. He crouched beside me as I lay Joe on the path.

"Emma called an ambulance," he said. "Her and George are trying to get Shadow into his stable. Is Joe okay?"

No.

"I don't know, kiddo." I took Joe's pulse. It was strong, but his breathing was raspy, and as I pushed his T-shirt up, the hoof print on his abdomen was horrifying. "Get a blanket. We need to keep him warm."

Toby darted away and came back with a horse rug. I laid it over Joe and held him against me to keep him off the damp ground. "Where's the ambulance coming from?"

"There's an ambulance station in town," Toby said. "But

you won't hear them coming. They know since Josef died not to come up here with sirens."

Joe's grandfather had died three years ago. The likelihood of an ambulance crew remaining constant enough to recall instructions like that struck me impossible, but twelve minutes later, a fast-response car crept up the lane. No sirens.

By then, Joe was shivering, his skin grey, and fading in and out of consciousness. I called his name over and over, but he was too out of it to hold my gaze.

The paramedic took one look at him and called for backup. A second emergency vehicle arrived as silently as the first.

"Blunt force trauma," the lead paramedic said. "We need to get him to Treliske ASAP."

It took everything I had to let them lift Joe from my arms, even though I saw shades of my own brother in each of them. Joe's hand fell limply from mine and I scrambled out of the way, but his agonised groan when they rolled him onto his back cut me to the bone.

Toby trembled beside me. I put my arm around him, hoping my terror wouldn't seep into him and upset him more. I couldn't articulate what Joe meant to me—I'd yet to make sense of it—but he was Toby's hero, the farm's fearless leader, and Toby's tears said it all.

The lead paramedic stuck his head out of the ambulance. "We need to go. Who's coming with him?"

No one was stopping me getting in that ambulance. Later, I'd perhaps reason that Emma had been nowhere to be seen, Sal was away, and Toby too young, but right then—right now—none of that mattered. "Me. I'm coming with him."

I got in the ambulance and we sped away from the farm. Joe was sick before we hit the main road, and the drive to Truro was one I couldn't describe. Three times his blood pressure bottomed out, and when we reached the hospital, he'd deteriorated so badly that he was whisked away to Resus.

A nurse directed me to a waiting area. I prowled the plastic rows of seats like a caged animal. Was this how Shadow felt in his stable? I'd watched Joe wrestle him up to the top field more times than I cared to admit and always enjoyed the moment Shadow gained his freedom, galloping away up the hill, his dark mane flying behind him. But as my incarceration stretched on and on with no news, those moments seemed like another world.

Two hours in, I lost my shit. I flagged a nurse down and asked her about Joe. "He was kicked by a horse," I said when her face showed no recognition.

"Wait here," she said. "I'll get someone to talk to you."

Twenty-minutes later, a doctor who appeared barely out of his teens came to find me.

"Are you a relative?"

Nope. "Yes."

The doctor nodded, perhaps too busy to care at this point. I knew how hospitals worked. "We've done a scan of Joe's head, and there's no significant injury there—a mild concussion, perhaps, but we're more worried about his abdomen at this stage. We'll be taking him for an ultrasound shortly to check for any ruptures or tears."

"Internal bleeding?"

"Yes. It's a concern with any blunt-force injury."

"Is he conscious?"

"In and out, but that's to be expected. We've stabilised him with fluids and oxygen, and we're monitoring his BP. After the ultrasound, we'll know exactly what we're dealing with, but for now, it's a watch-and-wait situation."

I nodded, understanding more than I wanted to. "Can I sit with him?"

"Of course. Come with me." The doctor walked me to the alarmed doors at the end of the corridor. He buzzed us through. "Don't expect much sense from him. He's pretty groggy, and we've given him morphine and anti-emetics. Come and find me if you think he needs more."

"Why? Where are you going?"

But the doctor was already gone—reminding me that NHS hospitals were nothing like the fictional emergency departments on *Sky Atlantic*—and I was left to track down Joe by myself.

I found him on a bed in the RESUS department. A nurse was monitoring him and the bed next door. I caught her eye. "Am I in your way if I stand here?"

"Not at all," she said. "Let me know if he wakes up."

That didn't seem likely. Joe was on his back, his face deathly pale and lined with pain, but there was no sign of him being awake. Oxygen tubes snaked into his nose and his arm was hooked up to an IV. I read the label on the bag, but it didn't mean much to me. My medical knowledge was limited to rehabilitation, and I was so far out of my depth right now that I didn't know what to do with myself.

Joe's hand seemed a good place to start. I took it and turned it over, checking for injury beneath the dirt ground into his skin, before I twined my fingers with his and squeezed, hoping for a reaction. But there was none. I touched his cheek, gently brushing away some dried mud, and squeezed his hand a little harder. "All right, mate. I'm here. You're not on your own."

Whether he heard me or not, I had no idea.

They took him for an ultrasound a little while later. Waiting in an empty space freaked me out, so I stepped outside to respond to the increasingly panicked messages I was getting from the farm. I called Emma. She answered on the first ring, breathless, her voice tight.

"He's okay at the moment," I said quickly, even though it was far from true. "They weren't sure if he'd hit his head, so they did some tests, and he's fine in that respect."

"But?"

I tilted my face to the sky and gazed at the stars, tracking an airplane as it passed Orion's Belt. "He took a nasty kick to his abdomen. The doctors are worried that it's damaged him internally. They've taken him for an ultrasound to find out."

Emma sucked in a breath. "What does that even *mean?* I thought he might have broken his ribs again—internal damage . . . shit, Harry. How serious is that?"

"I don't know. I guess we'll find out after the ultrasound. Have you called your mum?"

"I've left her a message. She doesn't get a signal at her brother's house, and there was no one in when I called."

"Okay. What about Shadow? Did you get him calmed down?"

"I got him in his stable, but I might have to get the vet back out if he doesn't stop booting his door. And he's still got that huge splinter in his leg. I can't get near him to take it out."

The splinter was news to me, but the amped-up stress lacing Emma's every word was horribly familiar. "Is George still with you? And Toby? Who's watching the ponies?"

"George is. He's moved them to the tack room so they're closer to the house and put the donkey's in the foaling stable, but he was up all night in the paddock, so I'll have to send him home soon. And I can't let Toby stay. He's not old enough to work overnight."

As I processed the dizzying influx of information, I found it hard to believe that George or Toby would leave the farm—or Emma—in an hour of need. But the fact remained that Joe worked so much it would take three pairs of hands to replace him. "Is there anyone else you can call for help? Friends? Neighbours?"

Emma blew out a breath. "There's only one person I can call, but Joe will go ballistic. I'll just have to manage."

"I'll help you."

"You're not going to leave my brother, Harry. I don't know

what's going on between you, but I'm pretty sure I won't see you until we know he's okay."

She wasn't wrong. "I'm going to go back in. I'll call you if anything changes."

"Okay. Harry, I—"

"Don't. I wouldn't have it any other way. Just take care of the horses so he's got one less thing to worry about."

There wasn't much else to say. Even if I wasn't bound to Joe by the inexplicable cord between us, the farm couldn't manage without Emma right now. We said goodbye and I started to drift back inside, but my phone rang before I got to the doors. I expected to hear Emma's voice again and didn't even look at the screen. "What is it?"

"Nice to speak to you too," Rhys said dryly. "Didn't wake you up, did I? It's only eight o'clock."

"No—fuck. I can't talk right now."

"Why? What's wrong?"

"I'm at Trelisk hospital with the bloke I'm renting my room from. He got kicked by a horse."

"Shit. How bad?"

"I don't know. They took him for an ultrasound."

"An ultrasound of what?"

"His abdomen."

"Probably liver or spleen then."

He sounded so matter-of-fact that I wanted to reach through the phone and punch him. "How bad is that?"

"Trauma to any organ is serious, bro. Even if it's non-penetrative."

"Non-penetrative? You mean like bruising?"

"Yes. Bruising is still bleeding. It's worse for older people—"

"Joe's not old. He's twenty-eight."

"Then he's got a good chance of recovery if they can figure out what the injury is. They can do all sorts surgically these days.

I shuddered, unable to face the prospect of Joe going under the knife. "Hopefully it won't come to that."

Rhys hummed his agreement, and I was glad he couldn't see me. While we'd talked, I'd leaned on a damp wall, so my clothes were now as soaked as my shoes. My legs were splattered with mud, and I didn't want to contemplate what my face looked like. "Anyway," I said, "I'd better see if he's back from the ultrasound."

"Fair enough. Are *you* okay?"

"Why are you asking me that? I'm not the one who got booted by a horse."

"No, but you're my brother, and I can tell you're stressing the fuck out. You're a healer—you don't do blood and guts like me."

It was true. Rhys and I had both fallen into the world of caregiving by accident, but our fields were vastly different. He didn't have the patience for my work, and I didn't have the stomach for his. "I'm okay, I'm just . . . fuck, I'm just worried about Joe, man. We're—uh—friends."

"Friends with benefits?"

"Don't start that shit," I snapped. "I'm not you."

"Whoa." Rhys chuckled, though any humour he may have been trying for washed over me. "There goes my attempt to cheer you up. Go back in and get things squared away. I'm working tonight, so I'll be up. Call if you need me, yeah?"

I agreed and hung up, already feeling guilty for growling at him, and went back inside to find a flurry of activity at Joe's bedside. "You're moving him? Where to?"

"AAU," the young doctor said. "The scan didn't show any ruptures, but there's some significant bruising around the spleen that we'd like to keep an eye on."

Bruising is still bleeding. I nodded slowly. "How long do you need to monitor him?"

"Overnight on the AAU. They'll give him fluids and pain relief. Then he'll likely be admitted to a ward for a few days."

"What about recovery time?"

"Long-term?" The doctor shrugged. "If the bruising doesn't manifest as something more serious, we're probably looking at a month or so for a full recovery. They'll tell you more when he gets to a ward, but I'd imagine he'll be out of action for at least a couple of weeks."

My heart sank. The tentative prognosis was as positive as I could've hoped for, but how was the farm going to cope without Joe for the best part of a month? The stables were bursting at the seams and there was no denying that Joe was the muscle around the place—

Cold fingers closed around mine, cutting my brain off mid-flail. I looked down, and Joe was awake, his bloodshot eyes fixed on me. Panic forgotten, my world narrowed to him.

I rubbed his hand, trying to warm him up. "Hey, you. How you doing down there?"

Joe shook his head, and the doctor took over, asking Joe questions he couldn't seem to answer, and explaining what was about to happen. I held onto Joe's hand as long as I could, but eventually, a porter came to move his bed to the AAU department, and I was left behind to update Joe's personal information. I was halfway through the form when I realised that the only thing I knew about him was his name, address, and the faint map of freckles on the back of his neck.

It took a while to catch up with Joe in AAU, and by then, he was asleep again. I sat with him until the early hours of the morning, but around two, when nothing significant had changed, another friendly nurse kicked me out.

I took a cab back to the farm. Emma was waiting for me in the yard. "Oh god, Harry. I've been so worried. Is he okay?"

"As okay as he can be. He hasn't been awake much, but that's a good thing, apparently."

Emma shuddered. "He's been kicked before—we all have—but never like this. What the hell happened?"

"I honestly don't know. Toby didn't see it either, so I guess we'll have to wait for Joe to tell us."

"You didn't speak to him?"

"He's out of it at the moment. The drugs are doing their job." *Thank God.* The brief moments Joe had been awake had been agonising for him. The nurses said he was better off asleep, and I believed them. "Where's Shadow?"

"In his stable."

"Is he calm?"

Emma nodded, her gaze sliding guiltily from mine.

I caught her arm. "What is it? Is he hurt?"

"No . . . actually, he's doing much better."

I was missing something, and despite the hold Joe had on my heart, it was none of my business, but I tightened my grip on Emma all the same. "Just tell me. No point hiding bad news, mate."

"My dad's here."

"Oh." I glanced around automatically, searching for the familiar face of a man I'd never seen. "Is that a good thing? Joe hasn't told me—uh—much about him."

Emma sighed. "I can tell by your face that he's told you everything that matters, but I had no choice, Harry. I can't handle Shadow on my own at the best of times, and we've got all these sick ponies to take care of too—"

I held up my hand to slow the flood of words falling from Emma as her anxiety peaked. "You don't have to explain yourself to me."

"I need to explain it to someone. Mum can't get back until lunchtime tomorrow, and I know she'll go straight to the hospital. Perhaps Dad will be gone by then, but even if he is, I feel like I need to tell someone so it isn't a bad dream."

I tugged Emma into a loose embrace. "I get it. Sorry, I've got daddy issues of my own, so I'm a bit shit when people try to talk to me about theirs."

"You're not shit at anything, Harry. We'd be lost without you right now."

I had nothing. Just held Emma until the tack room door opened and an older version of Joe emerged into the yard. He stared at me for a moment and then Emma. And then he plucked a hip flask from his pocket and took a sip.

"Just a drop," he said. "Keep me going till morning."

I didn't know what to say as he sloped off to the feed shed. I'd gleaned enough from my short time on the farm to know that he'd brought trouble to the farm over and over again, but who was I to say that he shouldn't be here now? "What's his name again?"

"What?"

"Your dad. What's his name?"

"Jonah. I know, I know…Josef, Jonah, Joe. We're an original bunch."

I tried for a smile. Failed.

"Look," Emma said quietly, "I can't expect him not to drink at all, but he's promised he'll stay sensible till Joe gets back."

I shook my head. "Emma, Joe's not coming home for a few days, and even when he does, he won't be fit to work for at least a few weeks. If your dad can't keep it together for longer than one night, you're going to have to think of something else."

Easy for you to say. The accusation was clear in Emma's tired face, but she didn't say it. "Let's get through tonight," she said. "Dad won't come in the house, and George is sleeping at the bungalow to keep an eye on things and help me. If Toby pulls some extra hours, the girls too, maybe it will be enough."

I hoped so, for their sake, because Whisper Farm was the end of the road for most of the horses here. If Emma couldn't find a way to care for them while Joe recovered, some of them would have to be destroyed.

With a heavy heart, I made Emma promise that she'd go to bed when George got up and then retreated into the house to try and claim some sleep of my own. But Joe's couch felt like a bed of nails without him, and I managed nothing more than a fitful doze.

It was still dark when I got up and peeped out the window, smiling in spite of myself as Emma kept her promise and swapped places with George.

The smile faded when Jonah appeared in the yard a few minutes later, and I couldn't make sense of how the sight of him made me feel. He was clearly nothing like the only father I'd ever known, but he'd hurt his family multiple times just the same. Did that make him as bad as mine? Better? Worse?

I was still puzzling it over sometime later when the landline in the living room rang. My hand hovered over the receiver. What if it was a horse rescue? The farm had no capacity to take any more horses—and no Joe to coordinate a rescue—but was it my place to refuse?

It wasn't, but I picked up the phone anyway. Whoever it was deserved a straight answer. "Hello? Whisper Farm."

"Good morning. Could I speak with Harry, please?"

I frowned. The chipper female voice was familiar, but I couldn't place it. "Erm . . . this is Harry."

"Hello, Harry. Sorry to disturb you so early. I'm Dawn, one of the AAU nurses at Truro hospital. I've been looking after Joe this morning."

My hand gripped the phone hard enough for it to creak. "Is he okay?"

"He's a little agitated," the nurse said. "I think it might be helpful if someone could come to the hospital and sit with him. Are you able to do that?"

"Of course." I started for the door before I remembered that the landline phone was connected to the wall. "I'll be there in half an hour. Tell him I'm coming."

I dropped the phone and blurred around the room collecting the T-shirt, socks, and shoes that I'd discarded earlier in an effort to convince my brain that it was time for sleep. Outside in the yard, I got all the way to the gate before I remembered that my car was still in the garage.

Fuck! I dashed back to the house and searched the kitchen for the keys to Joe's van, the horsebox, even the battered motorbike that George tinkered with from time to time—anything with wheels. Anxiety gripped me so entirely that I didn't notice Jonah watching me until I barrelled right into him. "You're not supposed to be in the house."

It came out fiercer than I'd intended. Jonah stepped back, his gaze mild. "I ain't coming in. Just poked my head around the door to see what's got you all fired up. Something wrong?"

"I'm looking for the keys to Joe's van. The hospital called and asked me to go back."

Nothing changed in Jonah's expression—not even a flicker of concern as he inclined his head to the dresser by the door. I followed his direction to a bowl, with half a dozen sets of keys in, and recognised Joe's van keys immediately.

I grabbed them. "Thanks."

"No worries. You going to be okay driving on these wet roads?"

"I'll be fine. What are you going to do?"

"Get back to work, I suppose, lad."

Jonah took another step back, allowing me to barge around him and shut the front door behind me, locking it. I jogged across the yard, feeling Jonah's eyes tracking me. I was in the van, the keys jammed in the ignition, when he called out.

I wound the window down. "What?"

"Tell the boy the horse is fine."

"Which horse?"

But Jonah was already walking away.

CHAPTER ELEVEN

Joe

It was like I'd been hit by a bus, and then the bus kept coming, driving over my abdomen again and again, crushing my insides. Squeezing them. Twisting them. And then clobbering me around the head with a hammer for good measure.

I'd always been shit at staying put when I was hurt. The nurses kept telling me to lie down, to rest and wait for the doctor to come back and give me more tramadol—whatever the hell that was. But I couldn't stay still. It hurt too much. Besides, however badly Shadow had fucked me, I couldn't blame him. He was wild—always had been—and I had to get back to him before someone else did something stupid . . . like walk into his field with a phone in their pocket.

For the hundredth time, I curled my arms beneath me and tried to push myself up.

For the hundred-and-first time, the butcher in my belly kept me down.

Someone touched my shoulder—a nurse. "Come on now, sweetie. You need to lie down and rest. You're going to hurt yourself more if you don't keep still."

I shrugged her off. Her hands were light but felt like spikes against my heated skin. My head swam and I gasped for breath, despite the tubes blasting arctic air up my nose. The panic that had consumed me when I'd come round amped up a notch. I'd been kicked by horses before—even knocked out by them—but I'd never felt pain like this. I was dying, I was sure of it.

Dramatic? Possibly, but it hurt so fucking much.

I curled up on the bed again, cringing against waves of cramp-wreaked havoc in my gut that spread through my torso and shoulders. *Jesus-fucking-Christ.* The doctor had warned me that it would get worse before it got better, but that didn't make it any easier to take. I buried my head in my arms and longed for Harry. The time between Shadow kicking me and waking up in this damn, fucking bed was a blur, but Harry had been with me for a while, I was sure of it, and I craved his touch now more than I ever had. *Harry, I need you.*

Sometime later, gentle hands cupped my face, stroked my cheek, and rubbed the back of my neck. The sound that escaped me in response was piteous, but I didn't care. Harry was inexplicably perched on the edge of the bed from hell, and nothing else mattered. My battered body was instantly drawn to him, seeking out his warmth like it could soothe every ache and pain. I collided with his muscular thigh and fumbled for any part of him that I could reach. He smelled like the farm, of horses and hay. He smelled like home. "Harry?"

"It's me. Easy, mate. I'm here."

"Harry—I can't—it hurts so much."

"I know." Harry found my hand and squeezed, then he spoke over me to someone else. "Is he up to date with his pain relief?"

"Yes," the familiar nurse said. "He can't have any more until the consultant has seen him again."

"When will that be?"

"Within the hour."

Horror coursed through me. I couldn't handle another

fucking minute of this, let alone an hour. I started to squirm again, but Harry held me still, his grip on me absolute.

He forced me to look at him, distracting me with his liquid gaze as he drove his thumb into a tender spot on my wrist. "Can you feel that? It's a powerful acupressure point, and I'm going to press down hard into it, okay? It won't take the pain away, but if you can focus on it—on me—for a little while, it will help."

"Harry—"

"*Trust* me, Joe."

HARRY

Listen, focus, faith. It was a technique I'd often used on patients with severe nerve and muscle pain, and I repeated it over and over to Joe until some of the agony seizing his body finally eased.

By then he was curled around me, his head in my lap. I thought the doctor might've made him move when he stopped by to prescribe more drugs. But he said nothing. Merely signed the order and moved on to his next patient.

A nurse shot more pain relief into Joe's IV. Another notch of tension faded in him—like a slowly deflating balloon. I rubbed his neck to see if he was awake. He blinked up at me, and for the first time in however long it had been since I'd found him in the field, I recognised the man staring back.

I chanced a smile. "All right?"

He grimaced. "I'm so fucking mashed."

"Better than the alternative, eh?"

"Yeah."

I helped him unwrap himself from me, even though I mourned the loss of his head from my lap, and eased him onto his back. The bed had been flat when I'd arrived to find him in such a mess, but I raised it up now, hoping the relative change of scenery would pull him another step out of the vortex.

It seemed to work. He lay propped up and gazed around like he'd had no idea of his surroundings before. I touched his cheek, brushing away some of the dirt that was somehow still there. "Do you need anything? The nurse said you can drink water if you can keep it down?"

Joe blanched. "No, thanks. What time is it?"

"Eight o'clock."

"In the morning?"

"Yup. You've been here all night."

"Feels like a week." Joe licked his dry lips, his head lolled to one side, and it seemed like he might doze off, but then he jerked awake again. "Shit. I need to get out of here."

I steadied him. "Nah. You're gonna be in here a couple of days, mate."

"Fuck that." Joe pushed my hands off his shoulders. "Shadow—"

"Shadow's fine."

"No, he's not. He's got a splinter . . . that's why I went into his field."

"I know. But he's fine now. Last I heard he was chilling in his stable."

Joe's eyes gleamed briefly, like he knew there was a giant gap in my reassurance, but then he brought his hand to his face and rubbed his eyes. "Even if Emma somehow has Shadow under control, there's still so much to do. Those ponies need round-the-clock care."

"And they'll get it. Everyone's pitching in. George is sleeping on your mum's couch."

Again, it was half the truth, but it seemed all Joe could handle right now. He dropped his head again. "My stomach hurts."

"I know, mate. I know."

IT WAS lunchtime when Sal woke me up. At some point, I'd laid my head on Joe's bed and somehow fallen asleep.

"Rise and shine," Sal said softly. "They're moving him to a ward in a minute. Visiting hours don't start until two, but they said I can stay with him a little while longer."

I sat up, dazed and confused. "What?"

Sal smiled. "Bless you. I should've sent you home hours ago but didn't have it in me to prise you apart."

I had no idea what she meant until I looked down and saw my fingers wrapped tightly around Joe's. A flurry of conflicting emotions hit me, but I pushed them aside as my gaze darted automatically to Joe. Who cared if I was caught between mortification and wonder? As I studied Joe's face, I certainly didn't. He'd always been magnetic in a way that made no sense—when he was aloof or rude, or silent and still, like now. I stroked his face, paying Sal no heed, and wondered if his mind was finally quiet. "Have you been home? He's been worrying about the horses."

"No need," Sal said. "Emma's much better at holding the fort than she lets herself believe."

I could second that, but whether Sal knew about Jonah's overnight presence on the farm, I couldn't tell. "How's he been? He was really sick earlier."

Sal reached around me and rubbed Joe's arm. "The nurses said that too, but I haven't heard a peep out of either of you since I got here."

"What about the doctor? Has he been round?"

"An hour ago," Sal said. "He's happy that the bruising isn't hiding anything worse, so Joe can go to the ward."

Relief flooded me. I had no idea how long I'd been asleep, but the hours I'd spent at Joe's bedside, trying desperately to keep him calm, to soothe his pain, would stay with me forever.

A porter arrived. I peeled myself out of my hard plastic chair and moved out of the way. Sal caught my arm as I passed her and tugged me into the corridor.

"Go home," she said firmly. "He's on the mend. There's nothing more you can do, and he'll be cross if he sees you in this state."

I scrubbed my face. "I'm fine."

"Aye. You'll be better after a week of sleep, though. Go *home*, luv. I'm his mum . . . I'm not going to let anything happen to him."

I'd have taken a lot more persuading if the sight of Joe's bed disappearing into a lift hadn't reminded me that I couldn't follow him up to the ward. I rummaged through my tired mind for what he'd ask of me if he was able and turned back to Sal. "Do you need anything? Have you got money? Charge on your phone? What about food?"

"Dear God." Sal shook her head. "You're just like him in your own way, aren't you? Stop worrying about everyone else, Harry. I'm fine. And if I'm not, I'll call, okay?"

It was all I could ask. I made sure she really did have money and tapped my number into her phone, and then I left. Walking away from Joe was *hard*, but when I got outside, perspective returned to me. If Joe needed anyone, it was his mum—his family. Who was I?

The dickhead who'd parked Joe's van in a loading bay, apparently.

I peeled the parking ticket from the windscreen and climbed behind the wheel. My sense of direction let me down, and the half hour drive to Newquay took nearly an hour. By the time I reached the farm, I was ready to drop. A compulsion to check around the farm warred with a desperate need to get my head down.

The what-would-Joe-do instinct won out, and I went straight to the top field. Shadow was in the far corner, stripping the bark from a young tree. He looked the same as he always did —feral and untamed—and didn't seem to notice me as my gaze was drawn to the patch of mud where I'd found Joe. I breathed deeply, trying to push images of him so badly injured from my mind, to draw on Sal's parting words instead: *"He's on the mend . . ."* But with the same mud still splattered up my legs, it was tougher than I could bear.

I turned away and left Shadow to his botanical afternoon snack. The rest of the farm seemed business as usual—aside from Joe's absence—and I was on my way to find somewhere to sleep when I stumbled into Jonah.

He smiled, apparently far more with it than I was. "You're back then."

"Yup."

"The boy okay?"

"Getting there. Sal's with him."

Jonah nodded. "Good lad. He coming home soon?"

"I don't know."

"Aye, well . . . you let me know. Can't imagine he'd be too pleased to find me kipping on the doorstep."

"So why did you come?"

The question fell out with little consideration for why I thought it was my business. But Jonah merely gifted me another watery smile. "There isn't much use left in me, but what I've got belongs to this farm."

A profound sadness washed over me as I stared at Jonah. From what little I knew of him, his fuck-ups were epic, but his love and loyalty, however faded by the burden he'd become, was clear to see.

The contrast with my own father almost broke me. I pushed past Jonah and went into the house. My body was reacting to the clusterfuck of emotions coursing through me like it always did—with adrenaline . . . a misplaced energy that had, in the past, led me to pounding the gym until I blacked out. But I was over that now, right? Besides, even the disquiet having a party in my empty stomach couldn't overcome the bone-deep fatigue from three days without real sleep.

I took a much-needed shower, and then admitted defeat, and passed out on Joe's couch.

I slept for hours and hours until George woke me sometime later.

"Dinner's up," he said.

"Huh? I sat up, rubbing my face, but George was already gone.

I found a sweatshirt and trailed him to the kitchen, expecting to find the usual suspects crowded around the table, waiting on Sal to dish up. But George kept going, and when I followed him out into the yard, I saw why.

Someone had lit a BBQ in a metal pit. A huge pot was above the glowing embers, and Jonah was stirring the contents. He caught my eye but said nothing.

Lacey grabbed my arm. "Sit with us, Harry. We haven't seen you for ages. Have you been with Joe?"

"Um, for a little while till Sal got back."

Lacey nodded, her eyes bright with the kind of excitement that came from dinner in the dark when you were that young, and her innocence soothed me. Her and Jemima hadn't been on the farm when Joe had been hurt, and I was glad of it. They idolised Joe as much as Toby did, and his tears had been enough.

George dropped down on the other side of me. His gaze was trained on Jonah, and I observed the both of them for a while in an effort to distract myself from wondering where Sal was. Hospital visiting hours usually finished around eight o'clock and it was way past that now. Was something wrong? Had Joe deteriorated?

My fretting was eased somewhat when Emma joined the circle around the fire. Joe's friend Dex was with her. He met my gaze impassively, and I tried not to stare back, remembering what Joe had said about him not liking men he didn't know. Dex seemed at ease with the Whisper Farm gang, but his presence reminded me that I was still an outsider, and considering that I only had five weeks left on the farm, would probably remain so.

The thought didn't sit well. I'd woken feeling refreshed, though worry for Joe still gnawed at my insides, but as the chatter around the fire continued without me, I felt like I was crawling out of my skin until Sal turned up, apparently from the bungalow, clutching a loaf of her homemade bread.

She passed it to Jonah without looking at him and came straight to me, nudging Lacey aside. "You're awake," she said. "You were dead to the world when I got back."

"Sorry. It's been a long few days."

"I'll say. Joe was worried when I told him how long you'd been up."

Joe worrying about me sent another rush of conflicting emotions sluicing through me. That he cared warmed my bones, but I wanted him, for once, to screw everyone else and focus on himself. "How is he? Did you stay with him all day?"

"Until he was awake enough to answer me back," Sal said with a smile. "The boy doesn't like hospital food, so I'd imagine we'll be feeding him until they let him go."

"Do you know when that will be?"

"A few days. He's still quite poorly, and I don't think I've ever seen him so tired."

The ache in my heart came back. Sal rubbed my arm. "Visiting is at ten tomorrow. I've got some shopping to do, and Emma won't drive to Truro, so I was wondering if you'd sit with him for a bit? I think he prefers your company to mine."

How she could be so sure of that, I had no idea. After the last few days, snogging Joe on the couch seemed a distant memory, and before that, our interactions had been limited to meal times and awkward encounters in the yard.

It was more than that. But I was distracted from arguing with myself by a steaming plate of the same spicy sausage stew Joe had cooked a few weeks ago. Jonah's interpretation had more beans and less meat, and as it occurred to me that I hadn't eaten a proper meal in days, it was the most delicious thing I'd ever seen.

The low murmur of voices in the yard faded away as I cleared my plate. The hot food hitting my stomach was like magic, and the jittery anxiety that had plagued me over the last few days began to ease. *Idiot. How many times have you lectured Emma on the effect of blood sugar levels on anxiety?* Too many, but with a full belly and Sal's presence beside me reminding me that I hadn't answered her question, my mind was too full of Joe to berate myself.

Jonah came round with the pot, doling out seconds with hunks of Sal's bread. I filled my plate again without much conscious thought and nudged her gently. "Of course I'll sit with Joe tomorrow. Does he need me to bring anything?"

Again with Sal's slow smile. "Just yourself, I'd imagine, luv. But I'll leave some breakfast in the fridge for him."

I rolled my eyes and kept eating.

CHAPTER TWELVE

Joe

I kept missing him. It was like my body knew exactly when he was coming and sent me to sleep on purpose. Two days in a row, I woke up to food parcels and a note on my pillow, and by the third day, I was feeling human enough to be pissed off about it.

A doctor came to see me as I was studying the latest Post-it I'd found stuck to a tub of something that looked suspiciously like lentils. I reluctantly set it aside and let myself be prodded and pressed, glad that I could now get through it without chundering.

"Your latest scans are encouraging," the doctor said. "How's your pain?"

"Better." Understatement. I hadn't realised how much moving around depended on an abdomen that wasn't trying to kill you. "Can I go home?"

The doctor smiled, and I wondered if I'd asked him already that day. Tramadol had left big gaps in my head. The only thing I could recall from the last few days with any clarity was gut-twisting pain and the fact that I was pretty sure my mother was hiding something from me.

"You can go home this afternoon," the doctor said, "*if* I'm happy with your bloods from this morning and you commit to an aftercare plan."

I squinted at him. "What kind of aftercare? I don't have to take my own blood, do I?"

"No, but you will have to rest for a considerable amount of time. Your mum was telling me that you work on a farm?"

"I *live* on a farm. It's not my job, it's my life."

"Well, it can't be for the next month. I want you in bed for a week, and then only light exercise for a few weeks after. No horse-riding or heavy lifting. No stress if you can avoid it."

I want you in bed for a week. I let my eyes fall closed and imagined it was Harry saying those words to me. Heat pooled in my groin—thank God. I'd worried that my dick was broken. "I can rest—probably—but I don't actually have a bed."

"Find one," the doctor said. "Or I'll have to keep you here until you do."

He was joking, I was sure of it, so I didn't bother relaying the message when I texted Sal to tell her I was being discharged. And it didn't occur to me that anyone other than Harry would drive to set me free either, so I struggled to contain my disappointment when Emma rocked up later that afternoon.

She met my scowl with one of her own and then rushed to me for a hug. I evaded, knowing that even her slender frame was still too much for me, and settled for slipping an arm around her shoulders. "What are you doing here?"

"Idiot. I've come to drive you home."

"Seriously? On your own."

"Yep." Emma hid her face in my T-shirt. "Harry's been helping me loads this week. And I'm smashing it, Joe. I even went to the gym in town with him."

"The what?"

"The gym. There's a yoga group there I want to join. He

came with me for my first session. He's *so* flexible. You wouldn't think it for someone that muscly—"

I silenced her nervous chatter with my hand over her mouth. Thinking about how flexible Harry might be was bad for my blood pressure—even if it had been dragging on the floor for the best part of a week. "I'm glad you're here."

Emma ducked away from me. "Liar. You probably wanted Mum to take you to KFC on the way home, and I'm not doing that, no matter how brave I'm feeling."

If that was what she honestly thought, I let her have it. Sal seemed to know that something was cooking between Harry and me, but she was my mum—not much got by her. "Can we go now? I need to get home."

"What for? We've managed just fine without you."

"Yeah?"

Emma held my gaze fiercely for a few seconds, then caved and shook her head. "Harry's been amazing, Dex too, but no one knows the farm like you do. We've missed you so much."

It was nice to hear. Sometimes it seemed like the years rolled by and no one noticed that I was still drowning. That we all were.

I started to get down from the bed. Emma giggled. I glared at her. "What?"

"You've got no shoes. The paramedics lost your boots."

"So?"

"Oh right . . . you're going to walk to the van in the rain in your socks, are you?"

The thought of walking anywhere was almost enough to make me faint, but I didn't care if I crawled home on my knees, I was getting out of this shithole.

Thankfully, Emma had thought of everything. She retrieved a pair of gym bunny trainers from her bag and slipped them onto my feet. "They're Harry's," she supplied like I didn't already know. "You're the same size. He left you some joggers and stuff on the bed too."

"The bed?"

"Yes. He's going to take the couch while you recover."

"Em, we can't let him do that. He's paid for that room." I didn't add that there was no way on earth I was sleeping in Grandpa's bed, because I didn't have to . . . right?

Wrong. Emma shook her head and took my weight as I eased myself onto my feet. "It was Harry's idea. We went shopping and got new sheets and stuff, and he got cross when me and Mum offered him our beds."

"You didn't think of getting cross right back and telling him no?"

"Of course I did, but it wouldn't have worked. Joe, he wants to be in the house with you, and it's probably for the best. Do you really want Mum helping you up and down the stairs."

I growled under my breath. Being the weak link wasn't my style, and she knew it.

We said goodbye to the nurses, picked up a giant bag of medication, and made a shuffling getaway. I felt like shit, but the wind and rain in my face when we got outside was magic.

"Wait here," Emma said. "I'll bring the van around."

I propped myself against a wet wall and waited. A thought occurred to me while she was gone, and I put it to her when she got back to distract myself from how difficult it was to climb into the van. "If I'm in the bedroom, and Harry's in the living room, where the fuck did you put all the tack?"

"In the trailer."

"What?"

"The trailer," Emma repeated like I was a moron. "It's been cleaned out and secured."

"By who?"

Emma pulled out of the hospital grounds, paying more attention to the road than strictly necessary.

"Please tell me you didn't let Harry do it?"

"Not exactly."

"Then who? Most of that old junk is too heavy for Toby and George, and you're scared of spiders."

"I'm scared of everything. Doesn't stop me pulling my weight on the farm."

"Never said it did. I—" I caught myself before the conversation descended into the type of sibling bickering that went round in circles. "Who did it?"

Emma shot me a worried glance. "You're not allowed to get cross."

"I won't."

"I mean it, Joe. Mum had a long conversation with that doctor this morning and he said you're not allowed any stress."

"Then stop pissing me about and answer the question."

Emma eased the van onto the main road, taking care to avoid the bumps and holes, which I appreciated. "Dad's been helping on the farm."

"He's been what?"

"Helping, Joe. Fuck's sake. Don't make me say everything twice. You didn't bang your head that hard."

The bang to my head had been the least of my worries. Concussion was a breeze compared to the disaster in my stomach. I took a deep breath and forced myself to at least try and sound reasonable. "What's Jonah been doing on the farm? He can't stay there."

"I *know*," Emma said. "The night you got hurt, Shadow was too much for us, so I called the Legion looking for him, and he was sober enough to come and help. He's stuck around since then, helping George nurse those ponies and working with Shadow. He cleaned the trailer out too, but he's gone now, I swear. He knew you wouldn't want him around."

I absorbed it all and sat back in my seat, closing my eyes as my overloaded brain processed it. Weird emotions ran through me, but confusion was loudest. I'd been angry at my father for most of my life, but I could deal with him. Emma was the one who'd ignored him all these years, seemingly content to pretend that he was pretty much dead. How could she call on him for help and then explain it to me like it was fucking *normal*?

It was a while before I felt steady enough to continue the conversation, and by then I was too tired to be pissed off. "You do realise that we told Dicky that Jonah was never on the farm? If he finds out he has been, he might come back and have another go at Mum."

Emma snorted. "I doubt it. George was in the Legion last week, and apparently Harry scared the shit out of Dicky. He hasn't been around for ages."

Nothing was ever that simple, and Dicky McGee wasn't the kind of man to leave his pride in the mud of my yard. I started to argue with Emma but ran out of steam before I'd managed a coherent sentence.

She frowned at me.

I shook my head. "I'm tired."

"I know, big brother. We're almost home."

I couldn't wait.

At least, I thought I couldn't until the bumpy lane to the farm almost killed me.

"Sorry." Emma winced on my behalf. "Perhaps I should've let Harry fetch you in the car after all."

"It's fine," I said through gritted teeth. "Thank you for coming to get me. I know how shitty it must've been for you."

"Actually, I enjoyed it."

"Which part? The driving or seeing me lose my shit over a pothole?"

Emma grinned. "Both. Now stop your whining. We're home."

And we were. Emma edged the van as close to the house as possible and turned the engine off. She gave me a look, which I ignored, and then poked me in the side just hard enough to make my eyes water. "Mum's mucking out the donkeys, but she said you're to go straight upstairs and stay there. No funny business."

"Funny business?"

"Don't be a dick, basically. I know it's hard, but try, eh? For her sake, if not your own. She's been so worried about you. It's only fussing over Harry that's kept her sane."

I couldn't help a smile. If there was one fella who appreciated my mum almost as much as me, it was Harry, even if he didn't roll over for her pie and mash. "I'll try, Em. I swear."

Emma snorted and got out of the van. She opened my door and jumped up to ruffle my hair. "Whatever. Are you going to be okay getting in? I was sweating all the way to Truro so I need a shower."

"Thought your boiler was on the blink?"

"It was. Harry got a new thermocouple when we were in town and fixed it. Got all the hot water we need now. Shame we can't afford to use it."

Guilt squeezed my heart. In the rare moments I'd been with it enough to let my mind wander, I'd pictured Emma and Mum traipsing across the yard with wet hair and wellies, and it had driven me half mad. Add-in the sick ponies I was damn-well checking on before I went inside, and I'd been pretty much beside myself.

Emma pinched my cheek and disappeared, apparently deciding that if I needed her help, I'd have said so. But as I shifted in my seat and stared at the ground, the prospect of getting out of the van was overwhelming. I wrapped an arm around my battered torso and willed my legs to hold me up. White spots danced in front of my eyes, and the energy that had propelled me from my hospital bed ran out.

Strong hands gripped my shoulders. "Don't go falling over on me. I've been looking forward to seeing you awake all day."

Harry. A switch flipped inside me. I raised my head and met his gaze, and it seemed like the world had changed since I'd last seen him. Maybe it had. "Define awake."

"Anything more conscious than I've seen you the last four days."

Four days? Shit. Somewhere along the line, I'd lost twenty-four hours. "Thank you."

"What for?"

I shrugged. "Everything? I'm too tired to list it all."

Harry smiled. "No need—for the thanks or the list. Let's get you inside."

"I can manage," I lied.

"I know," Harry lied right back. "Let me help you anyway. It's good for my soul."

He didn't need any help with his soul as far as I could see, but I let him slip an arm under my shoulders anyway and support me as I shuffled inside.

At the stairs, he followed behind me, his hand on my back, and seemed to sense when the sight of Grandpa's bed made me pause. "New sheets," he said. "The others were covered in dust."

"They were new a week before you got here," I said absently, because it wasn't the sheets that got under my skin—it was everything else. The curtains, the window, the pictures on the walls. Perhaps I should've stripped it all when we'd cleared it out for Harry, but would that erase the memories? The good and the bad?

Probably not.

Harry nudged me towards the bed. "Sit down, mate. Sooner you rest, the sooner you can stop."

"Right." I loved that he knew how much I hated this. That I didn't have to explain myself. Somehow I knew that it wasn't because he didn't care.

I followed Harry's direction and sat gingerly on the edge of the bed. He handed me the stack of clothes Emma had promised. "Why are you giving me a pile of sweatpants?"

"To rest in," he said. "I've only ever seen you wearing jeans, and you seem to sleep in your clothes."

He had me there. What was the point in pyjamas when I didn't have a bedroom? And even in the summer, the draughty old house was too cold most nights for sleeping in my birthday suit. Besides, I'd take softly worn joggers that smelled of Harry over a hospital gown any day of the week.

"Anyway." Harry had drifted to the door while I'd stared at his clean laundry. "I'll leave you to it. Your mum's around, but drop me a text if you need anything."

"I don't have my phone."

Harry jerked his chin at the bedside table. "It's over there. My number is on the pad."

"Did I need to get kicked by a horse to get your number?" I said it to myself as much as him, but the flush that coloured Harry's cheeks did something to me. The way he held my gaze —silent, but so intense I wanted to throw myself at him. Would've thrown myself at him, if I hadn't been sinking into the bed like a sloth in quicksand.

Harry took pity on me and came back to the bed. He crouched in front of me, his hands on my knees. "You didn't need to get kicked by a horse. But you do need to rest. I know things got a bit heavy between us before you got hurt, but don't worry about that right now. Just get better, okay? Everything else can wait."

I didn't want to wait. I wanted to pull him down for a kiss and then tumble him onto the bed so I could feel his skin beneath my palms again. When I finally let him up, we'd wander around the farm together, checking in on horses that hadn't been to hell and back before they'd wound up on my shit-hole farm, and plan a future that didn't involve red-topped bills and pisshead relatives.

But reality kicked in with a flash of cramp in my healing gut. The pain had lessened with each passing day, but it still hurt like a bitch when I least expected it. I inhaled sharply and Harry took my hands. His thumb dug into my wrist. I gasped again, but not because of the pain. He'd done that before—I was sure of it.

Harry smiled wryly, like he heard my thoughts. "You remember?"

"Remember what?"

"How to focus beyond what's going on in your body."

"Um . . . sure?"

Harry chuckled. "You do remember, on some level, at least. We absorb much more than we consciously hear."

I leaned forward, intending to kick Harry's trainers off my feet, but somehow ended up with my head on his shoulder. It wasn't a bad place to be, so I stayed there. He pressed harder with his magic thumb and rubbed my back, and the corkscrew in my belly faded a bit.

The fatigue remained, though. And when Harry disentangled himself from me a little while later, I could tell he meant business this time. "You need to rest," he said. "Get your head down for a bit."

I couldn't deny that taking a nap sounded like heaven, even if it did mean the loss of Harry's arms around me. "What are you going to do?"

"Work," he said. "Or try to. I've been a bit shit the last few days. My laptop is in the kitchen, but I haven't touched it."

"Why not?"

He shrugged. "Wasn't feeling it."

There was more to it, I could tell, but nothing that he seemed to want to share, so I let it go. He gifted me one more smile and then shut the door behind him, leaving me alone in the room I'd done my best to avoid since I'd found Grandpa dead in his bed three years ago. Cleaning it out had been easier than I'd expected—with Sal's nagging and Emma's heckling, I'd been too irritated to feel much else—but it was different now. I changed into Harry's sweatpants and lay down on the bed. The afternoon sun streamed through the window and hit my bare chest, reminding me of how I'd snuck up here as a little boy and sunbathed until Sal called me down for tea.

The sun wasn't as soothing as I remembered, but it put me to sleep all the same. And it kept me there long after dark until I woke with a jump, anxiety squeezing my chest. The horses. I hadn't checked on any of them.

Bracing myself, I swung my legs off the bed. My feet hit the hardwood floor, and for the first time in days, I felt no pain. I was halfway down the stairs before the spleen god kicked me in the balls, but I pushed it away. I'd been on my arse long enough —I needed to see my horses with my own eyes.

I made it to the hallway by kitchen before Harry's low chuckle stopped me in my tracks. He was behind me at the table, his work spread out in front of him, the only light in the room coming from his flashy MacBook. "Don't start," I said.

"Moi?" He spread his hands innocently. "I'm not your mother."

"Where is my mother?"

"Asleep, I'd imagine. It's two o'clock in the morning."

"What?"

Harry eyed me. "Joe, it's the middle of the night."

Damn. Despite my absolute certainty that I wouldn't sleep a wink upstairs, I'd lost ten hours. I turned away from Harry and continued to the back door. Somehow, he got there before me.

"I know I just said I'm not your mother, but do you think you should maybe put some shoes on?"

Fucking shoes. It was in me to argue, to stomp outside barefoot and to hell with the damp ground, but the doctor had warned me that my immune system would be weaker while my spleen was healing, and I didn't fancy a brush with pneumonia.

I found a random pair of boots by the door and stamped into them. "Happy?"

"Nearly." Harry unzipped his hoodie and passed it to me. "Put this on and you'll do."

The hoodie was warm and smelled even more of him than the sweatpants I was already wearing. It was too big as well, obviously, but I wrapped it around myself anyway and put my hand on the door handle.

Harry's was already there. I closed my fingers around his before I truly knew what I was doing, but it felt like something I'd done a thousand times over. Like the spark from the contact shooting through my arm would one day be ordinary. "I need to check the horses."

"I know."

But Harry didn't move, and neither did I. The hallway was so dark I could hardly see his face, but his eyes seemed to gleam in the dim light, and for the millionth time, I tried to recall what my life had been like before him. How my chest had felt without the flutter that seemed to keep my heart beating.

Pulse skipping, I licked my lips. He was going to kiss me like he had before—kiss me, and leave me, and nothing would change. I wanted more than a kiss, more than his hands on my face, on my hips, holding me upright.

I wanted him to kiss me and mean it.

So I kissed him first.

CHAPTER THIRTEEN

HARRY

For the longest time, I'd fought to control how other people made me feel, but I stood no chance with Joe. He stormed through my hard-won defences and stole my breath away, kissing me like he didn't have the remnants of the worst bruise I'd ever seen staining his torso.

I gasped in a breath, letting him briefly dominate me before instinct took over and I lifted him clean off his feet, pressing him carefully against the wall behind him. He'd lost weight in recent days, but the lean, coiled planes of his body were still intoxicating as the kiss went on and on until he shuddered in my arms.

Reluctantly, I eased him down and broke away with a nervous laugh. "How did that happen?"

Joe shrugged, his expression guarded. "I'm not complaining."

Neither was I. But getting physical with him hadn't been my intention when I'd come to the door. The heat between us could wait. Joe's beloved horses couldn't. "Let's go for a walk," I whispered. "I heard Mani call out a while ago. I think he's waiting for you."

Joe's eyes stopped flashing. He let go of my hand and opened the door. It crossed my mind to let him go alone, but the thought of not being nearby if he needed help made me nauseous.

We stepped out into the night. Joe walked slowly and I matched his pace, my hands itching to steady him. But I kept them to myself as we reached the tack room to check on the abandoned ponies. With the horses on his mind, Joe didn't need my help.

He opened the half-door and peered inside. A soft light was on in the corner, George's radio playing Fleetwood Mac beside it. The man himself was asleep in the hay, and so was one of the ponies. The other staggered to its feet and came to the door, ignoring Joe and butting my arm with her wispy nose.

I stroked her gently and fed her the softened ginger nuts I'd somehow begun carrying in my pockets. The mare and I had an understanding: I'd feed her all the biscuits she liked if she didn't show me her teeth. It was working out well, so far.

"She likes you," Joe said.

"I don't know about that. I'm just glad to see her up. Your—uh—George thought she'd die."

The mare wandered off. Joe waited for her to lie down close to her stablemate and then shut the door on the cosy scene. "Who needs me, eh?"

"Just about everyone, I reckon. It's taken three people to keep up with your usual workload."

"Uh-huh." Joe shot me a sideways glance. "I know Jonah was here, so there's no need to cover for him."

"I wasn't going to keep it from you."

"Didn't tell me, though, did ya?" Joe started for the main stable block.

I trailed him. "When should I have told you?"

"Dunno. Just now? When you put me to bed? I—fuck. I don't know. I'm just—" Joe stopped at the first stall and flicked some low lights on. "It feels weird knowing he's been here. I've spent so long trying to pretend he never was."

"He didn't come in the house, if that's what you're worried about. He used the hose to wash, ate outside, and slept in the tack room."

"That sounds like him even when he lived here."

"How long ago was that?"

"A fucking long time." Joe studied Tauna and Carric before moving onto the next stall, and then the next. Shadow was in the sixth one along, which seemed to take him by surprise. "This is Mani's stall."

"He's on the end," I said.

"Why?"

"I don't know. Sorry."

Joe frowned and turned back to Shadow, who was observing us from the back of his stall. I wondered if I should leave them to it—if there was a private moment that passed between a horse and man when one of them had hurt the other so grievously. But Shadow merely grunted and then shifted so his shoulders blocked the view of his face, and Joe moved on.

The private moment came at Mani's stable. He heard Joe coming and got to his feet, calling out with the rickety cry that even I recognised as his. He bumped his nose against the door until it opened and then snorted softly in delight as he finally laid eyes on Joe.

I stepped away as the old horse embraced his master. Joe hid his face in Mani's mane, his shoulders shaking, and I took my cue to go back inside. My knowledge of horses was still limited, but I knew when a man needed a moment alone with his best friend.

Back in the kitchen, I forced myself not to pace the stone floor or peep through the window, and brewed a pot of tea for when Joe came in. Then I sat at the table and stared at my work. It had been a few days since I'd even glanced at the book, and it felt like a year. With Joe in hospital, I'd found myself unable to sit still, and helping out on the farm had given me a healthier outlet for that than running loops of Newquay.

As a result, I'd spent some time with Joe's father. And fuck, if that hadn't confused the hell out of me. I wanted to hate him . . . but I didn't. And I'd yet to figure out why it mattered so much. Could Joe shed any light on that? I'd gone to the hospital every day to find out, but he'd been asleep each time. A sign for me to mind my own business?

Maybe.

Joe came back a little while later and leaned in the kitchen doorway, his eyes hooded and shot through with red. "Everything's different."

"Like what?"

He shrugged. "The stables, the feed shed . . . you."

"Me?" I made an executive decision not to angst over what he'd been doing in the feed shed. "How am I different?"

"I don't know. But you are."

"Maybe it's the fresh air I've been getting. I wasn't taking the piss when I said I hadn't done much work this week."

"Emma reckoned you've done plenty. Cleaned out the trailer, by all accounts. Wheeled it down to the paddocks."

"I didn't do it on my own," I said carefully.

"I know."

"Your dad," I started and then stopped. What was I going to say? That I knew his father had let him down in so many ways, but I kind of liked him anyway? "Your dad helped me."

"I know that too."

I searched for something to say that would ease the conflict in his eyes—a turmoil that seemed to make sense, even if I didn't quite understand it. "I've been thinking about that space around the old stud farm."

"Why?"

"Because your dad has been on my mind when I haven't

been thinking about you, and that led me to the empty field. You're at capacity, right? You can't take any more horses?"

Joe leaned heavily on the doorframe. "We don't have the space, manpower, or equipment, and we can't afford the horses we already have."

"So you need another income stream?"

"Is that a trick question?"

Everything about Joe seemed brand new—the way he glowered at me, said my name, and made me feel—but I could handle the sullen cynicism he was throwing my way now. Had expected it. "Have you thought about running a campsite on that field? Just tents to start with, maybe some trailers if you could get hold of any more. You could even convert the stud farm into a shower block."

"How? Build it with my bare hands and magic beans to pay for the materials?"

"You could get a business loan if you had a viable plan."

Joe snorted. "We're up to our eyeballs in loans already, and there's nothing viable about the way we do business here. That's why *you're* here—because we needed your money."

Inexplicably, the admission stung. Like my subconscious believed that it had been some romantic twist of fate that had brought me into Joe's life. "Fair enough. I didn't really think it through. It's just you've got that spare land and it doesn't make sense not to use it."

"Nothing around here makes sense, Harry. If it did, we'd have gone down the swanny years ago."

His pessimism was suffocating. And unfair. The farm survived because he, and his grandfather before him, had given their lives to make it so. Hard work, sacrifice, and dogged determination. They hadn't folded because they refused to. "What about a riding school?"

"Nah." Joe shook his head. "We had one for a while, but the insurance was a nightmare—all those kids coming and going.

Besides, someone's got to teach the little fuckers, and if Emma ain't in the mood, I haven't got time for that shit."

I'd heard fragments of that explanation before and mulled the new additions over in my mind before I realised that Joe had pretty much become one with the doorframe and my pondering was keeping him there.

I got up and went to him, easing him upright and taking his weight. "You ready for bed?"

"What kind of question is that?"

"A serious one. Total inactivity can be as bad for the body as doing too much, but you still need to rest."

Joe stared at me. For a moment he looked like he wanted to punch me, kiss me, or both, but he did neither. Just sighed and pulled away. "Don't come upstairs with me."

I stepped back, folding my arms across my chest to stop myself from instinctively steadying him. I hadn't consciously thought about following him upstairs, but now he'd asked me not to, it took everything I had to stay still.

Joe set one foot on the bottom step. I figured he was bracing himself, but then he turned back to me, his gaze fierce. "It's not because I don't want you to."

"Want me to what?"

"Don't do that!"

I flinched. Couldn't help it.

Joe squeezed his eyes shut and slammed his hand on the wall. "Don't *do* that, Harry. You know what I'm talking about."

I really didn't, but seeing Joe distressed hurt more than I could say. I caught his hand before he could strike the wall again, covering his knuckles with my palm. "If you want to fight something, I've got a punchbag in the boot of my car. Give it a couple of weeks and it's all yours."

"I don't want the fucking punchbag."

"Okay."

"Is it?" The fire in Joe's eyes faded. "I want you to come

upstairs with me, lie down with me, and kiss the shit out of me until I pass out on you, but I can't let it happen because I know you're going to play along and then leave me. How is that fucking fair, Harry?"

I opened my mouth. Shut it again.

Joe snorted in disgust and turned away, and the bedroom door upstairs banged a long time before I'd found my tongue again.

". . . PLAY ALONG AND THEN LEAVE ME." Was that what he honestly thought? The idea was horrifying as I paced the kitchen. Joe had left me at the foot of the stairs more than an hour ago, but I still couldn't make sense of his fury. Patient testimonials said my empathy made me a decent therapist, but I'd always been dense when it came to real life. To *my* life.

Dense. Oblivious. Incompetent. They all fit. It was why I'd never had a boyfriend—because beyond sex, I didn't have a clue. Angelo and Dylan's relationship was a balm to my soul, and I'd always wanted it for myself but never known how. Grindr got me laid when I felt so inclined, but I rarely saw the same bloke twice. Didn't need to when the app was flooded with new faces by the hour.

But, *fuck*, I saw Joe every damn day. And I wanted to. I wanted to do all the things he'd said—apart from creeping away from him while he slept, so why had I done it? If I hadn't, perhaps he wouldn't have gone to Shadow's field that day. Perhaps he'd have stayed on the couch with me—kissing, touching . . . *more*. And maybe after I'd have stuck around to figure out what it all meant.

I stopped pacing and sank into the nearest chair. My laptop glowed accusingly—the only light in the room—and I pulled it towards me. The chapter I'd been working on was almost done, but I had another window open that I'd been plugging at when Joe had come in from the yard. It was a self-help plan for Emma, using the same theory that I'd applied to graded exercise programs for years. An inch at a time, little by little. Things that took a long time to put right took longer to break. And every step, however small, meant something. Meant everything.

Just not to me.

The therapist in me knew I was being unfair—that I hadn't spent my adult life guiding patients through recovery with complete and total detachment. Of course I hadn't. How many nights had I sat up with Angelo and Dylan? Teaching Dylan how to help Angelo, and Angelo how to let him? Did I do that because they'd become my friends? Or because it was impossible for me not to?

I blew out a long breath and shut the computer with a bang, plunging myself into darkness. The tangents in my head rarely made sense, and no amount of waiting for this particular one to lead me back to Joe would change anything. I'd fucked up, and despite him having the weight of the world on his mind, he cared.

Work abandoned, habit took me out into the yard. Dawn wasn't far away and the horses knew it. A few called out as I passed their stalls, and even the ponies in the tack room were awake.

I poked my head in, expecting to see George still kipping in the hay. But George wasn't there and I found myself face-to-face with Dex. "Oh. Erm. Sorry. I was just seeing if George wanted a cuppa."

Dex eyed me over the top of the weakest pony's head. "That's okay. I heard you coming."

It wasn't exactly an invitation to hang around, but I leaned on the half-door anyway, watching the friendly pony lick Dex's neck. "How are they doing?"

"Not so bad," Dex replied. "I didn't think this one would make it, but Jonah's worked his magic."

Dex's opinion on Jonah was hard to gauge. He'd been around a lot while Joe had been in hospital but rarely spoke, and true to Joe's warning that he didn't care for strange men, he'd given me a wide berth. "What will happen to them when they're better?"

Dex shrugged. "Adoption, or a city farm, maybe. I'd take them myself, but I haven't the room. How's Joe? Sal said he was still banjaxed."

It took a moment to make sense of Dex's soft Irish brogue. "He's tired, but he'll be okay."

"What about you?"

"Me?"

Dex patted the pony and came to the half-door. He peered at me in much the same way Joe did, albeit without the heat. "You're a good gorger, eh?"

Gorger. It took me a moment to translate the term for non-gypsy. I dragged a smile from somewhere and chanced it. "I try."

"You're like Seb. I didn't see it at first, but you're still here."

"Where else would I go?"

"Home," Dex said like it made perfect sense. "This farm isn't the place for every man."

He shot me a final shrewd gaze and then returned to the ponies. I stared, unseeing, at his back as the mist in my brain began to clear. I'd never considered my London flat less of a home than I did right now, but what did that matter if Joe was alone upstairs while I lapped the yard like a lost lunatic?

I backed away from the tack room and took off for the house. At the stairs, I kicked off my shoes and jogged up to the landing. A pile of cats had found Joe's hiding place and were camped outside the bedroom, and the closed door gave me pause. Its earlier slam echoed in the tangled mess my mind had become— or perhaps always had been. *Be brave.*

Holding my breath, I eased the door open, half expecting to find Joe sitting up, his eyes still bright with the frustration I deserved, but he was huddled on the bed, fast asleep, and still dressed in my clothes.

I moved to the window and drew the curtains, blocking the outside world for the first time since Joe had shown me this room all those weeks ago. Then, as though this was my bed—*our* bed—I lay down beside Joe and touched his shoulder, tentatively at first, but then with more purpose as my hand slid naturally over his torso and beneath his borrowed hoodie. My fingers found his abdomen and he shivered.

"Harry?"

"It's me," I whispered. "It's okay . . . keep sleeping."

Joe hummed and rolled over, his head coming to rest on my chest as though we were made to lie together like this—my arms tight around him, his leg hitched over mine. I buried my face in his hair and breathed him in and, for the first time in days, let sleep carry me away.

CHAPTER FOURTEEN

Joe

My mum looking in on me woke me up. At first, I didn't notice anything different. Recent days and weeks faded away, and I was tramping it on the couch in my muddy work clothes. Then her knowing smile and wink broke through the haze and reality hit me like that bus I'd been running from in my dreams.

She shut the door, her footsteps somehow barely audible on the creaky stairs. I turned my head and there was Harry, sleeping beside me like he'd always been there. My heart stuttered. Grandpa's room became somewhere else, and in my head, I found an ounce of Harry's grace and rolled over to straddle his waist, to kiss him awake, and show him without words how happy I was to see him.

But my body was stiff from sleep, sore from the hoof-shaped bullshit in my gut, and the best I managed was a pained gasp. Harry stirred, and I clamped a hand over my mouth, but it was too late. His eyes fluttered open, his gaze met mine, and somehow I knew that nothing between us would ever be the same.

He smiled and reached for me, carefully pulling me close, his touch gentle and light, but consuming all the same. I pressed my forehead against his and searched his expression. "Why did you stay?"

"Because I wanted to."

"Are you sure?"

"Yes."

It was the reassurance I didn't know I so badly needed. I kissed him, and my body came to life in ways that parts of it didn't really want to. Heat flared in my veins, and my skin tingled. And as he deepened the kiss, shudders rippled through me.

My abdomen protested as I slid closer, but I hardly felt it as Harry met me halfway and eased me onto my back. His body covered me, but without his weight. His chest was a hairsbreadth from mine. So close, but not nearly close enough. I arched up and couldn't bring myself to regret it as the heat of him seeped into me.

Harry gasped and I swallowed the tiny sound and scraped his lips with my teeth. I'd never kissed anyone like I kissed him. Never felt it in every dark corner of my body. I shivered again, and my dick hardened in the sweatpants that still smelled of him. I moved my hands to his waistband and pushed his loose joggers down his hips. When I opened my eyes, they were as low as they could be without the money shot, but it was still clear that Harry packed some heat.

I broke the kiss, desperate to touch him, but Harry laid his palm flat on my chest and held me down.

"Easy," he said. "I'm not going anywhere."

Could I take that literally? Being cooped up on my own had left me plenty of time to think about things I'd likely have ignored otherwise, and the fact that Harry's time on the farm was dwindling had occurred to me more often than I cared to admit. With his hands gliding over my tender abdomen, it was hard to imagine that he wouldn't be here in a few weeks' time, but the fact remained that however close we became, it was temporary.

He kissed me again, more demanding than before. I dissolved into him, and it felt like hours had passed when he finally pulled away for real.

"I'd better get up," he said. "I want to help Toby with the hay bales when he gets here."

"Toby knows where the hay is kept?" The swift drop to reality made me chuckle. "That kid hasn't fetched a bale since he got here."

Harry smiled. "So I heard, but Emma made a list of all the jobs you do that someone else could do, and—uh—would it be the worst pun in the world if I said that he'd drawn the short straw?"

"Yes. It would be so fucking bad that I wouldn't ask you to stay and put your dick in my mouth before you went downstairs."

"Wow." A flush stained Harry's cheeks beneath his dark beard. "You're feeling better."

It wasn't a question. And as I considered the statement, I realised that it was true. My stomach was sore, but it finally felt like a bruise, not the apocalypse, and the fatigue lacing my blood was no longer nauseating. "Is that a yes?"

"You didn't ask me anything."

I sat up on my elbows and held Harry's gaze. "Lock the door."

Harry propelled himself fluidly off the bed and to the door. As he flicked the tiny catch that could barely keep the cats out, the irony that in less than a day I'd gone from not wanting to sleep in this room to getting busy on Grandpa's bed struck me funnier than it should have.

"What are you smirking at?" Harry came back to the bed and straddled my waist. "'Cause if you're about to tell me you were taking the piss about having my dick in your mouth, we're gonna have a problem."

"You think I'd joke about that?"

Harry raised an eyebrow and we stared each other down. The truth was, despite a crazy connection that wouldn't quit, we didn't know each other at all when it came to sex. If you'd asked me after the first week, I'd have pegged him as a submissive bottom, but the way his gaze speared me now said otherwise.

Fuck. Images flashed through my mind, each one filthier than the last, and parts of me I'd assumed extinct roared to life. I fisted his T-shirt and yanked him down to my level. "I wouldn't joke about it."

Harry took my hand and pried it off him. "Good job I'm not laughing then, eh?"

I couldn't argue with that. Didn't want to. Harry shucked his trousers and underwear and then slid mine down my legs with a swift tug. His cock was as long and thick as I'd imagined. I swallowed and licked my lips. Could I take a dick that big? Would he want me to? Or would he stay exactly where he was and ride me? As Harry walked on his knees towards me, either way was equally terrifying, because whatever happened, this dude blew my damn mind.

Harry pressed the tip of his cock to my lips. I took him down my throat. He groaned, and his grip on the bed frame above my head tightened enough to make the wood crack, my breath catch, and my dick throb so hard I saw stars.

My stomach still wasn't strong enough to hold me up for long, but it turned out not to matter as he fucked my mouth. Harry was a gentle soul—soft-spoken and kind—but a different man drove his cock down my throat. Urgent, demanding . . . *dominant.* How had it taken us so long to get to this point? As Harry reached behind himself to jack me, I had no idea.

His power over me in this moment was absolute. Rhythm,

pace, grip, I was gone. I moaned around his dick, and my teeth scraped his shaft, spurring him on. His growls went right through me. I tilted my head back to let him thrust even deeper, and his rhythm on my cock faltered.

"You're gonna make me come," he guttered out.

Like he had anything to worry about when I was winning that race like a fucking pro. The only bad thing about having his dick in my mouth was that I couldn't kiss him as my balls tightened and my screaming core muscles seized up. I thrust up into his hand, groaning with abandon until my voice cracked, and then I came hard, painting us both with come.

"You're so fucking hot." Harry's strong thighs quaked, and his dick pulsed in my mouth. "I'm gonna come."

And come he did, like a train, while I swallowed it all like a starving man.

It seemed like he was coming forever, but eventually, he pulled out with a soft sigh and manoeuvred himself to lie next to me. My chest was heaving. He laid one hand over my racing heart, and the other rubbed soothing circles into my belly.

I winced. It was too much. The pain I'd ignored when my dick had taken over my senses came back full force and nausea washed over me.

Harry frowned. "Are you okay?"

"Give me a sec."

"I'm here."

I sucked in deep breaths and curled into him. The ache in my abdomen peaked in waves but was so fucking worth it for the residual pleasure zinging through my veins. For the warmth of his touch all over me. For the trance he could put me in with just the graze of his fingers.

"Joe?"

I opened my eyes and gazed up at Harry, aware that time had passed, but no idea how much. The question in his dark eyes was obvious. "I'm okay."

"Sure?"

"Yeah. I'm good, but you'd better help me strip the bed before my ma comes up and tries to do it for me."

Harry laughed—a real deep chuckle that was warmer than any sunshine. "There's another new duvet set in the cupboard. I'll put it on for you if you want to take a shower?"

"You saying I stink?"

"No, I'm saying you should probably take a shower while I'm around to listen out for you."

Just like that, Dom Harry disappeared. I waited a hopeful moment for him to come back, but it didn't happen, and the Harry I was left with still made my heart skip a beat.

He helped me stand, held me up when I wavered, and walked me to the bathroom. I wanted to drag him into the shower and sink to my knees in front of him, but I settled for turning the shower as hot as it would go and kissing his cheek, feeling suddenly—and weirdly—shy. "Don't go before I'm out, okay?"

"As if."

And he kept his promise. When I staggered out of the bathroom a little while later, he was sitting on the freshly-made bed—the dirty sheets who knew where—and thumbing through his phone. He seemed uncharacteristi-cally irritated.

I treated myself to another pair of his sweatpants and steadied myself with his shoulder as I pulled them on. "Why the long face? Something wrong?"

Harry glanced up. "You don't wear underwear anymore?"

"What's the point when I'm in quarantine?" I eyed him. "And what's with the deflection? You don't let anyone else get away with that shit."

"Don't I?"

"Don't be cute."

Harry grinned wryly. "You're a perceptive motherfucker."

"Thanks. Are you going to answer my question? 'Cause it would be a lot quicker if you told me to jog on."

"Fine. Come here." Harry patted the bed beside him until I sat down. Then he held his phone out to me. "Take a look through this Instagram account."

Lacey and Jemima pissed around on Instagram all the time, but my knowledge of social media was limited to the long-ago abandoned Facebook profile I had before I'd returned full-time to the farm. Instagram was a mystery, and scrolling through some fitness fanatic's profile didn't do much to educate me. "What am I looking for?"

"Nothing in particular. I just want to know what vibe you get from it."

I looked again at the dude posing in the pictures—all muscles, weights, and protein shakes—and watched a brief clip of him shouting about meal plans. In the captions below, he'd listed the subscription prices for whatever it was he was trying to sell, and my eyes bugged out. "How much a week?"

"I know, right?" Harry took the phone back. "There's hundreds of PTs like him, plugging meal plans and diets when they don't know jack about nutrition. And don't get me started on the weight regimes they pimp. Put together with this protein guzzling nonsense and it's—shit. Sorry. It just winds me up."

"I can tell. Is this why you don't eat mashed potato?"

Harry stared at me like I'd grown two heads. Like he thought I hadn't seen him blanch every time someone put bread on his plate. "What?"

I blinked first. "Never mind."

"Anyway . . ." Harry said. "My point is that these media PTs are dangerous. You can't focus on the latest fad and hope it will build your wellbeing. You wouldn't expect those ponies in the tack room to recover by just feeding them bran, would you? Your dad told me that horses don't live well without emotional support. Perhaps there's parallels."

"Leaving Jonah out of it, if you'd compared it to horses from the start I'd have known what you meant. I have a limited imagination."

"I don't believe that, but I'm sorry for ranting at you. My mate Angelo usually deals with the fall out when I've been on social media."

It was the first time Harry had mentioned friends from back home—from his real life. I wanted to know more . . . to press him until there was no room left in the "Harry" part of my brain, but he got up before I could voice a coherent question, ready to go and break his back on my farm.

I grabbed his T-shirt and yanked him down for a kiss. It was rough and raw, and over far too soon. "You'll come back later?"

"Of course," he said. "We can go for a walk if you're feeling up to it."

"Thought I was supposed to stay my arse in here?"

Harry winked and gently bit my cheek. "Then we'll go after dark."

IT TOOK me three days to figure out who was fucking around with my stable plan. I sat in Grandpa's chair and watched Emma lead Shadow to Mani's stall and forced myself not to holler out of the window at her.

I kept it in until she wandered into the house for dinner. "Why are you fucking with my horses?"

Emma glowered at me across the table as Toby drifted into the kitchen and stopped—eying us both—and clearly considering whether to join us or not. "Fucking with *your* horses? What does that even mean?"

"It means you've got Mani in Shadow's stall, and Shadow kicking up a storm next to Ava and Jazz."

"Have you heard him kicking?"

Not that I could remember, but that wasn't the point. I was sleeping like a dead man at the moment, especially at night when Harry lay behind me, his chest pressed against my back—

"Why have you moved them?"

"Because isolating Shadow doesn't make him any happier. Yeah, he made a fuss at first, but he likes it now. I caught him nuzzling Ava this morning."

"Bollocks." I didn't believe her. Most of my days right now were spent staring out of the window, mentally cataloguing what the rest of them were doing wrong, to stave off the mind-numbing boredom of being too wired to rest and too tired to move, and I hadn't seen Shadow do anything in his new digs but heckle passing cats. "He can't stay there if he starts on the other horses. It's not fair on them."

"I know that. Don't talk to me like I'm an idiot."

Harry came in as Emma was speaking. Like Toby, he glanced between us, but there was no apprehension in his amused expression, and despite being *so fucking hot* for him, I kind of wanted to punch him.

At least until he dropped into the seat beside me and surreptitiously squeezed my thigh. "What are you two bickering about?"

"Shadow," Emma said. "Joe thinks the world is going to end because he doesn't like change."

"Fuck you," I shot back. "The world will end if he kicks one of those old mares. He'll break their . . ." I trailed off as I realised they were all staring at me. "*What?*"

Harry squeezed me harder, and Emma giggled, leaving Toby to nervously take his seat and explain. "Erm . . . it's just that we were saying this morning that we missed you shouting, boss. Welcome back."

"I don't shout." Beside me, Harry's shoulders shook with silent laughter. Emma broke into full-on cackles. I threw a digestive biscuit at her. "Bugger off, the lot of you."

Their obvious amusement didn't ease my worries about Shadow. After dinner, I called time on my daylight confinement and supervised the horses as they were brought in from the fields. Instead of saving Shadow till last, Emma led him down with the oldest girls. I braced myself for disaster, but nothing happened. He went into his stall like a lamb, only pausing to take a shit where it was least convenient for him to do so.

Harry was apparently responsible for the evening feeds now. I bit down on the urge to nitpick at him and dragged Emma inside. "Okay. You have my attention. What's the theory?"

Emma stuck her hands in her pockets. "Same as the one Harry uses on me. That nothing can change if we don't try. We want him to be more socialised, but that's not going to happen if we keep him away from all the others. I think he's lonely, and he acts like a prick to compensate."

Her scowl was so intense that it was hard to tell if she was having a dig at herself or me, but the theory fit us both, particularly if you combined the worst traits of our personalities. Had Shadow absorbed that from both of us? He'd always been a difficult horse, but had we made him worse? "What did Jonah think when he was here?"

"Why do you care what Dad thinks?"

"Why did you bring him here if you don't?"

"Because you were so messed up I was scared you wouldn't come back. When I called him, they were still saying your liver might be pulverised."

I winced. "Thanks for the visual."

"You're welcome. But seriously, I was scared, and I needed help, and that night was probably the only time he'll ever be able to help me. It might not mean much to you, but it meant everything to me."

I hadn't thought of it that way, and suddenly my father's opinion of my renegade horse ceased to matter. I pulled my sister close and hugged her tight. "You should work with Shadow more. Perhaps you understand each other."

Emma sighed. "Perhaps we do."

She went back outside, and after swallowing a couple of codeine, I followed her. The idea of Shadow being an anxious horse troubled me. I parked myself on an upturned crate by the tack room and watched him for the rest of the evening, all the while jonesing for the cigarettes I'd forgotten about until now.

Harry came to join me as the sun went down. "Something on your mind?"

I jerked my head in Shadow's general direction. "Emma's right about him. He's so chilled out shacked up with the ladies."

"Yeah . . . it's interesting, isn't it? How aggression can mask other things. You've said before that he's calmer when he's exercised—which works for humans too—but I'd never considered the social aspect of it. Stupid, really, because lots of my patients see a spike in their recovery when they come to my group sessions."

I couldn't imagine anything worse than trying to put myself back together with an audience, but that was me, and I'd already established that I was probably part of the problem. "Do you think Emma could ride him?"

"You're asking me?" Harry leaned against the tack room door, lazily playing with the mane of the pony who came to investigate. "I don't know anything about riding, and I've never seen Emma on a horse."

"But you know her," I said. "Or at least, you understand how her mind works better than I do. She quit riding because she became terrified of hurting herself. Seriously, it was like this phobia that appeared overnight after Grandpa died. I never connected the two, but that was around the time Shadow started acting out too."

"Was it sudden? Your grandfather's death, I mean?"

"Yes and no." I watched Shadow poke his head out of his

stall and call out to his new girlfriend next door. "He was old and getting frailer, but I thought we had more time. We all did."

"Waiting for the end is almost as bad as the event itself."

"Is that what happened to your dad?"

"My dad died of a heart attack in a taxi on his way home from a strip club. It was so fast, he probably didn't realise what was happening, and I hate myself for thinking that he didn't deserve to go out so easy."

I looked up at him, squinting in the murky evening light. "Does he deserve you hating yourself instead?"

"Probably not."

You complex motherfucker. I nudged him with my elbow and went back to my horse-watching. After a while, Harry dropped a subtle kiss to my head and wandered off.

With the farm winding down for the night, it didn't take me long to follow.

CHAPTER FIFTEEN

HARRY

Joe recovered, slowly, and the farm went back to my perception of normal, but nothing felt quite the same. For starters, I was sharing a bed with him every night, but it was more than that. Despite him returning to most of his duties sooner than anyone thought possible, an ominous cloud settled over my soul, and I couldn't shake it.

One late afternoon, I found Emma at Shadow's gate, feeding him Polo mints. "Don't tell Joe. He doesn't like them having sugar."

Keeping a wary eye on Shadow, I stole one from her half-empty pack. "He's probably got a point."

"A few won't hurt."

"Fair enough. What are you doing out here? Sal said dinner was nearly ready."

"That explains why *you're* out here then. You haven't had dinner with us in days."

"I'm weaning myself off," I said. "I'll be back in London in a few weeks."

"Bless."

Emma fed Shadow another mint and apparently lost interest, and I was glad of it. My appetite disappeared with every day that passed, and it was only Joe's watchful gaze that kept me from bringing out the meal replacement shakes I'd stashed in my car. The hypocrisy was mind-blowing, but that was the way of it —knowing it was so, so wrong, but seemingly unable to stop. Maybe I really was my father's son.

"Do you think I could ride him?"

"Hmm?" I glanced at Emma and then followed her gaze to Shadow as he pranced away. "Damn. I don't know. If Joe can, I don't see why you couldn't. He says you're a better rider than him."

"Technically, maybe, but Joe hates rules, and he has no fear. If he did, he wouldn't have been close enough to get kicked in the first place."

"There's nothing wrong with fear when it serves its purpose."

"And what's that?"

"To protect us," I said, though it sounded hollow even to my own ears. "It becomes a problem when we lose sight of what it's protecting us *from*."

"So . . . if I'm too afraid to go out because I'm afraid of being hurt, and then I become scared of being afraid instead, that fear is limiting me instead of protecting me?"

"Something like that."

"You don't sound so sure."

"I'm not the oracle," I said. "If I was, I'd be indoors eating my dinner."

Emma's gaze sharpened. "Do you have an eating disorder?"

"Yes."

"Does Joe know?"

"What difference does that make?"

She shrugged. "I don't know."

I didn't know either. And it didn't seem to matter when Shadow came back to us and rested his chin on Emma's head. It was the first time I'd ever seen him be overtly affectionate, and the quiet joy in Emma's eyes was a balm to the scratchy sensations in my brain.

When he'd wandered off again, Emma took my hand and tugged me gently towards the house. "Come and sit with your friends, Harry. It doesn't matter if you eat or not. No one will say anything."

"I'm all right, Em. Honest. I'll come in later."

"Joe's gonna come looking for you if you don't show up."

"I know."

"Please?"

"No." I reclaimed my hand. "I've never dragged you out of the house kicking and screaming, so don't do it to me, okay?"

Her face fell, and I felt bad, but not bad enough. I turned back to Shadow's field and listened to her footsteps as they faded away.

***

"IT'S GREEN, so you have to eat it." Joe set a plate on my desk, eyeing the sandwich like it was an unexploded bomb. "And I used that weird protein bread you stashed in your cupboard."

"Um . . . thanks, I think?" I drew the plate towards me. Sandwiched between the keto bread was a sliced hardboiled egg, what looked like houmous, and some raw kale—stalks and all. "What are you bringing me sandwiches for at this time of night?"

Joe shrugged. "Why not? I just ate a packet of Haribo, so . . ."

"You're a sugar fiend."

"Only because I've cut the fags down. I'd rather have a smoke than a bag of Tangfastics, but what you gonna do?"

Both vices were a mystery to me, but I held my tongue. Joe's days had been crazy as he'd caught up with work on the farm, and I'd got away with dodging meals. But it was late now, and he was in for the night, which meant that it had only been a matter of time before he'd come looking for me.

Not that I was complaining. The sandwich looked . . . interesting, and beyond that, I was pleased to see him. We slept together every night, but he was gone at dawn most mornings, and chasing my deadline had started to keep me busy well into most evenings.

I missed him.

And with his dry grin finally soaking into my soul, eating the strangest sandwich I'd ever seen didn't seem so bad.

Joe perched on the edge of my desk but didn't watch me eat. Instead he peered at my work, frowning as he read my words under his breath. "I don't get you."

"You don't get me? What's that got to do with mindfulness in the city?"

"Everything. You're talking about how people should be kind to themselves, but that doesn't fit with how you treat yourself."

"It's my job, mate. Not an autobiography."

"Yeah, but you don't say stuff you don't mean. That's why I don't get it."

With anyone else, the food in my belly would've turned to dust, but Joe had a way of saying things that made me think beyond my own harmful behaviours. "If it had been George who'd been kicked by Shadow, telling him to stay home and rest would've been much easier for you than trying to take care of yourself has been."

"George isn't responsible for the farm."

"No, but he's responsible for himself."

"That doesn't make any sense."

He had a point. I mentally crossed the words out and searched for replacements, but after twelve hours of typing, none came to mind. Besides, I knew exactly what Joe was saying —I just didn't want to hear it.

I shut my laptop and ran my gaze over him. He'd ditched my clothes since he'd returned to work and was back in his weathered jeans, but he'd claimed one of my hoodies as his own and rarely took it off now the summer heat had gone. I wound the cords around my fingers and tugged him closer. Kissing him was effortless and made the itch in my bones easier to ignore.

We found our way to the bed like we did most nights when we caught each other awake. Joe lay beneath me, submissive in a way he never was outside of this room, and I made short work of stripping him. His body was glorious—long and lean and hard in all the right places. His hands were rough from farm graft, but the rest of him was hypnotically smooth, and I lost myself tracing every inch of him with my tongue.

Beneath me, he gasped and arched up. A week ago, the movement would've made him wince, but not now. Now, his eyes were bright with arousal, not pain, and I wanted to fuck him so much my cock *hurt*.

I shed my own clothes and tossed them somewhere over my shoulder. Then I fell forwards, dropping my palms either side of his head, and grazed his lips with mine. "I've been looking forward to getting naked all day."

Joe smirked. "Me too. I had to think of my grandma when I was riding Mani, or I'd have hurt myself."

"You've been riding?"

That was new to me, and my heart warred between concern that he was pushing himself too soon and relief that he was back where he belonged.

Relief won out. He'd once told me that fucking wasn't that different to riding a horse, and if the scenes flashing through my mind played out, I had nothing to worry about. I dipped my head for another ruining kiss, then evaded his hands to slide back down his body. Joe had become an instant master at driving me insane with his mouth on my dick, but somehow, I'd yet to return the favour.

That was about to change. I bit his hip to distract him and then swallowed him whole, holding him to the bed as he reared up, digging my fingers into his lean thighs. His groans sent shivers down my spine as I slid his cock down my throat, and I stared up at him, revelling in his reddened cheeks and blown pupils. *This* was the Joe I craved when my mind was filled with nothing but him. When the memory of him shirtless and riding wasn't enough. In his unique way, he was as guarded as me, but not when we were like this.

Not when his dick straining and pulsing in my mouth was all there was.

Over and over, I took him to the brink while he thrashed and moaned beneath me. I gripped his thighs and opened his legs, pushing them wider as I deep-throated him. My fingers gripped the base of his cock, and I looked up at him again, and if I could've frozen the world in that moment, I'd have done it in a heartbeat.

But as the world kept turning, a soul-deep desire for him spurred me on. I slid a wet finger into him. His ragged cry pierced the air and his whole body trembled. That it was me turning him inside out sent my blood roaring in my ears, and the urge to add another finger and curl them, to make him come, was so strong I almost gave into it. But there was another urge coursing through me. I withdrew my finger.

"*Harry.*" Joe tangled his fingers in my hair. His eyes were clenched shut. "Fuck—"

A wailing siren shattered the heady air. Blue lights flashed through the window, and Joe leapt from the bed, launching himself over my head and to the floor to snatch his clothes.

He was gone from the room before I could comprehend it, and I staggered to the window just in time to see four police cars and a van pull up in the yard.

CHAPTER SIXTEEN

Joe

"How the fuck did you get this warrant?"

The CID officer somehow managed to look bored and smug at the same time. "We got it the same place we get every other warrant in the land, now step aside so we can search this property."

"You're not searching the stables."

"Yes, we are." The officer jabbed a pudgy finger at the warrant he'd stuck to the side of the house. "The warrant covers the house, the stables, and all outbuildings and land. I'm asking you nicely right now to let us work, but if you obstruct, I'll arrest you."

Cunt.

Harry came out of the house, dressed in a hotchpotch of clothes he must've found on the floor. Two policemen jumped on him, demanding to see ID. He shot me a quizzical glance, but I had nothing. *I'm so fucking sorry.*

A team of police officers started towards the stable block. I moved fast to block them again. "Wait. You can't just barge into the stalls. I need to get the horses out first."

"One by one," the CID officer said. "And we'll be watching every move you make."

They started with Tauna and Carric. I led the placid old mares out and stood in the lane with them, fury seeping from every pore as my mind worked to figure out how this was happening to us again.

It didn't have to work very hard. Raids like this had happened dozens of times before Grandpa had kicked Jonah off the farm for good, and we hadn't had one since . . . until now. *Bastard.* I could've killed him. Would've, if he'd been in my line of sight, and everything he'd done for Emma and the horses while I'd been in hospital evaporated. He'd taken advantage of us at our weakest, and now all that remained to be seen was how deep a hole he'd left us in.

My mother and Emma were escorted from the bungalow and made to stand by the police van while the houses were searched. Harry stood with them, his back to me as he comforted Emma. I longed to see his face, to ground myself in his eyes, to go back to where we'd been a split second before this latest nightmare.

I had to settle for whispering soothing words to Tauna that the stoic old mare didn't need.

One by one, the stalls were searched. When Sal and Emma were allowed into the house to wait in the kitchen, Harry came out to help me with the horses. I thought he'd never led horses out by himself, but apparently, I was wrong. Mani went with him easily, and then Ava, until finally we were left with Shadow.

Police surrounded his stall. I rounded on them again, but Harry pulled me back, his lips at my ear. "It was your father's idea to move the horses around."

The words were muttered. Barely intelligible. But the implication was deafening. If there was anything to be found, it was in Shadow's lair, and if we didn't bring him out, the police would call someone to do it for us.

Someone who couldn't handle him.

The idea of Shadow being tranquillised—or worse—poured water on the fire in my veins. I didn't give a fuck what my father had buried in that damn-fucking stable, Shadow was my priority —and as much my family as Sal and Emma.

"I'll come with you," Harry said. "He doesn't seem to mind me when Emma leads him."

I nodded. "Okay, but step back if he kicks off. I can't handle you getting hurt."

We advanced on Shadow together. I'd always approached him with absolute quiet, but Harry spoke to him in much the same way he had to me when I'd been losing my mind with pain. His voice was low, entrancing, and Shadow tuned into him almost as fast as I had. I slipped a head collar on him and then reins, and we walked him out of the stall.

"Stand back," I gritted at the waiting police. "He'll brain you if you startle him."

Shadow was a big enough horse for them to take me seriously. They moved aside, but even with them well out of the way, Shadow couldn't be trusted to wait patiently in the lane like the others had. "We'll have to take him to the top field," I said. "Turn him out and hope he doesn't get into mischief before morning."

Harry opened the yard gate. "Have you left him out overnight before?"

"Only when I haven't been able to catch him. Didn't sleep, though. Spent the night sitting on the fence like a raving lunatic."

"Oh well." Harry snorted softly. "You probably weren't going to get much kip tonight anyway."

I couldn't figure out if he meant because of the clusterfuck with the police or the fact that he'd been on the brink of banging my brains out when they'd arrived.

Either way, he was right.

We turned Shadow loose in the field. He took off like a bullet and we made our way back to the yard, but despite the pressing need to return to the other horses, I pulled Harry behind the large tree at the donkey paddock. "I'm so sorry."

He rubbed his hands up and down my arms. "What the hell for?"

"For dragging you into more mess. This isn't what you signed up for."

"I signed up to a break from my suffocating city life. Whatever's happened, I've definitely had that."

"Is your life really suffocating?"

Harry shrugged. "Ask me again in a few weeks. The longer I'm here, the more I seem to think so."

A policeman appeared on the path and shone a flashlight in our faces. "Come out from there."

My hackles rose, but Harry's touch kept me in check. We stepped out from behind the tree and returned to the yard. He darted inside to check on the girls, and I slouched against the tack room door and surveyed the scene. Shadow's box was still being searched, though I couldn't imagine what was taking so long. There were only so many places to look in a pile of straw and shit.

Someone came out and muttered to the bloke in charge. A gaggle of police converged on Shadow's stable, and I closed my eyes. I'd seen energy like that before in coppers when they caught a scent. What would it be this time? Dodgy number plates? Knocked off jewellery? Over the years, they'd found it all.

Or so I thought until the lead officer walked out of the stable carrying a sawn-off shotgun.

AS A CHILD, I used to wonder if my life was nothing but a dream. If I'd wake up one day and be someone else entirely. On good days that would scare me—who would take care of Mani? Ride him, and feed him his favourite horse nuts? On bad days, I didn't much care. Take my shitty life and fuck it up worse than Jonah had. Go on. I dare you.

Without Harry beside me, today was one of those days. I stared at the gun with as much surprise as if they'd brought out a severed head, and a prickle of real fear shuddered through me. *Guns? Seriously?*

The head honcho approached, his hands already reaching to restrain me. A couple of goonies joined him and I was face down on the ground before I knew what was happening.

A knee drove into my back, pressing my still tender abdomen against the cold ground. "Who does the gun belong to?"

I laughed. Couldn't help it. I didn't know the lead officer, but I recognised some of the other coppers as men and women who'd cried over dead horses with me over the years. Funny how they never seemed to remember that when Carter family bullshit brought trouble to my door. "If you knew to come here to look for it, then you know who it belongs to."

"Not good enough." The knee pressed harder. "If you can't explain how a sawn-off shotgun came to be on your property, I'll have to assume that it belongs to you."

Bastard. He knew it wasn't mine. Just like his predecessor had known the fenced TVs last time hadn't been mine either. But did they care? Of course they fucking didn't. They wanted a scalp, and mine would do.

Give him up. But even as the thought crossed my mind, I knew I'd never do it. My father didn't deserve my loyalty, but he had it anyway. I could no more give him up than I could one of the horses. *I hate him.* Finally, something that made sense.

The officer on my back ran through his methods of persuasion. My arguments lapsed into silence and handcuffs were slapped around my wrists. It began to rain as I was hauled to my feet, and I could almost smell the grubby cell I'd be spending the night in when the front door opened.

Harry appeared in the doorway, the light from inside framing him so he looked like a broad-shouldered apparition. "What are you doing? Let him go."

The officer ignored him and began to tow me away. Harry's footsteps had always been light, but I heard them now as they followed us. I wanted to tell him to back off—to go inside so he didn't have to witness the latest round of Carter humiliation.

But I was too fucking tired.

Harry caught up with us and grabbed the lead officer's arm. "I *said* let him go. Whatever you've found . . . it's mine."

CHAPTER SEVENTEEN

Joe

I had no words for how it felt to watch them arrest Harry. My protests that the gun was indeed mine fell on deaf ears, and as the lead officer closed the van doors on Harry, he turned to me with a smug leer.

"I suggest you get your story straight and then come and find me, because until then, I'm holding your friend. And don't think I won't charge him, because I will. Just like I'd have charged you if you'd coughed to it when I asked."

"You know it's not his."

"I only know what I'm told," the officer said. "And he's saying it is."

My fists twitched. I could smash this bloke's face in any day of the week and still sleep like a baby, but I didn't have time for that shit. If he was serious about charging Harry, then I had to find Jonah, Dicky . . . *anyone* who I could pin that damn-fucking gun on.

"Of course," the officer continued when I didn't respond. "I could take your new statement seriously and believe that the gun belongs to you, but I don't think you really want me to do that."

"Why would I say it if I didn't want you to take it seriously?" I spat.

"Because you haven't thought it through. I'm familiar with everyone who lives and works on this farm, Mr. Carter, but your record makes a more interesting reading than most. Add a firearms charge onto that and I doubt you'd see the light of day for quite some time. Think on that while I question your friend."

The police left the farm, taking Harry with them, and the yard was plunged into sudden darkness. Mani called to me. Dazed, I went to him and brooded fruitlessly against his neck until I remembered Shadow.

I trudged to the top field to fetch him in, but he wouldn't come. A month ago, I'd have hurdled the gate and chased him around. Now, I didn't have the stomach for it—literally—or the time to sit on the fence and wait for him.

"Joe?"

I tossed an unseeing glance over my shoulder. "Em, go back inside. There's no reason for us both to be out in the rain."

"Never stopped you putting me to work before." Emma hopped up on the fence beside me. "Why are you shouting at him? You know that makes him more stubborn."

"I don't know anything. If I did, we wouldn't be in this mess, eh?"

"That's not fair, but we can't let Harry take the rap for this. Even a minor charge could ruin his career."

"It's not a minor charge. Jonah stashed a sawn-off in Shadow's stable."

Emma's sharp intake of breath seemed unnaturally loud. "A gun? Where the hell did he get it?"

"Does it matter?"

"Of course it matters. If we know where it came from, then we're a step closer to getting Harry off the hook. He could go to prison for firearm possession."

"Do you think I don't know that?" My shout rang out across the dark field. Somewhere in front of us, Shadow snorted and stamped his feet. I sighed, and the sensation of wandering amongst nightmares returned. "I don't know what he was thinking when he said the gun was his. Or if he even knew that's what he was coughing for. But I won't let it stand. If I can't straighten this out with Jonah, I'll find a way of proving it's mine."

"Joe, they'll put you away for years with your record."

"So? That's better than Harry taking the heat."

"Neither of you should be taking the heat. It's Dad's gun—or, at least, he brought it here. Just tell the police that."

I shook my head. Even if I could bring myself to do it, the police had already decided that my word was bollocks enough to ignore. If they got their hands on my father, that was one thing, but I'd heard through the grapevine that he'd gone to ground—Dicky too. Which meant that while the coppers had someone already fessing up, they wouldn't much care about hearsay.

Emma whistled and then called to Shadow in a sweet tone I rarely heard from her. The bastard ambled over like a mother-fucking Labrador, and the defeat only added to the weight in my chest. I passed her Shadow's head collar and slid off the fence. "I'm going to find Jonah. If I'm not back by morning, I've probably killed him."

I'D SPENT MORE of my life than I cared to remember searching for my father, but I searched for him now with a new urgency. His bedsit was dark and silent, and I came up blank at his usual haunts, but where on any other night I might've given up and gone home, tonight I pressed on and drove northwards, out of town towards Bodmin.

Jonah had taught me to gallop on the moors—to loosen the

reins and set a horse free the way you couldn't in a fenced-off field. Over the years, I'd come to prefer beach riding or hacking through the woods, but I remembered the little shacks Jonah had sheltered us in when the weather had caught us out. There was one in particular that had been his favourite. Off the beaten hikers' path, it was perfect for an old drunk to hole up in.

Not so perfect for finding your way to it in the dark, but despite my many flaws, my sense of direction was pretty hot, and my father and grandpa both had taught me to recognise landmarks that were unlikely to change much as the years rolled by—ancient trees and the shape of the hills. With the help of the moonlight, I was set.

The shack I had in mind was a mile away from the road. I ditched the van at a tourist spot and set off on foot. Twenty minutes later, I saw the shack in the distance. No lights, but as I got closer, I smelled my father's cherry tobacco, and relief warred with dread in the pit of my stomach. Somehow, I knew that by morning, nothing would ever be the same.

I came up on the shack like a ninja and burst through the door. My father was huddled in a sleeping bag on the floor, a neat cluster of empty beer cans and an open bottle of vodka beside him. He looked up at me and his eyes held little surprise.

He'd been expecting me.

HARRY

So this was what it was like to be arrested. Rhys had often described his wayward younger years to me, but I reckoned that London police stations were nothing like the rural shithole I found myself in now.

For starters, the place was deserted. Aside from me, two plain-clothes officers, and desk sergeant, there were no other souls to be seen. I had no idea what had happened to the dozen officers who'd converged on the farm.

And no one seemed likely to tell me when I was the one answering the questions.

"Tell me again," the male officer said. "What are you doing on Whisper Farm?"

"Working," I said. "I rented a room through Airbnb. The receipt is on my phone. I already gave you the passcode."

I'd done that as a distraction, remembering a conversation I'd overheard Rhys and his friends having years ago when getting picked up by the police had been their regular weekend party trick. *"Give them everything they don't need. Keep 'em busy while you get your story straight."*

The useless data on my phone had kept the CID officers occupied for a couple of hours, but I'd yet to figure out the second part—the explanation for the first real gun I'd ever laid eyes on, and just why I'd felt the need to claim it was mine.

Yeah, that's right, because it had been clear from the start that the detectives knew full well that I was lying through my teeth.

"Why are you protecting Jonah Carter?" And I had no answer for them, because it wasn't *Jonah* Carter I was trying to protect—it was the rest of them. Even without whatever was between Joe and me, I couldn't live with the fear I'd witnessed in Emma and Sal when the police had thrown Joe to the ground.

"Not my boy."

"Not again. We can't lose him."

I hadn't known about the gun at the time. From what Emma had said up to that point, I'd imagined a haul of fake number plates or some knocked-off designer gear. If I'd seen the shotgun beforehand, would I have done anything different? Pondering it was a welcome distraction from my fate if the detectives began to take me seriously, but I wasn't any closer to an answer to that either.

The police called a timeout on the interview and I was led to the front desk to make a phone call. Lacking any better ideas, I called Rhys, but he didn't answer. So I called the farm.

Sal answered. "Joe's not here," she said before I could ask. "He's out looking for his father. I'm so sorry, Harry. We'll fix this, I promise."

I glanced around, mindful of the desk sergeant, and turned my back on him. "That's okay. I'm sure it will work itself out."

"If it doesn't, Joe will step up."

"I don't want him to step up."

"I know, sweet boy, but if you think he's going to let you do time for his father's mistakes, then you don't know him at all."

I closed my eyes to the hopeless gravity of it. My heart knew that the police weren't going to charge me for possession of a firearm. Joe's panic when I'd claimed responsibility for the gun had highlighted me as bait, and the detective who'd brought me in had been shrewd enough to see it. *I* knew they wouldn't charge me, and the detective knew it, but Joe didn't. And he couldn't deliver his father, he'd put himself in the frame, and I was getting the impression that the younger Carter scalp would do if Jonah couldn't be found. "Listen, Sal. They can hold me for twenty-four hours without charging. Tell Joe to do what he can with that time. Right now, that's all we can do."

There wasn't much else to say. If Sal knew that I'd put myself forward as a distraction, I couldn't tell, and I hung up with mixed emotions. One day I'd understand the instant bond I'd had for this family, but today wasn't that day.

I was towed to a holding cell and given the worst sandwich in the world and a bottle of water. The CID detectives informed me that they'd be back for me later, but when an hour stretched to two, and then three, I began to wonder if something had happened.

CHAPTER EIGHTEEN

Joe

The eerie peace of the moors was shattered by my father hitting the side of my van. He took the impact and rolled with it, letting momentum correct his equilibrium before he turned his bland gaze on me.

"Do you think throwing me around is going to change anything, son?"

"Does it matter what I think?" I spat. "If you gave a fuck about me, we wouldn't be out here."

"That's not true." Jonah straightened his grubby clothes. "If I didn't care, I'd still be on the farm. I wouldn't have let your grandfather sign it over to you, and life would be very different."

He was right about that, but I wasn't in the mood for his philosophical old man act. "I don't care about life being different. I just want you to own your mistakes and stop fucking me over."

"It's not you in the police cell, Joe. It's your . . . friend."

The pause threw petrol on the fire in me. I lunged at Jonah again and grasped his collar, propelling him around the van's bonnet to the passenger side.

I wrenched the door open. "Get in."

For reasons only he understood, my father obeyed.

I shut the door and got in the other side, locking us in. The van rumbled to life, and I peeled out of the car park. "I'm taking you down the nick."

"What for?"

"What do you think? To cough to that bloody gun."

"What do you think will happen then?"

I hadn't given that much thought. The child in me imagined that Jonah would be whisked away, Harry set free, and that would be the end of it. But life didn't work like that, particularly if you were a Carter. Simple things turned complicated in the blink of an eye. People got hurt, let down, and fucked over. And somehow my father always carried on. Always moving forward, but nothing ever changed. "I don't care what happens to you."

Jonah was silent, staring listlessly out of the window. My heart burned for a real reaction from him, but I knew it wouldn't come, and I wanted to throttle him for making me feel this way —angry, guilty, and so fucking alone.

We hit the A30. I found some cigarettes in the van door and lit up, exhaling the sweet smoke I'd barely missed until now. "Where did you even get it?"

"It was in Dicky's caravan."

"The one you owed him money for?"

Jonah shot me a sideways look. "You think I haven't paid for that?"

"You told me you didn't. And that you smashed it up on this fucking road. Don't start telling me now that it was all a big misunderstanding—and don't look at me like that. I can't figure this shit out if you talk in code."

"I don't understand why you always think you have to figure anything out, son. You know how the gun got into the stables, and you knew where to find me, so why are we here taking the long way to the inevitable while your friend takes the heat?"

I was twenty-eight years old and I had no idea why every

moment with my father had to be so complicated. So I said the one thing I was sure of. "Harry's not my friend."

More silence. Ants crept over my skin. My sexuality was fluid enough that I'd never felt the need to come out to Jonah. The rare hookups that turned into something more had all come before I'd returned to live on the farm, and he'd been gone by the time that had happened.

Jonah lit a pipe and cleared his throat. "I met Harry when you were away. I liked him."

"Is that supposed to matter?"

"Just making conversation."

"Why did you take Dicky's gun?"

A cloud of cherry tobacco smoke drifted across my face, fuelled by Jonah's heavy sigh. "Because he was going to shoot a horse with it."

He said it so matter-of-factly that I thought I'd misheard him. "One of our horses?"

"He wouldn't waste a bullet on our old nags, son. It was one of Buddy Pierce's thoroughbreds."

"Why?"

"Same reason he came after your mother, I'd imagine. Business."

I snorted. "Dicky McGee ain't no businessman, Dad. He's a fucking helmet."

"That's neither here nor there to me. I just did what had to be done."

I took my foot off the accelerator. The van slowed as I tried to piece together Jonah's latest version of events. "How does this tie in to the buggered-up caravan?"

Jonah sighed. "It doesn't, really. Least not on purpose. Dicky had stashed the gun in the caravan one night after we'd been on the whisky at the Legion, but he'd forgotten about it, see, 'cause his boy was home from the Navy. Then he sold me the van before he remembered."

"And you totalled it on purpose? So he'd think the gun was destroyed?"

"Aye, lad. I buried it under my mattress for a while, but then he caught on that I'd pinched it and came looking. Course he couldn't say what he was after to anyone that asked, but I knew."

"Why did you bring it to the farm?"

"Because I knew it'd be the last place he'd think I'd stashed it. He'd come after me all right, but he wouldn't think me daft enough to hide it so close to home."

"The farm isn't your home."

I lit another cigarette. After so long without smoking, doubling up burned my lungs, but I welcomed the distraction. Tales like these were why I hated Jonah. I wanted to shake the shit out of him and call him a cunt, but he'd saved a horse, and that was the reason I'd been put on this earth. "You had no business being on the farm while I was gone."

"Your sister asked me to."

"Well she shouldn't have."

"She needed me."

"Dex would've helped her."

"He did. But the lad's got his own stables to run."

Dex also had the money to pay for help, and I knew he'd never have let the weak ponies suffer, but what about Shadow? Jonah had worked with him for the best part of a week and coached Emma on how to handle him better. The difference in him was startling.

I hated Jonah for that too.

We drove in silence until we got into town. When the police station came into view, I slowed to a crawl and then swung into a deserted car park. "You have to hand yourself in."

"And say what?"

"That the gun is yours."

"It's not mine."

"It's not Harry's either!" My shout rang out and I punched the dashboard. "Jesus, Dad. Will you just do as I need you to for once in my fucking life?"

I expected more argument, more guilt tripping, and perhaps even a trace of Jonah's rare temper. But it didn't happen. My father merely nodded, got out of the van, and walked away.

HARRY

It was still dark when they let me out, but dawn wasn't far off. I collected my phone from the desk sergeant and accepted a caution for wasting police time, and then I drifted out of the station to meet the drizzly early morning.

Joe was waiting for me with the van. He saw me coming and met me in the middle of the road. There was so much to say, but I didn't know where to start. So I put my arms around him and held him close, inhaling the earthy scent that had grounded me from day one.

He returned my desperate embrace, his lean shoulders trembling. It wasn't the first time I'd seen him cry, but it didn't hurt any less. I tightened my grip on him but didn't speak. What could I say? That I was sorry the police hadn't believed me and given him more time? That I understood more than I wanted to how hard it was when your father let you down so badly?

"What happened?" I whispered. "Did you find your dad?"

Joe nodded against my shoulder, then pulled back, swiping at his bloodshot eyes. "Yeah. Can we go somewhere and talk about it? If I stare at the nick much longer, I'm going to burn it down."

Tired but wired, I readily agreed and took Joe's keys from him, following his directions out of town to a nearby village that, even in the darkness, wouldn't have been out of place in the south of France. "This place is so pretty," I said.

Joe smiled wistfully. "It is now the tourists are starting to fuck off. Crantock is my spiritual home. I love it here."

We drove through the village and out the other side. The air became salty and clean, and even my city boy senses could tell we were by the sea.

Joe guided me to a deserted car park. "Go right to the top by the railing. I'll tell you when to stop so we don't go over."

The newfound madman in me trusted him entirely. I pulled the van to a stop at the end of the world and parked at the angle Joe instructed.

"We can look out the back too," he said.

"Come again?"

"I'll show you."

I'd never seen the back of Joe's van. Far from the workman's van it appeared from the outside, in the back, it was, apparently, a home from home. "Wow. You could live in here."

Joe tugged at the double seat, laying it flat to reveal a bed. "I did, once upon a time."

"What happened?"

"The tragic obvious. My dad was fucking up the farm, so I had to go home and live with Grandpa. After that, I lost the time and the passion to do anything else."

I'd heard fragments of this story before, but not enough to picture Joe living out of his converted campervan. The heartbreak in his eyes when he'd mentioned selling the van if the farm's finances got worse, now made sense.

We spread an old duvet over the bed, and Joe brewed instant coffee on his tiny gas stove, while I looked on, fascinated.

"Got no milk," he said. "But there's sugar in one of these boxes."

"I'm good with it black."

"Sound." Joe passed me a metal mug of coffee and we lounged on the bed with the van's tailgate open, watching the sun rise over Crantock Beach.

It was breathtaking. The sky was a cloudless blue, the sand pristinely white. Without the chilly breeze, it could've been the Bahamas. I sighed and carded my fingers absently through Joe's messy hair. The night had been surreal, but this? It was as near perfection as I'd ever known. I stared at the waves and imagined Joe riding them on a surfboard, his eyes wild, his golden skin contrasting so beautifully against the moody sea. "When did you last go in the water?"

"To surf?"

"Yeah."

Joe put his chin on my chest, his legs were already tangled with mine. "The day Grandpa died. I came out here late in the evening and surfed until it got dark. He was dead in his bed when I got home."

It wasn't as shocking as it might've been a few months ago. I'd always known that I was sleeping in a dead man's bed, but it had oddly never bothered me until Joe had started sleeping with me. As he'd recovered from his injury, he'd become restless some nights, talking in his sleep, tossing and turning, until I took hold of him and held him against me. "Do you think it might've been different if you'd stayed home?"

"I used to, but I've come to realise if I'd been home, I'd have been out in the yard with the horses, so it wouldn't have changed anything. Besides, he was watching the sun go down over the fields, enjoying the peace and quiet with one of those stupid fucking cats on his lap. It wasn't a bad way to go."

"Some people get the death they deserve."

I hadn't meant it as sinisterly as it came out. Joe raised his head and stared at me, his gaze complex and searching. He touched my face, his fingertips like ghosts on my cheeks. "Tell me?"

"Tell you what?"

"About your dad. You said you hated him . . . Why?"

"Because he didn't love me." It wasn't the answer that I'd

parroted over and over as the years had rolled by or even the answer that had played out in my head for my ears alone. But it was the truth. "I thought it was my fault. It took me a long time to realise that it wasn't."

Joe nodded slowly, understanding, like he always had, even when I'd said nothing at all. "He really hurt you, didn't he?"

"He hurt all of us." I sat up and crawled towards the open tailgate, chasing the light . . . the sun, and its warmth.

Joe followed me—of course he did. "Did he hit your mum?"

"Yes."

"Your brother?"

"Yes."

"And you?"

"For a while."

"What happened?"

I shrugged. "Rhys is older than me, but I've always been bigger—stronger, faster, whatever. He's got the charm, I've got the brawn, you know?"

"I'd say you have plenty of charm." Joe's smirk was gentler than usual. "But go on . . . please. I want to know your story."

And for the first time, I wanted—perhaps needed—to tell it. "There's not a huge amount to it, really. My dad drank like an arsehole and kicked the shit out of my mum until Rhys and I got old enough to intervene. Then he kicked the shit out of us instead—but Rhys took the worst of it, because he was the oldest, and . . . well, like I said, I was bigger. And angrier too. I started playing rugby—and then I started hitting him back. It escalated until the neighbours called the police one too many times and he got sent down for domestic violence—for what he'd done to Rhys."

"How long did he get?"

"Four years. Felt like four days, though. I was away at uni when he got out, but my mum and Rhys were still living in the old house. They had to move in the end. My mum's a fucking trooper, but the whole thing messed with Rhys's head. He went off the rails for a while, and that was the hardest thing for me."

"Why?"

"Because I wasn't there. And I didn't want to be. I had a new life—and I loved it. I didn't want to go back."

Joe stretched his long legs out in front of him. "I know how that feels."

"Yeah, but you *did* go back. I didn't. I left Rhys in Romford, and so did my mum. She moved to Spain six months after Dad died. Rhys was sorting himself out by then, but I still felt like shit about it."

"Did he?"

"Hmm?"

"Did Rhys resent you for leaving?"

I mirrored Joe's pose, noting that he was wearing the trainers I'd given him when he was in hospital. "Nah. He encouraged it because it bothered him that he hadn't been able to protect me. He's never understood that taking the worst of it when I was so young gave me time to do what I had to do. That if I'd had my ribs kicked in when I was twelve like he did, my fingers broken, I might not have had the chance to make things right."

Joe hummed his understanding. "I hate that either of you had to get hurt."

I shrugged. "It was a long time ago. And Rhys is okay now. He works as a paramedic and parties in sex clubs."

"Wow."

"Yup."

Neither of us spoke for a while. Joe seemed to be digesting my tale of woe, and I didn't have the heart to admit that I'd barely scratched the surface. Besides, what was the point? Life had moved on, and the details no longer mattered.

"What's Rhys like?"

I turned my head at just the right moment to bury my face in Joe's hair. "Contradictory. On the surface, he's a bit of a lad, but he's a sensitive soul, really. I was happy enough on my own until I met you, but he's not like that. Sometimes it seems like he craves affection, you know? Even when it comes from the wrong place . . . *especially* when it comes from the wrong place. And he doesn't let anyone in. Not even me."

"Did he hate your dad too?"

I lifted my shoulders again. "Maybe. We stopped talking about him after a while, so I don't really know where he is on that."

"Are you close?"

"Yes and no. We're there for each other, but our lives are pretty much separate. Apart from—" I broke off with a chuckle.

Joe's earnest gaze turned curious. "What?"

I laughed again. "I shouldn't tell you this, but I've been carrying it around for more than a year now, and it's just about killing me."

"It can't be worse than anything else you've told me."

Another snigger tumbled out of me. "Oh, trust me, it can."

"Yeah?"

"Yeah." I turned on the bed to face Joe and automatically tucked some of his wayward hair behind his ears. "Remember what I said about Rhys and sex clubs?"

"How could I forget?"

I smirked. "Well, try forgetting this: I had a patient a year or so ago that became a friend. Angelo. Him and his boyfriend frequent the same club as Rhys. I know they've all been fucking, but they have no idea how we're all connected."

Joe's eyes widened. "That Angelo dude doesn't know he's fucking your brother? And Rhys doesn't know he's fucking your friend?"

"That's about the size of it. There's some kind of sex club *omertà*, so Rhys has never told me the name of the hot couple he hooks up with, but combined with what Angelo tells me, it all adds up."

"Wow." Joe shifted on the bed. "That's kind of hot, but terrifying at the same time."

I laughed. "It's not hot for me. I had such a crush on Angelo before I realised. His fella is gorgeous too."

"And your brother?"

"Piss off." I landed a playful punch on Joe's arm. "He's a slightly shorter, slimmer version of me—with better hair."

Joe ran his hand over the buzz on my head. "I like your hair. And I love how big and powerful you are. Makes me feel safe."

That there was even a moment when he didn't feel safe hurt my heart. I found his hand and tugged him close enough for a sweet kiss that went on and on until he pulled away, his gaze too serious again. "Can I ask you something else?"

I sighed. "Sure."

"You know what you said about building yourself up so you could defend yourself?"

"Yeah?" I knew where this was going. If Emma had worked it out, it had only been a matter of time before Joe did too.

"Did it ever take over? The training, I mean. The discipline?"

I nodded slowly. "Of course it did. Protecting my mum, and Rhys, was my priority, but it got out of hand, and it didn't go away, even after I didn't need to protect them anymore. Rhys dealt with what happened to us by going wild—I went the other way. Control, obsession, whatever you want to call it. It consumed me for a while."

"What . . . like an eating disorder?"

"Yeah. Probably not like you're imagining, though. It wasn't like I wanted to be thin."

"You wanted the opposite?"

"For a while, but ultimately, I think I just wanted to be perfect . . . like, from the inside out? And controlling what I put in my body was one way of achieving that. Or so I thought. All it actually meant was that I ate nothing but chicken breasts and protein shakes."

Joe's brow furrowed. I could see him recalling my time on the farm and wondering what that shit meant for me now. "You still eat a lot of chicken and drink weird, mushy shakes."

I chuckled. "I know. And I'm still carb-phobic when I don't check myself, but I'm so much better than I was. Stress fucks with my focus, and I do slip back sometimes, but I manage it these days. Writing helps, at least it did until I started getting paid for it, but the best therapy I've found recently is you."

"Seriously?" Joe's expression brightened considerably. "And here was me thinking I'd brought you nothing but hassle."

I couldn't deny that being on the farm had brought stresses of its own, so I didn't. I snaked an arm around Joe and lolled my head on his shoulder. "You lot are so casual about food—and yet, it means so much to you all. It brings you together every single day, twice a day, sometimes three times. Being a part of that has meant the world to me. I didn't realise how lonely I was until I came here."

"I don't want you to be lonely, Harry. I can't bear it."

I gazed at him and rubbed my jaw against his. "I'm never lonely when I'm with you."

Joe kissed me like he had a hundred times, but it felt different now. Like my night of incarceration had somehow set us free. He fused our mouths together and grazed his teeth over my soul.

"Joe." His name was a whisper on my lips.

And his answer was to pull the tailgate shut and push me down on the fold out bed.

I lay back and let him climb all over me. Kissing Joe—and more—had been a sporadic journey to oblivion, but his taste was so familiar that I wanted to weep. I tugged at his T-shirt until it disappeared. My hoodie followed, and as his chest touched mine, a new spark danced between us.

He sucked in a breath. The bulge in his jeans hardened against my leg, and I slid my hand to his belt buckle. His jeans went the same way as his T-shirt, and suddenly he was rolling over, pulling me on top of him. "Fuck me."

I'd waited a lifetime for him to finish that sentence. I fumbled for my wallet and the long-abandoned condom tucked behind my collection of store loyalty cards. By some insane stroke of fortune, a sachet of lube lurked there too.

Joe raised an eyebrow. "It's almost like you planned this."

"Let me check the expiry dates before I claim credit for that."

I was only half joking, but they were both in date, and my humour faded as I stripped away the remaining clothes between us. My desire for Joe had been electric from the start, but it was off the scale now as my heart beat a souped-up samba, thudding against my ribcage like it would never stop.

Joe shivered and arched up into me. "Don't go too hard."

"I'll be gentle," I whispered.

He smirked. "Not for my sake, mate. Just don't want to get nicked again."

In the haze of being naked with him, I'd clean forgotten about the fact that we were in a public car park, and any enthusiastic movements would send the van rocking. I paused for breath and fought for a glimmer of self-control. The prospect of fucking Joe was making me tremble with need, but I had to take care with him—in every sense.

I rolled the condom on and ripped open the lube sachet. Joe closed his eyes as I slicked us both, and he blew out a long slow breath as I brought his leg to his chest. I lined my cock up against him, pressing slowly inside him, tracking the glorious flush that stole over his beautiful skin. He clamped around me, resisting at first, but then welcoming me in, moaning, ragged and breathless, and digging his fingers into my shoulder.

"*Fuck.*" He bit my shoulder, his body tense and strained. "Give me a sec."

I'd give him the world if he'd let me, but now didn't seem the time to tell him. And I was kind of hoping he already knew.

I held my hips still and rubbed his chest, smoothing my palm over the lean muscle and up his neck to cup his face. "You okay?"

He hummed and wrapped his legs around my waist, his heels at my back, urging me on with infinitesimal pressure. I took the hint and rolled my hips gently enough to make my eyes water. His answering moan was fucking magical, and I found a crazy-slow rhythm that set me on fire, cell by cell, atom by atom.

Pleasure crept up on me, building like an inferno in the breeze. The contradiction between pace and sensation blew my mind. I sought refuge in Joe, in his kiss, in his neck, and eventually devoured every inch of him I could reach. Sweat slicked our bodies together, our pulses raced in time, and I swallowed his every gasp.

Joe's hands roamed my back. He scraped his blunt nails over my heated skin and growled filthy words in my ear. "Touch me."

His dick was like steel, trapped between us. I squeezed it and jacked him in time with the thrust of my cock.

"*Jesus!*" He jerked up, breaking the rhythm, and my dick slid into him harder. "I'm gonna come."

I bent down to kiss him again, driving my tongue into his mouth. "Do it."

"Harry—"

Joe's face contorted, and he screwed his eyes shut until I gripped his chin and forced him to look at me, my other hand still pumping his cock.

"Eyes on me," I whispered. "I wanna see you."

Joe's only answer was a frantic moan, and his gravelly cry shot through me like a spark on dry tinder. My own release roared to life, kept at bay only by the desperate need to watch him fall apart—eyes wild, skin stretched taut over his straining muscles. *Fuck, he's so beautiful.* I'd seen him come before, but not like this—with his whole body, every facet of him given over to the pleasure coursing through him.

Bearing witness to it tipped me over the edge. I rose up on my knees, clutching one of his thighs to me like an anchor, and fucked him harder, driving every shudder and shake from him until I exploded with a guttural groan.

For long moments, my world narrowed to my whited-out vision and Joe's laboured breaths. And it was perfect. My veins sizzled with aftershocks and a quiet peace stole over me.

It was a while before the van returned to my consciousness. Joe was still wrecked, so I cleaned us both up and tucked the condom in an old plastic bag, and then I lay down beside him, playing absently with his hair until he seemed to come back into himself.

His grin was sleepy and wonderful. I drank it in, but reality bit down hard. "You never told me what happened with your dad."

Joe's sigh was barely audible. "There isn't much to tell. I rounded him up, yelled at him for being a pathetic human being, then felt bad about it because he slapped me with a guilt horse."

"A what?"

Joe's hand drifted to his abdomen. I covered it with my own. "Does it still hurt?"

"Nah. Just feels a bit, uh, jumpy, sometimes. It's hard to explain."

"Tell me about the guilt horse instead then."

Joe sat up, wincing a little. "He reckons he took the gun from Dicky McGee to stop him shooting some other twat's thoroughbred. And he's probably telling the truth; it's the kind of arsehole thing Dicky would do."

"Why does that make you feel guilty?"

"Because I'd probably have taken the gun too."

I thought back to the random details Joe had let slip about his father over the past few months, usually after some whisky. "But you wouldn't have driven drunk and crashed the caravan. Or stashed the gun on the farm."

"Maybe not, but I've made plenty of mistakes that have hurt people."

"Haven't we all? Being hurt is part of being human."

Joe rolled his eyes. "Don't be so fucking reasonable."

"Sorry."

"Liar."

He had me there. We got dressed and Joe drove us back to the farm. I kept my hand on his leg the whole way and wondered what it would be like to lie back on the wide bed upstairs in the farmhouse and let him climb all over me—ride me, fuck me . . . own me.

"What are you smirking about?"

I glanced at Joe and then out of the window in surprise. I hadn't noticed the van pulling up in the yard. "Nothing in particular. What are you doing now? Fancy a nap?"

Joe's grin was weary. "And then some, but I've got shit to do. George is off this afternoon, and Toby's gone back to school."

"Already? Damn." The weeks were flying by.

"What about you?" Joe asked. "Are you going to bed?"

How could I with him out working? Though I knew he'd never let me help him after I'd spent a night in the cells. "I've got stuff to do too. Find me later?"

Joe nodded. "Sure."

"What's up?"

"Hmm? Oh, nothing. I was just thinking about your book."

"My book? What about it?"

"Are you nearly finished?"

The question was left field and totally out of the blue. Joe had always seemed bewildered when I talked about my writing work, and so I hadn't much. "I suppose so. It's a bit ragged at the moment, but I guess it's coming together."

Joe stared hard at something behind me. "What will you do when it's done?"

"Um . . . send it to my agent, I guess."

"No, I mean what will you *do*?"

"What I did before. The book thing isn't my normal, thank God, because I'm starting to hate it. I'm due back at the hospital clinic in a few weeks, whether it's finished or not."

"Right."

Joe's expression was unreadable, and the implication of what I'd said took a beat too long to sink in. But when it did, it was like the bottom had dropped out of my world. The last twenty-four hours had been so intense that I'd somehow forgotten my temporary status on the farm. That returning to my real job—my real *life*—meant that I'd be leaving for good in a couple of weeks.

Leaving Joe.

I felt sick. Joe took my hands and curled his fingers around them. "I don't want you to go."

"Joe, I—"

"Don't." He put his finger to my lips. "Don't say anything, okay? My head's fucked, the farm's fucked . . . I've got nothing to offer you, but I need you to know that I love you. I don't need you to say it back."

He got out of the van before I had a chance to respond. I watched him jog across the yard and disappear around the barn before the words formed on my kiss-swollen lips. *Oh, Joe. I love you too.*

CHAPTER NINETEEN

Joe

I didn't expect Harry to come after me—to chase me down and match my pound-shop declaration—but I was kind of taken aback when I came back from the barn to find his car gone.

"Peeled out of here an hour ago," Sal said. "Didn't say where he was going, but he had a bag with him."

My heart sank. Deep down, I knew Harry would never up and leave without telling me, but the fear was still real.

I spent the afternoon catching up on the little jobs around the farm that never seemed to get done. Keeping busy kept my mind quiet and my heart steady, but when I returned to the house that evening and found Harry still gone, the disquiet came back.

Exhausted, I threw myself into a chair at the table and slumped forward with my head on my arms. Sal brought me tea and rubbed my shoulders, but her comforting touch wasn't enough for me anymore, and she seemed to know it.

"Any news from your dad?"

As if on cue, the phone rang. I hauled myself up to answer it and listened to Jonah as he reeled off his dire straits. "So they're not giving you bail?"

"Nope. Just as well, though, eh? 'Cause I reckon Dicky will have burned my place down by now."

I couldn't figure out if he was talking metaphorically, and I didn't much care. Jonah had long ago lost, broken, or pawned anything that meant something to him. "What about the horse he was going to kill? Do I need to do something about that?"

"Don't expect so. Reckon the geezer had time to sell his horses while Dicky was coming after me."

Was that your plan all along? But I didn't bother asking. Jonah's plans never panned out. Any positive outcome was a stroke of pure luck. "How long will you be on remand for?"

"They didn't say."

"Do you need anything?"

"Nothing that they'll let me have down the prison, lad. Look after your ma, like you always do. Everything else will come right."

And then he hung up, leaving me with another rock of despair in my gut. I put the phone back and closed my eyes, trying to claw back the bliss I'd felt with Harry on the edge of the cliff. When he'd pushed inside me and speared me with a gaze so piercing I'd felt it scrape my bones.

But I couldn't find it, so I retreated to the table and went back to sulking until I remembered my own phone in my pocket. It was switched off, my newfound habit when I was with the horses. I powered it up and tossed it on the table to sort itself out—damn thing was running an operating system so old that it took about a week.

Sal came to the table with a sandwich and tutted when I pushed it away. "You're getting as bad as Harry, going off your food when you've got a flea in your ear."

"He doesn't have a flea in his ear, Ma. He just doesn't like food when he's stressed."

"Why's he stressed? Have you fallen out?"

"Hope not. I told him I loved him."

I hadn't meant to spill my guts to my mother, but sometimes it went down that way, and I wasn't ashamed. How could I be when my ma was a fucking angel?

Sal heard me out—I spared her the gory details—and said nothing until I'd talked as much as I was ever going to. Then she drew the teapot across the table and topped up my mug. "Sweetheart, I don't know much about romance these days—if I even ever did—but if that big boy doesn't love you right back, I'll eat my yard boots."

"You never wear your yard boots."

"So? Doesn't make them any tastier, does it?"

"You fucking loon."

Sal cuffed me playfully. "Don't talk to your mother like that. You know I'm right."

Perhaps I did, but was that really the problem? "I know he cares about me . . . about all of us. But he's got a life in London, Ma. A job at a hospital—patients and stuff. Even if we did some lame co-dependent, long-distance thing, we'd never see each other. He works as much as I do."

"What do you *want* him to do?"

I rolled my eyes, because if she didn't know the answer to that, she was as daft as me. "It doesn't matter what I want. It can't happen."

Sal gave me a look—*the* look, which meant that she was about to say something that I'd better not dare argue with. "Joe, this farm doesn't keep going with us thinking that things can't be done. If you want that boy to stay here and share this life with you, you've got to tell him. Give him the *choice*. Nothing is impossible if you want it enough."

"Bollocks. I want a new stable block and a credit account at the organic feed place. Can't have that, can I?"

"Not right now. But things change. If they didn't, none of us would still be here."

My ma could be a wise woman when she wanted to be, but

on this occasion, I couldn't see how she could possibly be right. Asking Harry to live on the farm was easy. I'd do it in a heartbeat if I didn't know how much it would kill him to refuse. Whether he loved me or not, I couldn't be sure, but—

The phone rang again, the ear-splitting peal startling me out of my introspective melodrama. Sal answered it and passed it over when the caller identified themselves.

It was Newquay police station and I couldn't help but laugh as they explained the reason for the call. "You've just locked my dad up for the foreseeable and now you want me to do you a favour?"

"If you wouldn't mind," the policewoman said. "The RSPCA can't come out until tomorrow, and there's all kinds of animals on this property."

"How many horses?"

"I'm not entirely sure."

"I don't have the space for more strays as it is. I'm still housing the last lot."

"I appreciate that, Mr. Carter, but if we can't round some of these animals up, we'll have to call a vet . . ."

And so it went on. Luckily for the nags, wherever I was going, two of our younger horses had been donated to a riding school the week after I'd come home from hospital, freeing up a couple of stalls if some old timers went back to sharing. Maybe it wouldn't come to that, but who the hell knew anymore?

I took the location down and relayed the message to Sal. "I'm heading out. Did George put diesel in the horsebox? It conked out on me yesterday."

"I don't think so, luv. He got caught up trimming hooves. Said he'd do it tomorrow."

Damn it. Though I couldn't really complain. Bending to trim hooves had been impossible for me in the weeks after Shadow booting me, and George had picked up the slack.

Keeping the vehicles running was my responsibility, and I'd fucked it up.

Again.

"I'll take the van," I said. "If there's anything to come back, I'll pick some diesel up on the way."

I left Sal in the kitchen and hit the road, driving out of town and all the way down to Redruth where the police waited for me at a sprawling property that was nothing like the shit holes they usually dragged me out to.

A sergeant showed me inside, and for the first time in years, I was truly shocked by what I saw. Most of the house was empty, but a living room that was larger than the entire ground floor of my house housed a gang of more cats than I'd ever seen in one place. Dozens of them, all in various states of health, and the room stank to high heaven. "Erm, you know I run a horse farm, right?"

"There's a horse here," the sergeant said. "Goats too. They're out the back."

I shook my head and followed him outside. In the garden were six pygmy goats and a gangly old horse. I clicked my teeth and the horse came to me like a dog, nosing automatically at my hands for treats. He turned up a hay cube and some stale biscuit crumbs, and when he was satisfied that my pockets were bare, dropped his bucket head on my shoulder.

Fucker. Like I needed another reason to take him home. With a heavy sigh, I fished my phone out of my pocket. A message flashed up, but I dismissed it without reading it and called home.

Emma answered. "How bad is it?"

"I've seen worse, but I've got an old boy to bring home and a load of pygmy goats."

"What?"

"You heard."

"Joe, we've only just got rid of the last goat, and that one ate my favourite saddle."

"Shouldn't have left it lying about then."

"*Joe—*"

"All *right*," I snapped. "They'll have to go in Ma's garden then. Just tell her I don't give a witch's tit about her vegetable patch."

"You will when there's no potatoes on your plate."

"Whatever. I'm going to see if I can secure the animals and then come back for the horsebox."

"Okay—" Emma broke off and spoke to someone else at her end. "Don't worry about coming back. George just rocked up with some diesel. He says he'll come to you."

It was the best news I could've hoped for. I tied the old horse to a sturdy tree and studied the lively goats. There was nowhere to herd them, so I'd have to round them up when it was time to go. *Brilliant.* Catching goats had never been my strong point.

I poked my head back in the house to tell the police that I was taking the horse. A woman from a local cat charity was scooping cats into carriers. "Where are you going to take them?"

The woman shrugged. "Home, I'd imagine. My husband is clearing out the garage."

"This lot is going to fit in your garage?"

"Not quite," the woman admitted. "But we'll make it work. Always do."

I liked her. I helped round up the stinky cats and loaded them into her van. When she was gone, I went back to the garden and stood with the cuddly old horse as darkness fell around us. The police ignored me entirely, and I was pretty much asleep on my feet when I heard the horsebox pull into the driveway.

"Took your time," I called out when footsteps approached

me from behind. "Hope you're feeling up to chasing goats in the dark."

There was a pause and then a low chuckle that wrapped around me like the warmest embrace. Harry reached around me and patted the old horse. "Knack to it, is there?"

"If there is, I've never found it. Where've you been all day?"

"I've been into town to poach Wetherspoon's WiFi. Yours is down and I had a lot to—uh—sort out."

"Sounds ominous."

"Not really." Harry grinned. "Let's get this squared away and I'll tell you all about it on the way home."

We rounded up the goats and led the old horse into the horsebox. He seemed unfazed by the gaggle of goats penned in beside him, and I shut the box with a rueful grin. If only all rescues were as simple as this one had turned out to be.

"Um, Joe?"

I glanced at Harry over my shoulder, my skin tingling at his close proximity. "Yeah?"

"I thought you said someone else had taken all the cats?"

"They did." I turned to find Harry with his big arms full of kittens. "What the fuck? Where did you find them?"

"In that shed. I think they're hungry. There's some kitten food in the feed store, isn't there?"

"Are you taking the piss?"

Harry smiled as one of the kittens scaled his broad chest and took up residence on his shoulder. "No . . . the police told me that you were taking all the remaining animals. We can't just leave them here."

"We have a bazillion cats already."

"So, a few more wouldn't hurt?"

My life had become a permanent reinvention of *The Twilight Zone*. I'd gone from chasing my dad around the moors to herding goats in a dead guy's back garden. And now the only person I'd ever truly fallen in love with was waving a bunch of kittens in my face like he wasn't going back to London in just a few short weeks. "Don't go."

Harry blinked. "What?"

"Don't *go*," I repeated, desperation suddenly spilling from me in a torrent of words I couldn't have stopped with a goddam mountain. "Don't go back to London, to your job, to your empty flat—to the gym that makes you feel like shit. Don't go back to the life that makes you so lonely. Please . . . don't go anywhere. Stay here . . . with me, with all of us. We love you—*I* love you—"

Harry deposited the kittens into a wire carrier I hadn't noticed at his feet and clamped his hand over my mouth. "Jesus. Stop, will you? Do you honestly think I *want* to go back to London? That I'm not completely fucking in love with you?"

I fought his hold on me, but I had nothing on his brute strength, and he backed me up against the horsebox with his hand still over my mouth, and his other arm on my chest.

"Joe."

The way he said my name terrified me. Like the end of the world loomed behind the single syllable. I stared at him, trying to read the molten eyes that felt like home. He loved me. Of course he did. I knew that—it was in everything he'd ever said and done for me. But what the fuck did we do now?

Like he'd heard the panic in my mind, Harry pressed his hand harder against my mouth and his forehead against mine.

"Joe," he said again. "I'm not going anywhere, okay? I mean —I have to at some point, to sort my life out . . . That's what I've been trying to do today, but I'm not leaving *you*, Joe. I— I couldn't even if you wanted me to."

His hand slipped from my mouth, but it took me a few seconds to process what he was saying. "You're not going back to London?"

"Not permanently. I've got some things to clear up, and I have to give notice at the clinic and find something else down here, but I want to stay on the farm—with you—if you'll have me?"

"What?"

"You heard me," he said gently. "And I heard you this morning when you told me you loved me. This trip has been a crazy experience for me in so many ways, but I'm not ready for it to end, and the harder I try to contemplate it, the less likely it seems that I will ever be."

"You're staying?" It came out as a whisper but was punctuated by a chorus of discontented meows from the carrier on the ground.

Harry laughed and swept me off my feet, spinning me in a dizzying circle until I didn't know which way was up. "*Joe*, for fuck's sake. I'm *staying*, so let's go *home* so I can feed those cats."

EPILOGUE

Joe

I impaled myself on Harry's dick, grinding down on him so hard that the bed shunted along the floor and hit the wall. *Fuck.* Having him inside me was insane every time, but never more so than when I caught him in the mood to lie back and let me climb all over him.

His dick was as huge as the rest of him, but it didn't take me long to adjust anymore. A warm hand at the base of my spine helped—like it helped with just about everything. Emotion filled me as we fucked bareback in the delicate spring sunshine. I'd never been with someone the way I was with Harry—where everything meant something . . . every word, touch, and kiss. Every heated stare and snatched breath. God, I loved him.

He reared up beneath me, pressing deeper inside me. I fell forward and gasped out his name before I regained some tenuous control. Riding him was always a quick game. My cock bounced between us, hard and weeping, and his gravelly moans and gentle snarl booted me over the edge so fast that I came without touching myself.

Harry laughed as I cursed and drove my fist into the mattress. "You'd think you'd have figured it out by now."

"Shut up." My face was muffled by a pillow. I looked up and scowled at him. "You did say you only had time for a quickie."

"And you never let me down."

As he shot inside me with a growl that sent my eyes rolling again, I couldn't deny it. We spent *hours* fucking at night when we had the time to kick back, but snatched daytime encounters were kind of a kink for me, and my lack of stamina when it came to Harry was a bonus.

After, we lay sprawled together. "What time is the yoga woman coming?"

Harry sat up and reached for his phone. "Three. I haven't got much to show her, but she seems keen."

Of course she was keen. Every alternative therapist in Cornwall had been keen when they'd found out that Harry was setting up a holistic recovery retreat on the old stud farm site. Hell, I'd do fucking Pilates if it gave me an extra half hour with him.

"What about the physiotherapy equipment? When does that arrive?"

"Next week. The floor will be down by then, and the chalets are nearly done."

I nodded, still awed by the progress Harry had made on the site since he'd bought it from me at the start of the year, using the money from his *wildly* successful book. Leaving his patients in London had wrenched his conscience, but having the retreat to focus on had brought him to life in a way I'd only dreamed of when I'd met him. And the financial boost to the farm had changed my life too. I now employed an accountant and a full-time stable hand, which meant the bills got paid, and I had time to stop for lunch and bang the love of my life.

We parted ways for the rest of the day. I tackled the perpetual chaos in the feed store, and Harry went down to the retreat site for a series of meetings I didn't quite understand. Around four, I plucked Clyde and Bonnie—the old boy from the crazy cat house and the last mare from the abandoned barn—and led them down to the retreat. Both horses had proved so affectionate that we'd had a hard time letting them go, and somewhere along the line we'd come up with a potential way for them to earn their keep.

Harry was waiting for me in the space he'd designated for outdoor therapy. Beside him was a slender, olive-skinned man with piercing eyes and killer legs. *Angelo*—the patient-turned-friend who was fucking Harry's brother at the sex club. *City boys*. He'd arrived last night, but I'd been caught up with spreading the muck pile to say hello. Such was *my* life.

I liked Angelo, though. I'd met him at Christmas when Harry had dragged me to London, and it was fucking hilarious to see his pristine designer kicks in my muddy field.

"Piss off," Angelo said when I laughed at him. "Can't look more freaked out than you in Lovato's."

He had me there. Harry and I had stayed in the sex club long enough for us both to decide that public sex wasn't our bag —even if the eyeful we'd caught of Angelo and his boyfriend was something we still talked about now, low and dirty, when we were—

"Joe?"

"Hmm?" I blinked at Harry. "Sorry, what?"

Harry rolled his eyes. "I was saying that Clyde and Bonnie are the horses we're going to use for balance therapy."

Finally something I understood when it came to the work Harry was planning for the retreat. "Aye. Well, you won't get any walking frames steadier than these two."

"That right?" Angelo dodged Clyde's curious nose. "I think we should test that theory."

It was only then I belatedly realised that Angelo was leaning on a pair of funky black crutches. I searched my brain for what little I knew about him aside from his sexploits. *Italian, dancer . . . ME.* Yeah, that was it, though my knowledge of the condition stopped there.

Harry took Angelo's crutches and set them aside while I fitted a special harness to Bonnie that would allow Angelo to lead her while she took most of his weight. It was a work in progress, but Angelo persisted as Harry and I looked on.

"We'll be here all day if that's how long it takes him to walk in a straight line," Harry said softly. "Angelo's a machine, even when he's relapsed."

"You'll have to explain that to me one day," I said. "I'd forgotten there was anything wrong with him."

Harry hummed. "That's why it's so cruel. Look at Bonnie go, though. She's so chilled."

"Or too lazy to misbehave." Not that it mattered. After three months training with a specialist equine therapist, Bonnie and Clyde had more than earned their place in Harry's grand adventures.

When Angelo had done a round with Clyde too, I took the horses back to the stables and gave them a rub down. After settling them with extra feed, I went inside and found Emma at the kitchen table with travel brochures spread out in front of her.

"Going somewhere?"

"Fuck off," she snapped.

Fair enough. I swiped a slice of Sal's fruitcake from the tin and retreated to the living room. The french doors were open and one of the pygmy goats wandered in with some socks it had stolen from the washing line. I was still trying to get them back when Emma appeared a little while later.

"Sorry," she said.

"What for?"

"The usual. Add it to my tab."

I grinned. "Only if you tell what you're up to."

"I want to go on a teaching course."

"Teaching what? Riding?"

"Yeah. My qualifications are old and out of date, so if I want to help Harry, I'll need some new ones."

"Okay. Why do you need to look at mountain resorts in Norway for that?"

"Because I think the only reason I'd get on a plane would be for something I'm passionate about, and I really, *really* want to do this, Joe."

"So do it."

"Right. Like it's that simple."

Of course it wasn't simple. Nothing for Emma ever was, but surely the last year on the farm had shown her that anything was possible?

She wandered off before I figured out if she did, and Harry showed up not long after.

I let the goat have the socks and stood to greet him. "Angelo gone?"

"Yup. Put him in a taxi back to his hotel. He's driving home tomorrow."

"Will he be okay on his own?"

Harry shrugged. "It's up to him to say if he's not. I gave him a cat for Dylan's dad, though, if it's any consolation."

It was. Thanks to Harry, the farm now had more cats that a Greek holiday resort, and the more of them he gave away, the better. "It wasn't Macky, was it?"

"Of course not. I know you can't sleep without him. Hey, are we going surfing tomorrow?"

I ignored the question—we went surfing every morning we could these days—and got up in his face. "Dude, you're the only fella I can't be without."

Harry smiled and wrapped his strong arms around me. "Can't see you ever having to be, so I guess we're both happy, eh?"

And then some. In his quiet way, Harry had turned my

world upside down. I had a life now, a future, and heart fit to burst every time I looked at him. Happy didn't even come close.

HARRY

The retreat opened almost a year to the day since I'd first set foot on Whisper Farm. Angelo and Dylan came down from London, Rhys too, but thankfully they'd somehow just missed each other.

"Shame," Joe said when Rhys's flying visit had come to an end, and Angelo and Dylan had just arrived. "I was looking forward to some mad drama and make-up orgies."

I rolled my eyes. "Angelo's a bad influence on you. Are you sure you don't want to try the club again?"

Joe shuddered, and I laughed, because for all his brass, Joe was a private soul. Fucking in public . . . sharing me with someone else would never be his bag, so as fun as it had been to catch a glimpse of the world my brother and our shared friends called home, we wouldn't be going back.

Didn't stop him beckoning me to the bedroom window later that night, though, and pointing across the farm to the retreat's chalet site. After a day of introductory outpatient clinics, Angelo and Dylan were the only guests staying over, and they were fucking with the lights on, blinds up, and the windows wide open.

Joe nuzzled my neck. "Do they know we can see them?"

"Probably not, though I reckon Angelo gets a kick out of making you blush."

"He does not make me blush."

"Liar."

"Valid." Joe shrugged. "Sorry. You know I love you."

"I do. And I don't blame you for gawping at Angelo. I've

424

told you before that those two used to turn me inside out just looking at me until I found out they knew Rhys."

"They don't—uh—play together anymore," Joe said. "Rhys told me in the pub that he's trying to quit the sex club, and smoking too."

"Interesting. Maybe I'll never have to confess after all. Did he say why he's quitting? The sex club, I mean. Not the fags—that won't happen."

"Oh, ye of little faith. But nope. And I didn't ask about either. I was enjoying my own smoke too much, and I wasn't drunk enough to talk about the sex club. He said something about helicopter training later on, but that might've been about something else."

"Awesome." I rolled my eyes, then let my gaze wander back to the window. Angelo was hauling Dylan onto his back and curving his body around him, slamming into him hard enough to make *my* eyes water. The physio in me was proud of how strong he was, given how tough the last few months had been for him, but the rest of me was torn between mildly mortified and horny as hell.

Joe was apparently happily settled in the horny camp. He dragged me away from the window and sat on the edge of the bed, lining his face up with my crotch. The man had a blow-job fetish, I swear, and my dick was in his mouth before I could blink. He swallowed me whole. My hips thrust forwards of their own accord, and my groan rang out in the thankfully empty house.

I didn't let Joe have his own way for long, though. He'd got the better of me a few times in recent days, and I was game for some revenge. I reclaimed my dick and pulled him to his feet while I stripped his clothes.

Then I shoved him face first on the bed and climbed over him, rubbing my lube-slick cock between his thighs, pressing against him. We'd stopped using condoms months ago, and it was in moments like these that I was grateful for it. When I felt his smooth skin against my dick, and then the tight, wet heat of him clamping around me as I slid home.

I fucked him slowly, revelling in his deep moans, my hands leaving imprints on his flawless back. His injured stomach was finally completely healed and I no longer had to be careful with him. Grabbing his hair and tilting his head back for a crazed kiss. Sinking my teeth into his shoulder. It was rough, primal, and so fucking dirty it was never going to last long.

Joe began to unravel. His entire body quaked and trembled, and his frantic warning poured petrol on the fire in me. I picked up the pace and fucked him harder, faster, deeper, and the answering bolts of pleasure made me lose my mind.

I came with a high pitched, breathless cry. Beneath me, Joe convulsed. He fisted the sheets and hunched his shoulders, his guttural shout muffled by the mattress. Blood roared in my ears, but I somehow found the equilibrium to rub his back and whisper in his ear. "I got you."

For long minutes, I lay on top of him, absorbing his laboured breaths like they were my own, but eventually, I rolled off him, and we sprawled out with our legs tangled together. Joe was shaking—with laughter.

I scowled at him. "What's so funny?"

He pointed at the window. "You do realise they can see us too?"

It hadn't even occurred to me, but when I tried to care, I realised that I didn't. How could I when nothing on earth mattered to me more than having Joe in my arms? Especially when he was naked, laughing, and staring at me from behind his sex-tousled hair.

I pushed the damp strands out of his eyes. "Thank you."
"What for?"
"For today, for yesterday . . . for tomorrow. I wouldn't be who I am now without you."

"Works both ways," Joe said. "I'd probably be doing time with my old man if it wasn't for you."

I shuddered at the thought. Jonah had been sentenced to six years in prison for possession of the firearm found in Shadow's stable, and the only blessing from that had been his extended sobriety. Joe had yet to visit him, but I took Emma every fortnight.

"Don't go to sleep on me just yet." Joe knocked his knuckles on the side of my head. "I want to ask you something."

I forced my heavy eyes open. "What is it?"

"You know how you made me keep back some of the land around the old stud? So the retreat is in both of our names?"

"Um . . . yeah?" I'd done that so the farm benefitted from the retreat as much as I did. The boost from the land sale and regular income from the rent had allowed Joe to take some much-needed time off—to ride Mani on the beach and ride the waves like he'd been born on a surfboard and not in a saddle. "You're not going to try and give it to me again, are you?"

"No, I'm going to give you my house."

"What?"

Joe sat up and reached over me to the bedside table. In the drawer was an envelope, which he tossed to me while chewing on his lip. "Don't get all huffy. It's only fair."

"*What* is?"

"That we share everything. You put half your business in my name, so I want to share mine with you—the farm, the house . . . everything."

"You can't give me the farm, Joe."

"I'm not giving it, I'm sharing it. Listen, will you?"

There was humour in his kaleidoscope gaze, but fire too. I took the envelope and scanned the documents inside. Everything was as he said—the house, the farm was mine as much as it was his if I signed on the dotted line.

"Please, Harry," Joe whispered. "I need this—I need everything we have to be ours."

I couldn't refuse him. I signed the papers and as I thrust them back at him, the final piece of our puzzle slotted into place. I'd had a life before Joe—before the farm and the new life we'd built together, but I'd never belonged anywhere like I did here with Joe. Over the past few months, I'd turned down a second book deal and gone back to blogging, and a weight that had dragged behind me since childhood had faded away.

His, mine, ours, it didn't matter. "Joe?"

"Yeah?"

"I love you."

THE END

BELIEVE

FOREWORD

Big thanks and love to Don, my sensitivity reader. Thank you for giving me authentic insight to your life as a British queer man of colour. Also to my own daughter for enlightening me to what it's like to grow up as a young POC in a very white town. We love you to the moon.

CHAPTER ONE

THE BEAT in Lovato's throbbed in time with Rhys Foster's pulse. He glanced around the club, searching for a prospective partner . . . or two. Perhaps a couple willing to have him join their fun. Men, women, whatever; he was down for it all.

An orgy in the corridor caught his attention—three girls and a dude. *Yeah, I could dig that.* But something made him walk on by, and it was a pattern that continued until he wound up back at the bar.

Disconcerted, he threw himself onto a stool and ordered a beer, anxiety simmering in veins that usually thrummed with excitement when he came to the club. Damn. Was he broken? Or just out of practise? After all, it had been more than a month since he'd last come out to play. *Fuck being a responsible adult if this is where it gets me.*

He drank his beer and a bottle of water, hoping the nagging sensation that he was in the wrong place would pass. But it didn't. And the longer he sat there, the harder it became to ignore. Nonplussed, he drifted to the locker room and retrieved his phone. His sometimes regular fuck buddy, Dylan, was still at the top of his contact list, even though Rhys hadn't seen him and his boyfriend in months. Was it bad manners to call someone up and moan about not feeling the vibe in a sex club?

For anyone else, probably, but Dylan knew the lifestyle as well as Rhys—perhaps better. It was only Angelo's ill health that kept them away from the club, and if anyone would understand Rhys's anxious discontent, it was Dylan.

Rhys bit the bullet and made the call. Dylan answered on the third ring. "Well, hello, you. Are your ears burning?"

"Nope. Nothing's burning. Cold as a wet fish over here, mate."

"Sure about that? Because it sounds like you're in a club."

"I'm in the club, as it happens, but my assessment still stands."

Dylan laughed, and the warmth in his throaty chuckle went a little way towards lifting Rhys's mood. He'd played with Dylan and Angelo more times than he could count, and it was moments like these that reminded him why. Acceptance and friendship combined with the hottest fucks ever, what more did a man need?

Everything, dickhead.

Rhys's humour dropped as swiftly as it had risen. He pictured the last time he'd hooked up with Dylan and Angelo, recalled the absolute love in Angelo's eyes as he'd fucked Dylan raw, and the answering glow in Dylan's gaze as he'd stared past Rhys in response.

Nice.

Not. As beautiful as to had been to witness, and as hot as they were together, by the third go around, Rhys had begun to feel a little lonely. And three months later, nothing had changed. Even Rhys's brother, Harry—who he'd always counted on to be as quietly miserable as him—was now disgustingly and nauseatingly happy.

Fuck my life.

"Um, hello?" Dylan sang. "Did you call me for a reason? Or

just to creeper-breathe down the phone? 'Cause, to be honest, I can get that at work when I man the consultation lines."

"People call Romford Citizens Advice to get their rocks off?"

"You'd be surprised. Or maybe not, given what you've told me about 999 call centres."

"True that."

"So . . . " Dylan said. "Not that I don't love you, but it's a school night. What do you actually want?"

Oops. Rhys hadn't even considered the time. Why would he when he was at the start of a blissful week off work? "Crap. Sorry. I'll let you go."

"That's not what I meant. I'm clearly awake and I'm quite happy to shoot the shit, but you've got to give me something to work with here. Why are you calling me from Lovato's? What's wrong?"

"Nothing's wrong." Rhys stared at his bare feet. "I'm just—um—not feeling it tonight."

"Not feeling what? The club? Hooking up?"

"Both, I guess, though it's nice to be out and about."

"The hooking up then," Dylan said. "Slim pickings?"

"Nope. It's not that." And it wasn't. There were plenty of familiar faces around the club Rhys had enjoyed spending time with before. "I'm just . . . tired of it, I think."

"Sounds like you should've stayed in with a curry and a cuddle."

"Right. Who the fuck is gonna cuddle me? We haven't all got an Angelo at home, you know."

"I do know, actually," Dylan said. "Before I met him, I was lonely too. I'd been hooking up with my best mate and his missus, and I fell in love with them by mistake. Breaking away from that hurt like hell, and the club was going to be my refuge until Angelo came along. I never got the chance to see if it would've done me any good, but I don't think it would have."

"How does you meeting your Italian stallion in a BDSM chamber help me?"

"It doesn't. My point is that if messing around in the club hasn't made you happy yet, it probably isn't going to. I love playing as much as the next fella, but sex can't be a crutch, Rhys. People get hurt—you get hurt."

"Yeah, yeah." But Dylan's words hit home more than Rhys cared to admit. Playing in the club had always been an escape . . . from work, from life, but it had grown to more than that recently, to the point where he'd started looking for the same satisfaction in the outside world—pubs and bars—and found it hard to live with the disappointment when it didn't match up. "I don't know what to do."

"Go home," Dylan said. "You remember what you told me about taking LSD?"

Rhys bit out a laugh. "What does me dropping acid when I was eighteen and raving have to do with anything?"

"Everything. I've never been into class As, but the theory matches up. You told me one of the reasons people have bad trips was because they take those kind of drugs when they're in a bad frame of mind—so the drugs amplify that and give them the worst night of their lives. Perhaps hooking up in the club is the same. You can't deny that it's a high . . . for all of us, not just you."

Ugh. Rhys hated it when Dylan got all psycho-analytical and hated it even more when he was right. Rhys's drunk-arse theory about popping tabs aside, anonymous hook-ups had become his drug of choice, and now it had stopped working.

"Go home, mate," Dylan said again.

Rhys groaned. "But I'm so fucking horny."

"Not the right kind of horny if you're having an anxiety attack in a sex club. Go home and have a wank."

The ridiculousness of the conversation hit Rhys all at once.

He laughed and covered his face with a hand. "Shit. I'm such a disaster. Sorry for chucking it at you."

"Don't be sorry. I'd much rather you called me than you do something you don't want to actually do. Club life is supposed to be fun. When it stops, it's time to chip off home."

The agitation burning Rhys's chest began to dissipate. He let Dylan go and got up from the bench to retrieve his clothes from his locker.

Dressing without the damp residue of a shower felt odd—he'd never left the club with dry hair—but when he got outside, the cool night breeze blew through his mind, taking some of the chaos with it and leaving behind a certainty that Dylan's musings had hit the mark. Since he and Angelo had taken an extended break from partying, Rhys's choice of playmates had varied so much that he could barely remember them—orgies, gangbangs, glory hole adventures, but despite being a regular at the club, the anonymity had grown, eclipsing the affection Rhys had so desperately craved when he'd wandered into the club that very first time. He thought of Dylan and Angelo again, of Harry and the true love he'd found with Joe down in Cornwall.

I want what they have.

Shame he'd have to settle for a solitary pint on the way home.

JEVON CAMPBELL STARED at the bottom of his third empty pint glass. Somehow, it seemed more interesting than the ones that had come before it, but that might've been because he hadn't had a beer in months. The first one hadn't touched the sides; the second had given him hiccups. And now? Well. Now he was that kind of tipsy that could send him to the moon or put him flat on his arse.

Another beer was a sure-fire path to the latter, but he

bought one anyway and went back to stealing furtive glances around the bar. The gay pub was his favourite haunt when he was in the country long enough to indulge his own queerness. Watching. Wishing. Wondering. Absorbing the vibe of men who were comfortable enough to touch and kiss at the bar. To tip each other a wink and leave together, sliding into a waiting cab, or worse, the grimy bathrooms at the back of the bar. Heat pooled in Jevon's groin as he pictured what the latest departing couple would do once they were alone. Kissing, sucking, fucking. *Damn it*. His imagination was a live porn feed that didn't match his proverbial balls.

Deflated, he retied the scarf around his escaping dreads and pushed his half-finished pint away, prepared to abandon it in favour of claiming a bed on his cousin's couch for the night. He had an early start in the morning, so another epic failure at picking up blokes was probably just as well.

"Aw, don't leave. You're the only fella in here under fifty."

Jevon blinked. Somehow, lost in the haze of his own misery, he'd missed the stool beside him becoming occupied. *Jesus. How did I miss him sitting down?* Tall, with inky hair and dark stubble that was just thick enough to be called a beard, the man was *gorgeous*. Jevon reached blindly for his glass. "I wasn't going anywhere."

"Good." The man's smile made his eyes gleam. "Because I've had a shit day and I could use a pint with someone who isn't cruising this place for a Grindr hook-up."

Grindr. Another arena that terrified and fascinated Jevon in equal parts. "I'm not cruising. Just having a beer, man."

The dark-eyed man nodded. "Awesome. I'll get you another. I'm Rhys, by the way."

"Jevon." They shook hands, Rhys's white skin alabaster pale against Jevon's own Brit-Caribbean complexion. Rhys's palm was warm and rough, and the heat of his touch spread through Jevon like wildfire. Like they'd met before, and the current zipping through Jevon's veins was a reconnection of something that had been there for years. *What the fuck?* Shocked, he shivered and knocked back the rest of his pint in a desperate swallow.

Rhys didn't appear to notice and turned away to attract the barman while Jevon inhaled a shaky breath and tried to get himself under control. *Christ. It's not like you've never talked to a bloke before.*

"IPA do you?" Rhys asked.

Jevon nodded, and a fourth pint of ale appeared in front of him. He eyed it warily, already half cut, but the reckless side he rarely indulged won out for once, and Rhys slid the beer closer to him. "Thanks."

"Welcome." Rhys clinked glasses with him and turned on his stool to face him, their knees a hairsbreadth from touching. "So . . . I haven't seen you in here before."

"Come here often?"

"Recently, yeah. I bought a flat up the road a few months ago."

"In Whitechapel?"

"Nah. Brick Lane."

"Where did you live before?"

"Romford."

Jevon nodded. "My uncle lives in Romford. Across the road from the sex club. Can't remember its name."

Rhys coughed through a mouthful of beer and wiped his mouth with the back of his hand. "Lovato's. Ever been?"

Jevon covered his flush with a swig of his own drink. "Can't say I have. So why did you move?"

"Work mainly," Rhys said with a shrug. "But other reasons too. I lived in Romford for fifteen years, man—since I was sixteen. That's way too long for a shithole like that. Same faces, same fucks . . . it wasn't doing me any good, you know? Habit draws me back there sometimes, but I'm getting better at fighting it."

Jevon ignored the comment about fucking—had to or he'd lose his damn mind—and did a quick calculation. Sixteen plus fifteen meant Rhys was thirty-one, older than he looked, and two years younger than Jevon. "I think sometimes we have to give life a kick to keep it moving."

"True that," Rhys said. "It's so easy to come home every night, be doing the same old shit, and not realise that the world's a different place when you step out the next day."

Jevon smiled wistfully. "I hear you. But it's not quite like that for me. I work away a lot, so sometimes months pass before I notice that I've fucked up at home."

"Where is your home?"

"I don't really have one at the moment. I sold my flat last year, so I crash with family when I'm in the city. Maybe I'll buy again someday, but I can't be bothered right now."

It was a shortened version of the truth, but Jevon didn't feel like explaining his eccentric way of life just yet—or even at all, if this came to nothing. Which it would, because even if he hadn't been getting on a plane the very next day, he had no idea how to ask someone like Rhys if he could see him again.

Luckily, Rhys's interest in the property market dried up. He bought a couple of tequila shots and slid one Jevon's way. "You know you're way too hot to be sitting in a gay bar on your own, right?"

"If you say so." Jevon toyed with the tiny glass. "I don't come to these places much, so I don't keep up with the etiquette. Is banging in the toilets the thing now?"

Rhys snorted. "It is around here. Ain't *my* thing though. I don't mind fucking in public but it's gotta be somewhere clean."

Another zap of heat buzzed through Jevon's veins, turning his body into a live wire of unfulfilled sexual tension. He imagined taking Rhys by the hand and leading him to a dark corner, dropping to his knees, and—*Right. Like you'd even know what to do with a cock in your mouth.*

Perspective returned like the grim reaper and Jevon almost laughed, but Rhys's questioning frown stopped him. Jevon shrugged. "Sorry. I'm a bit leathered."

Rhys nodded. "Fair enough. I'm halfway there myself. Fancy some fresh air? My place is five minutes away."

Jevon gulped. He'd heard propositions like that before but never from anyone he'd have considered going home with. *Am I tripping?* The suggestive twinkle in Rhys's dark gaze seemed like a dream, but the pounding in Jevon's chest was all too real. "You want me to come back to your place?"

"If you want to," Rhys said. "You seem like you've had enough of this place for the night, but I'm kind of enjoying your company, so . . ."

"What if I'm an axe murderer?"

Rhys shrugged. "There's been nights when I wouldn't have cared if you'd killed me in my sleep. You wanna do it now, I'd call that fate."

A shadow clouded Rhys's wry humour. It was fleeting—gone so fast someone else might not have seen it—but Jevon saw it. How could he not when his life's work was to chase shadows away?

He slid from his stool in a motion that could've been smooth three pints ago and closed his hand around Rhys's wrist. A spark flowed from where they touched to Jevon's already thumping heart, and he swallowed, gripping Rhys tighter and chancing a glance to find him transfixed by Jevon's hand on him.

Whoops. Jevon let go, but Rhys inhaled sharply and quickly reclaimed Jevon's hand, pulling him forward. Jevon stumbled. He collided with Rhys's shoulder, and they were inexplicably kissing.

The world exploded. Rhys smelled of beer and mint and

cologne. His lips were rough and unyielding, his jaw scraping Jevon's face, and Jevon's whole body caught alight.

But too soon, it was over. Rhys pulled back, his eyes wide, and panic seized Jevon's chest. Fear of rejection roared in his ears like a gathering storm and he willed himself to walk away first. But he couldn't. *I want this. I need this. Please, let it be real.*

"Fuck it." Rhys tightened his grip on Jevon's hand and yanked him outside. He pushed Jevon against a cool brick wall and kissed him again.

Jevon gasped. *This is madness.* It seemed like mere moments ago that he'd been disparaging men who apparently couldn't wait until they got home, and now he was snogging Rhys in a grotty alleyway. *How did this happen?*

As they kissed again, over and over, he had no idea, and the will to care evaporated. He slid a hand under Rhys's jacket, roaming the hard flesh there, then grasped Rhys's bearded jaw. The contact grounded him as Rhys bruised his lips, but did nothing to calm the inferno raging in his blood. Heat pooled in his groin. Tension fought the constraint of his tight jeans and a desperate moan escaped him.

A rumbling groan shuddered through Rhys too. He kissed Jevon one more time, then broke away, dropping his head onto Jevon's shoulder, breathing heavily. "Wow. I only meant to ask you if you wanted to get some cans and watch *Match of the Day*."

Jevon swallowed, his heart kicking the shit out of his ribcage. "Sorry."

Rhys chuckled darkly. "That's not what I meant."

"What *did* you mean?"

Rhys pressed harder against Jevon, the dark sweatpants he wore doing nothing to hide the bulge inside. "I've been trying really hard not to do things like this."

"Kiss blokes?"

"Pick up blokes in bars."

"Oh." Having spent most of the last year trying to find the courage to do just that, Jevon didn't know what to say. Disappointment warred with relief. Rhys was the bones of every fantasy he'd ever had, but his confidence and poise were terrifying. *I don't know how to be with a man like this.*

Rhys sighed and knocked his head on Jevon's shoulder. The outline of his cock against Jevon's thigh was distracting—consuming—but Jevon forced himself to meet his gaze as he traced Jevon's lips with the tip of his finger. "My brain's imploding," Rhys whispered. "But I'm not an axe murderer either. Come home with me . . . please?"

IT TOOK Jevon all of three seconds to decide to go home with Rhys. Nerves still raged in his gut, but the ever-rising booze buzz made them easier to ignore as Rhys kept hold of his hand.

They wove through the busy London streets. No one glanced their way, but Jevon felt their connection like a giant neon sign and kept his head down, not looking up until they reached a converted apartment block.

Rhys fumbled with his keys, laughing at himself as he dropped them multiple times. "Sorry," he said. "I'm not usually such a twat."

A slightly hysterical chuckle burst out of Jevon. "It's okay. I've made a living at being a bit of a twat."

Rhys shot him a quizzical glance, but the door swung open before Jevon could explain himself.

He followed Rhys inside and up a utilitarian staircase. "You don't use the lifts?"

"Nah. I like my food too much."

Made sense, though from behind, Jevon couldn't see what Rhys had to worry about. His legs were long and lean and led up to a perfectly round arse that begged to be touched, kissed, bitten . . . fucked—

Jesus. Had tequila always made him this horny?

Rhys's flat was on the third floor. He unlocked the door and beckoned Jevon inside, flipping the lights on to reveal a tidy studio apartment. "The sofa folds out to a king-size bed."

"Okay." Jevon gulped, cold sweat beading the back of his neck. Was he really going to do this? Hook up with a bloke so gorgeous it was hard to believe he was real? *What if—*

"Hey." Rhys appeared in front of Jevon and snapped his fingers. "We don't have to do anything if you're not feeling it. Things got heavy at the pub, but I meant it when I asked you back for a drink and some TV footie. I've got a wicked bottle of Grey Goose, and I genuinely enjoy your company."

Jevon swallowed thickly again. "I don't know how you figure that when we've only spent ten minutes chatting, but it's not— it's just—" Just *what?* Was he really drunk enough to reveal something so personal to a man he'd just met? "I—uh—haven't done this much."

"Ah." Understanding dawned on Rhys's face. "And here's me laying it all out like a professional or some shit?"

Another nervous chuckle escaped Jevon. "I didn't think *that.*"

"Good. Not that there'd be anything wrong with it. Rent boys get laid for kicks too."

"Are you a rent boy?"

"No. But I've hooked up a lot, so that's probably why I'm coming across a bit cold. Sorry, mate. It's habit. To be honest, I'm nervous too. It's been a long time since I brought someone home."

"Thought you said you hook up a lot?"

"I said I *have.* I don't anymore."

"Why not?"

"Because someone told me about two hours ago that it wasn't making me happy, and they were right." Rhys took a step closer to Jevon. "Wow. You're shaking. You really haven't done this much, have you?"

"I haven't done it at all."

Silence. Then Rhys's eyes widened. "You're a virgin?"

"Not exactly." Heat crept up the back of Jevon's neck. "I've been with women—lots of women—but I realised a few years ago that I was more attracted to men and that I was probably on the gayer side of bi. Just haven't had the balls to do much about it since."

Jevon braced himself for another round of awkward silence, or even amusement on Rhys's part, but Rhys merely shrugged and slugged Jevon's shoulder. "Makes sense. I'm bi too, so you're welcome to test the waters with me, but that's not why we're here, okay? Let's get the vodka out and talk. Don't worry about anything else."

It was the best offer Jevon had ever heard in his entire life. He poured vodka into tumblers while Rhys kicked off his shoes and unfolded his bed.

"More comfortable," Rhys said when he caught Jevon tracking him. "If we do get fruity, it's a pain in the arse to stop and piss around with levers and pillows."

The idea of getting fruity was still making Jevon dizzy. He tipped a shot of vodka down his throat and poured another, trying not to imagine how it would feel to have Rhys's solid body pressing down on him. They were pretty evenly matched in size, but everything about Rhys told Jevon that if anything physical happened, he'd be entirely at Rhys's mercy.

Rhys sprawled on the bed and eyed Jevon hovering in the doorway, still clutching the vodka. "Are you hungry?"

"Hmm?"

"Hungry," Rhys repeated. "It's pretty late, but the pizza place downstairs delivers until midnight."

It took a lot for Jevon not to be hungry, but being alone in a flat with a bloke who'd made it clear he wouldn't mind getting naked was probably at the top of the list. He shook his head. "Nah. I'm good."

"Are you staying?"

"What?"

Rhys grinned. "You look like you're about to scarper—which is fine, by the way. I wouldn't be offended, but leave the vodka behind. I've got a week off work and I plan on spending at least one night of it off my rocker."

He turned his attention to the TV and switched it on, grumbling at the SKY remote until it did what he asked. *Match of the Day* came on, and the familiar theme tune took Jevon back to his grandfather's house in Brixton. If he hadn't been sick with nerves, he'd have been able to smell the jerk chicken.

Chill, you fool. He's not asking you to bend over.

Another conflicted shudder ran through Jevon. He'd imagined himself doing just that so many times that it had begun to seem real—like something he'd done enough that it had become unremarkable. But at the same time, picturing it gave him goosebumps. Could he do that? Did he even want to?

Lacking any better ideas, he toed his boots off, ventured forward with the vodka bottle, and held it out.

Rhys closed his fingers around it. He didn't touch Jevon, but a spark hit Jevon all the same, and he leaned forward as though Rhys had tugged on a puppet string. The vodka bottle fell to the bed and Rhys was up on his knees before Jevon could blink. His hands ghosted to Jevon's face, his thumbs skimming Jevon's jawline. He closed his eyes and pressed his lips to Jevon's, gently at first, but then harder when Jevon tentatively responded.

The world shifted differently to the first time—in the pub and outside in the alleyway. This time, Jevon's limbs trembled, but Rhys held him steady, controlling him and controlling the kiss, like he sensed that Jevon was hanging on by a thread. Their chests collided, but gently. Their breaths shortened, but slowly

—casually—and Jevon didn't lose his mind, his sanity, or the hope that he could see this through.

Rhys pulled back with a low chuckle. "We're getting good at that."

Jevon laughed too. "Practise, eh?"

"If you like." Rhys winked and fell back on the bed, beckoning Jevon to join him. "Do you mind if I ask you some stuff?"

Jevon lay down, surprised by how natural it felt to stretch out beside Rhys. "Stuff? Sounds ominous."

"Not really. I just want to make sure I don't push you too hard."

"Sounds like you wanna be my coach," Jevon blurted with a vodka-loose tongue. "Like those porn films."

Rhys shifted onto his side. "Can you imagine? I mean, I don't think I've got time to teach you everything in one night, but still. I can't deny thinking about it is just about killing me."

For the thousandth time since Rhys had walked into the pub, heat crept up the back of Jevon's neck. "You're thinking about fucking me?"

"Amongst other things, but right now I'm wondering if you've ever been naked with a bloke at all. Like, just lie around with someone, shooting the shit. When I first figured out that I liked men, it took a while for me to relax around them, and until then, sex was awful."

"Awful?"

"Yup." Rhys smoothed a wayward dread back from Jevon's face. "I was so worked up about getting to touch a bloke's body for the first time, I forgot to enjoy it. Too busy shaking and shouting *Oh my god, it's a real-life dick* in my head."

Jevon laughed again, despite Rhys's touch and close proximity eliciting all the responses Rhys was warning him about. "The shit that goes through my head when I'm anywhere near a queer man is unbelievable."

"It probably isn't. We've all been there."

Jevon would have to take Rhys's word for that, as he couldn't imagine him being anything other than the beautiful, chilled-out man who was touching his face. "I haven't been naked with a fella outside of football training. Tried a couple of times, but it's never quite panned out, and I don't get much chance to put that right."

Rhys hummed, his hand travelling idly down Jevon's neck, lingering at his collarbone. "I'm going to take my T-shirt off. You can touch me if you want, or we can just watch the telly. Either way is fine with me."

His hands slid from Jevon and he rolled away, lifting the hem of his T-shirt as he went. Every inch it rode up revealed a swath of flawless skin, a muscular back, and broad shoulders. Jevon licked his lips, his hands tingled, and he was on his way to hyperventilating by the time Rhys turned back to him, treating him to the sight of his strong chest.

"Jesus fucking Christ," Jevon muttered before he could stop himself.

Rhys raised an eyebrow. "What?"

"*You're* killing *me*."

"Revenge," Rhys replied with a smirk, but he didn't advance on Jevon again. Merely lay back and left the ball in Jevon's court.

Jevon's heart pounded. Again. *Damn. Am I going to make it past this night without having a coronary?* But he battled his nerves and fingered his own T-shirt. He wasn't as broad as Rhys, but he was in good shape, lean and strong. What did he have to lose?

Sober Jevon could probably have written a list, but drunk Jevon fought hard to move past caring. He ripped his T-shirt over his head and tossed it over his shoulder before he could change his mind.

Something flickered in Rhys's dark gaze, but he didn't otherwise react, prompting Jevon to lean forward and reclaim his spot in Rhys's personal space. Rhys's bare skin was so close that it seemed to shimmer, like heat was rising from it. Jevon's hand hovered over Rhys's abdomen, fingers trembling.

"Go on," Rhys whispered. "Touch me."

"You want me to?"

"Yes."

Jevon let his hand fall. His palm connected with Rhys's ripped stomach and absorbed Rhys's answering shudder. He dragged his fingers over every ridge of muscle and slid up to Rhys's chest. Rhys's nipples were perfectly round and pink, and they puckered when Jevon grazed them.

Rhys moaned softly. "That's a jackpot spot for me. Goes straight to my dick."

"Really?" Jevon tried—and failed—to cover his fascination. "No one's ever touched me there."

"Let me?"

Jevon kept his hands on Rhys as he fell onto his back. Rhys came with him and leaned over barely enough to press their bodies together while still leaving room for him to touch Jevon's torso. He mirrored Jevon's hands on him, tracing a path from Jevon's abdomen to his chest, over the intricate tattoo etched on his skin, until he reached his nipples. Rhys skimmed his palms over the sensitive flesh and twisted them lightly between his fingers, grinning when Jevon gasped. "Imagine that with your dick down someone's throat. Or when you're getting fucked."

Jevon groaned. "Stop."

"Stop touching you? Or talking?"

"Talking. Don't ever stop touching me."

Jevon's gritted-out plea seemed to ignite something in Rhys. He wedged a knee between Jevon's legs and slid a hand down to Jevon's hip, raising Jevon's pelvis up from the bed to press against his. The friction was insane, and Jevon's eyes rolled as Rhys kissed him.

His body arched and began a slow, instinctive grind. Rhys

matched it, and the unfamiliar room faded away, taking with it the fact that they were strangers who'd met in the night and never kissed before. Taking with it that Jevon had never kissed *anyone* like Rhys was kissing him now.

Rhys's tongue stroked Jevon's. His teeth grazed Jevon's lips, and Jevon's every breath was lost to Rhys's velvet mouth. His head began to spin. He wove a hand into Rhys's soft hair, holding Rhys to his face, roamed Rhys's back, and eventually slipped below his spine to squeeze the softer flesh there. Rhys answered with a gentle thrust of his hips. The bulge in his sweats rubbed against Jevon's own hard cock, and Jevon broke the kiss with a strangled moan.

Rhys stared at him, his gorgeous chest rising and falling fast enough to reassure Jevon that the heat in the room wasn't all his. "What do you want?"

Jevon shook his head. "I don't know."

Rhys kissed him again and grasped his waistband. "I'm so fucking hard right now. Wanna see?"

"Yes."

"Sure?"

"Yes." Jevon wanted to see, wanted to stroke and taste, wanted to do everything he hadn't ever possessed the courage to do before this night. "Show me."

Rhys shoved his sweatpants down his hips. Jevon reached nervously for the boxer-briefs beneath and sent the underwear the same way as Rhys's sweatpants.

"Eager," Rhys said with a smile and shucked the rest of his clothes.

Naked, he turned back to Jevon and rose up on his knees, his hard cock jutting out from his glorious body. It was cut, and straight, and thickly veined.

Jevon's mouth watered. He scrambled to his knees too, gazed fixed on Rhys. "Can I touch you?"

"Please."

Please. The single syllable went straight to Jevon's own dick. He palmed himself, trying to ease the painful tension in his groin, but his hand didn't linger long. Couldn't when Rhys's cock was like a siren's call. He brushed his fingers from root to tip, revelling in Rhys's answering shiver. "I don't know what to do."

"If you've ever had a decent wank, I reckon you probably know more than you think."

Jevon bit his lip and closed his hand around Rhys's cock, squeezing and pumping slowly until beads of moisture appeared on the tip. He smeared it with his thumb, leaving Rhys sticky, and popped his thumb into his mouth, sucking it clean.

Rhys groaned. "Fuck, you're so hot, and you have no bloody idea."

Jevon released his thumb from his mouth. "I don't know what that means."

"It means get your fucking clothes off."

Rhys spoke gently, giving Jevon every chance to refuse, but Jevon's hands flew to his jeans of their own accord. He unbuttoned them and shoved them down with his underwear. His dick sprang free, rigid and weeping, and Rhys's eyes widened.

"What?"

"Nothing . . . but you have a pretty dick, in case you were wondering."

"Um . . . thanks, I guess? If that's a good thing."

"It is. I'm guessing you haven't seen many up close, but I have, and I can tell you that they ain't all as nice as yours."

The ridiculousness of the conversation briefly distracted Jevon from the fact that Rhys's hard dick was inches away from him, but it didn't last long. Rhys pushed Jevon back on the bed and straddled him, his thighs caging Jevon, his cock sliding along his abdomen.

His kiss was different now, more urgent. More heated. And his touch was more demanding. Jevon fell slack beneath him and gave into it, lost himself in it. His hips rose to meet Rhys, and soon their cocks were grinding together, building a friction that left Jevon dizzy.

He dug his fingers into Rhys's back and cried out, dangerously close to exploding as he wondered what it would feel like to have Rhys ride him, to impale himself on Jevon's dick, as he fucked him from beneath.

The thought was a departure from his usual fantasies, and too much. He broke the kiss, panting. "I want you in my mouth."

Rhys gazed down at him, still slowly thrusting his hips. "Sure?"

"Yes. Stop asking me that."

"Fair enough." Rhys walked up Jevon's torso on his knees and brought his dick to Jevon's mouth, smearing his lips with the sticky head. "Smack me if you want to stop though, okay?"

Jevon had no intention of stopping or of ever letting Rhys and his glorious body out of his sight. But Rhys's dark eyes were serious, so Jevon nodded. "I'll let you know."

"Good boy."

Though wry, the term of endearment was so sweetly erotic Jevon almost wept. Almost, because the emotion fast became a distant memory as Rhys's cock slid into his mouth.

Jevon flattened his tongue and took it all in. Sensation overwhelmed him—choked him—and swallowing around Rhys seemed surreal, like it was happening to someone else and he was watching from a balcony. *Am I really doing this?* Even as he scraped his teeth over Rhys's length, he wasn't entirely convinced until Rhys's gravelly moan invaded his introspection.

"Man, I don't believe you haven't sucked dick before."

Jevon gazed up at him, transfixed by his hooded eyes and flushed cheeks. A retort danced through his mind, but his mouth was crammed full of Rhys's cock, and he had no intention of giving that up.

He sat up slightly to give his neck more scope. Rhys groaned again and gripped the back of the sofa bed. "Yeah. That's right. Suck it. Show me how you want me to suck *your* dick."

The prospect of Rhys returning the favour made Jevon's cock throb. It jerked, and Jevon gasped, sucking harder and working Rhys with one hand while the other flew to his own dick.

Rhys threw his head back and thrust into Jevon's mouth, gently at first, but then with more force as Jevon opened his throat. "Fuck yeah. Jesus. You're good at this."

Jevon hummed on instinct and squeezed his hand around the base of Rhys's shaft. Moisture dripped down from his mouth, slicking Rhys's cock, and he imagined Rhys pulling out, shoving him down the bed, and easing inside him. Or pushing Rhys onto his back, nudging his legs apart, and—

Fuck. Where on earth was his head at now? He'd never pictured himself topping, but the reality of being with Rhys had blasted open a door he'd only had the nerve to peep around until tonight. For the first time since Jevon's attraction to men had made itself known, anything—*everything*—seemed possible.

I want him.

Jevon's composure began to slip as years of unresolved desires broke free, spilling out of him in every gasp and shudder —every groan and violent jerk of his hips as he fucked his own hand.

Rhys's moans grew louder, too, and more frequent, his muttered curses less intelligible. He tightened his grip on the back of the sofa bed and drove his cock mercilessly down Jevon's throat. "God, yeah. Like that. Don't stop."

As if Jevon could. As if he wanted to. He screwed his eyes shut and lost himself to the crazy duel sensations of Rhys swelling in his mouth and his own dick pulsing in his hand. Rhys was getting harder by the second, his thrusts erratic, and Jevon was barely holding on.

And then he wasn't holding on at all.

He lost his grip. Orgasm sluiced through him, and his body arched up from the bed. He came with a muffled scream, choking on Rhys's cock, swallowing convulsively as hot come splattered his belly.

Rhys shouted and fucked Jevon's mouth impossibly harder. "Shit, I'm gonna come, mate." He tried to pull back, but Jevon clamped down and gripped Rhys's hips, holding him prisoner in his mouth as Rhys exploded down his throat. *"Fuck!"*

It seemed to go on and on. Jevon's chest heaved, and his stomach caved in and out, but he couldn't bear to let Rhys slip from his mouth. He sucked and licked Rhys's softening dick until Rhys finally pulled out with a shaky groan.

Rhys collapsed sideways, landing in a heap beside Jevon, panting wildly. He muttered something that Jevon didn't quite catch and slung an arm over Jevon's chest.

Jevon's mind was in bits. His body was on fire, and the confirmation he'd been chasing all this time slotted into place so absolutely that he couldn't breathe. *I'm gay.*

Shit.

Not bisexual—like Rhys—and like he'd assumed himself to be for so long, but *gay*. His encounters with women had been wonderful, but as his heart thudded in his ears, he knew there would be no more.

I'm so fucking gay.

The relief was so intense he almost laughed until he realised Rhys was staring at him. "What?"

"You look like you're freaking out," Rhys said. "If it's because I shot in your mouth, don't worry. I got tested at work a month ago."

Jevon shook his head. "I wasn't thinking about that, and I'm not freaking out. But I'm clear too, in case you were worried. I got tested when my girlfriend cheated on me, and I haven't been with anyone since."

"You have a girlfriend?" Rhys's tone sharpened.

"No . . . I *had* one, a year ago."

Silence. Then Rhys blinked. "Sorry. I misunderstood. I'm all for sexual freedom in relationships—if it feels right—but cheating fucks with my head, you know? Sorry it happened to you."

Jevon shrugged. "It was my fault, really. I pushed her into it so I had a reason to bail."

"Because you were freaking out about liking men?"

"Something like that." Understanding and empathy warmed Rhys's face. Jevon wanted to touch him, but his hands were sticky with jizz. He settled for knocking his head on Rhys's shoulder. "Anyway. It doesn't matter now. I—um—I think I'm gay."

Rhys nodded slowly. "There are worse things to be."

"I'm starting to see that."

"Good. You can't expect the world to accept you if you don't accept yourself." Rhys yawned and flopped onto his back. "I remember when my brother came out, I was waiting for him to start walking tall, you know? Shoulders back, not giving a fuck what anyone thought. But it wasn't like that for him, and it took me a while to realise that labelling himself didn't change the fact that he still didn't know who he was."

"What about you? What happened when you came out?"

"I never bothered," Rhys said. "Because I don't give two shits what people want to call me. Bisexual suits me right now, but it might change. Or it might not. Does it matter? Not to me . . . and that's all that counts when it comes to *my* sexuality."

"I've never met anyone like you."

It wasn't what Jevon meant to say, but Rhys seemed to understand. He sat up on his elbows, sweat glistening on his chest, and nodded toward the tiny bathroom. "Go wash up. We can expand on that when you get back."

Needing a minute and grateful for the out, Jevon slid from

the bed and meandered across the room, legs still wobbling. He sensed Rhys's eyes on his back and tried not to imagine what he might be thinking as he took in Jevon's naked body. He was captivated by Rhys, but though his throat still ached from Rhys's cock and Rhys's guttural shouts still echoed in his head, it was impossible to know how Rhys truly felt.

Perhaps he was humouring him.

Or had a virgin fetish.

A friendly daddy on Grindr had warned Jevon about shit like that once, but as he wiped dried come from his skin and washed his hands, none of it seemed to fit Rhys. His kindness was too authentic, too real, and Jevon couldn't deny the insane heat that simmered between them even now, when they'd both come themselves hoarse.

"We can expand on that . . ." What did that mean? The desire to find out rippled through Jevon, jerking his briefly sated cock back to life. He left the bathroom and padded to the bed, the words to ask Rhys to touch him again dripping off his tongue.

But Rhys was asleep, sprawled on his stomach, naked and beautiful, and perspective returned to Jevon like the beginnings of an autumn rainstorm. Droplets of reality but then a downpour of cold hard facts: Rhys was a stranger asleep in his own bed, and Jevon was a hook-up with a plane to catch.

He gathered his clothes and dressed quietly. Then he kissed two fingers and touched them to Rhys's temple.

Thank you.

CHAPTER THREE

SLEEPING HAD BECOME the curse of the wicked. Torn between imagined monsters left behind in his waking life and the flickers of long brown limbs and innocent eyes of his dreams, Rhys couldn't catch a fucking break. He tossed and turned in his bunk until the crude blast of the base alarm woke him just before dawn.

Autopilot kicked in. He rolled to his feet, grabbed his kit, and dashed to the rooftop with the rest of the scrambled HELIMED crew.

He jumped onto the chopper. A flight doctor he vaguely knew was already on board: an ex-military medic who was satanically good looking and something of a legend when it came to trauma medicine.

Marc grinned and clapped Rhys on the back. "How's tricks?"

"All good." Rhys zipped up his orange flight suit. "What are you doing down here? Thought you'd stuck your boots in up north?"

Marc scowled. "I have, but there's been a cock-up with doc holiday time down here, and I wasn't going to let them ground the chopper, was I?"

"Bible," Rhys agreed.

Marc rolled his eyes. "Bloody young 'uns. Always with the wacky lingo."

"Yeah, yeah. How's Jamie?"

Like the rising sun, Marc's face brightened. "He's good, man. Haven't seen him since Tuesday morning though. Can't wait to get home."

Rhys nodded with as much pleasantness as he could muster, but the sight of someone else so nauseatingly in love turned his stomach. Marc and Jamie, Dylan and Angelo. Harry and his Cornish horseman soulmate.

Fuck's sake.

Rhys slapped his headset on and listened to the briefing as it came through. *Major fire incident. Multiple casualties. Location: Bedford.*

"Bedford?" Rhys glanced at Marc. "That's not in our jurisdiction."

Marc shrugged. "Must be a bad one. Check your kit, then sit tight. Windy out there today."

Great. Despite transferring to the air ambulance way back at the start of the year, Rhys had yet to get used to turbulent flights. Even the calm ones rolled his stomach when he didn't have a patient to concentrate on.

He ran through the pre-flight checks and took his seat as the chopper came to life, closing his eyes to the roar of the rotor blades.

Marc nudged him. "Really? Still? Guess I'm navigating then."

"Fuck off," Rhys muttered without opening his eyes. "You're the one who said it was windy."

And it was. The chopper took off less than two minutes after Rhys had rolled out of bed and was immediately buffeted by strong gusts he hadn't noticed when he'd sprinted to the helipad. He gritted his teeth, reminding himself that the pilots were ridiculously experienced at flying in all weather conditions, that they wouldn't attempt a take-off if it was truly dangerous, but when that didn't work, he settled for a method he'd come to rely on: fantasising about the one who'd got away, AKA Jevon. The charismatic dude who'd done a moonlight flit from Rhys's bed.

Like magic, the juddering helicopter faded away, even with the crew still chatting through Rhys's headset. He blocked their voices and pictured Jevon as he'd last seen him, padding to the bathroom, come splattered on his belly, his tattooed skin sheened with fresh sweat. He'd smelled amazing. Felt amazing, and his every nervous touch had set Rhys on fire, but it was more than that. Hooking up with Jevon had been nothing like Rhys had experienced before. Rhys was a natural bottom, and he'd never dominated a man like Jevon had invited him to. Until that night, getting dicked out had been his favourite escape, and he'd rarely called the shots.

Jevon's way had blown his mind. Three months later and he was still thinking about it. Obsessing over it. Imagining what could've gone down if he hadn't passed out drunk. *Idiot.* He was used to a hangover and an empty bed, but that morning had felt like the end of the world. Still did when he had time to stew on it—which was more than he cared to admit now he'd quit playing around at the club.

The flight out of London took twenty-four minutes. Thoughts of Jevon—his gentle, curious gaze and gorgeous cock— took up ninety per cent of the journey, but a couple of minutes before landing, reality kicked in.

"Jesus," Marc muttered. "That ain't no kitchen fire."

Rhys peered out of the window at the huge clouds of smoke billowing from the compound below. "Might've started as one."

"Nah. The fire doors would've contained it. If that shit ain't deliberate, I'll buy your lunch."

Marc always bought lunch, so Rhys let the latter comment

slide, and he respected Marc's opinion too much to disagree with him. "What is this place?"

"Immigration detention centre," Marc said darkly. "So either an inmate set the fire from inside—some kind of protest, maybe—or we're looking at an outside terror attack."

Rhys suppressed a shudder, but their time to speculate ran out. The chopper landed. Marc jumped out. Rhys followed, and they dashed to the pop-up control point to touch base.

Time ceased to exist. The detention centre housed families seeking asylum, and many of the injured were young. Chopper teams always copped the worst cases, and Marc was immediately assigned to a badly burned teenager. Rhys saw terrible things with such monotonous regularity that blood and gore went over his head. Screaming relatives affected him more, but the boy didn't seem to have any nearby.

Marc stabilised him for transport and they carried him to the helicopter, readying for take-off a mere half hour after they'd landed. With him on board, Rhys went back to collect leftover equipment, and it was only then he noticed a second child crouched on a kit bag.

"Shift up, kiddo," he said. "I need that bag."

The tiny girl stared back at him, apparently oblivious to the chaos around her. "Brother," she said.

Rhys glanced around. "Who is?"

"*Brother*," she repeated.

"Rhys! Come on! We need to go!"

Rhys acknowledged Marc's shout with a wave of his hand and, lacking any brighter ideas, scooped the girl up from the kit bag. He searched the immediate area for anyone with a fucking clue what was going on. Other paramedics and fire crews were all busy, but a G4S worker caught his eye. Rhys approached her, balancing the girl on his hip, the kit bag slung over his shoulder. "She was on her own," he said. "But I think we have her brother in the chopper. Get her taken care of."

There wasn't time to wait for a response. He started to pass the child over, but she dug her fingers into his flight suit and tightened her legs around his torso. "No."

"Come on, kiddo," Rhys said. "I've got to go. This lady will look after you."

"*No*," the girl said again in a perfect echo of their first exchange.

Her grip was fearsome and something in her eyes terrified Rhys, but there was little he could do but detach her tiny hands and force her into the waiting woman's arms.

He backed away and ran to the waiting chopper, slotting into his place opposite Marc. The helicopter took off and Marc shot instructions across the strapped-down gurney, but even as Rhys's mind switched back to autopilot, he found himself glancing out the window as the incident scene grew smaller. The young girl was impossible to spot, but somehow, he still felt her gaze all over him.

<hr>

"THAT'S IT," Marc said. "We're done for the day."

Rhys glanced up from the coffee pot he was surreptitiously emptying into the flight crew's travel mugs. "We're not going back?"

"Couldn't if we wanted to. Chopper's fucked."

Mixed emotions warred in Rhys's tired brain. They'd already made three runs to the fire incident and fatigue had begun to creep over all of them. Going off duty was a relief, but the helicopter was their ride home. If it was grounded, so were they. "What's wrong with the damn thing now?"

"No idea. Someone's coming to look at it, but even if they can fix it, it'll be awhile." Marc glanced at Rhys's handiwork. "Is one of those Pater's? I'll take it to him."

Marc departed with the pilot's coffee, leaving Rhys alone

in the staff lounge they'd been permitted to use. A doctor was asleep in an armchair in the corner. At first glance, he reminded Rhys of Jevon, but closer inspection revealed hair that was too short, skin that was too pale, and actually . . . he didn't look anything like Jevon at all. *Fuck. Will this never stop?*

Scrubbing his face, Rhys turned away and retreated to his own quiet corner to drink his coffee. A nap sounded good, but as the hospital java kicked in, sleep wouldn't come.

Restless, he crept out of the staff room and into the bustling A&E corridor. The department was still in major-incident mode on top of their usual patient numbers, and the quiet hum of civilised chaos got under Rhys's skin, reminding him why he'd become a paramedic and not a nurse. Disaster was a lot easier to face with the rain on your back, the wind in your hair. Indoors, there was no escape.

A nurse hurried past but doubled back when she noticed Rhys. "Did you come from the Smallwood fire?"

"The detention centre?" Rhys nodded. "Yeah. Three times. How's it looking?"

The nurse shook her head. "Horrendous. We have half a dozen fatalities and double that in unaccompanied children. No one speaks English, and we have no idea who belongs to who."

Rhys's mind flashed back to the little girl he'd plucked from the ground. The young man who was likely her brother had died in the helicopter, and he hadn't had time to ponder her fate before now. "Where are they all?"

"Over there," the nurse said, pointing to a curtained off area in minors. "Social services are here, but they don't know their arse from their elbow without an interpreter. Those poor kids."

She shook her head and disappeared in the direction of the unclaimed children. Curiosity got the better of Rhys and he followed her, expecting to be hit with a wall of noise as she pulled the curtain back. But there was none. Beyond the busy department, twelve or so young children were huddled on the floor, silent and staring.

Their haunted faces felt oddly familiar, and Rhys found the little girl almost immediately. She met his gaze, but there was no recognition there, and his heart sank, though he wasn't entirely sure why. He'd held her for mere moments before he'd passed her over. Why would she remember him? "What's going to happen to them?"

The nurse, who was handing out juice cartons, shrugged, but the arrival of a social worker cut her off.

"We found an interpreter at a local charity," the social worker said. "He's on his way, but he wants us to move them out of here and into a private room. Do you have anywhere big enough?"

"I doubt it," the nurse snapped.

She drifted away to find out for certain. Common sense told Rhys to go back to the staff room where Marc could find him, but he lingered anyway, glancing between the silent children and the brisk social worker, absorbing a dynamic that inexplicably made his skin crawl.

It was a while before he realised the social worker was wearing Marks and Spencer chinos. Beige. Wrinkled. And held up by a belt just thick enough to break skin. *Bend over, boy. It's time I knocked some sense into you . . ."*

Rhys inhaled sharply. His father's voice faded as suddenly as it had appeared, but disquiet bloomed in his gut all the same. He shifted his weight from one foot to the other, his flight suit suddenly unbearably tight. Sweat prickled the nape of his neck. *Fuck this—*

"There's a room upstairs," the nurse announced, stepping around Rhys. "It's got nothing in it, but we're rustling up some furniture. Maybe a TV."

The social worker and a couple of nurses mobilised to begin moving the children out of A&E. Rhys kept back as they directed the operation with hand signals, but the little girl he'd encountered at the incident site didn't move.

Rhys pushed past the seemingly inept social worker and picked her up. "Come on," he said. "I'll take you."

The girl showed no indication that she'd understood, but she didn't protest either. Rhys took it as a win and joined the line of exiting children. They passed the staff room to get wherever they were going. Marc spotted Rhys and came to the door.

"That's where you've got to. I've been looking for you."

"Do you need me?"

Marc shook his head, eying the little girl. "Nope. Where are you taking this little lady?"

"Upstairs somewhere. There's an interpreter coming from a local children's charity to help social services sort them out."

"Shame I don't speak much Levantine Arabic or I could've chipped in."

"Levantine Arabic?"

"The families in the block that caught fire were from Homs," Marc said. "Most of my Arabic is Iraqi."

He said something to the girl that Rhys didn't understand. She said something back and hid her face in Rhys's neck.

Rhys frowned. "What was that?"

"She basically told me to piss off." Marc smiled wryly. "And she isn't the first girl to do that, but . . . anyway. I was looking for you to tell you the chopper won't be fixed till morning. I'm going to jump on a train home, but there's another doc coming on shift here tomorrow who'll fly back into London with you."

"Am I kipping here?"

It wasn't unheard of for Rhys to spend the night in a random hospital, but Marc shook his head. "They've booked you and Pater into the Travelodge across the road. Grab what you need from the helicopter and check in whenever you're ready. Be safe, man."

Rhys knocked Marc's fist and continued on his way,

hurrying to catch up with the rest of the children. The trudge upstairs seemed to go on and on, but eventually, the front of the line began to file into an open door. Rhys shifted the child on his hip. "Nearly there now."

The little girl ignored him, but he hadn't expected a response, so it took him a beat to realise that she was staring over his shoulder at something behind him. Rhys turned and goosebumps rose on his skin, tingling on his forearms. He blinked. Refocused. But the reaction made no sense until *Jevon* rode past him on a fucking unicycle.

CHAPTER FOUR

JEVON SAT ON THE FLOOR, his most colourful building blocks spread out in front of him. Most of the children in the room were too old for the game, but experience taught him that distraction therapy worked best in young minds when the leap wasn't too great. Colours. Pictures. Songs. Even the unfamiliar seemed familiar when it was offered so simply.

The children closest—the youngest—were starting to respond. Light sparked in eyes that had been glazed with trauma when Jevon had arrived.

"Come on," Jevon said softly in Arabic. "I'm trying to build a den. Will you help me?"

A small boy inched forward, still out of reach, but further from the shadows than he'd been before. "What kind of den?"

"A safe one," Jevon said.

"Will it protect you from the bombs?"

"There are no bombs here, but yes, it probably would." Jevon laid another block on the brightly coloured wall he was constructing. The hospital officials had clearly thought him mad when he'd arrived with a sack of giant Lego, but as more children crept forward, Jevon stuck the officials an invisible middle finger.

"They're in A&E," the social worker had said when she'd contacted him. "Sitting on the floor."

Jevon had suppressed a growl. "Is that the best you can do? They've lost everything twice over and you can't find them a beanbag and somewhere quiet to sit?"

By the time Jevon had reached the hospital, a room had been found, but he got the feeling that he wasn't the kind of interpreter they'd expected. As he continued to work with the children, he sensed unease behind him. Murmurs. Shuffling paperwork. The clip of footsteps coming and going. At some point he'd have to appease them and extract the necessary information from the Syrian children, but not yet. They weren't ready to tell him, and despite a lifetime of this kind of work, Jevon and the goosebumps on the back of his neck weren't quite ready to hear it.

JEVON FILLED out the penultimate form and passed it to the waiting hospital official. In the hours he'd been on the floor with the Syrian children, more and more corduroy suits had appeared, clutching clipboards and stacks of paperwork. There were dozens of them now, all eying the makeshift shelter Jevon and the children had fashioned from Technicolour building blocks. The structure was small, but just big enough to hide a child as they helped Jevon fill out their forms.

Child by child took a piece of Jevon's heart as they gave up their names and drifted away with the waiting social workers. Many of them had been orphans before they'd fled to Britain. Now they'd lost whoever they'd had left—grandparents, cousins, brothers, and sisters. What would become of them now?

Jevon sighed and turned to the last child—a tiny girl with grubby hands and huge eyes. She'd grafted diligently on the building work but hadn't looked Jevon's way even once. Elsewhere, he'd perhaps have the time to leave her be, to wait for her to come to him, but it wasn't going to pan out like that today.

A pretty pink cloth was poking out of Jevon's play sack. He nudged it towards the girl with his foot. "Can you bring me that?"

He spoke in English, and finally, she cast him a glance. "Why?"

"Because I think we need a roof on this place."

"Why?"

"To keep us dry? It rains a lot here, doesn't it?"

The girl shrugged, and for a long, painful moment, Jevon feared she would go back to staring, unseeing, at the blank walls, but then something seemed to give. She got up and fished the cloth from the backpack. The flowered fabric wound around her wrist and her lips twitched in what—in another life—might've been a smile.

She brought the cloth to Jevon. "Here you go."

"Thank you." He began to drape it over the building blocks. The girl helped, correcting the hash Jevon deliberately made of it, and, little by little, revealed the scraps of information he needed to send her on her way.

With the shelter and the form complete, he scooped her from the ground and carried her to the doorway.

She came willingly enough. Jevon passed her to a social worker, but the girl kicked out and wriggled out of the waiting woman's grip. Her tiny feet hit the floor and she ran with an imaginary wind behind her, reaching the end of the corridor before Jevon could react, throwing herself at a tall, dark-haired man dressed in bright orange. She climbed up him and onto his back, winding her arms around his neck.

The man seemed as surprised as everyone else, and it took Jevon far too long to realise that it was the bloke who'd been haunting his dreams.

It was Rhys.

"JESUS CHRIST." Rhys leaned on the damp brick wall and closed his eyes. *What the fuck is this day?* He'd have struggled to invent a more bizarre chain of events, and as it was, he was struggling anyway. Jevon's sudden reappearance in circus form had nothing on the trauma of giving that little girl—*Haya*—up to social services, and Rhys was about done for the rest of the year. He wanted to go home, drown his sorrows, or find a club to get his dick wet—to screw away the carnage in his mind—but all he had was a scummy hotel room, the clothes he stood in, and a fuckton of unanswered questions about Jevon, the child whisperer.

A hysterical bark of laughter escaped Rhys. *I'm fucking tripping, I swear.*

"Rhys?"

Yup, definitely tripping. Because the voice calling Rhys's name was the one he'd heard in his sleep every night for the last three months—a voice that didn't belong in the drizzly evening outside a Bedford hospital.

"Rhys."

Rhys opened his eyes and Jevon was standing in front of him, his bow tie undone, a unicycle at his feet, and a sack of blocks slung over his shoulder. "You're not real," Rhys whispered.

"Aren't I?" Jevon stepped closer. "What makes you think that?"

"What the *fuck* are you doing here?"

"I might ask you the same thing."

Silence. A thousand replies danced chaotically through Rhys's mind, but nothing coherent formed on his tongue. How could it, when out of everything he'd seen today, Jevon's smiling face had kicked him hardest in the gut? "I don't understand."

"Understand what?"

"Why it hurts so much to see you here."

It wasn't what he'd meant to say, but it came from his heart.

Understanding flickered in Jevon's warm eyes. "I wanted to cry when I saw you holding Haya. All this time, I'd pictured you so happy and free; it fucked me up to know that you'd seen the same horrible side of the world that I have."

Something clicked and Rhys saw logic in the far-fetched explanation. Handing Haya over had cut him to the bone, but harder still had been to watch Jevon disappear with her, his kindness in every whispered word Rhys couldn't decipher. *He's seen what I've seen.*

Whatever that meant.

Right now, it meant everything.

"So you're a paramedic?" Jevon ventured when Rhys didn't respond. "It kind of fits now."

"How?"

"Because you're patient and gentle in situations other people might find ridiculous."

The instant heat that had sparked between them in the bar all those months ago flickered in Rhys's belly. Jevon's clothes, the rain, and the grimy hospital car park faded away, and Rhys saw him as he most liked to remember him—naked and on his back, eyes wide and curious, as Rhys fucked his mouth. Rawness tempered by innocence.

But there was no innocence in Jevon's eyes now, and perhaps that was the disquiet fizzing in Rhys's veins. His recollection of Jevon wasn't real, and the man who'd never been with another fella had lived far more than Rhys had imagined.

"Anyway." Jevon started to turn away. "It was nice to see you again."

Rhys's arm shot out like a coiled spring. He grabbed Jevon's wrist. "Wait. Um—I mean—do you want to get a drink or something?"

"You don't have somewhere to be? A helicopter to get on or something?"

Rhys shook his head. "Nope. Chopper's grounded. I'm stuck at the Travelodge for the night."

Jevon glanced over his shoulder, his expression giving nothing away, but he turned back with a smile. "Fuck that. Come home with me."

CHAPTER FIVE

IT WASN'T AS simple as taking Jevon's outstretched hand and leaving the hospital. Rhys had to collect his emergency overnight pack from the helicopter and tell Pater, the pilot, exactly where he was going.

Which turned out to be not very far at all. Jevon was renting a small house a couple of streets away from the hospital—the perfect distance, apparently, for unicycling home.

Still half convinced he was walking in a dream, Rhys traipsed beside him, trying not to get caught admiring Jevon's lithe, agile frame or notice the stares they picked up along the way. "Do you, uh, cycle this way often?"

Jevon chuckled. "No. Believe it or not, I don't spend much time roaming Bedford dressed like this."

"Why are you here? In Bedford, I mean. I thought you were from London."

"I am." Jevon expertly manoeuvred the unicycle up a kerb. "But I don't have a place there at the moment, and I wanted to save some money before I go away again."

"Away?"

"Yes. For work. I don't spend much time in this country."

Flickers of past conversations echoed in Rhys's head. "So, you're an Arabic speaking clown."

It wasn't a question, but Jevon snorted anyway. "I do some clown work, but not in the scary, painted-face sense. I'm actually a play specialist. I work for the Free to Fly Project."

"The what?"

"FFP—it's an organisation that provides play therapy for children traumatised by conflict and war—singing, dancing, art and crafts. Just generally being silly, really. Kids need to be kids, man. No matter what we've done to destroy where they were born."

"Wow. Do you work in Syria?"

"God, no. We wouldn't survive that even if we could get in. I've just come back from a camp on the Greek/Macedonian border. Lots of displaced people have been stranded there since Europe started closing entry routes."

"How on earth did you end up doing that?"

Jevon directed Rhys down a street lined with small terraced houses. "I did half a social work degree, then literally ran away to join the circus. An OXFAM guy came to a show one night with a big idea, and it went from there—from the trapeze to a war zone in less than a week. Oh hey . . . this is my place."

He stopped outside a house with a red front door and leapt from the unicycle like a cat. Then he took Rhys's hand again and tugged him up the path.

"You don't have to pull me everywhere," Rhys muttered dryly.

"I know. But you look a little lost. I don't want you to fall through the cracks in the pavement."

It made about as much sense as everything else in the last few hours. Rhys let it go and followed Jevon into the house. Inside was cosy and cluttered with circus paraphernalia. The bright colours drew Rhys in, and he wandered around the living room, fascinated, while Jevon went to the kitchen for beer.

Jevon returned with cans of Red Stripe and a bottle of Coruba. Rhys shuddered. "Don't give me any of that rum. I've got to fly tomorrow and I have enough trouble not upchucking on the patients as it is."

"You don't like flying?"

"Not particularly."

Jevon tilted his head sideways, his frown questioning.

Rhys shrugged. "There was a brief shortage of flight paramedics last year and I was offered the chance to be seconded from the NHS. Working on the road ambos . . . damn, we need the choppers in the air, you know? There's too many kids dying in traffic jams."

"There are too many children dying at all."

"Do they die in the camps?"

"Sometimes." Jevon's lovely face clouded with sadness. "People fleeing don't always have access to medical care on route to the camps. I've seen folk show up with limbs hanging off a few times. But the disease is the worst. Camps like that aren't exactly sanitary. There was a cholera outbreak a few months back."

"Wow."

"Yeah. It was pretty awful. I'd done some clown doctor work at Great Ormond Street before I signed up for FFP, but it's nothing like working in a DP camp."

The acronyms meant little to Rhys for a moment. He popped the tab on his beer and muddled through it. *Free to Fly Project. Displaced persons camp.* "What the fuck is a clown doctor?"

Jevon laughed. "I'll show you."

It took a bit of rummaging, but several boxes—and beer cans—later, Jevon unearthed a wooden stethoscope and yet another day-glo bow tie. "See? No Ronald McDonald shit. *Anyway,* kids get pretty lonely and frightened when they're in hospital, even if their parents stay with them. You'd be amazed what ten minutes with a fake doctor can do for that."

Rhys was already feeling amazed. He'd obsessed over the Jevon he remembered for months, but he could easily fall in love with the Jevon in front of him now. Instinct drew him forwards, and he closed the distance between them in one step, invading Jevon's personal space like he did it all the time. Like this was fucking normal. Like he'd kissed Jevon every day for the last three months instead of dreaming about it.

Their lips met. Rhys gasped, inexplicably shocked when it was him pushing Jevon against the wall, one hand on his chest, the other clutching the loose knot of dreads at the nape of his neck. *Him* wedging his legs between Jevon's, kissing him like he'd never stop.

Jevon's shaky intake of breath was sharp too. The wooden stethoscope fell to the floor, and he wound his arms around Rhys, pulling him impossibly closer. He'd flicked a speaker on when they'd come in the house, flooding the cosy space with a low, mellow reggae beat. Now, the rhythm pulsed between them, singing in Rhys's blood until he didn't know where he ended and Jevon began. He thought he'd remembered everything about Jevon, but fuck, he'd forgotten how good he smelled. His taste. How right their bodies felt crushed together. *I want—*

Jevon broke away with a low whistle. "Wow. I wasn't sure you'd want to do that again with me."

"What?"

He winced a little. "I know I embarrassed myself a bit last time."

"What?"

"Um—you know. With all the virgin talk."

Perspective returned to Rhys with a rush. He blinked and pressed his forehead to Jevon's, absorbing his wide gaze. Then he pulled back, releasing Jevon from his cage against the wall. "You're nuts."

"Excuse me?"

Rhys shook his head. "The only embarrassing thing about that night was me shooting my load in ten seconds flat and passing out on you. There's no shame in not fucking the whole world by the time you hit thirty."

"Is that what you've done?"

"Would that matter?"

"To me?" Jevon shrugged when Rhys didn't answer. "Of course not. It's just—I dunno. Makes me nervous I wouldn't measure up if something happened between us."

Rhys snorted. "Trust me, mate. You measure up."

"I wasn't talking about my dick."

"I know. I'm just trying to break the heavy, man. It's been a long day."

Jevon blinked. "Sorry. Yes, of course it has. Are you hungry? I can cook while you grab a shower?"

Aside from diving head first into Jevon's kiss again, a hot shower sounded like the best thing in the world. Jevon showed Rhys the bathroom, passed him clean towels, and left him to it.

Under the scalding spray, the steamy solitude was more welcome than Rhys had realised. He stood with his head bowed a while, then he gave in and sank to the floor, his favourite way to brood for as long as he could remember. Jevon was fucking wonderful, but what did they do now? Pick up where they'd left off before summer? Or have dinner as strangers and part again in the morning, leaving things to fate once more?

If someone had asked Rhys yesterday, he'd have told them his intention was to screw Jevon's brains out. To teach him how to feel good and own it—to *believe* it—but kissing Jevon had blown his fantasies out of the water. Suddenly it seemed that whatever happened next, it would never, ever be enough.

The hot water ran cold. Rhys hauled himself out of the shower and dressed in the scruffy jeans and Stone Roses T-shirt he kept in the chopper for overnights like these. In Jevon's colourful house, he felt kind of scuzzy, but it was all he had, and it suited his mood.

But when he got downstairs, Jevon's smile turned the world upside down. The cloud that followed Rhys when he wasn't sharp enough to evade it evaporated. *Goddamn, he's so fucking beautiful.*

Jevon beckoned Rhys into the narrow kitchen and sat him on a stool at the counter. "I've got the rice on, but I wasn't sure what you'd want with it. You like spicy food?"

"Love it."

"Winner. That's all I can cook. You want jerk chicken? Or fish? I've got some plantain around here somewhere . . ." Jevon wandered off and came back with the biggest bananas Rhys had ever seen. "*Plantain,*" he corrected when Rhys said as much. "You white boys are all the same."

"Sorry."

Jevon chuckled. "Don't be. I'm taking the piss. I didn't know what they were either until I was fifteen and my auntie Pearl came to stay."

"Stay where? Where did you grow up?"

"A tiny village just outside Reading." Jevon stirred the rice. "I was the only black kid in my school, but then we moved to Brixton when my parents got back together, and my world got real. I met all my dad's family and made friends with kids who looked like me. It changed my life—it really did."

Rhys could listen to Jevon talk all night. He folded his arms on the counter and rested his chin on them. "Do your family know about your sexuality?"

"Kind of. My grandparents in Jamaica don't, but I'm okay with that. My parents though . . . that was weird."

"How so?"

Jevon opened the fridge and retrieved chicken, salmon, and prawns, offering them to Rhys to choose.

"Fish all the way," Rhys said. "I don't eat chicken."

"No?"

"Nah. My brother was obsessed with it when he had an eating disorder. I gave it up to show him that life went on without it. Never wanted to eat it since."

Jevon chucked the chicken back in the fridge. "Valid. You'll have to tell me about him when you're done grilling me."

"Do you feel like I'm grilling you?"

"Of course not. I'm a clown, remember? I say silly things."

Jevon brushed a soft kiss to Rhys's cheek and went back to cooking. The gesture was so lightly intimate that Rhys couldn't speak. For long minutes, he stared, lost in Jevon—his flawless skin and elegant neck, the graceful way he moved around the tiny kitchen. It was a while before he remembered what they'd been talking about.

"So . . . what happened with your parents?"

"I got it wrong." Jevon poured something spicy looking onto the salmon and prawns. "As in, misjudged them. I figured my mum would be okay with whatever and my dad would lose his shit, but it was the other way around."

"Your mum freaked?"

"Totally. We got past it, but it took her a while to give up the hetero-normative future she'd planned for when I finally stop messing around for a living."

Rhys cocked an eyebrow. "That's what she thinks you do?"

"Probably. We don't talk about it much."

"Does that bother you?"

"What? That my mum hasn't got a clue what to make of me? Nah, son. It used to, but families are messed up. I don't know anyone who hasn't got issues."

"True that." Rhys thought of his own and shivered. Their drama had faded as the years had rolled by, but he hadn't forgotten. Couldn't. "But your dad was cool?"

"So cool." Jevon smiled fondly. "It helped that my cousin Efe had married her girlfriend a year before, but I swear down, I told my pops a while back that I probably wouldn't be bringing anymore girls home, and he didn't bat an eye. Just told me to find a dude who liked cricket."

Rhys burst out laughing. "Seriously?"

"Yup. He's obsessed. Keeps him out of trouble though."

"That's nice."

"Uh-huh." Jevon slid the fish into the oven and washed his hands. Then he came to Rhys's side, warmth spilling from his liquid gaze as he gently brushed Rhys's hair back. "What about your family? I remember you said that you never came out, but do they know you're into fellas?"

Rhys nodded. "It's not an issue with my mum and my brother. She just wants us to be happy, and Harry's as gay as Christmas, so he can't fucking complain."

"Do they live in London?"

"Nah. My mum retired to Malaga, and Harry lives in Cornwall with his boyfriend. Love's young dream, they are."

"He's happy then?"

"*So* happy."

"What about you?" Jevon leaned down, his face millimetres from Rhys's. "Are you happy?"

Rhys shook his head—not a no, but not a yes. How could he be happy when he was so fucking lonely? When Jevon's hand on his arm was the deepest affection he'd ever felt from someone without sharing blood? "I don't know."

"Try," Jevon whispered. "You deserve it."

He drifted back to the stove, sparing Rhys the pressure of an intelligent response.

<hr>

RHYS PUSHED his plate away and rubbed his stomach. "You've killed me. That was amazing."

"You've had enough?" Jevon hovered with his rice pot. "There's more."

"*Stop*. I'll legit explode if I eat any more." And Rhys was only half joking. Jevon had cooked jerk fish, rice and peas, and fried plantain, and Rhys had devoured every scrap offered until his distended stomach could take no more. "Seriously. I'm good."

Jevon relented and disappeared into the kitchen with the empty plates. He came back with civilised measures of rum and flopped onto the couch beside Rhys. "Wimp. I'm going to be eating leftovers for a week."

"Lucky you. I'll be back on the Maccy D's breakfasts and marmite butties tomorrow."

Jevon pulled a face that made him look about twelve. "All that shit you just said is disgusting."

"Yup."

"But you eat it anyway?"

"Yup. We don't get much time some days, and there isn't much scope for cooking on the airbase. Microwave and a toaster. At least it ain't Pop Tarts, eh?"

"Oooh, Pop Tarts." Jevon leaned back on the couch. "I loved them when I was a kid—the chocolate ones—but I tried one recently and they taste rank, man. I was so disappointed."

There was nothing about Jevon's face that didn't make Rhys smile. He traced his jawbone with his knuckles and coiled a loose dread around his index finger. "There's a picture of you over there with blue and white hair. Was it real?"

"Yes. I painted my head every day for two weeks straight. I lost a bet with a bunch of kids in Jordan."

"Jordan?"

"Yeah. Two camps before the one I'm at now."

The reality that Jevon's real life lay far away from his cosy Bedford living room cut Rhys deep, but he pushed it aside. They'd dealt with enough for one day.

"Where did you get your tattoo?"

"Hmm?"

Jevon was slouched on the couch, his glass of rum resting lazily on his belly. Rhys plucked it from his hand and set it aside, and Jevon didn't protest as he slung a leg over him.

"Your tattoo. I've never seen one like it."

"I got it when I went island hopping around the Pacific about a million years ago. Do you like it?"

"Fuck yeah. I think I dreamed about it a few days ago."

It was true. Rhys had thought about Jevon in every way imaginable since they'd last been together, though his imagination hadn't done justice to the sensation of sliding into Jevon's lap.

Jevon widened his legs, welcoming Rhys, reeling him in. Their first kiss had replayed in Rhys's mind a thousand times, but it had nothing on the slow, sensual heat that ignited as their lips touched now. Rhys clutched Jevon's face, his fingers sliding under the black headscarf Jevon wore around his dreads, and kissed him over and over, losing himself in the natural rhythm of Jevon grinding up into him. *Oh god, I remember this.* The way Jevon's body had responded so easily to him that it was hard to believe no one had ever touched him this way before. No one before Rhys. *God, I want him.*

A shudder ran through Rhys. He tightened his thighs around Jevon's body, like that—like *anything*—could tie him down to the world when Jevon's lips were on his. When Jevon's tongue was in his mouth. When Jevon moaned so sweetly that Rhys was left dizzy.

Rhys drove his body down, revelling in the answering hardness in Jevon's lap. After the day he'd had, it would be so easy to shed their clothes and sink down on Jevon's thick cock, screwing them both into oblivion. Until their minds were devoid of all else but what it felt like to lose yourself in another person. But

Rhys knew what would happen if he did that—if he used Jevon's body to soothe his battered soul.

Nothing.

They'd come, and Rhys would walk away, like he always did. Roll from the couch and leave behind a piece of him that he'd never get back.

Jevon deserved *better*.

Rhys broke their kiss, swallowing to catch hold of his heaving chest. "You know what feels good?"

Jevon licked his lips. "What?"

"Riding someone like this—fucking them real slow while your dick slides against their stomach."

"Someone?"

"Yeah, bloke or bird, it doesn't matter to me. Some of the best nights I've had have been with a woman who knows her pegging."

A flush crept up Jevon's neck. "I, uh, didn't think you would bottom."

"Why not?" Rhys punctuated the words with a wet kiss to Jevon's neck. "You think it's a woman's role? That a man ain't a man if he likes it like that?"

"*No*, god no. It's just . . . uh—fuck, I don't know. I don't know if I could top a man. I've thought about it, but it terrifies me, which is weird, 'cause I've never thought twice about it with women."

"Nothing about sex is weird, mate."

Rhys kissed Jevon again while he chased his thoughts enough to ponder what to do next. He wanted Jevon to fuck him —craved it—and he wasn't averse to things playing out the other way around. But every instinct not clouded by bone-deep desire screamed that Jevon wasn't ready for any of it . . . even if he thought he was, which Rhys had a feeling he might be if the heat between them rose another notch.

He slid off Jevon's lap. Jevon's eyes widened, but Rhys

grabbed his hand before he could question it. "Show me your bedroom?"

"What?"

"Your bedroom. I want to lie down and be naked with you again."

Jevon's throat worked as he swallowed hard, but his only answer was to rise from the couch and tug Rhys to the stairs.

His attic bedroom was the plainest room in the house so far —not much to it but a bed, a stack of crime novels, and a suitcase tucked in the corner. "I need at least one quiet space in my life when I'm in this country," he explained. "Otherwise my brain's too crowded when I go back to the camps."

It made sense. Rhys wanted to know more about what Jevon's life was really like—to devour every detail Jevon gave up —but there was something else they had to do first, or Rhys was going to explode.

He pulled Jevon close and fingered the hem of the white vest he'd been wearing under his Technicolour shirt. "I want to get naked again," he whispered. "If that's something you want? I can go to my hotel if you want to cool things down."

Jevon let out a breathless laugh. "I don't want to cool things down. I'm just so fucking hot for you, I don't know what to do with myself. It's like I've forgotten how to have sex completely, not just the stuff I never knew in the first place."

"There's no *just* anything." Rhys drew Jevon's vest over his head, his breath catching as he lay eyes on Jevon's perfect chest. "But don't freak out, okay? Nothing's gonna happen that you're not ready for."

Conflict shimmered in Jevon's warm gaze, and Rhys understood it. The horny bloke in Jevon wanted to do all the things he probably dreamed of when he was alone at night in this very bed, but a million things were stopping him. Some tangible. Some not. And some so nonsensical he'd probably never figure them out. *Christ, I've been there.* But Jevon wasn't Rhys . . . and Rhys didn't want him to be.

Slowly, they shed their clothes. Jevon's sheets were smooth, clean, and smelled of him. Rhys sank onto his back, pulling Jevon on top of him. Skin touched skin, and they both gasped. Jevon sank his teeth into Rhys's chest and kissed his way from nipple to nipple, remembering Rhys's kryptonite spots with military accuracy as Rhys dissolved beneath him, powerless to stop the mentor role he'd assumed slipping away. What Jevon lacked in experience was eclipsed by the instinctive way he played Rhys's body, and Rhys was a shuddering mess at his metaphorical feet.

Eventually, they found themselves in the reverse of the position they'd been in on the couch: Rhys propped up against the headboard, Jevon straddling his lap. Naked, it meant so much more. Meant nothing more. Meant everything. Jevon's cock was trapped between them, rucking against Rhys's abdomen. Jevon stared down at it, apparently fascinated as their bodies moved together. "I reckon I could come like this."

Rhys could believe it. He'd been ready to blow an hour ago. He thrust up gently, taking care to slide his own dick along Jevon's tender flesh, rather than jabbing it in. "We can do that if you like, but I had something else in mind if you're game?"

Jevon's eyes widened. "Like what?"

"Like paying you back for letting me fuck your mouth and pass out on you."

"You want me to fuck your mouth?"

"I want to blow you." Heat sluiced through Rhys at the mere thought of it. "It doesn't matter how we do it."

The cogs turning in Jevon's brain were conversely blank and visible, leaving Rhys no idea of what he was thinking as he slowly straightened up. Rhys braced himself for Jevon to climb off his lap, but he didn't. He lay back, arching his body like a graceful cat, and left their bodies entwined. His cock jutted up, sticky from rutting together. Rhys gazed at it, and his mouth watered. He scrambled to his knees and chased Jevon down, covering his body with his own and swooping down for one more kiss.

Then he crawled between Jevon's legs, nudging them wider apart, and swallowed him whole.

Jevon reacted like he'd been plugged into the mains. As though Rhys's tongue sliding up and down his length tapped into a brand new circuit. His back arched from the bed, and his limbs spasmed out, jerking and wild. "*Fuck.*"

The curse was whispered—hoarse—but the single syllable went straight to Rhys's dick. He sucked Jevon harder, working him with his hand. His loose plan had been to do this slowly . . . sensually, to build Jevon up a dozen times before he finally let him come, but a minute in and they were already derailing.

Jevon's hands flew to the back of Rhys's head, resting lightly there at first, but then with more purpose as Rhys urged him on.

"Do it," Rhys growled. "Do what you feel."

Jevon gripped Rhys's hair, his fingers tangling in it with just enough pressure to make Rhys's eyes roll. A year's old craving for pain kicked in, but he fought it and won, quickly losing himself in Jevon's building pleasure.

Sucking cock had always been Rhys's jam, but he regretted that now as Jevon thrashed beneath him, and Rhys's view was obscured. *I want to see him.* But he wanted Jevon to *feel* more. Wanted Jevon to let go of every single thought in his mind and give into the desires he'd hidden for so long. Rhys's life had disintegrated more times than he cared to admit, but hiding his sexuality from the world wasn't a problem he'd ever carried. Fuck, no. And he had the scars to prove it.

But Jevon had scars too, and if Rhys could heal them just a little, with the swipe of his tongue and a gentle graze of his teeth, he'd suck Jevon's cock all night long.

"Oh god," Jevon whispered. "I'm gonna come."

The soft plea hit Rhys harder than if Jevon had screamed at the top of his lungs. He flattened his own body, grinding his dick against the mattress, and took Jevon as deep down as he could. Jevon's cock scraped the back of his throat, and he unravelled, his body curling in on itself as he clutched Rhys tight against him. He erupted with a ragged yell, shooting hot come down Rhys's throat, and Rhys drank it all down, absorbing the spasms in Jevon's abdomen, revelling in them, believing them. Believing in himself if just for a moment. *This is what you're good at.*

Rhys's stomach rolled, but the bleak thought was fast eclipsed by his own pleasure. When he'd swallowed every drop of Jevon's release, he rose up on his knees, his hand a blur on his cock, and came quickly—and *hard*—on Jevon's chest, a guttered shout tearing from his lungs.

Exhausted, he fell forwards, his palms landing either side of Jevon's head, gasping, and for a long moment, the only sounds in the room were laboured breaths and pounding hearts.

Jevon gripped Rhys's chin and gently forced him to meet his gaze. He smiled, and Rhys blinked down at him, awed. Fell into his languid kiss like a warm summer lake and wondered how the fuck life had given him this.

Given him Jevon.

He pulled back, still staring, until a shiver racked Jevon, and Rhys remembered that he'd covered him in come. "I'll clean up."

Rhys stumbled from the bed and to the bathroom where he found a fresh washcloth. He dampened it with warm water and returned to the bed to clean them both up.

When he was done, he sat back on his heels. Jevon gazed at him drowsily. "Don't go."

"Go where?"

"Anywhere."

"No?"

"No." Jevon wriggled up the bed and drew the covers back. "Stay, Rhys. Stay with me."

As if Rhys could refuse. He crawled into bed as Jevon muttered something else and rolled over, his long arm stretched over his head, his fingers tangled loosely in Rhys's hair. His eyes closed, and the absolute peace radiating from him seeped into Rhys like a drug.

He slid his arm around Jevon and breathed him in. "I'm not going anywhere, mate."

RHYS WAS DEFINITELY *NOT* a morning person. Jevon steered clear as he stumbled around, gathering his clothes, and slipped downstairs to get the coffee on, trying to temper his amusement. Rhys's grumbling was kind of cute, but also scary. Jevon didn't stick his head above the parapet until the coffee was ready.

The bleary-eyed smile he got in return was well worth the wait.

"Thanks," Rhys said. "Sorry for getting you up this early."

"It's okay. I'm going to the children's home later to work with those Syrian kids some more."

"Damn. What are you going to do with them?"

"Play." Jevon peered out of the kitchen window. "Outside, hopefully, if the weather holds. I've never found a language that doesn't translate duck, duck, goose, so I'd imagine there'll be a lot of that."

Rhys took a thoughtful sip of his coffee. "Do you ever find they just don't want to play?"

"Sometimes. And it's a constant worry when you go somewhere new—that it's not the right place for us, that we're insulting them by invading the worst time in their lives with drums and feather boas—but at the end of the day, kids need to be kids, man."

"And I guess in situations like this, it's all you can do for them?"

"Exactly." Jevon slid off the kitchen counter. "I spend a lot of time paying outrageous compliments to pretty average artwork, and that's just for the adults."

Rhys's smile widened a touch. He was close enough to slip effortlessly into Jevon's personal space, and he did, his stubbled cheek scratching Jevon's jaw as he nuzzled his face. For a fleeting moment, it was like he'd always been here, that they both had, but too soon, he pulled away. "I'd better go."

"Okay." Jevon chewed on his lip and trailed Rhys to the hallway, tracking him as he shrugged into his coat. "Are you working all day?"

Rhys stamped moodily into his shoes. "Yeah. Seven to five on paper, but I reckon I won't get out till six. Never do."

"What happens if you get a call that goes over your time?"

"We keep going till it's done." Rhys straightened up, and flicker by flicker, the lightness Jevon had seen in him last night fluttered away, like the skin he wore to work was slotting into place. "Um . . ."

He stopped and scratched the back of his head. Jevon raised an eyebrow and waited, but nothing happened. Rhys shifted his weight from one foot to the other, and whatever he'd wanted to say seemed to desert him.

Jevon took a deep breath and opened the kitchen drawer where he'd stashed his new set of business cards. He plucked one free of the wrapping and offered it to Rhys. "The email address goes to the office before it gets to me, but the phone number is mine. Maybe, uh, you could give me a call sometime . . . if you want?"

Rhys said nothing. Just stared.

Jevon's heart skipped a beat and his fingers tightened

around the shiny card. Last night—all of it, not just the mind-blowing orgasm—had been incredible, like fate had stepped in and brought them back together, but what if that was it? What if last night had been nothing more than a convenient coincidence? After all, it wasn't like Jevon had shown Rhys a good time in the bedroom. *You didn't even make him come—*

Rhys took the card, and with it, Jevon's hand. He pulled Jevon into his arms and kissed him so soundly that the doubts cartwheeling through Jevon's mind evaporated like they'd never been there at all. They'd be back, but in that moment, there was nothing but lips bruising lips, grasping hands, and snatched breath. For Jevon, there was nothing but Rhys.

They stumbled against the fridge. Magnets fell to the floor, breaking the spell. Jevon, who'd fallen slack in Rhys's searching embrace, reluctantly pulled away. "You'll call me?"

Rhys took a deep breath and squeezed Jevon's hands. "Yes."

RHYS DIDN'T CALL. For a week, Jevon stalked his phone like a teenage girl, but nothing happened, not even a text. One week stretched into two, and by the third, he'd given up hope.

"Why don't *you* call *him*," Efe said when Jevon called her up to bend her ear.

Jevon rolled his eyes. He loved his cousin dearly, but listening to his *actual words* wasn't her strong point. "I already told you—I don't have his number. I gave him my card before he left and he said he'd call."

"You can't track him down on Facebook or something?"

"I don't know his full name."

"Oh."

"Yeah, *oh*." Jevon made a note on the paperwork he was wading through for his assessment of the surviving children from the detention centre fire. "All I know about him is his first name, his occupation, and that he doesn't eat chicken."

"Whoa, brother. Hold the bus. Man'dem don't eat chicken? What kind of monster is that?"

"Shut up."

Efe laughed. "Don't blow up my phone if you don't want to hear my chat."

Jevon grumbled under his breath, but in truth, just hearing Efe's voice had lightened his mood. He'd spent twelve hours with the fire children that day—his last session with them—and letting them go had hurt his heart.

Efe understood. She always did. "Come and see me," she said when she was done ribbing Jevon's forlorn love life. "I'm making patties tonight—sweet potato, beef, salt cod. All your favourites. I'll give you a box for the freezer."

It was a kind offer, but Efe's Vauxhall bakery was a mission on the train from Bedford. As amazing as her food was, Jevon didn't have the energy. "Nah, blood. Thanks, though. I'll come see you soon."

"You've been saying that since you got back."

"I know, and I mean it, I swear. I've just been busy with work."

"I thought you only did a few kiddie parties when you were over here?"

"I do, but something came up." Jevon's attention drifted back to his laptop screen as Efe said something else. "Sorry, what?"

She sighed. "There's a type of man who don't stop working, and it don't do him no good. There's a few of them round here, and it hurts me to see what becomes of them. Don't let life suck you down, cuz. Put your work aside and get out there living."

She hung up before Jevon could reply, and he absently set his phone aside. Haya—the little girl who'd attached herself to

Rhys in the hospital—was next on his list. Last on his list, in fact, by design, rather than fate.

He spread his notes out on the coffee table. Social services hadn't asked his opinion or even paid for his services beyond the interpreter fees, but he'd offered his assessments anyway in the hope that someone might read them. Haya's most of all.

Jevon collated his notes into a document that made his chest tight and his eyes sting. Most of the children he'd seen over the last few days had, despite their grief and trauma, made progress, but Haya was different. The brother who'd died in Rhys's helicopter had been her only living relative. She was alone in the world now, and the risk of her being deported was at an all-time high.

When his work was done, Jevon retreated to the kitchen to nurse the rum bottle. He was on his second shot when Efe called him back.

"Come over," she said. "I can't concentrate knowing that you're so down, and I like having you around my kitchen. Please, Jevon? Gloria's helping me out tonight, and she'd love to see you too."

Jevon sighed. The prospect of facing two Jamaican women who wanted to be all up in his business was daunting, but he couldn't deny the prospect of another lonely night was far, far worse. "All right," he said eventually. "But you'd better have somewhere decent for me to kip when you're done with me."

Efe giggled gleefully. "Only the best flour-covered couch for you. Hurry yourself up, son."

CHAPTER SEVEN

RHYS JUMPED off the helicopter as soon as it was declared safe to do so and charged across the roof to the second helipad. Another chopper was parked there, fixed and good to go when the next call came in, but he wasn't waiting for the next call. Couldn't because he'd been waiting for this chopper three long weeks already.

He hopped inside and scrambled immediately to where he'd been sitting when the chopper had returned to London from the Bedford job. It had gone out of service for essential maintenance half an hour *before* Rhys had realised he'd left something precious on board.

"Come on, come on, come on . . ." He rummaged between the seats and down the backs, praying that whoever had cleaned the chopper had done a piss-poor job. For long, terrifying moments, it seemed the maintenance crew had let him down, but then his groping fingers touched thin cardboard, and his heart threw itself against his ribcage.

He pried the creased card free and turned it over. Jevon's contact number jumped out at him, and his phone was out of his pocket with little conscious thought.

Rhys jumped down from the helicopter and tapped the

digits into his phone as he walked back to the base rest quarters. He felt sick. Three weeks. Three *fucking* weeks. Would Jevon answer? Would he tell Rhys to *do one* even if he did?

Jevon didn't answer. The call went to an automated voice-mail, and the nausea in Rhys's gut turned to despair. The email address on Jevon's card was the same as the one on the FFP's website. The one that had bounced back when Rhys had sent a benign message asking Jevon to contact him. *Fuck.* He crum-pled Jevon's card in his hand, then instantly panicked and flat-tened it out again, shoving it into his flight suit pocket for safekeeping, at least until his shift was over. He'd known it was taking the piss to expect Jevon to wait around the best part of a month for him to call, but he was sorely unprepared for how much that one unanswered call hurt.

His phone buzzed in his hand. Rhys's heart briefly leapt again but sank just as fast when he saw his brother's name on the screen.

H: *Where are you?*

R: *Work*

H: *Can you talk?*

R: *No*

In the past, Harry would've let that slide, but he'd become more persistent since he'd jumped ship to Cornwall. Like seventy-five thousand texts a week made up for the fact that he wasn't there. Like it perpetuated the myth that *he* was the older brother, distracting them both from the fact that Rhys couldn't be bothered to check in on himself, let alone anyone else.

H: *Stop ignoring me*

R: *I'm not. I'm at work*

H: *You're not on a run or you wouldn't be responding at all*

R: *Fuck off*

H: *No. What's wrong?*

R: *Nothing*

H: *Liar*

R: *Fine. I think I'm in love with a real-life clown who's blown me once. Happy now?*

Harry called instantly, but Rhys silenced him and turned his phone off. He justified his childishness when the base alarm went off a few seconds later, but by the time his shift ended in the early hours of the morning, he'd accepted that he was a moody prick.

He rescued Jevon's card from his flight suit and tucked it into his wallet, then he turned his phone on and sent Harry a GIF acknowledging his wanker status.

Harry didn't reply, but why would he at this time? And no one else had tried to contact Rhys either.

With a heavy heart, Rhys pocketed his phone and headed out to catch the night bus home. Staying awake on route was a struggle, but when he got home, he found himself irritatingly restless again. A packet of fags called his name, but a year-old promise to Harry kept him indoors, and eventually, he crawled into bed.

The TV droned in the background while he stared at the ceiling, willing himself to pass the fuck out already. He had twenty-four hours off work, but it came on the back of seven days straight, and he was so tired his eyeballs hurt. *Sleep, dickhead.* But the gods were against him. Under his pillow, his phone buzzed with a message. Assuming it to be Harry's response to his half-arsed apology, Rhys ignored it until it vibrated a second time, and a third.

"Fuck's sake." He shoved his hand beneath the pillow, prepared to turn the phone off again, but when he looked at the screen, the three new WhatsApp messages weren't from Harry.

And the sender was still online.

RHYS LEANED on the wall outside the pizza bar, eyes closed, his face turned to the fading afternoon sun. Inside, his heart was thumping, his mind racing, but like this, with the warmth of the late autumn seeping into his bones, his nauseating nerves gave him a break.

"Rhys?"

Or not. Rhys jumped and opened his eyes to find Jevon right in front of him, dressed in Timberlands, grungy black jeans, and a white tee, his hair held back by a tribal-patterned scarf. "Hi."

"Hi." Jevon's smile was cautious, and Rhys knew why. He hadn't got round to telling his tale of woe in the handful of WhatsApp messages they'd exchanged over the last couple of days. Lord knew what Jevon was thinking.

"Listen—"

"So—" Jevon said at the same time.

They both stopped, then Rhys threw caution to the wind and pulled Jevon in for a tight hug. *God, I've missed him.* "Let's go inside. I know I've got some explaining to do."

Jevon didn't argue. He led Rhys inside and to a booth at the back of the restaurant. Rhys sensed eyes on them as they manoeuvred around the tables, and his stomach flipped a little when Jevon waved at a member of staff working in the open kitchen. The woman was tall, statuesque, and utterly gorgeous. If she wasn't related to Jevon, Rhys would eat his damn shoe.

"My cousin," Jevon offered when he caught Rhys's questioning frown. "She's the master baker next door. That's why I'm in the city. I've been staying with her for a few days."

"Right." Rhys processed the information. Discovering that Jevon was in London and free to meet had made his day when they'd finally made contact, but the notion that he'd been there all along hurt. So much wasted time. "I think I've been here before."

"This place? Or—" Jevon cut himself off with a wave of his hand. "Sorry. Carry on."

Okaaay. Rhys took a deep breath. "Yeah. This place. I think I came here when it opened, and I've been back for work since. Someone passed out in the kitchen."

There'd been a little more to it if Rhys remembered correctly, but the details escaped him. All he could truly recall was feeling incredibly lonely as he'd watched the dude's mates take care of him like brothers. *I miss Harry too.*

"Rhys?"

Rhys blinked. "Sorry, what?"

Jevon smiled a little wider. "You look knackered."

"I am. It's been a long week."

"Is that why you didn't call?"

"Nah. I didn't call because I left your card on the broken chopper. It only came back into service yesterday."

"Oh."

A rush of something Rhys couldn't quite decipher seemed to leave Jevon all at once. He held his tongue while a server brought water and menus, then reached across the table to take Jevon's hand. "I was losing my fucking mind these last few weeks. I even googled that bloody circus place you work for, but the email address on their website is wrong too. It bounced back."

Jevon's eyes widened. "Seriously? They were supposed to have fixed that before I left on my last trip."

"Well, they haven't," Rhys said. "Trust me, mate. Short of sending up smoke signals, I did everything I could to find you, but even the landline number didn't do me any good. I kept sleeping through its opening hours, or it was engaged, and I—"

He stopped. Did Jevon really need to know he'd launched his phone across the room so many times it was a wonder it still functioned? That only the nuclear-proof case he used for work had saved it? *Probably not.*

Or maybe he did.

Rhys tapped Jevon's chin with his knuckles, forcing his gaze up from the table. "I'm sorry . . . I really am. I've been wanting to see you again so much."

"Really?"

"Yes. I've been slammed at work, but you've been on my mind every spare moment I've had."

More tension seeped from Jevon's shoulders, and he leaned forward like he was going to kiss Rhys.

He didn't, but the hand that wasn't entwined with Rhys's found his face, fingers grazing Rhys's rough cheek, thumb tracing his scratchy eyes. "I'd nearly given up on you."

"Only nearly?"

Jevon nodded. "I couldn't bring myself to let go entirely. It's too—too real, you know? If that doesn't make me sound like a thirsty bitch."

The cruel words were all wrong falling from Jevon's sweet tongue, from his kind lips, but Rhys got it. Jevon's easy poise, his sunshine smile, hid insecurities that only a man naked in bed with him would ever see. "I wanted to call, Jevon. I swear. I wasn't joking when I said I've been losing my mind. Shit, I don't think I've slept more than a few hours a night since I last saw you."

"It shows," Jevon said gently. "And ignore me. I just—um— I'm not a particularly insecure guy, but when it comes to sex these days . . . and you, I kinda lose my head a bit too."

Rhys nodded slowly. They'd talked about this before, and he was getting the feeling nothing he could say would do much good at this point. Jevon was fucking incredible, in *every* way. He just had to learn to believe it. "I hear you."

"I know." Jevon's smile finally cranked up to the mega-wattage Rhys saw in his dreams. "I always feel like you get me, even when I can't find the words to explain myself. I've never felt that with anyone else."

Rhys had never felt anything that came close to how Jevon made him feel. To hear that even a fragment of it was reciprocated blew the stress clean out of his soul. "You can talk to me, mate. And not just about sex. Do me good to listen to something outside of my own head."

"Introspective, eh?"

Rhys shrugged. "According to my brother, the fountain of all knowledge. He reckons I have one skin for work, one for hooking up, and neither is who I really am."

"Everyone's got skins, dude. You think I wake up in entertainer mode every day?"

Rhys chuckled but was saved from answering by the server coming back. "You order," he said to Jevon. "I gotta take a leak."

He retreated to the gender-neutral bathrooms, and by the time he returned, Jevon was alone again, twirling a straw in a rum and Coke. "So . . . " he said as Rhys reclaimed his seat.

"So, what?"

"How did you end up becoming a paramedic? It's a pretty intense career choice."

"It wasn't really a choice," Rhys said. "Not a conscious one, anyway."

"Curious."

"Scuzzy, actually." Rhys gulped some of the rum-laced drink Jevon had ordered for him. "I was a terrible teenager, and it spilled out into adulthood until I wound up doing community service at King's hospital. From there, I got a job as a healthcare assistant, then a place on a paramedic course. I quit briefly to work in a butchers—ironic, huh?—but I knuckled down eventually, and here I am."

Jevon tilted his head to one side, spearing Rhys with a quizzical frown. "What's scuzzy about that?"

Rhys shrugged. "It's not my calling, I guess. I didn't get into it to help people . . . I was trying to help myself. Save myself, I suppose."

"From what?"

"Everything. My dad died a little while ago, and before that, he was in prison for some shit that went down at home. It took me some time to get past that."

Jevon said nothing for a long moment. Just stared at Rhys like his bottomless eyes could burn a path to everything that had ever hurt Rhys. Like he wanted to take it away and set it on fire.

But he couldn't do that. No one could. Rhys had started plenty of his own fires, and somehow all the bullshit still lived in the ashes. "Don't look at me like that," he whispered. "I'm not one of your kids that needs saving."

More silence. But the server intervened with the food Jevon had ordered while Rhys had been gone. Two pizzas and a salad that looked like it belonged in the Tate Modern. And for the first time in days, Rhys was actually hungry. They dug in while Jevon explained between bites what he was doing with his life for the next few months.

"I swore down I'd only do a few birthday parties, but I've got four next week alone."

Rhys chuckled. "You don't like them?"

"It's not that. Any chance I get to act the fool is fine by me, but it just seems kind of—I don't know—hollow, I guess. Which is why they make us do it."

"Who does?"

"The team who look after the entertainers at the charity. There's a psychologist here in London who comes to visit us on site and checks in with us when we come home. He's the reason we're only allowed three-month stints in the camps now before they bring us home for a while. Before him, we had people bedded in for most of the year without a break, and not even soldiers do that."

There was beauty in the comparison. Jevon and his coworkers fought wars of their own with laughter instead of bullets, joy in place of despair. But at what cost? Rhys had seen enough medics go under to know the risks were real. "Do you ever feel like not going back?"

"Not really." Jevon toyed thoughtfully with a pizza crust. "It's hard sometimes—lonely too—but I can't imagine leaving those kids with nothing, you know? Even if all we give them is a few days of madness. It is getting harder though. Lots of governments are tearing the camps down."

"I thought that was a good thing? The camps I've seen on the news look awful."

"They aren't great, but where else do people go? At least in the camps, the aid organisations know where to find them. And, it's safe for them to look. We've done some street work, but I don't fancy roaming the Albanian countryside on my unicycle. Getting shot ain't my bag."

Rhys shuddered. He'd seen a few gun shot wounds since he'd joined the chopper team, and the thought of Jevon getting hurt turned the dinner in his belly to dust. "When are you going back?"

"Second week in December."

"Gone for Christmas then?"

"I've been gone every Christmas since the war in Syria kicked off."

Rhys traced lazy patterns on the back of Jevon's hand. He wanted to ask more, but at the same time, the thought of Jevon leaving the country in just eight weeks time made him feel sick. *This* was why he didn't do relationships. Because life always got in the way and fucked everything up, and he had no idea what to do with the ever-growing, bone-deep affection he felt every time Jevon crossed his mind. Every time they touched.

Kissed.

More.

I can't do this.

But I need him.

Rhys took a deep breath and leaned back in his seat. The

pizza place had filled up while they'd eaten and it was kicking. Staff flitted around with trays of food, and the hot guy manning the pizza oven seemed to be in constant motion. Rhys watched him work, absently admiring the flex of his tanned forearms and the concentrated expression that made him equal parts alluring and intimidating. The dude was hot, and Rhys was about to say so when another man approached the chef from behind.

This dude was half the size. Slender and blond, he reminded Rhys a little of Dylan. He climbed up the other man's back and wrapped his arms around his neck, kissing his cheek. The chef's answering smile was blinding.

"Nice, isn't it?" Jevon squeezed Rhys's fingers, breaking into his reverie. "I hung around here a lot when my sexuality first started making itself known."

"Just to watch them?"

Rhys could understand that. Dylan and Angelo's relationship made him jealous as hell, and Harry and Joe were so utterly perfect together, Rhys often wanted to puke in their presence, but the moody chef and his elegant partner were a joy to watch. Like the distance between them and Rhys made their love easier to bear.

"Not just them," Jevon said. "There's a few queer blokes around here—more than a few, actually—and being around them made me feel normal."

"You don't feel normal?"

"I do *now*, but I didn't for a while. There were moments when I was so terrified, I couldn't imagine how it would ever end well."

"What changed?"

"Lots of things over time. Work, family, relationships. Things that I thought were gospel turned out to be the opposite. My dad being sound was a big factor, and Efe is my best friend in the world, but something has always felt missing. I figured it was just the sex, but then I met you, and . . . well . . . it's more than that."

Of course it was. Rhys had pictured himself having sex with Jevon so many times, it almost seemed like they'd done it already. But it wasn't enough. Being with Jevon *was* so much more.

A new chef took over at the pizza oven, and the dark-haired man and his partner disappeared. Rhys watched them go, sensing Jevon's gaze on him but unable to face him, though he wasn't entirely sure why.

"I watched them fuck once."

That got Rhys's attention. He turned to Jevon and wondered instantly how he'd held out so long. "I'd let him fuck me."

If Rhys's candour offended Jevon, it didn't show. "Which one?"

"The darker dude."

Jevon shook his head. "It was the other way around."

"For real?"

"Yup. I didn't watch it all, so maybe they switched, but what I saw was so sensual and hot, I knew I'd like bottoming . . . if I ever found the balls to try."

If. A tiny word that held so much power. Rhys rarely topped, preferring the oblivion of having his own brains screwed out, but he wanted to fuck Jevon. Needed to. Even if it tied a bow around the heartbreak they were surely heading for.

Rhys caught the eye of their server and signalled for the bill. "Let's get out of here."

CHAPTER EIGHT

BEING with Rhys was the perfect contradiction. Jevon had never felt more like his true self, but with that peace came the relentless sensation that Rhys wasn't entirely happy. That he wasn't happy with Jevon.

Or maybe he wasn't happy at all.

Neither option sat well.

They left the pizza place and walked towards the Tube station. Rhys seemed on edge. Twitchy. Jevon grabbed his hand and tugged him into the nearest shop—a gentrified cupcake parlour. "You look like you need some sugar," he responded to Rhys's quizzical frown.

"I just ate my bodyweight in pizza and hipster salad."

"Humour me. You like chocolate, right?"

Rhys's expression evened out. "I do. Not white chocolate though. That shit tastes like soap."

"Noted." Jevon surveyed the options and picked out two cakes he hoped would put a smile back on Rhys's face. Then he took Rhys's hand again and held it tight, daring him to let go as they left the shop and continued to the underground.

Rhys didn't let go. They got on the Victoria line towards his Brick Lane flat and found a corner on the crowded train. Jevon half sat on a cushioned ledge and held Rhys against him, ghosting a subtle hand under his jacket, then under his clothes so his palm slid over Rhys's warm skin. Somehow touching him had become the easiest thing in the world. Would it feel that way when they got back to Rhys's flat? When their clothes came off and they were naked again? *I hope so.* But for once, screwing around was the last thing on Jevon's mind.

He dug his fingers into Rhys's muscled back, kneading the tension he found there. "Are you okay?"

The words were whispered, barely audible, but Rhys jerked like Jevon had shouted in his ear. "What?"

Jevon raised an eyebrow, waiting for the question to compute.

Rhys shrugged and scrubbed a hand down his face. "Shit. Sorry. I'm just knackered. I swear you're like a tranquiliser to me."

"That boring, eh?"

"The opposite. I meant that you chill me out."

"That's sweet, but you don't seem particularly chilled."

Rhys shook his head. "Sorry."

He didn't elaborate. Merely pulled Jevon off the train at Victoria and guided him onto the District line. The second train was even more crowded than the first, and an elderly lady got between them, her shopping bags piled at their feet. By the time they'd helped her off the train at Aldgate and carried her bags above ground, the moment had passed.

Rhys's flat was just as Jevon remembered it. Which was lucky, because he'd been so drunk that night, he'd barely recalled his own name the next morning. The bed was already unfolded though. *Wasn't it a couch last time?*

Rhys chucked his jacket and shoes in the hallway cupboard and returned to where Jevon was hovering in the living room doorway. "What's up?"

"Nothing. Just trying to remember the last time I was here."

"Ah." Rhys ducked under Jevon's arm. "Good luck with that. I was pretty sure I'd dreamt you until I found your sock under a pillow."

"My sock?"

Rhys rummaged in a fortuitously nearby basket of clean clothes. "Yeah. I don't think I could pull these off at work."

He tossed the sock to Jevon. It was black, covered in psychedelic unicorns, and belonged to his favourite pair. How had he not noticed it was missing? *Because you've had nothing but Rhys on your mind since he put his dick in your mouth.*

The devil on Jevon's shoulder was so on the money that he couldn't speak. Just took his sock and stuffed it in his pocket, willing away the random flashes of the ecstasy-laced panic attacks he'd floated through on Rhys's sofa bed.

Rhys sat down heavily. Jevon dropped the paper bag from the cake shop on the coffee table and joined him. "What's the matter?"

"Nothing's the matter."

"Liar. You're freaking out about something, and if it's me, I can easily go. St. Pancreas to Bedford and I'll be home soon enough."

"No! God, no." Rhys's hand shot out and he grabbed Jevon's arm. "Don't go. It's not that, I swear."

"Then what is it?"

Rhys shoved his free hand into his hair and tugged brutally on it until Jevon stopped him. "It's this. Us. I want you so much, but I don't know how to do any of the stuff that comes next. Or even if you want that, because you're leaving again soon, and I don't want to deal with that either."

"You don't want to deal with it?"

Rhys shook his head. "Fuck. That's not what I meant."

"Right." Jevon had a sinking feeling that he knew where this was going, but the distress in Rhys's face didn't match up with ditching someone because they were too much hassle.

Jevon didn't know much about making men come, but he recognised imploding self-esteem like he knew his own mother. *This isn't about me.* It couldn't be or everything Jevon had learned about human beings—about *Rhys*—didn't mean jack.

He slid from the bed and onto his knees, inserting himself between Rhys's legs before Rhys could protest. Their hands were still tightly entwined. Jevon brought them to his lips and kissed Rhys's knuckles as he tried to put words to what Rhys needed to hear. "You think you're not good enough."

It wasn't quite what he meant to say, but the flicker in Rhys's dark gaze said it was a start. "I'm not good enough for *you*, Jevon. I *told* you—I want you . . . I just—I— *Fuck.* Why is this so hard?"

Jevon had no idea. He held his tongue and Rhys's hands and willed him to continue.

Rhys took a shaky breath. "I'm not like you. I couldn't have waited all this time to explore liking men—liking *anyone*. I've fucked so many people I can't even count them. Am I really the kind of person you want to do this with?"

"You think we should get married first?"

"I'm serious."

"So am I," Jevon said gently. "Just because I've never been with a dude, doesn't mean I'm some kind of saint. I've been around the block, just not the same block as you."

"Jevon—"

"Shh. I'm not asking you to sweep me off my feet here, son. I'm not even asking you to sleep with me if it doesn't pan out."

"What if it does?"

"Does what?"

"Pan out," Rhys said. "Then what? I've never been emotionally attached to someone I've fucked, but it'll be different with you. Everything is."

"You can't have it both ways. Either you're too cold to ruin my precious little heart or too scared of getting hurt to dive in deep. Which is it?"

"Does it matter at this point?"

Jevon wasn't altogether sure, and Rhys slut shaming himself was more than he could bear, but Rhys's phone vibrating gave him a reprieve.

Rhys pulled it out of his pocket and glanced at the screen. Whoever it was made him frown. He silenced the call and tossed the phone aside, shaking his head at Jevon's questioning frown. "My mate Dylan. I used to hook up with him and his boyfriend in that sex club in Romford. *That's* who I am."

"Even if that's true, what makes you so sure I'd think it was a bad thing? You don't think I'd play in a sex club if I had the balls?"

The growing bleakness in Rhys's face stalled. "What?"

Jevon tapped his fingers on Rhys's knuckles. "It's a fair question. And by assuming the answer, you're putting words in my head that ain't there. I'm a butt-sex virgin. Not a fucking monk."

A wild laugh tore out of Rhys. Exploded out of him. Like it was the first emotion to escape and make a mad dash for the exit. "I don't know what to say."

"So don't say anything. I think you're a fella who needs to talk, but that doesn't mean the first thing that comes to your mind is the right thing." Jevon tapped Rhys's temple. "Just let it be. We can't change who we are, and I don't want to."

RHYS'S FINGERS grazed Jevon's hole. Jevon shivered, his skin jumping beneath Rhys's touch, like it had done every time his hands had strayed lower than Jevon's cock.

Most times, Rhys hadn't lingered, but he did now. "Has anyone . . . ?"

Jevon shook his head. "Never. Not even me."

Rhys absorbed the information with no comment. His fingers slipped away and he kissed Jevon again, driving his tongue into Jevon's mouth like he'd been doing for hours now, his hand palming Jevon's dick, squeezing, twisting, and teasing. Working Jevon up to the point of madness, only to pull back and return to languid kisses that melted Jevon to the bed.

But even Jevon had limits. Glass ceilings. And this one broke. Out of his mind, he reared up from the bed, wrapping his legs around Rhys's waist, caging him. Rhys's dick touched his, and they slid together with every frantic rock of Jevon's hips, the friction too much and nowhere near enough. *I need more.*

Jevon broke the kiss. "Please."

"Please what?" Rhys kissed him again, hard and searching. "What do you want?"

"Anything. Please."

Somewhere in the back of Jevon's mind, his desperation for Rhys was mortifying, but right now, he didn't care. He'd used up his skill points when he'd sucked Rhys's cock an hour ago. Life had moved on, and he needed *more.*

Rhys loosened Jevon's legs around him and moved down Jevon's body, hooking his arms under Jevon's knees. Jevon's cock protruded between them, rigid and weeping. Rhys stuck his tongue out and licked the very tip—a feather-light swipe that curled Jevon's toes—and in the dim light of the room, his gaze was contemplative.

Jevon caught his chin. "Stop thinking."

"Stop thinking about what?"

"About actions and consequences."

Rhys laughed softly. "I spent a long time not thinking about either and it didn't get me anywhere."

"This isn't like that. I'm not like that. Do what you feel. I can take it."

Take it. Want it. And *fuck*, Jevon wanted it. He wanted it all.

Rhys held his gaze for a long moment, then he took Jevon's cock in his mouth, his hands on Jevon's thighs, pushing his legs further apart, as Jevon arched naturally from the mattress, showing his body to Rhys in a way that no one had ever seen it.

Saliva dribbled from Rhys's mouth, trickling lower and lower until it coated Jevon's hole. "God," Jevon ground out. "Touch me, man."

Rhys hummed and his fingers drifted back to where they'd made Jevon jump before. Grazing again. Pressing. Dipping slowly inside Jevon.

The sensation was insane and Jevon's body instantly rebelled, rejecting Rhys's probing finger, but it was a war that couldn't be won. Rhys persisted and fresh nerve endings claimed his touch. Heat sluiced through Jevon with a violent shudder, and Rhys's entire finger slid inside him.

Rhys pulled his mouth from Jevon's cock and kissed his inner thigh. "Okay?"

"Yeah."

"Sure?"

"Yeah."

"How about if I do this?" Rhys swept his finger from side to side, curling it slightly.

Jevon bit his lip, his eyes screwed shut, and more fluid spilled from his dick. "Yeah. I like it."

"Good boy," Rhys whispered with just enough humour to lighten the blanket-thick air in the room. "Hold tight to your knees, man, 'cause I'm gonna make you scream."

His finger slipped from inside Jevon, and he crawled up the bed, sinking his teeth into Jevon's chest. Jevon jerked wildly and didn't notice at first that Rhys was rummaging for something under the mattress.

Then Rhys tossed a half-empty bottle of lube on the bed. The sound of it hitting the duvet seemed to echo in Jevon's head, the dull thud like a sonic boom. He stared at it, body tingling from the taster Rhys had given him already, and imagined Rhys coating his cock with it and sliding his thick length inside him. Anxiety seized his chest, but Rhys was right there.

He leaned over Jevon and kissed him deeply before pulling back and fixing Jevon with his hypnotic gaze. "Your turn to stop thinking. Nothing's gonna happen that you can't handle."

I don't know what I can handle. Jevon wanted Rhys—his body was crying out for anything he could give—but his heart trembled. And perhaps Rhys felt it.

He pressed his forehead to Jevon's. "Trust me. Please?"

"I trust you."

No more words. Rhys moved down the bed, taking the lube with him. He swallowed Jevon's dick whole, gagging on it, choking, as he distracted Jevon from his wandering fingers. But then he moved his mouth lower, and his tongue swept across Jevon's hole, and Jevon returned to that place where just one more notch of heat would trigger an inferno.

He rode Rhys's tongue, moaning softly as the ghost-like sensation intensified. It wasn't enough to make him come, but it pushed him closer to the precipice, dangling him over the edge and pulling him back to safety.

The click of the lube bottle pierced the air. Jevon tensed, but Rhys's slick finger sliding home again was like a dream. No pain or discomfort, just the toe-curling strokes of a devilish old friend.

Rhys finger fucked Jevon slowly, working him open with every scissoring twist. Jevon's groan rang out, and Rhys moaned too. "God, you're so hot. My dick feels like it's gonna explode."

Jevon's cock throbbed in sympathy. He opened his eyes and met Rhys's stare beyond his weeping dick. His body was on fire. His chest heaved, and his skin was sheened with sweat. Rhys curled his fingers and Jevon exploded, hot come spurting out of his cock without either one of them touching it. "Fuck!"

The plummet to earth went on and on as Rhys tortured

Jevon's prostate, wringing every last shudder of pleasure from him, but eventually, it was over. Rhys's fingers slowed and slipped out of Jevon altogether, leaving behind an emptiness that was eclipsed only by a desperate need to break Rhys into as many pieces as he had Jevon.

Panting, Jevon scrambled to his knees and pushed Rhys back on the bed. He ached to slide his fingers inside Rhys, to explore and unravel him, but his hands were shaking too much. He took Rhys in his mouth and scraped his teeth along Rhys's length, sucking hard until Rhys gasped and threw his head back, his hips jutting forward, jamming his cock further down Jevon's throat as he blew his load with a loud groan.

"*Jesus*, I'd forgotten how good you are at this. You could fucking bite me and I'd still come like a train."

Jevon crawled up the bed, noting the theory to make use of next time, and collapsed on top of Rhys, kissing him fiercely as his own thighs still quivered. Rhys wrapped his arms around him, his legs around his waist, and it was a while before they came up for air.

Inexplicably, Jevon was hard again. He tried to hide it, but Rhys's smirk told him he'd failed.

"There's a beast inside you," he said.

Jevon grinned. "One day soon."

Laughing, Rhys rolled onto his side. "Yeah. I think I can guarantee that. Pretty shocked I didn't put my dick in you this time."

"So why didn't you?"

A flicker Jevon couldn't quite decipher passed through Rhys's lazy, blissed-out expression. "Um, I guess I'm a bit scared."

"Scared?" Jevon shifted to mirror Rhys's pose and brushed imaginary hair from his face. "Of what?"

"Of messing it up for you. I didn't have the greatest experience when I bottomed the first time, and it stayed with me enough to make things, uh, difficult for a while."

"Did someone hurt you?"

Rhys shook his head. "Not on purpose. I think I gave them the impression I was more confident than I actually was, and things moved too fast. It put me off blokes for a bit."

"At least you had other options," Jevon said as lightly as he could manage around the colossal lump in his throat. *I wish I'd been there.* "I can't imagine being with a woman now."

"That might change. Sexuality has never been static for me."

"I remember." Of course he did. Jevon had every word Rhys had ever uttered to him mapped out on his heart. "But I really do think I'm ready, if it's any consolation, especially after what just happened. And I wouldn't be shy about changing my mind mid-fuck."

Rhys sighed. "I know that, deep down, because you're nothing like nineteen-year-old me, horny and brimming with daddy issues. I know you're sure of your own mind and you make good decisions. It's just hard not to judge every situation by my own shitty standards."

"You're not good at being kind to yourself. It's like you don't believe you can be happy."

"Happy with you?"

"Happy at all." Jevon swiped a stray bead of sweat as it trickled down Rhys's chest. "You have to love yourself before you can love anyone else."

"Do you?"

"Do I what? Love myself?" Jevon drew his gaze up from tracing circles on Rhys's bare shoulder. "Absolutely."

And he could love Rhys too. He *would* love Rhys if the day ever came when Rhys let him.

The conversation faded. They cleaned up in the bathroom and returned to bed. Rhys didn't ask Jevon to stay, and Jevon didn't offer to leave, but crawling under the covers together was as easy as breathing.

Sleep came fast for both of them, but Jevon woke early the next morning to a phone buzzing somewhere on the bed. Careful not to jostle Rhys, he sat up and felt around for the phone, coming up with Rhys's. *Huh, same ringtone.* He peered at the screen. A younger, thicker-set version of Rhys stared back at him.

Harry.

Jevon shook Rhys awake and showed him the phone. "It's your brother."

"Wha—" Rhys squinted at the screen and a scowl formed on his face. He silenced the call and tossed the phone aside. "Fuck that shit."

Jevon stared, eyebrow raised. "That's what you do when your brother calls you at six in the morning?"

"Especially when he calls me at six in the morning. He probably wants to talk me through a breakfast smoothie and FaceTime a yoga class."

That didn't sound half bad to Jevon, but something else niggled him. He reached for the phone. Three missed calls and a bunch of message alerts lit up the screen. "He must be pretty excited about it to hassle you this much."

"You don't know my brother." But Rhys took the phone as Jevon held it out and thumbed through his notifications with a sleepy frown that steadily morphed into something more awake, concerned, and confused. "Shit."

"What's wrong?"

"I don't know." Rhys sat up, already halfway out of the bed, his phone pressed to his ear. "But I need to speak to Harry right now."

CHAPTER NINE

"I DON'T UNDERSTAND." Rhys blurred around the bedroom, gathering clothes from the floor. "Why are you asking me to check on a patient in Romford when you haven't worked there for more than a year?"

"He's not just a patient," Harry said. "He's a colleague and a mate, and I'm worried about him."

"Why?"

"Because he's been out of touch for a couple of days."

"What about his family? Friends?"

"There's no one local apart from his fella, but he's in Germany on business right now. I'm sorry, bro. I wouldn't ask if I didn't have to."

"I know." Rhys yanked jeans up his legs and pulled on the T-shirt Jevon handed him. "Why are you so worried, though? The dude might have dropped his phone down the bog."

"He has severe ME. If he's collapsed or fallen, there's a good chance he can't get up."

"Got it. I can be there in forty minutes if I run for the train. Give me the address."

"Rhys . . ."

"What?"

Crickets. Rhys paused in the action of stamping into his shoes. "Spit it out, mate. If you want me to hit the road fast, you've got to give me everything right now. I'm on shift at midday."

"Okay, but don't get lairy with me till after you've been over there, right? Nothing matters until I know he's safe."

Jevon appeared in front of Rhys, somehow already dressed and holding out Rhys's coat, wallet, and keys. His gentle eyes held questions Rhys couldn't answer.

Rhys shook his head. "Jesus, Harry. Just tell me. This dude an axe murderer, or what?"

"No, Rhys. It's Angelo . . . Angelo Giordano."

Giordano. Rhys turned the name over and over in his mind, but it still took far too long to make the connection. And even when he did, it didn't make any sense. "How do you know Angelo?"

"I told you—he's a patient. At least, he used to be."

He's a colleague and a mate. The words echoed, repeating on a loop over and over, until links he hadn't known were missing began to slot into place. Angelo's condition fit Harry's specialties perfectly—Christ, Rhys had even talked about it with Dylan.

"Listen," Harry spoke over the chaos in Rhys's brain. "I know I've got some explaining to do, but we don't have time for that right now. Dylan's losing his shit, and I'm worried too. It's not like Angelo to go silent."

Outside of the club, Rhys didn't know Angelo well enough to know if that was true, but he'd seen him unwell before. A distant night a few years ago flashed into his mind: Angelo stumbling along the pavement, face pale, glassy eyes, his legs too weak to hold him up.

Perspective returned and the paramedic in Rhys kicked in. "Okay. I'm leaving now. Text me the address and I'll call you when I've found him. And, Harry?"

"Yeah?"

"I fucking hate you sometimes."

RHYS POUNDED on Angelo and Dylan's front door. A friendly neighbour had squinted at Rhys's paramedic ID and opened the exterior doors, but so far, there'd been no response from Angelo.

"Perhaps he's not here?"

Jevon leaned on the wall. He'd come with Rhys, despite being offered little explanation of where they were going. Of course he had. And it was only his calming presence that was keeping Rhys tied to the ground as his mind raced. *Harry knows Angelo. And Dylan. And he knew I did too.*

It didn't make any sense, but it wasn't important right now. Rhys hammered on the door again, then dropped to his knees and opened the letter box. The flat beyond was dark and quiet. *Too quiet.* Concern gnawed at Rhys's gut. Despite an active playmate connection, he'd never been as close to Angelo as he was to Dylan, but the prickly feeling on the back of his neck told him something was wrong.

He straightened up and glanced around the lobby. A lamp plugged into the mains caught his attention. He ripped it from the wall and disconnected the cable.

Jevon's eyes widened. "Whoa. What are you doing?"

"Breaking in."

"Do I want to know how you know how to do that?"

"Probably not. Can you hold the letter box open?"

Jevon shook his head but moved to help Rhys anyway. He held the letter box open while Rhys jammed his arm through and hooked the cable over the handle inside.

It took a few tries, but eventually, the lock clicked and the door opened. Rhys dropped the cable and pushed inside, jogging through the dark flat without waiting to see if Jevon followed.

A quick scout of the kitchen, bedroom, and bathroom found them empty. Rhys was coming down the hallway again when Jevon called out.

"Rhys, man. He's in here."

Rhys hurried into the living room and found Angelo on the couch, sprawled out with one arm dangling limply off the side. "Shit."

"He's so cold," Jevon said.

He moved out of the way as Rhys pushed past to touch two fingers to Angelo's neck. A strong pulse greeted him—*thank god*—but the pallor in Angelo's usually olive complexion was terrifying. The slackness in his limbs. His ice cold fingers as Rhys squeezed his hand and shook his chest.

"Angelo? Come on, mate. Wake up." For a long moment, nothing happened, then a faint groan escaped Angelo in a scratchy whoosh of air. His eyes twitched, and Rhys kept shaking him until they flickered open. "Angelo? It's Rhys. Can you hear me? Do you know where you are?"

Angelo's bloodshot eyes held no recognition. His blank gaze drifted to Jevon, and nothing changed.

Rhys squeezed his hands harder and tried again. "Angelo, mate? It's Rhys. I need you to wake up for me, okay?"

Finally, awareness seeped into Angelo's face. He blinked, then his eyes widened a touch. "Rhys?"

"Yup. It's me. Can you sit up?"

"Wha—what are you doing here?"

"Welfare check. You've got some people pretty worried about you. Where's your phone?"

"I—I don't know."

"I'll look for it." Jevon got up and left the room.

Angelo's bewildered gaze followed him. "Who's that?"

"A friend. Don't worry; he won't raid your toy box. Can you sit up?"

"No."

"Try. Wrap your arms around my neck."

Angelo obeyed and Rhys eased him upright, keeping hold of him as he swayed dizzily and his eyes drooped again.

Rhys gave him a moment, then reclaimed his focus. "What's wrong? Is your ME bad?"

"Yeah."

"How long have you been like this?"

"I—I can't think."

"All right, mate. Don't worry. It's okay." Rhys was familiar enough with Angelo's condition that he didn't expect any coherent answers just yet. He checked him for signs of genuine danger to life, then worked on getting him warm.

Jevon reappeared with a phone. "Dead. I'm gonna plug it in down here, man, okay?"

Angelo nodded. "Thanks."

Jevon glanced at Rhys, eying the way he was rubbing circulation back into Angelo's hands. "Should I put the heating on?"

"Please. Maybe the kettle too?" Rhys looked at Angelo again. "When did you last eat?"

"I don't know."

"On it." Jevon disappeared again.

Rhys moved onto Angelo's other hand. "What's the last thing you remember?"

"Um . . ." Angelo leaned back on the couch, frowning as he struggled to process the question. "Coming home from work, maybe? I was fine all day, then I fell off the bus."

"What day was that?"

"Friday. It's the only day I take the bus back from Stratford."

Friday. It was Monday now, which meant that Angelo had been ill and alone all weekend. "Where's Dylan?"

"Germany. Munich, I think." Colour was beginning to

return to Angelo's cheeks. "Some Brexit training thing for work."

"Sounds like Dylan."

"Yeah. Is he okay? I can't remember when I last spoke to him."

"He called me last night." Rhys ducked his head guiltily. "But I didn't answer. If I had, I'd have been here sooner. He had to call Harry in the end to wake my arse up this morning."

"Harry?"

"Yeah."

Angelo blinked slowly. "I'm so fucking out of it, I thought you *were* Harry when I first saw you. I'm so sorry you had a stranger dragging you out of bed."

Jevon came back as Angelo was speaking. He handed two mugs to Rhys, one with tea, the other with tomato soup. In his other hand was a plate of toast. He set it within Angelo's reach, and Rhys wondered if he'd leave again.

He didn't.

Rhys held the soup to Angelo's lips and helped him drink some, grateful that Jevon hadn't made it too hot, then he set it aside and took a deep breath. "Yeah. About that whole stranger thing."

Angelo accepted the mug of tea. "What about it? Harry's a good bloke. If he was shitty, it would only be because—"

Rhys held up his hand. "He wasn't shitty—at least no more than I probably deserve—and that's because he's my brother, man."

"What?"

"You heard. Harry Foster. Physiotherapist. Spinach freak. New-found horse fanatic. He's my little brother."

Angelo opened his mouth. Shut it again. "I don't understand."

"That makes two of us. If it's any consolation, I didn't know how we were all connected until this morning, and I still have no fucking idea how this happened."

"Harry was my physio before he moved away."

"I know."

"He was my mentor when I trained as an exercise therapist."

"I know that too."

"Rhys, he's like the best friend I've ever had."

"Yup."

Angelo took a bite of toast, life returning to his hooded eyes with every rotation of his jaw. When he looked up, Rhys finally saw something he recognised. "Does he know we're fuck buddies?"

"Uh—" Rhys winced and died a little inside. "I reckon so. He already knew we were connected when he called and put together with shit I've told him about my weekends and stuff . . ."

"Fuck. Me too. I never used your name, but we've definitely talked about you in front of him."

"I'm probably gonna kill him, just so you know. Once I've told him you're not dead."

"That's not fair." Jevon spoke for the first time since coming back in the room.

Rhys studied his face for horror, for any sign that he was about to leave Rhys to the soap opera his life apparently was, but found nothing beyond amused kindness. "How do you figure that?"

"Angelo was his patient," Jevon said. "Harry couldn't tell you anything about him without breaking confidentiality. And whatever freaky shit you kids have going on at that sex club probably falls under that too. Don't those places have some mafia code?"

Angelo started to laugh, but it turned into a cough, reminding Rhys of the real reason they were all there.

"Fuck. I need to call my darling brother and let him know you're okay. Has your phone come back on yet? You should call Dylan."

Rhys stepped out of the room, leaving Jevon to help Angelo with his phone, and went to the kitchen.

Harry answered on the first ring.

"He's all right," Rhys said quickly. "Fucked, but okay. I've checked him out, and I don't think he needs to go to hospital if he can get to his GP in the next couple of days."

"What happened? Relapse?"

"I think so. He's pretty confused."

"Yeah. He gets that way when his energy levels tank. It hasn't happened for a while though."

"How do you know that all the way from Cornwall?"

"Because we're friends," Harry said. "He picked up some of my London patients when he qualified as an exercise therapist, and he's been down here to work with me on the farm."

"Brilliant."

Harry sighed.

Rhys closed his eyes and pictured him prowling around Joe's farmhouse kitchen, rubbing his head like a deranged gorilla —his favourite tic when his anxiety was up. "He's okay, mate. Just exhausted. We'll get some grub into him and maybe get him up on his feet, see how he goes."

"Be careful. His balance is awful when he's been down— hang on a sec—" Harry spoke to someone else, then came back on the line. "Listen, Joe's going to drive the van up and get him. Bring him down to us until Dylan gets back. Do you think you can watch him until Joe gets there?"

Relief flooded Rhys. He hadn't relished the idea of leaving Angelo alone again. "Why can't you come?"

"Because I have eight residential patients waiting on me. If I could leave, I'd already be on my way. Seriously, Rhys, do you honestly think I'd have created this mess for you if it was something I could've sorted myself?"

"So you admit it's a bloody mess then?"

"Which part? Angelo needing us both right now? Or the fact that he was fucking you in a sex club long before the hospital referred him to me? Because from where I'm standing, bro, none of that is my fault."

"Are you saying it's mine?"

"No, I'm saying it's ridiculous, and it doesn't even matter anymore. Angelo needs help, and I'm asking you to give it to him until Joe can get there."

Rhys let loose a heavy sigh of his own. Angsty conversations with Harry always went like this—round in circles and making no sense until one of them blinked and played the part of the father they'd never had. "How soon can Joe get here?"

"He's leaving now."

Rhys glanced at his phone screen and his stomach sank. Harry and Joe's Newquay home was five hours away on a good day. Add in rush-hour traffic and motorway bullshit, and an afternoon ETA was wishful thinking. "Fuck. I've got to be on the chopper at noon. There's no way I can stay until Joe gets here."

"Can you leave a key? So he can get in if Angelo can't get up?"

Rhys stepped out into the hallway and stuck his head around the living room door. Jevon was holding the phone to Angelo's ear with one hand and rubbing Angelo's seized-up leg with the other. "Yeah, I'll do that if I have to, but I'll try and sort something else out first. Just tell Joe to put his foot down."

"Will do. And Rhys?"

"Yeah?"

"For what it's worth, you would've found out about Angelo and Dylan last Christmas when they were here too. But you didn't show up."

RHYS CAME BACK into the room with a face like Jevon had never seen. He crouched by Angelo and fixed him with what Jevon imagined was a mask from his paramedic skin. "Joe's coming to get you. Harry wants you to stay with them until Dylan gets back."

The defeat in Angelo was obvious, even to Jevon. "I can't let them look after me."

"Why not?" Rhys said. "They're your friends."

"They're *your* family and you don't let them look after you."

"How do you know that?"

Angelo raised one shoulder in a slight half shrug. "He doesn't talk about you much—which makes sense now—but I know he misses you. Joe's clan are awesome, but it's not the same as your own having your back."

Rhys's gaze sharpened. "I have his back. It's not my fault he fucked off to Cornwall, is it?"

"If you found someone who loved you like Joe loves him, you'd fuck off too."

There was no malice in Angelo's tone, but Rhys seemed to bristle all the same. "I can't fuck off. I work on the air ambulance, mate. I can't hand a car crash off to someone else because I fancy spending my summers on horseback."

"Okay." Angelo leaned back on the couch again. "But I think you're being a bit of a dick. Yeah, maybe he could've given you a heads-up about me and Dylan, but I don't know when. He's not my official physio anymore, but I don't think I've ever stopped being his patient."

Rhys said nothing, his expression clear he was done talking about his brother.

Jevon chewed on his lip. He was beginning to feel superfluous to requirements, but somehow stepping away seemed impossible.

He settled for excusing himself to the kitchen to make more tea.

Rhys followed him a few minutes later. "I'm so sorry."

"Don't be." Jevon chucked an extra spoon of sugar in Angelo's mug. "It's not my business, man."

"And yet here you are making tea in a stranger's kitchen."

"I've brewed up in worse places."

"Me too." Rhys knocked his head on Jevon's shoulder. "Listen, I need to ask you a favour."

Jevon put the kettle back on its stand and turned to face Rhys. "If you're going to ask me to wait with Angelo until your brother's fella gets here, it's fine. I was going to offer."

"For real?"

"Of course. You have to work and he needs someone here."

"But you don't know him."

"Neither do you, by the sound of it. Even if you have fucked him."

The words were out of Jevon's mouth before he was consciously aware of them forming in his head, but as soon as they registered with Rhys, it was clear he'd hit a nerve.

"You're right," Rhys said. "Until a few months back, I'd been mucking around with Angelo and Dylan for a good while, but I don't know Angelo. Just that he loves Dylan, and his health isn't always great."

"What about Dylan?"

Rhys shrugged. "Better. We talk on the phone, confide in each other, but I haven't seen him in months."

"Why not?"

"Does it matter? I thought you'd be pleased they weren't still fucking me."

One day Jevon would understand how simple conversations with Rhys could become the end of the world. "It's not my business if they're fucking you."

"No?"

"No. It just worries me—for your sake—that you have a relationship with them you seem ashamed of."

"*That's* what you're annoyed about?"

"I'm not annoyed," Jevon said, even as sharp scratches of temper buzzed through his veins. "And I'm not jealous that you had a life before you met me. I'm just sad it doesn't seem to mean anything to you. That you won't *let* it."

Whatever was stoking the fire in Rhys's dark gaze seemed to give up on him. He leaned heavily on the counter and shook his head. "I don't understand what's happening right now."

The bewilderment in his face was so complete that Jevon abandoned his tea making and pulled him into a tight hug. "What a day, huh? And it ain't even lunchtime."

Rhys rumbled something against Jevon's chest but didn't pull back to make himself heard, so Jevon let him be, rubbed his back, and tried not to wonder what on earth would happen next. He'd fallen hard and fast for Rhys in ways he couldn't describe, but despite seeming to function in the outside world, Rhys was a mess. Angelo was a mess. And Harry didn't sound too happy either.

What do you care?

Jevon couldn't answer that question, except to say that he did. He really fucking did.

Movement in the living room roused them. Rhys disentangled himself and hurried to help Angelo, who was trying to get up. "What are you doing?"

"Going to the bathroom."

"Come on then, I'll help you."

"Fuck, no. I can take a piss by myself."

"It's not the pissing I'm worried about. And you shouldn't be worried at all. It's not like I haven't seen your dick."

To hear Rhys joke about it was oddly relieving. And warming. Jevon sat on the couch and tried to decipher why that was—why the thought of Rhys being with anyone else made him feel good. And it all came back to Rhys—to the self-loathing that could only be eclipsed by acceptance. *He needs to feel good about this too.*

Rhys came back from the bathroom alone. "He's in bed. Figure that's the best place for him until Joe gets here. It's gonna be a long ride back to Cornwall."

Jevon could imagine. "Do you need to go right now?"

"Yeah. I've got to get back, shower, and get my arse to work by midday. Even if I don't eat, I'm cutting it fine already."

"Eat the cupcakes. We forgot last night."

Rhys smirked, but there wasn't much left to say. He gave Jevon a list of numbers to call if anything went wrong, then it was time to go.

He said goodbye to Jevon on the doorstep with a kiss that dragged them to the opposite wall, nipping Jevon's bottom lip until he pulled away with flushed cheeks and a hooded half grin. "I'm not off until ten, but I can meet you somewhere later?"

Jevon shook his head. "I have to go back to Bedford tonight. Got a party in the morning, then I'm doing some stuff at a school in the afternoon. Maybe the day after?"

"I'm working. My next day off is Friday."

Jevon groaned. "I'm going to Manchester on Friday. There's a big aid summit in the city. I'm crashing it in clown mode and telling all the big charities how shit they are."

"Seriously?"

"Well, I might not tell them they're shit, but I've got a whole list of things that they can do better."

Rhys chuckled. "You're surreal. Sometimes I think I've dreamed you."

"You might have to dream about me for a while. I'll be gone all weekend."

Rhys's humour faded. "That sucks."

Jevon couldn't argue with that, and they'd run out of time in any case. Rhys kissed Jevon once, twice more, then he was gone, leaving Jevon to the unfamiliar flat and a stranger in the bed.

ANGELO LIMPED into the living room, leaning heavily on the furniture for support. "Did you clean up in here?"

Jevon shrugged. "A bit. Sorry, did I disturb you?"

"Only when I couldn't remember who the fuck you were." Angelo ventured further into the room, moving slowly, like his body had forgotten how to walk. Jevon caught him when he stumbled by the couch and eased him down. "Thanks."

"Anytime. I think Joe will be here soon. You want to eat before he gets here?"

Angelo shook his head. "Nah. I've got too much tea in my belly right now to handle anything else."

"Do you feel better?"

"No."

Jevon smiled. Angelo had been asleep for a good portion of the morning, but what communication they'd shared had been brutally honest on Angelo's part. "Fair enough. You remember who I am now?"

"If your name and the fact that Rhys seemed to have trouble looking anywhere but at you counts for anything. What's the deal with you two? Are you together?"

"Would it matter if we were?"

"Only if he wasn't happy." Angelo gazed steadily at Jevon. "I heard you talking earlier, and you're both wrong about him and me. We're not exactly mates, but I do care about him."

"It's not my business."

"True, but if neither of you wanted it to be, you wouldn't be bickering about it in my kitchen."

"Bickering?"

Angelo shrugged but seemed to run out of steam. Jevon let it go and got to his feet. "You're gonna need some stuff packing if you're staying with Harry a few days. Tell me where it is and I'll get it for you."

"That's okay. You've done enough already."

"I haven't done much, mate. And it will save Joe a job, eh?"

Angelo relented and directed Jevon to a bag in the bedroom cupboard that was half packed already. Jevon stuffed in some more clothes and retrieved a toothbrush and toiletries from the bathroom.

When he got back, Angelo was squinting painfully at his phone. He grinned a little when he saw Jevon. "Hang on, I'll turn the camera round. Shit . . . I can't see it. Hey, Jevon? Come here . . . Dylan wants to see you."

Curious, Jevon put the bag down and rounded the back of the couch. He relieved Angelo's shaking hands of the phone and held it far enough away that both of their faces fit on the screen.

A blond man—Dylan, presumably—who was every bit as pretty as Angelo, peered back at him, his head tilted sideways. "Wow. So you're who's been hiding Rhys away?"

"Doubt it," Jevon said. "Until yesterday, I hadn't seen him for a few weeks."

"And yet you were still with him this morning?" Dylan's tone was playful. "Rhys doesn't do sleepovers with random fucks."

"Um—"

"Stop it." Angelo rescued Jevon with a mistimed wave of his hand. "Jevon isn't a hook-up."

Dylan eyed Jevon, but his expression was hard to read through FaceTime. Jevon recalled what Rhys had said about being closer to him than Angelo and wondered if he was being appraised.

"Joe should be here soon," he said when the silence had stretched on a beat too long.

Dylan seemed to shake himself. "Thank god. Jevon, can I have a quick chat with you before he gets there?"

Jevon glanced at Angelo, but he seemed to have zoned out. "Sure. Give me a sec, I'll step outside and call you back."

After getting Angelo comfortable, Jevon took Angelo's phone outside and called Dylan. "What's up?"

"Nothing, really. I just wanted to thank you without embarrassing Angelo. He hates people seeing him like this. It's probably why he didn't call anyone when he started to feel bad."

"It's no problem. To be honest, I haven't done much. He's been asleep most of the time while I've folded some washing and watched Peaky Blinders because I couldn't work your telly out."

"Peaky Blinders is awesome."

"Heh." Jevon remained unconvinced on that point. The main character was *hot,* but picking up midway through the second season had left him totally confused. "Either way, there's no need to say thanks. If Rhys needs something, he'll always get it from me."

"I was hoping you'd say that."

"Why?"

"Because he deserves to have someone there for him."

"You're not there for him?"

"Of course I am, but it's not me he wants, and it's not the same. Look, it's none of my business, but I reckon you've heard enough about everyone else's lives this morning to handle a little bit more."

"Go on," Jevon said warily. "Unless you're about to tell me he's a sound bloke who deserves to be happy, because I know that shit already."

"Then there's nothing to say. Just don't let him push you away. I don't know what the fuck's been going on with him and Harry, but I do know that Rhys's bad habits tend to kick in when he's convinced himself he was born to be lonely."

Jevon wondered when the world had started kicking out men like Rhys and his so-called not friends, and where the hell they'd been his whole life. "Listen, I can't promise what I don't know, but when Rhys is with me, I'll take care of him, okay? Just like he takes care of me."

"Thank you," Dylan said. "For looking after Angelo and letting me butt my nose in your business. Can we meet when Angelo's well again? We'd love to get to know you better."

Sex clubs and orgies filled Jevon's mind, sticking his tongue to the roof of his mouth. And then refugee camps, aeroplanes, and a three-month stint thousands of miles away replaced it. "Sure," he managed eventually. "I'll put my number in Angelo's phone. Call me anytime."

Dylan said goodbye, and as luck would have it, a battered Transporter van pulled up outside a moment later.

Yet another dark-haired hottie got out. This one had high cheekbones, flawless skin, and startling blue eyes, and Jevon made a note to ask Rhys if he knew any men that weren't ridiculously beautiful. And if he knew a way to slow the world down so their dwindling time together could last a bit longer.

CHAPTER ELEVEN

———————

R: *Sorry about Joe. No filter. Wasn't too rude, was he?*

Rhys flopped down on his bed while he waited for Jevon to answer and resisted the urge to sniff the sheets and see if the bed still smelled of their night together. The last twenty-four hours had been insane, and those precious few hours were all that made sense.

His phone buzzed.

J: *Just blunt. Nothing I couldn't handle. And he was good to Angelo.*

R: *He's a good man.*

J: *So's your brother by all accounts.*

Rhys scowled, despite the tickle in his belly that flared every time Jevon's name lit up his phone. After a lecture from Dylan and an earful from Joe—who usually stayed out of his business—he was sick of talking about Harry.

R: *I know Harry's good. He's a fucking superhero.*

J: *You should probably talk to him then.*

R: *How do u know I haven't?*

J: *Because you're talking to me right now . . . and Angelo told me.*

Angelo. News had filtered out of Cornwall that he was

safely in Harry's care, but while Rhys's conscience told him that was all that truly mattered, imagining him in the hub of Joe's cosy kitchen, more at home there than Rhys had ever been, still stung. *Idiot.* Did he seriously begrudge Angelo that? A cup of tea and a slice of Joe's mum's cake when his legs wouldn't hold him up?

R: *I'm sorry.*

J: *What for now?*

R: *For being an internalising wanker.*

Jevon didn't reply straight away. Rhys wondered if he'd fallen asleep and ventured off the bed to find some dinner. The bag of cupcakes was still on the kitchen counter—one chocolate, one lemon. Rhys ate them both in two bites and retreated to the shower.

When he got back, Jevon had replied with a photograph of a UNICEF camp who-the-hell-knew-where. There was no written message, but there didn't need to be. *Perspective, man.*

IT WAS Friday morning by the time Rhys's brood wore off. He called Harry when he got in from his night shift and turned the coffee machine on while he waited for the call to connect.

"You're not dead then?" Harry enquired when he answered.

Rhys sniffed the milk in the fridge. "Don't be dramatic. I've only ignored you twice."

"I guess that's not so bad, considering it's you."

"Don't start. You ignore me plenty when you've got your knickers in a twist."

Harry laughed. "True that. Are you still freaking out about Angelo and Dylan?"

"I was never freaking out."

"Liar."

"Yup." Rhys binned the milk. "And I'm sorry I ripped into

you about it. You just—I dunno—caught me off guard. I've been trying to move on from all that stuff at the club."

"Why? I mean, I get that you've maybe outgrown partying at the club, but Angelo and Dylan have always talked about you like you're friends."

Rhys didn't feel like dissecting his non-relationship with Angelo for the millionth time. He sighed. "It's hard to explain."

"Try."

"Why? So you can tell me I'm emotionally stunted?"

"I've never said that."

Harry's tone was mild, but Rhys caught the hurt. Always did. "I know. It's me that thinks that. Or, at least, I did until I met them."

"And you wanted more than just sex?"

"No. I just hated seeing them so happy. Before them, and you and Joe, I'd never seen blokes look at each other like that."

"Why would you when your only social interactions are in sex clubs and hook-up joints?"

Rhys winced. "Brutal."

"And true. But when it comes to Angelo and Dylan, I get it. I was so jealous when I first saw them together, lonely, too. I thought it was such a rare thing that it couldn't possibly happen for me."

"Yeah, yeah. Then you met Joe and lived happily ever after. I get it, bro. You don't have to sing me a song."

"And *you* don't have to pretend you're okay when you're not. Do you know how much it hurt to hear Dylan telling Angelo how worried he's been about you these last few months? To know you've been unhappy and I can't do a damn thing about it because you just won't *talk* to me? Jesus, Rhys, I—" Harry broke off with a frustrated sigh. "Look, I miss you, okay? Nothing else really matters anymore."

Rhys dropped heavily onto the couch, his sleepless night catching up with him. "I miss you too."

"What are you doing for Christmas? Do you have to work this year?"

"I don't know. I haven't seen December's rota yet."

"If you don't . . . come down, please? Maybe you can bring your, uh, new friend with you?"

That woke Rhys up. Somehow he'd clean forgotten that even Angelo was bound to have remembered Jevon and mentioned him to Harry. Not to mention Joe.

Rhys's brain swam with images of Jevon as he'd last seen him, smiling and waving from Angelo's doorstep before he'd turned away to do a man he'd just met a fraternal solid. Then he pictured them together at Joe's big table, enduring a rowdy Christmas. A real one. *Right. 'Cause life's just that kind.* "I'll let you know."

"Do it. Oh, and Rhys?"

"Yeah?"

"Just so you know, Joe gave me hell for not telling you about Angelo and Dylan, even though he knew I couldn't. Reckons I could've told Angelo and let him deal with it, but there's a reason I didn't do that."

"It'd better be a good one."

"It is—it was because you're my brother, and there's no way you were going to hear that shit from anyone but me, even if it did take two years and a crisis to make it happen. I love you, man."

"I know that."

"Good."

An awkward pause crackled between them, and for once Rhys felt compelled to fill it. "Listen, I've got to get some sleep before my eyes fall out, but for what it's worth, I'm glad it happened this way. Angelo's lucky to have a friend like you."

"Fuck off, Rhys. I'm the one who's lucky. No one else can call you their brother. Now get some sleep and take care of yourself."

SATURDAY EVENING FOUND Rhys wide awake, alone, and indulging in his new favourite hobby: staring at his phone and waiting for Jevon to call. He started at home, but eventually the walls closed in on him and he decamped to the pub where they'd first met.

The bar was busy—packed with men looking for a good time. Few were alone, and if they were, it didn't stay that way for long.

Rhys kept his head down as he pushed through the crowds, hardly noticing the swathes of bare skin and the distinct smell of any establishment stuffed with this much testosterone. He got a pint and settled in a corner, head down, thumbing through his phone, ignoring any fool who interrupted him.

The message thread between him and Jevon kept him occupied for a while. Jevon had been busy most days since they'd parted ways in Romford, but the evenings were a different story. Wherever Jevon was and whatever he was doing, the rum seemed to be flowing, and rum, apparently, made Jevon . . . chatty.

J: *Wish you were here*
R: *Why?*
J: *'Cause I miss you, and . . .*
R: *. . . ?*
J: *I wanna do stuff with you*
R: *Like what?*
J: *I want you to fuck me*

Heat crept up the back of Rhys's neck. Getting Angelo safely to Harry, and the realisation that it would be more than a week before he would see Jevon again, had put a pretty heavy dampener on the amazing night they'd shared. But when Jevon sent messages like that, the thrill of simply being with him—even when he wasn't there—returned full force.

Rhys licked his lips and carried on reading.

R: *How do you want me to fuck you?*

J: *Slowly. Maybe . . . I don't know.*

J: *How do you want to fuck me?*

J: *Assuming you do . . .*

R: *I want to fuck you. If u don't know that by now, we're doing it wrong*

J: *Doing what?*

And just like that, the recycled thrill dancing through Rhys fell off a cliff. Talking to Harry, and multiple texts from Dylan, had put the nature of his relationship with Jevon at the front of his mind, but he was no closer to defining it. No closer to wanting to because every train of thought stopped at the same station—the one where Jevon left. Just like everyone else that Rhys had ever cared about.

He put his phone away and bought another drink, trying to push the maudlin thoughts out of his mind. Jevon had never promised him anything, and Rhys had never asked. And dear god, if he wasn't tired of the wallowing loop playing in his brain.

Fuck this shit.

Downing his drink, he pulled his phone from his pocket and shot Jevon a message.

R: *Call me when you're free. I've got an idea.*

JEVON CALLED JUST AFTER MIDNIGHT. Rhys was in bed, awake and waiting. "Hey."

"Hey yourself," Jevon said softly. "Sorry it took me a while. It's been a mad day."

"Where are you?"

"The Holiday Inn near Canal Street. It's kinda noisy."

"I can imagine. Is that where clowns go these days?"

"Nah, it was just the cheapest room FFP could find without

dumping us at the worst B&B in the world. They like to look after us a bit when we're back on home turf."

Rhys sat up and reached for his well-nursed glass of vodka. "Do you have your own room?"

"Yes."

"Are you there now?"

"Yes. Why? You gonna FaceTime me something freaky?"

"Do you want me to?"

Jevon chuckled dryly. "If I have to answer that question, then we're *still* doing it wrong."

"Right." Rhys swallowed more vodka. "Hang on a sec."

He swiped at his screen until the FaceTime option came up and made the switch. Jevon connected the call, and his sunshine smile filled the screen.

Rhys's heart jumped. Missing Jevon was his normal these days, but he hadn't realised how real it was until he saw Jevon's face. Locked eyes with him. Heard his voice. Rhys touched the screen, like he could reach through the glass and feel Jevon's warmth against his fingertips. "Hey."

"Hello. How're you doing over there?"

Rhys rolled onto his belly. "Lonely, naked, and a little bit drunk."

"Me too." Jevon chuckled softly and flipped a lamp on beside him, treating Rhys to a clearer view.

He was naked.

And hard.

And so fucking beautiful Rhys wanted to cry, among other things.

The other things were less embarrassing. He licked his lips, heat already pooling in his groin. "What have you been up to tonight? Have you been down Canal Street?"

"A bit. My mate Jean was trying to hook me up with a go-go dancer."

"Oh yeah?" A flash of unearned possessiveness rippled through Rhys. "How did that go?"

Jevon tilted his head sideways. "It didn't. Despite the spell you cast over me the night we met, random hook-ups aren't my thing . . . even if I did have a clue what I was doing."

"You know what you're doing."

"Do I?"

Jevon's easy smile was clouded with insecurities that had no right to be there. The desperate need to touch him, to soothe him, caught in Rhys's throat, but all he had was a vodka-loose tongue and the truth. "I've never been with anyone who makes me come like you do."

They weren't the words of wisdom he'd imagined himself saying, but the desired effect was the same. Jevon's grin widened, chasing away shadowed doubt. "I love watching you come. I dream about it."

"Yeah? What are we doing?"

"Fucking . . . sometimes, but mostly just stuff we've already done. I like looking back at it—looking back at you."

"You could look back at me while I fuck you." Rhys snaked a hand beneath himself and squeezed his dick.

Jevon smirked, but questions danced in his eyes.

Rhys propped his phone up on the pillow so he could see him better. "What is it?"

"What?"

"What *is* it? I can tell you want to ask me something."

"How can you tell?"

"Psychic. Now spit it out."

Jevon bit his lip and sighed. "Are you fucking anyone else? I mean, I know it's not my business, but I feel like—I dunno—I need to know? Is that cool?"

"Of course it's cool." Rhys had never been so relieved he'd met Jevon when he had. "I'm not fucking anyone else, and I haven't been since a month before I met you."

"Seriously?" The surprise in Jevon's face would've been funny if it hadn't stung so much.

"Seriously. I told you when we met that I was trying to live a different life. I don't regret anything—or anyone—I've done, but it wasn't making me happy."

"Not even with Angelo and Dylan?"

"Especially not with them. Jesus, I've already had this conversation with Harry this week, but if you must know, fucking them was the worst. They're so happy and secure with each other that nothing else matters to them. They can go to the club and play around and no one gets hurt. But—"

"But it hurt you?"

"Yes. Jealousy is an evil thing."

"It's not jealousy to want happiness."

"Maybe not, but it felt that way at the time, so I stopped playing with them. Then I found I couldn't face being with anyone until I met you. There's no one else, Jevon. I swear."

"I believe you," Jevon whispered. "I just don't know if we can do this without one of us getting hurt."

Rhys had nothing because it was too late to save himself. Saying goodbye to Jevon would tear him apart whether he did it now or when he left the country. "I don't know either. I'm trying not to think too far ahead."

"Is that a plan?"

"An ill-advised one, I'd imagine."

"Uh-huh." Jevon lay back on a wide bed, his hair fanning out on the pristine white sheets. "It could work, though. I legit called you up with the intention of having some fuck-hot phone sex, but here we are angsting round in circles again. If I wasn't half lashed, I'd maybe think we should read something into that, but right now, I just want to be with you."

"I want that too." Rhys had spent most of his life practising the art of shutting down his emotions. At work, he still reached for that switch, but he'd never quite managed it with Jevon. Had never found a safe place to hide.

There was no safe place now, but they couldn't talk their way past the inevitable, so why bother?

Fuck it. The determination that had carried Rhys home from the bar returned with a couple of mates. He rose up on his knees and closed his hand around his hard length. His phone was propped just high enough to fit his whole body in shot, and he tipped Jevon a wink. "I wish I could fuck you right now, but as that's not going to happen, perhaps I can show you something?"

"Like what?"

"I don't know . . . you said you like watching me come. How about I show you how hard I can nut around my favourite dildo?"

Jevon swallowed. Even on the tiny phone screen, his throat worked convulsively. "You have no idea how much I want to see that. Um, out of interest? How versatile are you?"

"Very. I know you're nervous about topping, but if it's something you ever want to try, it's on the table. *Everything's* on the table."

Jevon's eyes rolled into the back of his head as he palmed himself. "You're gonna kill me. You're literally every fantasy I've ever had come to life."

Rhys wanted to be so much more than that, but right now, it was all they had. He left Jevon hanging a moment and rummaged under his bed. His box of tricks had been neglected in recent months and was covered in a thin layer of dust. He wiped it clean with a sock from the nearby laundry basket, then heaved it onto the bed and nudged off the lid. "Pick and mix. Whatever you want."

Jevon's rumbling chuckle turned throaty. "I don't know what half of it is."

"I do. Just ask and I'll show you."

"Show me?"

"Yeah."

"Wow." Jevon whistled through his teeth and sat up on his elbows. "Is it wrong that I want to know what that tentacle thing is?"

Rhys laughed and retrieved the Bad Dragon dildo from the box. "You'd think it was a novelty toy, but it's probably the most expensive thing in here."

"For real?"

"Bible. And it's a small one."

Jevon gulped. "Jesus."

"Yep. I've never really used it, and I'm nowhere near drunk enough to try now."

"Good job it's not my first pick then, eh?"

"Very funny. What *is* your first pick?"

"The black cock. I can't take the rest of it seriously—not yet, anyway."

Relief washed over Rhys. Most of the toys in the box were well used, but there weren't many that seemed to fit the burning desire in his gut for Jevon. Kink was kink, and he embraced it all, but getting off with Jevon wasn't like that. They still had so much to learn about each other.

Rhys claimed the toy and put the box on the floor. He lubed up the dildo and fucked himself with it while Jevon looked on. Coming under the weight of Jevon's gaze but without his touch was an odd feeling. Breathing his name without an answering kiss. "Oh, god, Jevon."

"You're so fucking beautiful."

"I miss you," Rhys choked out.

Jevon's answer was a whisper. "I know, baby. I know."

CHAPTER TWELVE

BIRMINGHAM CHILDREN'S HOSPITAL was as familiar to Jevon as it was brand new. The interior had changed beyond recognition, but it smelled exactly the same.

He took the lift to the oncology department and cycled down the corridor to the nurse's station. Wide eyes followed him. He smiled and waved, the exaggerated movements so natural it was a wonder he didn't do it to everyone he met. Wan-faced children waved back. Some even smiled, and Jevon's world narrowed to just them as he entertained them with a quiet magic show.

An hour later, he made his escape and ventured into the fracture clinic. Despite the plaster parade, the children in there were more mobile. For hours, Jevon played games and painted pictures. Laughed, sang, and danced. He knew *"Fee-fi-fo-fum"* in six languages. Today he used four.

"Can you come again tomorrow?"

Jevon glanced down at the small boy tugging on his sleeve. "I don't think so, kiddo, but you don't really need me to. You know all the tricks better than I do." He pulled a pound coin from behind the boy's ear. "Look at that. Who put that there, eh?"

The boy took his prize and wheeled his chair back to his bed, a look of wonder on his face that got Jevon out of bed in the morning. *I fucking hate hospitals.*

A smiling young nurse brought him a cup of the worst tea in the world. "He's not the only one who'd like to see you every day. You've cheered me right up too."

Jevon ducked his head under the pretence of packing up his plastic pizza kit. The woman had been following him around all afternoon, testing the waters with gentle flirtation. *Awkward.*

"Listen," she said. "I'm finishing at five, and a bunch of us are going for a drink. Do you want to join us?"

"Thanks, but I've got plans."

"With your, uh, girlfriend?"

"Nah. I'm gay."

The nurse seemed as surprised as Jevon by the admission he'd never voiced to a stranger outside of a gay bar. It had slipped off his tongue like honey, and damn if it didn't feel good. He'd already smiled so much that day his face hurt, but he left the ward with a spring in his step, his unicycle under his arm, and his phone in his hand.

J: *Guess what?*

R: *What?*

J: *I just told a complete stranger I'm gay*

R: *That's fucking awesome. Who was it? Some rando in the street?*

J: *A nurse. She was chatting me up*

R: *A nurse where?*

J: *Kids hosp in Birmingham*

R: *BCH?*

J: *That's the one*

R: *Ure taking the piss, right?*

J: *Um, no?*

R: *Where are you?*

J: *Told you. BCH*

R: *No. Literally. Where are u?*

J: *Gift shop by Xray*

R: *Stay there*

Nonplussed, Jevon put his bags down, and leaned the unicycle against the wall. He spun around, searching for any clue as to why Rhys wanted him to linger in the hospital and . . .

Found himself face to face with the man of his dreams. "Jesus!"

"Not quite," Rhys said with a grin. "But I'm hoping that means you're pleased to see me?"

"Pleased to see you?" Jevon enveloped Rhys in a bear hug, squeezing him as tight as he dared. "I'm over the moon. What are you doing here?"

Rhys pulled back and glanced pointedly at his orange flight suit. "Fancy dress party. Seriously. What do you think?"

"I think my costume is better than yours."

Rhys laughed. His face lit up, and his often-stormy eyes crinkled at the sides. "Yeah. I'm pretty sure I couldn't pull off Rupert Bear trousers and a pink dickie bow, but it looks awesome on you. I take it you're working?"

"I was. All done now and heading home. What are you doing here?"

"Dropping off a patient. We do transport sometimes as well as emergency calls. I reckon I'll have been halfway round the country and back by the time I get home tonight."

"I can't believe you're here."

Rhys's grin widened. "Me either."

They stared at each other, lost in a moment they hadn't expected. Since their drunken FaceTime sexting, they'd spoken only briefly, relying instead on texts and the occasional dirty GIF. Jevon hadn't expected to see Rhys until after the weekend. Another four days, at least. "What time do you—"

"What are you doing tonight?" Rhys blurted at the same time.

Jevon shook his head. "Damn. That didn't work out. You go."

"We're due back in London at eight. If nothing comes up, I should be home by ten."

Jevon nodded slowly, calculating his own timetable. He had a meeting in Bedford when he got back, but it would be the easiest thing in the world to reschedule it and get on a train to London instead. *Screw it.* "I can meet you somewhere . . . if you want? Grab a drink and a late dinner? I've got a key to Efe's place, so I can sleep on her—"

Rough lips cut Jevon off. The kiss was harsh, brutal, and brief. And Rhys's glare was fierce. He pressed a key into Jevon's hand. "You're not sleeping anywhere but with me. I've gotta run, but let yourself in whenever, okay? I'll be home as soon as I can."

He was gone before Jevon could answer, dashing away to get back on his helicopter, perhaps unaware that he was the only man on the planet who could make a tango-orange jumpsuit sexy.

Jevon shook his head, half convinced the entire exchange had been a dream, but the key in his hand was warm against his palm, and the curious stare of a nearby couple bored into the side of his head.

He spared them a glance, bracing himself for disgust or derision. After all, they weren't in Vauxhall now, and Rhys had been in uniform. But to his surprise, the elderly couple smiled and waved, and Jevon realised they'd been upstairs with him on the oncology ward.

"Wonderful work you do," the old man said. "We haven't seen our wee girl smile like that in months."

"Thank you."

It was all Jevon could say.

LETTING himself into Rhys's flat felt all kinds of weird. Jevon's gaze darted around the small space, half expecting Rhys to emerge from the kitchen or from the bathroom, wearing just a towel. But of course, he didn't.

Jevon dropped the key on the coffee table and stashed his stuff in the hallway cupboard. Then he sat on the sofa and twiddled his thumbs, feeling no more at ease doing naff all than he had in Angelo's flat ten days ago.

Shit. Has it been that long?

Yeah. It had. It really fucking had.

Jevon got up and paced the room. When he got bored with that, he opened Rhys's fridge, rolling his eyes at the bare shelves. *What does the boy eat?* He already kind of knew the answer, but the Pot Noodle and baked beans in the cupboards still struck him as sad.

Resolved, Jevon left the flat again and crossed the road to the Asian supermarket. He bought real noodles, prawns, green vegetables, and bird's eye chillies. In the spice aisle, he picked up ginger, garlic, and a hefty bottle of soy sauce. With a cheap wok under his arm, he made his way to the till. He was still wearing his bright clothes, but this was London, and no one gave a shit.

At the One Stop next door, he stocked up on bread and milk and all the things Rhys seemed to be lacking, then he went home—to *Rhys's* home—and put it all away.

The whole expedition had taken forty-three minutes, which still left three hours until Rhys was due home. Jevon sat on the sofa again, then on the bed when he unfolded it just for something to do. The TV held little interest, and Rhys didn't seem to read books. He was on the verge of searching for a porn stash when he remembered the box under the bed.

Wow. Jevon had seen most of the toys over FaceTime, but that didn't come close to seeing them in real life. Dildos, plugs, rings, and probes. Handcuffs, ropes, and about eighty-four gallons of lube. Inadequacy reared its ugly head, but Jevon fought it. And won. He remembered Rhys's face when he'd come with Jevon's name on his lips. And he believed him.

Setting the black cock from that night aside, Jevon rummaged through the box, searching for something *way* smaller. His hand brushed a civilised looking plug. He pulled it out and considered it, turning it this way and that. Its girth didn't appear to be much more than Rhys's fingers, but it had been a while since *that* night, and however easy Rhys had made it look to take something inside him, the small plug was halfway to terrifying.

Still, Jevon kept hold of it—and a bottle of lube—while he packed the box away and slid it under the bed.

He shot Rhys a text.

J: *Can I use your shower?*

R: *Of course*

Awesome. Or was it? The butterflies having a rave in Jevon's belly couldn't quite decide. He shut down WhatsApp and started to toss his phone aside, but a work email buzzed through at the last second.

Jevon opened it with most of his mind already in the shower, just him, the butt plug, and a bottle of Wet. He'd read the message three times before it made any sense and his soul sank through the floor.

Fuck my life.

CHAPTER THIRTEEN

RHYS DASHED up the stairs to his flat with seconds to spare. Jevon had buzzed him inside, and as he neared the front door, the delicious scent of something he'd never dream of cooking was everywhere.

The front door was on the latch. Rhys pushed inside and followed the smell to the kitchen where Jevon was tossing something around in a pan that definitely didn't belong in Rhys's kitchen. "All right, mate?"

"Rhys!" Jevon turned the burner off and set the pan aside.

Rhys pounced on him, kissing him, and backed him against the counter. "Fuck, it's good to see you."

The words were mumbled against Jevon's lips, and they lost a battle with his roving tongue. Gasping, Rhys shoved his hands past Jevon's clown clothes, roaming the smooth skin he found there, and unbuttoned Jevon's ridiculous trousers. Jevon was a tall bloke and not much leaner than Rhys, but lifting him onto the counter was easy. Swallowing his thick cock made sense, and minutes later, swallowing every drop of his come was a balm to Rhys's bitter soul.

"Jesus fucking Christ." Jevon banged his head on the cupboard behind him, panting. "You're a whirlwind."

Rhys straightened up, licking his lips. "I've been called worse."

"Not by me." Jevon seized Rhys's jacket and yanked him close, snapping his teeth in Rhys's face. "Now get your arse up here."

Minutes later, it was Rhys's turn to come with a startled yell, his fingers carving grooves into Jevon's skull as he clutched at his head. *Best day ever.*

He came back into himself with a happy sigh. The sound surprised even him, but he let it go and slid from the counter. Jevon steadied him, then turned his attention to whatever magic he'd cooked up in the giant pan, his trousers still undone and hanging low enough to give Rhys a second wind.

Rhys left his own jeans open and came up behind Jevon, wrapping his arms tight around him, burying his face between his strong shoulder blades. His still half-hard dick pressed between Jevon's cheeks, but he tried to ignore how amazing it felt and bit down on Jevon's neck, revelling in his squirm. "I can't decide what I'm most hungry for—you or whatever sorcery you have in that shiny thing."

"Dude, it's a wok."

"If you say so."

Jevon chuckled and drew the wok towards him. "It's just a stir fry. You had nothing but MSG-noodle junk in your cupboards."

"I wasn't expecting company, but if you ever meet my brother, do me a favour and don't gossip about the nutritional state of my kitchen cupboards. I don't need that lecture in my life."

Jevon said nothing. Just exhaled slowly, like he was bracing himself for a storm. Rhys frowned and spun him around. "What's up?"

"Nothing."

"Liar."

"Am I?" A hint of a smile played on Jevon's lips . . . a whisper of mischief, but there was something else too.

Something that squeezed the giddy feeling Rhys had carried since their surprise Birmingham encounter. "Seriously. You look like you have the weight of the world on your shoulders. What's on your mind?"

"Two things," Jevon said. "One you'll probably like, and one that if you feel anything like me will probably make you want to drown yourself."

Jevon wasn't a man given to dramatics. Rhys pulled himself entirely from his lust-filled haze and reclaimed the functioning adult he'd left at the door. "Give me the bad news first."

"Sure about that? 'Cause it's pretty fucking shit."

"Just tell me, man."

Jevon sighed. "You know how I'm due back overseas just before Christmas?"

A painful band tightened around Rhys's heart. "Yeah . . ."

"They've brought it forward. Someone on my camp needs to come home right now, so my troupe is going in early."

"How early?"

"Two weeks. We fly out a week from Monday."

A week from Monday. *Jesus Christ.* The wind left Rhys's sails in one harsh breath. His hands tightened like vices around Jevon's wrists, and the tic in his jaw rattled his teeth. For a horrifying moment, he thought he might cry, but then apathy set in, forced, as usual, by circumstances he couldn't change. He pushed the pain from his heart and forced himself to meet Jevon's broken gaze. "What was the good news?"

"What?"

"You said you had something to tell me that I might like."

The sadness marring Jevon's lovely face deepened. "Don't be like that."

"Like what?"

"Cold. It doesn't suit you."

"I'm not being cold, mate. I just need to hear something happy right now. Help me out . . . please?"

Jevon inhaled deeply, then seemed to find a smirk from somewhere and plastered it on his face. "Okay . . . well, while I was waiting for you, I had a rummage in your magic box. I hope you don't mind."

"My magic box?" It took Rhys's brain a second to compute. "Oh. *That* box."

"Yeah."

"And?"

"*And* . . ." Jevon stuck his hand in his pocket and withdrew a squishy purple plug that Rhys had never used. "I found something I liked."

Rhys took the plug from him and turned it over in his hands. "Did you try it out?"

"Yes."

"And you liked it?"

"Yes."

Rhys passed the plug back. "Show me."

THE SUN WOKE Rhys the next morning. Crisp, clean winter rays streaming through the blinds he'd forgotten to close the night before. He bathed in them a moment, enjoying the warmth, but then the solid body next to him invaded his dazed consciousness. *Jevon.*

Rhys rolled over. Jevon was still asleep, stretched out on his stomach. Smiling, Rhys trailed his fingers down his spine, counting the vertebrae, and slid his hand under the sheets that were bunched at Jevon's waist. Flashes of the night they'd spent together before they'd crashed out danced through his mind. They'd played around for hours, like they could use pleasure to block out the wrench of Jevon's news, and done everything under the sun except fuck. *Jevon* was ready—Rhys knew it like he knew water was wet—but every time the opportunity had arisen, he'd found himself backing away. Like fucking Jevon was the icing on a cake he didn't want to eat yet.

Like it was their pinnacle and nothing else could come after.

"You're gonna give yourself a migraine."

Rhys blinked. Jevon was awake and staring at him, his arm curled beneath his chin. "What do you mean?"

Jevon stretched like a luxuriating cat, exposing more of his sinuous body. "You look lost."

"I'm not lost. I'm right here."

"Are you, though?" Jevon sat up slightly, just enough that he could loop an arm around Rhys's shoulders and tug him into an embrace that felt like home. "'Cause I don't want you to spend the next ten days feeling like I've already gone."

"That makes me sound like a melodramatic bitch. Like I'm acting as though you've died or something."

Jevon snorted. "I know you're not a drama queen, son."

"Thanks, but still." Rhys shrugged helplessly. "It's so hard. I don't want you to go, but at the same time, I know it's so right that you do. I'm confused."

"Aren't we all?" Jevon kissed Rhys's forehead. His eyes were still hooded and sleepy, but empathy laced every gentle touch. "I wish you knew how much my heart is screaming at me not to go—to stay here with you—but—"

"Don't." Rhys stopped him with a kiss of his own. "I get it. It's killing me, but I know how important your work is—I've seen it."

"Seen it?"

"Yeah. I've been YouTubing the fuck out of you the last few weeks." A blush stole over Rhys's face but he held Jevon's gaze. "I saw the videos from Calais and Idomeni. What you do is amazing—it's part of you—and I'd never ask you to give it up."

Jevon shrugged. "I could contribute from here, in the hospitals and the detention centres."

Rhys's heart leapt as he considered the prospect but sank again just as fast. "I don't think you could. I'm not saying that side of it isn't important, but what about those kids getting off the boats in Greece? The ones that don't make it to the UK? There's plenty of clowns in this country, Jevon, but there ain't many waiting on the beaches at Lesbos."

"Wow. You really have done your research."

"Not on purpose. I just missed you and wanted to know more about you than what makes you come."

Jevon sighed, shaking his head slightly at Rhys's weak attempt at humour. "You're right. I can't give it up. Those kids, man . . . they *need* their childhood back, even if it's just a few moments of laughter. I'm not a one-man band—there's a crew of us, a troupe—but however much it's going to kill me to leave you behind, I couldn't live with myself if I walked away."

It was nothing Rhys hadn't known already, but it hurt all the same. All the more because he knew Jevon was right. A Jevon who left his life's work by the wayside wasn't the man who'd stolen his heart. The hard way was the only way. "Can I ask you something?"

Jevon sat up for real and tied his dreads back from his face. "Of course."

"How on earth did you end up being a clown? I mean, you've already told me how you got to working with kids and in the camps and stuff, but you never said how the clown skin became your vehicle for that."

Jevon smiled and shook his head. "I thought you were going to ask me why I chose the butt plug from your box."

"Nope. You don't need to verbally explain that to me. I've seen it."

"Git." Jevon rolled his eyes, but his expression fell serious again as he considered Rhys's question. "I s'pose I should probably start by clarifying that I'm not just a clown, and definitely not the type people have nightmares about. It's the easiest way to explain it when people ask, but I do other circus acts—acrobatics, trapeze, stuff like that."

Rhys groaned. "Stop. I've got such a fetish for acrobats."

"Lucky me. *Anyway*, it started when I was about six, I think? My sister was really ill for a long time. Clowning around and making her laugh was the only thing I could do to make her feel better. And . . . later, when I was at school and kids just wanted to touch my hair, throwing myself around was a good way of distracting them."

"And combining it with social work was a natural progression?"

"I guess," Jevon said. "It took a while because school didn't pan out, but I went back and got a masters from the Open University eventually."

"That's amazing."

"Not really. It's kind of sad we don't have an education system that works for children who don't fit in certain boxes, but that's a rant for another day."

I could love him. "What's your sister's name?"

The wry humour faded from Jevon's face. "Melody, but she died when I was fourteen. Leukaemia."

"Shit. I'm sorry."

"Me too," Jevon said. "She was a year older than me, but we were like twins until she got sick. After that, I grew up at her bedside."

"So you know first hand how much it means to make sick and sad children smile."

It wasn't a question. More a realisation of what made this incredible man tick. And in any case, Jevon shook his head. "What I do now isn't about me. It's so much bigger, but at the same time painfully simple. Every child has the right to be anything they want to be. My job is to help them believe that."

Maybe I do love him.

And maybe Jevon knew. He coaxed Rhys into laying his head in his lap and toyed with his hair, rubbed his neck, and stroked his face until Rhys's mind quieted.

He leaned down and put his lips to Rhys's ear. "Go back to sleep. I've got you."

CAMDEN WAS SO JEVON. Vibrant. Alive. Rhys ambled beside him, their hands brushing with every step, and tried not to stare as Jevon drank it all in.

"I should come here more," Jevon said. "I've got cousins around here, and I've always loved it."

"You've got cousins everywhere."

Jevon laughed. "Big family, on my dad's side, at least. My nan cooks Christmas dinner for thirty-plus people every year."

"We banned my mum from cooking. She's awful at it, and Harry didn't particularly like eating for a while."

Jevon shot Rhys a sideways look. "You never talk about your family."

"We've talked about Harry loads."

"Only because of Angelo."

Rhys hummed and stopped to buy some hot, spiced nuts from the Bolivian bloke who always seemed to be opposite the hemp stalls. Cradling the warm paper cup, they set off on their aimless wandering while Rhys pondered Jevon's words. "I guess I don't talk about them much because there's not much to say. Me and Harry were proper mummy's boys growing up, but it evolved into something else after my dad was gone. We didn't all need to protect each other anymore, so we didn't. We split off to live our own lives."

"Do you talk to your mum?"

"Not often. Harry does."

"And you don't talk to him either?"

"I *do* talk to him, just not when he's bugging me about stuff."

"What stuff?"

Rhys flicked a cashew nut at Jevon. "Just stuff. What's with the inquisition? You think my tragic childhood will make up for me being a wanker? Because it won't. Sometimes I'm just a wanker."

"No, you *think* you're a wanker, and you hide behind that when you don't want to admit something upsets you. Like your dad. I know he hurt you."

Rhys couldn't deny it. Didn't want to. But he didn't want to dissect it either. He scooped a handful of nuts out of the paper cup and crammed them into Jevon's mouth. When he was satisfied Jevon would be chewing for a while, he gave him the short version of the truth. "My dad was a nightmare. A big drinker, a bully . . . everything you don't want in a father. He kicked the shit out of all of us, and he went to prison in the end for breaking my ribs . . . stamping on my fingers, but by then Harry had grown into the Hulk and started hitting him back, so it didn't matter anyway. Happy now?"

Jevon swallowed. "I'm happy that you shared it with me. Not that it happened. Do you think that's why you became a paramedic? To regain some control over caring for people? Protecting people? Because you couldn't do it at home?"

"Not in the slightest. I told you before, it's just a job to me."

Jevon's scepticism was as obvious as the chill in the frosty air, but he let it go. And Rhys was relieved. They'd constructed an unspoken agreement to make the most of the time they had left. He wasn't going to waste a moment talking about his father or anything else he didn't give a shit about.

They walked past the markets and under the bridge. When they emerged, they found themselves surrounded by the kind of street performers you only saw in London. Beat poets fought for space with mime artists, jugglers, and buskers. Jevon drifted towards an old man playing a banjo, sitting on the pavement, his back to the wall of a burger bar.

"Whatcha playing, mate?"

"Marley, son."

Jevon eyed the collection of instruments piled up beside the man. "Got any bongos?"

Of course he had. The man seemed to have everything spilling out of his tatty bag. He supplied Jevon with a set of bongo drums and struck up a funky rendition of "Is This Love." Jevon played along for a while. Then he swapped his bongos for a more portable drum and began to dance.

The sway of his hips was the sexiest thing Rhys had ever seen, and his smile was glorious. Infectious. A small crowd grew as Rhys moved aside to lean on a nearby lamp post. Children were drawn to Jevon. He beckoned them closer and said something to the old man, who nodded. Instruments were passed out, and suddenly the whole street was in motion—singing, dancing, laughing.

Jevon got up in Rhys's face, brandishing a set of maracas, but Rhys shook his head. "I ain't Bez from the Happy Mondays."

Jevon's laugh rang out even over the impromptu party he'd started on Camden High Street, and he danced away, taking more of Rhys's heart with each step.

Three songs later, and Rhys had a chill in his bones that could only be shifted by a drink, a blowjob, or a hot dinner.

The burger bar offered two out of three, although the beer was the overpriced hipster slosh Rhys usually tried to avoid. "What's in a Brixton bap?"

"No idea." Jevon handed his menu back to the server. "Guess we'll find out, eh?"

Rhys shrugged and ordered the Thai chicken patty. When the server had gone, he rested his elbows on the table. "I'm glad we came out."

"Me too. As much fun as losing a day to your bed is."

Rhys sniggered and drank some expensive beer. "We do have fun, don't we?"

"We do."

Jevon stirred the ice in his rum and Coke. "It's nice to see you smile, too. I reckon we should—"

A panicked scream and the screech of chairs being pushed back cut him off. Instinct turned Rhys around, his gaze quickly zeroing in on a table six feet away from them. A child strapped into a high chair was coughing, and the adults at the table were losing it.

"He's choking!" A man lurched to his feet and moved to stick his fingers down the child's throat.

Shit. Rhys dashed across the crowded restaurant, his stool crashing to the floor behind him. He reached the man before he could blink and shoved him away. "No! You'll push the blockage further down."

The child had fallen silent, coughing cut off by whatever was lodged in his throat. Rhys unbuckled the high chair straps. "How old?"

"Ten months," the woman closest to the child gasped. "He's ten months."

Rhys pulled the baby from the high chair and laid him face down on his bent leg, supporting his head, and aimed five firm blows with the heel of his hand between the child's shoulder blades.

Nothing happened.

Rhys tried again, but whatever was blocking the baby's airway wouldn't budge. He tried to remember the last time he'd performed abdominal thrusts on a living patient this small but came up blank. He'd seen Marc do it, but Marc was pretty much God.

Focus. Rhys sensed Jevon behind him and drew strength from the calmness that seeped from him anytime he was nearby with his clothes on. He turned the baby over and found the breastbone, pressing down sharply with two fingers. Again, nothing happened, but on the second cycle, finally, something moved. The baby coughed. Rhys turned him over and gently knocked his back until the wadded lump of bread spilled out of his mouth.

The entire scene had unfolded in less than a minute, but when Rhys looked up, it seemed like a lifetime had passed. "You still need an ambulance," he said to the circle of adults around him. "There might be more that hasn't come out yet."

"I'm on the line with them now," a man said. "They want to talk to you."

Rhys took the phone and gave his details to the 999 operator, smiling inwardly at the relief in the baby's loved ones when they realised he was an actual paramedic, not some nutter who'd snatched their kid and lumped it one.

A street crew was on their way. Rhys could've passed the baby back and returned to his dinner, but he didn't, and he was still rubbing the tiny boy's back when the ambulance rolled up a few minutes later.

It was a crew he knew. He handed the baby over, debriefed them, and only then did he go back to his table.

Jevon was waiting for him, new drinks and full plates of food ready. He was smirking.

"What?" Rhys asked tiredly.

"Nothing, brother. Eat your dinner."

Rhys shook his head and did as he was told. Sometimes regaining control came from someone else taking the reins, and the burgers were *good*. Rhys was hoovering up the last of the chips when a tall, broad-shouldered blond man emerged from the staff door of the restaurant and approached the table with a bottle of ridiculously expensive champagne.

"Tom Fearnes—I'm one of the owners of Misfits." He

extended his hand. "Oh hey, Jevon. I didn't realise it was your table that saved the day."

"Not me." Jevon slapped the man—Tom—on the back. "It was Rhys."

"Well, whoever it was, trust me, you're not paying for your meal." Tom turned to Rhys. "Thank you. I can't even contemplate what could've happened if you hadn't been here. Our team are first aid trained, but I'm not sure any of them could've handled it the way you did."

Rhys shrugged. "Comes with the job. I can cook burgers at home, but not for a hundred people."

"Still." Tom held out the champagne. "We'd like to give you this as a tiny token of our appreciation. It's people like you that remind us what really matters."

He shook their hands again and walked away. Rhys watched him disappear into the kitchen, though he clearly wasn't a chef, then cast a quizzical look at Jevon. "How do you know that hottie?"

"Tom?"

"No, the other blond hunk handing out the bubbly."

Jevon laughed. "He's Efe's boss. He owns the pizza place we were at the other week, this place, and a bunch of others in the city. Urban Soul? Ever heard of them?"

"Nope."

"Fair enough. I don't know him that well, to be honest. Just that he's pretty awesome to Efe, and he has, like, two boyfriends."

"Two?"

"Yup. Cass and Jake. I've never met them, but Efe says they're every bit as hot as Tom."

A month ago, Rhys would've been fascinated, but his world had narrowed to just Jevon, and as sweet as the story was, he wasn't interested. He drained his beer and pulled Jevon in for a surreptitious kiss. "Can we get out of here?"

"Sure, but I can't come back to yours. I've got to go home and start packing my life up."

Rhys nodded, ignoring the dread that slashed through him. "I'll come to the station with you."

King's Cross was on Rhys's way home anyway, and they parted ways outside the over-ground platform that would take Jevon back to Bedford. "Look," Rhys said. "I know I'm a bit of a drag when I go into one, but you were right earlier—I don't want to waste the next few days sulking about you going."

"Make the most of it, eh?"

"For sure." Rhys tugged Jevon close and wrapped his arms round his waist. They kissed long and slow, but mindful of their public location, Rhys broke away before things got too hot. "I've got an early shift the day after tomorrow. Maybe I can come over?"

"Sounds like a plan." Jevon nuzzled Rhys's jaw, then backed off. "Bring that champagne. We'll have some fun."

He began to walk away. Rhys watched him go, lost in the elegant rise and fall of his lithe body. He almost didn't hear Jevon when he stopped at the ticket barriers and called his name. "What?"

Jevon dragged an oyster card from his back pocket and swiped the barrier. "I said, if that shit you pulled in the restaurant is just a job, then I'm quitting mine to sell car insurance."

CHAPTER FOURTEEN

GEARING up for an overseas deployment had always been a no brainer. The camps were where Jevon was meant to be, and he'd never questioned it. But it was different now. There was a line down his heart, blurred and cruel, and whichever way he turned, people got hurt. *He* got hurt.

It didn't help that time seemed to be slipping through his fingers. Two weeks had turned into one, and now he had only days left before he boarded the plane to Greece. Excitement warred with sadness, and the ominous dread in his bones got heavier with every passing day.

Still, he'd promised Rhys they wouldn't get bogged down in their impending separation, and that apparently meant pretending it wasn't happening. Pretending this wouldn't be Jevon's last trip to London before he left.

He got off the train at King's Cross and walked straight into Rhys's open arms, his smile wide enough to split his cheeks. "'Sup. You all good?"

Rhys hummed. "Nothing a week's kip wouldn't cure."

"You haven't slept?"

"Nah. The overnight ran, uh, over. I haven't been home."

Jevon stepped back, belatedly noticing the bag at Rhys's feet and the clothes he often wore to and from the air ambulance base. "Damn. What do you want to do? Go home and rest for a while?"

They had loose plans to visit Efe and go out for a few drinks before they returned to Rhys's flat for the night, but Jevon would be as happy to hold Rhys in his arms as he slept. Happy to be anywhere as long as they were together.

But Rhys shook his head. "I'm good. Just need a shower and a change of clothes and I'll be right as rain."

On another day, Jevon might've argued that a shower couldn't repair the damage from a twenty-four-hour shift, but this wasn't an ordinary day.

They made their way to Brick Lane. Jevon waited while Rhys took a shower but, when he'd been gone twenty minutes, braved the steam to check on him.

Rhys was standing beneath the hot water, head down, hands braced on the wall. Jevon hovered in the doorway for a blink of an eye before stripping his clothes and stepping under the spray to join him.

He stood behind Rhys, his arms around his waist, his face nuzzling the swathe of perfect pale skin between his shoulder blades. Even a glance across a crowded bar from Rhys was enough to make Jevon's dick twitch. Naked in the shower? Yeah. It was *on*.

Jevon's cock slid smoothly along Rhys's crease. He sunk his teeth into Rhys's tender flesh and revelled in the answering gasp. "I thought you'd got lost in here."

Rhys hummed. "If I had, I've definitely been found." He pushed back on Jevon, grinding himself lightly against Jevon's cock. "But it won't be for long if you keep doing that."

"Uh-huh." Jevon glided his hands down Rhys's wet skin. Over the past week, he'd learned how to play this part of Rhys's body with his fingers and tongue—committed every sweetly sensitive spot to memory—and had become so addicted that his dreams had shifted from Rhys fucking him, to Jevon's cock easing inside Rhys. Making his eyes roll and his body jerk. But then his fantasies would flip back again, and he'd imagine himself on his back, his legs flung open, and Rhys thrusting inside him, driving him into oblivion. *Man, I'm confused.* But of one thing he was certain. *I need him to feel good.*

Jevon shut off the shower and tugged Rhys out of the bathroom, water dripping on the floor as they went. He snagged a towel and haphazardly dried them both, then he pushed Rhys down on the bed and straddled him. In this new position, it was Rhys's cock teasing Jevon's hole, but he tore himself away from the entrancing pleasure and moved down Rhys's body.

Sucking Rhys's cock was like breathing now. Sliding his fingers inside him, searching out the electric spot that turned Rhys's moans into guttural shouts took more patience. But Jevon did it. He hooked Rhys's leg over his shoulder and made him come, only withdrawing when Rhys begged him to stop.

"Fuck, fuck, fuck." Rhys shook his head, his face flushed and beautiful. "You do something to me, man. I'm gonna combust one of these days."

Jevon laughed. His own dick was still painfully hard, but nothing compared to seeing Rhys like this. The world could wait because Jevon wasn't getting off. *That's a bad pun, dude.*

Rhys cupped Jevon's face. "What are you laughing at?"

"Myself. I'm fucking hilarious."

"Well, you *are* a clown, babe."

The casual endearment hurt Jevon's heart. He dragged himself back to Rhys's eye level and kissed him to numb the pain, but he still batted Rhys's hands away when he reached for his swollen cock. "Later. I gotta meet Efe and she'll deck me if I'm late."

"If *we're* late."

Jevon grinned. "Don't get too excited. She's a force of nature."

"Good for her."

They got dressed and left the Brick Lane flat behind. By the time they got to the bakery in Vauxhall, it was winding down for the night, but only out front. Jevon led Rhys behind the scenes where they found Efe gearing up for an overnight bake.

She tossed flour at him. "Are you here to help or eat me out of house and home?"

"Both." Rhys stepped between them before Jevon could retaliate.

Jevon raised an eyebrow. "Sure about that? You haven't slept since Wednesday."

"Shh."

Efe put an arm around Rhys, clearly as taken with him as Jevon. "I was joking, sweet boy, but seeing as you offered . . . if you can load up those sourdoughs for proving, I'll give you all the patties and coconut slices you can eat."

Efe's Jamaican lamb patties, wrapped in turmeric-spiced pastry, and the coconut-jam tarts Jevon remembered from school were among his favourite things to put in his mouth. If he hadn't had Rhys along for the ride, he'd have happily worked all night in exchange for a full belly.

As it was, the job she'd given them didn't take that long, though Rhys seemed to enjoy it. "Do you come here and do this often?"

"What? Give out free labour in return for stuffing my face? Yeah . . . kind of. I told you before that I liked being here when I first started to deal with my sexuality. It was a port in a storm, you know?"

Rhys carefully shaped elastic bread dough the way Efe had shown him and placed it in the proving basket. "Yeah. I get it. I reckon I could sleep in front of those ovens too."

"I think there's a couple of staff around here who do. Efe treats this place like her living room. It's open house once Nero's gone home."

"Nero?"

"The hot pizza dude."

Rhys nodded. "I remember. And I love that you had this place to come to. It beats whoring yourself around in a sex club for company."

"That's how you see yourself?"

"When I don't take the time to remind myself I did those things because I wanted to. I have no regrets, but loneliness does funny things to me."

Rhys spoke with a smile, but the shadows in his eyes were plain to see. *Hard* to see. Jevon couldn't bear it. He held out his hand. "Let's go eat."

Efe joined them for dinner, making good on her promise to bring them all the patties and jam tarts they could eat and setting up an impromptu staff picnic round the back by the main bread ovens.

Bakers trickled in to join them.

"It's like being in the engine room of the Titanic," Rhys whispered to Jevon. "If they had coal on their faces instead of flour."

Jevon laughed. "Trust me. There's nothing sinking about this ship. Efe's been voted London's top artisan baker three years running."

Efe elbowed Jevon in the ribs. "Shush. I want Rhys to think I'm humble."

It was hard to imagine that Rhys would think any different as they camped out on the bakery floor, sharing food she'd prepared with her own hands. And his smile said as much. "Let him talk you up, luv. Then you can return the favour."

Sneaky git. It was as if he'd known that Efe had a gazillion stories to tell about Jevon's awkward childhood.

"Honestly," Efe said on her third go around. "You could've heard a pin drop in that church, and this young one comes screaming in because he's poured gravy on his ice cream instead of chocolate sauce."

Rhys laughed. "Did he ever get over it?"

Efe took a breath to respond, but Jevon clamped a hand over her mouth. "God, make it stop. I've got plenty of stories about you, girl. Don't make me break open the vault."

Still laughing, Efe wriggled out of Jevon's grip. "You wouldn't dare. Who'd feed you? Give you a bed for the night in the city?"

"I would." Rhys reached for another tart. "But he'd be a fool to give up on this jam sorcery you've got going on, so I don't reckon he's gonna talk."

Jevon mock-glared at both of them, then excused himself to the bathroom. When he came back, Efe and Rhys were alone, only empty trays and crumbs left to show for the feast Efe had brought with her. Rhys was still laughing, but Jevon sensed the shift in his already forced mood. Absorbed it. Made it his own.

He caught Efe's gaze and she took the hint, bending to whisper something in Rhys's ear before she hugged them both, lingering a little with her embrace for Jevon while Rhys slipped away to give them a moment.

"I can't believe you're going already," she said. "It feels like you've barely been home."

"Where's home, cuz? It's not Bedford, and it's not kipping on your couch."

"Is it over there, though, J? Because I don't like the vibe coming off you right now. It's like you don't want to go."

Jevon shrugged helplessly. "I do want to go—I *have* to go— but it's so hard this time. I've never felt like this before."

"You mean how you feel about Rhys?"

Jevon nodded, the ability to verbalise the chaos in his heart fast becoming thin on the ground. "I've been pretending it's not really happening these last few weeks, but—shit. I don't know how I'm gonna do it."

"Think he feels the same?" Efe nodded without waiting for Jevon's answer. "Of course he does. He's a tough one, that boy, but even he can't hide how sweet he is on you. There must be a way?"

If there was, Jevon hadn't thought of it yet. He hugged Efe close, kissed her cheek, and pulled away. "I guess we'll either do the long distance thing or call it a day. And right now, I don't know which is worse."

"They both suck," Efe said. "But maybe you need to think bigger picture? Life evolves, man. So can you."

"Yeah, well, we've run out of rope. I'm heading out in the morning, and I don't want to waste the time we've got left hashing out something that hurts whichever way we turn."

"So you're going with denial?"

"Pretty much."

Jevon kissed Efe one more time, promised to eat all the vegetables he could find in a sodden refugee camp, then made his escape. Rhys was waiting in the bus stop, thumbing through his phone. He glanced up when he heard Jevon coming, and the gradual detachment was already there. They'd known each other a matter of months, but Jevon knew what he was doing: cutting the strings before circumstances did it for him. Shutting down. Shutting the gates. Five minutes on his own and he was already a million miles away. What would he be like after three months?

Panic seized Jevon's chest. In the cocoon of the warm bakery, denial had seemed the safest option, but as he stared at Rhys, he realised how wrong he'd been. Pain was part of living, and fuck if the short time he'd spent with Rhys hadn't made him more alive than he'd ever been. And there was still more. There had to be.

Jevon yanked Rhys to his feet, startling some light into his dark, dark eyes. "Take me home."

CHAPTER FIFTEEN

THIS WASN'T how Rhys had imagined the climax to their last night together. He'd pictured Jevon nervous, trembling, and even unsure, but as they stumbled across the city to Rhys's flat, it was clear Jevon knew exactly what he wanted.

Rhys's front door hit the wall with a sickening crack. Jevon yanked Rhys over the threshold and kicked the door closed, barely waiting for another loud slam before he shoved Rhys against it, his tongue plundering his mouth. Claiming it.

Clothes disappeared in a rush of torn T-shirts and shoved-away denim. Jevon kicked his underwear aside and gripped Rhys's throat. "Show me."

Show you what? But Rhys didn't say it because he knew the answer. Jevon wanted to know how much Rhys would miss him. How empty his bed would be without him. And how goddamn fucking much they could've loved each other if things had been different.

Rhys pried Jevon's hand from around his neck and twined their fingers together, moving slowly despite the racing tattoo in his chest. The animal in him wanted to throw Jevon onto the bed, pin him down, and fuck him senseless—from the top or the bottom, as he was still unsure what Jevon wanted—but there was more than one way to ravage a man, and if they only did this once, fuck, they'd do it right.

He led Jevon to the bed and laid him down, covering him with his body, kissing him, consuming him, swallowing every gasp that fell from his beautiful mouth. Every touch screamed the words he'd never said, but Jevon knew. He had to know. *I love you.*

Jevon rolled them over, hooking a leg over Rhys's hips so their cocks slid together as their bodies undulated like poetry. Friction. Heat. Rhys's senses imploded, and low, tortured sounds ripped from his chest. He held Jevon tighter, blunt nails digging into his back, and hid his face in Jevon's neck until Jevon wove his hands into Rhys's hair and pulled his head back.

"No hiding. I want to see you."

Rhys couldn't argue. Didn't want to. Just wanted to lose himself in every part of Jevon he could reach. He pushed Jevon onto his back and moved down his body, tracing the rise and fall of his abs until he reached his cock. Then he took him in his mouth and sucked him slowly, savouring every ridge and vein, every drop of fluid as it seeped out and coated his tongue. He reached up and found Jevon's hands, squeezing them tight, keeping his mouth around Jevon's dick even as Jevon yanked on his arms.

Flipping around was seamless, like they'd done it a thousand times. They lay on their sides, swallowing each other whole, tasting, testing . . . pushing closer to the precipice where one of them would break.

But Rhys pulled back before they fell and crawled up the bed until he found Jevon's mouth with his own again. They kissed like drowning men, rolling over and over again, before Jevon dug his heels into the mattress, caging Rhys against him in his sinewy arms. "Like this."

It took Rhys's Jevon-addled brain a moment to compute. Then it sank in. *He wants me to fuck him.* A million emotions warred in Rhys's crowded soul. The prospect of taking Jevon's thick cock inside him had kept him awake more nights than he cared to admit. He wanted it. Craved it. But he needed *this* more. Needed to be inside Jevon, to feel his tight, wet heat clamping around him, shielding him from the real world if only for one more night.

He found their trusty bottle of lube and drove his fingers into Jevon, searching out the live-wired spots he'd already committed to memory, his mouth once again sealed around Jevon's dick, Jevon's leg draped over his shoulder. He worked Jevon until his body trembled, his limbs quivered, and his moans became unintelligible.

"Rhys," Jevon gasped out. "Please. I need you."

I was born needing you. I just never knew it. Rhys tore his mouth from Jevon's cock, wiping it with the back of his hand. In the darkness of the room, Jevon's eyes gleamed, the fire in them matching the inferno in Rhys's blood. "Do you want me to use a condom?"

"No, fuck no." Jevon shook his head. "I wanna feel you."

Rhys's pulse stuttered. He'd been around the block more times than he could count, but never bare. Never naked to the sensation of hot pulsing flesh against the hardness of his throbbing length. "I want to feel you too."

Sliding inside Jevon came like drops of mystical rain after a lifetime of drought. Inch by inch, breath by breath, the burn of intrusion faded from Jevon's face, then the bliss came. The wonder. The hit of pleasure that eclipsed any drug you could buy on the street.

Rhys bit down on the ecstasy already roaring in his ears and fucked Jevon slowly, revelling in the sensation of Jevon clamping down on him, his legs a vice around his waist. He kissed Jevon deeply and tangled his fingers in his hair, gripping the black headscarf that was somehow still in place, fighting oblivion as his balls tightened to the point of pain.

He groaned and bit Jevon's chest. "You feel so good."

Jevon thrashed his head from side to side, his eyes clenched shut. "It's all you, baby. Fuck me harder."

Rhys obeyed, thrusting into Jevon with strokes that grew braver with every twist of his hips. The sofa bed shunted rhythmically across the floor, mattress squeaking. Rhys clutched the back like it could tie him down to the world, but just when he feared he'd lost his grip, Jevon ripped his hands free and rolled them over, straddling Rhys's waist.

"You said this was the best."

"It is," Rhys managed hoarsely. "But it's all fucking insane with you. It's never been like this."

Jevon stared Rhys down as he took his dick inside him again. "You've never fucked anyone else like this?"

"Never—oh god, Jevon. Ride me, please."

Rhys's incoherency seemed to gift Jevon the confidence he deserved. He impaled himself on Rhys's cock, then set a torturous, mind-blowing pace with slow, barely there undulations of his hips, grinding down with every crazy-hot trip around the block. His dick slid along Rhys's clenched abdomen, gliding through the lube and precome that seemed to be everywhere, and his eyes closed, his mouth hung open, and Rhys knew he was gone. Lost. Climbing so high he might never come down.

He wasn't alone. Rhys was with him for every shudder and moan. Every ripple of pleasure that threatened to free-fall them into a vortex so hot it scared even Rhys.

Jevon ground down harder, faster, and Rhys rose up from the bed to meet him, slamming into him until Jevon relinquished control. Rhys rolled them over again, keeping Jevon tight against him so his dick stayed buried inside him, then he let go—in every sense—and fucked Jevon the way he'd imagined the very first time he'd caught his shy gaze in the crowded bar.

Skin slapped skin and moans tangled in the air. Rhys rose up on his knees, Jevon's legs clutched to his chest, and a clean slate appeared between them—like this was the beginning and not the end. White noise fizzed in Rhys's brain and his body short-circuited.

Jevon jack-knifed from the bed in a perfect arch, sweat glistening on his skin. Rhys's name fell from his lips and a guttural shout ripped from his chest. "I'm gonna explode, I swear. Fuck!"

Rhys upped the pace of his thrusts to punishing, and something snapped. Jevon gripped his cock, jacking himself in time with Rhys's dick sliding home, and everything began to unravel.

"Rhys, I'm—"

Rhys cut him off with a fierce kiss, only ripping his lips away when his own orgasm knocked him off balance. Heat flooded every part of him, and his release pulsed out of him, filling Jevon with wet heat.

But every shockwave of pleasure paled in comparison to the innocent beauty of watching Jevon come. Of witnessing him come apart at the seams. Head thrown back, Jevon let out a gravelly cry, and his dick erupted, painting them both with hot come. The tendons in his neck strained, and his body convulsed, and for long moments it seemed like neither one of them would ever stop coming.

"Fuck, fuck, fuck." Rhys covered Jevon in kisses, then he fell slack, panting as Jevon clung to him, his heart hammering against Rhys's chest, his body trembling.

There is nothing else.

Only this.

Only him.

Rhys fought for breath and eventually found enough to draw back and brush Jevon's dreads off his face. "Okay?"

Jevon met his gaze and smiled, the agonising twist of orgasm fading from his face. "Yeah."

"Sure? I didn't go too—"

It was Jevon's turn to kill an unnecessary conversation with a kiss. He threaded his hand around the back of Rhys's neck and tugged him down, slicking his soft tongue into Rhys's mouth until they both needed more air.

All at once, fatigue hit Rhys like a train. Thirty-six hours with no sleep caught up with him, and it was all he could do to stay upright.

Attuned to him as ever, Jevon sat up, almost managing to conceal a wince. "Lie down," he said. "I'm going to clean up, then I'll stick the kettle on."

Rhys caught his arm. "Don't go."

Jevon stared at Rhys's hand clamped around his wrist, his face caught in a conflict of emotions that left Rhys dizzy. "Okay. Fuck the kettle, but let me clean us both up, all right?"

So many unspoken pleas and declarations danced through the air; Rhys had no hope of catching them all. He lay back, his body sprawled out with exhaustion, and counted the seconds until Jevon came back to the bed with a warm wet flannel.

When they were both clean, Jevon drew back the covers and they crawled into bed. Sleep pounded the door to Rhys's brain, demanding entrance, but Rhys fought it, clinging to consciousness as tightly as he clung to Jevon. *I love you.*

He didn't say it though. Couldn't. Even as Jevon held him close and kissed his temple, whispering words that chased him into his dreams. "Wherever I go, Rhys, this night will always be with me. Sleep easy. I've got you."

CHAPTER SIXTEEN

RHYS CLUNG to the helpfully placed handles as the chopper swung from side to side in the wind, buffeting his dinner around his stomach. Flying at night terrified him at the best of times, but rough night flights took the royal piss. Especially when he'd been nursing a hangover in the first place.

The helicopter lurched downwards. Rhys glanced at Pater, who seemed as unconcerned as ever, and tried to reassure himself that it meant something. A tough ask when the cool German pilot could smile through an apocalypse.

Rhys brought his mouthpiece closer to his lips. "How long till we land?"

"Twenty minutes, but I'm going to bring us in early at Oxford. No sense flying through this if we haven't got a patient."

Unscheduled stops usually got on Rhys's nerves, but he was glad of it tonight. They landed at the private flying club in Oxford and were immediately granted access to some pretty snazzy facilities. Shame Rhys had zero enthusiasm for anything that wasn't being dead asleep or something that would help put him there.

Pater and the flight doctor decamped to the club's swanky

cafeteria, which had stayed open for them, but Rhys declined dinner and lingered in the bathrooms, hiding out under a shower that made the one he had at home look like a school changing room.

Two showerheads pummelled Rhys's body. He closed his eyes and braced himself on the tiled wall, trying not to remember how it had felt to have Jevon come up behind him, wrap his arms around him, and slide his cock along his body. How it had felt to imagine Jevon was fucking him for real, driving into him with long, deep strokes, one hand on his hip, the other gently at his throat.

But he failed, spectacularly, like he had every night since Jevon had left. The ache in his gut expanded into his chest. He let go of the wall and slid to the floor. At home, he'd crawl out of the bathroom and find the bottle of rum he'd taken to keeping by the bed, but he couldn't do that here. Couldn't numb himself enough to sleep. So he did something he hadn't done in more than a decade.

He put his head in his hands and cried.

IT WAS dawn when the chopper made it back to London. Rhys drifted home and threw himself into bed, but he wasn't drunk enough to sleep, and with another shift rolling by in twelve hours' time, he'd run out of time to fix it.

He lay on his back, staring at the ceiling, his phone dormant on his chest, fingers itching for the scrap of paper that he'd carried everywhere with him since he'd woken alone ten days ago. He gave in almost immediately and retrieved it from his wallet, unfolding it, and holding it up to the light.

Rhys,

I'm sorry I didn't wake you, but I couldn't do it. Saying goodbye is wrong, and I don't want to believe it's true.

Thank you . . . for everything, not just the obvious. Leaving you is so hard, but I'm doing it feeling more like myself than I ever have before. I thought knew myself until I met you. Now I am myself.

I'll call you from the camp as soon as I can, but it takes a while for my phone to find a connection over there. It might be a couple of days . . . maybe longer.

I fucking love you, man. For real. Take care of yourself . . .

Jevon x

Rhys knew the words by now, had committed them to memory that dark morning when the crater in his heart had expanded with every breath. Jevon's words, and the scent of him on his sheets, had kept him together then—were still keeping him together, but for how long?

He eyed the rum bottle and rolled over, turning his back on it. Jevon's letter found its way back into his wallet, and Rhys picked up his phone instead. In recent days, he'd found himself calling Joe, particularly if he'd had a skinful, but he called Harry now and closed his eyes when his brother's voice filled the void Jevon had left behind.

"Hey," Harry said. "This is early for you. Just getting in or just getting up?"

"Getting in. Trying to sleep, but it's not happening. Can I ask you something?"

"Of course." A door closed at Harry's end. "Are you okay?"

"Don't start."

"Sorry. Go on."

Rhys scrubbed a hand down his face. His eyes were scratchy from his shower meltdown, and his head ached with all the tears he'd left behind. *Fucking idiot.* "How did you know?"

"Know what?"

"That changing your life to be with Joe was the right thing to do? I mean, I know you loved him and all that bollocks, but how did you *know*?"

"Are you drunk?"

"Harry."

"Okay, okay . . . it's just not like you to give a fuck about why I've done the things I've done."

"That's not fair."

"I didn't mean it in a bad way, bro. Just that you never ask me why. You accept everything I do without question because you believe in me . . . unless it really is because you don't care."

"I care."

"I know."

"So . . ." Rhys banged his head on his pillow. "Are you gonna answer my question or psychoanalyse me?"

"Is this about Jevon?"

"No. It's about you."

Harry sighed. "I don't believe you, but whatever. Okay, here's the thing . . . when it came to being with Joe, there wasn't really a choice to be made. Being with him was going to happen, and there was a big part of me that didn't care how. Like, I'd have done *anything* to be with him."

"Seems legit. You don't think he'd have done anything to be with you?"

"It wasn't the same for him. He loves me as much as I love him, but he was in a different place. Joe doesn't have the kind of life he can pick up and move to London. He has to be here, and I have to be with him, so that's what happened."

"But why? What made his life more important than yours?"

"Everything. There are thousands of dudes in London who could do what I was doing, but there's only one Joe in the world. Besides, I didn't want to go back to the city. I was miserable, Rhys . . . you know I was."

Rhys couldn't argue with that. Putting up and keeping on was in the Foster family blood, but Harry had never been able to hide how much he hated it. Wearing his heart on his sleeve there for the whole world to see. Loneliness had hit him far harder than it ever had Rhys, and no one deserved his new life in Newquay more than him. "I don't know what to do."

"So this is about Jevon? Angelo told me he's gone."

"How the fuck does Angelo know that?"

Rhys couldn't keep the growl out of his voice, but Harry didn't seem to hear it. "I'd imagine because Jevon kept in touch with him after you helped him out that time. Angelo's still here, by the way."

"I know. Joe told me."

"Because you'd rather talk to him than to me?"

"Shut up."

Harry laughed. "You're fucking impossible. Look, I don't know what the deal is between you and Jevon, but Angelo reckons he's the tits and that he's as into you as you are him. You just have to figure out how to mesh your lives together. If you love each other, what seems impossible is easier than you think."

"Shut *up.*"

"Dude, you called me."

"Yeah, yeah." Rhys said goodbye and hung up, pondering Harry's sage advice as he thumbed through his phone to Jevon's contact details. Eleven digits and a photograph. It didn't seem enough for the mark Jevon had left on Rhys's soul.

The phone vibrated in Rhys's hand, startling him enough for the phone to slip out of his grasp. He fumbled for it, expecting Harry and any words of wisdom he might've forgotten.

But it wasn't Harry.

It was Jevon.

Rhys sat up and swiped at the screen like a man possessed. The picture jumped like an eighties TV and froze before finally —*finally*—Jevon's smile lit up the world.

"Hey."

"He—" Rhys cleared his throat and tried again. "Hey. There you are."

"Here I am. Are you okay? Did I wake you up?"

"Nah. I'm good. Just getting in. God. I can't believe it's you." Rhys touched the screen. "Where are you?"

"Camp Moria, on Lesbos. Hang on, I'll show you." The picture panned away from Jevon's face as he flipped the camera and scanned the scene below wherever he was.

More tents than Rhys had ever seen filled the horizon. "Jesus Christ. It's huge."

"Not huge enough." Jevon returned the screen to his face and sat down on what appeared to be a sandy-coloured rock. "Four thousand people in a camp that was built for fifteen hundred. It's like the end of the world, man. And more keep coming. I've never seen so many kids . . . I can't even describe it."

Rhys crawled out of bed and drifted to the kitchen, though for what, he wasn't entirely sure. "What can you do for them?"

"With seven of us? Not a great deal as we don't have enough equipment to go around, but we've played a lot of football this week, and I got caught up in a Taylor Swift singalong last night."

Rhys cringed. "Ouch."

"Yeah. It wasn't pretty, but the older kids like that shit. It makes them smile, and that's why we're here."

"Where do you sleep?"

"In the Médecins sans Frontières tent. They're pretty awesome, and some days they need cheering up as much as the kids."

Rhys could well imagine. A long conversation with Marc a few days ago had confirmed his worst fears about disease and sanitation in the refugee camps. "*Hell on Earth*," Marc had said. "*And it doesn't get any better, no matter how many Guardian articles good people write. Only the governments can fix this now.*"

He hadn't seemed optimistic about that happening.

"I miss you," Rhys whispered.

Jevon smiled and ducked his head, his dreads falling into his face. "I miss you too. I'm sorry I left without saying a proper goodbye . . . you looked so peaceful, man. I just couldn't face it."

"It's okay," Rhys said. "I'm glad it played out that way. I probably would've taken you hostage otherwise."

"Some days I wish you had."

"No, you don't."

"I do, Rhys. You don't understand." Jevon covered his face with his hand and sighed brokenly. "This place is so much more than where I was before . . . it's too much. I can't—fuck—I can't see how I can ever leave while it's like this, you know? How I can ever come home, but then the idea of staying, of not seeing you or Efe or my family for months on end, is killing me."

Rhys was sorely unprepared to see Jevon so upset. He sucked in a shaky breath and tried to imagine what he'd do if Jevon was right in front of him. What he'd say. How he'd fix something that was so fucking unfixable. "It's not going to kill you. It can't because it's where you're meant to be."

"I know that. I just—it just feels wrong, Rhys. And it's so big, it's like it doesn't matter how long we're here, nothing gets better. We're not helping these kids because we can't. No one can while—*shit*. I only called to say hello. What the fuck's wrong with me?"

"You're overwhelmed," Rhys hedged. "The camp's bigger than you've dealt with before, and you can't see the difference you're making when the scale is so huge. It's like a mass-casualty incident when you scrape a couple of people up and patch them back together. It doesn't seem to mean much when double that number don't make it."

Jevon let his hand drop. His eyes were bloodshot but still warm. "But the people you saved still got to live. One life matters as much as twenty."

"I know that today," Rhys said. "Just never when I need to."

Jevon sighed. "I'm so fucking emotional right now. I've never felt like this before. Makes me wonder if I've been in some kind of bubble my whole life."

"Would it matter if you had been? You can't control how you feel."

"I wish I could."

Rhys touched his phone screen again. "So do I."

"Do you love me, Rhys?"

"Yes. But you knew that, didn't you?"

"Yeah. I think I did."

A silence fell over them. It wasn't the way Rhys had planned to reciprocate the sentiment in Jevon's letter, and the new conflict in Jevon's face tore him apart, but a layer of heaviness left him. Like confessing his love had set a sliver of him free. "Tell me something good," he said. "Tell me what's made you smile since I last saw you."

"Memories," Jevon said. "I keep seeing you and Efe huddled in that corner taking the piss out of me, and it makes me want to bottle you both and keep you in my pocket."

"I like Efe."

"She likes you too."

"What else?" Rhys pressed on before the conversation got lost in separation again. "What are the kids like?"

A smile no man could fake bloomed on Jevon's face. "Amazing. Sometimes we're the only ones there when they get off the boats. We take them to the reception centres and start playing games straight away, and some of them seem to forget that they've just spent twelve hours at sea. Kids are incredible."

"So are you."

Jevon rolled his eyes. "Not today. I'm supposed to be leading a juggling session, but I cried off to climb up this rock and catch a phone signal because I couldn't handle another day without hearing your voice, even though we've got some local engineers coming out this afternoon to install some Wi-Fi."

"And you think that takes away from all the work you've done already? Jevon, you're human, and you miss the people who love you. That doesn't make you less of who you are."

"Why are you never this nice to yourself?"

"We're not talking about me."

Jevon chuckled, and some of the tension in the air broke. "Maybe we should. My phone just pinged with a bunch of messages from Angelo. He says you're giving Harry the run around again."

"Fucking Angelo." It was Rhys's turn to roll his eyes. "He was never this up in my business when he was screwing me in the club."

A month ago, insecurity would've clouded any humour in Jevon's eyes, but not now. His grin widened to a smirk. "Well, perhaps you should've spent more time getting to know him than screwing him. Then you'd know that he cares about your brother enough to call you out for being a dick."

"I already know that. And I'm not being a dick to Harry. He knows I love him."

"Does he?"

"Yes."

Jevon frowned, apparently unconvinced, but let it go. "What are you doing today?"

"Sleeping until four, then I'm on shift all night from seven."

"So you'll be awake around five then?"

"That's the plan. Why?"

"Because the Wi-Fi will be working by then, and I'm running a circus session, and I was wondering if you'd like to come?"

"Come?"

"Yeah. As in watch. I can prop my phone up on something and you can see what we do. I know you've seen videos and stuff, but knowing you're watching would do wonders for my motivation right now."

"Then I'll be there. And Jevon?"

"Yeah?"

Rhys tried for a smile. "I'll always be here. I meant it when I said I loved you . . . 'cause I really fucking do."

"I love you too, man."

CHAPTER SEVENTEEN

JEVON WALKED UPSIDE DOWN around the makeshift arena, his gloved hands squelching in the mud. The dirt smearing his arms smelt awful and so did he after four days of no running water, but the laughter around him masked the grime.

He flipped over, landing on his feet, then fell into a deliberately clumsy cartwheel, falling in a heap by a clutch of young boys. "Come," he said, beckoning with a muddy hand. "You try."

The boys scrambled to their collective feet and joined Jevon in his makeshift circus ring . . . and successively put Jevon to shame as they hurled their nimble young bodies around with an ease he barely remembered.

He watched them a moment, head tilted to one side, then turned in a slow circle, studying each cluster of children as they worked with different members of the FFP troop. The acrobatic boys, the girls spinning flawless pirouettes, the opera-singing teenager. Jevon was used to children surprising him, but the group of Syrians who'd arrived overnight were something else. Most of them spoke better English than he did.

Jevon left them to it and retreated to the phone he'd left

propped up on a stack of crates. Rhys was there, like he had been every morning for the past week, eating what looked suspiciously like Coco Pops while he lounged in bed after a long night shift.

Grinning, Jevon jerked his thumb over his shoulder. "Are you seeing this?"

"Syria's Got Talent?" Rhys nodded. "Yeah. Weird that they're all so fly. Where did they come from?"

"Originally? I'm not sure. I know they sailed in from Turkey, but I don't know which part of Syria they came from."

"Ask them," Rhys said. "I read about the last performing arts institution in Aleppo being bombed a few weeks ago. Maybe they came from there."

"I doubt it. I can't imagine that anyone would be left in Aleppo by now."

But when Jevon left Rhys to sleep and struck up a conversation with the older children in the group, it turned out that Rhys's musing had been right on the money. "It's fucking criminal," Jevon fumed to the leader of the Médecins sans Frontières group they were sharing living quarters with. "Why are they still bombing civilian areas?"

Anton shrugged. "You're asking me to make sense of what's happening in Syria? We could talk about it for the rest of our lives and never understand."

Jevon growled and flopped down on the camp bed he'd claimed as his own. "Have you heard from your people at Idomeni? Ours got kicked out a week ago."

It was Anton's turn to growl. "We've got a team on the ground, but they're being kept back at the roadblocks while they clear the camp. God knows when they'll be able to link up with the DPs again."

DPs: displaced people. It sounded so clinical, and Jevon was glad he hadn't been around to see the Idomeni camp dismantled. To wave helplessly at children as they were herded onto rickety buses bound for who knew where. At least in Lesbos they sometimes got to the children before the authorities, smuggling toys and sweets into their sodden pockets.

Anton was called away. Jevon claimed ownership of his still warm cup of muddy coffee and lay back on his bed, itching to call Rhys again but forcing himself to wait until later. Rhys seemed to be working around the clock right now, and he needed rest. A lot of rest if the shadows smudged beneath his eyes were anything to go by.

Not that Jevon could talk. Local tensions surrounding the camp were spilling out every night now—protests, flares, soldiers, and police with dogs. Last night, it had got to the point where Jevon and his team had brought the youngest children into the staff tent, sitting up until dawn with half a dozen toddlers each to care for. Only the prospect of calling Rhys at sunrise had kept Jevon sane.

Sleep was his only true respite, but his dozing was interrupted a little while later by Anton coming back from the medical tents.

"Don't suppose you know how to stick an IV, do you?"

"Me?" Jevon cracked an eye open. "Nah. Sorry, mate. I've only done that basic Red Cross course."

Anton sighed. "Shame. I reckon you'd be a better nurse than you are a clown."

It was Anton's way to fill any time he spent with Jevon and his troop drolly informing them how distinctly unfunny they were. The banter passed the time when the generator failed and the water system clogged, but it was different now. The humour was laced with a graveness that drove Jevon to sit up. "What's going on?"

"The reinforcements I was expecting to arrive this week aren't going to get here."

"They're delayed?"

"Nope. They're just not coming. Something's kicked off

somewhere else so they've been sent there instead. There's no money to bring anyone else over, so we just have to make do."

"There's no volunteers?"

"None that we haven't taken full advantage of already. I might be able to rustle up a couple of docs in the next few months, but it's nurses I need and medical assistants, particularly ones with paediatric experience."

Jevon recalled the moment he'd spun around in the Bedford hospital to see Haya climbing up Rhys's legs. "What about paramedics?"

Anton nodded. "I'd marry one about now if it got them on a plane. Why? You know of anyone? Or a secret stash of paediatric antibiotics I could raid?"

"Maybe." But Jevon left it at that as madness began to take hold in his brain. Anton wandered off again, and Jevon retrieved his phone from under his pillow. The Wi-Fi wasn't working well enough for FaceTime, so he sent Rhys a message.

J: *Random long shot . . . MSF is in desperate need of medics and paediatric drugs. Any chance you fancy a change of scenery?*

R: *When do you need an answer? Got to find some info first.*

Jevon read the message for the thousandth time over the two weeks since Rhys had sent it, his heart skipping a brand new beat every time he considered the implications—the possibility that Rhys could join him at the camp in Lesbos. The application process for MSF took too long, but another NGO working with them on site had a faster system and had bitten Jevon's hand off when he'd passed them Rhys's details.

It seemed too good to be true. And there it was. Good. The word was so ironic it burned. The prospect of Rhys coming over filled Jevon with emotions he couldn't describe, but there was conflict too. Life on the camp was horrendous and growing worse every day. Did Jevon truly want Rhys to see the things he'd seen? Babies dying in tents? Dead children washing up on beaches?

It's Rhys's decision. But it didn't seem to matter how many times Jevon told himself that or even reminded himself that Rhys had seen plenty of horrors of his own, the war in his heart remained. A war that had sparked the moment they'd first kissed all those weeks ago. Months ago. A lifetime ago.

Jevon reflexively touched his lips, tracing them with the pad of his thumb. They tingled like they always did when he gave into memories that made his dick hard. Thankfully, he was alone in the living quarters, but he rolled over all the same, squashing the bulge in his trousers. He missed Rhys's touch like a drowning man missed air, but it ran deeper than sex, even with the sensation of Rhys finally pushing inside him still raw in his mind. *Fuck.* Jevon closed his eyes as desire pulsed through him. His yearning for Rhys was far more than physical, but the craving for that mind-blowing sensation haunted Jevon every free moment he wasn't distracted by something else.

Like talking to Rhys on the phone, on FaceTime, or texting him.

Jevon tapped out of WhatsApp and attempted a FaceTime call. The Wi-Fi failed for video, but the audio call went through until it failed to connect at Rhys's end. Disappointment weighed heavily in Jevon's bones. It was Saturday afternoon, and Rhys was on nights. Jevon would've regretted waking him up, but every snatched contact was precious. Missing one felt like the end of the world.

An inexplicable dread settled over Jevon. He sat up, boner forgotten, and rubbed his chest to disperse it, but agitation took hold of him instead. He'd been scheduled a rest afternoon, but suddenly the idea of spending the next four hours alone was awful.

He abandoned his bed, dressed in his least dirty clown

clothes, and left the tent. The FFP big top was a five-minute unicycle ride away—three, if he avoided the sludge, and when he got there, he found a rowdy game of stuck-in-the-mud in full swing.

The noise and the joy you only saw in children when they ran without a care in the world was a welcome distraction. Jevon ditched his unicycle and joined in, scooping up the smaller children and dashing around the tent with them, shouting, whooping, and celebrating tiny victories as though they were changing the world. Because laughter did change the world, if only for a moment.

After the third game, the session leaders called a timeout to distribute juice and snacks. Jevon sat with the acrobat children from Aleppo. He'd grown close to them in the fortnight since they'd arrived, and they seemed drawn to him too—and Rhys, when they'd worked out that Jevon was talking to someone whenever he retreated to the corner with his phone.

The oldest boy—spokesman for the tight knit group—nudged Jevon's arm. "Can we talk to the orange man?"

Jevon chuckled. He'd yet to tell Rhys about the nickname his flight suit had earned him. "You mean Rhys? I don't know. I think he might be at work."

The children continued to stare expectantly, reminding Jevon that Rhys being at work had proved no barrier to communication in the past. A tour of the rooftop base and the air ambulance had kept fifteen children crowded around Jevon's phone for forty-five minutes a few days ago, before they'd broken form to put on a show for Rhys and his colleagues. "Seriously, guys. We can try, but don't get upset if he can't talk, okay? Rhys has a very important job."

They made the call. Rhys didn't pick up, and the kids wandered off, but Jevon stayed on the floor, picking idly at a leftover packet of raisins, trying not to scrutinise the time and wonder what Rhys was doing to stop him answering the phone.

Jevon had told the kids he was probably working, but it wasn't like Rhys to let two calls go by without some kind of response, even if it was a one-word text.

And it wasn't like Jevon to fret over something so ridiculous either. He finished the raisins and hauled himself to his feet. *Daft twat.* There were all kinds of reasons why Rhys might not have called back. The fact that Jevon had lost the ability to think of any was irrelevant. Or maybe it wasn't. *Huh.* Perhaps he did need those rest hours after all.

Jevon was on his way out of the big top when Anton appeared, carrying a baby that had come off the same boat as the Aleppo acrobats. "Oh, hey." Jevon took the baby and fitted her to his hip. "I thought she was too poorly to come and play?"

"She was yesterday," Anton said. "But we got a surprise shipment of antibiotics overnight. A donation from The Royal London Hospital."

Royal London was where Rhys was based. Where the air ambulance he worked on took off from every day. Coincidence? Rhys hadn't mentioned talking to hospital bosses, but he knew about the shortages the camp medical teams were facing. Knew how a simple resupply would keep hundreds of people alive long enough to continue their journeys. *God, I love him.*

Jevon relieved Anton of the baby for a while and took her to the magic show he'd been planning on skipping. With many of the children tired from a rambunctious afternoon, the performance was light and easy and filled with gentle laughter that made the baby girl hiccup with glee.

She was still smiling when Jevon returned her to her family a little while later.

And Rhys still wasn't answering his phone.

J: *Everything okay?*

Jevon waited for two grey ticks to appear by the message to signal that it had been delivered, but for long minutes there was only one. Tired of fretting, he thrust the phone into his pocket and returned to his bed. His planned nap turned into a restless doze, and when he woke, the evening had turned into night, and temperatures in the camp had dropped. Jevon joined the medical staff passing out blankets and woolly hats to new arrivals, determinedly avoiding his blank phone screen. Camp officials liked children to stay in their assigned tents at night, but that didn't mean FFP's work was done.

It was close to midnight by the time Jevon had finished his rounds, sprinkling tiny foil dreamcatchers with "magic" dust. Anton was waiting for him, his face grave.

Jevon's forced good mood faded. "What's the matter? Did a boat come in?"

Anton shook his head. "No. It's not that. Load your news app, Jevon. Something's happened in London."

CHAPTER EIGHTEEN

RHYS HADN'T BEEN BORN with a gut instinct that carried him through a paramedic shift; it had developed over time, nurtured by each and every job. Every patient. Each life he'd held in his hands. Five years deep and he was still learning, but as he dashed across London Bridge, tracking the shouts of panicked police officers, every nerve he had was in overdrive.

"Is there anyone else on scene?" Tarryn, the chopper doc for the shift, shouted ahead.

Rhys tossed a glance over his shoulder. "No. Just the police. LFB are on route."

"Jesus."

Rhys concurred. It was rare that a helicopter crew were first on scene, but they'd been on another run when the call had come in, loading their patient into a road ambulance. With the incident just over the bridge from their location, they'd opted to approach on foot, leaving the chopper to take to the sky and find somewhere closer to land.

They reached the other side of the bridge. A policeman called out, and Rhys zeroed in on him, absorbing the carnage. Blood. So much blood. Rhys's stomach turned over.

He dropped to his knees, hands doing what they were

meant to even before his brain had processed the patient's injuries. "What happened?"

"Knife attack . . . like the last one," the policeman said. "I've got two down here, one at your six and more further into the street to your left."

"Where's the attacker?"

"At large. I'm surprised you got this far across the bridge, actually. They've just told me no crews are coming in until the area is secure."

Adrenaline was making the policeman talk so fast he was barely coherent, but Rhys collated the useful information: terror attack, lockdown, no other crews on scene. *Shit.* He'd worked through previous attacks on the city, but never on the ground with no back up.

He shot Tarryn an urgent glance. "Assess any casualties close by, but don't go far. We need to tag them and move on."

"Right."

Tarryn was ashen, reminding Rhys that it was only her second flight shift. Her anxiety laced the air, so thick he could taste it, but he pushed it away, grabbed her arm, and pointed to the next closest body on the ground. "Take the packs. Assess and tag. It's all we can do with no transport. The crews that come in behind us will scoop and run."

Five minutes later, they moved off, leaving three patients under the care of the policeman. Eerie silence greeted them in the next street. Restaurants and bars had locked their doors, and the usually bustling pavements were deserted, save the scattered bodies on the ground.

Rhys black tagged two—a young couple who'd fallen close together. The man had long dreads like Jevon's, and Rhys's heart tightened, threatening the barricades he'd thrown up when he'd clocked on shift this afternoon. Unease prickled the back of his neck. Logic told him the scene would burst to life at any moment, be flooded with blue lights and boots on the ground, but right now, even with Tarryn at his back, he'd never felt more exposed.

A noise to the left made him jump. In the distance, sirens wailed and car brakes screeched. Someone yelled for help, and the ghostly silence evaporated like it had never been there at all.

Pub doors opened. People streamed out, covered in blood and carrying people who couldn't carry themselves. A panicked crowd swarmed Rhys, and he had to shout to make himself heard. "Back up. If you need medical attention, find a safe place to wait and we'll come to you."

Eventually. As pieces of a grim jigsaw fit together, Rhys couldn't see how they'd ever get to everyone crying out for help, and another spike of terror reared in his gut. RTCs, fights, and gang wars had brought him a constant workload, day and night, since he'd hit the streets as a rookie technician years ago, but the sinister sense of something "big" unfolding around him was impossible to ignore.

A conveyor belt of truly horrible trauma unfolded. Rhys triaged one side of the street, Tarryn the other, and with each stab wound and trample injury, it became clear that whoever had wielded the weapon had intended to kill anyone who crossed their path. Neck slashes. Chest punctures.

"There were three of them," a woman gasped. "They had machetes and carving knives."

"Easy. You're safe now." Rhys repeated the mantra to every soul he touched but believed it less and less the longer he and Tarryn were the only crew on the ground. "We need urgent assistance," he pleaded into the radio. "There's too many wounded for us to help."

Again and again, the message came back: *Not yet. Standby.*

They cleared the first road. A policeman armed with a pepper spray and a thin baton accompanied them into the next. More bodies littered the street. A man was in the gutter, blood pouring from a puncture wound to his stomach. Rhys crouched down as the radio on his shoulder crackled to life, speaking in time with the policeman's, warning them to take cover.

Gunshots rang out, one after another. *Crack, crack, crack.* Rhys's whole body cringed, and the policeman grabbed his arm. "We need to get off the streets. Armed police are moving in."

Rhys pushed Tarryn towards a cafe that had seen them coming and opened its doors. "In there!" he shouted. "Let's go!"

He hauled the injured man up and dragged him towards the cafe as more gunshots pierced the air. A helicopter buzzed above them, and police cars screamed into the street. Rhys pushed Tarryn again, knocking her off balance. She grabbed him to steady herself. He tripped up the kerb, rolled his ankle, and whacked his head on the kerb with a sickening crack.

IT'S funny how the concept of time passing can change by the second. One minute, Rhys was stalking the city streets, stuffing stab wounds with gauze, the next he was sitting on a hospital ward with the worst headache in the world, having a meltdown over his misplaced phone.

"Calm down," Harry said. "We'll get you another phone."

Rhys ignored him and rummaged through the flight suit he'd found in a plastic bag by his bed for the hundredth time. Save his ID, his pockets were empty. No wallet, no phone. "*Fuck!*"

Harry stood and put his hands on Rhys's shoulders. "Easy. Do you need to call someone? You can use my phone."

More panic lanced Rhys's chest. "I don't have his number. It's in my phone."

"Whose number? Jevon's?"

Rhys nodded, his teeth chattering, even though he wasn't cold. "I haven't spoken to him since Friday."

"It's barely Sunday now," Harry said.

"Is it?"

"Yes. You've been here all night, and you've been awake from a concussion for an hour, so do you think you could lie down and stop losing your shit? I'll find your phone, or I'll get you another one, and we'll find a way of contacting Jevon, okay? Angelo has his number, right?"

It rang a bell, but the chaos in Rhys's mind was too loud. He let Harry tackle him onto his back and promptly fell asleep. When he woke up, it was afternoon and Joe had taken his place.

"This city is all kinds of fucked up." Joe unfolded his long legs from the crappy plastic chair he was wedged in. "Three dudes with machetes killed eight people last night. Why does shit like that happen?"

Rhys had no idea. He sat up and glared at the heavy strapping on his swollen left foot. "Have they said when I can leave?"

"Not to me, but I'd imagine they won't keep you any longer than they have to. The hospital is full."

"Why are you here?"

"To stop Harry crashing the van. I think a piece of him died when the police called yesterday to say you'd been hurt."

Guilt washed over Rhys. The last—fuck, however many hours it had been—had passed in a blur of headaches, swelling, and nurses with big syringes of drugs that made his head swim. And in his panic to find his phone, he hadn't stopped to wonder why Harry and Joe had appeared in London in the first place. "Sorry, man. I'm fine . . . honest. I didn't get hurt—I fell on my face and sprained my ankle."

"Uh-huh. You sprained it carrying a dying man across the street when you were the only paramedic on scene for more than an hour. Don't fuck with perspective, Rhys. Not today."

Joe was fierce. Always had been. Rhys was growing to love him like a brother, but nausea rolling in his gut stopped him from saying so. "I need to talk to Jevon."

"I know. My mum's helping Angelo look for his phone, and

my sister is trying to get in touch with the organisation he works for. We'll find him, dude. I promise."

There wasn't much else to say, and Joe wasn't one for small talk. He fed Rhys a Snickers bar, then fell silent, tapping his fingers against the bed rail until Rhys dozed off again.

Harry was back when Rhys woke the following morning—Joe had stayed at Rhys's flat to pack him some things.

"You're coming home with us."

"No."

"Yes." Harry's fists clenched at his sides until he folded his arms across his chest. "You can't be alone right now with a head injury. Besides, you're going to be on crutches for six weeks, need physio and rest. I'm not leaving you to rot in that flat by yourself when rehab and recovery are the only things I can do to help."

"Right. So you're going to collect me like you do everyone else who can't walk to the bogs by themselves? Save me from myself? Piss off, Harry. I'm not going to the arse crack of Cornwall with you."

"Yes, you are."

"No, I'm not."

Ten minutes later found Rhys huddled up in the back of Joe's cosy camper van. "Just take me home," he pleaded.

Joe stared stoically ahead while Harry shot Rhys an exasperated glare. "I *am*."

Lies. It was all lies, but Rhys was too tired to argue. To fight. And to worry over something he couldn't fix. Angelo had lost his phone too, and all of Joe's sister's attempts to contact FFP had come to nothing. Jevon would probably think Rhys had given up on him. Had changed his mind about quitting London for life on the road. Without a phone, there was nothing Rhys could do to make that right.

And without Jevon, nothing would ever be okay.

London slipped away. Harry and Joe talked quietly in the

front of the van while Rhys lost his mind in the back. Common sense told him he'd find a way to contact Jevon eventually, and that Jevon would understand about the radio silence—of course he would—but the anxiety demon having a party in his brain wouldn't quit. His ankle throbbed in time with the disquiet beating in his chest. Joe cranked the heat up, but still Rhys shivered.

"You're in shock," Harry said when they stopped for petrol. "I know you've got Jevon on your mind, but don't forget what you've just been through. You saved dozens of people, bro. By yourself."

"I wasn't by myself. Tarryn was there, and so were a bunch of coppers."

"Yeah, yeah." Harry put his arms around Rhys and held him in a fraternal embrace that meant everything and nothing while Rhys's head was in bits. "I'm just reminding you it's okay to be shaken up. Your supervisor said there'll be counselling and—"

"Jesus Christ, Harry . . . stop, will you? It was two days ago, and I'm fine."

Rhys disentangled himself from Harry as Joe returned to the van with more chocolate and sweets to make Harry scowl. Any other day, his face would've made Rhys laugh, but not today.

Joe was the only one capable of laughing, apparently, when they pulled up at the farm in Newquay, six hours after they'd left London behind. His chuckle came from deep in his belly, and he exited the van without explaining.

Harry watched him go, still scowling, but then something seemed to make him smile too.

He slid out of the passenger seat and opened the sliding door, holding out his hands to help Rhys to his feet, crutches ready to slip onto his arms. "I'd help you to the bungalow, but something tells me that won't be necessary."

Rhys didn't even look up. All he wanted was a shower, a bed

for the night, and a plan to fix the mess his life had become in the last twenty-four hours. Avoiding the news usually helped when he'd been on a clusterfuck call. Perhaps a stint in Newquay would do him good after all, of course, he'd found a way to—

"Rhys?"

"What?"

But when Rhys snapped his gaze up, it wasn't Harry in front of him. It wasn't Joe and it wasn't Angelo, who Rhys could somehow sense nearby. Harry's big hands were replaced by warm, elegant fingers carrying a current that travelled straight to Rhys's heart, straight to his soul, eclipsing every hurt in its path. Rhys blinked in wonder and lost himself in liquid brown eyes and a gentle smile. "Jevon?"

CHAPTER NINETEEN

"I DON'T UNDERSTAND." Rhys sat on the edge of the bed, his eyes hooded and bloodshot and his face so pale Jevon could see bone. "How are you *here* of all places?"

Jevon knelt in front of Rhys and eased his shoe off his good foot. "I made tracks to come home as soon as I got news of the attack in London and I couldn't get hold of you. I was at the airport when Angelo called this morning and told me Harry was bringing you home, so I switched my flight. Some crazy old dude picked me up in a horse box, and I got here ten minutes before you."

Rhys blinked, shaking his head. "This is mad."

"I'll say." Jevon brushed Rhys's hair back from his forehead, his fingers lingering on the tender bruise on Rhys's temple. "You have amazing family and friends, but I'm sorry you had to go through something so awful for me to meet them."

"Awful?" Rhys stared with dead eyes Jevon had seen in hundreds of traumatised refugees.

"Yes. Awful," Jevon said. "I know you're hardened to some pretty terrible things, but that doesn't make them okay."

Rhys said nothing. Just stared around the feminine bedroom

that apparently belonged to his brother's boyfriend's sister. "Where are we?"

"Joe's mum's bungalow. She's gone to stay with a friend, and Emma—Joe's sister—is staying with Angelo. They said you can use this place as long as you need."

"Oh."

"Uh-huh. Emma seemed pretty nice."

"She is."

Jevon squeezed Rhys's hands. "Help me out here, man. What do you need?"

"Need?"

"Yeah. Need. You hungry? Wanna shower? I can help you?"

Rhys shook his head slowly. "Nah, Jevon. I just need you."

***

FOR ALL THAT, it turned out Rhys did want a shower. Jevon held him up, then eased him into the bed Joe had slipped in and made up with fresh sheets.

Jevon saw him out. "Thanks, man."

"No worries," Joe said. "There's food in the fridge and cupboards, and everything the hospital gave us is on the counter. Harry will probably come by to check you're not dead, but no one else will bother you. Call me if you need anything—my number's on the side."

He left, and Jevon drifted back to the bedroom. Rhys was sitting on the bed, looking every bit as lost as he'd seemed since Jevon had practically shoved Harry out of the way at the van door. Flashes of the news reports Jevon had seen invaded his mind—blood, blue lights, horror, and death . . . things that were Rhys's constant companion when he was at work, but knowing they'd stemmed from hate this time made it all seem so much worse.

Jevon ran a towel over Rhys's wet hair. "Does your ankle hurt?"

"Hmm?" Rhys tilted his head sideways and studied his purple-black foot. "Um, not really, no. I can't feel it, to be honest."

"Numb, huh?"

"Yeah."

Jevon dropped the towel and slid his fingers up Rhys's neck and into his damp hair. "How about now? Can you feel this?"

"What? Your fingers setting me on fire? Of course I can."

Relief flooded Jevon's veins, and he persisted in his journey over every part of Rhys he could reach, retracing steps his hands had last made more than a month ago. Damn . . . was that all? It seemed like a lifetime had passed since he'd last put his hands on Rhys. Last felt his heated skin glide beneath his palms. Last heard his soft intake of breath as Jevon's fingers grazed a sensitive spot.

A spot that was marred by bruises from where Rhys had hit the pavement.

Jevon's fingers stilled. Adrenaline and relief that Rhys had made it through the horrible events in London relatively unscathed had carried him this far, but the reality that things could've turned out vastly different hit Jevon hard and fast. The attackers had been gunned down by police twenty feet from where Rhys had fallen. What a difference ten seconds either way could've made.

"Jevon?" Rhys had turned around and was staring right at him. "What's the matter?"

"I—uh, nothing. I'm fine."

"Liar."

There was no accusation in Rhys's tone. Only fact. In spite of himself, Jevon smiled and cupped Rhys's face, absently thumbing the dark smudges beneath his eyes. "I'm okay. Just struggling to believe we're both really here."

It was a vague version of the truth, and Rhys seemed to know it. He sighed and pulled Jevon into a tight hug. "I'm sorry it had to be this way too. I was supposed to meet my boss whenever Monday is to discuss if he could let me out of my secondment to join the NGO. He's a good bloke . . . I was hoping he'd say yes."

Jevon closed his eyes. Three days ago, getting Rhys to Lesbos had been everything. Now counting the thud of his heart against his own was more. So much more. "Don't think about that right now. You're going to be off your feet for a while."

"Foot."

"What?"

"Foot. My other one is fine."

"Dick."

"But you love me?"

"I do." Jevon leaned down and kissed Rhys deeply, reconnecting the wires that had been flailing in the wind for four long weeks. "Do you love me?"

"More than you know."

"Show me."

AN HOUR of shifting awkwardly on Joe's sister's bed, kissing the hell out of each other, wore Rhys out. After hustling Jevon under the flowery duvet, he knocked out. Jevon held him for a while, watching him sleep, like a creeper, while he poked around on his phone, but restlessness and a craving for Newquay's fresh air eventually drove him outside to take a walk.

It was dark and cold on the farm. Wind whipped up the lane and swirled around the yard Jevon meandered to. Close to midnight, he didn't expect to see anyone, but Joe was sitting on the doorstep of the main house, drinking whisky and smoking a cigarette. "Everything okay?"

"Think so." Jevon leaned on the cold stone wall. "Rhys is knackered."

"Harry too. He hasn't slept since it kicked off on the news."

Neither had Jevon, but fatigue seemed far away. He accepted the whisky bottle Joe held out and took a deep swig. The amber liquid burned wonderfully, scraping away some of the terror still scratching his soul. "Thanks."

"Welcome." Joe took the bottle back. "You okay? Must've been a hell of a day for you too."

Jevon shrugged. "I've had better."

"Not much for complaining, eh?"

"What's the point?"

"Truth." Joe looked as though he wanted to say something else, but Harry opened the front door, looking every inch Rhys's brother, though he was broader and his eyes softer.

Joe stubbed his cigarette out. "Don't start."

Harry smiled and kissed Joe's cheek. "I wasn't going to. The RSPCA are on the phone, though, so I hope you haven't necked too much whisky to drive."

"How dare you? I'd better call George, though."

Joe unfolded himself from the step and slipped inside, leaving Jevon with Harry, who regarded him with obvious curiosity.

"I've never seen my brother so attached to someone," he said.

"Attached?"

"Invested. Emotional. Sorry, I'm not good with words when I'm tired."

"Who is?"

Harry laughed quietly. "Not Rhys. Come inside. I'm making tea."

Tea turned out to be some herbal infusion that tasted like dusty flowers. Jevon sipped it and mourned Joe's whisky bottle.

Harry sat beside him at the kind of kitchen table that instantly made Jevon hungry. "It's nice to meet you. I was beginning to think the others had made you up."

"Others?"

"Joe. Angelo. They like you."

"I like them. It was nice to see Angelo looking so well. I barely recognised him when he came to meet the horse box."

Harry's weary smile widened briefly. "Amazing, isn't he? He works so hard to keep himself upright, it breaks my heart when it's not enough."

Before today, Jevon had only seen Angelo on his knees, so he could only imagine how tough it had been to crawl his way back to the lithe dancer who'd greeted him with a hug and a kiss to both cheeks. "Where's Dylan?"

"Romford. He's coming for Christmas in a couple of days."

"That's nice."

"Yeah. I'm kinda hoping you and Rhys will stick around too."

"For Christmas?"

"It's next week."

The festive season had slipped Jevon's mind. "I hadn't even thought about it."

"Don't blame you. Rhys usually works, but I guess that's off the table for now. What about your job? When are they expecting you back?"

Jevon's stomach tightened. "I don't know if they are. I literally ran out on them with ten minutes notice."

"Will they sack you?"

A hysterical chuckle burst from Jevon's chest. "I've had moments these last few weeks when I've wished they would, but, no. I'll have to go back as soon as Rhys is okay."

"You're welcome to stay here as long as you like. We have plenty of room."

"Thanks." Jevon toyed with the teabag in his cup. "I wasn't sure what to expect when I met you."

"Why? Does Rhys slag me off?"

Humour danced in Harry's dark eyes, but Jevon shook his head emphatically anyway. "No. God, no. I just got the sense that you have a complex relationship."

Harry shrugged. "Me and Rhys aren't particularly patient with each other when shit gets real. Old habits die hard, but basically, we just want the other to be okay."

"I see that," Jevon said. "And I know he loves you."

"So do I."

A comfortable silence stretched out. A cat appeared from nowhere and draped itself across Jevon's thighs while he tried to summon the energy to walk back to the bungalow. The warm mass on his lap didn't help, but the desire to be as close to Rhys as possible won out. He finished his tea and bid Harry goodnight and was crawling into bed behind Rhys before he could blink.

The heat between them roared to life as Rhys stirred in response. "Jevon?"

"Shh," Jevon whispered. "I'm here."

Rhys rolled over, his eyes blazing. "*Show* me."

CHAPTER TWENTY

JEVON KISSED RHYS, devoured him, and for once Rhys didn't lose himself in the madness that came with having Jevon's lips locked with his. Couldn't. Because he was too busy reacquainting himself with Jevon's taste. His warm skin. Every sound he breathed into Rhys's mouth. Committing it all to indelible memory for when they inevitably had to part again.

A month without contact had left Rhys starved, and he couldn't get enough. He drove his tongue wetly into Jevon's mouth and arched up into him as much as he could with his weighted left foot.

Their hips met clumsily, roughly, and it was perfect. Rhys unbuttoned Jevon's jeans and squeezed his dick, pumping his hard length until Jevon broke their kiss, eyes rolling back, a groan escaping from his hung-open mouth. He thrust into Rhys's hand, then drew back to pull his hooded sweatshirt over his head. His jeans disappeared, and he slipped into bed with Rhys. "Your turn."

Rhys's sweatpants and underwear followed Jevon's clothes. Naked, they clung to each other, kissing, hands roaming, the only sounds in the dark room their increasingly frantic gasps and moans. Jevon rocked his hips, his cock sliding in tandem with Rhys's, sticky with precome. Rhys had to taste him. "Fuck my mouth."

"Are you—"

"Do it."

Jevon straddled Rhys's sweat-damp chest and eased his thick cock into Rhys's mouth. Steady moans tore from him as Rhys sucked him, revelling in the suffocating bliss of having Jevon's cock crammed down his throat. Jevon's quivering thighs went straight to his own dick, and he jacked himself in time with Jevon's stuttered thrusts until he forced himself to pull back.

"More." He wiped his mouth with the back of his hand. "I need more."

"Easy." Jevon laid a heated palm over Rhys's thundering heart. "We've got no lube, dude."

Rhys got a hold of his racing mind, considered logistics, and his brain gifted him a last shot of reason. "We have. Joe fetched me the bag I brought to Bedford last time I came. It's over there."

"You're fucking magic."

Jevon leapt out of bed and retrieved the bottle of lube Rhys had tucked into the inner pocket of his overnight bag. He squeezed some onto his hands and reached for Rhys's dick, but Rhys caught him. Shook his head. "Not like that. Fuck *me*, Jevon."

Something flickered in Jevon's face that Rhys couldn't quite decipher. Doubt. Uncertainty? *No.* Not tonight. And not ever again. Rhys dug his nails into Jevon's wrists. "Please . . . I need you."

"You've got me, baby." Jevon freed himself from Rhys's punishing grip and slicked his cock with lube. Then he helped Rhys shift onto his side, his good leg bent to his chest. His probing fingers were sure of their path, sliding straight to the sweet spot that sprayed stars into Rhys's vision, like they had so many times before, but it was different now. Jevon moved with more purpose, stretching and sweeping.

Rhys couldn't wait a moment longer. "Now, Jevon. *Please.*"

"Okay, okay." Jevon withdrew his fingers and rubbed Rhys's back. His touch was soothing, but a moment later, the insistent press of his dick against Rhys's slicked up hole was electric.

The burn was incredible, and Rhys cried out, pressing his face into a pillow that smelled of grass and hairspray, his whole body clenching, straining . . . resisting, but desperate for more.

"Am I hurting you?" Jevon whispered.

As if he could. Rhys thrashed his head. "No. Just fuck me . . . please."

It was the third time he'd resorted to begging, and Jevon finally seemed to hear him. To *believe* that Rhys's desperation was all about him. That he'd never wanted anyone else like this, and he never would. That Jevon was everything to him and more.

Jevon dropped soft, wet kisses to the back of Rhys's neck, and drove his cock inside Rhys to the hilt. He stilled, giving Rhys a moment to suck in a breath and adjust to the sheer girth of him, then he began to move, and every man who'd fucked Rhys before him evaporated like they'd never been there at all.

Hands, lips, tongue, Jevon was everywhere, driving in and out of Rhys, rocking them both in a cadence so sweet Rhys could barely breathe. He moaned, fisting the pillow by his face, and pushed back on Jevon, seeking more friction, chasing heat that was too much and not enough rolled into one.

Jevon curled around him, screwing him just a tiny bit harder. "God, this feels so good. Why did we wait so long?"

Rhys couldn't fathom an answer, but despite the rosy haze clouding his mind, he knew they'd been right to hang tough for this moment. To have faith in their stars to align—*begin* to align, because they weren't there yet. Jevon was inside Rhys, loving him like they'd always known he could, but there was so much more to say. So much more to *do*.

But not now. It could wait—it could *all* wait, because Rhys was about to lose his fucking mind. He drove his fist into the mattress. "*Harder*," he ground out, and something—*everything*—changed.

Jevon pulled out and drew Rhys further down the bed, pushing him onto his front with oh-so-gentle hands. Then he drove back in, his cock nudging far deeper than it had before. Over and over, he thrust his hips, building speed and depth with each thrust, until his hypnotic, flexing pace faltered and the moans falling from him gained an octave. "Fuck, I'm gonna come."

"Do it." Rhys hunched his spine and braced himself, ignoring the lance of pain from his injured ankle. "I wanna feel you."

Jevon slammed their bodies together once more, twice more, then he seized up, and his movements became jerky as his cock pulsed inside Rhys. "Fuck, I love you, man."

"I love you, too," Rhys gasped out. "Don't stop, don't stop."

Jevon didn't stop. He kept moving, his dick still a steely rod buried inside Rhys as he screwed them both through his orgasm. He gripped Rhys's shoulders and fucked him harder, and the rhythmic pounding of his hips stoked a throbbing burn in Rhys so intense he forgot where he was. Forgot the bloody, ruined bodies that brought him here. Forgot the traumatised young faces that led him and Jevon back together in the first place.

Forgot everything except the pleasure building from somewhere so deep he couldn't trace it back. Couldn't follow a beam of light, even as it burst into blinding rays. Numbness had carried him out of London, but Rhys wasn't numb anymore. His ankle screamed again—like the pins holding him together were being screwed in *right now*—and as his release spilled out of him, so did any apathy Jevon had missed when he'd claimed Rhys's heart as his own.

With a ragged shout, Rhys fell apart. Gasps turned to sobs, and Jevon's arms were around him so fast Rhys barely felt his softened dick slip out of him. Jevon laid him on his back and moved a pillow under Rhys's injured ankle, propping it up. The bruise on his temple throbbed, but the ache in Rhys's sprained tendons eased instantly, even as violent shivers continued to shudder through him.

Jevon pressed his forehead to Rhys's, forcing him to meet his gaze. He offered no words of comfort, only himself. And it was enough. The abrupt vomit of emotion faded as Rhys's lungs won the battle for air. His limbs still trembled, but it made sense, even if he didn't know why.

He clutched Jevon's hands. "I'm sorry."

"Don't be. You wouldn't be human if the last few days hadn't fucked you up. Shit, I can hardly stand to think about what happened in London, and I wasn't there."

"Neither was I, really." Rhys closed his eyes and took a deep breath, letting the oxygen filter through his strained nerves. "And that detachment is likely the problem. I usually go back on base after a messed-up shift. Talk it out with Pater and whatever doc was with us or the next crew coming on. I didn't do that this time—I came round from this fucking concussion, shouted at Harry, then came here."

"Camaraderie is everything when life gets real."

"Yup. And I think I maybe need to speak to someone now I'm not going to have that for a while, but I'm okay at the moment. Maybe we can talk about it later?"

"Always."

Rhys knew he could count on Jevon to hold him to it. "What about you? How was topping a bloke for the first time?"

"Do I need to answer that? I think we scared the horses."

A genuine laugh bubbled out of Rhys. In his suspended

delirium, it was more of a giggle, and he slapped his hand over his mouth. When he'd composed himself, he pulled Jevon impossibly closer. "It was—*fuck*—it was amazing for me. I've never been with anyone like that."

"Never?"

"Never. I've told you before—fucking has always been fun for me . . . hot, exciting, whatever. But with you? Shit. It's all those things and so much more. I literally feel like I've been to the moon and back. You're everything, Jevon."

Jevon smiled. "I can't even describe how it was for me. For all the times I've pictured it, I figured I'd have some idea what it would be like, but I— Damn. You're amazing."

"I'm really, really not," Rhys said around a sigh that turned into a jaw-cracking yawn. "I'm as good as you make me feel."

"Whatever. We've got some time to work on that fractured self-esteem. Don't think I'm gonna go easy on you."

Rhys didn't doubt it for a second, and as he stared at Jevon through heavy lidded eyes, a renegade faction in his body came to life again. He was tired and sore, but even with the weight of the world crashing down, Jevon made him feel so fucking alive. His cock rose, and his body craved Jevon inside him again so fiercely that his heart stuttered.

Jevon read him like an open book and smirked. "Sure about that? You should keep your foot up."

"I will." Rhys widened his legs, canting his hips just enough that Jevon would be able to slide easily home. "You might have to hold me down, though. Everything about your dick makes me crazy."

"Just my dick, huh?" Jevon climbed carefully over Rhys's battered body until he was safely cradled between his legs. "What about my tongue?"

Without warning, he took Rhys in his mouth, and coherent thought was gone, replaced by Jevon's tongue, fingers, and eventually his cock. He fucked Rhys slower this time, the

desperate need from before calmed by the certainty that this
worked. That it was right for both of them, whichever way
they came at it, and all the final puzzle pieces were a perfect
fit.

Rhys climaxed with a soundless cry, then he fell limp, his
face buried in Jevon's neck, his lungs empty, and nothing left in
his heart but love.

⸺

RHYS WOKE to sunlight streaming through the gap in the
flowery curtains, Jevon's arm flung over his face, and gentle
knocking at the bedroom door. He sat up, wincing at the stiff-
ness in his strapped ankle. "Yeah?"

"Breakfast at the house if you want it," Harry called softly.
"Plenty of stuff right here if you don't."

Light footsteps padded away without waiting for an answer,
and the bungalow's front door clicked shut. Rhys shook his
head. Harry was a big guy, but he'd always moved like a ninja—
all silence and grace. Rhys pictured him leaping across the shattered living room in the old family house, tackling their father to
the floor, and keeping him there until Rhys could get away. It
hadn't felt right then, and it didn't feel right now. Harry was a
lover, not a fighter.

Jevon stirred. "What are you smirking about?"

"What do you think?" Rhys leaned down and kissed Jevon's
cheek. "I got lucky last night."

Lucky didn't begin to cover it, but it was all Rhys had. Jevon
rolled his eyes and pulled a pillow over his head in response,
and it was a few minutes before he deemed Rhys worthy of
more conversation. By then, Rhys was hauling himself back
from the bathroom on his crutches.

"You look better," Jevon remarked.

"Better?"

"Yeah. You've lost that corpse-like white boy thang you had going on."

"Nice."

"Not really. You're way hotter with some colour in your cheeks."

Rhys made it back to the bed and deposited himself in a heap of crutches and limbs. "Must be the salty sea air. I always look like a cabbage patch kid when I'm down here."

"Do you visit a lot?"

"Nope."

"Why? It's gorgeous."

Rhys flopped onto his back and pulled Jevon with him, more addicted to touching him than ever, if such a thing was possible. "I don't know, to be honest. When Harry asks, I tell him I'm busy, but I actually love it here when he's not nagging me to live a better life."

Jevon hummed. "I'd jump on that bandwagon, but I'm too hungry to think straight. Do you think we can rustle up some breakfast here?"

"Probably, but it'll be better up at the house if you're feeling sociable. Feeding time at the zoo goes on all day here."

Jevon's face brightened considerably. "Sounds like my kind of house. I've been living off stale pitta bread and dodgy chicken for weeks."

"Really? Is it that bad in the camp?"

Jevon shrugged. "Yeah. And it's getting worse with the weather, but it's much tougher for the people living outside the staff quarters. We have heaters and cooking facilities. Hot water when the system works. They don't."

"When are you going back?"

Jevon sighed. "Can we talk about this later?"

"Sure."

Rhys wasn't complaining. Still riding high on the euphoria of Jevon turning him inside out, facing reality all over again wasn't high on his Christmas list. Accepting that their time together was, as always, temporary, could wait.

They got dressed and ventured across the farm to the big old house Harry and Joe called home. In the cosy kitchen, they found Joe, Harry, and Emma—Joe's sister—sitting at the table while Angelo dished out breakfast to them and a handful of faces Rhys didn't recognise. Crispy fried eggs, sautéed polenta, and something with tomatoes and white beans.

Rhys smirked at Joe. "This ain't your mum's fry up."

"Angie reckons we're in Milan or some shit, but I'm not complaining. For all the mess he makes of the kitchen, the boy can cook."

Joe flashed Angelo a wink, earning him an eye roll in response, as Angelo dropped into the seat beside Rhys. "You think you'd get this in Milan? This is peasant food, mate."

"Suits me then."

Joe returned his attention to his plate. Rhys fumbled with his crutches until Harry reached a long arm around Jevon and leaned them against a nearby dresser.

Angelo chuckled quietly.

Rhys shot him a dead-eyed stare. "What?"

"Annoying, isn't it?"

"No more than usual. I didn't need to fuck my ankle to know my brother is irritating."

"I didn't mean that. I meant having to rely on other people to put one foot in front of the other. It's not Harry's fault you need help."

He spoke too quietly for anyone around the table to hear, but Rhys's glare intensified anyway before he caught himself and reined his petulant inner wanker in for good. "Yeah. I know. I'm just acclimatising to being on my arse. I'll stop being a dick soon, I promise."

Angelo chuckled again. "Let me know when it starts."

Twat. But Rhys struggled to mean it. If it hadn't been for

Angelo keeping in touch with Jevon, Rhys would be sleeping in Emma's bed by himself. And despite wasting so much time protesting otherwise, Rhys *did* consider Angelo a friend. He slung a lazy arm around Angelo's slender shoulders and raised his voice to normal levels. "It's good to see you looking more like the feisty Dom I know and love."

Beside Rhys, Jevon snorted, and across the table, Harry cringed. "Seriously? We're going to talk about that over breakfast?"

"If you want, bro. Wasn't me who wasn't ever talking about it."

Harry gave Rhys the finger, and the conversation moved on. And life did too. Joe and Harry went back to work, leaving Angelo to clean up and shoo Jevon away when he offered to help. "I'm good. I like to make the most of my usefulness when it's here. Makes up for all the times I'm surgically attached to the couch."

"You sure?"

Angelo wrapped his arms around Jevon's neck and kissed his cheek. "I'm sure. Take that grumpy arsehole back to bed."

Going back to bed had its merits, but Rhys didn't feel like retreating to the bungalow again straight away. Instead, they navigated across the frosty yard to a helpfully positioned bench and watched Joe and Emma work with the huge black stallion Rhys had always been warned not to touch.

"His name's Shadow. Only Joe, Emma, and their father can handle him, and even then, he nearly killed Joe a while ago."

"He's huge," Jevon said. "Does Joe's father live in the bungalow too?"

"Nah. He's in prison."

"I feel peaceful here," was all Jevon offered in return. "Like it's where we're meant to be right now."

"How long for, though?"

The question was out before Rhys could catch it, tainting

the easy air they'd ambled—hobbled, in Rhys's case—around the farm with. Jevon kept his eyes on Joe and the fiery stallion and tightened his grip on Rhys's hand. "I haven't been in touch with anyone from FFP since I bailed on them, but I can't stay much longer than Christmas."

"Christmas?"

"Yeah. There's an early morning flight out of Newquay the day after Boxing Day. I booked it last night when you were asleep. I'm sorry I didn't tell you."

It was on the tip of Rhys's tongue to point out he hadn't given Jevon much chance for talking the night before, but he let it go. Christmas was a week away, and that gave them far longer together than he'd feared. "Harry will want us to stay here."

"I know. He's already asked me."

"When?"

"Last night. After I'd booked the ticket, actually, but it all seemed to make sense when he did. I kind of assumed you'd want to stay . . . unless you want to go back to London?"

"What about your family?"

Jevon shrugged. "They don't know I'm here. And they've pretty much given up on me as far as Christmas is concerned. I usually make it up to them over the summer with a couple of mega barbecues. Trust me, it's easier than trying to get your head around pouring turkey gravy over your rice and peas."

"You've lost me."

"Have I?"

"Never." Rhys lolled his head on Jevon's shoulder. "And for what it's worth, I can't imagine a better way to spend Christmas than here with you . . . and my family."

"I was hoping you'd say that."

"Yeah?"

"Yeah. Family is important, man. You've gotta drop the lone wolf shit . . . I hate thinking of you being alone when I'm gone."

"It won't be for long."

"How d'ya figure?"

Rhys sat up as Joe took a tumble off the big black horse, waiting until he stood up and threw his helmet at Emma before answering with a theory that had been on his mind since he'd woken up. "Transferring my secondment from the air ambulance to the NGO needs a lot of paperwork shuffling I didn't really have time for while I was working. If my ankle heals right, I can probably wrap it up by the time I'm back on my feet."

"Wow." Jevon shifted on the bench so he was facing Rhys. "You could be on camp by February?"

"I reckon so."

"Do you think—"

He stopped. Rhys nudged him. "What? Go on, please?"

Jevon gazed steadily at Rhys. "You said last night you were thinking of talking to someone about all the shit you've been through. Are you going to do that too...while you're off your feet anyway?"

Rhys nodded. "I am. I've been dodging service counselling for years, but that's going to change. I need to be back on my feet in every sense before I embark on anything new."

"And your ankle will be okay?"

"Hopefully. I've got the best physiotherapist in the business for a brother, so I've every chance."

A smile burst slowly across Jevon's lovely face, like rays of sunshine eating up the clouds. "I thought it would take months and months. That we'd be apart until summer, at least."

"Fuck that noise." Rhys brought one of Jevon's hands to his lips and kissed it. "I'd quit my job before I let that happen. I want to be with you, but more than that—I want—fuck . . . I want to use the skills I have to make a bigger impact. These days, there's a waiting list of paramedics to get on the air ambulance team—dozens of people lined up to do my job, and I know it every time I put that damn suit on. Working on the camps feels more personal, you know?"

Jevon nodded slowly. "I get it. I worried for a while that I was being selfish by pitching you the idea, but then I saw the light in your eyes every time we talked about it and knew you'd make it happen with or without me."

"I can't be without you, Jevon. You know that, don't you?"

"As much as I know I can't be without you."

Rhys's own smile widened enough to hurt his face. "Then we'd better go tell Harry to order an extra turkey."

EPILOGUE

Six months later . . .

"I CAN'T BELIEVE you live in a minibus with blacked out windows. Thought you were supposed to be roughing it?"

Rhys gave Harry the finger down the phone and continued on his guided tour of the Sicilian IDP camp he currently called home. "A tour company donated a bunch of broken-down vehicles that were bound for scrap—warmer than tents come winter —and I think we got the mafia's cast-offs. I'm not complaining, though."

"Bet you're not," Angelo called out from somewhere behind Harry.

He left the rest of the sentence unsaid, but he wasn't wrong. The rusty gangster minibus had everything he and Jevon needed, including a facade of privacy they wouldn't get anywhere else on the sprawling camp.

"Anyway," Harry said when Angelo was apparently done heckling. "I have to go—I've got a bunch of new clients arriving today and I've left Joe to set up. But call me in a few days, okay? And email me if there's anything you need."

"I've got all I need, bro."

"Me too."

Harry treated Rhys to a smile that he usually saved for Joe and hung up, leaving Rhys with a goofy grin of his own. Because for all that the camp was proving to be hell on earth some days, Rhys couldn't deny that he was happy. That he'd finally found his place.

He tucked his phone into his pocket and left the bus behind. On his way to the makeshift field hospital, he passed Jevon's big top and couldn't resist peeking inside. Jevon was stood in the centre of a large circle. Dozens of children surrounded him, each one enchanted as he led them in a game Rhys had yet to get to grips with on the rare occasions he had time to play. *God, I love him.*

With a herculean effort, Rhys moved on. At the hospital, he found a team assembling by the only roadworthy vehicle.

Anton tossed him a lifejacket, and Rhys's good mood waned. "Boat?"

"Multiple," Anton said grimly. "One of them's already gone over."

He didn't need to say anymore. Rhys climbed in the truck, rode it to the beach, and hauled ass to the charity-funded lifeboat that scoured the ocean for drowning refugees.

Four hours later, he returned to camp with seven mildly hypothermic children. The adults had gone with Anton.

Jevon was waiting in the special reception area he'd constructed in the hospital for any youngsters arriving on camp. There was food and warmth and toys. Gentle smiles and, more than anything, hope. For most of these children, their journey was far from over, but Rhys knew a couple of hours with Jevon and his troop was a respite they desperately needed.

It was dark when they walked back to the bus, close enough that their hands brushed with every step. In the shadows by the water pump, Rhys pulled Jevon to him, wound his arms around his neck, and kissed him. "I love you."

Jevon smiled. "I love you too."

JEVON PRESSED his hand over Rhys's mouth and flexed his hips again, thrusting inside Rhys with enough force to make him sink his teeth into Jevon's palm, but not enough to send the bus rocking. Over and over he slid home, nudging Rhys's sweet spot, revelling in the sensation of Rhys's wet heat clamped tight around him. It was ecstasy, it was bliss, and he couldn't fathom how he'd survived so many years without it.

Without *Rhys*.

He fused their lips together, muffling Rhys's cries as he convulsed beneath him, then his own as his body poured all he had into Rhys—love, friendship, and so much more.

When the storm had passed, Jevon lay on his back with Rhys's head on his chest. Rhys dozed while Jevon played with his hair and thought of home. Two care packages had arrived from the UK that week—one from Efe in London, the other from Newquay, loaded with little gifts from just about everyone on Joe and Harry's farm. A rush of contentment warmed Jevon's bones. His own family had always had his back, but Rhys's was so much bigger than he'd seemed to know until he'd left them behind. Rhys spoke to Harry all the time, sent Joe and Angelo good-natured abuse, and talked with Dylan for hours when they both found the time. Jevon loved them all.

"What are you smiling about?" Rhys gazed sleepily up at Jevon, his too long, sex-tousled hair all over his face.

Oops. Jevon smoothed it back. "I was thinking about home—well, the farm really. I kind of miss them."

"They miss you too. Dylan wants to fall asleep in your lap again."

Jevon recalled that drunken Christmas night and laughed. "I wouldn't stop him. He's adorable."

It was true. All slender limbs and blond hair, Dylan was gorgeous and sweet and lovely, and nothing like Jevon had imagined when he'd first spoken to him on the phone. "I dreamed about him fucking you the other night."

That got Rhys's attention. The post-coital haze cleared from his gaze. "Why?"

Jevon shrugged. "No idea, though it might've had something to do with, uh, Christmas and you describing your club encounters to me in great detail."

"Both of those things were your idea."

"I know." Unbidden, borrowed images of Rhys riding Dylan's cock while Angelo fucked his mouth flashed through Jevon's mind. Heat rippled through him. "I'm not complaining."

"Right." Rhys didn't look convinced.

Jevon poked him. "I mean it—I don't think I would ever want to go further than what happened at Christmas when we were all kind of watching each other—but thinking about you with your friends is really fucking hot."

"*Our* friends," Rhys corrected as he tried to steer his mind away from *that* drunken night, when the line between new friends and old playmates had blurred just a tiny bit. *Jesus, Christmas was a mad one.* "And you know I played with loads more people than those two, right? But I get what you're saying. Dylan and Angelo are mesmerising, eh? There was a time when I thought I wanted to be just like them."

"You don't now?"

"Nah. I adore them, and their relationship is beautiful, but apart from the fact I wouldn't wish Angelo's life on anyone, I'm not the same as them. They've always played in clubs for healthy reasons—sex positive, you know? I wasn't doing it like that . . . and the reasons I *was* doing it don't exist anymore."

"Because you're happy?"

"Yes. The four of us? Yeah, I'd play for days if it was something you truly wanted to do, but I never think about it. I don't need it."

When they'd first met, Jevon wouldn't have believed it, but Rhys was different now—they both were. Jevon no longer worried that he didn't match up to all that had come before him, and Rhys believed in himself enough to simply be loved, and to love in return. With clothes on their backs and a safe place to sleep, they didn't need anything else.

The End

CROSSROADS — A CHRISTMAS NOVELLA

CHAPTER ONE

DYLAN PACED the draughty seating area of Truro train station, clutching a paper cup of cinnamon-spiced coffee from the dodgy Costa stand. It tasted like soap, but he hardly noticed. Back home, coffee was his drug of choice—lifeblood when the chaos of reality frayed his nerves—but he wasn't in Romford now. He'd left the city behind, and within the hour, he'd get his reward . . . *if* anyone ever showed up to give him a lift.

He circled around the glass entrance doors again, scanning the traffic outside for a familiar vehicle. When he found none, he pulled his phone from his pocket and scanned his message threads, wondering if he'd missed something—instructions to make his own way to Newquay or any clue who was picking him up. Over the past few months, he'd seen them all—Harry, Joe, Emma, even old George in the stinky horsebox. But the WhatsApp chats revealed nothing. Just a vague notion that someone he recognised would be there to meet his afternoon train. Someone who was either late as fuck or had clean forgotten.

Fuck it. Dylan eyed the taxi rank. He could've done without spending twenty quid, but—

"Hey."

Relief punched Dylan in the gut. He whirled around. Blinked. And threw himself into the embrace he'd been dreaming of all the way from London. Clutched the lithe, sinewy body against him, and buried his face in silky hair that smelt of *real* coffee and grass.

I've missed you.

I love you.

I know.

For a long moment, they simply held each other, until Dylan pulled back to check his Angelo-starved imagination wasn't playing tricks on him. "God, it's really you."

Angelo laughed. "Who else would it be?"

"Everyone. You've never come to the station before."

Smoky brown eyes clouded with guilt. "I'm sorry."

"Don't be. Shit. That's not what I meant—I just wasn't expecting to see you for a little while longer."

"Oh." Mollified, Angelo grabbed Dylan's hand to tow him out of the station. "Come on then. Let's get out of here."

"Wait! I need my stuff." Dylan doubled back and grabbed the hold-all and messenger bag he'd hulked on the train. He shifted the larger bag out of Angelo's reach but gave up the one carrying his laptop.

Harry's car was outside, but there was no sign of the man himself. Dylan cocked an eyebrow. "You drove?"

"Uh-huh. I do have a licence, you know."

"I know that, you just haven't driven for, like, a year."

Angelo rolled his eyes. "I don't need to back home when everything's on our doorstep. Down here I have to ask for a lift anytime I run out of lube, so Harry lent me his car for a while."

A while. Dylan's stomach clenched as he stowed his bag in the boot of the borrowed Ford Focus. It had already been a couple of months since Angelo had come to Harry's rehabilitation retreat to recover from a severe ME relapse. Dylan wasn't sure he could handle the prospect of a lonely train home in two weeks' time.

He slid into the passenger seat and shamelessly ogled Angelo as he slipped behind the wheel. It had been thirteen days since they'd last seen each other in the flesh, but the difference in Angelo—as Dylan was becoming accustomed to every time he made the six-hundred-mile round trip to visit—was maddeningly clear. "You look so well."

Angelo fixed him with a disbelieving frown. "Really? I had trouble getting up this morning."

Another kick to the gut. Guilt replaced frustration, and Dylan covered Angelo's hand with his own. "Fuck. I'm sorry. Do you feel better now? I hate it when you're in pain."

"I'm not in pain, babe. I promise. Harry had me doing yoga with the donkeys before I could think about it too much. It hurt then, but I feel good now."

And there it was—the elephant in the room, and the reason they'd wound up at the end of the world in the first place. Harry was Angelo's long-time physiotherapist, and the only one who could help Angelo when his ME made life so hard. The only one who could set him back on his fatigue-ravaged feet when all Dylan could do was angst himself into a migraine and make the fucking tea.

He left his hand where it was as Angelo started the car and backed out of the parking space. Truro disappeared and rugged Cornish countryside took its place. Dylan gazed out of the window, absorbing the familiar heat in his veins from Angelo's touch, and pondered what lay ahead. Spending Christmas on Joe and Harry's farm had seemed a no-brainer a few weeks ago. With Angelo on the mend, he'd looked forward to long, lazy days of eating, fucking, and just being together, but he felt antsy now, like he'd stepped into a puddle of quicksand. He'd avoided asking himself why while he'd been snowed under at the office, but with the end of his working year behind him, reality was hitting home. Angelo looked well because he *was* well. Because farm life suited him—healed him—and sooner or later, one of them would have to voice the idea that something in their current way of living had to change.

———

ANGELO TOOK Dylan's bags to the chalet he called home right now, and relief washed over him as he dumped them on the bed. *I miss him so much.*

"All right, mate?"

Angelo spun around.

Harry blocked the doorway with his large frame, handsome face amused. "Dylan got caught by Sal. She's taken him inside for tea and cake."

"Sal's back?"

"Only for the day. She came to tell Joe she's spending Christmas with Bob."

"Ouch." Angelo winced. "What did Joe say to that?"

"About his mother ditching him to shack up with her fella? What do you think?" Harry grinned, but his face said it all. "Put it this way, I'm glad we have a full house to distract him, even if she hasn't gone very far."

"Me too."

"I bet. You've been counting down the weeks, eh?"

"You know it." Angelo sat on the edge of the bed, the energy he'd ridden to the station suddenly deserting him.

Attuned to the entire world as ever, Harry frowned. "What's wrong?"

"Nothing."

"Liar. What is it? Something sore?"

"No . . . it's not that."

Harry waited, believing Angelo, as always, but giving him time to figure out the real answer.

"I'm scared," Angelo admitted when the silence became too much.

Harry knelt in front of him. "Of what?"

"Of telling him I don't want to go home."

Understanding dawned in Harry's gentle eyes. "So, you've seriously considered my job offer?"

Angelo nodded. "Of course I have. I'd be a fool to turn you down—and I don't *want* to—but I can't see how it's ever going to work."

"You don't have to decide any time soon," Harry said. "We'd be lucky to have you, so it's an open-ended offer."

"It's a ridiculous offer," Angelo muttered. Flexible hours, free accommodation, and a competitive salary, it was a disabled therapist's dream job. It was *Angelo's* dream job, and Harry was wrong about having unlimited time to decide. "My sick pay at the Blackberry Clinic is about to expire. They've said they'll keep my position open for a while, but if I'm not back by spring, they'll have to replace me."

"You've only been gone a few months."

"I know, but I didn't have a good summer. The heat got to my muscles and I couldn't get out of bed for most of August, remember? Besides, I wasn't coping there anyway. I love the job, but the commuting is killing me. That weekend Rhys broke into my flat, I fell off the bus on the way home."

"You never told me that."

"Yeah, well. I figured I'd embarrassed myself enough by needing your brother and his new boyfriend to babysit me, then pretty much dying in *your* boyfriend's mum's bed."

Harry grunted, clearly remembering the dark days a few months ago when Angelo had been so weak he could hardly raise his head. "That's whatever at this point. You needed help, so your friends helped you. It's not like you haven't returned the favour by working here for free."

"In exchange for your undivided attention, and I'm still getting a fucking good deal."

Harry opened his mouth to argue but seemed to think better of it. "We could ride this circle all day. Bottom line is you're as helpful to me as I am to you, but I know it's not that simple—hence the open-ended offer. Have you talked to Dylan about it at all?"

"Nope."

"Why not?"

Angelo shrugged. "Because he's super frazzled with work and travelling down here to see my sorry arse every other week."

"So maybe Dylan's life needs to change too."

"Right. 'Cause wouldn't that be a fucking fairy tale?"

"Cynic."

"Realist, actually. It's me stressing Dylan out right now. He could handle work if I was there to have his back."

"You are there for him, Angelo. Don't write your entire relationship off because circumstance has forced you apart for a couple of months. *Talk* to him. You might be surprised by what he has to say."

CHAPTER TWO

ANGELO ROLLED over in bed and, instead of cold, empty space, found warmth, love, and sunlight streaming through the open curtains.

He opened his eyes. Dylan was already awake and gazing at him, his blond hair a tousled riot, his bloodshot eyes the only hint of the bottle of rum he'd helped Joe and Jevon sink last night. "Hey."

"Hey." Angelo stretched carefully, testing his muscles, then sat up on his elbows. "What time is it?"

"Six."

"Six?"

"Yeah. Someone took the horsebox out about an hour ago. Woke me up."

"Lucky horsebox. It took me ages to get you into bed in the first place, you fucking hooligan."

"Sorry." Dylan grinned without an ounce of contrition. "Blame Jevon. He said I was as buzzed as a kid at the end of term, and I kinda felt that way after a couple of those fruity things he was making."

Angelo laughed. "You had about ten."

"Five, actually."

"Whatever."

"Is it?"

"Is it what?"

"Whatever," Dylan said. "I kind of got the feeling you wanted to talk last night, but we never got the chance. I didn't realise there would be so many people here—Joe and Harry usually leave us to it."

"That's because they go to bed at nine o'clock. Rhys can go all night, remember?"

The double meaning made Dylan laugh too, reminding Angelo—as if he needed it—how lucky he was to have lost his heart to someone who understood him so well. Harry's brother, Rhys, had been their playmate at Lovato's—*a place for every fantasy*—for more than a year before shifting planes had drawn them apart.

"He looked good, don't you think?" Dylan said. "Rhys, I mean, considering he just got caught up in a terrorist attack."

Angelo shuddered. "I don't want to think about that."

"Me either. Anyway," Dylan went on. "What's on *your* mind?"

"Nothing."

"Uh-huh." Dylan eased Angelo back down and stroked his hair out of his face. "Is that right?"

No. But with Dylan's morning wood digging into Angelo's thigh, it was hard to form a coherent thought, let alone put words to the introspective carousel he'd been stuck on since he'd first realised returning to city life would put him back where he'd started a few months ago.

Then Dylan kissed him and it was impossible to contemplate why any of it even mattered, because when Dylan's lips were on his, there was nothing else. They'd tumbled into bed naked the night before, clothes flung carelessly aside, and fallen asleep before appreciating the alchemy of skin on skin, entwined limbs, and roaming hands. But that magic roared to life now. Dylan covered Angelo with his body, slipping seamlessly between Angelo's legs as he fused his mouth to Angelo's sensitive nipples, one after the other.

Angelo's limbs usually took a little persuasion to wake up, but Dylan's touch was his kryptonite, and being without it for weeks at a time had amped up its potency. His legs quivered and his back arched from the bed. "Jesus!"

Dylan chuckled filthily and moved further down Angelo's body, kissing and nipping. Angelo's cock rose to greet him like an old friend, and Angelo braced himself for the dizzying sensation of Dylan swallowing him whole.

A knock at the chalet door shattered his dreams. Dylan cast a baleful glare over his shoulder. "Who's that at this time?"

"Joe." Angelo covered his face with a groan. "You lost that bet about how many Maltesers you could fit in your mouth, remember? One of us has to muck out the donkeys."

If the grief for a lost blowjob hadn't been so strong, the bewilderment marring Dylan's lovely face would've been funny. "I don't remember that."

"Lucky you." Angelo eased Dylan off him and slid out of bed, searching for something to cover his junk. "You spat them in my face."

"Seriously?"

"Pretty much."

Angelo snagged some sweatpants from the floor and pulled them on. He left Dylan in bed and padded to the door, opening it just as Joe was walking away. "Hey! I'm up."

Joe turned. In the crisp morning light, his olive skin and strong frame made Angelo feel like a pasty cripple. "So I see."

Angelo cocked an eyebrow, staring Joe down. In his hurry to get to the door, he'd forgotten his dick print was probably a fucking sculpture, but he knew Joe would break first. Away from the beautiful bubble he and Harry lived in, he was surprisingly shy about sex, considering how lairy he could be about everything else.

"Er, anyway," Joe went on when Angelo didn't blink. "I was gonna let you off the donkey bet, but George just brought in a mare and foal that need some TLC. Harry and Emma are doing the stables, but if you're up to sorting the donkeys, it would really help me out."

"I can do that."

"You sure? I can get George back if—"

"Joe, stop, man. I'm good."

"'Kay."

Joe spun around and jogged away, disappearing up the lane that led to the working farm. Angelo watched him go, jealous, as ever, of the easy elegance that laced his every step, then closed the door with a sigh.

Back in the bedroom, Dylan wasn't impressed with the prospect of shovelling donkey shit before breakfast.

"Stay in bed." Angelo swapped his sweatpants for the ripped jeans he wore on the rare occasions he did any real work on the farm. "It won't take long if Joe's left everything where I can find it."

Dylan's gaze narrowed, tinged with faint amusement that did little to conceal genuine irritation. "Since when were you a farmer's best friend? Last I knew, you were still scared of horses."

"I'm not scared of them—just never went anywhere near them until Harry built the clinic here. He uses horses all the time for balance therapy. Bonny and Clyde, remember? You know all this."

"Uh-huh." Dylan flopped back on the bed and closed his eyes.

Angelo took it as his cue to get his arse in gear and sloped off to the donkey barn. Unable to ever let anyone do him a complete favour, Joe had indeed left everything Angelo needed nearby, which left Angelo plenty of time to make a fuss of Ronnie and Reggie, the weathered old donkeys who were his favourite animals at Whisper Farm. Smaller than the horses—apart from the Shetlands—they were gentle souls who responded obediently to Angelo's bumbling attempts to move them around.

He gave them breakfast and then led them out to their paddock. On his way, he passed Rhys and Jevon who were heading into the house for breakfast, Rhys easing slowly across the yard on his crutches.

"All right?" Angelo called out.

Jevon grinned. "Yeah, man. Dylan up yet?"

"Just about."

"See you at breakfast?"

"For sure."

Jevon smiled again as they moved on. Rhys merely nodded, but Angelo was used to his fluctuating moods, and he'd thrown enough of his own angst Rhys's way in the past.

Angelo settled the donkeys in the paddock and drifted back to their stall. Mucking it out didn't take long, and his muscles sizzled with life by the time he was done, energy he never took for granted.

"Suits you."

Angelo jumped. Dylan was leaning in the doorway, wrapped up in one of Joe's old coats, his expression unreadable.

"What does?" Angelo slid the manger back to its rightful place. "Being covered in mud?"

"No, though it is weirdly hot. I actually meant being outside and working with your hands. I haven't seen you this mobile first thing in the morning for months."

"I think the clean air helps."

"And the freedom to move? I mean, like, really move instead of shuffling from place to place with the traffic and crowds?"

Angelo eyed Dylan, absorbing the speculative gleam in his

gaze, and found himself suddenly and irrationally irritated. "Are you trying to say I've looked like shit every time you've seen me before?"

"Don't be a dick."

"I'm not."

"Right."

Dylan walked away. Angelo stared after him, annoyance fading to bewilderment. He'd been so happy to see Dylan the night before that reality had danced just out of reach, but in the cold light of day, it was unforgivably clear that Dylan wasn't happy. And Angelo knew why—of course he did. Angelo didn't want to go home, but Dylan didn't want to stay.

Dread seized Angelo's chest. The idea of returning to London life terrified him, but Dylan being unhappy frightened him more. Devastated him.

You selfish fuck. Do you really want him to abandon his whole life just so you can have a job on your doorstep?

Angelo's brain had lost the ability to cope with stress. When shit got real, it emptied itself, leaving him dazed and confused and more useless than he was when his legs didn't work. The brush in his hand fell to the floor. He bent to retrieve it and blood rushed in his ears. He'd spent weeks with his head in the sand, taking his own recovery a day at a time, but while he'd been busy with his treacherous muscles, Dylan had been keeping their life together—a life that was as much his as Angelo's. *"Talk to him. You might be surprised by what he has to say."*

Right. Harry had been halfway there, but Angelo was fairly certain he knew what Dylan would say to the idea of spending the rest of their lives on a Cornish horse farm.

Heart pounding, he stood slowly and leaned the brush on the wall. Dizziness rushed over him, but it wasn't equilibrium-sucking waves that came with the worst of a bad day. No. This was pure panic, a gentle tornado of fear—of the future, of the past repeating itself, and of a present he couldn't escape. Angelo loved Dylan more than the moon loved the stars, but he couldn't go home.

———

"SIT DOWN."

Dylan glanced up, but it took a few moments to realise Rhys wasn't talking to him, even though he'd been the only one standing the last time he'd looked around the kitchen. Somehow he'd missed Angelo drifting in from the yard, muddy and cold, his lovely face marred by the mental fog Dylan often forgot about when Angelo's body worked like it was meant to. When his elegant frame carried him like the world-class *ballerino* he'd once been.

He's upset.

Guilt weighed Dylan's heavy step forward, but Rhys got there first, faster than Dylan, even with a dodgy ankle. He didn't even stand—just reached up from the table, grasped Angelo's elbow, and guided him to a seat between him and Jevon.

Angelo sat down and buried his face in his arms. Jevon, apparently the most empathetic dude on the planet, didn't look up from his plate as he draped a comforting arm around Angelo's shoulders, and Dylan was torn between falling a little bit in love with him and punching him in the face. *What the fuck is wrong with me?*

He was no closer to figuring it out when Joe came in, his face the fiery opposite of Angelo's blank distress.

Harry rose immediately. "What's wrong?"

"Fucking numbnuts accountant," Joe growled. "He's pissed off to the Maldives for six months without setting up the tax payment due in January."

"The big one?"

"Yeah, the one we'll get fined a bazillion quid for if we don't pay on time."

"Why didn't you pay it in April when he did your accounts?"

Joe shot Dylan a murderous stare. "Because he told us to earn interest off the savings, remember? And you said it was a good idea."

"It is a good idea if you set it up properly."

Joe pursed his lips, a failsafe clue that he was about to explode.

Dylan took pity on him—and Harry—and plucked the paperwork from his hands. "Do you know where he put the money?"

"Nope."

"No idea at all?"

"Emma reckons it could be in an ISA or some premium bonds, but I didn't know we had any of that shit."

"Okay." Dylan took Joe's arm and tugged him out of the kitchen to the small office Joe hated so much. "First, we'll find the money, and if we can't do that, we'll explain to HMRC that you might need some extra time."

"Tried that," Joe grumbled. "They're shut for Christmas."

"Nah, they just want you to think that. I've got a direct number."

It took twenty minutes to fix Joe's tax woes. The friendly accountant had set up the payment for the wrong year—a simple typo that was easily rectified.

Joe fell back in his chair. "Jesus Christ, this financial stuff is gonna kill me one day, I swear."

Dylan chuckled mirthlessly, his bones aching for the piece of his heart he'd left slumped at the kitchen table. "It's really not that bad. You just need to pay more attention so it doesn't creep up on you."

"About that." Joe's eyes—darker than Angelo's . . . wilder—were merciless as they bored into Dylan's soul. "Ain't it what you and Angelo have been doing for weeks?

Ignoring shit to the point where you can't even look at each other?"

"I can look at him."

"So why aren't you locked in that chalet, fucking like bunnies like you usually do when matey boy can walk straight?"

It was Joe's way not to waste his words, but after a lengthy spell of talking to no one outside the world of debt management and financial services, Dylan was unprepared for how deep they flayed him. "I don't know. I was kind of counting on us doing just that, so I'm not sure why things are the way they are."

"Bollocks. You know everything about everything."

"I really don't. Not when it comes to real life."

"You mean *your* life."

"Whatever."

Joe hummed. "Well, you'd better work it out, 'cause you know he can't."

Brutal, but true. The anxiety that had plagued Dylan most of his adult life had nothing on the ME-induced brain fog that impaired Angelo's thinking so much. Sometimes Angelo didn't make things right because he *couldn't*. Because he couldn't think around the complications Dylan's own bad habits had created for them.

This isn't your fault either.

But it didn't matter. None of it did. All that mattered was making things right.

Which meant figuring out what was wrong.

Dylan drifted back to the kitchen. Everyone had gone, leaving Angelo on his own with a pile of cats, some of whom were closely related to the feral queen who'd taken up residence in Dylan's own father's house.

He plucked the one who looked least likely to bite him from the back of Angelo's chair and dropped it on his lap as he claimed a seat. His legs slid instinctively to entwine with Angelo's, and Angelo finally looked up. "Hey."

Angelo smiled a little. "Hey."

"How are you feeling?"

"I'm okay."

"Really? Because you look a little rattled."

"Probably just horny."

A faintly hysterical laugh burst out of Dylan. "Me too, but I don't think we're gonna get around this by fucking."

"Shame."

"I know."

"So?"

"So . . ." Dylan found Angelo's hands and gripped them. "We have to figure out what we're doing. You don't have to tell me you don't want to come back to London because I already know. And I get it, I really do, but I don't know where that leaves me. I can't—" Dylan stopped and glanced around the cosy kitchen that seemed to be home to everyone but him. "I can't live here, Angelo. I'd lose my fucking mind."

"Why?"

"Because I'm not like you. Or like Harry. Or Joe. I don't work with my hands—I don't build things, fix things, teach broken people how to move again. I earn my living sat on my arse with a phone glued to my ear."

"That's not true."

"It is, and I'm not even saying it's a bad thing. Just that it's not how things work down here. You guys all move in sync like this machine of equine-fuelled efficiency, and . . . it's just not me. I don't fit in—"

This time, Angelo cut Dylan off with a strong hand clamped over his mouth. "Don't say that."

It's true.

Angelo's eyes were fire. *It's not.*

But he was wrong. Dylan loved Whisper Farm as much as Angelo, but that didn't make it home. He squirmed out of Angelo's grasp. "There's nothing I wouldn't do for you—you know that. You have to, or we're fucked anyway. But I can't drop everything and move down here without something more than horse shit and sausage baps to wake up to. It will destroy us, I know it will."

And there it was: the reality Dylan was so afraid of, laid out on the table like the pure damn selfishness it felt like as soon as the words left his mouth. "I'm so fucking sorry."

"Don't." Angelo shook his head. "Don't ever be sorry that my bullshit has screwed your life up too. It's not your fault."

"It's not your fault either, and you haven't screwed my life up. We're at a crossroads, Angelo. None of this changes how much I love you."

"No?"

"No!" Dylan pulled Angelo close and wrapped his arms around him, clutching him as tight as he dared. "I just miss you so much, it's made me so fucking crazy I can't think straight."

"Then I need to come home—"

"That's not the answer either. You'd be as unhappy there as I'd be down here without a fucking purpose, damn it. Why is this so hard?"

"Because you ain't got a plan."

The new voice in the room startled Dylan. He reared back from Angelo to find Jevon passing through on his way to the living room. "What?"

Jevon shrugged. "Sorry to barge into your drama. It's just you seem to be having the same conversation me and Rhys angsted over for months until he decided to come and work on the camps. 'Cause it wasn't about me in the end, or us, it was about him. He could've come over, kipped in my tent, and done a bit of volunteering to stay useful, but it wouldn't have meant anything until he found his own path. The NGO he's hooked up with have done that for him. Or at least, they will when he gets back on his feet."

Angelo looked bemused, but Dylan was up to date enough

with Rhys's love life to put together what Jevon was trying to say: that his place was right here if he searched hard enough to find it. "I suppose I could look for work in Truro."

Jevon shook his head. "Don't live to work, man."

He left the kitchen again, leaving Dylan with his words and the barest hint of an idea that made no more sense than anything else he and Angelo had been through to get to this point.

"I'm so confused," Angelo said. "I can't work out if you're leaving me or not."

There was humour lacing his weary tone, but Dylan hugged him again anyway. "I'm not leaving you. I'm trying to find a path that doesn't kill one of us. You can't live in London anymore—I know that, and I don't want you to when being down here is so good for you. I'm just trying to figure out how I fit into that, you know? Jevon's right . . . I can't just *be* here. I'd hate it, and you wouldn't be able to live with it any more than I can live with dragging you back to London."

The crack in his voice was a mile wide. Angelo mauled his bottom lip with his teeth until Dylan rescued it with a swipe of his finger, then he shook his head. "I wish I could be what you need."

Dylan sighed. "You *are* what I need. I *love* you. I just can't set us up for a fall. Please say you understand?"

"I understand."

With Angelo's eyes still hazed by a cloud they'd never escape, Dylan couldn't be sure it was true, but he'd run out of spoons to explain it. He kissed Angelo, slipping his tongue past that mutilated bottom lip, then pulled away with a hard-won resolve. "Come on," he said. "Let's grab breakfast and go back to bed."

"I NEED TO GET UP."

Dylan nipped Angelo's neck. "Maybe I don't want you to."

"Cute." Angelo let his head drop to the pillow and tried to lose himself in the sensation of Dylan's lips claiming every part of his body they'd missed the first time round. "You won't be saying that in an hour or so if you don't let me wash all this mud, sweat, and jizz off me."

Scowling, Dylan relented and let Angelo sit up. Then he stood and helped Angelo out of bed, his keen eyes zeroing in on the obvious tremor in Angelo's legs. "Wow."

"What?" Angelo snapped.

"Your legs. They weren't doing that an hour ago."

"So?"

"So . . . what's doing that? Stress?"

"Probably. I wouldn't want to eat me right now if I was a cannibal."

Dylan opened the bathroom door and switched the shower on. "Is that supposed to make sense to me?"

"No, just don't talk to Harry about stress hormones and factory farming. It's precious time you'll never get back." Angelo fought the spasms threatening his quivering thigh muscles and won. He took Dylan's outstretched hand and limped to the shower.

Hot water was magic. It pummelled his renegade body with heat and brought him back to life.

He leaned back on the tiles and gazed at Dylan through the steam. "Don't you ever get bored with it?"

"Bored with what?"

"With the constant nannying I need to function."

Dylan speared Angelo with a glare that didn't quite reach his eyes. "Do you get fed up with chasing my ridiculous anxieties round in circles?"

"No."

"Why not?"

"Because I love you and I don't care about any of that. I just want you to be okay."

"You want more than that—you want me to be happy, to feel loved and safe, even when life is hard, and I want that for you too, boo." Dylan punctuated his words with the kind of kiss that could easily put Angelo back on his arse if he lost his tenuous grip on his balance.

He widened his stance. Despite already coming like a train that morning, his cock rose, and Dylan was on his knees before Angelo could blink.

With his slick tongue and pillowy lips, Dylan had always known how to pull Angelo away from everything except the sensation of tight, wet heat and grazing teeth. He swallowed Angelo down, sucking his cock and playing merciless games with his fingers. Angelo didn't bottom much, but when Dylan teased his prostate like that? Yeah, he was down for just about anything.

Dylan pulled off Angelo's dick and stood. "Okay?"

"Yeah."

"You want more?"

"Yeah."

Smirking, Dylan coaxed Angelo away from the safety of the tiles and turned him around. "*Fox.*"

Angelo gasped out a laugh. They'd never had need to use their safe word, but they never forgot it, and Dylan's gravelly whisper went straight to Angelo's dick. He braced himself on the wall and dropped his head, his nerves already crying out for the assault Dylan was about to inflict on them.

And Dylan didn't make him wait for long before he dropped to his knees again and replaced his fingers with his tongue in Angelo's hole.

"*Fuck.*"

Dylan was the goddamn king of rimming, and it didn't take long for him to turn Angelo's limbs to jelly for all the right reasons. Angelo hung his head and gave himself over to the dizzying pleasure. Waves of sensation washed over him, and he clung desperately to the slippery tiles until he couldn't take another swipe of Dylan's devilish tongue.

Attuned to him as ever, Dylan rose and stepped briefly out of the shower for the bottle of lube they had stashed in every room. He moved fast, and Angelo had hardly caught his breath before Dylan was buried inside him, fucking him with short, sharp strokes.

Shower sex was always like this—quick and dirty, though it had been a while since Angelo had bottomed. Not that he was complaining. Dylan fucked like he did everything else—like a motherfucking dream—and Angelo fell to bits in two minutes flat. "I'm gonna come."

"Do it," Dylan ground out through clenched teeth. "I wanna feel you."

He didn't have to ask twice. Angelo let the pressured coil in his gut fly and came with a wild yell, spurting hot come everywhere without ever laying a hand on his dick.

"I love it when you come hands-free . . . you clench me so

tight . . . *fuck*." Dylan released inside Angelo, pulsing wet warmth where they were joined.

Angelo gasped and jerked forward. Alone in the shower, he would've fallen, but Dylan held him up, soothing him with gentle kisses until he could see straight. "Wow. If my shitty balance doesn't break my neck one of these days, getting fucked by you will."

"I can think of worse ways to go than in the shower with my favourite cock inside me," Dylan quipped as his dick slipped out of Angelo, but when he turned Angelo around, his expression was earnest. "I'd never let you fall."

"I know."

"Do you?"

"Yes."

They were talking about something far deeper than screwing around in the shower, and they both knew it, but Angelo's brain was too mushy to articulate anything intelligent.

So he let Dylan lead him out of the shower and deposit him on the bed, drying them both off the way only he could without making Angelo feel like a child.

It was kind of hot too, and Angelo itched to ask Dylan to crawl back into bed and write the whole day off to fucking and napping, but the restlessness in Dylan was impossible to ignore —his jittery gaze and tapping fingers. Angelo kissed him, then lay back and reached for the remote. "Go on. I'm gonna stay here for a bit."

"Do you need anything?"

"Only you."

"You have me, I promise."

Dylan pulled the covers up the bed and then left the chalet, leaving Angelo to his juddering legs and muddled thoughts. He dozed in front of shitty Christmas TV for a while, but eventually the solitude got under his skin. Over the last few months, he'd missed Dylan more than he could ever say, but he'd grown used to the constant company on the farm. Even on his bad days, laid up in this very bed, Harry, Joe, and even Emma had rarely allowed him to be alone.

When he was sure his legs had regrouped enough to hold him, he got up and dressed and ventured across the farm to the yard. Despite being up since the early hours with a rescued mare, Joe was still working, but he waved Angelo's admittedly limited help away. "Go indoors. Jevon's cooking something with those lava chillies he was talking about the other night."

Given the amount of rum that had flowed since Jevon had arrived on the farm, Angelo was surprised Joe remembered but heeded his advice anyway and went inside to find Jevon in Sal's customary place at the stove. "Where's Rhys?"

"Truro. He was going stir crazy, so Harry and Dylan took him out."

"Out?" Angelo had a misty memory of Dylan appearing by his bed and saying something about that. "To Truro?"

"Yup. Harry thought the city boys needed a break from the mud."

"Fair enough." Angelo bypassed his favourite seat at the battered table and peered over Jevon's shoulder into his bubbling pot. "What are you making?"

"Curry goat—without the goat."

Relief washed over Angelo. The farm seemed to have a revolving population of stray goats, and he wasn't sure he fancied eating any of them. "What did you use instead?"

"Harry's bottomless veg box and a tiny bit of mutton to keep Joe happy."

Angelo laughed. The regular food battles between health-conscious Harry and carb-addict Joe was a constant source of amusement on the farm. "It'll keep Dylan pretty happy too. He loves a ruby."

"Good man."

Jevon went back to his pot, and Angelo kept him company

while learning how to make a vat of rice and peas. When the food was ready for whenever the troops came home, they decamped to the living room to shoot the shit.

"Rhys is so different with you around," Angelo remarked while Jevon built a fire.

"You think?" Jevon glanced over his shoulder. "The last few months have been so crazy, it's hard to tell what's real sometimes."

"He loves you."

"I know. I'm a lucky man."

Angelo knew what lucky felt like every time he woke up to find Dylan beside him, and Jevon's easy affection when he spoke about Rhys was as warming as the flames licking the crackling logs. "When do you go back to your job overseas? I know you've already told me, but I forget stuff."

"I'm flying out the day after Boxing Day. I'd stay longer, but it doesn't really work like that."

Angelo searched the Jevon section of his brain. *Refugees, children, clowns.* "When do you think Rhys will be able to join you?"

"Not for a while. Even without his ankle injury holding him up, the paperwork takes months."

"I can see Rhys working in a refugee camp. He's way nicer than he thinks he is."

"Who's nice?" Joe ambled through the door and flopped heavily on the couch. "If you're talking about George, don't be fooled. He's a crafty old git."

"I was talking about Rhys."

Joe nodded slowly and scrubbed a hand down a face weary enough to make Angelo feel guilty for his afternoon in bed. "Fair point. He's as sweet as Harry beneath all the growling and sarcasm."

"Like you?" Jevon flicked a pinecone from the kindling pile in Joe's general direction.

Joe caught the cone with a shrug. "If you say so."

Jevon said nothing at all. Just stoked the fire high enough to cast an orange glow about the room and retreated to the other end of the couch while Joe slumped lower, his dark hair falling into his face.

Angelo nudged him before he fell asleep. "It's Christmas Eve tomorrow. Is there anything you need doing for Christmas Day? Harry said you've got eighteen coming for dinner."

Joe opened his eyes with a groan. "Fuck. I forgot to pick up the turkey."

"Get it tomorrow, man," Jevon said. "You've done enough today."

Angelo hummed his agreement. "I'll fetch it and anything else you need from town. Write a list."

"You can't read my tiny handwriting, remember? It gives you migraines."

"Get Harry to write it then."

Joe grumbled something unintelligible and closed his eyes again. Angelo let him be, and when he wound up stretched out with his head on Angelo's thigh, chucked a blanket over him.

"I like that," Jevon remarked softly.

"What?"

"How good you all are to each other. I thought it was a sex club thing with you and Rhys, but you're all like it."

"Are we?"

"Yup. And I get the feeling Joe wasn't the type to fall asleep in his mate's lap until you lot came along."

Angelo knew Joe well enough by now to believe that. The bloke was soft as shit beneath his fiery temper, but he'd been lonely before he'd met Harry—almost as lonely as Angelo's life before Dylan.

Disquiet sparked in Angelo's chest. A few hours of naked reconnection hadn't fixed the issues that had drawn them apart in the first place, and despite Dylan's reassurance that they'd find their way, Angelo was petrified. He'd move back to London in a heartbeat for Dylan—he'd do *anything* for him—but Dylan was right: one man falling on a sword would kill them both.

"Fuck's sake, mate." Joe groaned and covered his face with his arms. "I can hear you bellyaching in my sleep. You're going to give yourself a stroke."

Angelo scowled. "Nice."

Joe sat up, looking far too rumpled and cute for a farmer pushing thirty. "Never said I was. Are you still freaking out about going back to London?"

"I don't want to talk about it."

"Yeah, yeah." Joe slid off the couch and left the room. He came back a few moments later and dropped a dusty photo album into Jevon's lap. "Rhys told me you pulled a Nellie. Have a look at those—you might see something you recognise."

Jevon seemed as mystified as Angelo until he opened the album. Then his face lit up with the kind of smile that made it so fucking easy to see how Rhys had fallen in love with him. Rhys's shadows were complex—Angelo had missed them for the first few months they'd known each other—but Jevon's light was simple and free.

"Is this your grandfather?" Jevon turned a page. "Rhys told me he rode horses in Romani circuses."

Nelly. Elephant. Circus. Joe's nursery-rhyme slang clicked in Angelo's laboured brain.

"Yeah, that's him," Joe said. "I'm probably related to a few of the others too, but I don't know their names. My grandparents came here on their own."

Jevon was clearly fascinated. He tapped a page with his finger, tracing the skyline. "I've been here, but not with the circus. This is Macedonia, close to the Greek border. It's where I was before I went back to Lesbos."

Joe peered at the page. "What's it like now?"

"Hideous." Jevon's sunny expression faded. "But I'm trying to forget about work for a while."

"Good luck with that." Joe eyed the phone that seemed to ring for him every other night, dragging him out into the darkness to rescue more horses in need. "I'd drink a hell of a lot more if my old man wasn't a raging pisshead."

Jevon grinned. "Rum helps, eh?"

"It does."

Angelo watched the exchange like a spectator, switching his gaze back and forth. Then a page in the photo album caught his attention, and he elbowed Joe in the ribs. "Budge up."

"Piss off. Go round."

Rolling his eyes, Angelo clambered over him to sit beside Jevon. "I love acrobats. We used to have this bloke from Memphis come and train us every couple of weeks when I was with the English National Ballet."

"A Beale Street Flipper?"

"Yeah. He was *fit*."

Jevon chuckled. "Rhys likes acrobats. I'm thinking of doing backflips as foreplay."

"Seems legit." Angelo pictured Jevon and Rhys together, but intrigue outweighed the horniness of his imagination. "Thought you were a clown, though?"

"I'm a play specialist these days, but I started as an acrobat."

"Can you still do it?"

"Some days. I'm not as slick as I used to be, but I practice when I can."

"I'd like to see that. Harry had me doing cartwheels a while ago, but I don't think I can flip anymore."

"Nah, it's like riding a bike." Jevon closed Joe's precious photo album and carefully set it aside. "Let's go try."

"Now?" Angelo blinked in surprise.

"Where?" Joe said at the same time. "Harry will do his nut if one of you breaks your neck."

"Let's go to the clinic," Angelo said. "There's mats in there, and I have the keys in my pocket."

Joe sighed. "Jesus Christ. Okay then, but I'm bringing my beer, so don't get all sanctimonious and healthy on me as soon as we step over the dark side."

It was a running joke that Joe rarely set foot inside Harry's recovery clinic. He brought horses to the exercise yard for balance therapy and fetched and carried anything Harry needed, painted walls, and mended fences, but the mindfulness-themed indoor space pressed his rebel buttons, and it had been collectively decided it was best if he stayed outside.

And no one suited the outdoor life more than Joe.

They left the house and tramped across the farm to Harry's clinic. The exterior security system lit up as they approached, and Angelo unlocked the doors. Inside, he flicked more lights on and pointed to the exercise mats stacked up in the corner. "You can use those if you want."

Jevon laughed and kicked off his shoes. "Okay, mate."

Like he needed them. Jevon threw himself across the room in a series of flips and somersaults, and Angelo was fucking mesmerised. He'd seen some acrobats in his time, but something in Jevon's tumbling set him apart. There was perfection in the flaws, and Angelo's limbs itched with grief. He'd never had Jevon's skills, but he'd had his own.

Jevon came to a nimble stop in front of Angelo. "Your turn."

"Piss off."

"Nope. I can see it burning up inside you. Just move, man. Don't think about it so much."

"You don't understand." In Angelo's peripheral vision, Joe slouched on a bench—Joe who had scraped him off the floor and held his hand when Dylan and Harry hadn't been around. Joe who had no real idea of what Angelo's body had once been capable of. "I can't move like that anymore."

"But you can cartwheel? Walk on your hands?"

"Maybe—"

Jevon gripped Angelo's face in a way that might've been hot in other circumstances. "You know the difference between your physical limits and the roadblocks you've set up in your mind. Try it."

Even before ME, Angelo knew better than to throw himself into acrobatics without warming up. He escaped Jevon's encouraging grip and retreated to a treadmill at the back of the room, thankful he'd nursed the beer Jevon had given him while they'd cooked.

Running was among his least favourite things to do but warmed him up fast. A few gentle stretches later and he was ready to go, much to Joe's obvious amusement.

"You're fucking nuts."

"It's no crazier than galloping on that mad stallion," Angelo retorted.

"If you say so." Joe drank more beer and reclined on the bench until he was pretty much horizontal.

Angelo ignored him and considered the mats in the corner, but a rush of recklessness let him ignore them too. He eased his body into a slow cartwheel. His shoulders piped up a half-hearted protest, but Angelo was stronger than that. He rotated again and again until he was upright on the other side of the room.

Jevon nodded his approval. "Nice. You've got that dancer elegance, man. Don't you think so, Joe?"

Joe grunted, but his gaze was keen. "Do something else."

Angelo walked the perimeter of the room on his hands, then eased into a backwards walkover. His joints creaked and his muscles shook, but there was fluidity there—promise . . . hope. He shook his head as he came upright. "Wow. I haven't even thought about doing that in years."

"Throw some ballet shapes," Joe called out.

Angelo gave him the finger but accepted the challenge,

taking care to heed everything he'd learned about testing his body since Harry had set his life back on track. His legs lacked the spring they'd once had—the agility that clearly overflowed in Jevon—but despite the fatigue and pain, the natural flexibility he'd fought so hard to remember was still there.

Energy zinged through Angelo's veins. He spun and leapt around the room until his lungs gave up on him and he collapsed at Joe's feet.

Only then did he notice the new face in the room—Dylan, naturally, his sunny grin a mile wide, eclipsing the angst they were both dragging around right now. "I've never seen you dance like that before."

A flush crept under Angelo's skin. Performing had once been second nature, but these days he was more at home with his dick out in a club than prancing around a stage. "Jevon dared me to see what I could still do."

"Did it hurt?"

"No more than most things."

"Good." Dylan dropped to a crouch in front of him. "Because I'm gonna ask you to do that flippy-spinny thing for me pretty much every day."

Angelo kissed Dylan hard enough to fade their surroundings into nothing. Eyes closed, lips searching for the peace he only found when Dylan smiled at him like this. When he held Angelo like he was whole and strong.

Only the need to breathe made him stop, and when he opened his eyes, they were alone. "Where'd everybody go?"

Dylan blinked and gazed around too. "In for dinner, maybe? That's why I came up here—to fetch you all in."

Angelo's stomach rumbled, reminding him that he hadn't eaten since their shared plate of Marmite toast that morning. "Jevon made curry."

"I know. I smelt it as soon as we walked in the house. I'm starting to think that man was sent here to save us all."

"Perhaps he was."

Angelo had grown out of believing in a higher power, his Catholic roots long abandoned, but the spirit in Jevon stirred something in him—in all of them, perhaps. "Come on. Let's go eat."

They trudged back to the house. Dylan usually had something to say about the mud squelching around his favourite Vans, but he was quiet now—and apparently content. Hope tickled Angelo's heart. He nudged Dylan gently. "Where've you been all day?"

"Window shopping."

"And?"

"And what?"

Angelo rolled his eyes. "There's no way you managed to get Rhys to spend all day window shopping, especially on crutches."

Mischief gleamed in Dylan's gaze. "True, but do you think Harry would spend all day in the pub either?"

"Okay . . . maybe not. So what *did* you do?"

"A bit of both," Dylan said. "We genuinely did go to the shopping centre, but Rhys got tired, so we went to a juice bar, and *then* to the pub. I didn't drink, though. Harry said I could practice driving his car, so I got him drunk instead."

"You drove Harry's car?"

"Yup. I have a licence too, *you know*."

More hope danced across Angelo's soul. He took a breath to catch it, but Dylan kissed him before he could speak, then pulled away with a wicked grin. "No more angst today, babe. Just curry, beer, and banging."

He skipped into the house before Angelo could respond.

CHAPTER FOUR

"HOT ENOUGH FOR YOU?"

Dylan met Jevon's gaze across the table and countered it with a cheeky wink. "Just about."

Jevon smirked and went back to whatever he was doing under the table that was making Rhys squirm in his seat.

Dylan shoved his last bite of scotch-bonnet-laced curry into his mouth and flopped back in his seat, invigorated by the chilli heat spiking his blood, the cold beer washing it down, and Angelo's hand resting innocently on his thigh while his little finger brushed his cock with evil, feather-light strokes.

The sensation was driving Dylan slowly and deliciously mad. He sucked in a breath and replayed the afternoon he'd spent with Rhys and Harry—two brothers who were alike only in their dark good looks and deceptively gentle hands. Despite clearly knowing all about Dylan's current predicament, Harry had said nothing, but Rhys hadn't been quite so kind. "*Stop being a prick. There's no reason you can't pick up your work and move it down here. Whatever reason you don't want to do that has nothing to do with mud and horses.*"

He had a point . . . kind of. But what did that actually mean?

Dylan's job was more than a nine-to-five—had been since he'd left the banking world behind to work in community debt relief —but he was *tired*. Running Romford's sole advice centre had been a bigger challenge than he'd ever anticipated, and Dylan didn't have much left to give.

"So get off the damn treadmill. For you, as much as Angelo . . . he ain't the only one needs looking after."

Rich coming from Rhys when he was giving up a job as a flight paramedic to work in Europe's refugee camps with Jevon, but he was a hard man to ignore when he had something to say.

Dylan had known other men like that too, and he wondered what time it was in Poland—

"Hey." Angelo nudged Dylan. "You okay?"

"Hmm?"

Angelo stared at him. "You're miles away."

"Am I?"

"Don't be a dick."

"I'm *not*." Dylan hauled himself back into the present. The curry detritus had been cleared away and Emma, who'd joined them at the last possible moment, had dumped an overflowing plate of mince pies on the table. The scent of spiced fruit reached Dylan, and with it came the first hint of festive cheer he'd felt since he'd packed up work for the holidays.

He squeezed Angelo's hand. "Sorry. Was just thinking."

"About what?"

The worry in Angelo's earnest gaze broke Dylan's heart. "About how I told you we were done angsting for the day, and I meant it." He plucked a pie from the plate and shoved it in Angelo's sinful mouth. "Get your crimpers round that and pour me some rum."

For once, Angelo did as he was told, and the rum flowed. Emma disappeared, and eventually, Harry dragged Joe away.

"Behave," he warned as he pushed Joe towards the stairs.

"Christmas Eve is Joe's only day off all year, so I'm gonna need your help tomorrow."

Dylan laughed. "Hungover or not, how much help do you seriously think I'm going to be?"

"Enough help to get the breakfast on."

Fair enough. Dylan would take cooking breakfast for a dozen people over shovelling shit any day of the week.

Harry and Joe disappeared. Rhys tipped the last of his drink down his throat and manoeuvred himself to his feet. "As pervy as I am, I'm not up for listening to my little brother get busy. You guys want to come back to the bungalow with us?"

Dylan glanced at Angelo and was greeted by rum-lively eyes and a big smile. "You wanna?"

Angelo grinned. "I could go for a couple more, but we should probably take it to the chalet, if Rhys doesn't mind hopping over the mud. The horses don't rest when there's lights on in the bungalow."

It was as good a reason as any to take the party back to the chalet. There was no rum left, but there was vodka, and warm cans of Lidl lemonade.

They sat around the tiny living room and shot the shit. Well, Dylan and Jevon did. Rhys seemed preoccupied with burying his face in Jevon's neck, and Angelo had found a new place to hide his hand.

Desire rippled through Dylan, amping up with every graze of Angelo's elegant fingers along his cock. He bent his knee further, shielding his crotch from view, but Jevon smirked at him anyway.

"I thought this might be weird," Jevon said.

Dylan suppressed a pleasurable shudder. "What would?"

"Being here, lit and cosy with you two. I know you don't play around with Rhys anymore, but I still figured it could be awkward if we were ever all alone together."

Dylan couldn't imagine Jevon ever being awkward about anything, but he considered the point and realised it was one he'd never given much thought to before. Rhys was a friend, but they'd rarely seen him outside of the club until their real lives had revealed themselves to be coincidentally entwined. And Jevon? He was brand new—to Dylan, at least. "I don't feel awkward, but that doesn't mean you can't. We'd get it." Dylan nudged Angelo. "Right?"

"Hmm?" Angelo blinked. "What are we talking about?"

"We're talking about Jevon feeling weird about us all fucking before he met Rhys."

"Oh."

Dylan waited, but Angelo had nothing more, apparently too drunk and horny to articulate anything sensible. Another rush sluiced through Dylan. *Happy*, drunk, and horny Angelo was his favourite.

But he fought all thoughts of what might happen when he finally got Angelo alone and turned Jevon's words over again. "We don't get weird about playing—with Rhys or anyone else—because it's an intrinsic part of our relationship. We met at the club and built on what we found there. Rhys was part of that, so being around him is a slice of our normal, even if our friendship has moved on."

"Makes sense," Jevon said. "But I wasn't really thinking about it like that. I'm not jealous, man. It's just, I'm still learning about fancying fellas, so I was more worried about getting wood in the corner thinking about it."

Dylan burst out laughing, the booze and easy companionship unravelling another knot of tension in his chest. "Don't be shy about that. We love that shit."

"It's true," Rhys spoke up for the first time in a while. "And we should probably go if you don't want to see these two put on a show. Angie's got that look going on."

Jevon's gaze was more curious than anything, and he made no move to get off the armchair he and Rhys were reclining on. He slid his hand absently along Rhys's thigh. "I don't mind if they don't?"

Dylan didn't mind, and he had absolute confidence Angelo didn't either. He turned away from Rhys's obvious surprise and pulled Angelo on top of him for the real kiss he'd been craving since the last one they'd shared at the clinic, when Dylan's brain had been turned so inside out by Angelo's graceful dancing, he'd barely been able to speak.

Their lips met, and love and desire wove together, creating a melting pot that was set to boil over any moment if Dylan didn't get a grip on his tenuous self-control. Because when it came to Angelo, he'd never had much. Every time they touched, the very first time came rushing back to him, that rollercoaster night in the club when Dylan had chased oblivion and instead found his heart.

Fuck, I love him.

I want him.

I need him.

Like the resting Dom in Angelo had heard Dylan's call, Angelo came to life. His gently exploring hand disappeared, and he crawled over Dylan on the couch, his arousal clear through his worn-soft sweatpants. He kissed Dylan again, harder this time—searching . . . questioning. *Are we gonna do this? Here? With them?*

Dylan didn't know the answers, but when he forced himself to glance over Angelo's shoulder, he found Rhys and Jevon were engrossed in each other—demanding lips and wandering hands. Jevon seemed dominant, but it was hard to tell with Rhys restricted by his strapped ankle.

Thrusting his hips to catch some beautiful friction, Dylan brought his lips to Angelo's ear. "Bedroom," he whispered. "But leave the door open."

Jevon didn't appear a man easily led, even after a night on the rum, but putting some distance between them with an open invitation seemed a safe compromise with the filthy orgy playing out in Dylan's brain.

Angelo's too, if the reluctant glance he tossed over his shoulder as they slipped out of the room was anything to go by.

In the bedroom, he threw Dylan down. "Strip."

"Yes, sir." The term was playful and not one they often used when they occasionally dabbled in BDSM, but combined with the thrill of being watched, it dripped throatily off Dylan's tongue.

Angelo's eyes darkened in response. He helped Dylan undress and tossed the clothes aside, shedding only his own T-shirt to add to the mix. "On your knees."

Dylan obeyed and lowered his chest to the mattress, leaving himself open to Angelo's mercy.

Or not. Angelo was the king of edging, and as his tongue swept over Dylan's hole, light and teasing, Dylan knew he was in for a hell of a ride. He chanced a glance up and met Rhys's sultry gaze.

Game on, motherfucker.

"HARDER," Dylan gritted out. "Fuck me harder."

Angelo grabbed Dylan's hair and pushed his face into the mattress. "Quiet."

As if that would ever happen, but he said it anyway because Dylan fighting back, squirming out of his hold so he didn't miss a moment of Jevon riding Rhys, lit Angelo on fire. He held Dylan firm a few moments longer, then set him free, fucking him with abandon while the party was just getting started in the other room.

Or maybe it wasn't. Maybe it had been going for hours and

Angelo had been too wrapped up in Dylan to notice. Either way, he knew Rhys's come face well enough to guess he was about to blow. Angelo fucked Dylan harder and tracked Jevon's muscular back as he rolled his sensual hips. Rhys's head was thrown back, his eyes screwed shut, but their hands, like Angelo's and Dylan's, were tightly clasped, like they couldn't let go, even if they wanted to.

Years ago, watching loved-up couples fuck each other's brains out had scratched Angelo's soul, but he adored it now, sucked up the warmth and mixed it with the burning love he carried for Dylan. Sex was sex, but love was love—there was nothing like it.

"Angelo."

Dylan's desperate plea broke through the pound-shop poet in Angelo's brain. He squeezed Dylan's hand ever tighter and gave into the pleasure building inside him. Heat coiled in his belly, tighter and tighter, and blood roared in his ears as Dylan unravelled, his guttural cries loud enough to pull Rhys out of his Jevon-induced trance.

Rhys met Angelo's gaze and thrust up into Jevon, catching Jevon off guard. Jevon's groan was fucking beautiful, and combined with the ecstasy in Rhys's face and the wonder of being inside Dylan, Angelo was undone.

He lost his rhythm as he jammed his hips forward, and the coil in his gut snapped, tipping him over the edge. A ragged moan escaped him and he toppled over, landing on Dylan's sweaty back as his cock pulsed his release. *"Shit."*

"Fuck, yeah." Dylan convulsed one last time, then stilled, his fingers wrapped tightly around Angelo's. "I love you."

Angelo had eyes for only Dylan, but instinct told him it was all over in the other room too.

Smirking, he gently pulled out and rolled Dylan over, falling in love with his flushed, blissed-out face for the thousandth time. "I love you. Do you think we should shut the door?"

Dylan sniggered. "Nah. They'll figure it out."

Just as well because Angelo didn't plan on letting Dylan out of his arms anytime soon. He retrieved the duvet from the floor and threw it over them, then, despite plans to bang Dylan all night long, passed the fuck out.

CHAPTER FIVE

"WHAT IS IT? 'Cause it looks like a giant teacake."

Angelo scowled and set the fruit-studded round loaf on the counter with undue care. "It's panettone. You told me to get bread for stuffing."

"Bread*crumbs*," Dylan huffed. "How am I supposed to make sage and onion stuffing with that mutant hot cross bun?"

"Who said we were making sage and onion stuffing?"

"I did, when you told me you were taking an emergency client and abandoning me in the kitchen all day. You think I know how to make all your weird-arse Italian shit on my own?"

"It's not weird-arse, and I'll be gone an hour—perks of living at work. Don't be so dramatic."

Dylan resisted the compulsion to stick his tongue out and turned away to consider the ginormous turkey Angelo had also brought home from his morning dash to the shops, all the while absorbing the spring in Angelo's step at being so productive. Dylan was usually at his own job when Angelo went out to work, so he rarely saw him in therapist mode. After a night on the booze and banging, it was a startling change. *Why is he so fucking hot?*

Angelo scribbled down the recipe for his precious stuffing

and left Dylan to it. Dylan prepped the turkey, peeled potatoes, and wrapped a million tiny sausages in bacon. He was finishing up when he heard movement above him, so he knocked the leftover bacon into a sandwich and took it upstairs to Joe with a mug of sugar-sweet tea.

"You fucking diamond." Joe slurped the scalding tea. "Harry hides the sugar from me, I swear."

Dylan slid onto the bed. "Wouldn't put it past him. Angelo goes through phases of doing stuff like that, but I can usually get round him with rimming."

"Noted." A faint flush stained Joe's cheeks, but it could've been the tea. "What did you lot get up to last night? Please tell me you didn't have an orgy at my ma's house?"

Dylan laughed and stretched out on his stomach. "As if. I didn't even set foot in the bungalow. Rhys and Jevon came back with us for a bit, but they were gone when we woke up."

Silence. Joe's face was a study in apathy, but the tick in his cheek gave him away, and Dylan was feeling kind.

"We didn't have an orgy at all," he said, "if it's keeping you up at night thinking about it. We are capable of having fellas over for just drinks, you know."

"Didn't say you weren't." Joe eased his legs out in front of him. Well rested and dressed only in Harry's slightly too big sweatpants, he was the picture of hard-earned relaxation. "I just recognise the gleam in your eye from when you two have been on it."

"And you're feeling nosy?"

"If you say so, but I can live without knowing if you don't want to talk about it."

"There's not much to talk about," Dylan admitted. "I think Jevon's curious about playing but too wrapped up in Rhys to explore it."

"What about Rhys? I wondered if it might be different for him now he's with someone."

Dylan shrugged. "Hard to tell. I don't think he's turned off by the idea, but if he plays again, it'll be for better reasons."

Joe nodded. "Makes sense, but I think I've reached my limit on understanding you lot and your sex clubs. How's it going downstairs? Harry reckons I'm not allowed to get up until lunchtime, but if I sleep any more I'll probably die."

"Drama queen."

"Fuck you."

Dylan would *so* have fucked Joe for real if the opportunity had ever arisen, but there was more chance of him turning vegan than coming around to Dylan and Angelo's way of life.

Sighing, Dylan rolled onto his back. "I'm pretty much sick of handling raw meat products, but I think tomorrow's dinner is going to be epic . . . if you like fruitcake in your stuffing."

"Say what?"

"Ask Angelo. He's gone crazy Italian mama on me."

Joe chuckled and set his plate aside, then he stood and drifted to the window, surveying his ramshackle kingdom. "Did the donkeys get done?"

"You're asking me?"

"Yes."

"What the fuck for?"

"Because you always know what everyone's doing, even if you don't know why they're doing it."

Dylan sat up. "That's not true."

"Uh-huh. Where's Harry?"

"Mucking out the stalls."

"George?"

"Measuring out the feeds for tomorrow so you don't have to."

"Emma?"

"Wrestling that mad, black beast you call a horse in the top field."

Joe's grin widened, though he still wasn't looking at Dylan.

"What about Lacey and her mate from uni? I know they didn't rock up until late—"

"They didn't stay," Dylan cut in. "Lacey was hungover, so she called Toby instead. He's with the donkeys, Angelo's at the clinic, and Rhys and Jevon, in case you were wondering, are still in bed . . . hanging too, I reckon, unless they're freaking out because Jevon saw my dick, which is too bad if they are, because they're next on my breakfast route."

Laughter burst from Joe, deep and warm. He turned away from the window and flicked a stray bread crust at Dylan's head. "See? You've got that shit covered."

"What shit?"

"Keeping tabs on everyone . . . on the details that matter. You can't help yourself, and I wish I'd had you around years ago when I first came back here to run the farm. I'd have saved myself a lot of aggro if I'd had someone who knew one end of the business from the other."

"I don't know anything about running stables, Joe. I barely know one end of a *horse* from the other."

"Not about the nags, though, is it? It's about the money—everything is—and there's loads of farmers around here who need help with that."

"If this is your roundabout way of suggesting I go into farmyard financials, don't bother. I've already halfway thought about it, but I don't think it would work."

Joe came back to the bed and sat down. "Why not?"

"Because I don't know enough about farming to offer workable advice. Domestic finances are easy—I know exactly what's going to happen if someone doesn't pay their gas bill or their mortgage. It's different for businesses, particularly agricultural ones, and I don't have the knowledge to be truly helpful to anyone."

Dylan figured Joe would understand, but the challenge in his eyes remained.

He pulled a notebook from a drawer and scribbled something in it. "That's Emma's number if you can't catch her in the yard. She's got the knowledge you need but not the tools to distribute it. Maybe you can help each other."

Dylan took the number without comment and left Joe to his forced morning off. The idea had legs—serious legs—and a glimmer of hopeful enthusiasm carried him downstairs, merging with the vague Truro-based idea he'd been floating to himself since his afternoon with Rhys and Harry.

Brain buzzing, he cobbled breakfast together for Jevon and Rhys and braved the mud to deliver it.

At the bungalow, he found Jevon in the shower and Rhys still in bed. "You okay?"

Rhys yawned. "Just letting the last few weeks catch up with me. Apparently falling on my arse during a terrorist attack is more traumatic when you sink all that booze."

"I did wonder if it might be. You haven't talked about it at all, and you're usually good at that with me."

"I'm good at most things with you. You're a positive influence." Rhys held up the covers and nodded for Dylan to slide in beside him. "But yeah . . . I hadn't really talked about it enough, and because me and Jevon were both twatted, it took all night to hash out."

"But you did, though? Hash it out? Because I've got some numbers somewhere for stuff like this, and I'd imagine your employers do too."

"I know all that, mate. I'm not some rookie, and this isn't the first time I've seen horrible crap."

"It is the first time you've come close to getting stabbed by a marauding terrorist, though."

"You don't say." Rhys shifted awkwardly onto his side. "But I'm okay, honest. I flipped my shit when I first got here, but I guess I wasn't done—that I needed to let off some more steam—

and I reckon being around you and Angie helped me out with that."

"I hope so. How's Jevon this morning? Not hiding in the bathroom, is he?"

Rhys snorted. "Doubt it. I don't think he'd be up for the club anytime soon, but fucking around in front of you was his dynamite."

"He's beautiful, Rhys."

"I know that too."

Of course he did. The bathroom door opened and Jevon stepped into the bedroom, dark braids bundled at the nape of his neck, a towel wrapped around his trim waist. He grinned at Dylan like the long-lost pal perhaps he'd always been. "Morning, gorgeous."

Dylan smiled too; so comfortable in their bed he could've happily stayed all day if not for the mind-map exploding in his brain. "Says yourself. Don't worry. I'm not staying. Just brought you some fuel so you can hole up for the day."

"You don't need help in the kitchen?"

"Unless you can save me from Angelo's best Carluccio impression, nah, we're all right. Stay here and be naked."

"Fine by me," Rhys said.

Like a moth to a flame, Jevon's gaze left Dylan for Rhys and stayed there, transfixed. Dylan took his cue and crawled out of bed. He kissed them both on the cheek and left them to love each other.

Back in the kitchen, Angelo had returned, eyes bright with achievement.

Dylan kissed him too, but on the lips, devouring him like he'd been gone a week. "Good session?"

"Really good. Harry's given me a couple of ME patients to work with who have the same symptoms as me."

"Relapsing and remitting? I thought that was quite rare?"

"It is, but Harry has a few because he's the best. The ones I saw today are a girl about our age and her grandmother. Weird, huh?"

Nothing about Angelo's vicious condition surprised Dylan anymore, so he nodded for Angelo to go on.

"Anyway," Angelo said. "They both have random shitty days, like me, but we managed to ward one off today for the girl, and it reminded me what I can do for myself when things get tough."

"You already work like a dog on your recovery."

"I know, but I don't always believe it's worth the effort. It's good to be reminded that it is. I think—um, I think I'd be okay if we went back to London. I'm scared of it because not having Harry around is daunting, you know? Because he's such an amazing physio, but working with other people is good for me too, especially when I'm the one with the knowledge."

Dylan nodded slowly. "You do have something that Harry doesn't, though—a view from the inside—and I want to talk more about where we're going with this, but there's something I need to do first."

"Something back home?"

"No, something here. Can you hold the fort for a little while? I need to find Emma."

Angelo seemed mystified—and more fearful than Dylan could bear—but took over the mammoth meal preparations without protest and kissed Dylan's hand. "Hurry back. I miss you."

GINO GIORDANO'S sausage and panettone stuffing was the only good thing Angelo recalled of family Christmases. Spiked with chilli, sage, and lemon, it had brightened an otherwise painful experience, and he had fond memories of stealing the leftovers with his little cousin Ludo and hiding in the cellar of the big old Romford house until it was all gone.

Life had moved on since then, of course—Angelo hadn't seen Ludo in years—but the smell made him smile as he retrieved it from the oven and set it on the counter to cool; a welcome break from fretting over where Dylan had gone. *What the fuck does he want with Emma?* Two hours into Dylan's absence, and he still had no idea.

"What on earth is that?"

Angelo jumped. Somehow he'd missed Joe coming downstairs. "Stuffing. And what are you doing in here anyway? You're supposed to be sleeping."

"That was this morning. It's nearly tea time now, and if I sit in that room any longer, I'm going to smother myself with a pillow."

"Try spending a month in bed, then tell me how you really feel."

Joe gave Angelo a one-armed hug on his way to the fridge. "I know, mate. I know. That shit smells amazing, by the way. When can we eat it?"

"Tomorrow. Harry's ordering pizzas tonight, and he left some custard creams in the office to keep you going. He said you had some invoices to pay or something?"

"Wow. It must be fucking Christmas." Joe sloped off to the office.

Going on past experiences, Angelo expected him to reappear fairly quickly, raging about needing a secretary. When he didn't, Angelo stuck the kettle on and foraged for another packet of biscuits, but Dylan came back before he could resupply Joe, and Emma was a heartbeat behind him.

"We have a plan." Dylan's eyes blazed. "A pretty sketchy one right now, but if we can make it work, it should keep both of us busy for a while."

"Both of us?" It took Angelo a moment to realise Dylan was

talking about *Emma* and him. "Busy doing what? You're—uh—*we're*—going home in a few days."

"Yeah, but not for long if we can pull a long-term plan together before then."

"I literally have no idea what you're talking about."

"Then listen." Emma pulled up a chair at the table and dropped a stack of paperwork in the middle. "And tell us if you think of something we haven't."

"Are you taking the piss?"

"Just listen," Dylan said. "Please."

So Angelo did.

Managing money wasn't his strong point, and he knew even less about farming, but as Dylan and Emma hashed out a plan to provide financial advice to farms and agricultural businesses all over South West England, his bewilderment faded away. "So Emma would run the contact centre from here, and you'd go out into the community?"

"That's the basic plan." Dylan sat back in his seat. "I mean, Emma can come out with me anytime she wants, but the point is, she doesn't have to if she's having a shitty time."

Angelo nodded. Emma's anxiety disorder was as crippling as ME—every day a constant work in progress. Hoping for the best but planning for the worst was far more practical. He nudged her gently. "Is this what you want? I thought you were set on going to Norway to do that teaching course?"

She nudged him back. "As if that's ever going to happen—and don't give me a positive attitude pep talk, it doesn't help. I want to do this, Angelo. Me and Joe have nearly lost this place so many times, there's not much I don't know about keeping a farm above water, and other farmers call us for advice all the time. Trouble is, most of them need face-to-face communication —hours and hours to pour over their paperwork and get things in order, and I just . . . I just *can't do it* some days, and that's not fair when people are relying on you."

Angelo understood that all too well. How many times had he let patients down when he couldn't get out of bed? Too many to contemplate right now. "How would you get paid—" He stopped and shook his head, searching for less crude phrasing in his jumbled brain. "I mean, if you're providing a service for struggling farmers, how is it funded?"

"DEFRA, if I can secure it," Dylan said. "Similar to the funding system we use at Citizens Advice. It's basically the government outsourcing support services like they do everything else."

"Like the NHS paying Harry to take private patients?"

"Something like that."

It didn't make much sense to Angelo, but nothing about public funding ever did. He let it go and flicked through the list of businesses Emma already had on her list. "These are people you've worked with before?"

"Some of them for web design and marketing, but most of them are friends and acquaintances—the ones my dad hasn't pissed off over the years. They're not interested in fancy websites and social media campaigns. Right now, they need help just to stay above water. Farming isn't what it was twenty years ago, and if you're not producing artisan hipster crap, you just can't survive without help."

Dylan made a noise of agreement, and Angelo glanced between him and Emma, absorbing their shared enthusiasm all over again and finally allowing himself to contemplate what it actually meant. If Dylan had a project in Cornwall—a project he cared about as much as his work in London, could it be that—

"Hey." Dylan kicked Angelo gently under the table. "Did you have a stroke?"

"What?"

"You're going all *Walking Dead* on your lips again."

"Sorry."

"Don't be. What are you thinking?"

Angelo shrugged. "I'm wondering if this means you're actually *wanting* to quit your job in London and move down here instead of doing it for my sake."

"Aaaand, that's my cue to go and annoy Joe." Emma abandoned her paperwork and slipped noiselessly from the room.

Leaving Angelo mauling his bottom lip again.

Grinning, Dylan rescued it. "We've been over that a million times. Even the cats must be fed up with it by now, but to answer your question . . . yes. There's a lot to do to get this project off the ground, and it'll take a few months to wind down my work in London, but I'm really fucking excited about it. I think what we want to do—the service we can provide—could make a real difference to the farming communities around here."

"I love it when you talk dirty."

"Shut up." Dylan laughed and drew Angelo closer. "I want to ask you about something, though. Emma said Harry offered you a permanent job at the clinic. Why didn't you tell me?"

Angelo shrugged. "Because it's an amazing opportunity for me, and I didn't want you to make any decisions based on that. That's how it started, anyway. Eventually, I just couldn't find the right moment."

"And me having a meltdown every time we talked about it didn't help, I bet."

"You didn't have any meltdowns."

"On the outside, maybe." Dylan tapped his temple. "But to be honest, it seems like we've been chasing this solution for months, and I feel a hundred times lighter now we've got this idea on the table, even though there's still so much to do."

Lighter. Angelo turned the word over in his mind and it fit. "We don't have to literally live on the farm if you don't want to. Harry always planned for the biggest chalet to be for on-site staff, but it doesn't have to be me."

"We don't have to make any decisions about that right now."

Calmness that had been missing for weeks laced Dylan's gorgeous gravelly voice.

Fuck, I love his voice.

"But," Dylan went on. "It would make sense to live on the farm with me and Emma working together too. I don't want to live in a chalet forever, but it seems like a sensible place to start."

"What about the flat?"

"We can rent it out. Sam and Eddie mentioned coming back to London next summer. Maybe they can live there."

"Orgy BFF? Got it."

Dylan flicked Angelo's ear. "Stop it. I've never fucked Sam, and I haven't fucked Eddie in years."

"Not that many years."

"What's your point?"

Angelo grinned. "That I'm horny?"

Dylan ran his tongue over his full bottom lip, untouched by anxious, renegade teeth, but his retort was cut off by Harry coming in from a long day of hardcore farm work.

He left his boots by the door and glanced between Angelo and Dylan. "You two been on the rum already?"

"Nope." Dylan released Angelo from his smouldering stare. "Just making plans. Angelo's going to accept your job offer, and I'm going to work with Emma in agricultural debt relief, so I'm going to need a pair of those wellies you threatened to buy me yesterday. I'm not ruining any more shoes."

Harry's smile was a mile wide. "Seriously? You figured it all out?"

"Joe did, actually," Dylan said. "He fed me the idea this afternoon."

"He's a fucking dark horse," Harry said with obvious surprise. "He never mentioned it to me."

"That's because you've been busy planning other sneaky things," Emma snapped from the hallway that led to the office. "Get in here . . . *now*."

She disappeared as abruptly as she'd arrived. Harry rolled his eyes and ambled after her. At the door, he stopped and turned. "In all seriousness, I'm really happy for you. I get that leaving London behind is a massive wrench, even if things aren't perfect there, but life's different down here—it's for living, not just surviving."

"He'll be lucky if he survives the next ten minutes," Dylan remarked when he was gone. "Emma looked pissed."

"Yeah, well, you've got that to look forward to if you're going to work with her every day. Her and Joe are fucking wild."

"It'll be fine. If we're as busy as I hope we'll be, she won't have time to lose her shit. Now . . . didn't you say something about being horny?"

CHAPTER SIX

"WHAT THE ACTUAL FUCK?" Rhys growled.

Dylan turned his wide eyes to him, glad it was him who'd broken the stunned silence. After a day of tipping the world upside down, shaking it, and searching for an answer, he hadn't been entirely sure if he'd imagined what Emma had just said.

"You heard me," Emma said calmly, though the jitters in her hands gave her away. "My brother and your brother have decided to make honest men out of each other, right here—right now, in actual fact. The registrar will be here in half an hour."

More silence. Dylan took in the faces around him. Rhys's expression was hard to gauge, and Angelo was blinking, clearly bemused, but it was Jevon who came to life first. His half smile broadened, and he pounded Rhys on the back. "What about that, eh? Good job I brought my favourite bow tie."

Rhys glowered at him. "You did not bring a bow tie."

"You reckon?" Jevon shoved a hand in his pocket and came back with a pink and yellow dickie bow. He fastened it around Rhys's neck and thumped him again. "Just as well too. Can't have you showing your brother up."

Reality crept slowly into Rhys's stormy gaze. The edgy

confusion faded, and real joy seeped in. He tore his eyes from Jevon and looked at Emma. "You'd better not be shitting me."

Emma beamed. "As if I would. Now come with me . . . all of you. We've got about an hour to make this awesome."

Dylan pushed his chair back, as stunned as everyone else apparently was. A couple of beers and a double pepperoni pizza had been the only things on his radar, perhaps some lazy fucking if Angelo had been game. A wedding? Damn. He'd have been less surprised if Emma had burst into the kitchen with newly grown horns.

Beside him, Angelo was slower to his feet than everyone else. Dylan broke ranks to look at him, but there was no pain in his face, only a smile that threatened to split it in half. "I knew they were up to something with that barn."

"What barn?"

"The one with half a roof down by the stream. Harry said something about cleaning it up for summer weddings, and he's been over there loads the last few months. I figured he was planning some renovations in the spring."

"You never said."

"Didn't I?"

Dylan shook his head. "No, but I didn't ask either. Joe's barns have never been high on my list of things to grill you about."

Angelo started to say something else, but Emma got between them and grabbed their arms. "Come on." She tugged them towards the door. "We've got a derelict barn to make nice, and someone has to convince Joe to do something with his hair."

Emma was a force to be reckoned with when she took control of her nerves. And as she herded them to a corner of the farm Dylan had never been, he wondered if that was why Joe and Harry had sprung a wedding on the world like this, with little time for anyone to do much more than turn up.

And when they got to the barn, it was clear that whatever

was going down tonight had been given more than a few hours' thought. The broken-down barn had a new roof, new floors, and a bar installed at the back. A warm glow bathed the rustic space, and simple, vintage touches finished an intimate venue any Pinterest board would be proud of.

"Wow." Dylan spun in a slow circle. "What the fuck is even happening right now?"

Harry's deep chuckle came from somewhere behind him. "Don't get too excited. We didn't do all this for us. It's for the farm, to raise money for a new stable block. You're the one who said Cornish weddings were big business, remember?"

"I was drunk-reading Vogue. That's not the best time to take me seriously, mate."

"Noted." Harry laughed again and slung his arm around Angelo who was still painfully bemused. "I was kinda surprised *you* didn't figure it out, though. You answered the phone to the registrar last week, and she thought you were me."

Angelo shook his head. "I remember that, but I thought I'd misunderstood, then I lost my phone when we were trying to find Jevon, and . . . fuck, I don't know." He shrugged. "Give me a break, Harry. I never have a clue what's going on around here."

"Neither do I, apparently." Emma joined them. "When you said it was happening in the barn tonight, I pictured us all huddled up in the rain in our coats. Harry, this place is incredible. How have you *done* this without anyone noticing?"

Harry shrugged as Joe appeared seemingly out of nowhere and wound his arms around him from behind. "It was easier than you'd think, actually. Angelo, by his own admission, is pretty oblivious, and you don't come out this way. Toby and George were in on it from the start, and we did most of the work at night."

"Were you planning your own wedding all along?" Rhys asked.

"No." Harry shook his head. "That only came up a few

weeks ago when you said you'd try and get here for Christmas. With Dylan coming too, we figured it was probably the only time we'd get with all of you here. That Jevon's with us too is more than we dared hope for."

Rhys beamed and gave his crutches up to Jevon to hug his brother. Warmth bubbled in Dylan's gut and threatened to burst out of his chest. He clutched Angelo's hand, eyes burning, and yanked him away from the touching scenes.

Outside, concern marred the happiness lighting Angelo's gaze.

Dylan frowned. "What's the matter?"

"Nothing."

Dylan pulled him close and found solace in Angelo's neck, burying his face there a long moment before he found the composure to look up again. "I'm just so happy for them, you know? Harry was so lonely when we met him, and Joe is everything to him. It's how life should be."

"You don't think life is like that for us?"

"Of course I do." Dylan sniffed. "It's the reason I know Harry was lonely. Because he told me once that he wanted to love someone like you loved me . . . like I didn't already know I was the luckiest man in the world."

"Dylan—"

"Don't." Dylan clamped a hand over Angelo's mouth. "Don't tell me you're the lucky one, that you'd be nothing without me and all that *bollocks*, because I'm *tired* of it, Angelo. People don't find what we have as a given, and it wouldn't mean anything if it wasn't hard sometimes."

Angelo freed his mouth from Dylan's hand. "I bloody know all that, you fool. I just forget sometimes, like I forget everything else except the fact that I love you more than anything."

"Stop it. You'll make me cry for real."

"You started it."

"Not true. *They* did." Dylan jerked his head at the barn. "I feel so emotional right now, I might literally cry for the rest of the night."

He was joking . . . mostly, and Angelo seemed to know it. He kissed Dylan like it was their wedding night and then took his hands, entwining their fingers together like ivy clinging stubbornly to weathered bricks. "I'm so happy for Harry and Joe, it just makes me love you more. I *am* hard work, Dylan . . . perhaps we both are, but it's worth everything to be with you."

"I know, baby."

"Good." Angelo kissed the very tip of Dylan's nose. "Now let's go inside and watch our best friends get married."

LAUGHTER, tears, and joy—there was plenty of all three as Harry and Joe married each other in front of their family and friends. Even Harry's mother got a look in through a carefully placed phone camera.

Angelo sat between Dylan and Sal—who'd arrived at the last possible moment, crying and swatting Joe upside his head—passing tissues and trading hugs when emotions bubbled over.

"My precious boy," Sal said. "All I've ever wanted for him is to see him so loved."

Angelo smiled. "I think he loves Harry just as much."

"Of course he does. He wouldn't understand if he didn't. You can't take that kind of love from someone without giving it back."

"I know, Sal. I know."

And Angelo did. The last few months had been a train wreck, but loving Dylan had never been so easy, because Dylan loved him back, and together they were stronger than anything else life threw at them.

The ceremony drew to a close. Joe, dressed in jeans, a white shirt, and braces, tossed his grandfather's hat into the air. It landed on Rhys, and Jevon's uproarious laugh filled the barn to the rafters, seeping into every soul in the room, filling what little space Joe and Harry's love had left behind.

Angelo laughed too, turned to Dylan, and kissed his cheek. "I wish I'd caught it."

"Why?"

"Because it's a good hat."

"Dick." But Dylan's smile told Angelo he'd heard the words unsaid: *One day, baby. One day.*

Maybe, at least. Marriage had never crossed Angelo's mind before the twenty minutes of pure joy he'd just lived through, but he wanted the smile on Harry's face to be Dylan's, and the smouldering happiness in Joe's roguish eyes to be his. Dylan deserved it—they both did.

The party moved to the bar. Jevon and Dylan helped Emma fetch long-forgotten bottles of homemade wine from the house and order enough pizza for a small army while Angelo sank into a couch with Rhys, watching the world turn around them.

Angelo knocked Rhys's arm. "All right?"

"Think so." Rhys shook his head slightly. "Is it me, or have the last few weeks been totally fucking bananas?"

Up until a week ago, Rhys had been working on an air ambulance, so Angelo was willing to bet Rhys's life had been crazier than anything that had happened on the farm, but he nodded anyway. Insanity was subjective. "It's all good now, though, right? You and Jevon know what you're doing, me and Dylan are getting there . . . Emma too. And those two goons?" He jerked his head at Harry and Joe who still fended off emotional relatives. "Like we didn't already know they were made for each other."

"Disgusting, ain't it?"

"Yep."

"I've been meaning to have a proper conversation with you,

though," Rhys said after a protracted silence. "And I probably should've done it before we got busy in your living room."

Angelo snorted. "We've never worried about shit like that before. Remember the Mother Love Bone night last Christmas? I don't think me and you exchanged more than two words before then."

"Yeah, well . . . that's gonna change, mate. I—uh—I'm a pretty shit friend, and I'm not going to be around much once I'm back on my feet, but I'm hoping you and me can fix it all up before I go away. Harry said you're good with ankles, so I was wondering if you'd help me out with some physio?"

"You don't have to pretend to like me to get some physio."

"I do like—" Rhys began to protest before he caught Angelo's grin and flicked his ear. "Prick. Dylan's way nicer than you."

"I know, but of course I'll help you out with your rehab. I was going to offer anyway, but I thought you might want Harry to do it. And, I'm not a physiotherapist—not yet, anyway. I do rehab programmes and muscle recovery."

"You know as much as I need," Rhys said. "Besides, me and Harry would kill each other if we had to spend regular, forced periods of time together. I love him more than anything, but he gets on my nerves."

Laughter burst out of Angelo's chest. "How can *Harry* get on your nerves? He's the nicest bloke in the world."

Rhys gave Angelo a comically flat-eyed stare. "My point exactly. He's so fucking reasonable I want to brain him half the time."

"Then *you're* the prick."

"Tell me something new."

Angelo laughed again as someone somewhere turned some music just loud enough to amp up the party without disturbing the horses on the other side of the farm. An old rock beat filtered out of hidden speakers and into Angelo's veins. His muscles twitched, desperate to move, and in a moment of reckless abandon, he didn't question it.

He nudged Rhys again. "Can I dance with your boy?"

"Sure." Rhys waved his hand. "It's only fair, seeing as I've had *your* boy's balls—"

Angelo sprang from the couch before Rhys could finish his crude sentence and crossed the fast-filling-up barn to where Jevon was setting out pizzas on the bar. "Wanna dance?"

Jevon didn't take much persuading, and Dylan, Toby, and Lacey soon joined them, though Jevon was the only one who could keep up with Angelo.

"Stop," Dylan growled in Angelo's ear. "I'm so fucking horny watching you two throw each other around. Do you want me to screw you right here?"

Angelo wouldn't have complained, but he got the feeling Joe's friendly neighbours might've. He whirled away from Dylan and straight back into Jevon's waiting arms. Somewhere behind him, Rhys heckled something crass, but Angelo barely heard him. To move was to be free. And to be loved by Dylan on top of that was all he'd ever need.

ANGELO WAS GLORIOUS. Dylan could've watched him dance all night if the need to hustle him into bed wasn't so strong, though it was the early hours by the time someone turned the music off.

They emerged from the barn to a crisp, clear night that promised a frosty morning and trudged across the farm to the chalet they'd committed to call home in the very near future. Though sure of his path, nerves had plagued Dylan even as he'd planned up a storm with Emma, but tonight's festivities had washed them away. Home was where the heart was, and Dylan's heart belonged to Angelo.

"Are you hungry?"

"Hmm?" Angelo glanced up from navigating the potholed path. "Nah. I ate all that pizza."

"Yeah, but I'm pretty sure you danced it all off."

"Then I'll have plenty of room for stuffing tomorrow."

Dylan acknowledged the innuendo with a smirk, but Angelo's answering smile was too sweet to be dirty, so Dylan let it go and guided him around a puddle. "Remind me to call my dad in the morning."

"Is he spending Christmas with Tammy?"

"Yup. I don't think she goes home much anymore. He wants us to visit after the New Year, which should tie in well with telling him we're moving down here permanently."

"Will he be upset?"

Dylan shook his head. "Doubt it. He might've been a year ago, but he's got a whole new life now—and a cat. He doesn't need me in his face all the time."

"At least he gives a shit."

"Your mum cares."

"Uh-huh."

There was no challenge in Angelo's tone, but Dylan heard it all the same. "She does," he insisted. "In her own way."

Angelo snorted. "Her own way sucks donkey dick."

Dylan let him have that one and pushed all thoughts of anyone else aside. Tonight had been about nothing but love, and they still had a few more hours to enjoy it.

They reached the chalet. Angelo unlocked the door, but Dylan stopped him before he could go inside and caught him in the kind of kiss they didn't often have the patience to wait for. Tender and sweet, it was a slow burn and reminded Dylan of the very first kisses they'd shared after their explosive first encounter at the club. Those kisses had been such a perfect contradiction that Dylan had known from the start he was falling in love with this beautiful man.

My beautiful man.

Angelo's back hit the doorframe, and he gasped, his legs shaking, perhaps as much from Dylan's touch as his wild night on the dance floor. But it didn't matter how hard Angelo's illness ever shook him, Dylan would always be right here, arms tight around him, holding him up.

Finally breaking their kiss, he slipped an arm around Angelo and guided him inside. There weren't many places in the chalet they hadn't fucked, but right now, the bed was calling their names.

Dylan eased Angelo down onto his back. "Did you clean up in here?"

"Yeah . . . when I came back from work. I know you get all horny for fresh sheets."

"I get horny for *you*, but it's so much more than that, baby."

"I know."

Angelo pushed Dylan's coat off his shoulders and set to work unbuttoning the shirt Emma had forced them all into at the last possible minute before the wedding. It joined Dylan's coat on the floor. They kicked off their shoes, and Dylan stripped Angelo of the rest of his clothes before standing to remove his own jeans.

Naked, he came back to the bed and crawled over Angelo, covering him with his body until there wasn't an inch between them. He fused their lips together and hooked his arms around Angelo's legs, lifting them gently until they were draped over his shoulders. "Okay?"

Angelo sucked in a shaky breath and nodded. "I'm so hard for you. Fuck me, Dylan . . . please?"

As if Dylan could refuse. As if he wanted to. He reached over Angelo's head and found lube in the bedside table, then he slicked his fingers and worked Angelo open, all the while still kissing him like a drowning man.

Beneath him, Angelo trembled and his gasps rose in pitch to frantic moans. "*Dylan.*"

"What?" Dylan thrust his fingers harder, holding Angelo down with his other hand as he jerked from the bed. "What do you want? What do you *need*?"

"Love me," Angelo gritted out. "I don't care what you do, just love me."

"I do love you. Always." But Dylan heard the plea in the ragged words, and it matched the desperation building in his own veins. He reclaimed his fingers and coated his throbbing cock with more lube. Then he rolled Angelo onto his stomach to give his legs a break, lifting his hips from the mattress just enough for Angelo to grip his own dick.

Their bodies came together as Dylan pressed inside Angelo's tight, wet heat. Seamless and smooth, it was like they'd been formed from the same mould, two halves of one coin. Lava pulsed where they were joined, and Dylan's control began to slip. He gripped Angelo's hair and tugged his head back, sinking his teeth into Angelo's neck as he thrust inside him. "I love you so fucking much."

Angelo cried out in response, muscles tight and straining, pushing back on Dylan as though it didn't matter how absolutely Dylan filled him, it would never be enough.

Taking his cue, Dylan hunched over and began to fuck him, slowly at first, taking care to gauge the pain points Angelo seemed to have forgotten about, but when Angelo's cries held nothing but pleasure, Dylan set them both free.

Over and over, he drove inside Angelo, the crazy heat sweeping through him and flooding every vein. Fucking Angelo was always like this, but it was . . . more than that now. Like something had shifted between them, solidified, even though they'd never tangibly known it was loose. Pressure built in Dylan's gut, expanding with every thrust until his eyes rolled back and flickering dots obscured his vision.

He dug his nails into Angelo's leanly muscled back. "I'm gonna explode inside you."

Angelo groaned, deep and loud, and threw his arms out in front of him, his hands scrabbling for purchase on the clean sheets. "Do it. I'm going to come so fucking hard."

A frenzied urgency stole over Dylan, robbing him of what little sense he had left. One hand moved to the back of Angelo's head, pressing his face into the mattress, while the other kept balance at his spine, and then he let go, fucking Angelo with the abandon his heart desired, flesh slapping flesh the only sound in the room beyond harsh groans and squeaking bedsprings.

Angelo came first, releasing with a series of breathless cries that unravelled the swelling knot of pressure in Dylan's belly, and then Dylan came too, his rhythm deteriorating with every jolt of pleasure until one last erratic thrust.

Dylan shot inside Angelo, shuddering through every pulse of his release until his body could give no more. Panting, he withdrew and pressed a clumsy kiss between Angelo's shoulder blades. "I love you."

"... love ... you, too."

Angelo's exhausted mumble was barely audible. Dylan smiled and ruffled his hair. "Don't fall asleep there. You'll be stuck to the duvet when you wake up."

Angelo groaned and lifted his head. "Don't be so fucking practical."

"Not sorry." Dylan helped Angelo sit up enough so he could pull the covers back. "Wait a sec."

He dashed to the bathroom for a warm, wet cloth and cleaned them both up, then he moved to the window to draw the curtains. "Hey ... it's getting light."

"Leave them open then," Angelo said. "We can watch the sun come up."

Dylan left the curtains and padded back to the bed. He crawled under the duvet and lay on his back with Angelo curled against him, his head on Dylan's chest, and together they watched the dawn break through the clouds and bathe the frosty fields in ethereal winter sunshine.

"Merry Christmas," Angelo whispered.

Dylan smiled and held him impossibly tighter. "Merry Christmas, baby."

FURTHER READING

Gorgeous Toby is getting his own book! The Sex Coach is out October 1st 2020 and can be preordered HERE!

Angelo is also mentioned in Kiss Me Again. Ludo is his cousin. Tom, who pops up in Believe, has his very own story in Misfits.

Dylan features in What Matters, where you get to read Sam and Eddie's story. And Dr Marc is a secondary character in Between Ghosts, and has his very own story in Soul to Keep.

NEWSLETTER

For the most up to date news and free books, subscribe to my newsletter HERE.

This is a zero spam zone. Maximum number of emails you will receive is one per month.

PATREON

Not ready to let go of Angelo and Dylan? Joe and Harry, or Rhys and Jevon? Or looking for sneak peeks at future books in the series? Alternative POVs, outtakes, and missing moments from **all** Garrett's books can be found on her Patreon site. Misfits, Slide, Strays...the works. Because you know what? Garrett wasn't ready to let her boys go either.

Pledges start from as little as $2, and all content is available at the lowest tier.

ABOUT THE AUTHOR

Bonus Material available for all books on Garrett's Patreon account. Includes short stories from Misfits, Slide, Strays, What Remains, Dream, and much more. Sign up here: https://www.patreon.com/garrettleigh

Facebook Fan Group, Garrett's Den... https://www.facebook.com/groups/garre...

Garrett Leigh is an award-winning British writer, cover artist, and book designer. Her debut novel, Slide, won Best Bisexual Debut at the 2014 Rainbow Book Awards, and her polyamorous novel, Misfits was a finalist in the 2016 LAMBDA awards, and was again a finalist in 2017 with Rented Heart.

In 2017, she won the EPIC award in contemporary romance with her military novel, Between Ghosts, and the contemporary romance category in the Bisexual Book Awards with her novel What Remains.

When not writing, Garrett can generally be found procrastinating on Twitter, cooking up a storm, or sitting on her behind doing as little as possible, all the while shouting at her menagerie of children and animals and attempting to tame her unruly and wonderful FOX.

Garrett is also an award winning cover artist, taking the silver medal at the Benjamin Franklin Book Awards in 2016. She designs for various publishing houses and independent authors at blackjazzdesign.com, and co-owns the specialist stock site moonstockphotography.com

Connect with Garrett
www.garrettleigh.com